Colin de Silva was born in Ceylon (now Sri Lanka) and grew up there. He is an entrepreneur, in addition to being an author. He has also been an international trader, a member of the Ceylon Civil Service, a commissioned officer in the British Army and a diplomat. In 1962 he emigrated to Hawaii, where he now lives.

His first published novel, *The Winds of Sinhala*, was published in 1982 and quickly became an international bestseller, followed by the equally successful *The Founts of Sinhala* (1984), *The Fires of Sinhala* (1986), *The Last Sinhala Lions* (1987) and *Taj* (1989).

D1142610

By the same author

The Winds of Sinhala
The Founts of Sinhala
The Fires of Sinhala
The Last Sinhala Lions
Taj

COLIN DE SILVA

Alhambra

Arena of Assassins

Grafton
An Imprint of HarperCollinsPublishers

Grafton
An Imprint of HarperCollins*Publishers*
77–85 Fulham Palace Road,
Hammersmith, London W6 8JB

Published by Grafton 1992
9 8 7 6 5 4 3 2 1

First published in Great Britain by
HarperCollins*Publishers* 1991

ISBN 0 586 20805 4

Set in Times

Printed in Great Britain by
HarperCollinsManufacturing Glasgow

Dedicated to

my sister and brothers

the late

Rose Constance Winifred de Silva
(the Rev. Sister Mary Rose)

William Stanley Hamilton de Silva

Merl Conrad Hazelton de Silva

'Slaves in the realm of love
Are the only truly free men.'

Ibn Ammar

Contents

Author's Note	9
Acknowledgments	11
Prologue	13
Part I The Arena	23
Part II Assassins	265
Part III *Auto-da-Fé*	481
Part IV Councils of War	631
Postscript	703

Author's Note

Alhambra is not history, but a montage of historical names, events and places melded into fiction, even the Alhambra palace mosque being based on the grand mosque of Cordoba.

The characters portrayed bear names such as Yusuf ibn Nagralla, Ibn Gabirol, Pedro the Cruel, Charles the Bad, the kings of Catalonia, Aragon and Portugal, Maria de Padilla, Prince Ahmed, Prince Juan and Princess Beatrice. But these people did not participate in any of the events I have described, their presence in the novel is fictitious, so any resemblance of my characters to persons living or dead is purely coincidental. My own creations include Zurika, Princess Mathilde, Count Gaston, Aaron Levi, Bishop Eulogius and the minor characters, including nobility and spies, police and assassins, all woven into the ancient legend of Prince Ahmed al-Kamal.

As for my framework of events, the first Spanish *auto-da-fé* was really held in Seville as late as 1481 A.D., the gypsy migrations into Spain took place a century after the period of my story, Granada did not experience the Black Plague, nor was white Christian unity achieved at this time. Despite anachronisms, I hope I have conveyed the robust flavour of the times, and of the Spanish people who, above all other nations, know passion in their lives, reflected vividly, as with no other race, in their literature, music, painting, drama and architecture. If this passion is also revealed in my montage, the novel will have come to Spanish life.

All who lived in the Alhambra throughout the centuries have been touched by its beauty. Some heard the ghosts which still whisper or wail in its deserted buildings. Its occupation by the Christian King Ferdinand and Queen Isabella neither removed nor destroyed the dream of its creator or that of those lovers of beauty, the Muslim rulers. The plots, the betrayals, the romantic loves, the loyalty and sacrifice, the assassinations, the barbarism and the refinements of a remarkable civilization were embodied in their buildings.

Your own sigh, your tear, your laughter and delight will not waken the dead, but might stir their sleep.

Colin de Silva
Honolulu, Hawaii, 1990

Acknowledgments

My deep appreciation and thanks go to:

HarperCollins for its continuing faith in me.
Anne Charvet, who as my editor at the time advised me
to select Alhambra as the subject for my next novel.
The staff of every department of HarperCollins for their
past and present professional support.
My secretary, Marcia Krueger, once again almost my
local editor, whose devotion to typing and producing this
novel went beyond the line of duty.

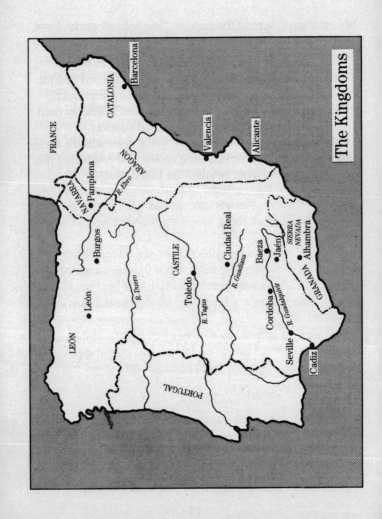

The Kingdoms

Prologue

My informers, spread throughout the civilized world, have sent me news that William, the northman, Duke of Normandy, descended from the warlike Danes, has decided to make preparations for an invasion of England, using the excuse of birthright through the Norman Emma, mother of King Ethelred, known as the Unready.

The Christian year is 1061 A.D. and I am Yusuf ibn Nagralla, Vizier or Chief Minister of Abdullah, the king of Moorish Spain known as the Caliph. Now Ibn Gabirol, poet and son of my adoption, and I rein in our grey Arab steeds on the high ground jutting out like a long spur from the Sierra Nevada mountains. We ride identical horses, and our clothing too is matched: black suits and robes today.

Evening light slants golden into the ravine below us, picking up a mystic vermilion from its clay mounds. Ibn Gabirol is a beardless youth. Curly black hair hanging to his shoulders frames a feminine, olive-skinned face dominated by large, intense brown eyes. I know his every mood so well, especially when he stares into nothing, lost in the world of his poetic creations. My plan has sent him into a trance of poesy, as his imagination soars with the beauty I intend.

'There shall be a full sea, matching Solomon's sea,
yet not resting on an ox,
but there are lions, in phalanx on its rim, seeming to
roar for prey, these whelps
whose bosoms are like wells gushing forth to water
the myrtle garden, fragrant from its white blossoms . . .'

He turns to gaze at me, taking in with affectionate eyes the hawklike visage, the square grey beard covering a lantern jaw, the huge beaked nose straddling my dark, unfathomable eyes. Beneath the black *yarmulke* my head is completely bald. 'It is well for us both to dream, my lord,' he addresses me soberly. 'But how will our Caliph, King Abdullah, react to your having a palace more impressive than his, rising above his own residence, cresting even the great city of *al-Birah*?'

Sure of myself and of my indispensability to the king, I laugh confidently. 'He should be pleased that his servant, the Vizier, has created a residence that is proof of devotion to him, total dedication to his welfare and,' I drop to a whisper, 'a rare genius for making a silken purse out of a sow's ear!'

'Sacrilege!' The poet lifts a hand in mock protest. 'You call our king the ear of a sow?'

'Because he always hears but will not often listen!'

'A sow is as odious to a Muslim as it is to us Jews.'

'You are the poet. Why do you not change the metaphor then?' I am full of the silent amusement of a man who knows himself to be the superior of his master but never openly displays that knowledge.

'I would rather say you have put a potential Muslim beggar on the fine Arab steed of a prosperous kingdom.'

'Very well then, poet, you keep the metaphor and I shall retain my truth.'

'But, lord, a man may still not stand taller than his king in audience.'

'In Jahweh's great audience hall, the earth, any man can stand taller than another if he has the height. Does not the eagle soar high above the Emperor?'

Ibn changes direction. I am aware of his thoughts and love him the more for his precociousness in debate. 'Why must you choose this most difficult site, my lord?' The title is interposed to convince me of the humility of his approach, but he is not a humble man! 'How can you possibly build on it?'

Now I can feel the passion of my mission making my dark eyes gleam. I have never divulged to him what I am about to say. How does a mature man share a fantasy with anyone? 'When I was in Rome last year, I was conducted through the villa built centuries ago by the Emperor Hadrian. I fell in love with it, and I have dreamed of owning such a residence ever since.' I cannot prevent the obsession showing in my expression. 'You, a poet, must know better than anyone else what it is to be consumed by a dream.'

The tremor of passion in my voice becomes uncontrollable. 'When I saw that villa, I knew why I had toiled so hard these many, many years. Most Viziers of the Caliphs have been of our race. Why? Because we are men of rare intellect, often of genius, of honesty and dedication to our masters. What is our reward? Constant insults as a race. We are always looked down upon, even by the masters we serve so faithfully.' My eyes drift downwards to the ravine below. 'A palace built here will be like the eyrie of an eagle, isolated, well above the reach of petty mortals, be they kings or beggars.'

'Will you not develop a god complex, lord?' The concern in Ibn Gabirol's voice robs the question of any offence.

My smile becomes enigmatic. 'Are we not all the children of God and therefore gods?'

'If the palace is separated from the rest of the city, would it not be a target for any invader?' the poet persists. Then, perceiving the strength of my motivation, he starts visibly, his hands tightening on the reins. His horse stamps an impatient foot, the hoof scraping against granite rock. 'You would be willing to take that risk in order to spend one single night in your creation, well above the scorn of men,' his brown eyes widen, 'lying above them on the bed of your own contempt for lesser mortals.' The words of comprehension come out slowly. 'Even one single night of superior bliss.'

'Yes.' My answer is a hiss.

Convinced at last that it would be futile to try and shake me through fear of consequences from the Caliph, my adopted son attacks from another angle. He has the privilege, my sole beloved, for I have no other family. 'How could you possibly build a palace on such impossible terrain, lord?' He grins boyishly. 'Will you, like Aesop, have eagles carry baskets and boys in the air?'

He is referring to the dwarf Aesop, writer of fables, who built a temporary structure in the air to win a wager against the Pharaoh of Egypt and freedom for his country. I glance down again at the evening sunlight, fascinated by the vermilion it picks up from the clay mounds in the ravine. A red tower! That is it; my tower will turn to red each evening. An eastern breeze rustles through dark green cypresses, brings the scent of myrtle to distend my nostrils. I shall have a myrtle garden in my entrance courtyard. A covey of grey partridge scuttle across a small, green glade on the slope immediately beneath me. The setting sun shafts a ray of silver gold sideways to rest on the dark branches. 'An omen!' I exclaim. 'My palace shall rest above the ravine like a huge boat, the bows anchored just beneath us, the sides nestling between those two spurs,' I nod downwards, 'while the stern thrusts towards the flatlands yonder.'

'You would show your backside to the king?' A raucous laugh escapes Ibn Gabirol.

'What more fitting than that, having served the Caliph faithfully for over forty years, I should turn my back on him?' I am so easy with this poet, the one person I trust, even with my life. 'As for my . . . our,' I smile, 'safety, what I contemplate is a *hisn*, a fortress palace that will one day become a great city. The only problem I foresee

16

is that our water supply, coming from the mountains through aqueducts and cisterns, will make us vulnerable, but there is no reward without risk. Besides we shall be virtually impregnable from the north, where our Christian enemies lie, but open to the help of our friends, the Caliphs, from the south, across the seas.'

'What will you call your *hisn*, lord?'

Knowing me so well, the poet is certain that I already have a name for it. A gush of tenderness for him sweeps through me. 'I do indeed have a name, one that should insulate the *hisn* from the effects of the king's envy!' My lips curl in a cynical smile. 'I shall call it the Fort of God, *Allah Hamra*.'

Five years later my informers bring me the news that William of Normandy had invaded England, defeated King Harold in battle at Hastings and is now the conqueror and ruler of that country. King William's fortunes and mine seemed to coincide, for my *hisn* is finally completed.

The year is 1066 A.D.

Having removed my gold shoes, I stand at the threshold of my fortress palace, facing its entrance doors surrounded by attendants. Morning sunlight lies bright silver on the white flagstones of the courtyard and the line of fountains in the long narrow pool behind me. The stone sill is sacred to us Jews. I hold a bunch of hyssop in my hand, ready to sprinkle blood on the lintel, though it is many months after the Passover season. Affixed to a post of the huge ornamental wooden door is a small metal box, the *mezuzah*, containing on parchment the words of Deuteronomy 6: 4–9, 'Hear, O Israel: The Lord our God is one Lord; and you shall love the Lord your God with all your heart, and with all your soul, and with all your might . . . And you shall write these words on the doorposts of your house and on your gates.' My devotion

17

to Jahweh is complete, for He alone had led me to this, the threshold of my dream.

A faint clatter at the entrance gates reaches my ears, makes me pause. I half turn to gaze down the roadway. The clatter swiftly increases to the drumming of fast-cantering hooves.

Who dares disturb my peace on such a solemn occasion? It could not be bandits; my gate guards would have dealt with them.

I soon have my answer. As the group of horsemen thunders round the bend, I note the huge black-bearded figure wearing a gold tunic and gold turban, topped by a feather, leading them. My eyes gleam with pleasure. 'My cup runneth over!' I declare. 'For my lord, the Caliph, has made a special journey to honour me and my new abode with his pleasure!'

With a grinding of hooves, the group draws to a stop in front of me. The contrasting quiet is startling despite the pawing and snorting of horses.

As a young page leaps off his bay and runs to the king's side, I note my ruler's black eyes fixed on me. Why the malignance? A flicker of apprehension filters through me as the page helps the king dismount. One can never be certain of a king's disposition.

King Abdullah, dressed in cloth of gold, the great, curved royal scimitar dangling at his side, makes no attempt to come forward. He stands beside his horse, a huge sombre figure, legs wide apart, arms akimbo, exuding menace. For once in my life, I am nonplussed. With the blood-soaked sacred hyssop in my grasp, I cannot advance to kneel before the king and kiss his hand. I am quickly saved the need to make a decision.

'You see before you a beggar off his horse,' King Abdullah grates. He has a curiously husky voice. 'Or should we say, the sow's ear you tried to convert to a silken purse.'

18

A chill cold as the tombs runs through me, carrying within its grim shroud the anguished knowledge of betrayal. This is how my son, the young poet, earned my king's patronage two years ago. When he left me to join the king's court, I had been overjoyed, but it was not his talent for poetry alone that had won him the coveted prize. Betrayed, dear Jahweh, betrayed by the boy I raised from the gutters, betrayed by the only person I have ever trusted completely.

'We have waited two years to give you our answer to your insults, Jew!' The deadly quiet of the king's voice is more menacing than his words. 'We decided to let you build your eyrie, your *hisn*, using all the immense wealth you have accumulated through us combined with your boundless energy to complete it.' He laughs low, pauses then advances until he towers directly in front of me. I must confess that I tremble before his controlled wrath. He has possessed the knowledge for two years and I, the great genius, obsessed by my dream, never realized it. This king is more clever than I had imagined. The sharp scent of his musk, smudging the delicate fragrance of myrtle, sickens me. 'We have now come to take over your eyrie, for you are no eagle but a vulture.' White teeth bared in an evil smile, he slowly nods his head, the peacock plume on the turban shimmering.

At that moment, a miracle occurs. I clearly see Jahweh's will manifested and humbly accept it. I have presumed to challenge more than a Caliph with my dream. I have been arrogant before God. I have dared to permit a dream to consume me. Fierce Jahweh has led me to the threshold of the dream's realization before denying me even one day in its reality.

'Hear me a moment, O Caliph!' The words emerge from me with such quiet authority that King Abdullah pauses. 'It is the ancient law of my people and yours that a man wronged may extract vengeance from the wrongdoer. You are therefore right to be my executioner.' I pause, fixing deadly dark eyes on the massive figure before me. 'When you have taken my life, however, you will have robbed me of my most precious possession, more precious, as I see now, more important by far than the dwelling I have created for its shell, my body.' I raise the hyssop in my hand and shake it for effect. Tiny droplets of red blood flutter down to the stone apron beneath me. 'My spirit shall therefore remain at this spot to claim vengeance on you and your successors.' I pause again, hearing in triumph the deathly silence that has fallen on the entire group. 'I lay my curse upon this abode. All infidel rulers who dwell here shall, while they hold it more precious than life, know violent death or exile, for, like me, they will have placed these portals above Jahweh.'

I take one last look at the roadway, the courtyard I have built, the gardens splattering with the silver sparkle of fountains. I breathe the scent of the myrtle garden I created close to the entrance doors to commemorate that evening when I sat on my grey Arab charger above the ravine beside the poet-son who has turned out to be my betrayer. 'Whoever adds to my creation without humility shall pay the price, as I am about to do.'

My dark eyes widen with vision. Fanned by sudden unyielding anger, my voice rises. 'My *hisn* shall become a great city, Caliph, revered by all men for its beauty, when you have been forgotten. However, any ruler who challenges Jahweh's omnipotence when adding to my *hisn* shall be laid low within its walls, again and again, until my curse is lifted by those matchless enemies of Moorish rule, the Christians. Know, Abdullah, that you are about to turn my beauteous abode into the Arena of Assassins.'

The great scimitar swishes, thwacks, the last sound I hear. I know a moment of excruciating agony as the blade tears through flesh, bone and gristle. Not with sightless

20

eyes, but with the sudden stark vision of the dead, I see red blood spurting, the black *yarmulke* sliding off a bald head. The body that has been Yusuf ibn Nagralla begins to topple on the threshold of his Fort of Allah, Alhambra.

As the first eternal consciousness takes over, I hear the terrible voice of Jahweh thunder through the firmament:

By my decree all living things go, upon death, to their last living thought. You selected vengeance, foolish mortal. Even when you faced death, your wicked arrogance did not cease, for the revenge you sought was against My laws of cause and effect. You therefore transported yourself to the perdition of a senseless revenge against people who have not harmed you. This estate you willed for yourself will not cease, under My inexorable laws, until no one dwells in your hisn *as its master. Only then will your perdition cease, and allow you to enter the peace of My abode.*

By my own last words had I been condemned.

You who have come after me these many centuries and have witnessed the beauty and perfection of the dream I could not enjoy, read the words that emerge from my spirit through the pen of a true lover of beauty as he recreates my tale.

No crowned head rested in peace within these Allah Hamra portals, even though the scent of myrtle remained. Fearing my curse, for nearly two centuries few of the successors of King Abdullah did much to embellish my abode. Indeed, one of them, more fearful than the rest, even partially destroyed it.

Then came a new breed, more addicted to creating beauty than to the dictates of good sense: the Banu Nasr dynasty which claimed descent from Sad-bin-Abada, a companion of the Holy Prophet and chief of the Khazraj tribe. The first Nasrid to make Granada his permanent home was Mohamed I, in 1236. His successor Mohamed

PART I

The Arena

Chapter 1

King Yusuf had tried for years to protect his only son, whom he had named Mo-Ahmed al Kamal, the Perfect One, from the malign influence of the planets conjoined at the time of the boy's birth. Caliph of Granada since the Christian year 1333, he was the first ruler of Granada to bear the name of Yusuf. Prince Ahmed was now eighteen and had been reared in the Gen al Arif palace, which had been built especially to keep him in isolation for the past sixteen years.

Why should Prince Ahmed's Chief Tutor, Abou bon Ebben, who was virtually his warder, request an immediate audience, especially when he, King Yusuf, had returned only that morning from his victorious strike against the King of Castile?

Seated cross-legged that night in the lotus pose on the red-cushioned dais-throne ottoman in the private audience chamber of the Daraxa, the living quarters of the Alhambra palace, after the victory celebration dinner, King Yusuf contemplated the question while he waited for Abou bon Ebben to be ushered in. Every Moorish ruler who resided in the Alhambra palace knew of the curse laid upon it by Yusuf ibn Nagralla and had reacted in their own way. His own father might well have named him Yusuf to appease the dead Jew.

Had the death of his beloved young wife, Mariam, been a product of the curse because he had begun to add to and embellish the palace soon after ascending the throne, even though he had tried to keep humility in his heart? In his own case, there was yet another source of guilt. His Prime Minister, Farouk Riswan, had organized his suc-

25

cession by arranging for his brother, King Mohamed IV, to be stabbed to death by the poinards of a band of Christians. Dear Allah, the things one does when one is young! He could not have anticipated that his brother's remains, naked and mangled, would be flung into a ravine without even a decent burial. He had feared, increasingly as he grew older, that Allah would punish him through his son and heir, a succession denied for one obtained through murder was typical of the Almighty's justice.

His thoughts were interrupted when Abou bon Ebben was announced. The old man hastened into the room with a rustle of black robes and knelt to kiss the royal hand. When he arose and squatted on bended knees, buttocks on heels, before the marble table, King Yusuf observed in the golden light of the scented oil lamps that his wrinkled cheeks were trembling and there was even a limpness to his flowing white beard. Why?

It was good to be back in the luxury and routine of his palace after three months of Spartan existence in the field, though like all Moorish kings he carried a miniature palace of tents into battle. He had enjoyed an excellent dinner and was now granting an audience in his favourite chamber. The room was supported by slender columns, the cornices joined in graceful arches of filigreed arabesques. Crystal oil lamps lined the walls, their glow falling on carved gold and marble ornaments in wall niches, the arches of which were decorated with rich mosaics of gold- and silver-threaded Damascene ceramic chips. His attendants had placed on the table a gold pitcher with slender curving handle and spout containing his favourite wine – Allah forgive him the transgression! – a fresh, young Valdepeñas straight from its large earthenware *tinaja*. What more could he want? And yet apprehension was curling around his well-filled stomach, even though his spies had already reported to him before dinner that Prince Ahmed was in good health.

One of the lamps sputtered, as if in derision at his fears, wafting the scent of frankincense to his nostrils.

As was his usual custom, King Yusuf opened the conversation with courteous generalities. 'What think you, Sage, of our victory in battle against King Pedro of Castile and the capture of his son?'

'Argh, it is a most memorable event, Your Majesty, the first Moorish victory since your illustrious predecessor negotiated a ten-year truce with King Alfonso XI following our ignominious defeat at Salado. Granada has never been conquered by the white Christian infidel Spaniards, not even when they retook northern Castile and Aragon that had been Moorish for five centuries. Your bold strike has sent a message to all the Christian kings that the Andalusian kingdom of Granada will remain invincible, its capital impregnable.'

'Indubitably, for our kingdom is protected by Allah, who placed it within the sunburnt summits of mountains mottled with the variegated colours of marble and granite that form the entrance to southern Spain.' King Yusuf found himself waxing poetic. 'Lush valleys planted with wheat, rice, figs, oranges and citrons, myrtle and rose, wind long and narrow below these stark tops, making Granada an oasis which we Moors have ornamented not only with our buildings but with our control of water to create gardens, which in the desert land are synonymous with Paradise.'

Both men knew that the capital, also named Granada, was approached through the frontier of Loxa, an unassailable fortress built along the face of an arid mountain, with the River Xenil washing its base. The royal palace formed only a part of the capital, which was a fortress, its walls overlooking the city within studded with towers, stretching irregularly round the whole west side of a hilly spur of the Sierra Nevada, the Snowy Mountains. Viewed from outside, one saw only a rough collection of towers and battlements. Once inside, however, unbelievable grace and beauty greeted the senses.

'It is no wonder that the Spanish kings have always panted for Granada,' King Yusuf continued euphorically. 'Small wonder too that they could never grasp it. When they were close to seizing it, Almighty Allah intervened by hurling the Black Death at White Christian Europe.' He needed to get to the subject of the audience. 'We and our son, Prince Ahmed, are therefore safe from outsiders in Granada. It is against the foes within the kingdom that we must maintain our security. We trust that your ward, our only son and heir, is safe and well?' He deliberately used the words 'your ward', injecting them with menace, to remind bon Ebben of his responsibility for the wellbeing of the heir.

'Prince Ahmed is indeed safe and well.' The sage's dry, crackly voice became nervous.

'Good.' King Yusuf eased his cramped right leg forward for comfort. Elbow on knee, finger to chin, he became more expansive now that he had been reassured as to his son's wellbeing. 'You arrived in our palace from the Court of the Pharaoh of Egypt on the very day Almighty Allah blessed us with the divine gift of a son. We considered this a sign from Allah, since our famed astrologer, Siddi el Ziman, had on that very day warned us of danger to our son, whom we named Mo-Ahmed al Kamal, the Perfect One. The Siddi foretold that Prince Ahmed would have a long and illustrious reign if love did not destroy him before his twenty-first year. You advised us not to worry, for you would take over care of Prince Ahmed and protect him from love, if we would only build him a luxurious new palace, complete with pleasure gardens, on the mountain across the ravine from our Allah Hamrah, to isolate him from any contact with other human beings.' An inquiring eyebrow cocked at bon Ebben invited a response but brooked no contradiction.

28

By restating the facts, King Yusuf sought to cast full responsibility for any problem on the sage, for all the good it would do.

'And you did build the Gen al Arif palace high above the Alhambra for Prince Ahmed and had it completed within two years, Sire,' bon Ebben commenced. 'It is as unsurpassed in the beauty of its gardens and bowers as it is secure from intrusion. Prince Ahmed has lived there since he was two under my personal supervision – sixteen years now – isolated from all possible sources of human love. His attendants have been old, ugly, black deaf mutes. His tutors, though the finest in religion and deportment, languages, mathematics, astronomy, history, politics, government, equestrianism, military strategy and the martial arts, including wrestling and acrobatics, have been wrinkled veterans. I have personally ensured that the prince has had no communion of an emotional nature with any man or woman, boy or girl. He has never even had direct exposure to human youth and beauty.' The parchment voice cracked. 'With the greatest effort of self-control, I have held back my own affection for the boy.'

Was the sage trying to build up credit against ill news? 'We ourselves have not seen Prince Ahmed for over sixteen years,' King Yusuf grated. His tone conveyed enormous sacrifice, but he well knew that time and separation had resulted in little or no personal feelings for his son. 'To a parent, that is a sacrifice of historic proportions. It must not have been in vain!' He shot a chilling glance at bon Ebben. 'For his personal safety as well as for the nation, any ruler needs a worthy son and heir. If the traditional line of succession is not ensured, the king becomes a target for men of ambition.' He refrained from adding that ambitious heirs, such as he himself, had always been a more deadly source of danger to a monarch than his worst enemies.

The kneeling bon Ebben quailed visibly. 'Now, more

than ever, in view of your victory over King Pedro the Cruel, it is essential to safeguard Your Majesty's sacred person. But Almighty Allah is on our side.'

'Yes indeed. We have already sent word of our victory to our brother in North Africa, King Abu Hasan of Morocco, requesting him to despatch an army so that we can spread the Holy Koran throughout all Spain, using fire and sword in our *jihad*, holy war. This will also honour our ancestors.'

'The Nasrid dynasty is better known throughout the world than any other, Sire.'

'Yes indeed. Our ancestors conquered nearly all of Spain because they were vastly superior in birth and religion to the mongrel collection of Celts, Iberians, Goths, Visigoths, Romans and other European riff-raff that formed its native population. Our decline started only in the last century.' His dark eyes narrowed; his dark voice rang out. 'But make no mistake. We shall end that decline and re-establish Islam throughout Spain and bring civilization back to it.' His eyes smouldered. 'Today Spain, tomorrow Europe, and then the world, with an Islamic Empire that stretches once again from the Atlantic to the Indian Ocean. A legacy for our son.'

'You will create a mighty legacy for him, Sire.'

The sage's words brought King Yusuf back once more to the main purpose of the audience. 'Indubitably.' He jerked an impatient finger at bon Ebben. 'Tell us why you requested an audience. Tell us, tell us.' He had developed a habit of repeating urgent words for emphasis when he was impatient. He now added his fingers, rapidly gesturing inwards.

'Prince Ahmed's spirit is confused, Sire, by a yearning that has made him rebel against his routine.'

'Yearning? For what? For what?'

'Argh, I am sure he does not know himself, Sire.'

King Yusuf chuckled with relief. 'It is the nature of

youth to rebel for things it cannot identify, sage. Or are you so long past your own youth that you have forgotten? Yes indeed, when the physical health is good, some rebellion is to be expected from men of spirit.' Another chuckle escaped him. 'Rebellion, which is also the privilege of youth, is part of the innate independence essential in a future ruler.'

The ancient sage did not seem reassured. He cleared his throat. 'The situation is a little more complex than a display of independence, Your Majesty. I'm afraid that we wrongly assumed from the beginning that the physical senses, communion with humans and attraction by their beauty or kindness are the main causes of love. Prince Ahmed's recent conduct has made me realize that love exists even when it is not directly inspired by outside entities, being an inherent force within all beings that clamours to surge forth, normally towards a parent, a child, a friend, a lover, a wife, or even an animal, as the effect of a multiplicity of causes, tangible and intangible, identifiable and undiscovered. Need for a home, a nest, a lair is part of it. These repressed urges within Prince Ahmed have finally erupted. Since he cannot even identify them, he is directing them elsewhere.' The sage stopped with bowed grey head, sweat beads rolling down his wrinkled cheeks.

'What is *elsewhere*?' the king demanded harshly. 'Speak up. Speak up.'

'All of Nature, Sire.'

'You mean, Prince Ahmed loves Nature?' King Yusuf's voice indicated his hope that this would be all.

'Yes, Sire,' bon Ebben murmured. 'He has directed his love force to Nature, adoring its beauty with a sensitivity that transcends any in my experience. He is his father's son, the true aesthete, worshipping at beauty's shrine, needing to give expression to his adoration.' He raised grey eyes to the king at the proper level, just below the

31

royal gaze. 'Soon after you left three months ago to give battle to the Spaniards, Prince Ahmed abandoned his studies. He took to walking in the walled gardens of the Gen al Arif palace daily, expressing his love for trees, shrubs and flowers in poems and songs of his composition. Yesterday, for instance, he serenaded a rosebush, accompanying himself on his lute.'

The king's laugh rang free. He reached for his wine pitcher, raised its spout to his lips and took a swallow. The smooth liquor added to his relief. 'Our son is a poet and a musician who loves Nature. Since he has also displayed extraordinary prowess in his military training, all is well. No bush, tree or flower can harm him.' The smile had reached his hard, dark eyes at last. 'You are being over-conscientious, sage, for which we commend you.'

A lizard chirped its warning. King Yusuf felt a tremor in a superstitious gut.

'I am relieved, Sire,' bon Ebben replied, but his voice lacked conviction.

The people of the kingdom of León y Navarra, which King Charles II ruled, included an ancient race antedating even the original Iberian tribes of Spain, who had for centuries been free peasants, shepherds, fishermen, navigators, miners and metalworkers giving allegiance only to their own chieftains, the Counts. Even to Rome the Basque country had been subject only nominally. The native Basques were hardy, cunning, fierce warriors, whom it took special qualities to lead; even the powers of their rulers were circumscribed by their Cortes, the assemblies of the people. Their independence had been immortalized in the *Song of Roland*, which celebrated one of the twelve original peers of Charlemagne who died in battle at the strategic Pass of Roncesvalles, between France and Navarre in the Pyrenees.

Not being a Basque, deep, deep down inside him, King Charles felt an interloper. His royal family had ruled the kingdom only for four generations, commencing with Louis I, followed by Philip II and Charles I. His own mother, Joanna II, had been the niece of Charles I and had succeeded to the throne because the Salic law forbidding the succession of female descendants or their heirs did not apply in Spain. His father had been Philip, Count of Evreux, who was therefore Prince Regent while Charles was growing up.

All of this and his mother's intense preoccupation with plotting to become Queen and thereafter with affairs of State, made him very lonely as a boy, determined to achieve fame in his own right regardless of right and wrong. So he had been Prince Charles the Bad, he frequently reflected, with a snicker at the word, even before he succeeded his mother and became King Charles the Bad, the estate of kingship having merely expanded the territory in which he could practise badness. After all, what was this badness but the way in which a timorous world perceived the independent gratification of his ambitions and desires!

The only person whom King Charles treated with deference was the Princess Mathilde of Beauvais. She had come to Pamplona, the capital of the kingdom, forty years earlier from Paris, to marry his uncle Prince René; but the prince had died suddenly of a stroke two days before the wedding. Although the marriage had been an arranged one, the seventeen-year-old princess had fallen in love with her dashing betrothed the moment she set eyes on him. So, moved by a grief she never displayed, she had elected to remain in Prince René's residence in the Pamplona palace. This was a time when kings built palaces large enough to provide luxurious quarters for princes and nobles, encouraging them to live in Court, where they could be easily detained, rather than in their feudal homes, where they might plot against their king.

Princess Mathilde had not left Pamplona since. Here she endured her continuing private heartache with commendable fortitude. 'After all, my dear,' she once remarked to Charles, 'an orgasm is no more than the culmination of a succession of strokes, while my poor René had only one!'

The one person King Charles had loved as a boy was Princess Mathilde. A small, silver-haired woman with the most elegant facial bones, delicate white skin and ever-merry black-pointed grey eyes, her manners were always as impeccable as her clothes and in sharp contrast with her unassuming personality and unpretentious ways. She had treated him as a human being from the first day he had been presented to her and had immediately become his French teacher and eternal friend.

By the time he succeeded to the throne, King Charles had grown so close to Princess Mathilde that he not only permitted her to remain in Prince René's quarters, which had virtually become hers by right of possession, but had them expanded and decorated. He was soon treating her as his unofficial adviser. After all, was it not she who had manoeuvred him to the throne by her charming wit and seemingly guileless cunning?

Wearing a long dress of light blue, tight at the waist and with a pink collar against her white skin, she knelt and kissed his hand in her large reception room. He made it a point to visit her every evening before dinner, and frequently had luncheon or dined alone with her whenever his duties permitted. He not only enjoyed her company, but found her quarters, which he had personally helped redesign, soothing. The loveseats and centre tables were ornate gilt, upholstered in black and white striped satin, with white Flemish carpets on black marble floors. Crystal glass lamps, gold-plated to match the furniture, shed a soft golden glow on the room and on the large oil paintings, the one above the mantelpiece being of Prince René in the pink-white, dark browns and golds of the northern painters. Though it was a hot summer evening, a log fire embered red-gold, highlighting a copper fire-screen, tongs and pokers and somehow enhanced the black and white swagged curtains adorning the two huge bay windows opening out to a balcony, beyond which he could see the dark outline of chestnut trees against a deep blue sky. Incense braziers emitted grey wisps of smoke tinted with a delicate sandalwood fragrance. All very soothing.

King Charles sat on his usual loveseat, while Princess Mathilde took her place on a settle opposite him. He never used the royal plural when he was alone with her. 'I love the peace and subdued elegance of this room,' he declared quietly.

'You should,' she responded brightly, her voice golden as the lamp-glow. 'You created it. People generally feel comfortable with the things they create. Just surroundings, not necessarily children!'

He laughed. Why did he never guffaw with this woman? he wondered for the umpteenth time. How did she bring out in him all the refinements of the ruling class which had been inculcated into him since his earliest days, when his more natural inclination was to shock and dominate? 'The stillness is your very own,' he declared, sounding as if he had delivered a quiet edict.

She picked up his thoughts. 'You are yourself with me,' she responded. 'This is not necessarily what you want to be all the time. It is *you* with *me*. We have always been the way we want to be with each other. You know that if you had ever wanted to stand on your head in this room, I would simply have enjoyed it. Even if you had not done it well, I would have applauded the impulse and the effort, and what went on here would have been for us alone, never to be shared with anyone else. That is the true basis of trust, the ability to be completely honest with someone else and not fear consequences.'

'Like a baby with its mother before all the teaching and the corrections start,' he observed wonderingly, for they had never discussed this before.

'Exactly.'

'God's body! Is that how you have thought of me?'

A light trill of amusement escaped her. 'Heavens, no, my dear.' Her face turned serious, her head tilted on one side as she was wont to do when she was thinking. 'I have always thought of you as you,' she finally said.

'Just Charles.'

'Not even that, for Charles gives you, the real you, a sort of identity. Human beings are like chefs, forever needing to paint labels on their ingredients: saffron, cinnamon, pepper and the like. Since they only look at the label, they sometimes reach for pepper when they want basil. With people the labels are wife, mistress, lover, friend, enemy, and . . . er . . . baby, or Charles! We paint the labels and *trust*, trust, mark you, those who are beneath any title to perform accordingly. When they do not, we call them unreliable, perfidious, more labels.' She wrinkled her pert nose. 'Such dreadful, common things, labels. Redolent of mongers who mark their fish fresh even when it stinks of putrefaction.'

'Are you saying that you label nothing then, dear Princess?' he demanded incredulously.

'I do not have to label fish to know it is rotten,' she retorted, a flash of white teeth removing any hint of acerbity from the remark. 'I just know it is inedible without resorting to vulgar analysis, such as that my nose, or my eyes, or my mouth tell me so.' Her smile broadened and she tickled the side of her mouth with a delicate white little finger, the nails painted silver to match her hair.

'In just the same way that you know when *I* am rotten?'

36

'There is no such thing as rotten with people, my dear. And if there were, you would never be rotten in *my* eyes.' She paused. A mischievous expression crossed her face. 'But only because I do not apply labels, remember?'

Knowing that this last was her way of removing sentiment from the loving statement expressed to make the love more definite, he was deeply touched. Some instinct made him want to run to her, kneel down and place his head on her lap like a little boy. Some deep love for her held him back. Stunned by the revelations, he merely gazed at her, his normally fierce eyes melting.

'I am glad you did not do what you wanted to, my dear,' she said with great quietude, only the slight pause before the last word betraying her great emotion. She nodded slowly at his astonishment that she had known what he was thinking. 'You should not be amazed at my perception, for I was created from your fifth rib, though you took so much longer than me to arrive.' Her voice sank; the slender nostrils dilated once. She stared across the room into the distance. 'What other joys there would have been if I had only arrived after you,' she whispered. 'And yet, that might have spoilt everything through the possessiveness that runs with such unions. Who knows? This was the way God intended it, so we could be what we have been to each other all these years. Otherwise,' she straightened her slender shoulders, returned twinkling grey eyes, quizzical now with their crinkling sides, 'we might have been nothing to each other but labels.'

A hidden sadness about her told him that she would have preferred the experiment to forty years of solitude, yes, solitude, he knew with a spurt of savagery at life. For he had realized in a blinding flash of knowledge that he wished the same. At that moment, he was tempted to ask her to marry him, but he immediately rejected the thought. The proposal, the event, the estate would debase her, even if she accepted it, which he knew she would not.

Once again she picked up his thoughts with that uncanny sensitivity to him. 'No labels, please, my dear, dear you.' Yet had her voice broken slightly at the word, 'please'?

'No labels,' he promised. And the moments were over, leaving him curiously fulfilled with the knowledge, curiously empty with the reality.

'Although you are so different in features and build to my dear René,' he heard her say, 'there is something of him within you. My recognition of it tells me that I am fated, by God's will, to lost causes.'

He stared at the painting above the mantelpiece, trying to work out what she meant. 'What was his ambition?' he finally inquired. 'Did you ever determine in the short time you knew him?'

Her grey eyes drifted to the picture, as if the answer lay there. 'To be the Emperor,' she replied quietly. 'That is one of the things you have in common with him. You want to be the Emperor of all Europe, ruler of Spain, Portugal, Italy, the Swiss *cantons*, the German States, France, the Flemish and Nordic countries, even England, not just of a fictitious, farcical Holy Roman Empire.'

His head jerked towards her. He was hard put to hold his jaw firm. He gripped his black beard fiercely. 'How did you know?' he demanded almost harshly, though he felt only a great wonder, brightened by a ray of relief that somebody understood at last. 'I have not spoken . . .' he paused, recognizing the futility of what he had been about to say. He wriggled his bull head on neckless shoulders.

She returned his look. 'Your mind carried the thought to your breath, your breath to your lungs, which touched your fifth rib with the news which I have known a long time. That is why I plotted the course that made you

38

king.' The grey eyes grew hard for a moment, 'Even had two contenders . . . removed for the purpose.'

'*You* did?' He could not believe his ears. Then suddenly it all fell into place, the way Prince Philip and Count Alfonso had died suddenly, one of food poisoning, the other thrown from a galloping horse when his saddle strap broke unaccountably. 'You did all that for me?'

'For you, anything, my dear. Anything you achieve, *I* achieve. Any heart's desire you satisfy, satisfies me.' Raising graceful fingers, she stroked back a wayward strand of hair from her white brow. 'Which is why you must take some short cuts.'

'Short cuts? Why?'

'They make the attainment of ambitions easier. You need to commence your programme while you are young enough to campaign and to enjoy the fruits of your endeavours. It would never do for you to become Emperor at sixty; by then you would have forgotten why you wanted to be there in the first place!' A decisive note entered her voice. 'You must become the ruler of white Christian Spain without delay, and take over the Moorish kingdom of Granada immediately after. You will then be powerful enough to conquer Portugal, by which time I will have set in motion the forces that will unseat that seedless water melon, John II, who has just succeeded to the Portuguese throne and then help you take over my beloved France. Next, you will free His Holiness the Pope from his Babylonish captivity by Avignon and, with his grateful help, become ruler of Italy and Switzerland, after which you will be able to dictate terms to the German States.'

'That is an extremely ambitious programme,' he asserted, shaking his head to clear it. Yet the realization began to dawn on him that what this remarkable woman said was not only possible but what he desired with all his heart.

'You are a man of phenomenal ambition,' she countered, the steel in her voice matching her grey eyes. 'Charlemagne did it. You can do better. *I* will provide the plan, the timing. *You* furnish the drive.'

'What a team we would make.' The words escaped him without thought as the future opened before him. 'You with the beauty and brains. I, with the ugliness and bull force. Irresistible.' For the first time ever with her, he guffawed. 'Is this how empires are created?'

'Empires commence with a thought. One moment there is nothing, except perhaps for a vague dissatisfaction or longing, the next there is the thought. Where does it begin? Who knows? With Alexander the Great, it may have been his bastard birth. What does it matter when, where or how an Empire is created, any more than it matters how you and I came together. What is important is that your Empire commenced even before our first consciousness of each other.' She paused. 'The Emperor Charles I. I like the sound of that. No Charlemagne II for you, as if you were some kind of left-over pudding!'

He grinned hugely. 'What's my next step?'

'The shortcut to ruling a united white Christian Spain. You must marry Princess Beatrice, who is heir to the Castilian throne.'

'What?'

'You will soon receive intimation of a tourney which King Pedro of Castile intends to hold for all eligible princes and counts of Europe, the prize being the hand in marriage of his daughter, Princess Beatrice, whom King Pedro has named his heir. I have engineered this, as part of my plan for you through King Pedro's mistress Maria de Padilla and King Pedro himself, though they each believe the idea to be their own! The winner will of course succeed to the throne of Castile . . . in due course, which is definitely too long and obscure a timeframe in your

40

case. You will accept the invitation, win the tourney and the . . . um . . . fair maid and take over Castile.'

When King Charles left her suite, Princess Mathilde walked to the great bay windows and thoughtfully surveyed the quiet scene.

Pamplona had laid its hold on her heart soon after she crossed the Roncesvalles Pass forty years earlier, even before she saw Prince René for the first time and he captured all her heart. Lying at the foot of the Pyrenees, though enshrined within lonely peaks, it was surrounded by pine trees, wild roses and water cascades, all so idyllic in comparison with the more undulating green lands, great woods and low hills of her native Beauvais in northern France. She even preferred the cathedral here to that of Beauvais, which was reputed at that time to be the tallest in Europe. Her marriage to Prince René was to have helped strengthen the alliance between France and Navarre, King Philip IV of France having acceded to the throne of Navarre in 1305 upon the death of his wife, Queen Joan of Navarre, Countess of Champagne.

God had spared her and Prince René the consequences of being part of the centre of an alliance troubled by King Philip's aggressive European ambitions. She smiled at recalling how self-willed she had been at the time. Even at seventeen she was capable of manipulating people and events to her desires.

She had loved the Pamplona court with its lesser degree of formality and its more relaxed people. The thought of returning to cold Beauvais, an eligible but unlucky female, to become a marital pawn once more in the international power game had been totally abhorrent to her. So she had manoeuvred King Philip and his successors into letting her remain in Pamplona, at first with the excuse that she was considering becoming a nun in the convent there.

41

She had influenced successive rulers in the reconstruction of the palace and Court life, but soon realized that she could never wield that kind of power with Queen Joanna, King Charles's mother. The woman was not only aloof and domineering, she was very French and did not need another French woman to teach her anything. Princess Mathilde had wisely decided not to risk the security of her stay by antagonizing the queen, whose heart condition would take her away some day. Instead, she came to find enormous satisfaction in the affection of the heir to the throne, the young, bull-like Prince Charles, with whom she shared an unspoken detestation of his mother. Princess Mathilde had never discouraged Prince Charles's silent rebellion against the rigidities of court life or his naturally fierce independence. Being cunning but not too intelligent, he could be manipulated by a greater intellect towards the fulfilment of his dreams of power, so she bided her time, knowing her day would come.

And it did come. By the time Queen Joanna died and Prince Charles ascended the throne, he was virtually in her power, though neither he nor anyone else for that matter, including the sagacious Chancellor, Count Gaston, suspected it. The badness was exclusively Charles's, and her acumen became ascribed to him. His rough, bluff exterior made a wonderful front for her sleek, smooth plotting. She was probably the one person in the world whom he trusted completely and to whom he would give uncompromising loyalty, but she never put these to the test. She was content to let him be himself and always be there for him. Were they not two of a kind? Each for the other, like night-dews on desert plants, she now reflected.

What did she feel for him? On the rare occasions when she asked herself the question, she skirted it, as now. She planned for him, wanted him to achieve whatever he desired, preached to him maternally. That was enough.

Nightfall, a magic time in a magic country. How hard it was to believe that this warm, gentle air was being breathed by such a fierce, indomitable people. Monuments of battle were enfolded for many a mile in the darkness. At Calahorra, Sertorius fought Pompey, at Numantia, the Basques defied Scipio Aemilianus's eight-month blockade.

She could barely discern the elaborately laid out gardens, their straight water courses supplying cascades and great fountains, segmenting rectangles of dark cypress, pruned bushes and multi-coloured flower beds.

Her attention was caught by the splash of a fountain. As her eyes fell on the silver water gleaming through the darkness of the great square courtyard, she recalled that it had been she who encouraged King Charles to follow the Moorish tradition and have the canal bringing water from the mountains improved to serve the entire capital, including flush toilets and steam baths copied from the Alhambra for the palace.

Within the huge palace itself, there was not much she could have done to improve on Queen Joanna's artistry: marble floors, painted ceilings, many of them adorned with frescoes, gilded moulding on birch panelling, huge coloured tapestries and carpets from newly emerging Aubusson, Belgian crystal, gold plate, African ivory ornaments.

Mathilde had also convinced King Charles that he should continue his mother's policy of making the royal court the centre of all the country's pleasure, so he not only hunted frequently with his courtiers but also continued to give grand balls, fêtes, firework displays, plays, concerts and river rides. Apart from its impact on the people, these splendid events were essential to keep the nobles, living away from their country mansions, from being bored. Also, she openly advised King Charles, such occasions required grand clothes and ostentatious jewellery, which placed many of the nobles, already absentee landlords, in such debt that they did not have the means to raise the rebel troops.

No one should of course outshine the king. Since her Charles loathed ostentation, she persuaded him that he liked to wear black all the time, adorned only by glittering jewels appropriate for the occasion, his clothes thus serving as a background for a dazzling effect, the bull draped for *fiesta*, as he once remarked.

Having laid the foundations well, the time had finally arrived to build the monument. Excitement tingled through her veins as she turned back from the night to face the chamber again. It was symbolic. Under her guidance, King Charles II would emerge from the beauty of darkness to the splendour of light.

Chapter 2

Black thigh boots clacking on the white marble floors, King Pedro strode towards his study in the Toledo palace. In a vile mood, he deliberately avoided reducing his pace to accommodate his companion, above whom he towered, finding savage satisfaction in forcing the plump, purple-robed Bishop Eulogius to twinkle along beside him on short legs.

He caught his image in the lamp glow of one of the gilt mirrors lining the walls as an extension of the power and ferocity of his inner being. Not even defeat could diminish him. No wonder men call me the Cruel, he reflected. I look a monster and I *am* a monster. My build is massive, my shoulders are powerful, my huge waist is solid without an ounce of fat on it. My ruddy complexion matches my red beard and my fierce blue eyes, gifts of the devil himself! I personally hacked off the heads of twenty of the seven hundred men who came with Don Fadique to rescue Blanche, my discarded queen. I have laughed in the face of those civic commissions that have dared to question my libertine actions and express disapproval of my delight in torturing and brutally slaying anyone who opposes me. Let all men fear me, for my path is strewn with blood. I don't need their love.

When he heard that King Yusuf had sallied forth from the Granada capital immediately the ten-year truce period had ended, he had in his usual fashion unhesitatingly advanced to meet the enemy. His defeat had been humiliating, but it was not the end of the world, especially as the heretic Moor had withdrawn to his base after battle. The capture of his son, Prince Juan, was an added humiliation, but it did not bother King Pedro as much as it would have done before he declared his illegitimate daughter, Princess Beatrice, his heir in place of his only son.

As he strode along, King Pedro tried to tell himself that he had nothing to fear. The capital city of Castile, Toledo, located on a granite hill protected on three sides by a gorge of the River Tagus, was virtually impregnable. Of pre-Roman origin, now surrounded by partly Gothic, partly Moorish walls, it had finally fallen to the Romans only in 193 B.C. The Alcantara bridge across the River Tagus provided the only major approach into the city, so he had good cause to feel secure. Why then did he not?

Was it because a voice within him questioned, Are not the enemies within the Church, your fellow white Christian kings and the little cleric walking beside you? It dawned on him that, while he was merely cruel, Bishop Eulogius was evil. He wanted to be ruler of a Spanish Empire. What did the bishop want? Realizing that he did not know the answer, fingers of unease gripped King Pedro's heart.

The Bishop of Toledo had white sweaty skin covering a cherubic, innocent face, the plump cheeks ever ready to crinkle and dimple in the smile he now gave, the merry ice-blue eyes vanishing into their folds. Yet something else lurked behind those eyes. This man who had clawed his way from the obscure origins of his petty merchant ancestry to become primate of the five Catholic bishoprics of Spain must be dangerous.

Leading off the main palace hallway, King Pedro's study was a small, oak-panelled room lined with shelves containing brown leather-bound manuscripts, the covers inscribed with gilt lettering. Though he was not a scholarly man, being given more to battle, jousting, drinking, carousing and love-making, King Pedro loved this room. Yet his one real love was Maria de Padilla, who had gently led him into real love-making, instead of merely lusting for female bodies. Having found true caring in the arms of his Maria, who had once been a lady-in-waiting to his former queen, he longed for her welcome in her bedchamber tonight, as soon as he had finished with Bishop Eulogius.

Unlike the princesses he had married and cast off at will, harlots who, having sold their birth for his royal marital bed, remained cold and indifferent upon it, Maria of the pale hands and face, of the tender heart, truly loved him and expressed her love in every glance, every word, every action. When he discarded his wife, Blanche of France, he had married Juana de Castro, sister of the Portuguese king. She had given him his only son, Prince Juan, but now, eighteen years later, he acknowledged only Maria as his queen, though uncrowned, and had even made his oldest child by her, the sixteen-year-old Beatrice, of bastard birth, a princess and named her his heir.

Strangely enough, the tall red-haired Prince Juan had accepted his disinheritance in a spirit of sweet charity. Now, that same self-righteous Christian prick was the prisoner of the circumcised prick, King Yusuf of Granada. God had certainly dealt King Pedro some severe blows in recent years.

The comforting glow from the hanging glass lamps, tinctured by the barely perceptible reek of burnt oil, and the large paintings of bullfights normally soothed him. One in particular of a matador administering the *coup-de-grâce* to a great black bull, was a symbol of those triumphant moments when he himself dealt the death-blow, not to animals, but to men. Tonight, nothing eased King Pedro's restlessness.

He sat on the curved wooden chair, indicated the matching one across the great oaken desk to the bishop. He placed elbows on the arms of this chair to slide it back

47

and stretch out his massive legs. 'Fuck everything!' he growled, pleasantly opening the conversation.

'You are troubled, Your Majesty.' Bishop Eulogius had a soft, husky voice, gentle of expression, the words always incanted as if part of a Latin liturgy. 'And with good cause. You have just suffered the first defeat of Christian forces since your father, King Alfonso XI, smote the heathen hip and thigh at the battle of Salado in 1340. The Moorish son of Satan, King Yusuf, barely allowed the ten-year truce to expire before he advanced across the peace zone. Unknown to us, he had been preparing the thrust all this time, probably since the Black Plague peaked two years ago causing us hellish destruction.' His sweet smile did not blunt the threat.

King Pedro knew that the cleric was angling for position, by driving a poinard in his back. It did not improve his mood, but he would not give the little ponce of the Church the satisfaction of showing any reaction. 'In truth, our father should never have accepted the truce. He should have driven the heathens back to North Africa, whence they came,' he responded, deliberately mild.

'Ah, but if he had done so, he would have weakened himself by having to govern all of South Eastern Spain, causing his allies the Kings of Aragon and Navarre to resent and fear his seeming power. What your royal father did achieve was the assertion of Reconquista, the re-establishment of Christianity in once conquered territories of our beloved country.'

Mule-shit, you hypocrite, King Pedro thought, with a return of savagery, but he was still determined not to react to the bishop's needling. 'We should have awaited our own allies this time before venturing to meet Yusuf when we received news of his advance three months ago,' he declared, adding piously, 'There is nothing like Christian unity.' He noted the bishop's eyes vanishing within the crinkle of amused cheeks. 'We would have turned the

48

tables on Yusuf too, if only he had pursued us. When we were beaten back by the sheer weight of the numbers of his mercenaries, we planned to retreat to the defiles and ravines of the hill country, trap him there and massacre his men. But he was too clever. He made his strike and withdrew.'

'All he wanted to do then was to test our mettle?'

'Curse him, yes,' King Pedro growled. 'God forsook us. The battle lost, we returned with our army to Toledo this afternoon to regroup, leaving Prince Juan a prisoner.' He wiped his brow with a linen cloth he pulled out from his sleeve. 'This damnable heat!' he cursed softly. 'How will our people take the reversal?' He drew his legs back and leaned forward, pounding the desk for emphasis so hard that it rattled upon the question. 'What will our Christian brother kings do? Turn round and rend us because they think we are the enfeebled lion? How will the Holy Father, Pope Clement VI, react from his exile in Avignon? And how will history judge us? Prithee, enlighten us.'

'The solutions to your situation are undoubtedly what you desired to speak to me about in private tonight,' Bishop Eulogius responded blandly.

'You are right, Bishop, but fuck it all, we could not even prepare you for the event with a good dinner.' He scowled at the recollection. Everything was going wrong.

'You certainly avenged our disappointed palates when you summoned your head cook and emptied the contents of the huge silver serving dish, complete with an entire roast calf, on his head.'

King Pedro roared with laughter in one of his mercurial changes of mood. He pointed a finger at the bishop. 'Did you notice how funny he looked, with white fat and brown gravy dripping down his grey locks and bits of spice littering his face?' He paused. 'But it didn't help our appetites, did it, having only chicken, bread and wine.

49

Ha!' He jerked his head up. 'The Rioja was good though, was it not?'

'Excellent, Your Majesty.'

'Wine does not go well with warm, summer nights, however.' King Pedro reached inside his black leather doublet, scratched a hairy armpit, wet with sweat. 'Fucking heat. Even makes the crotch itch in these tight black pantaloons.' He had a sudden thought. 'Easier for you though, because all you have to do is reach under your robe, like the Moors.' He laughed uproariously again. 'Tell us, Bishop, does a circumcised prick itch less than yours and mine in this heat? Or is your holy prick cool beneath that robe?'

A prim expression briefly crossed the primate's face. He was obviously unwilling to discuss anyone's private parts. Well, fuck him. King Pedro knew of Eulogius's secret lust for young maidens. The man was a voyeur who derived his satisfaction merely by looking at naked female bodies. That way, he could perhaps make the sign of the cross between ejaculations!

Suddenly, physical weariness overtook King Pedro. It had been a long, gruelling day. When he reached Toledo that afternoon, it had been after a tedious withdrawal and he had been met with accumulated problems from this three-month absence in the field.

The bishop's small mouth opened in a forced smile. Thin red lips parting sideways to reveal yellow teeth, he changed the subject. 'I presume, Sire, that you are already planning countermoves against King Yusuf and Granada?'

He pondered the question awhile, anger mounting within him. 'Why did our son, Prince Juan, allow himself to be taken prisoner?' he fumed. 'It inhibits our options. Miserable little coward! He should have impaled himself on his own sword rather than submit.'

'Suicide is a mortal sin,' the bishop reminded him.

'Ha!' He held back the blasphemy that rose to his lips, but it triggered a thought. 'Vengeance is not,' he ground out. The extension of an act of vengeance struck him. 'Like us, King Yusuf has an only son,' he declared.

'And heir,' Bishop Eulogius reminded him, following his trend of thought.

'We already have plans for the father.' This time it was a stark fact that hit him. 'So this Prince . . . Prince . . .'

'Ahmed, his full name being Mo-Ahmed al Kamal.'

'Prince Ahmed is now about eighteen years old. He would be our real rival for the throne of Granada. We should kidnap him.'

'It is reported that Prince Ahmed is virtually a prisoner in the ivory tower of the Gen al Arif palace. It would be extremely difficult to kidnap him from the tight security around him.'

King Pedro grinned ferociously. 'Always remember *this* about security, Eminence. Prince Ahmed's security measures must surely have been designed to keep him in, prevent him from running away. In such circumstances, the security to prevent ingress is more lax.' He paused, reflecting. 'Besides, our worthy Ruy de Vivar has many secret connections in Granada in general and the Alhambra in particular.'

He was referring to the head of Toledo's *Hermandad*, Brotherhood of Citizens, who guarded the city. De Vivar was also his secret police chief throughout the kingdom.

'If anyone can achieve it, de Vivar can,' the prelate agreed thoughtfully.

'A raid would be more to our liking.' King Pedro gloated a few moments over the gouts of red blood that would be spilled and the mortal pain inflicted in a raid, wishing he could participate. 'But that is impossible. We must aim to have the father assassinated and bring the son to Toledo. Since the son is our chief rival and enemy, we must destroy him personally. As luck would have it,

51

de Vivar is due here tomorrow morning to deliver his weekly report. We shall command him to proceed with his task immediately.'

'Your thirst for revenge is *so* un-Christian,' the bishop remonstrated, his cherubic grin belying the accusation.

King Pedro grinned wolfishly. 'Revenge should be slaked, lest it lose urgency,' he retorted. He held up a beefy hand, anticipating the bishop's counter. 'Oh, I know all about the Christian ethic, Eminence, fight for the Cross, not for revenge. But make no mistake, even the Reconquista of the past centuries, since the Moors first invaded Europe in the seventh century, is a creed of revenge motivated, like the Crusades, mostly by greed and ambition. We reconquistadores do not spread the gospel. We reconquer captive territories to slay the heretic and spread his wealth among ourselves!'

'In truth, to chastise the heathen is no sin. Our Lord Jesus took the whip against those who desecrated the temple.'

'Do you really believe that Jesus did so with Christian kindness in his heart? He may have desired to restore and cleanse, but his whip was a symbol of vengeance and punishment.'

'You are close to blasphemy, Your Majesty.' The bishop remained on comfortable clerical ground, a twinkle in the eyes continuing to reveal his apparent shock to be all pretence.

King Pedro was certain that the bishop had no great reverence for religion in his own heart, but had only turned to the Church as a means of improving his lot in life. He had reached the pinnacle of the Church by guile, deceit, bribery and every other means at his disposal, while demonstrating the two essential ingredients of seeming rectitude and pretended fanaticism. Beneath the jolly mask was a cold, calculating brain, the instrument of greed and ambition. King Pedro also believed that inquisition, torture of heretics, burning at the stake, would give Bishop Eulogius a delight so sexual that he would probably have orgasms from seeing the poor, wretched Muslims, Jews and witches die in agony.

King Pedro had held the bishop back. The laws of Toledo were based upon the *fueros*, a Castilian modification of the strict Gothic code. They were precise, minute in all details of crime and punishment where personal and civic life were concerned, right down to the dress of women, the social status of people, marriages, baptisms and funerals. The laws were strictly enforced, Moors and Jews having their own judges except when Christian interests were involved. This was where the monarch could come in, lay down his law. King Pedro knew that power to be one of his bargaining tools with Bishop Eulogius. He alone could decree Inquisition.

'True, but being close to anything, especially blasphemy, is good enough so long as it does not overtake us,' King Pedro responded aloud. 'After all, we have frequently been close to death and are still alive, by the grace of God.' He added the last words hastily, as a concession to form and secret superstition, even crossed himself piously. 'Religion apart, the Moors are invaders and our hereditary foes. We should send them packing back to the Meccas of their birthlands or the Paradise of their beliefs as an act of vengeance for desecrating our temple, Christian Spain.' God, how pious could one get to achieve a purpose!

The bishop raised plump hands in deprecation. 'We should first attempt to convert them. Are we not all invaders here in Spain, from the days our Celtic-Iberian ancestors, the herdsmen and agriculturists, arrived with their iron ploughshares and pruning hooks? They were followed by the Carthaginians under Hamilcar Barca, Hasdrubal and Hannibal. Then came the Romans in 218 B.C., the Germanic Visigoths under Alaric in the fifth century A.D. And finally the Cimbrians, Teutons, Franks, Alemanni, Ostrogoths and Suevi. This hodgepodge of races can only be united by Christianity and Holy Church.'

'A hell's brew of peoples with fornicating seed intermingled in our very bone. Even the Guzmans and de Ponces are not of pure blood, yet we Castilians pride ourselves on a pure bloodline. Faugh!' He laughed shortly. 'No matter. The truth is that we must all unite as Spaniards against the Moor.' He was deliberately inviting the reaction he desired.

'I beg to disagree, Sire. I repeat, only Christianity and Holy Church can truly unite us, else the divisive forces in our own white ranks, which exposed us to Moorish domination in the first place, will remain greater than those which separate Spaniard and Moor.'

'In the final analysis, however, it is the skill and daring of generals which alone can unite people, combined with the ferocity of the common soldier that determines the victor in battle. Muslim belief in Koran and sword has given them brilliant generals and fanatic fighting men.'

'Yet they have also brought our world their mathematics, astronomy, chemistry, physics, especially after their hero, Mohamed I, gave rebirth to the Nasrid dynasty and recaptured Granada in 1236. Their learning and culture are the devil's disguise, but they too have only been at their most ferocious whenever gnawing poverty made an instrument of their religion. In times of prosperity, right here in our beloved Spain, these sword and Koran zealots were frequently emasculated,' he paused to give the metaphor emphasis, 'by ease and our more equable climate in comparison with their blazing deserts.'

'Or when we cut off their balls.' King Pedro was not given to subtle phrases. 'Which leads us to the subject of our discussion tonight. We need a cause to bring our warring Counts together and . . . er . . . fire all our soldiers.' He had chosen the word 'fire' with deliberate cunning.

Bishop Eulogius reacted immediately. 'Ah, fire, forsooth! What better cause than religion, what better spur to all Christians than the cleansing fires of Inquisition.'

King Pedro deliberately ignored the implied suggestion. 'We are of like mind then as to the need for Christian unity to purify our unChristian motives?' His smile was bland.

'Of course. And my reward?'

'Shall be in heaven.' King Pedro rolled reverent eyes upwards.

'I prefer my heaven on earth.' The plump cheeks creased and dimpled in their smile; the ice-blue eyes disappeared.

'That can be arranged too.'

'Your words are manna from heaven.'

'Manna is but the droppings of locusts on tamarisk trees beside the Red Sea!' The king grinned, cynically this time.

'Perhaps we should discuss details of my heavenly reward on earth concurrently with your plans to bring the Christian Counts together here, in your palace, for discussions about unity. Shall we commence with the fiefdoms of certain villages desirable to me?'

Having always bartered thus with each other, they were finally on easy, level terms. 'Of course. And certain desirable maidens too,' King Pedro added.

'Ah yes, maidens! The bliss of heaven forsooth. Virgins are closer to God than any other living beings. Those of us who have taken the vow of celibacy should not despoil virgins but cherish them.'

'Do you then experience an orgasm just by looking at them, Eminence?'

'When the female body is naked, beautiful and virginal, it is Eve recreated for man, not to have sex with, but as

55

in the beginning, to adore. Orgasm thus becomes a Blessed Sacrament.'

'You are close to blasphemy, Eminence,' King Pedro quoted.

'As you just said, close is enough, though not with an orgasm!' The primate grew serious. 'To fire Christians to Islamic fervour, we need another weapon.'

'What do you suggest?' He knew the answer.

'You already know.'

Another source of orgasm for you, King Pedro thought coolly. Aloud he said, 'We are sending messengers to our brothers in Aragon and Navarre tomorrow. It might help them make up their minds if Holy Church endorses our invitation with a stirring call for Reconquista.'

'You are well on the way to earning my endorsement, Your Majesty. What is now needed is an incentive fcr Holy Church.'

'What do *you* suggest?'

'Blazing zeal needs blazing fires. You alone can permit the Inquisition.'

A tremor ran through King Pedro at the words, though he had known all along what Bishop Eulogius was driving for and had decided merely to make the primate believe that he would grant it.

The main thrust of any Inquisition would be against Moors and Jews. The Moors had become a part of the life of Spain, and for over three hundred years now, the Jews had not been the persecuted Hebrews of Visigothic times. Certain *fueros* granted to Jewish communities in the 1200s even protected Jewish orthodoxy and set punishments for Jews who did not observe the Sabbath. In neighbouring Aragon, many Jews were royal judges as well as leaders of every conceivable craft, including the women mourners at Christian burials, for no one could match a Jew at breast beating! While the proud, native Castilians

56

despised work, the Jews, a race of survivors, took over everything the Castilians did not deign to undertake.

Most importantly, however, Jews were the bankers, moneylenders and international traders of Europe. This made them both envied and hated. As for King Pedro, he believed in allowing all races of people to be as productive as possible, to make as much money as they could because some of their riches ended up in his Treasury.

Inquisition threatened serious problems. He did not want it. At some point, he would have to confront Bishop Eulogius and the Church, but for the present he would allow his cherubic primate to believe he was fucking an ambitious king.

She had been virtually imprisoned in her luxurious quarters in the Toledo palace by her father, King Pedro, since she attained maidenhood at the age of twelve. The decision made, that she would rule Toledo some day, she had to be protected from lovers to ensure that only a powerful prince or count would become her consort.

For four years now, Beatrice had been free only to roam the beautiful courtyard gardens, to have communion only with female slaves and the old men and clerics who were her tutors. Apart from her immediate family, any contact with the outside world, including her step-brother, Prince Juan, to whom she had drawn close as a child, was forbidden. Prince Juan had remained in touch with her, however, by using the secret tunnel that led from the main highway outside the city under the river and into the women's quarters. He had visited her once every month to keep their friendship alive. She had often thought how appropriate it was that the secret escape route for women and children against invaders should be providing her with an escape for her emotions, Prince Juan being so sensitive and understanding a human being that she could share her innermost thoughts and yearnings with him.

Now Juan was a prisoner of the hated Moors and she could not even look forward to the regular solace of his presence. God was cruel at times.

King Pedro had elevated her to the rank of princess, and had even named her his heir, displacing Prince Juan, but all such prestige was merely sham to one who was a prisoner and had no real significance for her. What Beatrice de Padilla's heart yearned for was love, the kind of love that her mother, Maria de Padilla and her father, King Pedro, knew for each other. She was a great romantic.

News of the defeat of her father's army had reached the palace two days ago, but it was only at dinner that night that she had learned of Prince Juan's fate. When she imagined the slim youth, fair, grey-eyed, with the fine features of his French mother's ancestry, manacled, chained, starving in some rat-infested dungeon in Granada, she had gagged over her food. She could not wait for dinner to be over so that she could say her special prayers for the intercession of the Blessed Virgin Mary on her step-brother's behalf. These were her first as she knelt on her *prie-dieu* before the blue-robed ceramic statue of the Virgin Mary in its grey grotto placed on the altar ledge. The face of the Blessed Mother came strangely alive in the flickering light of the two white candles on their ornate silver stands when she prayed for Prince Juan's safety, comfort and return home.

'Oh Mother Mary, virgin most mild, hear a virgin maiden's prayers,' she continued. 'You conceived our Lord Jesus of the Holy Ghost, before Saint Joseph took you for wife. You had to endure the scorn of men but not the process that leads to conception. My mother, Maria de Padilla, conceived me out of wedlock, without the sacrament of Holy Church to anoint her union with my father. Yet I believe their union to have been sanctified by the same true love which the Holy Ghost had when he

58

entered you, which alone is true marriage. If this be not so, I beseech you, as I have done daily these many years, to forgive them their sin and to have mercy on me, the product of that sin.' Tears stung her eyes. She raised her hands in supplication.

Your large, blue eyes are sunlight on the Mediterranean when they glisten with tears, my child. The statue of the Blessed Virgin had a gentle voice. *God gave you blonde hair, delicate features and a slim, tall body, so you would look like the angel you are. I shall intercede with Our Father for you.*

In the light of the two candles, the gaze of the statue intensified, overflowed with kindliness.

'Oh thank you, thank you, Holy Mother,' Beatrice breathed. Somewhere deep inside her, she wondered for a moment whether she was not committing a mortal sin in ascribing her own hopes and feelings to the Blessed Virgin. She carefully wiped the tears away with the tip of her forefinger. 'I want to remain a virgin until I can give this precious gift to the man I love. I see him in my dreams, though not his face, and I feel his love vibrating through me. My father, King Pedro, desires the continuation of his own rule through me, because he believes me to be the offspring of his sacred union with my mother. He insists that I marry a prince or a count so that I can rule Castile with the protection afforded by a royal Christian husband. I want to be an obedient child, but I would rather die or take the veil than submit my body to anyone except in such a union of love as my mother has revealed to me as my example. I may not take my life and I do not have the vocation to become a religious. So I am trapped. Help me to escape, Virgin Mother. Send the prince of my dreams to my rescue before it is too late, I beseech you . . .'

She had barely finished her Hail Marys and risen to her feet when the door opened and her mother glided into the room. Beatrice loved her gentle mother and thought her the most beautiful woman in the world, not because she had pretty features, but from the tender spirit that shone through her eyes, their light brown with black pupils vivid against a pale skin. Maria de Padilla was nearly forty at this time, but looked ten years younger, her complexion unwrinkled and the corners of her soft mouth tilted upwards. Beatrice stood taller than her mother, but they both had the same slender build, full breasts and delicate bones.

Beatrice ran across the room and was clasped in her mother's arms, breathing the fragrance of a lilac perfume. Palace trumpets blared the hour of ten in the distance. 'Oh *Madre*, isn't the news about our dear Juan dreadful?' Her mother did not know of Juan's visits.

Maria released her. 'Yes it is, my love.' She paused and Beatrice noticed a strange expression flit across the pale face. Had it been compassion? 'It's not a good time for us. Thank the Lord your father returned safely. We need God's protection desperately.'

A thrill of alarm shot through Beatrice. 'You think the Moors will invade Castile?'

Her mother sighed. 'Who knows? But things will never again be the same as they were during the ten-year truce.'

'Is that all that worries you, Mama?'

Her mother hesitated, then made up her mind. 'Have you said your prayers?'

'Yes, *Madre*.'

'Get into bed then. I will tuck you in. I need to talk to you.'

As far back as Beatrice could remember, her mother had tucked her into bed every single night, even when she herself was sick. Being an only child, Beatrice grew up having all the maternal attention she needed and it had certainly made the imprisonment of the last four years more bearable. Of late, however, Beatrice had felt an

60

increasing desire to break loose and find the other world of which she had read and heard, especially the world of love, romance and adventure contained in the manuscripts she devoured such as the ballad of the English troubadour Thomas, entitled *Horn*, which had touched her deeply.

Her maid had chosen pale blue silk for her bed linen to match the lace canopy. Blue is the colour of the Virgin Mary, so she will keep me safe on this bed, Beatrice thought as she removed her white silk robe, carefully placed her cloth sandals side by side and slipped under the covers. The silk was cool wherever it touched her body, even through her long white silk nightdress. Her mother lovingly tucked the light covering sheet around her, though it would not be long before she flung it aside because of the summer heat that would cause her to start sweating.

Maria sat beside her as usual, stared into space and then began to speak, avoiding Beatrice's gaze. 'As you know, you have been named your father's heir,' she stated. 'This honour brings duties and obligations. We have just suffered a stinging defeat in battle. Although it seems to be only a warning from the Moorish King Yusuf, we must assume that it was also a test of strength before escalation into a full-scale invasion of Castile, Aragon and Navarre.'

Beatrice dug her elbows on the bed, leaned up higher on the pillows. 'What is my father going to do?'

'He rightly believes that the time has come to unite the Spanish kingdoms against the common foe.'

'Holy Church provides us with the basis for such unity.'

'Certainly.' Her mother hesitated. 'But it is not enough to create unity through the Church or through race and nationality, or even from the needs of security alone. True unity lies in the family ties we call alliances.' She glanced at Beatrice, blinked once and looked away.

Beatrice's heart began to pound. 'You mean matrimonial alliances? But Prince . . .'

'Not Prince Juan, *muchacha*. You well know I am referring to the Princess Beatrice.'

The pounding had reached Beatrice's ears, her stomach felt weak. She had known this day would come but had hoped that the time would be stretched out until the prince of her dreams arrived. She knew he was there, somewhere out in the world. He just needed time to get to her. 'I would rather flee than endure such a fate,' she burst out.

'And how would you do that?' her mother inquired with unwonted grimness.

'By the secret trap door that serves as the escape route for us women and children from the palace should the city ever be taken, through the tunnel beneath the river and into the countryside.'

Her mother's face hardened, the mouth tightening. 'You will do your duty by your father and your country,' she directed harshly. Beatrice had never seen her so steely-tough. 'Especially your father, to whom you owe so much.' The brown eyes she turned to Beatrice were cold as tourmalines.

Beatrice was stunned, then heartsick.

This is a stranger, not my mother. She would sacrifice me, she would sacrifice anyone, anything, for her man. Why, she would even renounce her God for him. This is not love, it is utter selfishness clothed in the raiment of selfless devotion.

At that moment, for the first time ever, Beatrice hated her mother. The feeling terrified her. In a trance, the words escaped her. 'Horn was a child when his father, the King of Suddene, was killed by the Saracens who had landed on the coast and ravaged the country. Horn was so handsome that the Saracens could not bring themselves to kill him. They placed him and twelve other noble boys on a boat without oars or sails and set the vessel adrift. It landed safely in the country of Westernesse, where King Ailmar received them, treating them as honoured guests. Everyone came to love Horn, including Rymenhilde, the king's daughter. Their love was discovered and Horn was banished from the kingdom by King Ailmar.

'Before leaving, Horn asked Rymenhilde to wait seven years for him, after which she could marry someone else. She gave him a gold ring in token that she would wait and they parted. The oath being sacred, King Ailmar waited the seven years, Rymenhilde in vain. The day ended, King Ailmar forced her to accept the hand of Madi, King of Ryenes . . .'

Her mother did not seem to have heard her. 'Your father King Pedro, will hold a joust shortly, to which all eligible princes and counts who can strengthen our military might will be invited. Heralds leave with the invitations tomorrow. They will go as far as France, Germany and Italy . . . Invitees will include eligible dukes and counts owing allegiance to the Emperor Charles IV of Luxembourg and King Rudolph II, ruler of the Rhine Palatinate. The winner will be given your hand in marriage. What a romantic way to find a husband!'

Beatrice was not listening to this history lesson. 'On Rymenhilde's wedding day, Horn entered the palace disguised as a pilgrim,' she continued, still in the trance which was her temporary refuge against the terrible news. 'He had blackened his face and looked like a beggar. When he gave Rymenhilde the gold ring, she imagined that he was a messenger, come to tell her that Horn was dead.

> 'Heart, now thou burst
> For Horn thou hast no more . . .
> She fell on her bed,
> There her knife is hid.

63

Chapter 3

The invitation to the tourney had reached the Pamplona palace almost at the very moment that Princess Mathilde mentioned it to King Charles, who regarded the coincidence as an omen that he would win every joust. It had called for a celebration dinner in the great hall, at which he presided with his Chancellor, Count Gaston, on his right.

King Charles preferred the mealtime camaraderie generated in the great hall to the formality of elegant private dining. The glow cast by the brass lamps and the sputtering tapers on their huge silver sconces which lined the walls, produced a colour and texture that was home. The lofty wood-beamed ceiling rose over two storeys in the centre of the hall. Mezzanine verandahs on the upper floor, supported by Gothic arches, roofed three sides of the hall, beneath which servants in royal red and gold livery stood at attention, one behind each guest.

The two dozen counts and nobles sitting around the U-shaped solid mahogany table were all gorgeously dressed in red, green and blue tunics of cloth of gold or velvet, white knee breeches and hosen, their jewelled necklaces, armlets and rings sparkling in the golden light. King Charles wore his customary black, with three gold necklaces of red rubies, green emeralds and grey pearls. The head of the table fronted the great black marble fireplace, meant to warm the king's back in winter but unlit tonight. They had all paid for being well dressed, sweating in the sweltering summer heat until copious draughts of wine had rendered everything painless.

Course followed course: lampreys, roast mutton, lamb

stew, pheasant, at which stage King Charles lost count. The odours of roast meat clung even after the table had been cleared and the gold flagons of fruity red Navarre wine were refilled, when raucous laughter and shouting began cascading around the hall.

Bleary-eyed, King Charles suddenly remembered the cause of the revelry. He reached over and nudged Count Gaston with his right elbow. 'Good newsh about the tourney, eh?' The question was a statement. He studied the count's lean hawk-like face. The slightly hollowed cheeks and high forehead beneath flowing black hair were shiny with sweat, but the trim black moustache and beard gave the nobleman a haughty look, heightened by dark, intense eyes under jutting brows. Those eyes! Though he was near-drunk, King Charles paused at the eyes, while mouthing the words. 'We sh . . . shall accept the invitation, win the hand of the fair young maid and add Cashtile to our kingdom without firing a sh-single arrow.'

Count Gaston glanced coolly at him. 'You would still need to fire arrows, though on your nuptial bed,' he asserted dryly. 'Every right brings a duty. Should you come to enjoy that particular conjugal duty you will forfeit your free access to love and licentiousness, which could be rather trying for one such as you, Sire, who practises debauchery with the dedication of a choirboy singing his first solo.'

King Charles knew that his cynical Chancellor never stooped to sycophancy. A proud Basque, he held himself the equal of all men, merely giving rank its due respect.

When he became king, Charles had deliberately selected Count Gaston as his Chancellor to strengthen ties with the Basques, but one of the many things he had been unable to discover during the many years they had known each other, was where the man's own ambitions lay. Often too, he had wondered what the elegant Count's views were on the rowdiness and vulgarity he had deliberately brought to the Navarre court as a reaction to the refinement that had been the hallmark of his haughty French mother, Queen Joanna, and her consort, Count Philip of Evereaux.

'God'sh body! You mean we shall have to take the virgin fort by sh . . . storm?' King Charles inquired.

Count Gaston looked him over as if he were an ox at the auction. 'Well, Sire, you are not the most attractive man in the world,' he declared. 'You can hardly expect a virgin maiden to welcome to her bed an obese giant with a bull neck, florid features and dingy brown eyes. Since you have always gained your prizes through brute strength, I swear to God you are justifiably called Charles the Bad. History may well . . .'

'Fuck history,' Charles growled. He never liked to be reminded of his ugliness.

'That is what history is, Sire. The product of the systematic copulation of the human race.'

'We don't care pigeon's shit for what people say about us now, or what history will say later.'

'A good sentiment, Sire, for pigeons do just that on historical monuments.' Count Gaston nodded. 'Which reminds me, our Bishop Albano hinted again today that he would like a statue in his honour to be erected opposite the cathedral at our expense.'

'Fuck the Bishop too. He's too old for any kind of erection.' King Charles guffawed, in rare good humour again at his own wit.

'It might pay you to restrain the effects of your own when dealing with the Princess Beatrice.'

'Now why the fuck would we do that? God'sh body! Ram the bitches, we say. That'sh how to take a fort. And do we have a battering ram!'

'Women of refinement would trade a kingdom for respectability.'

'You've never been married, how the fuck would you know about cunts?'

'I don't have to father a child to recognize its sex, Your Majesty.'

The statement fuddled the king. 'There's a catch somewhere in what you sh-say.'

'Only if you catch it, Sire.' Count Gaston grinned faintly.

'You don't get drunk, you don't fuck, who the hell are you?' the king roared, exasperated.

'A student of the human race. One who does not have such a lust for life that he has to live a life of lust.'

'Sounds more like a fucking pedagogue to me.'

'Then let the pedagogue urge you to be gentle with Princess Beatrice should you win the joust.'

'Why?' King Charles was so astounded he forgot to swear.

'Princess Beatrice must have inherited some of her mother's qualities. And Maria de Padilla is surely a very special woman to have earned and maintained King Pedro's love all these years.'

'Love, love. Who gives a flea's fart for love?'

'Can fleas do that, Sire?' The count was his cynical self again. He raised a supercilious eyebrow.

'Why don't you go out and check? There are enough on the palace dogs.' A dangerous edge had entered King Charles's voice. He was becoming infuriated with this superior bastard.

A slim pageboy bearing a gold flagon of wine came between them. Dressed in red silk, the youth had straight golden hair, cut shoulder length, and a pink and white complexion. His features were girlish. King Charles took the opportunity to change the subject. 'Such a pretty boy,' he declared, reaching out with a finger to lift a lock of the page's hair, observing its sheen with a stirring of interest, though he was not given to homosexuality. 'You're new, aren't you?' he enquired, carefully articulating the words.

The youth flushed. Delicate tints of rose mantled his flawless cheeks; the large blue eyes, with the longest dark lashes, widened with fear. 'Yes, Your Majesty.'

'Whose sh-son are you?'

'Both my parents died years ago. I l-lived with my grandmother, Countess Isabella Alcazar, who g-got me into your royal service b-before she too died a f-few weeks ago.'

'You have no relations?'

'None, Sire.'

'H'mm. What is your name?'

'Jacques.'

'God'sh body, you are prettier than a woman, Jacques. Let's sh . . . see whether you are really a man.' King Charles reached over, grabbed the boy so roughly by the crotch that some of the wine spilt on the royal tunic. 'Damn you, you have sh-soiled my new tunic. You shall pay for it.' He snatched the flagon from the boy's grasp with his free hand, slammed the container on the table, spilling more wine. He pulled the boy on to his lap. The terror in the staring blue eyes, the trembling of the slim, hard body excited him, while Count Gaston's unexpressed contempt dared him to defiant extremes.

'Are you man enough to give the lad an erection, Your Majesty?' the chubby-cheeked Count Rafael drawled from the lower end of the table. 'If not, you may call on me.' A known homosexual, he ran a pink tongue over sensual red lips.

King Charles turned his head sideways to look at Jacques, noted the soft, curving red mouth quivering like a woman's. His royal organ pulsed, but he was too drunk to summon an erection. He fondled the boy's genitals. 'Flaccid as a frog's pouch!' He swore under his breath. 'You a fucking virgin?' he demanded irritably.

69

Staring eyes fixed on the king's face, the boy nodded, speechless with fear.

'Talk, damn you, when your king addresshes you. Else I'll cut your cock out.'

'Y-yes . . . yes, Sire,' the boy managed to croak.

'Fucking no good, virgins,' King Charles muttered. 'They only make the penis sh-sore.' He paused. 'You're going to have an erection tonight, Jacques.' He darted a malevolent glance at Count Gaston, meeting the chancellor's look of well-bred contempt. 'Being our Chancellor, Count, you are also chief ponce of our Court. We command you have our youngest lady-in-waiting brought to our bedchamber. We'll sh-see whether she can't persuade this young prick to rise to the occasion.' He roared with laughter, pleased once more at his own maudlin humour. His guests tittered. He directed a drunken gaze at the page. 'What did you sh-say your name was, boy? Hic!'

'J . . . Jacques, Sire.'

'Well, Jacques, you are going to fuck that young lady and when you are ready to come, I'll fuck you, then her.'

'You haven't given the boy an erection though, Sire,' Count Rafael called down the table. 'If you *must* do it by proxy, why don't you let *me* have a try?'

'Fuck you, Count.'

'I prefer the boy to do it, Sire.'

Enraged, King Charles reached for the object nearest him, the wine flagon. He flung it at Count Rafael. It missed, crashed on the floor. He joined in the drunken laughter that exploded around the hall.

'Another near miss from you, Sire,' Count Gaston murmured.

At that moment, the terrified pageboy, still on the royal lap, wet his pantaloons.

'I swear to God, a touché for Jacques,' the Count concluded.

* * *

As she sat on a flat red sandstone rock outside her cave in Granada, the surroundings were glamorized by dusk. The truth was that the gypsy caves puncturing the bare mountain slope were dirty, smelly, ill-ventilated and generally hung with smoke from the cooking fires. People defecated around the caves like their goats and donkeys, so it did not even need the breezes blowing across the ravine to bring the stench right into the cave. Many were the nights when Zurika had cried herself to sleep in sheer helplessness at her lot.

Majo would try to have her some day. There was nothing she could do about it, except stab him to death with the long knife she always carried hidden at her waist when he approached her. She had better kill herself too then, for Majo, being the chief of her tribe, could take any woman for whom he lusted and the tribe would kill her if she murdered him. May the Blessed Virgin intercede with God to save her from Hell or Purgatory for any mortally sinful act in consequence of which she would not even be given a Christian burial and take her straight to heaven for having protected her virtue from a beast.

Zurika was fifteen. She had feared and loathed Majo ever since she became conscious of her womanhood. Like most of the small band of gypsies who occupied the caves of the rugged mountain opposite the Granada palace, above the rapid noisy River Xenil, she had sung and danced from her earliest days. After she attained maidenhood and her breasts and figure began to develop, she noticed Majo's growing interest in her and saw the desire flaming in the dark eyes whenever they fell on her.

Young as she was, people already acclaimed her one of the best dancers in Andalusia. With her slender, lithe body, long legs, olive skin, glossy raven hair hanging down straight and free and dark brown sultry eyes, she looked the classic priestess of gypsy dance. And when she

71

danced, she was possessed. She did not express herself
with wild abandon as many others did, but with inner
passion, her upper body rigid, her arms and legs free,
eyes contemplative or challenging, all of it expressed from
her very soul, the pride, seductiveness and hauteur that
was normally hidden beneath a mask of humility flowing
unfettered.

Zurika had never known her parents. Her mother had
died in childbirth and her father had been killed in a knife
fight shortly after. It was his knife she carried, as a
sentimental gesture when she was young, but now as her
defence against molestation. Her grandmother, Pilar, had
given her a home and looked after her. Since Pilar too
had no relatives, she and Zurika had been drawn together
by bonds of caring and a need for each other.

There were those who called her grandmother a witch.
Once, when a ten-year-old gypsy boy who flung invective
at Pilar had inexplicably become ill and died, there was
talk that Pilar had laid a spell on the boy and threats that
she would be tested by the water ordeal. Flung into the
river, if Pilar drowned she would not have been a witch.
If she floated, she was indeed a witch and would be
burned at the stake. No one dared take further steps
against such a one, however, in case she commanded the
powers of the Devil. Also, Majo had stood against it. His
dark eyes had told Zurika why. Some day he would claim
his reward. No one spoke ill of Pilar thereafter.

Zurika knew that Pilar, being a Christian, did not
practise either devil worship or black magic. She was not
a member of a coven, nor did she attend sabbats. She was
not a sorceress either, but a seeress and an enchantress.

Grandmother Pilar too was aware that it was only a
matter of time before Majo raped Zurika or seized her
and carried her to his cave to join his other women, when
Zurika's life would end in squalor, abuse, beatings and
childbearing. Majo was an uncouth monster. His lean,

very tall figure, erect for his seventy years, appeared in Zurika's nightmares, the hatchet face cruel, white hair contrasting with fierce brows which were strangely black above wrinkled cheeks burned dark brown by the sun. And the devil's hot eyes. Zurika shuddered at the recollection.

Her longing to escape was not from Majo alone, but from the filth and degradation of her surroundings and the hopelessness of her lot. In this she knew herself to be unique, so she grew apart from the other gypsy children and became a loner. Though she had spent all her life in the caves, she had noticed the way richer people lived in the fortress city of Granada and in the fringes of the palace within it, where even the humblest servants seemed to have a better life than hers. Seeing the fine ladies who drove by in their coaches, rode in their sedan chairs or attended church in rich silks, with their auras of heady perfume, had increased Zurika's soul-hunger for cleanliness, sweet smells and fine clothes. She wanted to be like them. She dreamed of a prince who would rescue her from this sordid state.

From where she now sat she could barely discern the other families gathered outside their caves to enjoy the cooler air, but the murmur of their voices reached her, punctuated by an occasional laugh or the shriek of a child. The falling shades of night could not mute the squalor, even the sounds, never the smells. A guitar tinkled sweet and virginal from a ledge higher up. Her feet tapped *punta-talon*, toe-heel, . . . *punta-talon* to its rhythm. Golden lights pricked the mass of the palace on the Sabika crest across the ravine, its red sandstone walls vermilion in the twilight, but only a few windows of the Gen al Arif towers above it glowed. She thought of the lonely prince virtually imprisoned in the Gen al Arif and wove her usual fantasy around him. He would rescue her some day.

73

The stars overhead, in a sky as pure and blue as the Blessed Virgin's robe, were God's sparklers, the scent of honeysuckle wafted up from the fertile valley below by a sudden breeze, His sweet breath. Even the faint hoot of an owl from the groves below was part of God's music, all of it the purity of His creation. Her own life lay in the squalor of her surroundings.

What was that rustling in the darkness? Was Majo coming to get her?

Heart pounding, she sprang to her feet, ready to flee.

The short figure shuffling up the pathway winding up the mountainside, walking with a limp, brought instant relief. It was Grandmother Pilar. She raced to embrace the old woman.

As always, Pilar smelled of unwashed clothes and the peculiar odour of the untended old. But she loved her grandmother fiercely. 'Oh, *Madre*, I'm so glad it's you,' she breathed. 'I was beginning to be afraid that something had happened.'

The old woman grasped Zurika's arms, loosed them gently from around her. 'Always remember, Grandmother Pilar never leave her precious baby alone after dark.' Her normally hoarse voice was grainier than ever as she recovered her breath from the climb. She hawked and spat. 'I delayed at Great Bazaar buying what I need for this night.' She dropped her voice, glanced around her furtively to make sure that none of the cave-dwellers was within earshot. 'Tonight is auspicious time. We find out what future hold for you.' Her low cackle reminded Zurika of a witch.

'You will look into the crystal for me?' Zurika's blood had quickened.

Pilar nodded. 'I look see what future hold for you, dearie. No need fear. If Majo in crystal, I put curse on him.' She cackled, baring blackened teeth. 'I good witch but I know curse too. Come into cave now. We eat, then

74

make all ready for midnight.' She patted her bag and shawl. 'I have what I need in here.'

The gypsy forefathers who originally came from the distant East had handed it down that the river below once reached above the top of the mountain. As the waters subsided throughout the centuries, underground streams that fed the river ran dry. These underground channels became empty tunnels, which earthslips turned into caves and caverns. The gypsy caves were stifling hot in summer and cold and damp during the rainy months. Living in them was even more difficult than residing in towns and villages was for the poor. Water from the city's fountains was denied the outcast gypsies. They had to draw theirs from wells that had been set aside for them in the valley below and carry it up the mountain in pitchers and pots; the women did this because gypsy men were lazy, except when they danced. A few wealthier gypsies used their donkeys. Women were the donkeys of the poor.

The roof and walls of Pilar's cave were part of the red sandstone of the mountain, the roof averaging about fifteen feet from the ground. The cooking area was at the front with a large clay water jar on the side, a stack of firewood and sacks of grain, flour and other foods in sacks beside it. A metal tripod hung over a wood fire, the smoke from which was drawn upwards and into the open air by a natural vent above it. When the wood was wet, smoke could not readily escape, so it loitered within the cave, infecting everything, even the body, with its odour. That was a clean smell, however, in comparison with the combination of stale urine, asafoetida, garlic and garbage that frequently infested the cave, as it did tonight.

The entire cave was lit by two smoking oil lamps hanging from the roof. A curtain of hides sewn together separated off the sleeping area. The furniture in the front consisted of a low table created by a wooden board on sandstone bricks. Apart from a rickety wooden bench, there were no seats. Clothes hung on pegs hammered into the looser gravel portions of the walls. In the inner space, a pallet bed with a yellow mat and a dingy cushion were placed on one side beneath a rough wooden crucifix hung above an altar covered with a blue linen square. Two white candles on red clay stands stood on the altar. Across the room, in a niche carved out of the mountain, a small grey grotto contained a statue of the Blessed Virgin wearing a blue robe. Zurika had placed a white lily she had picked from the valley that morning in front of the statue, for Mother Mary was her one refuge and hope.

Zurika and Pilar ate their simple meal of gruel, ladled directly from the cooking pot on to brown clay platters, at the trestle table in companionable silence. Zurika had learned not to interrupt her grandmother's thoughts or concentration before a ritual. They finished off the meal with cold water from a bronze pitcher, probably stolen by one of Pilar's family long ago, then wiped the platters with a damp rag. Water was too precious to be wasted on washing utensils.

The air had turned cooler, causing the lamps to glow more clearly as Pilar assembled all she needed. Black candles for the two sacred circles, and two wax figures which would be assigned to Zurika and Majo as godparents to provoke love or death. Pilar mixed male semen and menstrual blood from separate ceramic containers, poured the mixture into a tiny mortar containing the blood of a bat and thickened it with white flour. She raised her skirt, picked three grey hairs from her own pubis, placed them beside the mortar, then strung together a mock rosary of lizard vertebrae and dice to represent the gamble that is life. She poured some powdered human bones into a small bowl. Finally, she produced the cage containing a small white pigeon she had bought in the Great Bazaar that evening. She had carried the bird concealed in her shawl, since exposing

76

the white pigeon to the gaze of her fellow gypsies would
have betrayed her purpose.

The crystal for the prophecy would only be removed
from its hiding place in a little hole at the far end of the
cave at the right time.

The mountain was silent and still as the grave. The
entire hillside village was fast asleep. Pilar changed into a
loose white garment. She sat cross-legged on the floor and
began muttering incantations. Zurika squatted on the
floor in front of her, mind bright but slowly succumbing
to Pilar's mood, awaiting the magic hour.

The hoot of the owl, closer than before, was ghostly. A
distant church bell tolled a knell. Someone had died.

Zurika shivered in the warm air. Suddenly the cave
seemed like a tomb.

Chapter 4

The previous day his father, King Yusuf, had returned to Granada from battle, victorious over King Pedro, the white Spanish Castilian.

This morning before dawn Prince Ahmed's personal attendant, Tarif, had come to his bedchamber as usual. Kings and princes always woke to the sound of music, but Prince Ahmed generally remained in bed until he heard Tarif's respectful knock on the door. There was still time to wash and be ready for the muezzin's call to *subh*, morning prayer, resounding from the main palace tower. Prince Ahmed could hear that call clearly in his own eyrie in the Gen al Arif palace that had been his abode for the past sixteen years. He had only a vague recollection of where he had been during the first two years of his life. He guessed it was in the main palace, which to him was only a collection of rooftops and bowers, towers and gardens below his window.

While the past years had made him thoroughly familiar with his prison, only those parts of the king's palace and the city which he could see meant anything to him. He had discovered from plans which had been shown him, that the sandstone battlement walls studded with towers stretched irregularly round the whole crest of the high hill, on which it stood. The snowy mountain range of the Sierra Nevada and the city's capacity to accommodate an army of 40,000 in its outer precincts, made it a stronghold against rebellious subjects or a foreign invader.

Some day he, Prince Ahmed, would traverse the city freely, see its streets and alleys, the convent, the church, the main street known as Zacatin, the Great Bazaar and the square in which tournaments were held. It would be a special joy finally to participate in the jousts against all comers.

Washed and scented, he sat before the mirror for Tarif to comb out his long, glossy raven hair. Most of the scented lights in the Granada palace were not extinguished until daylight, some burning perpetually. He could see Tarif's hunchback figure, clad in a long white linen robe, reflected behind his own in the mirror, an ebony hand with long shapely fingers and curiously pale palms moving downwards in graceful strokes. Tarif's wrinkled cheeks, leathery as old black boots, shone in the lampglow. Hardly a day went by without Prince Ahmed noting the contrast between the old black deaf-mutes in the Gen al Arif and his own youthful appearance in the mirrors.

He had read in his manuscripts about youth and age. Somewhere beyond the palace confines there was youth other than himself. Were other young men like him in appearance, with tight olive skin, fine-drawn over the regular bone structure of the face, the high bridge of the nose and the nostrils firm, with never a wrinkle? The mirror revealed to him the difference between the sparkle in his black, brooding eyes and the faded gaze of his personal attendant. It was strange to reflect that Tarif had once been slim and tall with a skin that would have looked like polished ebony, the near black eyes set in heavy features beneath high brows sparkling and alive. What had Tarif felt at the moment of his castration sixty-four years earlier? Prince Ahmed had surges of feeling for the black Moroccan which he could only identify as pity.

'I had the wet dream last night, Tarif,' he sign-languaged.

'So I noticed from your robe, Prince.' Tarif formed the Arabic words with his lips.

'I have never been able to get used to the horrible

79

sticky liquid, cold against my thighs when I wake, and the dreadful raw odour.'

'Did you have the same dream?'

'Yes. I remember it distinctly this time. There was this strange tree in the garden, beside the main fountain, more graceful than any other tree, perfect in every feature. Its twin branches stretched sideways like arms, its base had two legs. Birdsong trills and whistles were its voice, the fragrance of its blossoms was so enticing. Its shade enfolded me, caressed my skin with each breeze. I longed to clasp it to my bosom. And when I did, oh, the ecstasy of feeling its body against mine, the vibrance of every pore of the bark against my private parts. In some strange way my penis suddenly penetrated it. Wetness spurted immediately like a jerking fountain, thrilling me, cascading through my whole being, but I awoke to disgust. And yet the tenderness of the union remains.'

The black deaf-mute was strangely thoughtful, but he continued with his comb-strokes, more mechanically now. 'I remember your first wet dreams, Prince,' he finally mouthed. 'You were so terrified, you couldn't wait until I arrived in the morning to robe you, so you could ask me what it was all about.'

A low laugh escaped Prince Ahmed at the recollection, and he could not help the sigh that followed. 'That was when you told me your own story, Tarif.' He watched Tarif's rheumy eyes clouding and shifting away. 'You were a ten-year-old pageboy to General Husain when you landed at Tarifa in 1275 with Sultan Yusuf's 100,000-man army in support of King Mohamed II's campaign against the Walis of Malaga.' Knowing that it helped the old man to speak about it, he paused for Tarif to tell the rest. This had become almost a ritual with them, the repetition in some way a solace to the eunuch.

'I proved myself to be devoted and capable. When I was your age, I saved my general's life and came to King

Mohamed's notice. The general gifted me to the king. Oh, I was young, lusty and romantic in those days.' Though no one could hear, he raised a quick hand to his mouth and looked around at having mouthed the word 'romantic', forbidden in any context other than poetry. 'The king found me so intelligent and trustworthy that he decided to assign me to his harem. Inevitably I had to be castrated to receive this high honour.' His mouth trembled. He shrugged his shoulders, the humped one moving awkwardly. 'Such is life. You always have to give up something for what you get. You prune a bush on one side if you want it to grow on the other. That was sixty-four years ago. I was twenty-one at the time.'

'And the sadness has never left you.'

'The anguish eased, but kept returning, less and less frequently as the years went by.' Tarif smiled wistfully into the mirror. 'It never quite leaves you.' The smile widened. 'But for the side that was pruned, I had abundant growth on the other, when our present King Yusuf, your father, appointed me to be your personal attendant.'

Instinctively, Prince Ahmed reached back to lay his hand on the old man's humped shoulder. 'Oh Tarif!' he mouthed, then quickly withdrew his hand. One never knew what hidden eyes spied. Even secret mouthings might be spotted in his gilded prison. Its marble floors, gold platters, ivory ornaments, scented lamps and magic gardens were all the abode of tale-carriers. 'I remember your telling me when I had my first dream that it was natural for one growing into manhood. The sensations of the lead into ejaculation were so intensely vibrant, the final spurts so ecstatic that you risked your life and taught me how to do it to myself in the privy, then to take the fluid and wash it away so no one would know.'

'Except that Lord bon Ebben smelled it once,' Tarif reminded him drily.

'Dear Allah, he sniffed like a hound on the scent and

searched everywhere to find the substance. One would imagine that he was looking for the original Koran. But it was gone and only his suspicions remained. I learned to disguise the odour with sandalwood paste and camphor incense after that. I even ran out of the perfumes at first because I needed them so often!'

'You made yourself sick one day from going at this secret delight with wild abandon. You vomited and purged, reminding me of an overworked rabbit.' Tarif paused. 'I had to pretend to the old *hakim*, physician, that it was some over-salted meat you had eaten. He gave you an antidote while I administered what you really needed, a stimulant.' He picked up a gold turban from an adjacent table, placed it on Prince Ahmed's hair. 'There now, you look like one of the Arabian Nights princes, the handsomest in the world.'

'Thank you, Tarif.'

The muezzin's call to prayer reached them through the open windows.

'*Come to Allah!*'

For what? The question exploded in Prince Ahmed's brain like the burst of a giant firecracker.

He had been in his twelfth year when he first ceased to accept his imprisonment. The early herald had been a vague dissatisfaction which he could not identify except as a suspicion that there must be more for him than his lot permitted, that he was missing something. Then he began to have physical urges, to touch and be touched, mental and physical erections which left him restless. He thought these were all sinful, but could not help expressing them by caressing objects, such as his sword, touching the walls of his personal suite of rooms, speaking to his black charger, Ibn, stroking its glossy side.

I feel something for you, and of you. You must have a

82

life and a spirit of your own to be able to inspire my communion.

He had obliquely broached the subject with bon Ebben.

'Anyone who believes that beasts and material things have life is a heretic,' the sage had declared decisively. 'He would be considered mad and cast into a hospital for the insane, because according to Islam, a man shall not be punished when Allah has driven him mad.'

That effectively silenced Prince Ahmed, but not his yearning for beauty and the need to express himself poetically. Nor did it end his growing rebellion or his secret actions. Soon, however, he was longing to receive what he was giving. The house, the sword, his black Egyptian war charger could only speak to him with silent voices, like Tarif. He needed to hear the words. He longed to be touched in return, so desperately that at times it seemed to create a vacuum on his skin.

Then the questions began to emerge. What sort of life did the king, whom he was being trained and groomed to succeed, lead? Why was the king so much above his subjects, a near god, bon Ebben had told him, that he could not even see his only son, but would finally grant him an audience when he reached the age of twenty-one?

Would he, Prince Ahmed, too, be a near god some day?

It is not for you to ask questions. Obey first, do your duty, then you will have learned to rule. That was bon Ebben's creed.

It was all very confusing. His mind was too dense to discover and hold the truth, his days too full, with never a pause so that he was always dead tired at bedtime, to permit deep thinking.

He learned to control the questions, the urges, the thoughts and the unidentified yearnings when they began to pile upon him however tired he was in the secret recesses of the night.

83

The more difficult task was to ignore the increasingly frequent oddities he discovered in events and in his routine, when he read of something, for example, and a word would hit him. The word was there, he knew what it meant. It was important, but since it was not translated into an experience in his own life, it had no significance.

'A future king must know all,' bon Ebben explained, 'but need not experience all. For instance, he does not have to partake of the food of common people to know what they eat.'

By the time questions as to how human, animal and plant life were created arose within him, Prince Ahmed did not even bother to ask bon Ebben. The tutor would give him dialectics, but not the truth. Tarif, who would give the truth, was not allowed to tell him. So there was no one to whom he could turn.

Three months ago, when he heard the trumpets and drums resounding in the capital shortly after *subh*, he was told that his father was going to war against the Castilians. The news charged him with excitement. War was one of the final fulfilments of all he had learned. Useless for him though, like his own life. He was told he could not experience it yet. Loyalty, patriotism, duty, were all concepts that had been drilled into him, but they had to stagnate within him. Not for him the thrill of battle, the exultation of killing, of facing death or gaining glory. That had to be in the future. So the promise of the future was a distant river while he was confined to the arid stream bed of a narrow gorge, such as he had once seen in a painting.

The day his father rode out of the city at the head of the army, something broke loose in Prince Ahmed and he finally rebelled.

Refusing to do his studies, he began walking around the palace gardens all day, bestowing emotions he could not identify on trees, plants and shrubs, touching petals and leaves. He expressed his feelings in melodies of songs he composed and the sweet, tinkling notes of his lute. If he could not find fulfilment in battle, he would find it in beauty, which he adored.

Was that all he really wanted? No. But he did not know what he wanted at present – only to find out what he really wanted! And his natural intelligence told him that he would not know even that until he was free to discover all about life beyond the confines of his prison. At present he could only exercise the freedom blindly to express his delight at the free things of life, such as the vibrant grace of a tree, the sweet fragrance of its blossoms, the gentle rustle of wind through its clothes, the leaves, the music of its voice, the song of the bird at its breast.

'*Come to Allah!*' For what?

His father had returned yesterday, but far from reverting to obedience, Prince Ahmed had another idea. He could not wait for *subh* to end to give it effect.

He hurried through breakfast with bon Ebben in the small private courtyard that served his quarters, allowing the drone of the old sage's voice to pass over him like a dry, overhead wind, paying no more attention to it than to the humming of a bee that was busy sucking honey from the African tulips bordering the courtyard.

'Your royal father commands that you rigidly follow the daily schedule I have set for you,' bon Ebben insisted, pounding the white marble table so hard with his fist that the breakfast platters rattled. 'Now that he is back from battle, you had best put an end to this nonsense of mooning around the gardens spouting poetry and song and return to your studies.'

Such displays of strength by proxy, without firmness, were so much frumenty pudding and it was difficult for one so old as bon Ebben to be convincingly firm. The now familiar stubbornness stiffened inside Prince Ahmed. 'You may hurt your hand, revered tutor,' he warned

85

coldly, glancing at the gnarled fist on the table. 'Besides, it is rude to pound tables and, as you have so frequently admonished me, an argument that requires the strength of physical power to support it must be inherently weak.'

The sage's jaw dropped. He raised dark eyes to the pale blue sky above in resignation. 'Allah give me strength,' he quavered. His gaze dropped to Prince Ahmed. 'It is you who will be hurt if you anger your royal father.'

'You too, so you will not tell him!' Something within Prince Ahmed suddenly clamoured: You and my royal father have already hurt my mind and spirit so much that whatever you may do to my body can never matter. The realization startled him, filled him with an implacable resolve to put himself where he need never again submit his stifled mind and spirit to any man, whatever torture was inflicted on his body.

Ignoring all the sage's pleas and admonitions, he rose from his white marble seat and walked out into the silver air, so pure in contrast to his foul imprisonment. Its limpid cool meant another warm sunny day ahead, but felt good on his body. His long cloth of gold tunic, the belt encrusted with blue lapis lazuli and red rubies, the marble and gold palace, the surfeit of splendour without substance, all sickened him so much he suddenly wanted to vomit.

His shoes clacked rapidly on the red flagstone walkway between the great green cypresses, sculpted bushes and wide flower beds rioting with the pinks and reds of petunias, yellows of marigolds and white daisies. The contrast of water, pristine pure, splashing crystal in the great alabaster fountain at the centre of the long pool with its artificial excess of carved stonework seemed to splatter him with a revelation. Man would even filigree God's simplest, most exquisite creation, the white lily. The sweet innocence of an earth just awakened from its dewy sleep by the sun hit him, birds singing free, flowers freely casting their fragrance upon the air, even the light breeze that caressed his face, free. Free, free. Only he was a slave.

Hatred for his captors burst forth within him. He hated his father, the king, bon Ebben, his warder, his jailer, life. For the first time ever, he knew real hatred. And it terrified him.

He did not *want* to hate, least of all with such beauty cascading all around him.

He wanted to . . . he wanted to . . . dear Allah, what was it he wanted?

He did not know, but suddenly he longed to break loose from the two prisons, this palace outside him and the hatred that was enveloping him from within. Gold shoes with their upcurling points clacking more urgently, he strode purposefully towards the object he had selected.

As he approached the magnolia tree, a breeze rustled its leaves. Its branches swayed forward, reaching to caress him, the scent of its white blossoms enticing. He paused, nostrils quivering. The warmth of the silver sunlight tingled his skin.

He gazed spellbound at the spirit of the tree emerging in human form, white, wraithlike, with never a wrinkle on it. So different from man, so soft, gentle, tender . . . so young. Trembling, he dropped to his knees, arms instinctively raised from feelings that had no name. Words began pouring from him to the tree, in a chant.

> 'Man alone is cruel, harsh
> Governs by the rod
> Lost in evil's slimy marsh,
> While you are close to God.
>
> My admiration surges
> In most unusual fashion,
> As your spirit with me merges,
> I shake with holy passion

These strange desires in me
Why do they have no name?
And who can answer this my plea
When no one feels the same.

O tree of beauty and of grace
You never will enslave me
Your spirit never stern or base
To chain the life God gave me.'

From the holy ecstasy of his adoration of beauty, the sight, the sound, the scent enshrined in pure air, from the sweet joy of beauty's clean spirit symbolized by the tree, holy lust emerged. He rose, stepped forward to embrace the smooth bole with never a wrinkle on its body. His organ swelled, became erect.

Dimly conscious of bon Ebben's presence, he answered the instinct to move his loins, thrusting, thrusting.

The breeze became a wind, caressing him and the tree standing together in holy union, Allah's blessing. The tree swayed, tenderly returning his passion. Eyes closed, cool in the sunlight, warm in the shadow, ecstasy dawned, thrilling within his crotch. The slow quiver-fire reached into his eager-answering consciousness. A branch groaned. *Oh Allah, it responds to my ecstasy.*

Ecstasy peaked. The raw smell of his semen smote his nostrils.

Chapter 5

Tonight the Great Hall of the Pamplona palace was to be used exclusively for dancing to the accompaniment of a thirty-piece string orchestra playing from one of the mezzanines above. The mahogany dining table had been moved to a large adjoining chamber, as the centrepiece of several tables lining the walls beneath huge containers of red, white and pink roses. All the tables, covered in snow-white linen, gleamed with silver and gold ware, glittered with crystal. The dining table now held large silver-ribboned baskets of fruit: golden German apples, huge yellow Italian peaches, Andalusian oranges, red Spanish plums and cherries, in a colourful display surrounded by a border of candied fruit and caramels in crystal bowls. One adjoining table offered gold dishes containing miniature pastries filled with cod-liver or beef marrow, meat in a thin cinnamon sauce, beef marrow fritters, eels in a thick brown spicy purée, roach in a cold green sauce flavoured with spices and sage, large cuts of roast and boiled meat. The other had capon pasties and crisps, bream and eel pasties, yet another frumenty, venison, lampreys with hot sauce, roast bream and darioles, sturgeon and jellies. A table across the room was laden with sweetmeats of every kind, including some from Persia. Next to it was the buffet containing iced waters and a variety of rosé, white and burgundy wines in great crystal goblets sparkling beneath the flames of tapers on silver stands placed around them and the glow of the overhead oil lamps. Beneath the vault of pale pink, soft blue, white and gentle green frescoes on the ceiling, the feast might have been spread in heaven.

Princess Mathilde surveyed her glittering, artistic creation for King Charles's Christmas ball with great satisfaction. Servants in green and gold-braided livery standing erect behind the tables and uniformed attendants with gold and silver trays in their hands waiting to serve the revellers, gave animation to the scene. The guests had arrived and awaited their ruler in the Great Hall. Dear Charles would be pleased in spite of his normal impatience with adornments.

'Your Royal Highness has excelled herself,' Countess Isabella, her chief lady-in-waiting, remarked. 'Pamplona has never seen the like even in the day of Queen Joanna.' A haughty Spanish aristocrat, she was old enough to know. 'But the most exquisite feature of the hall is you.'

'Thank you, Countess.' Princess Mathilde knew that the proud Isabella, of the tip-tilted nose, the scornful black eyebrows and the dark eyes, cold as deep water, was more given to supercilious comments than to flattery. 'Coming from you that is praise indeed.'

But she knew it to be true. Her own boudoir mirrors had revealed it. She had personally designed her long-sleeved white dress of Luccan satin, sheer and tight at the breast, waist and hips, but flowing out in pleats from below a silver belt slung low. The upper part of the dress, cut square, low in front and at the shoulders, had a four-inch silver border studded with black pearls, the grey of which matched her eyes, and red rubies, with which her six-inch belt was also studded. Her shoes were plain silver and her headdress studded with diamonds set in silver.

'You will stand out amid the ostentation of the popinjays attending the ball like a single lily in the profusion of a multi-coloured flower-bed.' Countess Isabella's tall, gaunt figure, was conservatively clothed in pale blue, with dark blue sapphires for ornament.

Princess Mathilde laughed. 'Together we shall be like the blue forget-me-not and the white lily, but not to be forgotten!' She turned to enter the Great Hall, followed by the countess. She was greeted by the great orchestra she had assembled tuning up, an unrehearsed composition of tinkling viols, Moorish and Latin guitars and lutes, light clinks of small cymbals. The little essays of clacking castanets pierced the three-stringed hurdy-gurdy operated by two players who turned its wheel and crank, one string playing the melody, the other two acting as drones. The tiny, two-stringed rebec, the Arabian fiddle and the triangular stringed psaltery squeaked melodically, transverse flutes, trumpets and horns piped harmonious notes, while drums sounded an occasional deep beat.

The transformation she had effected in the Great Hall had turned out so magnificently she could not restrain a thrill of pride. The entire balustrade running along the side of the mezzanine floor verandah overlooking the Hall below was festooned with greenery interspersed with fresh red and white roses, the motif carried through under the verandahs which formed the ceiling right down the walls to the pink marble floors. Gilt chairs with small matching tables lined the walls. Small oil lamps of red and white glass had been cleverly nestled amid the greenery and flowers in such a way that they would not cause a fire. The effect was simply magical, the scent of roses mingling with that of the perfumed lamps to charm the senses.

A blazing log fire roared orange-red in the fireplace on the fourth side of the Hall. Above the huge marble mantelpiece was draped King Charles's royal banner, surrounded by the spectacular display, in the order of precedence protocol dictated, of the flags of all the princely and noble families in the kingdom. A red-carpeted platform for the king's throne had been erected immediately in front. Huge brass stands containing red and white roses lined the sides of the platform, the four corners of which contained multi-tiered brass candlestands, the wicks in each tier flickering with tiny yellow points of light.

The high-backed throne of intricately carved mahogany was lined with gold, upholstered in red velvet. The arms were a mosaic of mother-of-pearl and black ebony chips, encrusted with red rubies and green emeralds. The royal footstool matched the throne exactly, except that the royal sceptre and the great sword of the Kings of Navarre in a gold scabbard, the hilt studded with rubies and emeralds, had been placed upon it. Here, the king would receive only fellow kings and ambassadors from other countries. Since the ambassadors represented their own monarchs, they ranked equally with their host and did not have to kneel to him but bowed low three times as they approached the throne, where they would kiss the royal hand. The smaller matching chair at the left of the throne was for Princess Mathilde, as senior lady of the Court. Count Gaston would stand behind the throne and to its right, while other senior officials would stand directly behind it.

She crossed the room, graciously bowing to the gorgeously uniformed attendants and footmen who backed away and acknowledging the compliments of the brilliantly dressed officials. A hum of conversation from the ante-room greeted her as she entered the long, wide marble corridor leading to it. A chamberlain hastened to her, bowed low and announced that His Majesty was due to arrive. On this signal, the senior princes and counts began to line the corridor. They would kneel as the king walked slowly towards the throne followed by his immediate entourage, headed by herself and Count Gaston.

Beneath a sparkling array of lights from torches, candelabra and taper-stands, the crowded ante-room, its semi-circular high-vaulted roof covered with bright coloured frescoes, presented a glittering scene: jewellery of the women in their long, close-fitting gowns of blue, purple, burgundy, green or gold, some with hoods or mantillas of matching Spanish or Brussels lace, rivalling the large gems adorning the men. All the princes, nobles and their ladies had outdone themselves in magnificence.

'Our tall, voluptuous Princess Leona looks so ravishing tonight that it will not be long before she is ravished,' Princess Mathilde remarked behind her fan to Countess Isabella.

The men wore tight-fitting belted tunics of different styles, glittering with jewels, some with long tippet sleeves and under-tunics covering the torso above sheer nether-hosen of darker colours. Since it was winter, many wore brilliant surcoats though these had disappeared from fashion for normal wear. The handsome Prince Ferdinand, whose olive skin, fine bones and dark moustache made him look like a Spanish brigand, was dressed in a light brown tunic with borders of brown tourmaline and dark brown nether-hosen. He bowed low to Princess Mathilde as he made way for her. She despised his mocking smile, which reminded her that she had been an easy conquest, though on just one night.

The babel of voices was interrupted by the blare of trumpets sounding the royal fanfare. The gigantic Chief Herald stood at the door to the ante-room. He rapped sharply three times on the marble floor with his gold-mounted ebony staff. A hush quickly descended. 'Make way for His Majesty King Charles Champagne, Supreme Ruler of the Kingdom of León y Navarra!' His stentorian tones would have risen above rumbling thunder.

The crowd parted, clearing a passage along the wide corridor, down which the senior princes and counts hurried to take the places allotted to them under the rules of protocol.

Princess Mathilde calmly walked to the entrance to the ante-room, Countess Isabella following. She paused when she saw the king approaching, the hatchet-faced, proud

Count Gaston in shining white immediately behind him and followed by a glittering entourage. Bull-like, his huge head resting on enormous shoulders, the king was dressed in a black velvet tunic so liberally studded with red rubies, white pearls, green emeralds and blue sapphires that it seemed like a jewelled coat. His white nether-hosen sheathing massive limbs made a startling contrast. His long black hair was neatly combed beneath a gold crown, a huge stone of one of the nine precious gems at each point, a blazing white topaz in the centre. He walked with slow dignity.

Before she knelt to him, as always on such occasions, Princess Mathilde was awed by the sheer majesty of King Charles the Bad.

At midnight yesterday, when the palace trumpets had resounded faintly across the ravine announcing the hour, Pilar had abruptly become a shrouded figure emerging from the swirling mists of her own incantations. Black-shawled head raised attentively above hunched shoulders, she had looked like a great bird. 'The time is not right,' she muttered. 'The spirits are in another house. We must try again tomorrow night.'

Sick disappointment had tugged at Zurika's stomach, but now it was that tomorrow night and the palace trumpets were blaring once again. Standing within her circle of seven lighted black candles, Zurika stared fearfully through the invisible mists of her grandmother's incantations lest Pilar should emerge from them once more to announce another postponement. That would be more than a bitter disappointment, it would be frightening, in case it was Zurika's own presence that was keeping the spirits away.

Pilar's sessions were only performed in the homes of the afflicted, a misfortune to be lifted, a dire ailment to be cured or harrowing fears to be set at rest. She always took Zurika with her on these visits, but did not permit her to be present at the actual ceremonies.

Men said that Pilar sometimes slipped away at dead of night to perform rites in the graveyard on the other side of the mountain, but Zurika never believed such stories and no one, not even the Catholic priests or the Muslim *imams*, would venture into a graveyard after midnight to check their veracity. It being her first experience, Zurika had spent the intervening period since the previous night in a state of mixed emotions suspended by time, anticipation, curiosity, apprehension, occasionally an unreasoning terror. What would the crystal reveal? Would the ceremony somehow affect her sanity? Subjects had been known to fall sick, to be driven mad or even to die from the effects of such events. Would she be consigning her soul to the Devil by participating in what might be regarded by God as an evil rite?

Each time Zurika had managed to set aside her fears through faith in her grandmother. Pilar loved her and would never expose her to harm. But the black candles! Why black?

So when the distant blare of trumpets reached her ears, Zurika felt she had existed only between two sets of trumpet calls, bridged by these swirling mists of Pilar's incantations, those that had ended last night and those that began tonight but which had kept ringing in her ears even during the intervening hours.

The cave had suddenly turned so cold, Zurika shivered as she stood in the centre of the seven black candles of the right hand circle, within yellow flames flickering and smouldering with each hint of breeze that slid through the cracks at the sides of the curtain of hides. A figurine representing a godfather, which could become Majo if the need arose, occupied the centre of the other circle of seven candles. Her mind swinging this way and that,

Zurika's identity slowly slipped away and she became a puppet on the string of Pilar's dictates.

Pilar stopped her chanting and stretched herself out across the mattress of the pallet bed. Her grey head, extended over one edge, was supported by a pillow placed on the wooden bench which had been turned upside down. Her spindly legs hung over the other edge of the bed. A white napkin, with the cross removed from the wall placed on it, covered her wrinkled breasts. A small silver chalice rested on her naked belly.

A few moments of silence ensued, heightened by Pilar's heavy breathing. Like a jagged scar across dry parchment, Pilar began crackling the conjuration in high-pitched, quavering tones.

'*O spirits of dead, O Og, Gog, Magog, O Peter, John, James, O Virgin Mary, receive supplication of this true believer who has power of force, of light, power of the direct rays of divine Jesus.*'

Zurika's gaze was clamped on the crystal. Then it began to glitter, occasionally winking at her. Pilar's incantations, surging through the confined space, soon dominated Zurika to become her entire world, the sound jagging through aching eardrums into her brain. The winking of the crystal slowly emerged from eyes, countless tiny eyes, all nodding, smiling the same invitation. To what?

'*Reveal me what lies within eternal crystal, within rainbow colours of heaven. Bestow the sight on me, sightless sight, reveal the fountains of truth I seek . . .*'

Zurika heard the words as from a distance. The earth was receding from her. She was no longer a body, just a soul staring through a pair of eyes that did not belong to her but were a part of the thousand glittering eyes of the crystal.

The hoot of an owl screeched through Pilar's sudden silence. The whirring of bats' wings serrated Zurika's eardrums, a death stench filled her nostrils. But she was not afraid, for all of it emerged from that mixture of semen, menstrual blood and the blood of bats. The clear tinkling of a liquid brought a breath of fresh air, absorbed the stench, replaced it with the fragrance of camphor. It was Zurika's soul, not her mind, that told her Pilar had poured holy water from the chalice to dispel the foulness from evil spirits attracted by the mixture.

'*O, divine joy! Blessed Mary, Holy Jesus, all saints have cleansed my rite of evil spirits enticed by filthy mixture of blood and semen in the hope of turning sacred into sabbat.*'

Zurika's soul soared with ecstasy. Mine is a virgin body, a virgin mind, a virgin spirit. Pure and clean as holy water.

'*O Jesus, Mary, O Holy Disciples, O Blessed Saints, give this virgin body, this virgin mind, this virgin spirit gift of inner sight. . .*'

In some incredible way, Pilar has penetrated my thoughts, Zurika realized, or else my thoughts have penetrated Pilar, who has cast a spell over me. The power to reveal is hers. The gift of sight is mine. It is not Pilar but I who will read the future.

The thousand eyes of the crystal began to spin, dazzling Zurika. The spinning lights converged and became one. A hollow appeared in the core of the glittering, spinning mass. Within its centre a human form took shape. A man clad in fine raiment, a golden robe lined with jewels, a gold turban with a huge red ruby at its centre, a great curving scimitar gleaming golden at his side. His feet were shod with gem-studded shoes. His glitter outshone the mass within which he stood.

He has no face.

Tears streamed down Zurika's soul.

Nothing has changed. Here is the prince of my dreams, but he still has no face.

'*Reveal him her . . . reveal his face to handmaiden . . . reveal who he is to servant . . . Accept tears of a virgin's*

*heart, crystal as they crystal, as reward. Let soul-tears melt
your heart . . .*'

How did Pilar know what I have seen? How has she
known of my soul's tears? Why has she risen from her
bed?

The death screech of the sacrificed white pigeon rent
Zurika's eardrums. Pilar's sharp gaze pierced her seeing
eyes. The spinning stopped. The figure of the prince
emerged crystal clear.

I do see his face. At last, I see his face.

Oh joy divine.

'Dance for me,' the prince said. His voice was clear as
the crystal from which he had emerged, gentle as dew on
the grass.

Another face appeared in the shadow of his body,
older, gaunt, white-haired, somehow more compelling.

How may this be? Is my prince two people? Does he
have two faces?

The ecstasy exploded in Zurika's brain. She fainted.

By midnight, the Grand Ball was in full swing, with
increasingly loud conversation providing a background to
each dance. Raucous laughter from the corridor and ante-
room into which guests flushed with wine and sated with
good food had spilled, fractured the air; the giant Count
Fernando in particular had a belly laugh that grated on
Princess Mathilde.

She had arranged for the formal dances, the elegant
volta, the solemn and stately *danse basse*, the *cotillion* and
even the *caudrilla*, to take place in the first half of the
night. Now it was time for her bold innovation, the
Andalusian *fandango*, an ancient Spanish dance of Moorish origin which had not yet reached white Spain and the
rest of Europe.

She was standing on the platform chatting with Count
Gaston when the palace trumpets blared the hour. Before

the last echoes died down, the orchestra broke into the triple time of the *fandango*. A nasal voice began singing from the mezzanine. The couple whom she had hired whirled on to the cleared ballroom floor and began to dance, singing while they danced. The woman wore a long dress with black and white bands, the skirt swirling with each step. The man wore tight-fitting black pantaloons, a short beaded tunic and high boots. Whenever the music halted abruptly, the dancers remained rigid, like proud statues. She had taken the trouble to arrange for some of the courtiers and ladies-in-waiting of the Pamplona palace to learn the steps earlier, so couple soon followed couple on the floor to the accompaniment of castanets, guitars and singing. When the onlookers began clapping to the beat of the music, wildly applauding each pair as they ended their dance, she knew that her innovation had been instantly successful.

'Inspirational, Princess!' Count Gaston murmured, his deep, dark eyes sparkling.

'I thank you, Count.' But her mind was on something else.

Through all these years, she had seldom met Count Gaston alone and then only briefly each time. His official life was an open book in the glare of the Court. He had been married to a Nordic princess named Ingemar while on his travels and was known to have loved her devotedly. She had died in childbirth ten years earlier, leaving him completely alone. For him, as it had been for her with Count René, this had been the one love of a lifetime, so they were alike in their fidelity to true love. The similarity, however, ended there for, unlike her, Count Gaston had withdrawn from people. He performed his duties towards his tenants and region punctiliously, attended Court as always, but no one could reach him, still less fathom the person he had become. If he was haunted by the ghosts of his lost love, he never showed it. On the contrary,

Princess Mathilde, unlike anyone else, had always sensed a great inner peace within him which could only be the product of terrible torment fought to submission, though not necessarily overcome.

The time had come for her to probe this enigma, because both reasoning and instinct had told her that Count Gaston could play a pivotal role in the achievement of her goals for King Charles, not merely as Chancellor, but as a man. The count was the soul of honour and a brilliant administrator, just the sort of aide the Emperor Charles would require later to govern his far-flung territories. It was her intention to select all King Charles's highest officials, not only because she trusted her own judgment – even the appointment of Count Gaston as Chancellor had been made by King Charles on her personal advice – but also because it would give her the reins of power. While she would gladly concede the imperial role to her favourite person, she knew that all King Charles craved for was the glory and was convinced that she alone would wield power in his best interests.

The soul of honour! This tall, hatchet-faced aristocrat, his sword-blade body clad in white satin, was the soul of honour. Would he be prepared to participate in some of the courses of action she had in mind, such as eliminating King Pedro after King Charles married his daughter Princess Beatrice and the Moorish kingdom of Granada had been conquered? While she experienced an occasional pang at the thought of her Charles having a permanent bed-partner, she had no fear that a seventeen-year-old virgin, even the daughter of one like Maria de Padilla, who had been capable of arousing incredible loyalty and devotion from King Pedro, could acquire any influence over her husband or become his confidante. Women that young provided company, never companionship.

Count Gaston bowed. 'Would you do me the honour of this dance, Princess?' he inquired.

He was a graceful dancer who obviously knew and responded to inner rhythm so she would have loved to dance with him, but she had other plans tonight. She wielded her fan of grey dove feathers more vigorously. 'I would love to,' she responded. 'But do you know what would do *me* honour?'

'I am at your command, Princess.'

'It has got very close in here and I need some fresh air,' she smiled at him, 'even of the cold winter variety outside. Would you walk with me in the private courtyard, please? I promise you a turn with the *fandango* as soon as we get back.'

He bowed again. 'I would be honoured, Princess. Pray, let me get some cloaks.' He signalled to an attendant as if her request had been the most natural thing in the world.

King Charles was in the centre of the ballroom, dancing with the woman dancer she had hired. He had been taught to dance from boyhood and, like most burly men, was tremendously light on his feet. His face flushed, he was having a marvellous time.

They were followed by curious glances as they threaded their way through the guests. Count Fernando came up to them, bowed, kissed her hand. 'Fabuloush . . . er tremendoush ball!' he declaimed loudly, a huge hand to his heart. He was well in his cups and she steeled herself for the great guffaw. It came. 'Your sh . . . ch . . . choice of *fandango*,' he placed thumb and forefinger together, pushed them away from him. 'Terrific.' He paused, trying to focus down on her face. 'Will you marry me, Princesssh?'

This was a stock joke between them, well known in Court. She gave him her usual response. 'Certainly, Sir. Name your . . . er . . . weapons. My seconds will call on you to arrange for the duel.'

'Ha! ha! ha! ha! ha!' His great laugh, reeking with wine breath, smote her as she bowed and passed on, followed

101

by Count Gaston. She led the way through the ante-room, down the side corridor that led to the royal quarters which had its own private courtyard.

It was cold and clear outside, a typical winter night with a frosty blue sky and scattered crystal stars above the tracery of stark, winter-worn branches. The pure air was tinctured with the winter odour of wood ash. A wild leopard coughed from the king's private zoo about a hundred yards along the white flagstone walkway. 'He is feeling the cold, poor thing,' Princess Mathilde remarked as they paced towards the dark outline of the cages. 'He is from the East, as you know, and the climate does not exactly suit him.'

'Any more than the captivity, I am sure.'

The words were lightly said, but they arrested her attention. 'You disapprove of caging wild animals?' she inquired, taking his arm.

He stopped, half turned to look down at her. 'Do you want a serious answer, Princess, or shall we keep this light?'

A serious conversation was certainly what she had intended. 'It was a serious question, Sir Count.'

'Very well then. I try not to approve or disapprove of anyone or anything.'

She was puzzled. 'Your likes, dislikes, tastes?'

'Can be given expression, enjoyed – even my aversions – without the judgmental quality needed for approval or disapproval.'

King Charles had told her how serious Count Gaston could be, but this statement was profound enough to make her wonder whether she had not missed something by not making it a point to get to know him better in a court which, like all others, tended to be superficial. 'Do you like or dislike wild animals in captivity then?'

'I like all animals. They are more predictable than

people. I do not like captivity for anyone or anything. Both animals and people should be free as God made them.'

'You really believe that? Are not all things upon this earth meant for the delectation of man? And are not serfs the captives of their villages for the benefit of their feudal lords?'

'You of all people would not sincerely believe that, Princess. You have too much respect for human beings.' His lips parted, showing white teeth beneath the black moustache. 'Though not necessarily for people.'

A tremor ran through her. Did this man know her better than she knew him? She did not like that, because it meant she was not in control. She stared up at him, searching the hatchet face. Had she detected a hint of the old torment within him? 'It never quite leaves you, does it?' she enquired gently, changing the subject.

'Nor it does,' he replied directly and steadily, with no attempt at pretence. 'As you well know.'

She looked away, stared through the gloom, remembering Prince René, feeling one with the count. 'There are times, just occasionally, thank God, when it seems to have happened only yesterday.'

'I well understand the harshness of yesterday's tragedy as opposed to today's, for the reality strikes only later.'

'We should have had this conversation years ago. I am sorry I did not take the initiative.'

'It could only have happened today,' he replied enigmatically.

Now what did he mean by that? Did he know of her plans, her motives. No, no, that was impossible.

'Do you ever get lonely, like me at times? I mean soul-lonely for the right human being beside you, just beside you, not even to talk.'

'No. Solitude is my true and constant companion. I try not to want the things I have decided not to need.'

'*You* decided not to need?' She could not keep the incredulous note from her voice.

'*Ciertamente*, Princess. Do we not always decide what we need and do not need? Our main problem is when we do not keep our needs within the confines of whatever we can attain. An even greater problem arises when we drive ruthlessly to satisfy unnecessary needs, not because of the pain we inflict on those we stamp out of our way, but because of what we do to ourselves. Nearly eighteen hundred years ago, a wise Eastern philosopher who called himself the Buddha, or Enlightened One, observed that desire is the cause of suffering, because desire brings clinging and clinging causes suffering.'

'You accept such heretical beliefs?' There was no criticism in the question. A sudden gust of wind brought faint echoes of music from the ballroom. She shivered, drew her cloak closer with her free hand. Was she also hearing the gust of Count Fernando's belly-laugh?

'Heresy is any opinion contrary to the orthodox doctrine of our Church. I cannot say that the Buddha's teachings are contrary to our doctrine. Some of what he has said closely antecedes Our Lord's Sermon on the Mount. Some of it supplements our doctrines without contradicting them.'

'What is your religion, Sir Count?'

'I am labelled a Christian. But that is just a label.'

He had struck home without realizing it. 'Ah, labels. The hallmarks of the insecure.' She had taken some of his measure, but there was much that she would never discover, not because he was secretive, but because it would not occur to him to open up.

'I try not to be introspective either,' he remarked, uncannily picking up her thoughts. 'So I do not even have answers as to who I really am. It is not important. I *am*. That is all.'

104

How like her own thinking. 'I agree,' she responded, remembering her conversation of a few months earlier with King Charles.

'I simply strive for perfection in everything I think, say or do,' he added, courteously saving her from the need to ask questions to fill one of the gaps in her exploration of him. 'Even the simple things, like the way I wear my sword. So it is *my* idea of perfection, one that I offer God in the hope that it is acceptable by God's divine knowledge of who I am.'

'Do you like yourself, love yourself? We are told that these are the first essentials to liking and loving others.'

'Do you seriously believe that, Princess?'

'No.'

'Nor do I. On the contrary, I think that if I like myself, or love myself, I would personally become so preoccupied with myself that I would not have enough affection or giving for others. I find all self-analysis utterly boring. I leave introspection to saints, who are generally the products of their own sense of inferiority which has created insecurities, courtiers and . . . er . . . lovers.'

A trill of laughter escaped her. 'Spoken like one of the truly strong,' she declared. 'You and I do not need such introspection, let alone the deplorable self-love that follows it, from which it sprang in the first place!'

'I am honoured to be included with you . . . er . . . under such a *label*, Princess.'

'*Touché*, Sir Count.' It was enough. She would have to enjoy Count Gaston as a human being, use him for his talents and qualities. She could never manipulate him and he would always follow the dictates of his own personal code. 'You are a remarkable man, Count Gaston.' She meant the words. 'It is getting colder. Shall we return?'

His grin was almost boyish, the sides of his eyes crinkling. '*Ciertamente*, Princess. I would hate you, like that captured leopard, to be the cold air's captive.'

105

Chapter 6

Pedro the Cruel glanced almost with affection at the scarlet-robed Bishop Eulogius seated primly opposite his carved wooden desk in the small study of the Toledo palace. The dumpy prelate had fulfilled his part of the bargain, consummating the temporary marriage of Castile with Christian Navarre, Catalonia and Aragon speedily and effectively by bringing their rulers to Toledo, all of them assembled here for a discussion this morning. The little bishop-prick has certainly earned the promised fiefdoms and certain desirable maidens, King Pedro thought.

'Your Majesties are here today by the grace of God,' the Bishop intoned. 'Forsooth, we are all united by Christian faith, through my personal intervention as the instrument of Holy Church.'

You had to take personal credit for it, King Pedro reflected, making out that it is you and not Holy Church that has achieved unity. And of course, 'intervenes' is a good word, for Holy Church never interferes! Well, perhaps you did effect Christian unity, but I alone shall lead it. King Pedro deliberately excluded the cleric's incanted tones from his ears while his eyes sought the men seated in his study. The oak panelling gleamed rich in the silvery morning sunlight pouring through the open window, which made the large oil paintings of bullfights more stark. In contrast, the twittering of sparrows and the warbling of a dove outside were mellow, muted, soothing.

Though they were only six in number, the three Christian rulers and their Chancellors, all of whom had arrived at the Toledo palace the previous evening, packed the small room. Charles the Bad of Navarre, his great bulk encased in red tunic and pantaloons, dominating the room horizontally, was an open book of aggressiveness. In contrast his Chancellor, Count Gaston, lean and smooth as a sword blade, was an enigma. Dressed in white silk, the slim Basque was as elegant as his royal master was gross.

'Which is the real *Deus ex machina*, Your Eminence?' Count Gaston riposted. 'Holy Church or yourself? I would swear to God that intervention was really that of Holy Church as *your* personal instrument!'

Bishop Eulogius smiled cherubically, the blue eyes vanishing into the folds of their crinkled sides. 'You have a truly droll wit, Count Gaston,' he chuckled. 'Some might, however, consider such a remark sacrilegious . . .'

'But not you, Eminence. Neither you nor Holy Church would declare the truth to be sacrilege.'

'Dam' right,' King Henry grunted, thrusting out a black-bearded chin from his massive chest. 'We for one would never have answered a call from just any prelate, nor even from the Holy Father in Avignon.' The ruler of Aragon was well-known for his bluntness. A gorilla of a man, almost wider than he was tall, his huge head squatted on heavy thickset shoulders with no neck to support it, like the rump of a man squatting to relieve himself. He had arrived with Count Rafael, the pink-cheeked homosexual of the lazy smile whom he had recently appointed his Chancellor. 'In truth, it is your eminence, Eminence, that commanded our present presence here.'

King Pedro found Aragon's attempts at wit as simian as his build, but Bishop Eulogius dimpled with genuine pleasure.

A sniff was the only contribution of King Philip of Catalonia. The ruler of the small Mediterranean kingdom dominated the room vertically, being the tallest man present by far. His long, thin body was topped by a long thin neck with a prominent Adam's apple wobbling up and down beneath a long thin face. Thin cheeks thrust a prominent hooked nose even more sharply forward. Alert eyes darted here and there so sharply that one expected them to have yellow rims, completing the appearance of an eagle. His Chancellor was a bird of a man, obviously full of the cleverness and self-importance characteristic of little men, a Count whose name King Pedro had already forgotten. As Count Gaston had once remarked, it was more important to forget the names of self-important people than to remember those of the truly important.

'Forsooth, Your Majesties' unanimous vote of confidence gives me confidence to go forward with my proposals,' Bishop Eulogius continued blandly, adopting King Henry's vein. He smoothed his scarlet robe with a small plump hand, symbolically removing any possible wrinkles in the royal accord. 'For some inexplicable reason, God, in His infinite wisdom, chose to spare the heretic Moors from the scourge of the Black Plague. I rather suspect that this is because He had fewer vacancies in Hell than in Heaven.' He crossed himself piously at having presumed to divine the divine reasoning. 'Meanwhile, I have just received word from the Holy Father that the white Christian nations of Europe have lost over twenty-five million people to this scourge.' He paused to savour the effect of this startling statistic on those present.

King Pedro was aghast. He knew that the Pope was taking a census of Black Plague deaths, but never dreamed that the figures were so disastrous. He resisted the desire to swear. He always practised decorum in public. After all, cruelty was most effective when exercised beneath a mask of refinement.

'Our population in Catalonia alone has declined from 450,000 to about 350,000,' King Philip interjected gloomily. His voice was curiously deep and disembodied, seeming, as with most tall, cadaverous men, to emerge from the nether regions of his belly. 'Barcelona alone is down from 50,000 to 40,000. Any contribution we make to Christian unity will of necessity be limited.'

'We too have had our reverses from the Plague,' King Henry asserted. His yellow-toothed smile revealed no personal feeling or concern. 'Many of our artisans and small traders have fled to the south, to Italy and even Sicily, to avoid the scourge. But we shall not allow cowards to deter us. Aragon needs to get its economy back into shape . . . er . . . so it can contribute the more to Christian unity. What are our rewards for participating in this adventure?' He directed a penetrating gaze at King Pedro. 'Other than the prize of the fair hand of your beautiful daughter, Princess Beatrice, offered to those of us who, like our brother King Charles of Navarre and ourself, are single.'

'And survive the tourney,' King Charles the Bad interjected succinctly.

King Pedro's spies had told him that the ruler of Navarre had been bragging that he would be the one to win the joust. What King Henry had just asked, however, was the very question which had been concerning Pedro since Bishop Eulogius first sent out the invitations to the conference. All these rulers were men of greed and ambition. Only the ten-year truce had prevented them from waging war against the Moors since 1340. When the Black Plague followed in 1348, their countries had been drained of men, money and even the willpower to plan what they would do when the truce ended. Now King Yusuf, whose kingdom had not been affected by the plague, had taken the initiative and struck and they all saw the need for action, but only the promise of wealth would move them.

'Christian unity, white Spanish supremacy, national pride in Iberia are merely concepts to which we pay lip-service before our people, the Church and history, Your

109

Majesties.' Count Gaston was echoing King Pedro's own sentiments. 'We create these ideals to drum up support from our noblemen and their vassals for the attainment of our own true goals. Let us at least be honest among ourselves and admit that our principal motivations are wealth and power.'

'*En verdad*, Count Gaston is right,' King Pedro averred. 'I need not remind you of the vast wealth of the Moors, amassed through ten years of peace in Granada, which is but the outpost of a Muslim federation that stretches from North Africa to the Middle East. Granada's gold, silver and jewels are the ingredients of prosperity. Our soldiers will have loot and we kings will have the treasuries of the Moorish potentates to share in proportion to our contribution to the cause.'

'Of Christian unity,' Bishop Eulogius thrust in smoothly. 'On account of which Holy Church would of course be entitled to its tithe.'

Fuck you, King Pedro thought irritably. But he curbed his temper because it was the call for Christian unity that had been the excuse for these kings to come together in the first place.

'Since our subjects can neither amass wealth nor pay for the salvation of their souls, they need causes for which to lay down their poverty-stricken lives.' This time it was Charles the Bad who echoed King Pedro's own views. 'They must be offered the hope of plunder on earth so they can buy a heavenly reward with Peter's pence extracted from the heretic! A commendable irony, but who will physically rule the conquered territory?'

'Granada spreads below our own borders,' King Pedro responded, his voice decisive. 'It has always posed a direct threat to Castile, which has suffered most for over five centuries from Moorish incursions northwards. The policing of a conquered Granada had best be left to the rulers of Castile.' Thinking that a rather neat way of staking his claim, he smiled with his mouth at King Charles the Bad, then glanced at King Henry. 'Castile would of course share its rule with whomever wins the hand of our fair daughter, Princess Beatrice.'

He raised a hand as the wrangling started. 'Hear us out, brother monarchs. Since you want some of the Moorish territory only for what you can extract from it, not for power, nor the right to police a few more acres of land, the continued sharing of Granada's resources can also be arranged.' He noted Bishop Eulogius's quick glance of appreciation at his cunning.

'Who will lead the expedition?' It was typical of human nature that it was King Philip of Catalonia, which was virtually a satellite of Aragon, the man who would have the least right, having made the smallest contribution, who should ask the question.

'Castile, making the largest contribution and taking the greatest risk, should provide the leader,' King Pedro retorted. 'In truth, however, it would be a shared responsibility.'

'Alliances are sickening things to establish and once formed are as difficult to hold together as the droppings of a flying bird,' Count Gaston murmured.

True, but the alliances had to be made, for they were King Pedro's only hope of security if the Moors did invade Castile. He wanted power: they wanted wealth. These men were also his source of future power; he could bring them wealth. Charles the Bad was not being his usual raucous, demanding self, however, and even King Henry seemed more compliant, probably because each of the two bastards thought he would win the joust, become Prince Consort to Princess Beatrice, assassinate the king her father and seize supreme power. Being a king was a lonely business. You could trust no one. He at least had Maria de Padilla who would give her life for him. Would Beatrice give the same loyalty and devotion to whomever became her husband? Would she betray him, her father, for her husband's benefit?

'Your Majesties, may I remind you that, in addition to Reconquista, we are here today to save our hides from stripping by the Moors,' Bishop Eulogius incanted. 'King Yusuf's recent foray into Castile signals his intentions. Yesterday, a blow at Castile, tomorrow at all of Spain. Never forget that the Moors once occupied most of Iberia. I swear to God, they will do it again if we do not unite and attack first. King Yusuf has all the motivation he needs, a son and heir, reportedly due to come of age in two or three years, the end of a humiliating armistice following the even more humiliating defeat of his predecessor at the Battle of Salado, a prey weakened by dread disease and undoubtedly a burning ambition for a place in history, with an assured welcome to the Muslim Paradise when he dies. I for one doubt that King Yusuf is moved purely by religious zeal.' He looked around him for reactions.

Only King Charles nodded, his square jaw moving vigorously on its neckless axis, but none of the other rulers demurred. Encouraged, the bishop proceeded decisively. 'I suggest you first discuss the basis of your alliance. What contributions in men, money, armament, supplies and transportation will each of the four kingdoms make? It is only then that questions of who will lead the expedition, the sharing of the spoils of war and the wielding of power upon success can be intelligently settled.'

'The art of life is to live beyond other people's means,' Count Gaston murmured.

'Catalonia has more than men, a united front and debts to offer,' Count Rafael stated. 'Remember, Barcelona would be an essential port of embarkation for sending supplies south or for a naval expeditionary force to take the Moors on the eastern flank or the rear.'

'In truth, from Barcelona nowadays, it would undoubtedly be the rear.' King Charles guffawed at his thrust against the homosexual Count Rafael.

'The only front that can cause a man real pain is indeed the rear.' Count Rafael did not feel the need to be defensive about his sexual preference. 'But is there not always a price for peerless pleasure?'

'Let us stop duelling and get down to details of the army we can mobilize for this enterprise.' A man of action, King Pedro had no time for the frippery of diplomatic sparring. 'You may call it anything you like, a crusade, a holy war, rape of the Moors, but it is Holy Church and white Spain, a two-horse carriage, that brought us here.' His smile was feral. 'Now we have arrived, let us not debate as to why we mounted the vehicle but where we go from now.' He directed his gaze at the cleric. 'Bishop Eulogius, would you please act as our scribe on this occasion, since we do not wish to summon one of our own and run the risk of having our plans betrayed.'

The primate's pink chins moved vigorously in assent. 'Let us fix the date for assembly of our forces, determine how much in men and material each one of Your Majesties will contribute and proceed to preparing a plan for what will follow the tourney for the fair hand of Princess Beatrice.' He beamed. 'You will go down in Christian history for your fourteenth-century Crusade, powered by Holy Church.'

There was an unusually placid smile on Pilar's face when she returned home to the cave from the city that evening and Zurika, who was tuned in to her grandmother's every mood, was quick to notice it. Zurika had spent the rest of the night following the seance and all the next day dreaming of her handsome prince, whose face she had finally seen in her vision. She occasionally puzzled over

113

the identity of the second face, but since Pilar had no explanation for that part of the vision, she did not let it dim her excitement.

Pilar obviously had some important news, but it would be useless to question her, so Zurika waited impatiently for her to broach the subject. They were finishing their salt beef stew, seated opposite each other in the outer room of the cave in the fitful yellow light from the single white taper, before the knowing look returned to Pilar's rheumy eyes, indicating that she was ready to impart.

'Maybe your dream yesterday come to pass sooner than you think,' she declared, breaking the silence of the cave in her hoarse voice. She wiped her platter clean of the remaining gravy and slurped the contents into her mouth through blackened teeth.

Zurika's heart started to beat faster. Even Pilar never knew that her real dream was not from yesterday but had been with her for as far back as she could remember. Yet, kindly though she was, Pilar would never respond to over-eager curiosity, having always trained Zurika to self-control, so Zurika confined herself to a lift of the eyebrows. 'Really?' she inquired.

Pilar's face wrinkled even more in a smile that said she was aware of Zurika's studied reaction. 'You shall see your prince,' she stated flatly.

Zurika could not hold herself back any longer. Her platter rattled on to the earth floor as she leapt to her feet. In two strides she was kneeling beside her grandmother, her hands clasping Pilar's bony arms. 'Oh *querida*, beloved grandmother, when? Where? How?' Her brown eyes were sparkling with the excitement tingling through her whole body.

Pilar patted her affectionately on the cheek. 'Now, now, little one, no rush me.'

Zurika rubbed a cheek on Pilar's bony thigh, then looked up at her. A spark of delight brought out the

114

gypsy girl mischief. 'I *am* holding back, otherwise I'd be shaking the truth out of you, *abuela*,' she cried, crinkling her eyes.

'Such disrespect,' Pilar cackled. 'You were always imp, not of Satan but of angels. Yes, you angel-imp.' She wiped her mouth with the back of her hand, set her platter on the ground. 'When I in market today, messenger from palace come see me, knowing I sit by bird-cages shop every day, telling fortune. He ask me follow him secretly to palace where important person wait to talk with me. "And who earn my bread while I go from here?" I ask him. Without no more word, he give me one gold coin. One *gold* coin!' She reached into the fold of her blouse, pulled out the coin, held it gleaming to the light, bit it. 'More I can earn one month.' She giggled happily.

'Tell me more, *abuela*, grandmother,' Zurika urged.

'Man lead me to palace and from there to Gen al Arif.' Another cackle escaped Pilar. 'No woman ever been there. Only I, Pilar the Gypsy, have now see it. What do you think of your *abuela* now, my beauty?' She preened herself.

The child in this ancient woman never failed to charm Zurika. She clapped her hands, sprang to her feet and stamped out a *golpe* rhythm. 'Olé!' she cried, flinging one arm up. 'My tribute to Pilar, the Gypsy Queen.'

Pilar's face wrinkled even more with pleasure. 'Sit down and I tell you what I see. Tall tower and white walls of Gen al Arif on the other side of valley build on breast of palace mountain. Beautiful gardens, long pool, great fountain, huge cypresses, terraces, all like heaven. Even though I take to outside court only through servants rooms, I smell flowers, hear birds sing all around. The sage who want to see me called Abou bon Ebben. He meet me in Hall of Pictures. But when I get there, everything so like heaven I not see any picture. Oh

115

daughter, you never see anything like that. Gold, marble, ivory, jewels, like magic also.'

'Did you get to see Prince Ahmed?' Zurika demanded eagerly.

'Wait, wait, dearie. You wait now?' Pilar paused, chewed on blackened teeth, her cheeks folding into wrinkled pouches. 'Abou bon Ebben even older than Pilar, must be over eighty. He have white hair, clever eyes. He tell me everything, promise kill me if I tell secrets anyone! But to you I talk. All story we have hear of Prince Ahmed in Gen al Arif palace, true.' She slowly nodded her white head. 'Now prince be eighteen, they have trouble.'

'He is not sick?' Zurika inquired anxiously.

'Health fine, but mind not so good.'

'Is it?' Zurika's breath caught. 'Is he mad?'

'The wise peoples, dearie, they think they knows everything. They knows nothing of heart and sicknesses that hurt heart. Prince never know about love, but need love, so hungry heart break loose.'

Zurika listened with astonishment as Pilar unfolded the story of Prince Ahmed's revolt, commencing three months earlier and ending with his adoration of the magnolia tree the previous morning. 'So what does Abou bon Ebben think *you* can do to help Prince Ahmed, *abuela*?' she finally inquired, secretly admitting how thrilled she would be to give her own love to the love-hungry prince.

'He think I make Prince Ahmed not mad again. I find out by magic what wrong with Prince, then cure him.'

'Can you do it?'

Pilar cackled. 'Of course I do it, even if no can. I know what wrong with Prince Ahmed. How can old fart sage, who never know his own seed and no have no seed, find cure for heart sick without love?'

116

How can an old crone know about a man's need, Zurika wondered.

As usual, Pilar picked up her thoughts. 'Women knows things because women earth,' she declared. 'Men have seed, some men. They only plant seed in us.' She cackled again, dryly this time. 'We grow plant.'

'Did you see the prince?'

'I said to this Lord bon Ebben, I must see prince if I to help him.'

'And did you see him? Did you? Did you?' Zurika could have shrieked with excitement.

'Indeed.' Pilar paused to fix a solemn gaze on Zurika, binding her with its spell. 'He be prince you saw. He so handsome I want for myself.'

The last words passed over Zurika's head. 'Describe him to me, please, *querida* darling,' Zurika pleaded.

'He tall, slender, wear cloth of gold tunic with emeralds and diamonds on border. He have great red ruby centre of turban. His skin, colour of ripe olive, smooth, tight like gypsy. He eyes, very lover . . . dark brown, hoods of eagle, hard outside, very soft inside, like doe.'

Zurika's indrawn breath ended in a sigh. She barely noticed that it was echoed by Pilar's own 'Oh!' for Pilar had described the prince of her vision.

'I have some part of prince somehow,' Pilar muttered.

Zurika did not understand. 'What will you do to help him? When will you do it? Can I come with you?' She laid a hand on Pilar's bony arm. 'Please, *abuela*. You *always* take me.'

'I arrange for tomorrow evening, dearie. I go palace and be alone with Prince Ahmed. I ask for tallest tower of Gen al Arif, where Lord bon Ebben prison him after he make love to tree last morning.'

Zurika's stomach flopped with disappointment. She could have screamed aloud. Pilar had said 'I', not 'we'. Cunning intruded, however, and she calmly said, 'You

117

seem to have planned to go alone. I suppose I'm not good enough to go with you to such an important place as the palace.' She held up a cautionary hand. 'Don't worry, *abuela*, I understand.' Then, even more cunningly, 'If Majo comes for me because it is evening and you are not here, I shall kill him.' She reached through the folds of her dress, drew out her knife. It glittered in the pale light. 'With this!' she hissed.

'No need for play-act, dearie,' Pilar replied calmly. 'You not come inside palace, but I have plan for you.'

'What? What?'

Pilar told her.

He did not know why he had agreed to see the old gypsy from across the valley yesterday, except that he had been ashamed at what had occurred in the garden. Serenading the magnolia tree seemed natural to him, but the orgasm and emission, in public too, had humiliated him. Experiencing it in his dreams was one thing, but in reality it was shameful, especially when bon Ebben's only reaction to the disgusting episode had been a pitying glance and a quiet command that he go to his chambers and wash himself discreetly. No one must know of this, the sage had added, and Prince Ahmed's cheeks had burned with shame.

Prince Ahmed was not merely bewildered, he wondered whether his mind had become unhinged. Had there been insanity in his family? Was this the curse of Yusuf ibn Nagralla, the Jew? Confined by his tutor to the apartment in the Gen al Arif's tallest tower, Prince Ahmed had paced agitatedly up and down all day and tossed restlessly on his bed most of the night. Anger at his father, the king, and at bon Ebben, whose execution he could order when he became king, alternated with apprehension that he might never be fit to rule. His one unwavering determination was never again to submit to the authority of either of those monsters who were responsible for his present plight.

It was Tarif who had finally persuaded him to agree to bon Ebben's request that he see this crone – what was her name, Pilar? After all, what did he have to lose? If you are sick in body, Tarif's black fingers had sign-languaged, you see the physician. Your sickness is in your mind. Perhaps this Pilar is a mind physician.

Am I mad then?

Tarif's version of a laugh had escaped him. No, the deaf-mute had mouthed. The gypsy may be able to see whether someone has placed a charm on you and if so to exorcize the evil spirit. She is also well known for being able to tell the future.

So here he was, Prince Ahmed, the eighteen-year-old heir to the throne of Andalusia, seated on a filigreed ivory ottoman, awaiting a gypsy sorceress in the living chamber of his gilded prison. The room had been cleared of all furniture save for a white marble table between two matching ottomans. The one on which he now sat faced the open window of the chamber, through which he could see afternoon sunlight bathing the distant, snow-capped Sierra Nevada mountains and the clear blue skies above them. The other ottoman, opposite him, was for the old gypsy woman. The trilling of birds from far below the tower was the only sound, reaching his ears so faintly that a sense of unreality gripped him and was heightened by the heady camphor scent from the gilded incense burners lining the walls. Not even the clarity of white-gold sunlight pouring through the windows onto the pink marble floors could dispel the feeling.

He stood up, walked to the window, stared at the flat black rock on the barren escarpment immediately below him. How had that rock been formed? The creation of Almighty Allah, no doubt, but how and when had Allah created it?

The heavy door behind him creaked open. He swung round. An old crone hobbled in, baring blackened teeth in a smile that creased wrinkled cheeks. She wore a red linen robe reaching to her ankles. Her feet were bare. She carried a large bag of some yellow weave. The door creaked shut behind her. She hobbled up to him, genuflected and kissed his hand. He was revolted by the smell of her unwashed body. The sense of unreality heightened. A door had creaked open, an old witch had hobbled in, the door creaked shut. It was like something out of a nightmare.

Prince Ahmed watched as Pilar placed the bag on the floor, sank on both knees before it and began removing its contents, which she placed on the marble table, muttering some strange incantation. Two white ceramic containers, three black hairs, a rosary of small vertebrae and dice, a little bowl, a silver cup into which she poured some liquid from a goblet, a large crystal, a candle, a silver crucifix which Prince Ahmed was tempted to seize and fling out of the window as the symbol of an infidel faith.

'Sit here, Prince,' Pilar finally commanded, pointing to the ottoman that faced the windows. 'Look at crystal on table. No look anywhere else.'

He was about to rebel at being ordered about by a commoner, a gypsy at that, when he remembered Tarif's admonitions and meekly obeyed. As Pilar's muttering changed to an incantation, the sense of unreality slowly dissipated to fascination. She placed a small red pillow on the floor, stretched her body across the centre of her ottoman and rested her white head on the pillow.

Pilar began her conjuration in a hoarse voice, yet each word was clear as a bell-note.

Prince Ahmed stared at the crystal. Some trick of the shafts of sunlight pouring into the room made it glitter with countless eyes, all winking back at him. They converged to a single shaft of light which brought unity to his own two eyes. Pilar's incantations rose to a single volume of sound that rang in his ears. A hideous stench seeped into his nostrils. All senses captive, the rest of the world receded.

The tinkling of water reached through his captivity.

'You evil spirit, this be holy water. Go away, go away.'

Pilar's command reached him faintly, yet he understood its meaning and responded. The chamber was suddenly pure; the crystal eyes began to wink in triumph.

'Reveal to eyes of thy servant cure for what ail him.'

The words were repeated again and again, beating at his eardrums until they penetrated his brain.

'Reveal . . . reveal . . .'

The crystal eyes began spinning. Faster and faster. Separating, converging to become one. Now they were a single eye whirling, whirling . . . slowing down . . . slowing, grinding to a stop.

This is a mirror.

A figure slowly took shape within the mirror. Its outlines sharpened. What is this? No, who is this?

A human being in gypsy clothes, dancing. Could this be what they meant in the books when they spoke of a young woman, for this was a younger version of old Pilar?

How gracefully she dances, upper body erect, moving only from the waist down, long black hair tossing free with every stamp of the shapely feet.

She has no face. I simply must see her face. Dear Allah, grant me sight of her face.

'Reveal to thy servant sight of . . . face . . .' The plea was repeated, again and again.

How did she know I could not see the face? Did she hear my silent prayer?

The blur beneath the masses of hair began to clear slowly, as if in response to each repeated plea.

Dear Allah, what exquisite beauty. Olive skin, tight

drawn over fine bones, soft mouth, red as pale rosebuds, dimpled cheeks. The eyes, the dark-brown sultry eyes, latent with passion, the soul of all sorrow, the throb of a smile. Dear Allah, what exquisite beauty.

'You gaze on beauty of young girl. No more you need trees and flowers. No more you need horse, sword, walls of tower. Now you have tree, flower, song of bird, perfume of blossom, power of horse and sword, all in one . . . young woman.'

He gazed spellbound, moved to holy heights, totally the captive of face and form, grace and movement. Dear Allah, this is what they hid from me. Why? Why? Why?

'Open eyes, prince. Go to window.'

No, no, no. I want to remain here, enraptured by this crystal window, forever.

'Go to window . . .'

No, no, no.

A sharp click of fingers. The face in the mirror began to fade, the figure became blurred. Oh no! He reached out blindly for the crystal. Don't go. Please don't go. It was snatched away before he could grasp it.

In despair, he rushed to the window. He had suffered enough. He would throw himself out to end it all. Some deep-rooted teaching of Islam intruded. No suicide if you want to enter Paradise.

He hesitated, but only briefly.

He stood by the open window, sunlight warm on his chilled body. He trembled, began to shake. He grasped the window ledge to steady himself. Looked down. The drop was great, to jagged black rocks below. Sweat prickled his body. Dear Allah, help me.

His gaze slipped to the further distance of the flat slab of black rock, riveted back to the depth, grasped the sight, flashed back to the slab.

Merciful Allah!

There she was in the flesh, her gaze fixed on the

122

window, dancing. Her back was to the sun, so her face was in shadow, but he knew from the crystal what her eyes looked like.

'You now have flesh and blood. You no more need tree, flower, horse, sword. You now mine.'

Enthralled by the beauty he was witnessing, he barely heard Pilar's cackle.

Chapter 7

The girl had danced for almost half an hour, ending with a final *golpe* stamp and long moment when, chest heaving with her breathing, her gaze remained locked into his. She blew him a kiss, ran across the slab of rock and vanished into the surrounding boulders and undergrowth. Emptiness where she had been, so vibrant in beauty. He would tear his heart out to replace her image. In a daze of longing for the miracle to return, for just one more glimpse of this revelation of loveliness, he had turned to plead with Pilar.

'You see Zurika every single evening, if stand at window just before the sun set,' the old woman had promised. A cunning gleam crossed her eyes. 'But only you do work proper, so Lord bon Ebben know Pilar cure you. Also must keep Zurika dancing secret from everyones.'

Prince Ahmed had readily promised and Zurika had danced for him each evening, remaining in his consciousness every second of the day and serving as his inspiration to adhere rigidly to his daily schedule and do all he undertook perfectly, as if she were watching him. Noticing the gradual evaporating of his tutor's concerns, he strove even harder to set them at rest, because this was essential if he was to keep his evening trysts without exciting suspicion. As for his imprisonment in the tower, he now welcomed it for giving him the freedom of romance.

Meanwhile, Zurika haunted his dreams and exquisitely filled his waking moments. He wrote a poem to her every day and composed many a song, when his rigorous timetable permitted. All of it a secret, which he dare not share even with Tarif, if only because he had given his oath of secrecy to Pilar.

Without knowing what love was, Prince Ahmed had fallen in love with a dream figure. He stopped serenading trees and when he had wet dreams it was merely a passage of unused fluid unaccompanied by dreams. His entire adoration was transferred to the living object of his adoration and his daily life centred on the evening assignation.

'I have just returned from giving your royal father my report and he is well pleased with the progress you have made, Prince,' bon Ebben declared as they sat at breakfast in the tower that morning. 'His Majesty even summoned me to attend *subh* in the palace mosque and granted me an audience for this very purpose. Now that you have returned to your normal routine, we may soon be able to let you resume your previous life as well.'

Prince Ahmed fought against the old anger that began mounting in him. 'Normal routine, normal life!' he grated. 'What is *normal*? What is normal about my routine? And what is this *normal* life to which you are referring?'

'Aah! There is no such thing as a normal life in the absolute, Your Highness,' bon Ebben responded calmly.

'You have the skill of an expert swordsman with speech. It infuriates me at times.' Prince Ahmed leapt to his feet.

'Fury is normal only for barbarians!' bon Ebben twinkled at him with a superior lift of grey eyebrows. 'It is a luxury that people of quality cannot afford! Sit down decorously and then tell me courteously what is normal in your life that is not normal to a prince. Breathe the scent of camphor from those gold incense burners at the entrance to this room, look at these floors of marble, at the black and red of the Bokhara rug on which you stand, at the mother-of-pearl inlay on the arms and back of the chair you have just vacated with a lack of decorum that is certainly not normal for royalty, and tell me how much of this chamber will ever represent normalcy to the poor Flamenco gypsies living in the caves across the ravine.'

The reference to the gypsies calmed Prince Ahmed more than his tutor's admonitions. He resumed his seat. 'You are confusing me again with words,' he muttered sullenly. 'Also, you are very clever. You ask questions instead of giving answers. There are fallacies somewhere in your thinking, but you hide them beneath these questions so my brain cannot identify the real truth.'

'Then develop your brain first, Prince! Is that not what I have been urging you to do?' His yellow teeth showed in a conciliatory smile. 'Come now, you have less than three years to go before you and I can both savour other aspects of the normalcy that exists outside the Gen al Arif. Why not make a gracious acceptance of your present restricted but luxurious lifestyle your normalcy for the present? Why not accept the will of Allah?'

'I am trying, am I not?' Prince Ahmed gestured with a futile hand. 'Something within me impelled me to behave as I did before, but I have changed since that old gypsy, Pilar – is that her name? – treated me. I don't know what was wrong.' Then, cunningly, 'But she certainly cured me, so I must have been the victim of a spell.'

'Were you possessed then?' The rheumy grey eyes were amused.

'The rules imposed on me were burdensome to my spirit, which rebelled against them.'

'Rebels are executed. You were not a rebel, merely possessed.' Bon Ebben paused, grinning. 'Now that you are cured, your royal father has agreed to my suggestion that you should be rewarded by being given a new companion to help lighten your loneliness.'

Prince Ahmed's interest quickened, but only momentarily. He was probably being offered another old man like Tarif.

The tutor must have picked up his thoughts, for his

grey beard parted to reveal the yellow-toothed smile once more. 'It is no ancient black deaf-mute I shall bring you, but a young, white Castilian of royal birth, just two years older than yourself. He is Prince Juan, the son of King Pedro of Castile, who was captured during the recent battle in which your father defeated King Pedro.'

Prince Ahmed leapt to his feet, his face flushed with excitement. He could hardly believe his ears. 'Really? You mean I shall have someone I can actually converse with at last?' This was incredible.

'Not exactly.' The sage looked down at his slippered feet. 'Prince Juan was rendered a deaf-mute about four weeks ago for the express purpose of being made your companion. Having now recovered, he will join you today.'

'No . . . ooo!' The roar of a wounded animal escaped Prince Ahmed. Oh, the unspeakable cruelty of it all. And he was responsible. This time, he had not merely inherited a deaf-mute, the maiming had been deliberately done for him. God's creation brutalized by man once again. Blood pounded in his head. The room started to spin around him. Pity for Prince Juan seized him by the throat, choking him, rendering him deaf to the flow of words emerging from the cruel, cruel old man seated before him and dumb with anger.

A new-found emotion for his father emerged, hatred. 'God's curse is already on you and my father, for there is a cancer within you. And what of Prince Juan's anger? Will my new companion not loathe me for what I have done to him?'

'Why should he loathe you? It is the king's decree that has maimed him.' Bon Ebben had picked up his thoughts again. 'Besides, are not such punishments . . . er . . . normal, Prince?'

Minutes passed while Prince Ahmed gazed down at bon Ebben, shaking, fighting the urge to seize him by his scrawny throat. Could this man be so unconcerned about the suffering of a fellow human being? Would not Almighty Allah, the All Compassionate, strike him dead?

Finally, Prince Ahmed regained control of himself. The deed had been done. It was totally irreversible. It must have been Almighty Allah's will. All he Prince Ahmed could now do was to comfort and succour his new companion. He would teach Prince Juan the language of deaf-mutes. He would be responsible for someone else's welfare at last. That at least was a wonderful thought.

'Prince Juan will be joining us at luncheon today.' Bon Ebben's words were somehow the heralds of the future in Prince Ahmed's mind.

Having devoted his entire energy to his study routine throughout the morning, Prince Ahmed had been too busy to wonder what his new companion, Prince Juan, would look like. His was a vigorous schedule, commencing with the first call to prayer and interrupted only by the daily four calls to prayer, seven days a week. The cool hours of the first half of the day were devoted to vigorous physical training: equestrianism, tilting with lances, wrestling, acrobatics, archery and swordsmanship. Then he had just enough time to prepare for the tutors who would arrive before noon to teach him languages and for the later afternoon lessons in history, politics, administration, mathematics and astronomy. The pre-sunset hour, his only free time, was now devoted to Zurika. The *imam* who discoursed to him on Islam came after dinner.

His tutors always kept him at his studies without mercy. 'Shaitan creeps into empty hours, filling them with evil,' a Muslim philosopher had once said. Bon Ebben was given to repeating such dull fallacies with unfailing regularity, as a filler for conversation gaps. By noon that day, Prince Ahmed would have traded his aching body for a touch of evil from an empty hour.

Their food had been laid out on the white marble table

inlaid with circular mosaics of mother-of-pearl and dark mahogany chips in the small private dining chamber of the Gen al Arif's tower. The salt mutton had been cooked to perfection, the palace cooks having used oatmeal in a white linen cloth suspended in the cauldron in which the meat was simmering to absorb the excess salt. The pepper, ginger, saffron, cinnamon, cloves, mace and oregano used as spices combined with the meat's delicious smell and the fragrance of warm wheat cakes to remind Prince Ahmed that he was hungry. The puréed beans seemed a fitting accompaniment to the splendid main course. His favourite pudding, frumenty made of whole-wheat grains and almond milk enriched with egg-yolk and coloured with saffron, was the dessert. Goblets of red melon juice tinctured with honey would quench their thirst.

Prince Ahmed's first impression of his new companion was of a very white skin and then the neck-length golden hair on the head bowed in greeting. Never having seen golden hair before, he could not make up his mind whether he liked it or not, his immediate reaction being that it was odd. The prince was slim, but strongly built, the white silk hose, soled to make shoes unnecessary, covered slim, muscular legs. The laces through the eyelet holes that kept the hose in place matched the short, elegantly cut tunic of rich burgundy velvet reaching just below slender hips, the long sleeves of which hung in the jagged edges Prince Ahmed knew to be in vogue with white Christians. The tunic was braided with gold, continuing all the way round a collar full enough at the back to serve as a hood.

Prince Ahmed felt a flash of gratitude towards the grey-robed bon Ebben who had stood up beside him, for having provided Prince Juan with clothes befitting his elegance and rank rather than a prisoner's rags, before he found himself gazing spellbound at the only blue eyes he had ever seen. They are the light blue of the spring sky, he thought with wonder. How extraordinarily beautiful in a human being. Oh, Allah, how could anyone still the voice, extinguish the hearing of one on whom You have bestowed such eyes?

Then he saw the unspoken suffering in the blue depths and his heart melted with pity within which guilt erupted. He knew the cause of that suffering. He alone was responsible. He searched for hatred of him in Prince Juan's eyes, found none, only an unutterable sorrow which tore at his heart. His gaze drifted to the lean drawn face, the gold down of the upper lip, the clean-shaven chin, the thin, aristocratic nose. The skin white as the underbelly of a mouse, reminded him of people who had leucoderma, white leprosy. If this skin were only tinged with pink, it would be as pure and lovely as the marble of Greek Pharos, he thought, before bowing courteously in acknowledgment, hand to heart, lips and head. Knowing how to deal with deaf-mutes, he smiled his greeting and was rewarded by the even, white teeth of an answering smile that reached to a crinkling at the sides of the eyes.

'*Buenos dias.*' He formed the Spanish words with his lips while nodding.

He was rewarded by a slow mouthing of the greeting in response. Since bon Ebben stood at his right, as was proper, he gestured towards the chair on his left.

Prince Juan walked across the green marble floor with the practised grace of a courtier. A raven croaked hoarsely outside the high grilled windows. Unusual. Was it an ill omen? The bird must find the noonday sun as pitiless as Prince Juan has found life to be, Prince Ahmed thought with a fresh surge of pity. How can people be so inhuman? How could anyone mutilate a human being, even a tree? Suddenly the odours of the food nauseated him. He had lost his appetite.

As the meal proceeded, Prince Ahmed had to force

himself to eat. But how does one converse over a meal with a deaf-mute? He did not know. The deaf-mutes in his life were all palace servants, with whom he had never broken bread, while he had naturally given Prince Juan the place of an equal.

A companion, bon Ebben had said. So be it. When the black deaf-mute attendants brought in a silver platter with a knife, fork and goblet for Prince Juan, Prince Ahmed served his visitor. He noted bon Ebben's obvious disapproval of this gesture with cold satisfaction. Strange, he thought, the result of your cruelty to this beautiful creature is a stirring of urges within me from the same source that made me compose poems and songs to plants, flowers and trees and somehow connects with what the gypsy girl makes me feel. Is this the same urge that once made me embrace the graceful tree and sent my juices spurting? No, that experience was the physical product of physical sensations. What I am experiencing now is intangible. Prince Juan's beauty, which I appreciate with my eyes, does not stir any physical desire in me.

Since it would not be mannerly for Prince Ahmed to talk to bon Ebben when his guest could not hear, the meal proceeded in a silence broken only by an occasional grunt of satisfaction from bon Ebben – who taught better manners than he sometimes practised – and the raven's querulous croak.

The interview with her mother had left Princess Beatrice feeling very much alone. She knew that Maria de Padilla could not possibly care as much as she did about Prince Juan's captivity: he was not even her legal stepson. After she was placed in virtual imprisonment in the female quarters of the Toledo palace, Princess Beatrice had shared everything with her mother, except Prince Juan's secret visits to her. Now, with her mother a stranger, she had no one to whom she could pour out the pity she felt.

She also recognized that it would be useless for her to expect that Maria de Padilla would use her influence with King Pedro to work out some plan to save the prince. Her mother probably did not want Prince Juan to return. The thought fanned the flame of her newborn hatred of her mother. Try as she might, she simply could not overcome it. Honour thy father and mother was the Commandment. She begged God daily to forgive her this terrible sin.

The Blessed Virgin, whom she regularly implored to keep Prince Juan safe, now became Princess Beatrice's only source of comfort, the only being with whom she could share her fears for her own future.

Other doubts inevitably crept in. Why was Maria de Padilla so intensely loyal to King Pedro? Was love the cause, or was it the self-preservation of a cunning mind? Her mother had certainly bettered her lot from the union, having become virtually queen of Castile.

What was worst now was her own pretence. God forgive her, but she had had to keep pretending to her mother that she had not changed, that her filial love remained as tender and gentle as before and that she herself was the same sweetly subservient daughter she had always been.

Alone and helpless, with no one to whom she could turn for help or with whom she could share her desperate worries, each night, when her mother's knock sounded on the door, she heard it as a traitor's call to betrayal. Tonight, as she rose from her *prie-dieu*, to stand beside her bed, for some unaccountable reason, she was finding it specially difficult to bring her resentment under control. Was it the storm rising outside? The casement windows, shuttered against the moaning wind, rattled with each gust. An occasional howl brought the creak of branches and an acrid smell of firecrackers. The chamber was close and stifling.

Immediately she glided into the room, Maria de Padilla

must have sensed her daughter's feelings, for her pale face lifted slightly, the brown eyes revealing concern in the golden light of the tapers on their wall-sconces. 'What is wrong, *queridisima*?' She came up to Princess Beatrice and held her. She wore a lilac scent.

'Nothing, *muy Madre*,' Princess Beatrice murmured. 'Unless it is the storm outside and a persistent intuition I have had for nearly two months that my brother, Prince Juan, is either dead or being tortured.'

Her mother released her, gripped both her arms, stared deep into her eyes. 'Sit down, my child,' she gently directed. Pressing Beatrice lightly on to the bed, she sat down beside her, placed an arm around her, slowly tilting her face sideways to meet a commanding look.

A chill tremor ran through Beatrice, tightened her throat so she could not even ask the question that was hammering inside her brain.

'I have the most terrible news about Prince Juan,' Maria de Padilla stated, her vibrant voice flat and colourless.

'He's dead . . .' Princess Beatrice began rising from her seat but was held back by her mother's arm.

Maria de Padilla shook her head. 'No, he's very much alive, thank God.' She paused. 'But I wonder whether death would not have been preferable.'

Beatrice's face contorted. 'What has happened to him?' She could barely whisper the question. 'Have they tortured him?'

'Worse. Now hold steady, please.' Her mother's voice carried a note of such authority that it brought back the child in Princess Beatrice and she automatically steeled herself not to react.

'The Moors are a cruel and barbarous people,' Maria de Padilla said soberly. 'King Yusuf has made Prince Juan a deaf-mute. Be sure that all true Christians will unite to avenge this abhorrent deed.'

At first it did not register, seeming so much less than death or torture. Then the significance of it, the utter irrevocability of it, smashed into Princess Beatrice.

The strength of a demented mind brought release from her mother's restraining arm. Her chest heaved in a single breath. She sprang to her feet, a hand flying to her throat.

'No . . . oo . . . !' The cry that escaped her was that of a wounded animal.

Seventeen years of seeing her naked body every night he slept in the Toledo palace yet it still excited King Pedro. Why? He had wenched, had fucked his queens and tired of them all pretty soon, some in a single night. The wenches were either professionals, whose artificiality he sensed – some little word from the best of them, a gesture, the moan that should not have been there or was exaggerated – or nymphos who went for him with sheer animal lust. Others were so bored by the whole performance you almost expected them to be looking at their hand-mirrors while you kept jabbing them. As for the 'Fuck me, fuck me, you great stud!' type, they made him want to puke after it was over. Blanche, on the other hand, had been frigid, giving her lifeless body to him like a martyr dutifully on her way to execution with the certain knowledge of beatification.

King Pedro knew that the world saw him as a lusty, lustful man, whose only real joy from sex was to plunge his penis into a female and hammer away at her until he climaxed. No one knew of his secret yearnings. He had not identified them himself until Maria de Padilla revealed to him that sex was only a part of love-making. Maria it was who bestowed on him the gentleness, the tenderness, the caressing care when he first took her to bed that had made a blessed sacrament of sex. As she had later confessed to him, it was the only way in which one as religious as she was could justify the otherwise mortal sin

134

of adultery. She made love to him, accepting his love-making because she loved him. And from the deepest part of him, unfulfilled from his earliest childhood, was born a love that had been proven to the world by his actions, but the nature of which, the poetry, grace and delicacy, he would never reveal to anyone because it would make him less than Pedro the Cruel.

His mother had been a shadowy figure until she died when he was only four. His father, King Alfonso XI, the leader in the Reconquista of Spain from the Moors and victor at the Battle of Salado, never had time for his only legitimate son. And since his whoring had produced a row of bastard sons and daughters, Pedro had had to claw his way to the succession through sheer ferocity. Political expediency had forced him into a marriage with Blanche, the daughter of Pierre, Duc de Bourbon, which had lasted but a few months.

As always, Maria personally opened the door of her bedchamber to him that night. No one else would ever see the love that lit up his face when he entered and took her in his arms, holding her as gently as if she had been made of fine porcelain. In the golden glow of the candle-light, the ethereal look on her face showed how much she loved him – the glow of a bride on her wedding night – and it awed him.

He never used the royal plural when they were alone together. 'I have waited breathlessly all day for this moment,' he murmured, gazing deep into her eyes, feeling the merging of his soul with hers that he experienced unfailingly at this moment every night. Her pink silk nightgown revealed the slender contours of her body, the brown patch of downy pubis, full breasts with their large round aureoles which never failed to move him. Mother breasts, he called them at times.

Her eyes shone with love. 'And I, liege lord of my soul.' She stepped up to him, cupped his bearded face in

135

long, slender pink fingers. She reached up and kissed his lips, her own so soft, moist and yielding that a groan of joy escaped him.

He held her against him. The silken feel of her abdomen, the soft, almost transparent tissue of fat over her pliant body, brought an instant erection. Yet, with a sensitivity totally foreign to him save with her, he instinctively knew that something troubled her. He gently moved her away from him, lifted her in his arms.

'Oh!' The surprised exclamation escaped her.

He strode to the pink canopied bed, placed her on the silken sheets, sat beside her. '*Te ruego*, tell me, what's wrong,' he softly bade her.

'Noth . . .' Her white teeth gleamed in a smile, the brown, doe-like eyes misted. 'You always know, don't you?'

He nodded, moved as always by the depth and totality of their knowledge of each other.

'First, there is this dreadful thing the barbaric Moors have done to poor Juan,' she began. 'You must be heartsick and furious.'

'No more furious than I would be if it had happened to any of my subjects. You know that Prince Juan is a Christian who has qualified since boyhood for a crown in heaven, not on earth. *En verdad*, he has been a great disappointment to me. He only accompanied our army against the Moors because I commanded him. He took no part in the battle and when he was surrounded by the enemy, he meekly surrendered, not out of cowardice, but from a reluctance to kill and cut his way back to our lines. He is unbelievable. He is either a man or more than one, certainly not less. While I would never have wanted this fate for him, now that it has occurred, I can't help but see the benefit of it to our daughter, whose right to the throne no longer has a legal contender, while the joust will save her from my bastard half-brothers.'

136

'You are a hard man, beloved Pedro.'

'In truth and before God, I am. But I prefer to think of my attitude in this case as practical. I refuse to waste sentiment or emotion on any situation, especially one I cannot change.'

'How about on me?'

'I can never change my love for you. It is eternal; therefore, its sentiment is never wasted.'

She reached up and touched his cheek, sending a thrill through his face. It brought the realization that his erection had subsided. 'What else is bothering you?'

Her smile was sweet. She took his hand and pressed it against her own cheek.

'Your skin is cool as cool water on a summer day,' he said.

A blush began at her neck and rose to mantle her face. 'You can make me feel sixteen again,' she whispered.

'Instead of sixty,' he joked.

'I'll give you sixty lashes for that insult,' she threatened, 'for I'm a *hundred* and sixty.'

'When we are through with talking, I'll give you six hundred and sixty lashes,' he retorted. 'With you know what.'

Her eyes drifted to his crotch. 'How can you when he's fallen asleep again.'

'He's a light sleeper when you're around.'

'Oh, *queridisimo*, most beloved Pedro, how I love you.' She reached out and began fondling his testicles.

'I know, it is those balls you love.' He paused. 'Now, tell me what's wrong.'

'I wish I could. It's our daughter, Beatrice. She worries me. She was so torn with grief when I gave her the news about Prince Juan she became almost demented. How could she feel so deeply for him when they have been separated for over four years? Besides, I have sensed a difference in her since I told her about the tournament and warned her that she would have to marry whoever

137

won it in order to create a political alliance. Even if it is only a false hope, I know she is waiting for something to happen, for some opportunity to escape her fate, as she considers it. She is so romantic, she is dangerous.'

'She is probably waiting for a prince of her dreams to rescue her.' He laughed shortly. 'But apart from the Spanish princes who have entered the tournament, there is none in all of Christian Europe who would want her. And that event is but three months away. She will be married immediately it is over, and we shall be ready to go to war against the Moor by then.'

'She's a beautiful girl . . .'

'Whom I have taken care to shield from public gaze,' he reminded her. 'So even if she has hopes of some romantic rescue, they will never be realized.' He gazed at her longingly, began caressing her. His organ, which had already started to swell at her touch, became rock hard at the feel of her breasts, soft as curds. Mother breasts.

He bent down and kissed her. Mouth to her lips, he half rose and removed his pantaloons. His huge organ shot out. She grasped it firmly, began stroking it. She pushed him away, slid out of her nightgown. He barely had time to gaze at her naked body before she turned from him, went on her hands and knees. 'I need you to ride me tonight,' she whispered.

Their love gave an infinite variety to their love-making, ordained it to fit every mood. He knelt on the bed, entered her from behind. The feel of her buttocks thrilled against his haunches; the wet and slippery inside of her was sheer ecstasy. He grasped her long brown hair with both hands like reins and began riding in an easy motion. She came easily, one of the great delights of her. He rode her three orgasms before exploding inside her.

While she slept in his arms, he lay awake, somehow troubled by the thought of possible conflict with his daughter.

Chapter 8

Prince Juan proved himself an adept student at the sign language of the deaf and the dumb. Since he was already well versed in Arabic, which he had studied in the Toledo court, and since Prince Ahmed knew Spanish, within six weeks Prince Ahmed found himself communicating easily with his fellow prisoner. During this period, the two young men became constant companions.

Far from harbouring any resentment against Prince Ahmed for the atrocity committed on him, Prince Juan showed unrestrained friendliness and was soon permitted to participate in Prince Ahmed's daily study routine, except for the night classes in Islam which, as a Christian, he declined. This suited Prince Ahmed well, because it left him free each evening to enjoy his dancing dream alone.

On the other hand, he had invited Prince Juan to walk with him on the battlements of the tower every morning after breakfast, discovering the very first time they did so the prince's fear of heights. Nevertheless the walks became a rare pleasure for him, since his attendants and servants had never been permitted such association with their prince. Besides, Prince Juan proved to be the gentlest, most forgiving of people, full of rare compassion and charity without a resentful bone in his body, imbued with what Prince Ahmed knew to be a true Christian spirit, all springing from a great inner strength. The battlements, being open to the air, afforded the two princes, Prince Ahmed for the first time in his life, the opportunity to 'converse' openly. Abou bon Ebben permitted it as a special concession to Prince Ahmed, holding withdrawal of the privilege as a threat to ensure good conduct. The sage seemed to be well pleased with Prince Ahmed and even confided in him that he had secretly sent Pilar the Entrancer a small bag of gold, making her rich for life, as a reward for the miraculous change she had wrought on his ward.

With this companionship every morning and silent communion with Zurika each evening, for a short spell Prince Ahmed found his life fuller and more satisfying than it had ever been. Since first meeting Pilar and seeing Zurika dance, something had been struggling within him. He knew there were males and females in the world, though he had never seen a female until then, and that females produced children. How? Why were they differently formed? What were the differences, other than of the physical form, between a man and a woman? Some instinct told him that there was a link between the two and his vision of Zurika produced unidentifiable urges that had no relationship with his wet dreams. What was the connection?

It did not take long for two aspects of his new inspiration to begin to nag him. The first was that he could never see Zurika's eyes, hear her voice or breathe the fragrance of her. Zurika had animation and humanity, but it was all still objective. Allied to this was the fact that for all practical purposes she was not only deaf and dumb but had no eyes. In some respects, she was no different from the changing faces of the earth from dawn through night, except that he could not physically bestow on her the fruit of his own adoration; he dare not sing aloud to her, recite his love poems or serenade her with his lute. This frustration slowly crystallized in his mind until its focus became the eyes. He needed to see her eyes for her to become real to him.

The other frustration arose from a dawning knowledge within him that all he felt towards Zurika was merely the

140

product of some deeper instincts which he needed to identify and define. Perhaps Prince Juan, who knew the outside world, could help him.

'It is now autumn,' he signalled Prince Juan as they leant on the battlements that morning. 'There is more snow on the Sierra Nevada peaks.' He nodded towards the distant mountain range, shimmering white in the sunlight. The scent of orange blossoms, wafted to his nostrils by a cool breeze from the valley of the Darro, and a nightingale's song fluting through the air only increased his dissatisfaction. 'The sky is a paler shade of blue, the hillocks below us are more stark and dry. All this is a background for the living things of the earth. The trees and plants blossom in the spring. Even the birdsongs sound different. Do you know why, my friend?' He fixed an intense gaze on his companion.

A faint smile touched the sides of Prince Juan's face. He turned away and looked into the distance, reflecting. Prince Ahmed guessed that his hesitation was somehow caused by a reluctance to make revelations forbidden by bon Ebben.

Prince Juan turned to face him. 'To answer you, I would have to touch on a forbidden subject,' he gestured, regret in his eyes. 'And I am honour bound not to speak to you of it.' He paused. 'It grieves me.'

'I understand,' Prince Ahmed signalled back. He paused, moved by cunning. 'Of all living things, only the hawk, the owl, bats and an occasional swallow reach up here, because this tower is so high above the ground. But one morning last spring, a beautiful white dove came fleeing to these battlements, pursued by a brown hawk. It fell panting at my feet, while the pursuer, robbed of its prey, soared back towards the distant mountains. I picked up the dove and nestled it against my chest. I could feel its rapidly beating little heart, even before I began stroking its feathers. I put it in a golden cage, gave it the whitest wheat and the purest water, but the dove would touch neither. It sat in the cage, shivering and drooping. When I finally released the bird, it flew away on grateful wings, alive again. Why? Was it through knowing freedom at last from the imprisonment to which I had consigned it, I asked myself. My mind said, yes, but my heart contradicted my reason, because that dove had an obvious purpose in its flight away from me. It was going somewhere. Where?' A pleading expression crossed his face, for his whole future seemed to hang on Prince Juan's answer. 'Prithee, tell me where the dove was headed.'

'Not where,' Prince Juan responded. 'But to whom.'

'To whom then?'

The breeze stopped, the world seemed to stand as still as Prince Ahmed's senses, all awaiting the answer.

'To its mate.' Prince Juan mouthed the words. He placed a finger to his lips, indicating that he could not say who a mate was. A pitying look entered his blue eyes. He shook his head from side to side, as if to say: You have been rendered more deaf and dumb than I. He seemed to make up his mind, opened the top button of his tunic to reveal a small golden locket hanging from a gold chain around his neck. He looked down at the locket silently.

Prince Ahmed touched his arm, causing him to look up again. 'Where did you get that locket?' he inquired.

'I had it with me when I was taken prisoner.'

'They let you keep it?'

'Yes.' Prince Juan seemed undecided whether to say more. 'The locket has a secret catch. If your tutor knew that, he might have confiscated it,' he finally volunteered.

'Why?'

Instead of responding, Prince Juan pressed one of the sides of the locket. A lid sprang open. He proffered the locket to Prince Ahmed. 'This is my sister, Princess Beatrice.'

Prince Ahmed took the locket, glanced at the miniature

painting inside, then his eyes widened. It was the painting of a girl, like Zurika, but her colour was that of snow on the distant mountains when it is tinctured by the pink of the setting sun. Her hair was the spun gold of afternoon sunshine, framing an oval face with exquisite bones.

But it was her eyes that had filled Prince Ahmed with awe.

Blue eyes, more beautiful than the skies, because they were crystal mosaics of different colours of blue. They had depths to them, and yes, a soul.

His eyes were beholding the soul of a maiden at last.

Here at last was the connection. By some incredible magic of human knowledge, he understood what Prince Juan meant when he spoke of a mate. Shattered by the revelation, Prince Ahmed could not take his gaze off the image of Princess Beatrice, for now he understood why the dove had pined in its gold cage, why its very soul had rejoiced in its flight away from its gilded prison.

Suddenly, Prince Ahmed, the prisoner, knew what he would do, for the surges of his rebellion had reached the fruition of a purpose.

'She is the heir to our throne,' Prince Juan indexed.

'I had heard that from my tutor, bon Ebben,' Prince Ahmed replied, 'that you, the son, had been disinherited? Why?'

'My father is so infatuated with his consort, Maria de Padilla, that he would do anything she asks. I for one am convinced that it was she who suggested it to him, but subtly, because he must always be made to feel as if *he* has made the decisions.'

'What sort of person is this Maria de Padilla?'

'I have not met her often, but I assess her to be a strange mixture of the insecurities of her life, not just her early life, but even her present one and her undoubted love for my father, for whom she would sacrifice anyone or anything, even her daughter.' He paused, vivid blue eyes gazing into an unseen distance. 'It has just struck me that for King Pedro, Maria de Padilla would even sacrifice God. He must know this too and he clings to it as his only lifeline. He acceded to the throne when he was only fifteen and immediately engaged in a ruthless struggle for the succession with his five illegitimate brothers. He drenched Castile in blood and has personally murdered many, including the archbishop, friends and relations. He can trust no one and nobody can trust him, except Maria de Padilla. I am thankful that he has at least one such person in his life.'

'You say that when he has dispossessed and shamed you?' Prince Ahmed demanded, incredulous. He was certainly learning a new angle to life from his mutilated friend.

'I am a Christian first and last. Worldly things are not so important to me as my immortal soul. Would being the heir have saved me from being taken prisoner and,' he smiled to rob the words of offence, 'having my hearing and speech impaired? What good is any of it, my very dear Prince?'

Prince Ahmed fought back the tears that sprang to his eyes. 'It is the will of Allah,' he declared, but could not keep his voice from breaking.

Prince Juan reached out and touched his shoulder. 'You must not feel guilty about me or grieve for my loss,' he signalled. 'For whatever we lose, God's laws bring us compensation. It is part of the balance of life. Since I lost my hearing and speech, my eyesight has improved enormously and my sense of perception has magnified.' His face softened. 'And when I lost my freedom, I found you, God's richest gift to me, a true friend.'

This time, Prince Ahmed could not hold back the sob that racked him. His throat ached and his mouth went dry. It was all he could do to resist the urge to embrace Prince Juan. 'And you do not hate your sister?'

'No, I love her with all my heart. She has been my true friend and confidante and I hers. She loathes her position but she also loves her mother and will not accept that it is Maria de Padilla's desperate need for security that made her imprison her own daughter in the Toledo palace.'

'You are sure that this is what drives the mother?'

'What would the mother's position be if my father died? She has allied herself so totally with him that even if someone forgiving succeeded to the throne, there are others who would wreak secret vengeance on her. The one way in which she can be totally secure and wield power from behind the scenes, she thinks, is by having Princess Beatrice succeed.'

'Would you not have fought for the succession?'

The handsome golden head was slowly shaken from side to side. 'That would have defeated the very foundations of the laws of succession which, amongst other things, I would have sworn to uphold as king. Unlike other European countries which forbid succession by or through a female line, in Castile every ruler has the right to name his successor, so long as that successor has a legal claim. Your Moorish laws, Prince Ahmed, are different. The eldest son automatically succeeds. If I became king, it would be my duty to safeguard all our rights, traditions and institutions. How could I do that if I commenced my rule by violating the fundamental of succession?'

Prince Ahmed gazed at Prince Juan in amazement. Then the sincerity and goodness of the young prince struck him, turned amazement to awe, rendering him incapable of expression.

'My father wants to be the ruler of all Spain, including Aragon, León y Navarra, Catalonia, Portugal and Granada,' Prince Juan continued, gesturing. 'He will attack Granada first. The next time he will not do it alone, but with the assistance of the other white Christian kings and Holy Church which always meddles in lay affairs. If he takes Granada, he will turn on his allies and slay them, one by one.' His face tautened. 'I am convinced that he sees you as his most dangerous rival. What King Pedro cannot achieve in battle, he will accomplish by stealth, treachery and betrayal. Now that his ambitions are winging in your direction, he will come after you. You are in mortal danger.' His eyes closed. 'If I had the gift of prophecy, I would say that he is already planning to destroy you. I beg you therefore not to trust the security system you have always enjoyed in this beautiful tower. Be alert, for King Pedro makes a deadly rival.'

The blustery late autumn weather had not helped King Pedro's hangover. The attitude of the two Jewish leaders of Toledo, seated across the desk in his study in the palace, had aggravated it. So this morning the room with its oak panelled walls and oil paintings brought him no comfort, but seemed as gloomy to him as the leaden skies he could see through the windows.

When he had received news from his spies the previous evening that his fellow Christian kings were not proceeding as expeditiously as he had hoped for with the assembly of men and material they had promised for his campaign, he had decided to enlarge the size of his own contribution to the cause of Christian unity by hiring a contingent of German mercenaries. But since his own coffers would be heavily drained by the campaign, he had resorted to the prime source of funds which all European kings used, the Jewish moneylenders.

The Jewish community of Toledo was among the most affluent in Europe. It had acquired its wealth through trade, commerce and financing. Knowing that their wealth was an unfunded part of his Treasury, he had not only been tolerant of the Jewish religion, holding back attempts of clerics like Bishop Eulogius to persecute the Jews, but had extended many concessions to key members of the community, especially in respect of monopolies, preferences, licences and lower taxes.

He had therefore summoned the two Jewish leaders of Toledo late the previous evening for this morning's audience, then spent the rest of the night drinking. Not even the tender arms of his beloved Maria had relieved the hangover. His head ached, his mouth was dry, his breath tasted of the vomit he had not brought up, his mind felt vacant, without balance and his body stank so heavily, because he had refused his monthly bath last night, that even the amber scenting his brown leather jerkin had retreated in defeat. 'Are you telling me that the Black Death has stripped your resources so clean, that you will not be able to extend us all the support we need?' he demanded, glowering at the two men.

For some reason of pre-arranged strategy, Rabbi Azor had been the spokesman. A tall, cadaverous man with the characteristic high forehead, deepset eyes, prominent nose and flowing black beard of his race, he was dressed in a robe of blue fabric bordered by scarlet pomegranates alternating with golden bells, which tinkled occasionally. Over the robe, extending from armpit to waist, he wore an *ephod* or vest of white linen. Around his neck was a rosary of brown beads and on his head the customary rabbi's mitre. 'I am only saying that times have been hard for my people these past two years, Your Majesty.' He had a deep rich voice, but it seemed to wobble out of his prominent Adam's apple. He shifted in his chair, the tinkle of one of his bells jarring in the king's sore head.

The familiar reflex of cold cruelty that gripped King Pedro whenever he was thwarted now seized him. 'You are of the seed of Adam, so why is it that your Jahweh has caused your voice to emerge unsteadily from your Adam's apple?' he demanded rudely. 'Can it be that your Jahweh has smitten you with some affliction for the lies you have always uttered?' His voice was a growl, his smile through

147

bared teeth. 'Especially when you purport to speak for your people, rabbi, remember that it is not only your God's punishment that you will suffer if you lie to your earthly king.' He deliberately charged the look in his blue eyes with menace.

'Your Majesty, both Rabbi Azor and I and indeed the entire Jewish communities of Toledo and Castile are well aware of your power.' Lord Joram entered the discussion for the first time. A direct descendant of the house of David, his people addressed him by the title Lord. A small, trim man, with regular features save for the large nose and a black beard, he was soberly dressed in black, his headgear a black *pilion* skull cap. He was one of the richest Jews in Spain, but neither his attire, nor his pale, strangely yellow eyes, nor his demeanour, revealed it. 'On the contrary, it is your gracious treatment of us, your protection of our freedom of worship, your tolerance of our way of life and your many economic concessions to us that command us to be your staunchest, most loyal supporters. Did not our Sem Tob, Rabbi of Carion de los Condes, dedicate a work to you, his *Counsels to King Pedro* or *Moral Proverbs*?'

Though never taken in by such unctuous praise, King Pedro could not help recalling some of Rabbi Sem Tob's words. '*The exterior world is not only doubtful and fleeting, but the Jew's place in it gives rise to literary despair,*' he quoted. 'Have a care lest your despair extend from the literary to the social and economic world.' He grinned ferociously. Then, to demonstrate his appreciation of the beauty of Sem Tob's prose, he proceeded with the quotation. '*The rose dies and leaves behind its sweet rose water, which is its finest value. Does man leave behind a wake that lasting?*'

'*The whole world is an endless play of opposites, and even the crown may turn into a worn-out shoe,*' Rabbi Azor finished the quotation with a triumphant smile.

Fuck you, King Pedro thought angrily, though I would not be the one to do it. A distant roll of thunder rumbled into the room. He glanced outside briefly. One of Rabbi Azor's bells tinkled as he shifted in his seat. Dark grey clouds were scudding towards each other. The air had become oppressive. King Pedro recalled the rest of the quotation. *'The rose loses nothing by being born on the thorn and good* exempla *do not lose by being recited by a Jew.* See to it, honoured Jews, that you lose no more than good *exempla* do!'

'We will do everything in our power to finance your enterprise fully,' Lord Joram replied. 'If we do run into difficulty raising the millions of *reales* in gold which you need, please be assured, Your Majesty, that it is not for lack of deep and humble appreciation of your gracious justice and mercy. We beg you to extend to us, the most downtrodden of your subjects, your renowned Christian charity, which has always been our only source of hope.'

You make me sound like a fucking Christian martyr in a den of lions, King Pedro thought mercilessly. The ache at the base of his skull increased; pulses began to throb at either temple with his effort to hold back his mounting anger at being baited by these Jews. It would never do to explode openly. What he had to do to these two sons of bitches required guile. 'You know the rich rewards that await you,' he volunteered. 'You will receive more than the return of your principal and interest when we have taken Granada.'

'You will succeed in anything you undertake, Sire, but we must all be prepared for God's will,' Rabbi Azor slanted in. He seemed completely unperturbed by King Pedro's vicious attack on him. 'So please understand that my brethren are prepared for the risk of failure.'

You fucking bastard, you are trying to remind me subtly that my campaign may not succeed, in which event your brethren stand to lose their money, because I am gambling with your wealth. He decided to launch into the attack. 'You are obviously a bastard, rabbi, but prithee, tell us, are you a *fucking* bastard?' he demanded pleasantly. 'We mean, do *rabbis* today fuck as your ancestors fucked up our Lord Jesus Christ?' He crossed himself piously, then pointed a warning finger at Lord Joram. 'You should select a spokesman who has more to lose than a rabbi,' he warned. 'None of you will fuck *us* up. *En verdad*, if there is to be any fucking in this kingdom, we alone shall do it.'

He could sense Lord Joram blanch invisibly, but the rabbi's expression remained cordial. 'Your Majesty has the power of life and death over us,' he stated unafraid, his voice steady, though he had lowered it. 'But our souls belong to Jahweh, Who protects the helpless and has the kingdom of heaven awaiting us.'

For all his ill-temper, King Pedro could not help admiring the man's calm. He simmered down. 'God has commanded that we be your protector in the kingdom of Castile,' he conceded mildly.

'Your Majesty is most gracious,' Lord Joram stated, a conciliatory note in his voice. 'We shall certainly consult our community and do everything in our power to meet your needs.'

'Good, but time is short. How long will this take?'

'Would you kindly give us one week?'

King Pedro thought rapidly. The Jews needed the Saturday Sabbath for their consultations. Sunday was his own holy day, on which it would certainly not do to receive Jews in audience. 'Be present here next Monday then, at the same time.' He rose to his feet and his head seemed to split with the sudden movement. Towering over even the tall *rabbi*, he tugged at the sash that would summon his attendant. '*A Dios*, God be with you,' he said. And meant it, for both these men would need God before the week was out.

* * *

150

Ruy de Vivar claimed to be a bastard descendant of the famous man who had borne the same name, El Cid Campeador, the Castilian who had reached the Mediterranean in 1094 A.D. and whose exploits had inspired the *Cantar de mio Cid*. As luck would have it, de Vivar's regular weekly audience with King Pedro had been scheduled for that very morning.

De Vivar was the man to whom the king had already entrusted the task of having King Yusuf assassinated and Prince Ahmed kidnapped. He would not be satisfied with Prince Ahmed's death. The mutilation of his son did not bother him in the least but he owed it to himself to repay the insult. He would have Prince Ahmed's cock and balls for his son's speech and hearing. He also needed de Vivar to implement his plans for the two Jews who had just left his study, and he would have risked the exposure of his part in the plan even if de Vivar had had to make a special visit to the palace. The gates were more open to public gaze than the entrance to a public lavatory.

He had received de Vivar, his spymaster and the head of the town brotherhood, in his study, and the man had just concluded his report, which had been less clouded than the sky outside. The actions of the *Hermandades*, with their right to give criminals summary trial and sentencing, were often more oppressive than autumn skies, but kings countenanced them for the organizations represented a powerful segment of the population and a buffer against over-ambitious nobles. The *Hermandades* were citizens' organizations for maintaining public peace. The first of them had been formed in 1295, with a revival as recently as thirty-five years ago. Since maintaining public peace was one of the king's feudal duties, their formation relieved the royal Treasury and also provided him with a secret police arm whenever necessary.

An extremely thin, bald man, with a thin, bald face, and a tight-fitting brown tunic scented with amber, the

151

smile de Vivar gave was wintry, the thin nostrils distending. King Pedro knew him to be a firm believer in white supremacy. A petty landowner, he had no time for Jews, blacks, or Moors. 'Your Majesty must surely be joking,' he remonstrated in answer to King Pedro's question as to whether he knew the Rabbi and Jarom. 'I do not consort with Jews, heathens, stray cats or mongrel dogs.'

King Pedro's hangover had been lifting as the alcohol was slowly absorbed into his body. 'How well do you know *of* them then?' he inquired, smiling an understanding he did not feel, because he had no time for people who were so weak that they had to exploit their prejudices. He needed to humour this upstart today.

'Such as what, Sire?'

'What we have to tell you is most secret. Do you swear on the body of Jesus that you will not divulge our personal involvement to a living soul?'

The small blue eyes came alive with interest. The man sensed some advantage coming to him. 'I do swear by the body of God. Your Majesty has always received my uncompromising loyalty.'

Because it has never compromised you, King Pedro reflected cynically. 'Yes, we are well aware of that,' he responded. 'And the matter of which we are about to speak to you will earn you some substantial reward if it is successfully accomplished.'

De Vivar straightened his bony shoulders, his finger tightened on the black hat he was gripping in his hands. 'I am yours to command, Sire.'

'Tell us then what you consider to be the weaknesses of each of these men.' He never used his usual 'prithees' and 'in truths' with commoners. 'Family members loved too well, scandalous liaisons secretly pursued, suspicious activities.'

The pale blue eyes gleamed with understanding. 'The rabbi is reportedly devoted to his housemaid, a young

152

woman named Ruth, a niece whom he formally adopted as a child. There is no evidence of any sexual misconduct, but the rabbi would give his life for Ruth.'

'Good.' Disgorging someone else's fortune would be a smaller price for the rabbi to pay than the loss of such a niece. 'And Lord Joram?'

'Collects old lyres that he treasures even more than he does his family.'

'This young woman, Ruth, goes to the market daily to buy food, clothing, luxuries perhaps?'

'Yes, Sire.' A knowing look crossed de Vivar's face. 'Such a young woman, housemaid to a poor rabbi, would be easily tempted to steal. She can be found with the goods on her, arrested immediately and taken to prison.' A very perceptive man this de Vivar, a true secret agent.

'A fitting punishment for such a crime.' The cruel streak made King Pedro's eyes shine with glee. 'A little torture to extract a confession might also become necessary.' He paused, grinning evilly. 'What of Lord Joram's weakness?'

'He could be arrested for stealing lyres.'

This man may be perceptive, but he was crude in his thinking. 'That may not be wise. Lord Joram is a well respected member of the community. His arrest could rebound on you. Since he probably loves his ancient lyres even more than he loves himself, would it not be more productive for you to seize the most rare of his lyres on an official complaint that they were stolen?'

'You are so wise, Sire.' De Vivar nodded his appreciation.

No, I am not wise, King Pedro thought, only cunning and cruel. 'You may want to hold this housemaid – what is her name, Ruth? – on threat of torture to extract a confession and then allege blasphemy while she was in the dungeon. Lord Joram may be informed that his confiscated lyres could be smashed at any time.'

Nobody fucked with Pedro the Cruel. He would teach

the two circumcised pricks that the king's mercy did not mean they could trifle with him. 'Have it done immediately,' he commanded. He would await the Jews' appeal for his intervention and do so at the proper price.

'Certainly, Sire,' de Vivar readily responded. 'Do you have any other orders for me today?'

'What progress have you made with the assassination of the Moor Yusuf and the kidnapping of his son?'

De Vivar blinked. 'Sire, those commissions are more difficult to execute.' He grinned humourlessly at the use of the word. 'We are dealing with a separate kingdom, far removed from Toledo, and a well-fortified, royal palace actively guarded . . .'

'History is replete with examples of rulers whose murders have been accomplished from far away,' King Pedro interrupted impatiently. 'The trick has been to work with those who are their enemies within their palaces and have them do the deed.'

'Agreed, Your Majesty. But we have an added problem in the Gen al Arif tower, where the entire staff consists of deaf-mutes. I have already made contact with King Yusuf's enemies. We are setting up the necessary organization to ensure that the deed is done.' He grinned apologetically. 'All this costs money too.'

'You have free access to our Treasury for any funds you may require.' King Pedro thought awhile. 'Especially to kidnap Prince Ahmed.'

'That is the most difficult assignment I have ever undertaken. Having failed to find deaf-mutes that I could have infiltrated among Prince Ahmed's staff, I have set in motion a contingency plan. Have no doubt about it, Your Majesty, it is only a matter of time before I fulfil your desires.'

Chapter 9

Other than the hour when Zurika danced for him, dinner shared with Prince Juan had become the most satisfying time of the day for Prince Ahmed. Although Abou bon Ebben was generally present and the study hours before bedtime still lay ahead, Prince Ahmed had come to love the sense of spaciousness afforded by a good meal in satisfying company. Unlike Prince Ahmed, Abou bon Ebben did not know the deaf language, so being unable to participate in discussions with Prince Juan, he was generally a silent observer, his rheumy eyes watchful only for any sign of intimacy between the two princes.

His tutor seemed to be rather tired tonight and therefore preoccupied. What thoughts were going on within that cunning grey head, Prince Ahmed wondered as they sat down to dinner. In addition to his grey robe, bon Ebben wore a black cloak tonight, to ward off a slight chill in the air. Prince Ahmed had made it a point for the past four years to withstand rigours of climate, whether it was extreme heat or cold, without protection, anticipating the need to toughen himself in order to reach his ultimate goals, which were to succeed to the throne of Granada when his father died and then to bring Castile and Catalonia, Aragon and León y Navarra under the Moorish banner again. Strange how these aims had begun finally to crystallize in his brain only after he met Prince Juan. Until then, his entire world had been the Gen al Arif palace in his early years and the need to break loose from its confines recently. Prince Juan's arrival had brought a new world of reality to him in a startling fashion and their discussions had revealed to him the ambitions

155

of the rulers of the peninsula and stirred his own. He had been a frog trapped in what he had thought to be the infinity of a large pond, not just physically but mentally and emotionally. Now he had discovered the river of the outside world and in its mirrored waters he had found himself, the future man.

The dining room glowed with the golden light of the ceiling lamps, musk-scented tonight; tapers on wall-sconces flickering occasionally caused highlights on dark mahogany, on gold and silver tableware. Scents of roast lamb and mutton spiced with oregano and basil tinged the air after the uniformed deaf-mute servants had cleared the table and departed soft-footed to bring in fruit juices that would complete the meal.

Abou bon Ebben pushed his chair back, stretched out his legs, rubbed his stomach slowly in a circular motion with a bony hand. His loud belch was followed by a second, less militant, after-belch. 'Thanks be to Almighty Allah for another good meal,' he murmured.

'Talking of Almighty Allah,' Prince Juan, seated on Prince Ahmed's right, signalled to him, 'I find that the Muslims are as devoted to their religion as Jews and Christians, but far more meticulous in its daily observance. As a Catholic, I am not permitted to learn about other religions, as you have been warned. But I have come to believe from my experience of your faith these past weeks, that your religion is good and I would like to know more about it; not from the *imams* and teachers, but from you as a practising Muslim.'

Prince Ahmed's eyes widened. Here was yet another dimension of Prince Juan. His goodness frequently produced such surprises. A taper's sputter rested gently on his ears. He cleared his throat, toyed with a knife, contemplating what he should say, then let the knife clatter back on the table in order to commence his answering gestures. 'Muslims believe that Islam is the

156

code of life that God, the Creator and Lord of the Universe, has revealed through our Prophet Mahomet for the guidance of mankind. For proper development, man not only needs resources to maintain life and to fulfil the material needs of the individual and society, but also knowledge of the principles of individual and social behaviour for self-fulfilment and the maintenance of justice and peace in human life.'

'And God has provided for these needs?'

'In ample measure. All the resources of Nature are available to satisfy man's material wants. To provide for man's spiritual, social and cultural fulfilment, God raised His prophets from among men and revealed to them the code of life which can guide man's steps to the Right Path.'

'Your prophets include Adam, Noah, Abraham, Moses and our Lord Jesus Christ.'

Prince Ahmed smiled. 'Yes indeed. *Our* prophets and *your* Lord Jesus Christ. Islam is an Arabic word meaning submission, obedience, commitment and peace. If we submit to God's will, obey his laws and commit ourselves to His charge, we will have peace within ourselves and on earth. Having created the Universe, God sustains it. Having created man, He appoints for each a fixed period of life on this earth. Having prescribed a correct code of conduct for man, He has given man freedom of choice to accept or reject this code. One who accepts the code is a Muslim, one who rejects it is a *kafir*.'

'Like we Christians, you believe in the one God.'

'Yes. The Oneness of God is *Tawhid*, the central pivot around which the whole doctrine and teaching of Islam revolves. It means that all men are equal.' He looked pointedly at Prince Juan. 'Discrimination based on colour, class, race or territory is not for the Muslims.'

'The last prophet was Mahomet?'

'Peace be unto him. He gave us God's code of conduct,

157

which we call *Shari-ah*, revealed to him through his spiritual senses, by the Angel Jibril, Gabriel.' Prince Ahmed looked up as the door opened.

A dark, grey-bearded deaf-mute, dressed in the purple and gold satin uniform, walked into the room bearing fruit juices in silver containers on a solid gold tray. Prince Ahmed had never seen the man before. Probably a new servant to replace one of the ancients who had been retired. He glanced at Prince Juan in order to resume his exposition. The blue eyes fixed on the servant were puzzled but Prince Juan quickly looked away from the man and stared into space.

The servant placed the tray on the table, poured red pomegranate juice for them all and departed. The door clicked shut behind him.

'You looked puzzled and thoughtful when you saw that servant,' Prince Ahmed stated. 'Why?'

Prince Juan looked away again. He was obviously in deep thought. Finally his face lightened with the dawn of knowledge. He nodded slowly, looked directly at Prince Ahmed. 'Yes, I do know that man,' he mouthed. 'I once saw him at a spy trial in Toledo. He was a government informer. He is no deaf-mute, but an assassin.'

The assassin had been apprehended immediately, but the truth of Prince Juan's warning that King Pedro the Cruel regarded him, Prince Ahmed, as a rival for the rulership of Spain struck home with shattering force. He recognized for the first time the strength of his own ambitions. He wanted to become the Emperor of Spain. In this, he would clash with King Pedro the Cruel, King Charles the Bad, King Henry of Aragon, King Philip of Catalonia and the Catholic Church. The first conflict would be over Princess Beatrice. King Pedro needed his daughter as a means towards achieving his goal of conquest. He, Prince Ahmed, had already determined to free Princess Beatrice because he had fallen in love with her the moment he saw her portrait, but he could not deny the advantages in the fulfilment of his own ambitions if he could take her for his consort.

When Prince Juan had told Prince Ahmed that, like him, the Princess had been a prisoner in the Toledo palace since she was twelve, Prince Ahmed's heart had gone out to her. Such a beautiful, beautiful bird, caged, as he was by the ambitions of a royal father. Every hitherto unidentified chivalrous urge in Prince Ahmed clamoured to ride to her rescue.

How to rescue her, when he himself was a prisoner?

Although he had refused to speak, the assassin's screams under torture, as bon Ebben had reported to Prince Ahmed, proved that he was certainly not dumb. He had finally died in the torture chamber with no one in the Alhambra palace any the wiser as to the identity of his masters, but Prince Juan's statement confirmed that he must be an agent of King Pedro and had immediately earned Juan a better prison cell and more freedom.

Although the internal security of the entire palace had been tightened after the assassin had been discovered, Prince Ahmed's decision to escape and go to the aid of another prisoner, this one a beautiful maiden in far-off Toledo, had only intensified. He lived the days that followed in a turmoil of excitement at the prospect and terror at the consequences of failure. He well knew that if he was caught in the attempt, his father might have him executed or maimed. An eye for an eye was the rule of Islam and even an heir to the throne who ran away from imprisonment could have his legs chopped off, leaving him physically fit to rule. Prince Ahmed found the prospect of being a legless king singularly unattractive.

He had actually taken his momentous decision the morning he saw the miniature painting of Princess

Beatrice in Prince Juan's locket. Without knowing what love was, he had fallen in love with the princess. Somehow that small portrait had made her more real to him than Zurika, the dancing girl he saw each evening from the window of his tower apartment. It was the eyes. He had actually seen Princess Beatrice's eyes, whereas he knew only Zurika's gaze. A belief of the ancient Greeks had once slipped out from Abou bon Ebben. They believed that an invisible ray darted from the brain of a person through the eyes to the centre between the eyes of another and established an instant link. When he inquired from his tutor as to the nature of that link, bon Ebben changed the subject. Now he, Prince Ahmed, had experienced the phenomenon.

True, the gypsy girl was alive while the image of Princess Beatrice was only a collection of coloured paints, but the ways in which those paints were put together in human form appealed to Prince Ahmed's every aesthetic sensibility. Each feature, each colour, every texture of the princess was so perfect that he had even been tempted to ask Prince Juan to give him the locket. In the final analysis, Princess Beatrice's picture had had the impact of a thunderbolt on him, filling him with a strange sense of destiny. *Kismet!* Another form of the will of Almighty Allah.

How to rescue her, when he himself was a prisoner?

Since that day, Prince Ahmed had made a careful note of the movements of sentries in the towers and battlements, had studied their rosters. He discovered that the entire system of protection was the product of the years of peace and even the new measures regarding staff were directed towards preventing an enemy from infiltrating. They need not deter someone within the citadel from escaping. His own guards were localized in the Gen al Arif, the protective screen extremely thin, because it had been planned years earlier for a little boy and had never

160

been changed. He came to the conclusion that the shortest way out would be the easiest. If Zurika could get to her rock slab undetected daily, all he had to do was reach the slab. Once there, he would filter into the city and leave by the 'needle' wicket gate on the side of the main north gates like an ordinary citizen. Patrolling of the Gen al Arif tower battlements only commenced after dark and continued until dawn. He would slip out at dusk, before the night sentries arrived.

Having escaped from the city, he would still have to find his way to Toledo, which lay north over the snowy mountains. Finally, he had to get into the Toledo palace. He would need a guide to avoid leaving a trail of inquiries and, the obvious choice of a guide being Prince Juan, he took the captive prince into his confidence immediately. One of his rewards had been the way Prince Juan's blue eyes lit up at the prospect of escape.

Prince Ahmed became proud of the cool, methodical way he was evolving his plan, yet it did not surprise him. Were not his ancestors and his people among the most superb strategists and tacticians the world had known?

Once he determined that the gap in the guard roster combined with semi-darkness made dusk the best time for the escape, he manoeuvred bon Ebben into giving approval for Prince Juan to share his late evening private studies and dinner, leaving his apartment just before the nightly classes on Islam that followed the meal. In this way, Prince Juan's presence in the apartment on the night of the escape could not arouse suspicion. This meant that he now had to share Zurika, the dancing girl, with Prince Juan, but by now Prince Ahmed was so infatuated with Princess Beatrice that, though he had once found himself extremely possessive about Zurika, he no longer minded sharing her with his companion.

He finally selected 28 November for the escape. Being the night before the new moon was due to appear, it would be very dark, and since it was a Sunday most people would remain in their homes, for even Muslims took some advantage of the Christian holiday.

The evening of the escape finally arrived. As the fateful hour approached, his heart began to constrict with fear each time he thought of what lay ahead. Suddenly the whole adventure appeared mad and he wanted to give it up. Even the prospect of rescuing the fair princess did not seem so attractive. It was pride alone that kept him from faltering. He could not let Prince Juan think him a coward, which made him doubly glad that he had shared the secret with his friend.

By the time he stood at the window of the apartment waiting for Zurika to appear, Prince Ahmed knew that he had finally become a man. He had faced terror and overcome it, substituting resolution for cowardice. He possessed true courage, the ability to master fear.

He had taken the added precaution of pleading a headache to bon Ebben, so that he would be excused from dinner and his lesson on Islam. It aroused no suspicion. The old sage had by now been lulled into a sense of false security from his ward's totally co-operative attitude towards confinement. Once he was satisfied that there was no homosexual relationship between the two princes, bon Ebben had even encouraged their friendship, which he imagined had helped Prince Ahmed to sublimate his natural desire to love and be loved. He readily approved of Prince Juan keeping company with his sick friend for the night.

Many thoughts raced through Prince Ahmed's mind as he and Prince Juan watched Zurika dance that evening, against the last rays of the setting sun slanting red-gold from the west, shedding amber hues on the snow-capped mountains in the distance. Would he ever see Zurika dance again? She had changed his whole outlook. More, she had risked death to keep their tryst unfailingly each evening. Though he still could not pinpoint the undefined emotion in his mind, he loved Zurika, but had fallen in love with Princess Beatrice. Zurika must have strong feelings for him. What would she think when the window that had been the focus of her attention for weeks now was just a dark, blank, empty rectangle? Would she dance every evening regardless, hoping that he was only ill and would turn up, until she learned of his escape from town gossip? The questions filled him with sick guilt. Yet what he had planned was his destiny and he had to follow it, regardless.

Kismet, the will of Allah.

Zurika finished her dance, blew him a kiss and was absorbed by the fading light amid the rocks and bushes.

Prince Ahmed turned to Prince Juan, who had watched in silent fascination. 'Time to go,' he signalled with deft fingers.

The blue eyes, charged with excitement, crinkled in the sweet, ever-ready smile. 'God be with us,' Prince Juan signalled back.

'Merciful Allah guide us,' Prince Ahmed responded grinning. 'May your God be Allah to protect you as he will assuredly protect me.'

His private apartment occupied the entire top floor of the tower. The battlements were reached from the floor immediately beneath, and his plan was to clamber down the battlements, helping Prince Juan who had a terror of heights. Once they reached the high ground beneath the battlements, they would make their way up the slope to the slab of rock where Zurika danced, then vanish into the boulders and bushes following her own obvious route to town.

'*Por favor*, would you help me with the bags?' Prince Ahmed signalled. He turned on Prince Juan's nod and led the way to his bedchamber, a large room, the brass oil lamps of which had already been lit for the night. He stuck a plain dagger in his belt and seized one of the two brown leather saddlebags that he had laid on the white silken quilt of his wide divan-bed at the far end of the chamber. He handed the other bag to Prince Juan and took one last look at the room that had held his secret hopes and fears, his choking frustration and unshed tears these many months since his revolt first began.

In the golden glow of the lamplight, the black and red Bokhara carpets on the white marble floors seemed softer in hue, the low filigreed marble table and the two gold cushioned divans on each of the side walls more subdued. As he breathed the familiar pungent fragrance of frankincense today, from the oil in the lamps, he realized with wonder that this room was no longer a prison. He fought back the tears that prickled his eyes. 'At long last, this room becomes my home, just when I'm leaving it,' he mouthed to Prince Juan. 'We are going out to the unknown, both of us homeless.' He tossed the prince a black cloak.

'It is always the way,' Prince Juan replied, then smiled mischievously. 'Even my dungeon in your father's palace was home to me, though I was in chains, but I was glad to leave it.'

Light dawned on Prince Ahmed and most of his regret fled. 'I too shall be sorry to leave this, but I now know that a cell is never a prison if freedom is our true home, which the dove I told you about could not find in its cage.' He patted his saddlebags. 'There is a change of clothing for each of us in the bags, with enough gold and jewels to pay a king's ransom. Little did my father guess when he kept building me a huge private treasury as a sop to my imprisonment that it would some day be the source of my freedom.' He paused, reflecting. 'I wonder what the king will do to Abou bon Ebben when he discovers that you and I have both escaped?' He picked up his own black cloak.

'Abou bon Ebben will be tortured and executed even if we are apprehended and brought back.' A serious expression crossed Prince Juan's face. 'As a Christian, I have compassion for him, but speaking frankly, his punishment will be well deserved, for it was he alone that first conceived the plan to make you a prisoner.'

'Retribution,' Prince Ahmed muttered. He had mixed feelings about the old sage's fate.

'Cause and effect,' Prince Juan countered. 'God's inexorable law that causes the wheel to turn full circle. Your tutor dared to rob you of God's freedom; now he must meet the consequences.'

'We are never free. Not even my father the king is free. Amongst other compulsions, he is the slave of his royal estate and his desire to ensure a safe succession.' Prince Ahmed shrugged. 'Enough of philosophy. Let us hasten.' He paused. 'I shall surely miss Tarif. I know he'll miss me.' He turned and made for the living chamber. He took one last look round, sighed. He glanced out of the high window at the open sky now turned to dark rose and gold and made for the solid oaken door that gave entrance to the narrow stairway winding down to the battlements. He resolutely grasped the handle, turned it and pushed.

It would not give. He shoved. It still held firm. With a sinking heart, and guts gone cold, he pounded impotently on the door. 'Dear Allah, it is barred on the outside for the night,' he whispered.

He did not have to see Princess Mathilde's expression this evening to know that she had some plan of action in mind. King Charles's consciousness of her was so acute that he could sense the flow of her energy as if it were his own. The beautifully coiffed silver hair, the lightly made up white skin, the wide grey eyes with their impenetrable black points, the poise, were all the same as she rose from kneeling to kiss his hand, but there was something new within her.

He leaned forward slightly on the love seat and looked at her intently. 'You have a special plan in mind today, dear Princess,' he stated. Throughout the years, they had loved to surprise each other with this remarkable perception. Although it had ceased to be surprising long ago, it remained a tender expression of intimacy.

She raised her pink and gold fan, matching the dress she wore this evening, to her chin. 'Now whatever makes you think that, my dear?'

The old familiar formula never failed to touch him as he gave his habitual response. 'There is nothing about you that escapes me.'

'Really?'

'Really, not even your self-confessed fates worse than death.' He had purpose in these words today.

The usual trill of laughter escaped her. She pointed her fan at him. A blazing log crackled and sputtered in the black marble fireplace. 'Did you hear that? My fire expresses its disdain at your words.'

He was feeling fit and alert from the day's military exercises in preparation for the tourney. 'God's body, that's a vulgar way of expressing disdain. You ought to teach your fire better manners.'

'You sound like your mother.'

'Fuck my mother.' He could not avoid the relapse into vulgarity, unique in the presence of the princess.

She arched delicate eyebrows. 'That is what you would like to do, is it not, dear boy?' she inquired seriously.

Her insight stunned him. 'How did you know?' he demanded.

'There is nothing about you that escapes me.'

His guffaw filled the room. '*Touché.*'

The laugh had heightened his breathing. The delicate fragrance of honeysuckle from the scent she was wearing reached him. It brought the memory of his mother's favourite scent, a distillate of myrrh unlike anything the Princess Mathilde ever wore. It filled him with new wonder. Knowing how much he loathed and sexually desired his cold, haughty mother, the princess had deliberately avoided any clothing, hairstyle, scent, words or actions that would remind him of his mother. What a wonderful, wise woman.

Did it mean that she did not want him to desire her sexually either? The question confused him and he shied away from it. If there was one thing in life that he feared, it was to say or do anything that would offend Princess Mathilde, or could sully or end his communion with her. He actually became terrified whenever he thought of her dying. He had no fear of death for himself. If God proved to be an adversary at that time, he would face God as he did any other foe, with valour. If it was the Devil that he finally confronted, he would engage the fiend on any terms. And yet, the certainty that he would soon have a woman permanently in his life, the Princess Beatrice, as his queen, had during the past weeks slowly brought possessiveness of Princess Mathilde to the fore.

'Which brings me to the question of the fire within you, dear Princess,' he declared abruptly.

'Oh!'

He shifted his bulk awkwardly on the love-seat, eased the bull-neck on which his huge head suddenly seemed to sit awkwardly. 'Now that it is likely that I shall have a permanent wife, your fates worse than death must cease.'

'If that is a royal command, you should have used the plural.' She did not seem surprised, merely amused, the grey eyes twinkly but their black points sharp with comprehension.

'It is not a royal command.' To his utter surprise, he became seized by a most unusual humility. 'It is the plea of your most humble, obedient subject.'

'Oh!' For the first time ever, he had really amazed her. The grey eyes went moist. She looked down at the white Flemish carpet, while he waited, watching her delicate eyelids with the long fair lashes, strangely hearing his heart thudding. 'That is certainly an ironic request, couched in . . . er . . . ,' she cleared her throat, 'most unusual and . . . er . . . moving terms, my dear. Let me get this right. *You* are to have a permanent wife, therefore I am to cease having impermanent lovers. H'mmm. Most unusual, but not entirely unreasonable and,' she raised a clear, level gaze to him, 'not exactly unexpected.' A faint smile crossed her beautiful face. 'Very dear too, besides being a tribute to how totally *one* you feel with me.' She frowned. 'But what am I supposed to do about the calls of my own flesh?'

She had not rejected his plea, nor had she accepted it. At least they were discussing the question. His heartbeat slowly subsided. 'What do nuns do?'

'Never having been a nun, dear boy, I really do not know!'

'Some of them probably masturbate, others are known to find release with each other. Most of them must, however, be celibate in their fidelity to Christ, whose brides they are.'

'You have really thought this out, haven't you?'

'Yes.'

'I have not the slightest inclination to either of the sexual alternatives you have mentioned and I am certainly not a bride of Christ.' She looked down at the carpet again.

'You are *my* bride and always have been from the day we first met.' The words came out fiercely impulsive, without thought.

Her startled head jerked up in a flash of silver. They stared at each other, almost blankly, while time stopped for him. Finally, her grey eyes began to melt. 'Oh Charles,

168

dear, dear boy,' she whispered. A tear-drop formed on each lower lid. 'What a wonderful thing to say.'

He stared at her speechlessly, vulnerable from the knowledge he had never identified.

'Yes,' she finally declared. 'You have certainly taught me something tonight that I had never realized before. I have been and always will be, your bride, in a marriage that like those of the nuns to Christ will never be physically consummated. So I have no choice, now that you have identified it, but to give you the same fidelity, even if you have a wife.' She shrugged elegant shoulders. 'After all, Jesus has all those brides, does he not?'

'Thank you.' His dry mouth could barely form the words, let alone utter them.

She hesitated, looked away at the fire, reflecting, then back at him. 'I am going to say something just once and I shall never say it again.' She paused to get his complete attention. 'I have never liked my fates worse than death after they were over. They were no different from the process of eating. One absorbs the goodness, then eliminates the residue. Just a bodily function, this fate, not really necessary, merely a product of desires that could be rejected. While your own cohabiting took place without my knowledge, I simply did not have to think about any of it. Now, by my arranging it, you are going to share your bed with a specific woman. That I cannot ignore. The very thought fills me with such loathing, it makes me want to vomit.'

He choked up with emotion. 'I will refuse to attend the tourney. I will fight and deliberately lose. I will do anything to prevent your being hurt.'

'You would do that for me?'

He cleared his throat. 'I thought there was nothing about me that escapes you,' he said, trying to control his feelings.

She smiled then, white teeth showing, moist eyes crinkling in the sweetest smile he had ever seen. A nun's smile, sweet as Jesus. 'You absolutely amaze and delight me, dear, dear boy.' She nodded, took a pink lace handkerchief from her sleeve, dabbed at her eyes and cheeks, replaced the linen. She collected her composure, as if the weight of the emotions they had been generating were too much for a lady of breeding. 'The one cardinal rule of diplomacy is reciprocity,' she observed lightly. 'You have reciprocated by being willing to make the sacrifice for me and remain my champion, as you have always been from boyhood.' She paused. 'I can now unfold to you the specific plan I have evolved, to which you referred before forgetting it in this entirely unseemly display of heart, for which I adore you all the more.'

He drew a deep breath, realized with wonder that he had forgotten about his first perception that evening and that through it all he had never once wanted even to hold her. If he was the Christ to whom she was wedded, she was the Virgin Mary, to whom he was bound. Somehow the thought made him feel better. 'God's body, now *you* sound like my mother. Tell me your plan.'

'It is very simple really. You must arrange for Count Gaston, who knows all about tourneys, to visit King Pedro, who has never conducted one, in Toledo, to advise the king about the procedure and protocol. This will not only earn you King Pedro's favour but will also place Count Gaston in an inside position where he will have all the advance information you need about what is to take place and, more importantly, who your chief opponents will be, so we can send spies rapidly to investigate their styles, strengths and weaknesses.'

'Know your enemy. What a brilliant idea.'

'While he is there, Count Gaston can also confer with King Pedro about the forthcoming campaign against the Moors and place you in the position of being King Pedro's chief ally, while gathering all possible intelligence as to

King Pedro's plans and those of the other white Christian rulers. You must become the leader of the . . . er . . . crusade in fact, if not in name.'

'In other words, make Count Gaston virtually King Pedro's chief-of-staff, so I can be the commanding general. Count Gaston is ideally suited for the role and will be amused by it.'

'He must never know what you have in mind,' she flashed.

'Why not?'

'Always remember his sense of honour. He must not be made to feel that he is a spy in the camp of either a friend or an enemy.'

'God's body, you speak truly. I am so fortunate to have you in my life.'

While they discussed details of her plan, the blazing fire died down. Finally, she shivered once with the cold, reached for her gold mantilla. 'It is your dinner time, dear boy. I suppose you must go now.'

'Yes.' He rose to his feet.

'*Bon appetit.*'

'*Buen provecho,*' he responded, wondering whether she would eat tonight. As for him, his heart was too full for food.

King Pedro had never before held a tournament on the scale he now contemplated, and he wanted it to be an affair that would set him so pre-eminently above the other kings of the Iberian peninsula that it would establish his reputation with all the rulers of Europe and help him to further his ambition to become Emperor of Spain and Portugal. He had therefore requested King Charles, now generally known as Charles the Bad, to send his Chancellor, Count Gaston, on a visit to Toledo, ostensibly to discuss the progress of the plan to assemble a united army against the Moors – Aragon and Castile being the two largest of the Spanish Christian kingdoms – but really to seek the count's advice on the conduct of the tournament. With his experience of the French, German and Italian courts, the count was an acknowledged authority on such events.

During dinner in the great hall on the night of Count Gaston's arrival in the Toledo palace, King Pedro had come increasingly to like the Basque aristocrat. All else apart, he discovered that they both shared a cynical approach to life, circumstance and people, though the count expressed himself in speech with a rapier and a smile while King Pedro himself was wont to use a battle-axe and a glower.

The next day, being Sunday, a formal welcoming lunch-eon had been served in the Great Hall. Now, the long siesta hour over, it was nearing sunset and King Pedro had summoned Count Gaston to his small study for a couple of hours of private conversation before supper.

King Pedro was still in a mellow mood from the excellent luncheon. The young roast pheasant had been unusually tender and the red wine from the Penedes, specially served for his guest who was known to have Epicurean tastes, of rare flavour. Besides, only an hour earlier, King Pedro had received a visit from Rabbi Azor and Lord Joram, both anxiety-ridden from the calamities that had befallen them soon after they previously reported their inability to raise the funds he needed. The king had of course blandly offered to intercede, with no expressed conditions, but, as he had expected, the two Jews had assured him that they would raise the needed funds somehow if the niece and the antique lyres were restored. Giving no sign of the savage satisfaction he derived from the abject terror, no less, of the two Jewish pricks and their total surrender to his will, the king had blandly assured them that he required no reward for doing what was right by his subjects, a generalization that left unsaid

172

his intention that he would do what was right only in return for receiving his military funds, a reservation that both parties understood. The capitals of Europe might have become suburbs of Jerusalem, but the palace still ruled Toledo's suburbs.

The presence of the count, seated opposite the oaken desk in the golden light of the lamps that had just been lit, was comfortable to King Pedro. Here at long last was a man to whom he could talk freely. The subdued tu-whit, tu-whoo . . . tu-whit, tu-whoo of an owl filtering through shuttered windows blended mellowly into the atmosphere of the room.

Tonight is for general matters, the king suddenly decided. Substantive discussion of the pre-war effort could wait for the morrow.

He pushed back his chair, stretched out massive legs, surveyed his black thigh boots. 'Prithee, tell us your views on life, Count Gaston,' he suddenly demanded.

Only a lift of black eyebrows signalled the Count's surprise at the sudden entry into matters personal. A smile crossed his hatchet face revealing white teeth between trim black moustache and beard. He ran a deft fingernail below his right moustache. 'That would be difficult to answer, Your Majesty, because I really have no views on life.' He hesitated. 'I only believe in God, the God of my perception.'

'You are a practising Catholic, are you not?'

'I swear to God, one needs to be, in order to enjoy modern conveniences, but my practice of religion has not made me perfect, nor do my religious habits accord with my beliefs or actions.' The dark eyes became challenging. 'If I may venture to say so, this is something I have in common with a few women and most men.' He paused, eyeing King Pedro coolly. 'And especially *you*, Sire.'

Taken aback, King Pedro cleared his throat, then decided that he liked such frankness. 'You had better not say that openly,' he warned, 'especially to such as Bishop Eulogius.'

'We in Navarre also have tribulations from our own bishops, Sire, who believe that it is important to sin only in private, with propriety, and to receive rather than make confessions.'

'Do you not believe in Christian virtues?'

'No, but I adhere without thought to those that are or have become a part of me and consciously practise those that are necessary for maintaining my . . . er . . . civilized existence.'

King Pedro knit shaggy red brows in puzzlement. 'What do you mean without thought and consciously?' he demanded.

'Well, Sire, like the birds of the air and the beasts of the field, human beings are born with certain traits that men say are necessary for survival. Some call them instincts, but I do not believe in instincts; nor do I agree that we follow instincts in order to survive. We tend too much to draw design and purpose from results. Fallacious *ex post facto* human reasoning, the equivalent of saying that elimination is the cause of our eating and drinking. There is cause and effect, that is all.'

'Are you saying then that we just *are* at birth – and certain consequences result from what we are?'

'The consequences are not just from what we *are* at birth, Your Majesty, but from breeding as well. We have to be the professional children of amateur parents. At each level of society, based upon arbitrary assessments of what are deemed to be the essentials of each level, our parents, friends, teachers, peers and social groups consciously breed us with the inexorable precision of dog-handlers training hounds for the hunt.' He smiled faintly. 'They too simply follow the old rules of the herd. Meanwhile, our own consciousness directs us deliberately to practise conduct that we deem would give us immediate or future benefit. To that extent, we too end up as professionals, professional survivors.'

'The king pleasing his subjects even when he loathes them, the fawning courtier placating his master?' King Pedro had suspected that the count could expand his horizons of thought, but not to this extent.

'We are all thieves of life, learning our profession.'

'Are there no fundamental elements of human existence called virtues then?'

'Human beings possess or cultivate distinctive traits, Your Majesty, which we extol as virtues or execrate as vices. Excesses of virtues are deemed saintly, while excesses of vices are called inhuman. I for one consider any excess deplorable. Excess of goodness robs living of its salt. It could culminate in the death of sin, which would be disastrous, because we would then be perpetually swallowing the communion wafer of life.

'None of our acts are divine or devilish, only singularly human, even those we characterize as inhuman, yet we keep referring to *godly* virtues and *devilish* humour. How can there be godly virtues when a Creator can never have virtues? As for devilish humour, surely the Devil can have only a divine sense of humour! The devilish humour belongs surely to our God; what other explanation can we give for One who has placed man in creation with an egoistic clinging to his own home, while storm, flood, drought, famine are his environment? Is that not a devilish joke? I rather think that, having created heaven and earth in six days, God spent the seventh laughing at His joke of Genesis before going on to other things. And yes, a Creator would certainly not rest forever after the puny labours of a few days. Can you imagine Him sitting back so satisfied with His handiwork that he contents Himself thereafter with merely managing the world, a common bailiff of His own possessions?'

175

'Without even a Chancellor,' King Pedro interjected, grinning.

'But seriously, do you really think that a God Who creates Universes, rules Creation as we do our puny, human institutions, Sire? How dare we expect His reward of perpetual heaven for belief in a Saviour Son and adherence to the Ten Commandments during a single minuscule span on earth? Eternal bliss for the tiny shred of a single lifetime, less than nothing in the realm of the eternal. And all of it for an individual man who is less than a speck in Infinity. Such crass presumptuousness is also God's joke recreated by man's devilish conceit!'

King Pedro put up his hands in mock horror. 'Blasphemy!' he exclaimed. Count Gaston was becoming more and more a person after his own heart. 'You are a heretic through and through!'

'Burn me at the stake then, Your Majesty. Only join me there yourself, because you share my views!'

King Pedro could not help a surge of delight. 'Do you express yourself so freely to others?' he inquired.

'No, Your Majesty. I would . . . er . . . humbly, do you the honour of saying that it is to you alone and to my mastiff that I can express such thoughts.'

King Pedro roared with laughter, then, growing immediately serious, he abruptly changed the subject, as was his wont. 'Now as to the tournament, Chancellor.' He had intended slyly tapping Count Gaston's knowledge without revealing his ignorance, but now felt free to ask the questions openly. 'We have never held one of such magnitude before and our protocol may be different to that of other European nations. You, Chancellor, are reputed to be an expert on such matters. Before we issue our commands to those responsible for its organization, we would greatly appreciate your telling us all you know, as if we ourselves knew nothing. He moved his chair forward, drew in his legs, placed both elbows on the table

176

to signify his attention. 'Begin at the beginning. When and where did it all start?'

A twinkle appeared in Count Gaston's eyes at these signs of unwonted humility. 'The idea has its parallel in the Olympiad of Greece.'

'*En verdad?* Pray begin with the Olympiad then.'

'According to tradition, the first Olympiad, named in honour of Olympian Zeus, was initiated in the seven hundred and seventy-sixth year before Christ. The Games were held every four years until the Roman Emperor Theodosius I discontinued them in the fourth century A.D. They were so much part of the nationalistic spirit of ancient Greece that the States are reported to have been prouder of Olympic victories than of winning battles. This meant that women, foreigners, slaves and dishonoured persons were forbidden to compete.'

'*Incredible.* Did the women accept this?'

Count Gaston smiled faintly. 'Women have never taken discrimination lying down, Sire, as they may take sex if they are flaccid! They have always fought back with their own weapons. In this case, within about two hundred years, women held games of their own every four years, called Heraea, founded by a lady named Hippodameia, which the Romans also continued after they conquered Greece.'

'The Romans were barbarians.'

'Perhaps there was truth in the saying that the Greeks conquered their conquerors?' Count Gaston paused. 'To continue with the Olympics, the original Games were confined to running. Coraebus was the official winner of the first race in the year 776 B.C. The marathon race was inaugurated in 720 B.C., when the loincloth was abandoned and athletes began appearing naked.'

'The Greeks had to have been barbarians too if they ran about displaying their cocks.' King Pedro could not help slipping into the vernacular.

177

Count Gaston cocked an amused eyebrow. 'Do public displays of private organs make barbarians, Sire?'

King Pedro guffawed, reverted to his subject. 'When were other events added to the Olympiad?'

'The pentathlon in 708 B.C., boxing in 688 B.C., chariot racing in 648 B.C., contests for boys in 632 B.C. and the foot race with armour in 580 B.C.'

'How do you know all this?'

'From the works of Greek and Roman writers, such as Pindar and Pausanias. We even have lists of Olympic winners from 776 B.C. to A.D. 217 drawn up by Julius Africanus and presented to the Emperor Eusebius.' He reflected a moment. 'The glory of the Olympiad was heightened by the introductory procession, the call of the trumpet, religious festivities and banquets.'

'From which the ceremonial of our tournaments derived, though ours are of Germanic origin, are they not, the Goths being part of our own mongrel ancestry, a warlike people who adored feats of arms?'

'The Roman writer Tacitus speaks of a dance of arms among the Germans. Henry I of Germany is credited with making them *turnier* or tournaments. In England, tournaments were undertaken by the Norman knights during the reign of King Stephen. They were forbidden by Henry II, but re-introduced by Richard the Lion-Heart, so that he could display his skill with arms and also use the events to raise revenues by levying huge taxes for permission to hold them.'

'Pity we cannot do that ourselves,' King Pedro interjected.

'Not in this case, Sire, unless you impose the tax on yourself!' The count eased back in his seat. 'In France, the origin of *tournai* is attributed to Gaufroy de Preully, a knight who died, appropriately enough, in the year of the Norman invasion of England, 1066. Tournaments in Italy and our Iberian *torneo* are of uncertain origins, but they

178

probably commenced after they were held in France.' He sat back, ran a thumbnail beneath one moustache, then the other. 'That, Sire, is a thumbnail sketch of the history of tournaments . . .' He smiled apologetically at the pun.

The tu-whit, tu-whoo of the owl intruded into the silence of the room, more clearly this time. Count Gaston is a remarkable man, King Pedro reflected, erudite, sophisticated, an expert swordsman. Then sourly, why can't I find someone like this? He had deliberately refrained from appointing a Chancellor, preferring to handle all his affairs himself directly through various officials, for want of someone he could like and trust implicitly. 'A tournament can only be proclaimed by a king, a prince, a high baron or a banneret?'

'In Germany, the Knights of the Empire, Franconia, Swabia, Bavaria and the Rhine are authorized to do so.'

'Ours will not take the usual form of a challenge from us, so, having issued the invitations and named the reward, we shall not despatch a herald to the combatants with a tilting sword.'

'The contending parties have to do that, Sire, once we know who they are, which will make them Appellants and Defendants respectively. After the challenge is accepted, the Defendant has to select four *juges diseurs*, as the French call them, out of a list of eight knights and four squires whom you will have named. He will also have to present the herald-at-arms with a costly garment, embroidered with gold or made of scarlet satin. At the commencement of the tournament the herald will receive a large sheet of parchment from you, the four corners of which display the armorial bearings of the judges. The parchment will contain pictures of the contending Appellant and Defendant portrayed in the act of tourneying. Placing the parchment on his shoulders as his authorization, the herald will appear before the judges, who will determine where and at what time the tournament will be celebrated. In the case of your tournament, the venue being your court, the rule that the king shall be informed of it will not apply and it is your court that will have the judges assembled. There being more than a few contests, the time of each combat will be decided by the respective judges.'

'It is still the rule that combatants renounce their personal and national antipathies?' King Pedro was on more familiar ground now.

'Yes, Sire. That way the vanquished does not end a martyr.'

'Since we expect many contenders, the combatants shall engage each other *en masse* at first.'

'The Germans call it *Behord*.'

'*En verdad*. And only those who participate in the – what did you call it? – *Behord*, will be permitted to joust. The weapons will be blunt and it will be unlawful to injure unprotected parts of the body, though death or dangerous wounds may still result. We have chosen only the lance and the sword, excluding clubs, batons or battleaxes. We do not want a son-in-law with bludgeoned brains. The blade of each lance will be no more than four inches wide and it must be one inch thick lest it penetrate the visor of the opponent's helmet, and it may not exceed the length of the arm. The breast or the body must be struck, so skill at avoiding the lance or letting it glide will be all important. When the lance is properly aimed and strikes the body, the adversary will be unhorsed and the weapon shattered. If a combatant falls or his lance remains unimpaired while that of his adversary is broken, he is considered vanquished.'

'You may also wish to include the German *Gesellen-stechen* as a preliminary, if you have too many contenders, Sire. Combatants will attack each other in groups until only a single victor remains, after which the winners of the group combats will joust each other for the prize.'

'Good idea. And speaking of prizes, despite the presence of kings and princes, it is the ladies who will award the honours. We are certain that your King Charles will be the victor of the *tournai* and become betrothed to our Princess Beatrice. The houses of Navarre and Castile thus united, your king and we shall take advantage of the *tournai* to deliberate upon and plan our Christian crusade to drive the Moorish ruler from Granada.'

Count Gaston bowed his head in acknowledgment.

'A pity you have decided not to participate,' King Pedro added impulsively. 'We should have liked you for a son-in-law.'

Only a flicker of dark eyes told him that Count Gaston was touched. 'I am honoured, Sire, but you would be better advised to have a ruling monarch added to the family stable,' he declared lightly, to hide his emotions. 'Besides, you would probably make an extraordinarily difficult father-in-law!'

King Pedro was taken aback, but only for a moment. 'Fuck you, Count,' he declared affectionately.

Chapter 10

Never having used the stairway leading to the battlements after dark, Prince Ahmed had not been aware that the entrance door was always barred at night. He had been even more of a prisoner than he had imagined. His first reaction was despair. His shoulders slumped, his hand flopped down from the door handle. All his hopes had been dashed in an instant. He was trapped.

Resolution flared. And determination. He would never give in, never, never, never. Heart thumping in his chest, he turned. Should he go through the front door of the apartment and seek the regular entrance to the battlements? No, that would be too risky. There were attendants and guards everywhere. The only private place was his apartment.

The harsh croak of ravens intruded, followed by the muted cooing of a dove. Was it the same bird he had once released from its cage, the dove that had flown to freedom through the open window?

The open window. That was it. He beckoned to Prince Juan, signalled his new plan. Grabbing Prince Juan's saddlebag, he hastened to the window. In the distance, the rosy hues of sunset had turned the Sierra Nevada mountain tops to sheets of red-gold flame.

He leaned over the windowsill. The late autumn air was cool on his face but he imagined that he could smell the fragrance of orange blossoms. He dropped one of the saddlebags, swirling it to make for a lighter landing. It reached the white flagstones below with a thud that sounded like thunder. Heart pounding, his eyes scanned the battlements. No one had heard. He sighed with relief, checked for Prince Juan's reaction to the drop. The large blue eyes were fixed, staring down in horror at the battlements below. He had taken Prince Juan's affliction too lightly. Apprehension gnawed at his guts again. Would his entire plan fail because of his companion's vertigo? Would the weeks of planning, the hours of hope and fear come to nothing because of one single item he had failed to consider? He had no alternative but to proceed. Resolutely, he tossed the two black cloaks down.

The beautiful Princess Beatrice, the maiden of his dreams, was languishing in her own prison. He needed Prince Juan to free her. He would escape with the prince if he had to throw the young man bodily out of the window and down from the battlements. He thought swiftly, glad to be calm in the face of the crisis. He passed his hands slowly before Prince Juan's eyes. The prince blinked once, then gradually raised them. Smiling reassuringly at him, Prince Ahmed turned him then firmly gripped both his shoulders. A tremor passed through Prince Juan's body.

'I'm sorry,' he mouthed. 'I must get a grip on myself.'

'More importantly, you shall get a grip on me.' Prince Ahmed smiled, determined to make light of the situation. He indicated to Prince Juan how he would go through the window.

The prince obediently faced the room, gripped the window sill behind him with both hands. He raised one leg, placed it on the sill, then the other. Now he was crouching on the sill. He shifted one leg down, then the other and hung from the sill. Prince Ahmed gripped his wrists. Prince Juan let go his hold on the sill. Suspended only by Prince Ahmed's grip, he gazed up apprehensively.

'Don't look down even for a second,' Prince Ahmed mouthed. 'Keep looking at me. Trust me, I'll not let go.'

A slight nod of the golden head was his reply. He leaned forward out of the window slowly lowering Prince

Juan, a dead weight now. Thanking Allah for his strength and acrobatic practice, he leaned further down as far as he could go without losing his balance. When he was stretched to the limit, he gently let go his left hand and grasped the window post with it, twisting to lower Prince Juan a foot more. His upper right arm began to ache, took fire, the agony licking his shoulder. His arm felt as if it were coming out of its socket.

'Now!' he mouthed to the pale upturned face. And let go.

Prince Juan landed safely on his toes, crouching forward in the proper manner and remained crouched to avoid observation. Prince Ahmed heaved a sigh of relief, gently massaged his aching shoulder. He clambered out of the window, hung from the sill and dropped to the white flagstone floor of the battlements, landing with practised ease, like a cat.

'Thank you,' Prince Juan framed the words. He began trembling uncontrollably.

'*De nada*, not at all,' Prince Ahmed responded, deliberately casual. He scanned the battlements, then the distant tower. Nothing moved. The silence was ponderous. He grabbed one of the saddlebags, crawled to the battlement wall, straightened, leaned over and gently dropped the bag. It landed on wild grass with a soft thump. Another thump told him that Prince Juan had dropped the other bag. The two cloaks followed, like great bats' wings. Prince Ahmed thanked Allah again, this time because his companion was functioning normally. Prince Ahmed's heart began beating rapidly. They faced a repeat of the window performance with the battlement wall, but this time, because of the longer drop, he had to hang from the wall so that Prince Juan could use his body to clamber down, clinging to Prince Ahmed's ankles for the final jump. A thud told Prince Ahmed that the manoeuvre had been successfully completed.

184

The blood began sparkling in Prince Ahmed's veins. His heartbeat easing, he stooped to pick up his saddlebag. He came erect, the winter air chill in his nostrils.

Oh the blessed, blessed feel of freedom. His feet were firmly planted on free soil for the first time in his life. His hands held money, the stuff of freedom, in the saddlebag.

He raised his eyes to the darkling heavens. 'I thank Thee for Thy mercy, Great Allah,' he whispered.

Free earth extending beneath his feet, free sky stretching above him endlessly, free air from a breeze caressing him. He longed to raise his arms to the heavens and scream his delight.

Sheer exhilaration and the inability to express it brought a sudden dizziness. He deliberately steadied his saddlebag in his hand, pointed questioningly at the flat rock slightly higher up the hill. Prince Juan nodded assent.

Ah, that rock, the first symbol of freedom on which a maiden had danced. They donned their cloaks. With a nervous glance towards the nearest sentry towers, Prince Ahmed followed Prince Juan towards the shelter of the cypress trees bordering the open ground, once cleared for fields of arrow-fire from the battlements but over-grown with shrubs and bushes during the ten-year armistice.

They wound their way through the sparse grove, climbing steadily and reached the rock. It was on this black granite that Zurika's feet had trod so free. Prince Ahmed now took the lead, following Zurika's departure route through rock and bush. Concern for Zurika suddenly stabbed again. Having made use of her, he was flinging her away like a worn sandal.

A dry leaf crackled. He came alert, felt a light tap on his arm. He swung sharply. Prince Juan had paused, warning finger to lips, alert as a mountain goat. The silence was suddenly oppressive.

Prince Ahmed's breath caught. Prince Juan, who had

been watching the rear, had signalled, We are being followed.

It seemed to King Yusuf that Abou bon Ebben looked totally smug this evening as he presented his report on Prince Ahmed in the king's private chamber immediately before the dinner hour. The gold light from the frankincense-scented oil lamps that had been lit in preparation for the night made the sage's deep-set eyes seem darker in contrast with his white hair and beard. In the kneeling position as usual, bon Ebben's long buttocks were more firm on his heels and the upper body in its loose-fitting grey robe more erect and steady than it often was.

'An excellent report, sage,' the king remarked. 'Your idea that Prince Ahmed should have a companion seems to have worked.' He searched for a sweetmeat from the gold filigree box on the low, white marble table. 'We are pleased that all is finally well after the storms. Did we not tell you that Prince Ahmed's rebellion was that of youth?'

'Aah, Your Majesty. As always, you were right.' Bon Ebben could not keep his quavery voice, the product of old age, steady. 'May I presume to observe, Your Majesty, that Prince Ahmed's outburst of poetry is part of his inheritance from you, misdirected only because of his confinement. You are a renowned poet, Sire, if I may humbly remind you, and you have devoted all these years of peace to the arts. You have unfailingly advanced painting, literature, architecture and music in the realm, while nonetheless encouraging science as well. You have enlarged and beautified the Alhambra, even having our great Babal-Shari gateway constructed, creating also the Royal Baths, the Puerta-de-la-Justica and the Casa Real.'

King Yusuf could not help but be pleased by this recital, which he knew to be true. 'We but do our duty, sage, under the guidance of Divine Allah, with the tools He has bestowed on us. Not every ruler is privileged to possess artistic gifts and able to help those of similar talent to blossom. We are glad our son has this inheritance for it is more precious than spun gold.'

'You are also uniquely progressive in governing, Sire,' the sage continued. 'You built the Alcazar and have supplied Granada with sweet water, stored in marble reservoirs, from the Sierra Nevada through lead pipes. You have provided every village with schools where free education is imparted to all, regardless of race or creed. You completed the College of Granada, with full research facilities in botany and natural science. You have reorganized the police department of the kingdom and instituted night patrols. You have caused municipalities to provide the people with better service. You have bestowed equal justice under your laws to persons of all religions, Jews, Christians and those of the true faith. What more can a ruler achieve? By the divine grace of Almighty Allah, whose Chosen you indeed are, you will go down to history as Spain's most noble, enlightened, civilized and puissant monarch.'

I pray that I retain humility in spite of all these achievements, the king thought grimly, for I do not want to be yet another victim of the Jew's curse. If I have bestowed equal justice on the infidels, Jews and Christians, it is because I need the support of them all to secure my rule against the white kings of Castile, Aragon and Navarre. I dislike Christians because most of them hate us of the true faith in Spain. Like most of my fellow Muslims, I despise Jews, whom the Prophet declared accursed for refusing to support him when he needed them. The Jews in turn despise everyone of any other religion because they believe themselves to be the Chosen People. Once I start my *jihad*, holy war, all these animosities will spew forth. 'Summarized as you have just done, it does seem as if we have indeed been blessed with a lifetime of achievement!' he exclaimed aloud.

'You certainly have, Sire.'

King Yusuf paused, reflecting, then darted a swift question as was his wont. 'You are sure there is no homosexual attraction between the two princes?'

'I'm absolutely certain, Sire. The friendship of the two princes is based solely on a companionship which has had such a steadying influence on Prince Ahmed that he has become more diligent than ever before, even in his regular studies as against matters military.'

'Only two and one-half years longer and we can set the prince free. Why, we ourselves might then be able to enjoy the son we never had.' He moved his right knee up, gestured with a heavily jewelled hand. 'We could even begin to assign certain responsibilities to him.' His dark eyes glittered at the prospect. 'There will be many more duties to be performed by that time, for by next year we shall have extended our dominion to the kingdoms of Castile, Aragon and Navarre.' He paused, debating whether to divulge his news. Why not? 'We have received word only today from our brother in Islam, King Abu Hassan of Morocco, that he will support us with an army of a hundred thousand faithful, including mercenaries, for our invasion of the Christian north.'

'When will the invasion begin, Sire?' bon Ebben inquired eagerly.

'It takes time to assemble a force of such vast numbers. Remember, the logistics do not merely involve trained men and animals, but arms, artillery, engineers, supply, medical and transport services.' He was so buoyed up by the prospects, however, that he knew a burst of supreme confidence. 'But never fear, for we shall be in Toledo by this time next year.' I will need to curb the expression of my brother's hatred of Christians and Jews, he reflected. Hating them is one thing, persecuting them another. The Muslims of North Africa have never needed to hold back their intolerance of infidels, who are such minorities in their kingdoms. When they come here, they will want to massacre all enemies of Islam.

'And from the way your princely son and heir is now progressing, he will join you there eighteen months later,' bon Ebben stated.

Elation gripped King Yusuf. 'We wish we could see Prince Ahmed at this very moment,' he declared impulsively, then paused. 'But we realize we must be patient.'

'You could not see him tonight anyway, Sire, because he is sick in his chamber.' Bon Ebben threw up pale palms. 'Nothing serious, just a bad headache, probably from being out too much in the afternoon sun. Yes, even a winter sun can be oppressive, but Prince Ahmed does not permit anything to interfere with his military training. Such a pity he cannot join Your Majesty in the campaign. There is nothing he would like better. A skilled horseman, a tireless, strong, devoted, aide and a superb fighting man, he would be a real asset to you. I swear no one but Your Majesty could unseat him in the joust.'

Suddenly moved by a thrust of feeling for his son that he had never before experienced, King Yusuf searched for some personal token he could send the sick young man. The jewels, coins, gold, silver, ornaments he had heaped on the boy, were all from his mind, partly as compensation for what he knew was imprisonment, however desirable. Now he was impelled to give something from the heart.

His eye fell on the gold box he had received that very evening. It contained assorted coloured sweetmeats from Arabia, the Turkish delight all the way from Arabia, by caravan across the Middle East desert through North Africa. A fit gift for a sick prince.

He leaned forward, took the gold box in both hands. 'These delicious sweetmeats have been sent to us as a special, personal token, all the way from Turkey and Arabia. Our son shall have it as an expression of our lo . . . er . . . concern for him. Since we have eaten but one sweetmeat, we shall be truly sharing the contents with him, something entirely personal shared for the first time ever. Tell Prince Ahmed so when you deliver this box to him. Say it is not from the king to his subject, but from a father to a son.'

The sage lowered his white head. 'I would be honoured to deliver such a touching gift, Your Majesty. Prince Ahmed shall have it first thing tomorrow morning.'

'Deliver it tonight,' King Yusuf insisted, pounding the marble table so the gold box rattled. 'Immediately you have finished dinner with us.' He clapped his hands for the attendant.

Apart from himself, only two other people knew of his complete plans, Ruy de Vivar and his beloved Maria de Padilla. Having received word from de Vivar just that evening that one of the three assassins, pretending to be a deaf-mute, had been securely installed in the Gen al Arif tower as a member of Prince Ahmed's staff while the other two were in contact with the Prime Minister of Granada, Farouk Riswan, to arrange for more ambitious prey, King Pedro could not wait to bear the news to Maria de Padilla.

He seldom visited Maria before bedtime. This evening, her slender figure in its long blue silk dress seemed to vibrate at the near contact with him and the way her limpid brown eyes lighted in the golden glow of lamps when she greeted him in her reception room, spoke of a love that was renewed each time they saw each other. Over seventeen years now and the excitement at seeing each other still remained. Marvelling at her beauty, he realized that Maria was the only vulnerable part of his life. If anything happened to her, he would be lost, demented by grief.

It had not been an easy road to reach what for him was

the Holy Grail of love, an ideal that would cause his rivals and enemies to laugh at him if they knew. From his earliest years, he had been a womanizer, a rapist if that was what it took to satisfy his lust. Maria had loved him exclusively, single-mindedly from the day of their first meeting, when she had been one of the ladies-in-waiting of his queen. Never once had she remonstrated with him or made him feel guilty, by a look, a word or a holding back. Instead, she had given him her virginity and there-after her body, her companionship and, yes, finally her soul, through every grief and horror, every torture she must have endured. Over the years, by slow degrees, he had come to depend on her, until the day he realized that *she*, not a place, was his home. He marvelled at the knowledge that all else was dross and that he did not ever want to stray from the home they had created for each other, the home that was ever-presently his, even when the two of them were not physically together.

This was his secret, shared with her. It had made it easy for him to shed his queen, ruthlessly murdering, with his own hands, those who had been sent to rescue her from the confinement he had decreed for her. He had defied Holy Church to take Maria for his consort, to give her his child and to declare that child heir to the throne of Castile. His reputation for being a womanizer would remain, but he himself was cleansed, his life secure in the arms of a devoted woman when so many of the others could easily have assassinated him in bed.

'You have news, Sire!' she exclaimed now, rising to her feet from offering him obeisance.

'*En verdad*, indeed, I do!' he declared, reaching for both her soft hands, the full fingers as always giving him a strange comfort. He bent to kiss her lips, fought down his erection at the way they melted.

He led her across the dark red Tabriz rug, which he had bought for her when their daughter was born, at great cost because it had 1200 stitches per square inch. He seated her on a gold upholstered love couch facing the marble fireplace and probed the red embers of the logs into yellow flame with a brass poker, sending up a tiny shower of sparks and wisps of smoke towards the chimney. The tinge of its eucalyptus wood pleased his nostrils. A log sputtered in protest. 'You have been given some immature wood,' he remarked. 'I shall have it set right tomorrow.'

He turned to face her, his back warmed by the fire, his eyes crinkling happily at the way her face had softened. 'I have just received some good news from Ruy de Vivar,' he declared. 'Our assassin is finally installed in the Gen al Arif palace as one of Prince Ahmed's deaf-mute attendants.'

'But he is no deaf-mute, *querido*, beloved Sire.'

He guffawed. 'I have many deaf-mutes in my Court who can hear and speak,' he stated. 'Being a deaf-mute is a question of perception.'

'Oh!' A long, delicate finger flew to the side of her chin in a gesture of comprehension which he loved. 'He is pretending to be a deaf-mute.'

'*Ciertamente*. What is significant is that we have finally penetrated the nest.'

'Your purpose is to kidnap Prince Ahmed?'

'Yes, having him killed is not part of my plan. It would defeat my purposes. Besides, I must follow the Muslim code.' He bared yellow teeth in a ferocious grin. 'An eye for an eye, a tooth for a tooth, a severed cock for Prince Juan's throat, two balls for his ears.'

'You have never told me that Pedro the Cruel feels so fiercely about his son's mutilation.'

The words 'his son' warned King Pedro of the one area in which Maria was irrational, although she always curbed her reactions to her continuing jealousy of his past marriage. 'On the contrary, you well know that I find delight

192

in people's torture,' he assured her. 'I only care about you, beloved, and for our daughter, the offspring of our love, bone of our bone. I would personally tear anyone who harms a single hair of your heads limb from limb.' The very thought of harm befalling Maria filled him with rage, but he quickly sobered down. 'As for the fate that has befallen Prince Juan, Pedro the Cruel takes no note of it. As I have already told you, I would prefer the young man had fought to the death rather than allow himself to be taken prisoner. But I must react as the ruler of Castile, one of whose subjects has been harmed. Our people are entitled to punishment and vengeance for the crime.'

'You think Prince Ahmed is responsible?'

'It was for him the deed was done.'

'At the command of the father.'

'*Ciertamente*, but it was for the son.'

'You will kill the father, why not the son, who is your future adversary?'

King Pedro had a flash of knowledge that Maria wanted Prince Ahmed dead. It ended before he could wonder why. He licked his thick lips, stroked his red beard. 'I want the delight of having him mutilated in public,' he stated softly. 'Oh yes, it will be something to savour and a spectacle for the people. Bread and circuses. Our people are not wanting for bread.' He laughed shortly. 'Prince Ahmed has probably been kidnapped at this very moment.'

He glanced at Maria for her reaction. She was staring into space as she did on the rare occasions when she had a revelation. 'Prince Ahmed will not be kidnapped.' The words came out as if from another space. 'Your plan has already been foiled.'

At Princess Mathilde's suggestion, King Charles had invited Count Rafael, the homosexual, to visit him in his palace at the capital of the Navarre kingdom while Count

Gaston was away with King Pedro in Toledo. The princess always advised him as to how he could keep ahead of everyone else in the march of political ambitions. In the present case, Count Rafael, being Aragon's Chancellor, would have up-to-date information about King Henry's prowess at the joust and his intentions regarding King Pedro's forthcoming campaign. He, King Charles, would thus have more knowledge than any of the other three kings. For his own part, far from minding the general opinion that he was merely Charles the Bad, not possessed of cunning, therefore incapable of exercising it, he fostered this illusion in order to deceive his peers, competitors and enemies.

His personal garden in the palace was King Charles's favourite place for secret or private conversation, his favourite time, the hour before his daily talk with the princess. So the entire earth was now mute. The shrill cries of ravens, the last of the birds to nest for the night, protesting at approaching darkness, which always brought the many hours during which they could not satisfy their insatiable appetites, had become hushed. It was not the beauty of the earth's silence during these moments between the sound of daylight ending and those of night commencing that King Charles welcomed, as he paced the flagstone walkway bordered by beds of rose bushes, pruned for winter, with Count Rafael, a dandy in burgundy velvet tunic and white hose. Nor was it the scent of eucalyptus from the darkling trees beyond, or the chill breeze that suddenly fanned his florid cheeks, trickled through his beard and cooled his bull face.

He had no patience with the appreciation of beauty. He had left such stupidity to his mother, the elegant French Queen Joanna, and look where it had got her, a fucking crypt for her mouldered remains and perhaps a place in heaven for her soul. Heaven, where she must be dreadfully frustrated because she could never alter its decor, dictate its manners or ordain its protocol.

No, King Charles liked this hour that was neither day nor night in the courtyard because its silence and seclusion invited intrigue.

A contemptuous laugh escaped him at the recall of his mother, the royal bitch.

Count Rafael turned chubby cheeks, pink even in that uncertain light, sharply to him. He had developed an empathy towards the count since that night many months earlier when he had tried to fuck the pageboy, Jacques, and failed to get the necessary erection. He had to admit that the boy's rounded pink bottom had aroused desire in him, and it was only pride that prevented him from re-trying the experience when he was more sober. It would never do for his nobles and subjects to regard him as a confirmed bi-sexual. Nobles were a collection of pricks, bent on fucking whomever was king.

King Charles had to admit that Count Rafael had an uncommon perception, as now. 'That laugh was savage, contemptuous and bitter, Your Majesty,' Count Rafael declared lightly. 'May one inquire as to its cause?' The normally blue eyes were of indeterminate colour in the semi-darkness, but the look, though seemingly light, was penetrating.

He halted, a detaining hand on the count's elbow. The palace building now sprawled behind his visitor, a dark three-storey mass surmounted by turrets and chimneys, with a mosaic of regularly spaced rectangles of gold from the lighted windows. Moving shadows behind the drapes told of people getting dressed for dinner. Above the black spread of the roofline, a rose-gold sky shaded upwards to its pale blue vault, the silver evening star winking above. A bull-frog croaked from one of the palace pools. Others picked up the sound until it crackled around them. Mating calls! Am I too a bull-frog ready to croak my emotional

195

secrets to this man? Why not? 'You are right, we just remembered our late royal mother,' he responded. A hungry tiger roared from the royal zoo.

The count's pale gold eyebrows arched. 'And that recollection evoked contempt and bitterness, Sire?'

This man was not only perceptive, he also had the ability to draw people out. Recognizing this, King Charles deliberately decided to play the fish to Count Rafael's bait, the better to win his confidence. There was nothing like pandering to a man's pride to make him betray other people's confidences without ever realizing it. And how better to be a pander on this occasion than by proffering the truth? 'Our royal mother had so much aesthetic sensibility, as she called it, that she worshipped aesthetics almost as much as she worshipped herself.' He shook a raised finger for emphasis.

'Report has it that she did so with the single-minded devotion of a pre-Mosaic Jew prostrating before an image of Baal,' Count Rafael remarked. He ran a pink tongue over his sensual red lips, the chubby cheeks creasing in a smile.

'God's body, you are right again, Chancellor.' King Charles could not help warming towards the man. He absent-mindedly scratched an armpit, reflecting. 'Do you know when we deliberately set out on a course of so-called badness?'

'No, Sire.' A silver fountain behind the count fizzled out, recovered.

'In our earliest childhood we discovered that there is no reward for goodness on earth. One was supposed to wait for heaven to receive that. And supposing one finally qualifies only for Purgatory, or even Hades? What good,' he bared yellow teeth in a cynical smile at his choice of the word, 'would the acts of goodness on earth have in such an event?' He nodded his huge head sagely. 'Waste of fucking time, right?'

'Most unusual line of thought, Sire, but you may have a point there, though our theologians will say that those good deeds could make the difference between Heaven and Purgatory, or Purgatory and Hell.'

'Do you really believe that God runs Purgatory like a reform school, permitting us to enter his kingdom only after He has consulted ledger clerks who maintain our debits and credits, like Jewish moneylenders or His Holiness the Pope overlooking the Vatican's tithes?'

'I do not permit my *beliefs* to stray into the realms of blasphemy or heresy, Your Majesty.' A prim note had entered Count Rafael's husky voice.

'You are a fucking liar, Count,' King Charles declared pleasantly. 'Your fucking *actions* – and I mean whom you fuck! – are in essence heretical.'

'Ah, Your Majesty, we live in an ecclesiastical world that does not permit us to equate our actions to our beliefs. Otherwise every sin would be heretical, every cry of deviate sexual ecstasy, blasphemy. It is the *expression* of beliefs and the malpractice of *religion* that provide the religious powers-that-be with human material to scourge, vilify or burn at the stake.' Count Rafael's eyes had lost their colour in the darkening air, but there was no mistaking the twinkle in them.

King Charles could not prevent his jaw dropping. He closed his mouth with a click of his teeth. 'Our royal mother, on the other hand, maintained such a ledger in her golden head, even after it became streaked with silver.' His massive jaw tightened. 'Goodness received no reward from her. It had to be a reward in itself. Taking goodness for granted, she swept through life and the Court, supreme in her own conceit, a being apart.' He paused. 'Only badness could bring her back to earth. Yes, Count, we discovered that the one way to attract her attention and to keep it for any brief period of time, was by being bad. We had confirmation of this when we were but ten years old.' His eyes flew into the distance, remembering, then alighted on the windows of his mother's former upstairs suite.

Count Rafael remained expectantly motionless.

You are a cunning son-of-a-bitch, King Charles decided. You really do know how to draw people out. 'We crept into the vestry of the palace chapel one evening and stole the Mass wine.' He chuckled at the recollection.

'Were you discovered?' The tone of Count Rafael's voice betrayed his surprise, though he was normally imperturbable.

'Of course. That is how we planned it, to check out our assessment of Queen Joanna.'

'Did it have the desired result?'

'*En verdad*, certainly it did. Our royal mother suddenly discovered that she had spawned a soul of the damned. Whether it was fear of her mortal sin in having conceived such a one in her womb, or concern that she would not be able to enjoy the cool bliss of Heaven if her son was roasting in Hell, she took us under her wing. We saw her daily thereafter, until she became convinced of our penitence and absolution, a conviction which we deliberately fostered in her in order to release ourself of the supervision our misdeed had spawned.' He shook a knowing head. 'We believe that the ultimate sin is hypocrisy. God, Who in his Wisdom knows our innermost secrets, must abhor hypocrisy more than murder, blasphemy, or sacrilege.'

'A most unusual concept, Sire. Would you not say there is a little touch of heresy in your own views?'

'There never is a little *touch* of heresy, any more than there is but a hint of the Black Death.' King Charles's grin was cynical. 'All this goodness must be abhorrent to God. Its worst manifestation is martyrdom. How embarrassing it must be to explain to God why people are dying like flies for their Saviour with the firm conviction that it entitles their souls to pound at the gates of Heaven. Can you imagine the conversation, Count. God tells Jesus: "Not another of your fucking martyrs surely, Son. Where are we going to put them up? What the hell did you do down there? I wanted you to teach people how to live and you have taught them how to die!"'

The count's laugh rang freely through the cool air. 'And Jesus responds: "Was it not you who made a hell of an earth and sent me there to repair the damage? I discovered that the only way to make people good on earth is to render them stupid. This I accomplished in good measure. Humanity has been clamouring for martyrdom ever since, just to follow my example."'

'Jesus set a hell of an example, so earth could be an example of hell,' King Charles riposted.

His frankness had the desired result. The count had become totally relaxed. 'You have a quality unique in rulers, Sire,' he observed. 'You have a clarity of vision unobscured by your Olympian heights.' He glanced sideways at a rustle beneath the bushes. 'A common or garden rat sees more even at night than many a royal . . . er . . . rodent.' He turned his head to grin at the euphemism.

King Charles smiled back. 'We shall see many of that variety at the joust,' he remarked, skilfully bringing the conversation to where he wanted it.

'My royal master is of course in a category by himself, certainly not of the rodent variety. But he will be participating in the joust.'

'Oh? We thought he was married.' He would shiver his lance and unseat the son-of-a-bitch.

'He has separated from Queen Sophia, Sire, and expects to obtain an annulment from His Holiness.'

'On what grounds?'

'The Vatican is so far removed from earth that . . .'

'It can find "*casus belli*" in an ill-timed fart!' King

199

Charles interrupted. He slapped his great thigh, laughed uproariously.

'Any boon will be granted by the Vatican for the right price, Your Majesty, so long as it is not politically inexpedient.'

'So it would seem, Count, from Peter's pence for a poor widow's plea to a king's ransom for the annulment of an inconvenient marriage. And you are right about political expediency. Forcibly quartered in Avignon, His Holiness could never sell any favour that would be objectionable to his gaoler, the French king.' He drew a deep breath. 'Oh well, we are all the victims of our systems, and your master, King Henry, is no exception. Does he expect to win the joust and ally Aragon with Castile?'

'Certainly, Sire.'

'Well, fuck him.'

'I'd rather you did, Sire. I prefer young boys!'

King Charles guffawed, slapped his thigh again. 'You have a nice wit, Chancellor. We should love to have you in our Court.'

'I would be honoured, Sire. Like His Holiness, at the right price.'

'We would certainly be able to afford that when we have won the joust, allied our kingdom with Castile,' then, deftly, 'and driven the Moorish bastards from Granada . . . er . . . with the support of all Christian rulers of Spain, including the quota of men, arms and material from your royal master.' This ploy had been Princess Mathilde's suggestion.

'King Henry has no intention . . .' Count Rafael stopped abruptly, cleared his throat, 'of . . . er holding back on his support should he lose the joust, Sire.'

Smooth recovery, you pink-faced queer, but not smooth enough, King Charles thought triumphantly. Would I have been a queer too if I had fucked the pageboy, Jacques, or is a man permitted one or two entries before he is granted full admission to your fair courts?

By the time they headed for the lighted entrance doors of the palace and he returned the halberd salutes of the uniformed guards on either side, King Charles had extracted all the information he needed from the wily count, including details of King Henry's jousting style. I am not merely Charles the Bad, he reflected. People call me that because I fornicate right royally and spit on personalities, institutions and the niceties of protocol. What they do not know is that my own craftiness and guile, guided by my mentor, Princess Mathilde, make me Charles the Really Bad!

Chapter 11

He reached for his dagger, swung round, keen eyes first darting up the track, then at the dark bushes and grey boulders beside it, for signs of movement. The feel of the weapon eased the thudding of his heart, but also made his blood sparkle with excitement. He would not be taken alive. Let his father have a corpse for an heir, but there would be other corpses too before he died.

Nothing stirred. Calm brought back reason. If the king's men were following, the alarm would have been sounded by now and armed guards would be pouring down the track. Whoever followed them was doing so furtively. He glanced questioningly at Prince Juan. Standing motionless on one side of the track, the prince repeatedly jabbed a finger in the direction they had come. Could a brigand be tailing them? Unlikely, for criminals would avoid a heavily guarded place like the palace. Had Prince Juan mistaken some movement of shadows for a person?

A dry leaf crackled again.

Signalling to Prince Juan to hide behind a boulder, Prince Ahmed backed into the bushes. He would take the intruder in the rear. Heel to toe, he began circling back, cat-footing to avoid making the slightest noise. Finding himself near-breathless with tension, he steadied his breathing. After years of military training, here was the real thing at last. An expert with knife, sword and dagger, he was stalking a live prey. What would it feel like to kill his first man? No pity, for an enemy was an enemy and had to be destroyed.

When he hit the track again, he paused behind a dark

green juniper bush, eyes darting up and down the track. The silence was eerie. A pleasant odour wisped into his nostrils. He could not identify it.

He crept back on to the track, moved cautiously towards a bend. It would be good to catch whomever it was between Prince Juan and himself. He rounded the bend. Not ten paces away, a hooded figure in a dark cloak loomed before him, moving stealthily on tiptoe. Ever so slowly, one step at a time. Another slight bend in the track hid the rock behind which Prince Juan waited.

Was his first kill to be a stab in the back, the assassin's dagger? Kill or be killed. No time for niceties. Here was the enemy. Dagger raised for the downward feint before thrusting upwards, Prince Ahmed stepped lightly forward. When he was close enough to the enemy, he sprang, swift as a mountain lion.

Gravel crunched beneath his right foot. The figure swung round on the instant, whipping out a long knife. Prince Ahmed reversed his dagger hand in mid-air, saw the enemy's face beneath the black hood, gasped, slashed wide. The opposing knife blade remained poised in mid-air.

Left shoulder leading, Prince Ahmed crashed into the figure. They sprawled together on the ground, the opponent beneath him. The softness of the body sent thrills through him. He stared down in shock at the face, took in the wide, staring eyes, the distending nostrils. The eyes at last.

'Why did you not strike?' he demanded, breathing hard.

'Because I saw it was you,' Zurika replied. 'You had a narrow escape.' A curious expression crossed the large brown eyes. They fluttered once, the fine nostrils beneath them dilated.

Excitement surged within Prince Ahmed. 'You too,' he replied shortly, his penis, vibrant upon her soft thighs, had begun to enlarge. That wisp of scent had been hers, now full and enticing.

He gazed into her eyes. Brown, not blue! *It is the Princess Beatrice I love. Why does this young woman inflame me, when her eyes are not blue?*

'What are you doing here?' He was trying hard to sublimate the feelings and desires flaming within him.

She seemed to recover. 'I am a bird doing my ritual dance at sunset.' Her faint smile, revealing even white teeth, was elfin. 'What are *you* doing here, Prince, outside your cage?'

He laughed then, heard the soft tread of footsteps, remembered Prince Juan. He looked up and saw the prince approach. Somewhat ashamed, he did not know why, he disengaged himself from Zurika. He rose to his feet, replacing the dagger in his belt, reached out a hand for her. She turned towards Prince Juan, who had stopped in his tracks, looking at her as if thunderstruck. He tried to speak, but only the usual glug . . . glug escaped him. A tortured expression flitted across his face. Prince Ahmed sensed the undercurrent of agonized frustration before Prince Juan looked away sadly.

'Why did you not return home after you danced this evening?' Prince Ahmed inquired of Zurika.

'My grandmother Pilar saw in her crystal that you would try to escape,' Zurika explained. 'She knew that on foot you would not get far before the guards caught up with you. She had received a small bag of gold from your tutor, Abou bon Ebben, for having helped you when your mind was not right and decided that the most fitting use for the gold, which she had hidden away and could not use immediately, was to help set you completely free. So she spent some of it to buy two horses which she stabled just outside the north needle gate of the city. Guessing that you would plan your escape for the darkest Sunday this month, she instructed me to remain here after my dance this evening, to lead you to the horses.'

Once he knew where Zurika's words were heading, Prince Ahmed had been finger-translating for Prince Juan, but he could not hide his incredulity. 'You mean to tell me that your grandmother saw all this?' He shook his head in disbelief. 'She must be a witch.'

Anger flared momentarily in Zurika's dark eyes. 'She is no witch, Prince, but an enchantress who is trying to help you.'

Prince Ahmed was immediately contrite. 'I am sorry,' he responded with unwonted humility. He realized that Zurika had been treating him as an equal so far, not as a prince. He had heard that some gypsies were proud; this must be one of them.

'I understand, Prince.' Zurika calmed down. 'Now I shall lead you both by a secret path to the north entrance, where we can slip through the needle gate without being challenged.' She grinned faintly. 'The stupid sentries only stop and question people who want to enter the city after dark, not those who leave it.'

Joy from hope renewed surged through Prince Ahmed. 'How can we ever thank your grandmother?'

'You will have the opportunity of doing so in person.'

'How?' Prince Ahmed began. He certainly had no intention of interrupting his flight to visit gypsy caves.

'Do you remember the story of the three beautiful princesses who were captives of their father, King Mohamed the Left-handed?'

'Ye . . . es.'

'We shall be repeating history tonight.'

Light began to dawn. 'You mean . . .' He pointed a finger at Zurika. '*You* will be accompanying us?'

'Certainly. My grandmother Pilar too.'

'B . . . but, you can't come with us . . . I . . . I mean . . .' He floundered.

'Why can't we?'

'I forbid it. I absolutely . . .'

'The horses are ours, aren't they? And you need them, don't you?' Her smile was wide with mischief, the eyes crinkling. 'Besides, would you want us to remain and be executed for helping you escape?'

'I shall pay your grandmother for the horses,' he declared stiffly.

'They are not for sale. Since neither my grandmother nor I can ride and both you princes are expert horsemen, we can ride behind you. My grandmother has also decided that we will not take the Toledo highway, which is what the king will expect you to do since Prince Juan is with you. Instead, we shall head for Cordoba, along the route taken by the three Spanish *caballero* prisoners who escaped with two of the princesses and their *dueña* using but three horses. Once we cross the border, we can change direction and make for Jaén, which is in the Castilian kingdom. Pilar will remain behind there and use her remaining gold to buy a place where she can practise her . . . er . . . fortune-telling. I shall ride on with you to Toledo.'

'You can't do that!' He knew the words were in vain even before he uttered them to this very determined young woman.

'Of course I can. My grandmother's crystal told her you will need me in Toledo.'

'Why would we need you?'

'The crystal did not say.'

Perplexed, Prince Ahmed glanced towards Prince Juan, who had somehow comprehended what was being said. The prince nodded assent.

Pilar smelled of musty clothes and an unwashed body. Knowing that Prince Juan's sight and sense of smell had sharpened with the loss of his voice and hearing, Prince

206

Ahmed, wanting to spare his companion the discomfort of such a strong odour, had volunteered to let the old crone ride behind him, while Zurika rode behind Prince Juan. He was now regretting his unselfishness with every hoofbeat of his cantering horse.

The three of them had slipped through the flare-lit needle eye of the northern gate with surprising ease. Even the precious saddlebags across Prince Juan's and his shoulders had not aroused interest. Mingling freely with people had been a totally new experience for Prince Ahmed. While enjoying it, he made a mental note to change the system of guards when he became king. When he became king! He was further from *that* than ever. Pilar had awaited them at the stables of a rough inn further up the Cordoba highway, with two horses, a tall bay which he selected for himself and a smaller chestnut. Pilar had packed a week's supply of bread, cheese, sausage and wine for them. Prince Ahmed had seen the grey-haired entrancer before, but he was not prepared for the devouring look she gave him in the light of the stone-paved courtyard of the inn before they mounted and set off. Now he had to overcome a triple aversion, her dreadful smell, her obvious delight at riding with him instead of with Prince Juan and her cackling laugh.

Determined to put as much distance as possible between themselves and the palace as quickly as possible, they had set off immediately, riding side by side towards the Pass of Lope which led through the mountains to Cordoba.

'They look for two princes, they no care four people, two women's also,' Pilar had quavered. 'Why you hurry?'

'They will look for anyone who left the city,' he had flashed back. Then, imperiously. 'We leave immediately.' Having had enough of dictation, he had slung the saddlebags across the horses for emphasis, mounted the bay and reached out a hand for the old lady.

Cantering briskly down the highway, used as he was to the well-trained thoroughbreds of the palace, mostly Arab, he found his horse's gait hard and awkward. As they clattered along, Pilar, gripping him closely around the waist, took every opportunity to press a wrinkled cheek against his back whenever the horse's gait wavered. Thanks be to Allah that she was downwind; even so she was too close for someone accustomed to the unfailingly sweet scents of a palace.

What am I doing here, riding through the chill night air along a cobbled highway flanked by dark cypresses, heading for I know not where? Erect in the saddle, moving only from the waist down with the horse's canter, he saw the dark mountains ahead, a clear sky above pricked with bright silver stars. Ah, I am following my own star, Princess Beatrice, the star of my soul. But what would it be like if it were the soft yielding body of Zurika with her woodsy fragrance riding behind me, holding me, instead of this bag of bones perched at my rear? He looked to the stars for help against the wrongful thought. Princess Beatrice was starlight. Zurika was the dusk. He had to give his all to the princess, all his loyalty and something else for which he had no name.

The first time she had had physical contact with a man and it had to be someone deaf and dumb! As she clung to Prince Juan while they rode along the dark highway, Zurika could tell that he was a superb horseman. Yet the ride was bumpy for her because she had never sat on a horse before. And was she not holding on to a prince, after all, even though she would have preferred to be riding behind the other prince on the taller horse beside them?

Was this really happening to her, Zurika, a sixteen-year-old gypsy dancing girl who, only last night, at this same time, had been sleeping in a smelly hillside cave?

Since she started dancing for Prince Ahmed, she had lived in a dream world that was nonetheless half-reality, a step towards the realization of her earlier dreams. She had been destined to leave the gypsy hillside and Majo's grisly aims for her. Had not Pilar seen that in the crystal too? Strangely, she had been very much at ease in conversation with Prince Ahmed, but he had somehow closed up after those brief, exciting moments when he had lain atop of her on the track. Now she had a more indefinable silent communion with this white Prince Juan.

The contact with Juan's body had not only pleased her with its warmth and physical closeness but had also created a stirring beneath her pubis. But she would rather have been riding with Prince Ahmed. He looked so dashing with his brown skin and tight face bones, cleft chin and dark, brooding eyes beneath straight black brows. After the first flood of speech on the hillside that evening, she had been smitten as dumb as this Prince Juan, barely volunteering a word, merely responding when she was asked a question. Once Pilar came on the scene, of course, she had no opening for speech! Glancing sideways at Prince Ahmed across the dark highway, she could just make out his profile. It was set and determined. She had been in love with him before they even met. Now, all that he was, tall, wide-shouldered, slim-waisted, elegant, exuding royal breeding, confirmed that love.

Looking up at the vault of the blue sky and the stars, for the first time she comprehended a oneness in all things, and somehow knew she would never return to the caves. Unaccountably, she shivered. Was it the chill air that caused it? Not entirely. What then? Was it a sudden realization that the future was still uncertain for her? Her situation was more than fantastic. It was unreal. Here she was with two princes, one the heir to the Granada throne, the other possibly to the kingdom of Castile. Where would she end up? As a concubine of Prince Ahmed?

That was as far as one of her station in life could expect. No matter, if Prince Ahmed took her into his harem, she would ensure by every means in her power that she alone was his love. She was already fiercely possessive of him.

When would he take her?

An unidentifiable premonition caused her to shiver again.

They crossed the Vega, reached the foothills of the rocky mountains of Elvira and began their ascent in silence save for the clattering of hooves, the creak of leather and an occasional snort from one of the horses, the sounds now echoing off the granite on either side of the highway. As they rounded a sharp bend, excitement gripped Prince Ahmed. The cleft of light in the dark mountain was the pass.

Even as he stared at the outlet to freedom, two fires sprang to life on either side of the gap. He reined in his bay, pointing. 'Can you see those fires?' he threw back at Pilar over his shoulders. 'They have been lit suddenly. What do they mean?'

Pilar craned her head around his body, muttered a curse.

'Well, what are they?' he impatiently demanded.

'They bale-fires from watch-towers.' She swung her head to the left, then the right. 'O Blessed Virgin Mary, O Peter, James, O John, help us.'

'What do they mean?' He sensed danger.

'Look round. You see many. They start from Alhambra palace to tell next one, then next one tell next one, so they burn and burn, one after other.'

'You mean it is a chain of signals from the Alhambra battlements?'

'Aiyee, yes.' Her body began trembling.

His heart sank. 'Dear Allah, they have discovered our flight at the palace. How?' He paused. 'No matter. They

210

are signalling the outposts to intercept us.' He had counted on a whole night's travel before their flight was discovered. Now they were barely gone three hours in all. Thanks be to Allah for the horses, but what good were horses now, with interception ahead and fast cavalry undeniably in pursuit behind them? He was hard put to control his trembling.

He glanced at Prince Juan, who had reined in alongside him. Through the gloom he noted that the prince, having observed the lights, had grown tense.

Prince Ahmed had studied all the escape routes thoroughly. The famous bridge of Pinos lay just ahead of them, spanning a ravine through which a stream rushed. Once across it, their only hope was to veer into the mountains, skirting the guardposts at the pass. He pointed ahead, clenched his fist and made the follow me sign. Prince Juan nodded.

'Hold on!' Prince Ahmed commanded Pilar. He clapped his legs into his bay's flanks. The animal refused to respond. He dug fiercely with his heels, urging the horse forward with his seat. The nag moved, began a faster canter. Soon they were pounding along the dark highway, hooves drumming, echoes flying back off the rocks. Prince Ahmed prayed to Allah that neither of the horses hit a loose cobblestone.

The air became cooler with the speed of their passage. Since he rode with erect body, cavalry fashion, he tightened his cloak around him so that the air would be cold only against his face. They clattered around a bend, then another.

'O Allah!' Prince Ahmed exclaimed, pulling in his horse.

The bridge lay just a quarter of a mile ahead, but the tower beside it blazed with light. Dozens of red-gold glares on the bridge itself glittered on the weapons of guards blocking the way.

* * *

King Yusuf was alternating between rage flaring in his head and undefinable apprehension in the pit of his stomach. He had been in the *baño*, the royal bath, when Abou bon Ebben brought him news of the escape of the two princes. Moorish people of consequence, unlike Christians, normally bathed during the day, but he, King Yusuf, had added hot and cold rooms when he extended the royal bath and liked the relaxation the steam room brought him at the end of each day, especially the gruelling ones, because it enabled him to sleep better.

He had added a beautifully decorated meeting hall, which was where he had received the sage, and an undressing room, a passageway from which led to the hot and cold rooms. While not as magnificent as the Khirbat al-Mafjar, with its magic carpet mosaic decorations, was reported to be, his own creation was more distinctive in that it could be reached only through the living quarters in the lower part of the Daraxa, with access to the Courts of the Myrtles and the Lions through the high windows of the second floor of the baths' main hall, which had required an elaborate tower-like cupola.

Was it a message from the dead Jew that he should receive the astounding news of the escape while making use of his own improvements to the Alhambra?

Abou bon Ebben had seemed so agitated that he had remained standing while talking to the sage. He had then sat on a settle, the white linen towels pulled closely around his naked body, gesturing to bon Ebben to kneel before him. Always slow to anger, he calmly reasoned that since Prince Juan had fled too, the fugitives would be heading for Toledo, the closest border being that along the Toledo highway, so he must stop them before they crossed into the safety of Castile. Snapping his fingers at his chief aide, a gigantic, black-bearded Moor, he calmly issued orders for their apprehension. 'Light the bale-fires on the battlements, have trumpets sound the alarm. Have

Captain Husain of the First Cavalry Regiment attend us so we can give him orders for the pursuit.' He smiled grimly. 'They are to be brought back alive . . . or dead.'

He would question Abou bon Ebben closely now. Should he alert his Prime Minister? Some instinct made him decide to keep Farouk Riswan in the dark for the present.

Had it not been for his gesture of paternal affection in sending the sweetmeats to his son and insisting that Abou bon Ebben deliver the box that very night, it would have been early morning before the flight was discovered. By then, it would have been too late to intercept the princes. The escape had certainly been well planned and boldly executed. He even knew a moment's grudging admiration for his son. What an heir! All the more reason to have him brought back. That was when the fear intruded. A ruler without a legal heir was a fortress without walls. The flash of feeling towards his son for the first time he could remember had been divinely inspired. Merciful Allah was looking after him. His son and Prince Juan would be apprehended and brought back. It must be Prince Juan who had inspired his son to escape. Otherwise why now, after all the years of confinement accepted by Prince Ahmed, apart from the one recent revolt? He would torture the white Castilian pig, cut off his manhood, then disembowel him.

Now it was Abou bon Ebben's turn to explain how this had happened. The grey-haired, wrinkled sage was kneeling, buttocks resting on heels, head lowered, white beard on chest, eyes downcast, awaiting the king's order to speak. The frankincense scent from the oil lamps began to overpower King Yusuf, the tinkling, clanking bedtime music of his orchestra reaching him faintly was dissonant in his ears, but still he remained outwardly calm. 'Your explanation, sage, for this outrageous event,' he quietly demanded.

213

The sage did not raise his eyes. 'I tried to explain this to you some time ago, Sire, when I spoke to you about Prince Ahmed's revolt the night you returned to Granada after your victory over King Pedro. I said then that we had both failed to recognize certain factors of human nature that are stronger than physical constraints.' The grey eyes finally lifted just below his gaze were steady. 'I know I have failed in my duty and my life should be forfeit.'

A short-cut without the need for explanation or recrimination. While he would normally have paused before such courage, the old man's calm merely infuriated King Yusuf. 'That shall be for us to decide,' he roared. 'We demand your explanation as to why this happened.'

Bon Ebben lowered his gaze. 'As to that, we have already told Your Majesty,' he murmured. 'Now it remains to ask ourselves, how.' He paused, contemplating the white marble floors. 'My most recent mistake was in confining Prince Ahmed to his apartment in the Gen al Arif tower when he first revolted against his situation. The human need to be free is far greater than any man's ability to conquer. Witness the freedom movements of people throughout history. As for the surging of love, it is divine, because it flows from Great Allah's love for all Creation. So I erred when I increased Prince Ahmed's imprisonment to a smaller cage within the large cage against which he had rebelled, instead of giving him more freedom.'

King Yusuf was becoming increasingly impressed by the sage's calm. Here was a man in the direst peril who had suddenly found peace within himself. How had he done it? 'We approved your decision,' he conceded gruffly.

'It is generous of you to say so, Sire, but the solution at the time was mine alone and I accept full responsibility for it. You merely endorsed my proposal.'

'Why did you permit Prince Juan to be our son's companion? You should never have even thought of that?'

'Aah, Sire, that was to fulfil Prince Ahmed's need for real companionship. We feared homosexuality, but that never occurred and Prince Ahmed did not succumb to love for Prince Juan. I personally doubt that it was Prince Juan who conceived or influenced Prince Ahmed's escape. On the contrary, I would say it was the other way around.' The wrinkled cheeks twitched in amusement at a secret joke. 'After all, Prince Ahmed is his father's son! I humbly beseech you, Sire, to consider what would have happened if the roles had been reversed and it had been Your Majesty that was confined.'

'Presumptuous wretch!' King Yusuf grated, then stopped in wonderment. What indeed would he have done? Conflicting thoughts began racing through his mind. Could his whole plan for his son have been ill-conceived? What else could have been the solution? Had he erred in not giving his son personal love and companionship? How could the escape have been prevented? What more could he do to apprehend the escapees and bring them back? How had they dared to flout his authority?

'Pray forgive me, Sire, but you well know that presumptuousness is not one of my attributes. I have been trained in many royal courts to respect the king's authority, indeed to respect all men and institutions.' The cheeks twitched again. 'It was over eighteen years ago that I really failed, when I first recommended to Your Majesty the solution to the possible tragedy the astrologers had predicted could await your baby son, from love. I overlooked two vital forces.'

'And those?' King Yusuf demanded sharply, though he already guessed the answers.

'First the desire of all living things to be free, second

215

the biological compulsion to love and be loved. Those are Almighty Allah's laws of the Universe. Why, the need for freedom even causes a star to break away from its position in space and shoot across the sky. As for love, I need not give Your Majesty examples.' He sighed. 'We must all pay for our misdeeds.' His smile was sad.

The fluttering of a moth's wings intruded upon the silence. And we are like that moth before our biological urges, King Yusuf thought. The moth's exercise of freedom impels it towards the flame, and the warmth which draws it is as inexorable as human love. In a kingdom, law and justice are equally inexorable. Those too are the causes created by man as an extension of the effects of Allah's laws, with their own attendant effects. All of it constitutes *kismet*, destiny.

'We have taken note of your words, Abou bon Ebben,' King Yusuf declared. 'All is the will of Allah. Yet it is also God's will that kings shall rule, creating laws for the people they govern. You have broken the king's law and shall be punished for it. The king's justice, however, remains to decree the nature of that punishment based upon all the circumstances you state and the king's own complicity in your actions.' He revealed white teeth, not clear in his own mind as to whether his smile was feral, benign or non-committal.

The sage's grey head drooped. 'Argh, a most wise and merciful . . .' he began. His jaw sagged. A gasp escaped him. He desperately clawed for breath. His wrinkled face lifted, the eyes wide, agonized. One hand flew to his chest. 'A . . . a . . . ar . . . r . . . r . . . gh,' he croaked. His eyes glazed. Like a floundering boat, he slowly careened over on his side.

King Yusuf had already risen from his seat, releasing his towels. They fell to the floor leaving him clad only with the towel around his waist. He became conscious of the cold marble beneath his feet. Abou bon Ebben's

216

contorted face was just as cold when he touched it. The sage had uttered his last 'Argh'.

Almighty Allah had intervened with His own justice before the king's law could operate. King Yusuf had never felt more *alone* in his life. Yes, he was now totally *alone* to face the consequence of his actions as a ruler after heeding the advice of a sage.

What had bon Ebben called those actions? Misdeeds! He recalled the inscription near two of the baths' lion-head spouts: 'Is there anyone like Abou al-Hajjaj, our sultan, who does not desist from triumph and great victory.' Was the dead Yusuf ibn Nagralla sending him a message?

Chapter 12

Hands on the pommel of his saddle, barely conscious of the heaving of his horse's ribcage and the snort that escaped Prince Juan's chestnut, Prince Ahmed stared down at the scene in stupefaction. They were trapped at the bridge, the only escape route. Though they were still too far away to be noticed from below, he even imagined that the faces of some of the guards were turned upwards towards them.

Guards in front, cavalry obviously pursuing them from the rear. What could they do?

Wild thoughts intruded, reaching his fevered brain. Should they try to crash through the bridge? Should they cut into the wilderness to live like bandits until the pursuit ended? The beautiful face of Princess Beatrice as he had seen it in Prince Juan's miniature floated into his mind, expanded to life size. Princess Beatrice, his inspiration, the angel of pink, white and gold, of delicate bones, thin fine nostrils and noble brow who haunted his dreams. The urgency of the rescue mission pushed all other thoughts aside.

He cast anxiety from his mind, began to think clearly and coolly. They had to get over the bridge somehow. But how to do it? Not over, you idiot, but past it, the logical part of his mind insisted. How? The fragment of history to which Zurika had referred that evening intruded, raced forward to the forepart of his brain, formed a distinct image. He clicked his fingers as details of the legend of the three princesses came into focus. Tarif had told him the tale a long time ago. Three white Christian *caballeros* who had been captured in battle against the Granada kingdom, had escaped with two of three princesses, daughters of the Moorish king, Mohamed the Left-handed, a tyrannical father who had imprisoned them and their *dueña*; the third princess had planned to accompany them too but had faltered at the last moment. Now the legend came to his rescue. He glanced at Prince Juan's pale, taut face. Prince Juan had more to lose than he if they were captured, so did Zurika and Pilar. Torture and hanging awaited them. No wonder the air was vibrant with their anxiety.

A laugh escaped Prince Ahmed. 'This is the best thing that could have happened,' he declared quietly, signalling the words to Prince Juan with deft fingers and hands, exuding a confidence he did not really feel. 'We shall strike off from the highway, thread our way down the hillside, proceed hidden by the rocks and trees until we hit the stream. We shall ride along the bank until we come to a ford, then get across and proceed west through the wilderness towards Cordoba, until we get to the border and cross it.' His upraised arms pointed left. 'To freedom!'

'We should not have feared. Peter, Paul, Mary protect Prince Ahmed,' Pilar stated, hugging him from behind, much to his revulsion. 'Crystal tell we no be captured.'

Prince Ahmed could sense Zurika's adoring gaze, but avoided looking at her. A delighted ughh . . . ughh from the depths of the larynx was Prince Juan's response as he wheeled his chestnut into the rocks and scrub scattered between dark trees.

Prince Ahmed reined his own bay, headed left, leaving only Pilar's low cackle of triumph floating on the highway, her terrible breath in his nostrils.

His eyes had fallen on the young woman that morning as he walked in front of his entourage down the aisle of the Gothic cathedral of his capital, Pamplona, after High

Mass. She stood apart even in the crowd facing respectfully inwards for his passage. Desire for her had instantly blazed within King Charles the Bad. She was tall, cold and haughty looking. Her pink cheeks, slender features, curving red lips and roguish blue eyes adorned a slender figure, topped by a swan-like neck. This type of beauty never failed to captivate him. He freely acknowledged the cause of the attraction to himself. He was pursuing the likeness of his mother, Queen Joanna. Each time he took such a woman, especially from the rear, he revelled in doing so by force, for he was raping and ravishing his own mother, a punishment the dead bitch richly deserved. He occasionally wondered what it would have been like to fuck that cold proud beauty in fact instead of by proxy. Body of God, he would have enjoyed that!

Count Gaston was away in Toledo. The vice-chancellor was deputizing for him. Count Garcia was always ready to do his bidding, especially when it came to procuring women. Good thing Count Gaston was gone, for he would have disapproved. A fucking celibate monk! Now there was an incongruity. How were you celibate if you fucked! Yet he tolerated Count Gaston because he was one of the most powerful nobles in the joint kingdom, a great soldier and, yes, a good restraining influence at a time when the organizations of nobles and people were increasingly curtailing the unbridled powers of kings.

King Charles beckoned to young Count Garcia, who came up smiling through a ginger moustache, revealing red gums and a few blackened teeth. As he quietly stated his wishes, the count's small eyes disappeared in the shiny folds of ruddy skin above wide cheekbones. 'Your slightest wish is my command, Sire,' he softly lisped between gums and teeth. He paused, letting the royal party flow past him. King Charles knew that Vice-Chancellor Count Garcia would get the young woman to his master's bedchamber that night by hook, crook, or force, and so it had proven, as Count Garcia reported during dinner in the great hall that night.

'How did you do it?' King Charles inquired, though not with any special curiosity or amazement.

'Very simple really, Sire. Fortunately she had come to Church alone. I followed her home and engaged her in conversation at her door by pretending that I was trying to find a residence in the neighbourhood. That was when I also very respectfully inquired as to her name and where she was from. A singularly trusting girl.'

'Dealing with a plausible rogue.' King Charles had deliberately thrown the count a sop.

'Thank you, Your Majesty. Thank you indeed.' Count Garcia was well pleased. 'She told me she was French, a Parisienne.'

'Ah! She is French. Wonderful!' He would enjoy fucking and sodomizing this youthful recreation of his French mother the more. 'What is she doing in Pamplona?'

'Her name is Renée Latour. She is eighteen years old and betrothed to a young Spanish artist named Manuel Avilla, whom she met in Paris. She is here to marry him. Reportedly a virgin, she now awaits you in your bedchamber, Your Majesty.' The half-empty mouth was bared in a lascivious smile.

'How did you get her here?' King Charles was immediately concerned.

'I told her that you were my master and that you buy paintings. If she would bring one of her fiancé's paintings to the palace, I would greet her at the entrance and personally escort her to your private chamber where you would view it. If you liked the picture you would buy it and assure her fiancé's professional career.'

'You fucking stupid oaf, you divulged our identity to her?'

'Ah yes, Sire, but on the condition of absolute secrecy.' Count Garcia paused for effect. 'Your name and the royal palace established credibility, and she followed my strict instructions not to tell anyone and to come alone, cloaked and hooded. No one but you and I knows of her identity or her presence in your chamber. I even suggested to her that she should tell her fiancé and his parents only that she had a prospective buyer for the painting and wanted to keep the outcome a surprise. This permitted her to make the journey alone so late in the day. When I got her into Your Majesty's private ante-room, it was after the attendants had left for the evening. The paintings on the walls of the room reassured her! I drugged the glass of wine she had while she awaited you, then carried her into your bedchamber and locked the door.' He shrugged. 'The routine of Your Majesty's private quarters is highly conducive to abduction and . . . er seduction.' He shrugged again.

'Brilliant! You are a rascal, a rogue, cunning as the devil and absolutely brilliant. You have a great future ahead of you.'

'I endeavour to please Your Majesty with discretion. As I said, your slightest wish is my command.' Count Garcia paused for effect. 'Unlike many in your Court, Sire.'

A low ceaseless roar was the first herald of the stream. It heartened Prince Ahmed as he let his mount find its way down the rocky hillside. He had to trust the nag in this terrain, because the darkness was impenetrable. Prince Juan followed, an occasional slither of his chestnut's hooves revealing it to be less sure-footed than the bay. The air was cold and damp, causing both horses to sneeze occasionally. Prince Ahmed was doubly glad that they were heading away from the highway.

The stream's roar increased, accompanied now by a splash and gurgle that told of water fast-speeding over rocks. When he finally saw the lighter dark between the tree trunks and undergrowth that announced the bank, Prince Ahmed said a silent prayer of thanks to Almighty Allah.

They broke from the slope and found themselves on a flat, grassy bank. Pilar's low cackle once again applauded progress. The cackle's link with the one she had left floating on the highway had been her tight hold on him during the ride in the darkness and her nauseating odour, worse than her own breath, or a camel's.

The stream was about a hundred feet wide at this point, surging waters flowing swiftly. To their right, in the distance, Prince Ahmed could distinguish a glow, scattered with flarelights, that was the bridge. Veering left, he walked his horse along the bank, making for a bend in the river that would hide them from the bridge. The drier air here, the open space between the dark rock and the tree-lined banks and the blue vault of the sky studded with twinkling stars once more brought an exhilaration at having broken free. The total silence, except for the river sounds, was blessed.

Once they cleared the bend, Prince Juan trotted alongside him. The stream had begun to narrow, and reason told Prince Ahmed not to go too far before effecting the crossing, for, the narrower the stream, the greater the force of the water. When he spotted a place where cattle had probably gone down the bank, he decided literally to take the plunge.

Turning his mount to the right, he made for the water, directing the horse downslope. The track, as it proved to be, was muddy. The bay shied, slipped as he forced it forward.

'Hold on!' he cried to Pilar, leaning backwards as they began slithering almost on the animal's rump towards the rushing water. Pilar's grip around his waist tightened. She cannot be a witch because she does not fear the water, he thought inconsequentially before they hit the stream with a tremendous splash. The icy cold soon began seeping in through his boots and pantaloons, soaking him. Within seconds they were being carried rapidly downstream.

The bay started swimming. Keeping cool, Prince Ahmed angled the horse diagonally across the river, edging it towards the opposite bank. Another great splash told him that Prince Juan had hit the water in exactly the same manner. He glanced back, saw that the prince was following his lead. He waved once and Prince Juan waved back. In less than five minutes both horses had clambered up the opposite bank, where they halted, legs spread, flanks heaving, snorting and shaking water off dripping bodies.

Both princes began laughing with relief. Zurika giggled. Pilar cackled.

After the conversation with Count Garcia, King Charles had drunk less than usual at dinner, positively drooling at the prospect awaiting him, a rich dessert to give his mother her own rich desserts.

His bedchamber was a large room on the second floor of the Pamplona palace, another Gothic building dating back to the brief period centuries earlier when Charlemagne had ruled Navarre. The chamber overlooked the central courtyard, but the shutters had been closed against the chill night air. Tapers lining the walls and great bronze candelabra on rich mahogany tables cast bright golden light on the burgundy drapes bordered with gold braid and the matching Venetian rugs scattered on the pink marble floors. Bronze braziers trickled out grey camphor incense which tried vainly to overcome odours of a closed room and linen dank from humidity.

The tall young woman, dressed in dark blue beneath a long white woollen cloak, stood beside the great red-canopied bed, served by three wide steps and covered with pink silken bedlinen. She had her back to the door; her hands were clasped in prayer. She had obviously recovered from the effects of the drug and knew what lay ahead for her. She turned as the door clicked shut behind him. She exuded such a clean virginity in contrast with his own rough bull-like appearance, his high body odour and the reek of alcohol and garlic on his breath, that it gave King Charles an immediate erection, so stiff that it hurt. She of the swan-like neck, he, Charles the bull. She would offer him her pride before he penetrated her with . . .

Drink-bright eyes fixed on her, he slowly approached the bed. To his surprise, her glance was level, but there was something else in it he could not identify at first because her large blue eyes were in shadow.

He stopped before her. She was almost as tall as him. Good. His mother had been about the same height. 'They tell us your name is Renée Latour,' he said in French. 'Welcome to our bedchamber. We are glad to have you here.' Pleasantries first, before the brutal assault, the stunned surprise and excruciating agony inflicted. The plan alone was cause enough for a near orgasm.

'My name is indeed Renée Latour, Your Majesty. I am French and cannot say that I share your pleasure at my presence here.' Her voice was silver, cold and haughty. 'As a French citizen, I am under the protection of my king and demand in his name that I be returned safely to my abode. As a human being, I humbly beg for your mercy.'

He could not believe his ears. 'Fucking bitch,' he roared, shaking a huge fist at her. 'For that you shall pay a double virgin's price, first your rear, then your front.'

He could sense her blanch, but she continued to display no fear. 'I am indeed a virgin,' she declared. 'I intend to remain so until I give my virginity to my betrothed.' Her glance became contemptuous. 'You don't frighten me with your bull's roar.'

225

'Then I shall frighten you with my bull's charge,' he shouted, forgetting the royal plural in his rage.

He sprang upon her, bore her to the ground. Pinning her with his body, he sought wildly to place slobbery lips on hers. Eyes closed in utter disgust, she avoided him, moving her face from side to side. He pulled back and slapped her hard across the face. A gasp escaped her, but she gave no cry. One white hand flew to her mouth. A trickle of blood appeared on her red lips.

Continuing the motion of the hand with which he had slapped her, he pulled aside her white cloak. He grabbed the blue dress at the neckline, tore it off with one mighty jerk. Her white breasts were revealed, mounding above a pale blue bodice.

White breasts. Mother breasts, waiting to be suckled.

He ripped her bodice. The generous white mounds spilled over. Making animal sounds, he buried his lips on a pale pink nipple. An acrid smell prickled his nostrils. Was it smelling salts? Why smelling salts? He felt her body stiffen, arch, heard a rattle in her throat. Her soft flesh went limp, stiffened.

The animal noises emerging from him slowly subsided as the nipple beneath his mouth lost its resilience. He raised a shaggy head to stare at her.

Her face was stiff, held awkwardly at an angle. White froth mingled with blood smeared the sides of her mouth. He sought her eyes. They were wide and staring. She had fainted. Fucking bitch. The smelling salts. He had to get her awake before he raped and ravished her. He couldn't wait to get at those rounded white buttocks.

The acrid smell smote him again. What was it, this familiar odour? Not smelling salts. His eyes swept sideways to its source. An open glass phial of poison, which he always kept beside his bed, lay by the dead woman's face.

He sobered in an instant, sprang to his feet. The

dreadful consequences of the situation smote him. A French virgin had committed suicide in his bedchamber! Trouble with France, trouble from the parents, the citizens, loss of prestige for his prowess. Fucking bitch. He savagely kicked the dead body.

Keep cool in an emergency. He had always done so. Yet his brain raced feverishly. No one but Count Garcia and he knew of the woman's presence here, not even his personal staff. He had the whole night in which to dispose of the body. Not he, but Count Garcia would do that. The secret would remain.

Suddenly he recognized the expression he had not been able to identify on the dead woman's face. It had been hatred.

Something nagged. He could not identify it. He needed help, a clear head to advise him. Late though the hour was, he stumbled out of his quarters, closing the doors behind him. No one would dare enter while he sought advice from Princess Mathilde, his bride.

King Pedro gazed in consternation at his sagging member. It normally became stiff and erect just from the love that flowed between him and Maria de Padilla even before he shed his cod-piece and stockings. Tonight, for some unaccountable reason, the penis would not rise to the occasion. Was it that he had drunk too much wine? He had never had this problem before, however drunk.

His eyes moved slowly upward to meet those of Maria, expecting surprise, disappointment, even scorn. In the golden lamp-light her expression was one of unutterable love. Still holding his gaze, she rose slowly from her bed, covered tonight with white silken sheets. When she was at her full height, she slowly unbuttoned her pink bed-gown. Her youthful figure was revealed, the flesh glowing through a pale pink nightdress. Nipples with large dark-brown aureoles, colour-matching the patch of pubis between soft, rosy thighs. Mysteries beneath sheer silk. She shook her long hair loose.

King Pedro knew the answer even before he looked down again. Still no erection. An ugly sag nestling in a fierce black bush supported by thick hairy legs.

His gaze, now pitiful, drifted up to Maria once more. Her eyes were hypnotic with adoration. She slowly crossed her hands, gathered up her nightdress, eased it above her head. Pink-brown breasts spilled out, her open eyes still luminous on him, long hair a shining cascade around soft shoulders.

He did not have to look down to know that in spite of the spurts he desperately pushed out from his scrotum to his penis, it remained flaccid. He closed his eyes, hung his head in shame. Moments passed. Trumpets outside sounded the hour. He barely heard them. Was he being punished for his cruelty?

It was the familiar lilac scent of her that first made him aware that she was near. He opened his eyes. She had sunk to her knees before him, her beautiful face uplifted to him. As he looked down at her, she lovingly took his limp organ in a gentle hand. Her eyes still raised to his, she lowered her face and took him in a soft mouth.

Something stirred at the love flowing from her mouth, her eyes, her entire being. Within two minutes, he became hard and erect.

'I love you, beloved liege lord of my soul,' she whispered.

'You did it!' he exclaimed in wonder. 'You made it come right.'

The roguish expression he loved so well briefly crossed her face. '*Ciertamente*, but you have a while to go, however, before I let *you* come,' she countered softly. 'And it is not I that did it, rather my deep, deep love for you.'

Moved beyond belief, words escaped him without

228

thought. 'When a woman or a man can find joy in ministering to the mutilated, sagging or lifeless flesh of another, a restoration of pride emerges from the greatest of God's gifts to humanity, love. For is it not God's love that restores an earth wearied by fire, flood or tempest? When such love is bestowed on another person, that is surely divinity, for anyone who can bring the dead to life must be divine. Such a love comes from the immortality of past Heavens, Maria de Padilla, and it will surely waft us both to the immortality of endless Heavens to come.'

Two tears poised like dewdrops on Maria's eyelids. 'People who love make so many mistakes because they do not identify the real truth, my beloved Sire,' she whispered. 'Too many people consider a man's erection an end to be reached, something to be achieved. Surely it is not the erection that matters. Love may create the desire to give and receive an erection, but it is the intimacy of seeing and fondling secret places that is the product and the real consummation of love. So communion with a man's flaccid organ or a woman's unfeeling breasts or unresponsive bud are the real end, the true sharing of love.'

The two tears coursed down her soft cheeks.

When they coupled, it was as never before.

He was completely sober by the time he reached Princess Mathilde's quarters. No one had dared question him as he strode through the wide corridors of the palace. It brought the comforting reminder that he was King Charles the Bad, a ruler not to be crossed. Stationary guards at every intersection merely gave him the halberd salute. They were from his own, specially selected palace contingent anyway. Even the slightly rumpled ladies-in-waiting who answered his insistent knocking on the great double-doors of Princess Mathilde's second-floor suite and ushered him through the white marble-floored ante-room into the reception chamber betrayed no surprise. Were they well-trained to receive night visitors? He thrust the question aside before the recollection of his own peril.

When she entered through a side door with the rustle of silk and knelt to kiss his hand, Princess Mathilde looked no different from when he had last seen her that evening. Her silver hair was immaculate, her make-up as perfect as her poise. She acted as if a midnight visit from her king was a regular occurrence. The fire had died down in the fireplace, so it was chilly in the chamber. She drew her *mantilla* more closely around her shoulders, the long, slender fingers very white against the black, and waited with grey eyes lowered for him to open the conversation.

'I am here because I need your immediate advice.' He came directly to the point with an apology only implied.

She lifted her gaze to him. 'I am always at your command, dear boy.'

She lowered her eyes again, did not once move as he told her his story bluntly, with no excuses. 'My predicament is that here is a French subject, a young woman, a virgin, who has committed suicide in my bedchamber. I can make excuses for that, but what about the blow to my manhood?' He was glad he could be frank with her. 'I thought that since my deputy Chancellor, Count Garcia, had got me into this, he should get the woman out. It would be relatively simple to dispose of the body in the underground tunnel. But something is wrong with that. Can you discern what it is?'

The eyes she raised to him were calm. 'Of course. Such an action would place you in Count Garcia's power.'

He clicked his huge fingers. 'That's it. You are absolutely right. I knew there was something amiss.' He paused, eyeing her steadily. 'What should I do?'

'Exactly as you have planned.'

'B-but . . .' He began and stopped, puzzled.

'You will assist Count Garcia to dispose of the body

secretly. No one but you and he will know of the incident.'
Her voice was steady and calm as her look. 'When you
have done so, you will still be in the tunnel, alone with
Count Garcia and no one any the wiser. What you have
to do then is obvious.' She shrugged elegant shoulders, as
if she had implied that he should dispose of an importun-
ing beggar at the palace gates.

His shaggy eyebrows arched and creased at this first
evidence of her calm ruthlessness. As always, she picked
up his reaction. 'I dare anything for your safety,' she
declared quietly and his heart lifted. 'The ancient Thebans
believed that the price of honour is death, so when
necessary the king had to die. In the present case, you
can retain your honour through someone else's death.'

Holing up in wooded copses by day to sleep and travelling
at night using the stars for guidance, they neither encountered anyone nor heard sounds of pursuit, except for
some woodsmen on the first morning and a hunter,
fortunately without dogs, the second day. Hidden as they
were, they were not discovered.

On the sixth night, they descended a steep mountain,
crossed another stream flowing through a gorge, ascended
the opposite hill face and found themselves on a grassy,
wind-swept plateau scattered with gnarled trees. The
starlight revealed low hills, pricked here and there with
dim lights. These signs of habitation made them progress
more cautiously, although Prince Ahmed knew that they
would have to stop that night or the next to replenish
their stock of food, for they only had one day's supply
left. The horses seemed satisfied with cropping grass and
whatever greens they could reach for, but the alternative
for the four of them, which Pilar had already suggested,
was to steal from a lone farm when they came upon one.
What bothered Prince Ahmed more than the approaching
shortage of food was the lack of small streams the last two

days. They were all thirsty, smelled dreadfully of stale sweat – while Pilar stank – and they all looked unkempt. How ironic, he thought. We are tired, dirty, with aching bodies, living like mountain bandits, though we have a king's ransom in my two saddlebags!

They veered right now, heading east, with the north star to their left. It was almost dawn on the seventh day when Prince Ahmed noticed the cultivated land with well-kept groves and low bushes. Hope surging within him, he reined in his horse to survey the scene. Soon satisfied, he laughed aloud with relief. 'We have escaped!' he shouted excitedly, signalling at the same time to Prince Juan. 'Those are olive groves and vineyards. We are no longer in Granada, but in the sub-kingdom of Jaén, which belongs to Castile!' He crossed his right leg in front of him and slipped off the saddle. Prince Juan quickly did likewise. They helped the two women down.

Standing beside each other, they began shaking with laughter. 'Ha, ha! Ha, ha!' The sounds broke through the silence of the half light. A bird grumbled from its nest in a neighbouring African tulip tree. A dog barked not far away.

Pilar was the first to sober up. 'How you know?' she demanded, suddenly cautious again.

'Those are indeed olive groves and vineyards,' Prince Ahmed repeated. 'Jaén's best known industries have for centuries been olive oil and wine. The city itself is an ancient one. It was capital of the Moorish sub-kingdom of Andalusia, complete with a fort, about a hundred years ago, when the Castilian King Ferdinand III re-conquered it in the year 1246. He strengthened the fort and built a palace there. It has belonged to Castile ever since. We must have crossed the border at the ravine. We shall come to the main highway from Granada soon and can then head north again for the capital.'

'No more have move only night time like bat and owl,' Pilar cackled.

'Or an entrancer,' Zurika reminded her. She glanced at Prince Ahmed. 'Can we eat and bathe today?'

'Certainly,' Prince Ahmed responded, glad that a gypsy girl could have the same priorities as his own. 'But let us ride through the day until we get close to Jaén, so we can make just a single stop.'

In spite of its fear and discomfort, Prince Ahmed had found the entire journey like a visit to another world. Now, as they plodded along, dawn broke and he felt himself wafted to another land. The sky he well knew in all its moods and times, but he was seeing the natural countryside of people for the first time. Neat green hedgerows, relieved by tall trees with screeching black birds darting from them, fronted rectangular patches of brown fallow land interspersed by low light-green spreads of mustard and the taller more drab green of the vine-yards. The scent of honeysuckle mingled with odours of dung and manure. Labourers wearing wide-brimmed hats and carrying sickles and spades began to appear, the men riding donkeys or pulling wagons stacked with produce. No one failed to call out '*Buenos dias*.' Small whitewashed farm houses with yellow brown thatched roofs showed across the fields. The tiled roof of an imposing mansion nestled in a green grove on a distant hillside. A monk in a brown habit plodded towards them. He made the sign of the cross as he passed by and murmured, 'God be with you.' Prince Ahmed felt like an infidel for accepting a heretic's blessing and immediately recognized that he had better adjust to this new order from the orientation of a prince's life in a Muslim palace.

They shared the remainder of their food beside a roadside rivulet, then hastened on towards Jaén. There were fewer pedestrians on the highway, but more carts and coaches. Everyone looked at them curiously. Four people on two horses was hardly normal. They crossed two knights on bay chargers, staring straight ahead as if mesmerized by their own dignity, and an occasional horse-drawn litter with a lady inside. Ahmed wondered how far it was to Jaén, but resisted the urge to ask passers-by.

By noon the bustle on the highway began to diminish. Zurika had noticed it too. '*Siesta* hour,' she called out.

Prince Ahmed nodded. This was the first time they had travelled by day and he had forgotten about the siesta, just as he had not unfailingly observed the prayer times. Besides, they would only attract more attention if they kept on going with a glaring sun overhead. Although they were outside his father's territory, he did not deem it wise to run the risk of word being carried back to the king, who was not above sending assassins to kidnap him. The thought brought Abou bon Ebben to mind again. He wondered what had happened to the old sage.

He saw the distant spires gleaming dark against a brilliant blue sky in the fierce noonday sun's glare almost at the same time that his eyes fell on the small roadside inn.

'Look!' he bade Prince Juan, pointing to the sign.

They rode into the cobbled courtyard and paused at the wooden trough to water their sweating steeds. They then off-loaded the precious saddlebags and directed a loutish stableboy who came up, picking his nose, to feed and rub down the horses.

Even to the ignorant Prince Ahmed, the inn was obviously a converted two-storey farmhouse. It was built of whitewashed adobe and yellow thatch. They filed into a red tiled entrance foyer which opened to a tap room with a fireplace on one side and a dining room on the other, from which the aroma of roast lamb, basil, oregano and saffron emerged, accompanied by loud conversation, raucous laughter, the clatter of mugs and the clank of tankards. The innkeeper rolled up, rubbing his hands together. He was a large pot-bellied man, swarthy, with a shiny round face slashed by a thin black moustache. Oiled black hair and a gold earring in his right ear gave him the appearance of one of the pirates whose picture Prince Ahmed had once seen in a manuscript. This particular pirate wore a white smock, with brown leather knee gaiters, crossed leggings and an unctuous smile.

'*Buenos dias, Señores,*' he glanced at the two women, hesitated before adding, '*Señoras.* Welcome to the Rosarita Inn. I am Miguel, its owner and keeper. What may I do for you, my . . . er . . . lords and . . . er . . .' he gave the two women another appraising glance, 'ladies?'

His hesitation before referring to the two women as ladies irritated Prince Ahmed, but he held back his anger. 'We have travelled long and hard, from Badajoz, inn-keeper, and are headed for Jaén.' Finding himself instinctively mistrusting the man, Prince Ahmed made his words imperious. 'As you can see, we need everything, two rooms, baths and food.' He caught the flicker of doubt in the man's eye and fished out a gold coin from his belt pocket. 'Here is something in advance for your services.'

The flicker changed from doubt to avarice as the man took the proffered coin. He bowed as low as his pot-belly would permit. '*Muchas gracias.* As luck would have it, the two best rooms in my humble inn have just fallen vacant. If my lords would please follow me upstairs I shall lead you to them and have hot baths brought up. The kitchen will be kept open to serve you, if you will come downstairs when you have bathed and changed.'

'Have the baths prepared only in the ladies' room,' Prince Ahmed interposed. 'My cousin and I will bathe at the well, so all we will need are scrubbing stones, scented soap and towel linen.'

'Whatever you please, my lords.' Miguel glanced at the saddlebags, reached out a huge hand to Prince Juan. 'Permit me to relieve you of these.'

Prince Juan shook his head.

'No, thank you, *posadero*,' Prince Ahmed cut in. 'We shall carry them ourselves.' He did not need the innkeeper's lifted eyebrows to realize that this was an admission that the saddlebags contained more than a change of clothes and that asking to bathe at the well had also been a mistake, for they would have to take the saddlebags with them. 'On second thought, it is so hot outside that my cousin and I too will bathe in our room.' The inscrutable look in the innkeeper's dark eyes rang warning bells. He realized that he had made another mistake. There was no way in which Prince Juan could be his cousin.

The room into which they were ushered was a medium-sized loft with two small high uncurtained windows through which white sunlight glared. It had two truckle beds on either side, with a commode in the centre containing soap and scrubbing stone on a shelf, a white porcelain washbasin and ewer; doubtless the matching chamber pot was in the lower cabinet. For a moment, Prince Ahmed sighed for the cleanliness and luxury of the Alhambra palace.

'You will be very comfortable here, my lords,' the innkeeper stated. 'I shall have the maids bring up a tub and plenty of water immediately.' As he bowed and backed out of the room, his eyes flickered towards the saddlebags.

Prince Ahmed and Prince Juan agreed that they would take turns at their meal, so that one or the other would always be in the bedroom with the saddlebags.

'You almost look a prince again,' Prince Ahmed joked, when Prince Juan had bathed and changed and the maids had removed the tub to bring him his own bath.

'And you still look like the scruffy beggar who accompanied me.' Prince Juan grinned to rob the statement of offence. He held his nose. 'You smell like a sewer rat though, so I cannot quite place you. What am I, a prince of royal blood, doing with the likes of you?'

'Benefiting from the contrast, which is the only way you will look like anything,' Prince Ahmed retorted. He grew serious. They had already discussed the entire situation, including Miguel's unhealthy interest in the saddlebags. 'We can neither keep alternating as guards nor defend our treasure with only one dagger between us. We must buy swords for us both and a dagger for you.'

'Such weapons will help us defend the treasure against a few men,' Prince Juan mouthed, to the accompaniment of nimble fingers. 'But what if they are many?'

'Should we leave the inn and make for the city proper where we would be safer?'

'Now that the *posadero*'s greed has been aroused, he may have us followed. He appears to be a man of some consequence.'

'He is obviously a rogue, a thief and a . . .'

Prince Juan interrupted him with a slap on the thigh. 'I have it. I should have thought of it earlier.'

'What?'

'The Jewish moneylenders! They are bankers with strongrooms they call vaults, well built and guarded. If we go to the street of Jews, we can deposit the contents of the bags with one of them this very afternoon.'

'What good would it do us on the journey to Toledo and after we get there, to have the treasure in a Jew's vault in Jaén?'

'The Jewish bankers issue what they call letters of credit, signed and sealed, with amounts stated which allow the depositer to draw on other Jewish bankers of their fraternity anywhere in Spain. Each amount drawn is registered in the letter, signed and sealed. Knowing Jewish enterprise, I wouldn't doubt our being able to draw on such letters anywhere in the world.'

'We do not want to go anywhere in the world!' Prince

Ahmed pondered awhile. 'The tenets of Islam prohibit moneylending,' he asserted primly. 'Besides, our Prophet commanded us of the true faith to abhor Jews.'

'Because they refused to support him in his campaign against the powerful Quereshi,' Prince Juan retorted. 'As a True Believer do you always follow the precepts of Islam?'

'Certainly.' A hen clucked from the yard below.

'Why then have you not unfailingly performed your ablutions, faced Mecca and said your prayers five times a day since we left the Alhambra palace? Why did you not remain in the Gen al Arif tower, where you could do it all?'

Prince Ahmed prevented his jaw from dropping in time. 'It was not possible.' His fingers dithered. 'I mean, the interests of freedom, of safety . . .'

'Precisely!' Prince Juan cut in with deft fingers. He grinned. 'The interests of safety demand that we bank these treasures with the Jews. You are not borrowing from or lending to them. You are merely storing your money with them, paying them well for their services. No interest is involved. It is *your* money. If the treasure is stolen, you may have to return to your father alone.' A gentle smile brightened his blue eyes. He ran a hand through blond hair, his smile suddenly knowing. 'My poor sister will then have to suffer the tortures of the damned from a cruel husband.'

Though he suspected that he was being manoeuvred, that clinched it in Prince Ahmed's mind. 'You are right,' he agreed. 'We shall visit the Jews this evening.'

The thump of footsteps on the stairs accompanied by a clanking told of the maids' return with his bath. 'Go down now, cunning prince and enjoy your meal if you can stomach it in good conscience,' Prince Ahmed exclaimed. 'When you come back, I shall be bathed and musk-scented and I doubt that I shall acknowledge an infidel such as you.'

Unused to communal eating, Prince Ahmed found the dining room of the inn strange. It consisted of two long narrow tables of brown Spanish oak, littered with earthenware platters and mugs, two great dishes containing the remains of now greasy roast lamb at the centre, the odours of which spread even outside the room. The dirt floors were sprinkled with pale hay, marred by ugly dark splotches from spilled wine and bones cast to dogs. Two black hounds, low-growling occasionally with satisfaction, heads to one side, were gnawing contentedly in front of a stone fireplace embellished with a copper bin containing a poker and tongs, a neat stack of firewood at one side. Clay statues on the stone mantelpiece flanking a grotto with a blue and white statue of the Virgin Mary strove vainly to exude an air of dignity. The ceiling was bare except for great oak beams supporting the upper floor, which must be that of his bedroom. The whitewashed walls were discoloured by crude drawings. The one that evoked his immediate disgust was of a man drinking wine from a flagon while passing water. Since the windows were closed against flies and other insects, the air was warm and stuffy and he could almost smell the urine in that offensive drawing. Like the taproom, the dining room was a crude place, obviously catering to the passing traveller.

The single redeeming feature of the room was a gnome of a man sitting at the further table facing the entrance door. His long black robe and the *yarmulke* on his head would have proclaimed him a Jew even if his features had not betrayed it. From the high forehead through the beaked nose bridging dark eyes in sunken sockets and the thin-lipped mouth to the jutting chin, he was clearly of the brotherhood. It was the first time that Prince Ahmed had encountered a Jew at such close quarters. No sooner were the deep dark eyes raised to his than he had a moment's poignant vision of the suffering of the entire race since its origins. When he tried to grasp it, the revelation fled, mostly before the man's even white teeth flashing in a beautiful smile.

'Shalom!' The voice was unexpectedly strong for a man past middle age. 'I am Aaron Levi. You must be of my race, for you do not respect the sacred siesta hour either.' The smile had mischief to it, for Prince Ahmed was clearly Moorish. 'Will you not partake with me of the crumbs that are left on our master's table?'

Infidel he might be, but Prince Ahmed warmed to the man. '*Inshallah!*' He bowed, giving the hand to heart, mouth and head greeting. 'I am indeed of your race, for you are undoubtedly an *imam*, Muslim priest, and we both worship Almighty Allah.'

Aaron's eyes twinkled merrily. He clapped bony hands once in glee. 'What better end to a meal of stale fruit than a fresh young jester.' He grew mock-serious. 'Since the sun has passed its zenith, I hope you have already answered *adhan*, the calls to prayer, faced *giblah*, the direction of Mecca, and said *zuhr*, the early afternoon prayer.' He reached beside him and brandished a long staff that had lain on a bench beside him hidden by the table. It had a spike at one end. 'Defaulters like you should be punished by your *imam*.' Laughing quietly, he laid the staff back on the bench.

Prince Ahmed knew a flash of resentment. How dare this man laugh at his religion, which he had been rigorously trained all his life to venerate. Some invisible fountain from his newfound freedom, however, extinguished the holy fire. Treat religion seriously, but earnestness with a smile, a small voice within him urged. It was such a totally new thought, it startled him.

'You are debating whether to use your dagger on the

roast lamb or on the sacrificial lamb, a Jew.' Levi had picked up his reaction with uncanny perception. He chuckled. 'Since you have obviously rejected *zuhr* today, why should you not commit the ultimate sacrilege by accepting my call to break bread with me?' He waved a graceful hand towards the bench opposite him. 'This meat and bread are not *kosher*, so I may not eat them, but the flesh is not that of a forbidden animal so you may feast on this wonderfully . . . er . . . greasy food.' He paused until Prince Ahmed sat opposite him. He smelled of some sharp incense, a scent of Edom, Prince Ahmed guessed. 'You have not told me your name, *amir*.'

'How did you know that I am an *amir*?' Prince Ahmed blurted out the question without thought.

'Ah! It is in your bearing. Birth and breeding cannot be hidden from the discerning man by a commoner's clothes. A real prince is born to each family, regardless of its station, once every four generations; so even if you were not born a prince, you were born to be one. Now take me, for instance, what do you think is my profession?'

Prince Ahmed cocked his head to one side, and eyed Aaron. 'You are of a noble family,' he finally decided, then caught the infection of the kindly Jew's innate mischief. 'You are indeed an *imam*, Muslim priest, by profession,' he lied.

A single clap of the hand again and the same merry sparkle of the eyes like sunlight on a dead sea. 'You are wrong, *amir*,' Aaron declared with a surprising change of sobriety. 'I am a banker, and I believe you are going to need me.'

How in Allah's name . . . ? The question that shot through Prince Ahmed's shocked brain was interrupted by the thudding of feet from the floor above, followed by a crash.

What was that? The noises had come from his room upstairs.

Chapter 13

Since Count Gaston was to leave for Pamplona early the next morning, Bishop Eulogius had invited King Pedro and him to a private luncheon at the primate's palace located between the cathedral and the Alcazar, the capitol in Toledo. The cathedral was not only the greatest in Spain but also one of the richest Gothic churches in Europe. It had been a mosque until 1087, when Queen Constancia expelled the Moors and consecrated the building as a Christian church.

The bishop's private dining chamber was a small room that opened out to the central courtyard. King Pedro sat on a high chair on the right of the chunky scarlet-robed bishop at a long, narrow table of dark mahogany facing the white flagstone courtyard, which was strewn with scattered sunlight on dead brown leaves. He could just discern the glaring post-noon sun through the stark, seared branches of a Spanish maple. It was shady and cool in the room, but the king was sweating from having drunk heavily of the sun-kissed wine from Jerez de la Frontera on the southern tip of Spain, made famous by Hannibal's discovery of that wine region. Too much of this kind of wine generally gave him a headache, especially if he drank it during the day, but he loved its flavour and was prepared to pay the price for it.

En verdad, the servants of the Holy Church make up for whatever mortification of the flesh they may not practise in bed by having a splendid board, he reflected cynically. As for Bishop Eulogius the only flesh he mortifies is that of his virgins and then by his lascivious glance. The luxury of the bishop's palace, with its fine marble, exquisite stained glass, glittering crystal and elegant furniture matched the splendour of the great cathedral. The delightful odours of the meal they had just finished, *mortreurs*, boiled white fish pounded to a paste, reboiled until stiff and sprinkled with pepper and ginger, *blamanger* of shredded pheasant, flavoured pasties, pies and fritters were hardly the fare enjoyed by Our Lord's first disciples. 'Our planning for the joust and the Reconquista to follow is as complete, thanks to the Chancellor here,' he glanced affectionately at Count Gaston sitting erect facing him, 'as complete, *en verdad*, as this luncheon has been, thanks to your hospitality, Eminence.' He bowed slightly to the bishop, toyed with his gold wine cup. 'As for this sherry, it is nectar for the saints which Our Lord's disciples never tasted.'

Bishop Eulogius's chubby cheeks, rosy from the wine, creased into his cherubic smile. 'I am always honoured to have my liege lord at my poor board, Your Majesty.'

'And it is to reward saints such as you, Lord Bishop, that God provides such nectar,' Count Gaston put in, raising his own wine glass in a toast.

The primate's striking blue eyes vanished into their folds. 'Ah, Count, you should not number me among the saints,' he protested.

'Anyone who can serve such a divine meal must be numbered with the saints.'

The blue eyes emerged, searching. The quick glance which Bishop Eulogius gave Count Gaston to determine whether or not he was being played with took King Pedro back several months to that day in the corridor of his palace when he had returned from his defeat at the hands of that Moorish bastard, King Yusuf, and wondered whether Bishop Eulogius were not the real enemy. He always liked to know what drove a man or a woman. Once he discovered that, he could use the knowledge to defend himself or to manipulate the subject.

244

He knew that Bishop Eulogius strove for power, wealth, the hope of becoming Pontiff some day, not to mention certain desirable maidens. He did not know in what order, but wealth brought power, both were needed for the Pontificate, which in turn would bring the desirable girls!

He had yet been unable to fathom Count Gaston, but during the past few days had veered towards the conclusion that for the first time in his life he had come across someone who had neither ambition nor motivation towards any goal, but only one aim, to do anything he undertook perfectly. Perfection to the Count seemed to accord with his love of beauty. The Basque was undoubtedly a successor of the early Greek aesthetes and it was enough for King Pedro that he had come to like and respect the man enormously.

'Would that sainthood could be acquired by serving a simple meal.' The bishop was his incanting self again.

Count Gaston grinned mischievously. 'Perhaps sainthood is not acquired, Eminence, but is a quality of birth,' he murmured. 'After all, Our Lord had divinity in spite of feeding the multitude with but five loaves and two fishes.'

King Pedro knew by now that this was just the count's easy bantering style, taking nothing seriously, but Bishop Eulogius shot the Basque another keen glance.

'Let us return to the . . . hrrmph . . . equally important subject of the Reconquista,' King Pedro intervened. 'We shall hold our tourney three months from now. Our Proclamation is ready and we shall issue it next week, summoning contestants to attend our Court in Toledo on the fourth day of June in the year of Our Lord 1351. Since this is a Saturday it will give those near enough the entire week to travel without defiling our Christian Sabbath. The tourney shall last three weeks, so we expect to announce the name of the victor on the twenty-fifth day of June, leaving the rest of the month for feasting and enjoyment.' He lifted shaggy eyebrows at Count Gaston.

'Agreed, Sire.'

'Meanwhile, preparations for the attack on Granada will proceed under cover of the tourney while the heretic Moorish king is lulled to a sense of false security,' Bishop Eulogius put in. 'And the campaign will commence on two fronts, by land and sea, on the Monday following Mass at the Cathedral on Sunday the 3rd of July.'

King Pedro smiled. 'We rather like the idea of taking the Moor with a landing in the rear.'

'Our plans have been drawn up accordingly,' Count Gaston declared.

'You are sure that the losers at the tourney will not back away?' the bishop inquired.

'It is more likely that the losers will remain, even if less whole-heartedly than the winner,' the count responded. 'It is a matter of honour.' He smiled faintly. 'And since my own master is certain of winning, His Majesty here is assured of the support of the most powerful contestant.'

'Then, Your Majesty, it is timely for me to seek your immediate protection for Holy Church,' Bishop Eulogius declared, half-turning in his chair to face King Pedro.

'Against what, Bishop?' The king was taken aback by the unexpected change of subject.

'There is a move in our sacred capital to print and publish the Holy Scripture in the vernacular. I believe it is secretly financed by Jews.'

Now startled, King Pedro shot Count Gaston a keen glance, found only amusement in the lean hatchet face. 'Do you know anything about this, Chancellor?'

Count Gaston shook his head. 'No, Sire.'

'This sacrilegious attempt,' the bishop continued, 'which I understand has commenced in England and now spreads to Europe, to translate the Bible into the languages of each country so that the people may understand its meaning more directly, is a most despicable attempt to undermine the sanctity and eminence of the clergy.'

'In truth it would greatly diminish your power, would it not?' King Pedro inquired bluntly.

Bishop Eulogius flushed. 'The power of Holy Church is divine since it comes from God through Our Lord Jesus Christ,' he intoned. 'It may not be challenged by temporal forces. That would be heresy of the most profound order.'

Do your glances fuck your virgins in Latin? King Pedro thought savagely. Why did this little prick have to spoil good planning, high hopes and a fine luncheon by bringing contention to the scene?

'It is worse than heresy or sacrilege,' Count Gaston observed.

'What could be worse?' the primate inquired.

'The most unfortunate thing that could happen to Christianity is the publication of such a book,' Count Gaston stated. 'Anything that is readily understood, like common sense for instance, is the privilege of the masses and will of necessity be vulgar. If the masses familiarize themselves with the scriptures, Christianity will lose all dignity and become . . . er . . . vulgar.' The count casually picked up a slice of cheese from the gold platter in front of him and airily placed it in his mouth.

For once, Bishop Eulogius seemed at a loss for words. 'Why? . . .' he began.

'Ah, the primordial question, Why?' Count Gaston ran a deliberate thumbnail beneath each neat moustache. 'From creation to the resurrection, we are always asking ourselves, Why? And when we think we have the answer, the question pops up again like the head of a turtle.'

'Like why do I want to piss right now?' King Pedro slapped his thigh, roared with laughter.

'If I may answer that question, Sire, it is because your bladder is full and sends the message of its discomfort to

247

your brain, commanding you, Empty me. But is that discomfort the real cause? Is it not the wine you have drunk that is the real Why? If so, then why did you drink the wine? The simple question can take us back to creation, or,' he paused for effect, 'forward to the resurrection of our bodies and the life everlasting.'

King Pedro suddenly realized that the Count had deliberately diverted the conversation to a safer channel. 'What is truth then, Chancellor?' he inquired with feigned interest. For himself, he did not give a fart.

'There is no Why, Sire. Of all living creatures, we humans alone seek to know why and come up with answers circumscribed by our senses and our puny brains. We observe and deduce. Yet our powers of observation are limited by our humanity, and our ability to make correct deductions is in truth non-existent. We pit all our non-substance against what *is*, for we cannot comprehend a no beginning and a no end in which *nothing is*! We began to know less than the birds of the air and the beasts of the field when we started to reason. As for me, all I know is that I am of a creation that *is* God. I do not even consider whether or not I am a *part* of it, because the idea of part is a purely human concept. We, all of us, *are* only because that is our reality, when we might not even *be*.'

'Reason is God-given,' the bishop asserted sharply. 'Any assertion to the contrary is tantamount to blasphemy. Your utterances are at variance with the teachings of Holy Church, Count, and I shall forget that I ever heard them.' He turned to King Pedro. 'Which brings us to the real burden of my request, Your Majesty.' He rose to his feet, placed pudgy pink knuckles on the dark mahogany table, leaned forward. 'For our campaign against the heretic Moors to be successful, it must have the power of Holy Church behind it. Our soldiers shall be Christian soldiers, imbued with the teachings of our Lord

Jesus, marching to war. So we must first weed out evil in our own territory.'

'How do you propose that?' King Pedro already knew the answer with resignation.

'By Inquisition, Sire,' the bishop thundered. 'By converting all non-believers, especially Muslims and Jews, to the true faith or cleansing them at the stake.'

'The Jews are backing our campaign with vast sums of money,' King Pedro protested. 'We cannot set fire to the mine that produces our gold.' He directed his gaze to Count Gaston. 'What do you think, Chancellor?'

'The Jews have a stake in Toledo, other than the one at which they may be burned,' Count Gaston responded. 'Backed by the great historian, Josephus, they claim that they founded Toledo in the year 590 before Christ, giving it the name Toldoth. Even your cathedral, Eminence, was once a mosque. In the year 1087 Queen Constancia and Archbishop Bernado, the Abbot of Sahegum, took advantage of the Christian king's absence to expel the Muslims from and dedicate the building to Christianity. Hearing the news, the king decided to return to Toledo immediately to punish those responsible. One of the Muslim leaders, Alfaqui Abu-Wahid, went out to the king, met him in the village of Magan and begged that he pardon those who had committed the offence against his own Muslim religion. Moved beyond belief, the king granted el Alfaqui's request, so even the date 24th January is consecrated to Our Lady of Peace.' He nodded. 'I make no apology for repeating a story of which you are well aware, but it is sometimes necessary,' he shrugged elegant shoulders, 'to remind ourselves of such monuments of Christian tolerance.'

'We are not dealing with past history today, Count.' A note of asperity had entered the bishop's voice. 'Reconquista will *create* new history.' He faced King Pedro squarely, causing the king, who guessed what was coming, to squirm mentally. 'You and I have a pact, Sire, which you are in honour bound to keep. That pact was not made between two individual leaders, but by and between the kingdom of Castile and the kingdom of Christ. Inquisition in exchange for Christian unity, Inquisition as the spur to the gallant steeds of Christ. I have delivered Christian unity to you. Only you have the power to maintain it.' The threat was obvious.

Furious though he was at this little prick, King Pedro could not deny the truth of the statements. 'But you just don't say "Inquisition" and set it in motion,' he temporized. 'It requires careful thought, detailed planning. Let us start planning now.' He was playing for time.

'The planning has been completed, Sire,' Bishop Eulogius declaimed triumphantly, one stubby pink finger raised. 'While you were planning your military crusade, my own crusaders and I have been planning our religious crusade.'

King Pedro sensed the conflict, hanging in the afternoon air as tangibly as the odours of fish and pheasant, the smile of the dumpy cleric and Count Gaston's amused expression.

An instant of shocked surprise was followed by the explosion of sick dismay. Prince Ahmed's immediate concern was for Prince Juan. Was his comrade dead? He rushed to kneel beside the still form. Before he could reach out to touch the golden head tainted with red blood, Prince Juan stirred, his blue eyes opened, the lids fluttered. He raised a hand to the back of his head, went 'Urargh!' in pain and sat up nursing his wound. He looked at his bloodstained fingers.

Prince Ahmed supported him by the shoulders. 'Are you all right?' he mouthed.

Prince Juan nodded once. His long white fingers began gently checking his wound again.

'What happened?'

'Someone crept in and hit me on the back of the head as I stood by the bed looking out of the window.'

'Where are the saddlebags?'

In a moment, Prince Juan had leapt to his feet. The sudden movement made him dizzy, for he swayed and held on to Prince Ahmed's shoulder. Wild eyes searched the room. 'Gone!' The croak tore out of his mutilated voice box so forcefully that Prince Ahmed almost recognized the sound.

While springing to his own feet, Prince Ahmed's feverish gaze reconfirmed the truth. His heart sank. Their entire future was gone. He had to recover the saddlebags at all costs. But how? The thieves could not have gone far. 'How many of them?' he inquired.

'Only one, I think.'

As before in a crisis, Prince Ahmed reasoned calmly. The door to the loft room led directly from a small landing at the top of the staircase. The room occupied by Pilar and Zurika was the only other one in the loft, so the robber must have come up the stairs. It was logical for him to have gone back the same way. But . . . yes indeed, if the man had gone downstairs carrying two saddlebags, he would have risked being spotted. There was only one other way he could have gone, through one of the two open windows. Both were large enough for a man to wriggle through.

Reasoning that it would not be the window that opened on to the main courtyard, he ran to the other, Prince Juan stumbling behind him. He was vaguely conscious of a burnt blue sky beyond the bright glare of sunlight. The rear gable of the downstairs roof, no more than three feet below the window level, sloped down to a small private enclosure containing two chicken coops and a pig-sty. The clucking of a hen and the 'oink' of a pig reached his ears before his astonished gaze took in the most extraordinary sight.

A lean figure dressed in a brown peasant's smock and crossed leggings lay flat on his back in the grey dust. His hair was dishevelled, his eyes wild. And no wonder. At his throat was the spike of a long staff, held by a figure clad in a black robe, a *yarmulke* on his bald head, a hunched gnome of a man.

As he watched in amazement, Prince Ahmed detected a shadow move from beneath the roof's overhang. His gaze flickered to the pot-belly before the rest of the huge figure emerged. Miguel moved slowly, stealthily forward, light-footed as fat men can well be. He was weaponless, but there was no mistaking his intent as he stalked the gnome whose back was turned on them.

Prince Ahmed saw the brown saddlebags flung to one side of the enclosure and stifled the warning cry rising in his throat.

The report he had received from his chancellor that morning had been most satisfying. King Charles the Bad knew that Count Gaston generally succeeded in his missions, which was one reason why he put up with the manifestations of the Basque's superior intellect, fierce pride and strange sense of morality. He could trust the man.

Charles the Bad wished that his chancellor could have been present at the private interview this afternoon with the French ambassador to his court, Manuel Avila, the fiancé of the dead Renée, and the young artist's parents. He had decided that it would be prudent to grant the audience in his private chamber in the palace, a room he loathed for being as French as his dead mother, because it had the right atmosphere for the French ambassador, gilt furniture, Flemish carpets and Belgian crystal. The son of Blanche of Castile, Louis IX had been a votary of

Gothic architecture and had constructed great cathedrals in Amiens, Beauvais, Bourges, and Chartres, for which he was eventually canonized. He had also built the first French navy and established a great university at Sorbonne. Charles the Bad hoped that the influence of the good Christian monarch, reflected in his room's classical design, would mollify the French ambassador.

The Comte de Poitou was ambassador to King John 'the Good', a weak king who had just succeeded his father King Philip VI. The French had been maintaining a low profile after their crushing defeat by the English at the Battle of Crécy, four years earlier, but with the path to his ambitions in Spain opening, King Charles himself was more anxious than ever to have France as an active ally.

The ambassador was a small bird-like man with a neat black moustache, a pointed beard and piercing grey eyes. Dressed in burgundy velvet with white Belgian lace, he sat elegantly on his gilt chair. Young Manuel was a typical painter, his long, untidy hair, straw-brown in colour, matching a tight-fitting tunic and the recently out-of-fashion surcoat. He was slim, tall, had regular features and dreamy eyes still swollen from weeping. His parents were nondescript citizens, the resemblance of the father to the son striking, right down to his clothes, except that his hair was neatly combed. Both men were obviously more meek in the presence of the matronly wife and mother, dressed in a black robe and mantilla, the veil thrown back to reveal a pudgy red face and a self-important expression, than they would have been merely in the presence of their king.

'Your Excellency has already stated the reason for your request for this audience,' King Charles began, leaning forward slightly in the high gilt chair placed on a low platform covered with a red and green Flemish carpet that served for a throne in this small, windowless audience chamber. Having avoided drinking any wine during luncheon in order to remain sober for the important interview, he was clear-eyed but grainy. 'We deeply sympathize with this young man, reportedly the fiancé of your subject, Renée Latour, who has disappeared.' Secretly he thought, Serve the young cocksman right, for she probably allowed him to fuck her, or at least to play with those generous white breasts, while she gave me nothing. Or is that wrong? After all, she gave me her life, didn't she? The thought cheered him. 'Even if the young lady had not been a subject of our brother, King John, to whom we hope Your Excellency will convey the assurances of our highest consideration, esteem and affection, the resources of our kingdom would be available to search for her.' He made his voice ring with sincerity. 'For after all, our subjects are our family and we are responsible for their security.' A nice turn of speech on which he congratulated himself. He must remember it. The Comte de Poitou bowed in his chair. 'We deeply appreciate Your Majesty's concern.' He stroked his pointed beard. 'When . . .'

'We want our daughter back!' the woman burst in. A peasant, built like the bell of a parish church and with a voice that pealed like one, offending his ears.

'So do we, madam,' King Charles responded suavely. 'So do we.' He paused. 'But the problem we face is that the young lady has simply disappeared without a trace. If her body had been found we might have tracked down the murderer.' He turned towards the young artist, hiding the cruelty of his thrust beneath a compassionate glance. 'As matters stand, she may even have eloped with some-one else. After all, a young woman who could journey alone all the way from Paris to be with a lover . . .' A shrug of beefy shoulders told the rest.

'No, no, Your Majesty. My Renée loved only me,' the young man cried. 'It was love, our pure, radiant, romantic love that drew her to this city, a virgin breeze from Paradise that had never blown upon this earth before.'

So she *had* been a virgin. Damn, damn, damn the bitch. 'It is all so sad.' He gestured with beefy hands, then directing his glance at the matron, cunningly inquired, 'Do you have any evidence at all regarding this disappearance?'

'We do, Your Majesty.'

A throb of apprehension vibrated his diaphragm. Had that stupid dead bastard, his vice-chancellor, blundered? 'Tell us all the details,' he commanded.

'She told our son that a man came to our residence that morning and spoke to her on her return from the cathedral. He offered to sell one of our son's paintings to a wealthy benefactor, who, if he liked it, might become Manuel's patron. She took Manuel's best painting and left by herself that evening, because she wanted to succeed, to make a wedding gift for him. He gave her his framed oil painting of our cathedral at sunset, with the stained glass windows glowing their exquisite colours of red, blue, yellow and green. Such a beautiful painting, Your Majesty. Our son is a talented artist, worthy of your royal notice.'

King Charles glanced at the Comte de Poitou, who acknowledged the woman's obvious garrulity with a barely perceptible lift of fine black eyebrows. The gesture relieved King Charles because it meant that the ambassador had no suspicion of him. 'Has the painting been found?' he inquired blandly of the woman. Its remains were in the fireplace of his bedchamber!

'No, Sire.' She paused deliberately. 'But we have identified the caller.' She raised a large double chin without effort.

This time the throb of apprehension was more persistent. 'And his name?'

'Count Garcia, your vice-chancellor.'

Was the look in the matron's eyes almost accusing? A curse on his own bad reputation. 'Godsbody, *our* vice-chancellor?' he found himself playing for time, before inspiration dawned. He clicked stubby fingers, noticing the black hairs on the back of them. 'That's strange,' he declared, pretending reflection. 'Did you say this young woman, Renée Latour, met the man after Mass?'

'Yes, Sire.' The woman sat savouring the moment.

'Last Sunday?'

'Indeed, Sire.'

He nodded slowly. 'Our vice-chancellor also disappeared without trace last Sunday night.' Well, the traces would be there if one looked beneath the right paving in the secret underground escape tunnel that led from his bedchamber beyond the walls of the palace. He had decided that it would be safer to kill the count himself immediately after the man had disposed of Renée Latour's body in that tunnel. A simple sword thrust, safer than hiring an assassin.

'We had heard a rumour to that effect, Your Majesty,' the Comte intervened. He shrugged elegant shoulders. 'Please accept our condolences. These disappearances are occurring everywhere. Nobody is safe nowadays.' He addressed the woman. 'So you see, madam, the one person who might have thrown some light on the mystery has vanished too.'

Madame Avila was obviously flabbergasted. 'But, but, but,' she began.

She must be disappointed to be denied a confrontation with Count Garcia. Well, fuck her. On second thought, somebody else had better fuck that fat sow. 'It would seem that there is really no mystery,' King Charles declared smoothly. He turned an openly cruel gaze on Manuel. 'We know the culprit. Count Garcia, despite having recently lost most of his teeth, has the ability to charm even the devil's paramour. He obviously persuaded Renée Latour to elope with him.'

Manuel's anguished cry, quickly stifled, was the reward

for his cruelty. And he had just exacted his revenge on Renée Latour, for Manuel would now begin to despise her. As for his own dead mother, who was probably making common cause with the young woman wherever they both were, she was probably in despair at this very moment at the dreadful product of her womb!

Their host, Bishop Eulogius, had excused himself temporarily to answer a summons conveyed to him by his secretary, a black-robed Castilian abbot. King Pedro noticed the amused smile still hovering around Count Gaston's hatchet face. 'Well, fuck the little prelate prick,' he said pleasantly under his breath.

'You are going to have to do something of that order to him, Sire, if we are to proceed to war against the Moors without unhappy elements at home.'

'We cannot afford to antagonize him,' King Pedro remonstrated. 'We shall have to provide him with something else to satisfy his lust for cruelty, something that will give him those orgasms for which he craves. Having voyeured scores of desirable maidens' – he had already confided much to Count Gaston – 'he is seeking variety.'

'I rather suspect, Sire, that he needs to satisfy his ambition as well as his lust. Anyone who starts an Inquisition and conducts it with zeal and fervour will not only qualify for the highest church office and a place in history but also for canonization.'

'Canonization?' King Pedro raised shaggy eyebrows incredulously.

'Yes, Sire.'

'We had never even considered that.' He tapped a huge forefinger thoughtfully on the table. 'You are right,' he finally declared. 'The Bishop has come from nowhere into eminence.' He smiled at his own pun. 'Once a man drives himself to get so far, like a bolting horse, he cannot stop. His momentum takes over. Bishop Eulogius seeks all the concomitants of his present high office, wealth, fiefdoms and those desirable maidens I have told you of.' He bared his teeth in a smile. 'He has wealth and will have supreme power. What comes next? Perhaps you are right, only canonization.'

'And that might assure him of eternal life, even after death.'

'How would he realize it by Inquisition?'

'Canonization is achieved by miracles or by martyrdom. Since he is incapable of miracles other than those of cuisine, which are in reality the product of his chef, he resorts to martyrdom.'

King Pedro's eyes widened. 'You mean he hopes that some Jew or Muslim will assassinate him?'

'No, Sire. I doubt that he will ever be ready for that dubious estate. After all, martyrs are those who lay down their lives to avenge themselves on those who do not accept their beliefs, a practice that the early Christians converted into a profession.'

'You mean there is no virtue in it?'

'Hardly. I wonder whether martyrdom is not a form of spite at times. Is it not better to live for one's beliefs than to die for them? And what harm is there in pretending acceptance of another faith to avoid death in order to live for one's own strong ones. What better vengeance can one wreak on one's enemies than to be a victim, a constant thorn?'

Even to King Pedro, who enjoyed an outrageous stand, this was unbelievable. 'Would you not be prepared to die for a cause then, say, on the field of battle?'

Count Gaston shrugged. 'If I died on the field of battle, it would be because I was there on one side or another, not for any cause but in the pursuit of perfection. You on the other hand, when the times comes, will undoubtedly martyr your royal self to your conviction.'

'Us?' King Pedro demanded incredulously. 'Us, achieving martyrdom for our convictions? You must be joking, Chancellor.'

'No, Your Majesty. I was referring to your conviction that a certain course of action is in your own best interests.'

King Pedro's jaw dropped, then a guffaw escaped him. 'You are a rascal, Count Gaston.'

'And you, Sire, are avowedly cruel when you are crossed or thwarted and you glory in your cruelty. My own master is avowedly *bad*. A man can be bad without being cruel, but there has to be a consistency to badness which is not required of cruelty. My King Charles exercises that consistency with the dedication of a flagellant mortifying the flesh or a would-be martyr seeking canonization. Cruelty demands a cause! You should be canonized for your dedication to your conviction.'

For a moment, King Pedro was tempted to share the one area of unfailing gentleness in his life, his love for Maria de Padilla, with Count Gaston, but he instantly rejected the idea as a sign of weakness. '*En verdad*, the Jewish bankers are essential for the fulfilment of our . . .' he grinned, 'Christian aims. We cannot allow them to be the martyrs of an Inquisition when it is their treasuries which should be martyred to the cause of their peaceful existence.' He grew thoughtful. 'We shall have to find a half-way house.'

'Between the Christian martyr's Heaven of canonization and the Inquisitor's Hell of Jewish gold lies the Moralist's Purgatory of his life, Sire! That is what lies ahead for you.'

Within seconds, Prince Ahmed had crawled through the window. He sat on the roof. The glaring sunlight had warmed it. He swiftly slithered down the slope. Miguel was now within touching distance of Aaron Levi. Scream-

259

ing aloud, Prince Ahmed launched himself through the air. Startled, Miguel stopped, turned in his tracks.

Feet first, Prince Ahmed smashed into the innkeeper's head and chest, sent him sprawling before twisting in the air as he had been taught, to land on his feet. Miguel lay on his back, a stunned sloth amid the dirt.

Levi had swung round at the interruption. In a trice, his opponent knocked aside the staff, scrambled to his feet, darted towards the gate.

Before Prince Ahmed could go after him, he heard a thud, spun around. To his amazement, Prince Juan, having landed beside him, sprang forward and dived for the man's legs. The flying tackle brought the thief down with a yelp. In an instant, Juan straddled the man, pinning him down. Prince Ahmed resisted the urge to go and help.

'I thank you for saving me,' Aaron Levi said pleasantly. He shouldered his staff, glanced at the innkeeper's still form, then at the henchman's struggles. 'You arrived from heaven above to help an old Jew, so you must indeed be Jahweh's aides.' His eyes twinkled. 'By the way, your saddlebags are safe.' A very self-possessed man, this Jew.

A lighter thud. Prince Juan had banged his opponent's head in the dirt. The man's struggles ceased immediately.

'I thank you for saving our saddlebags,' Prince Ahmed responded. 'You must be an agent of Merciful Allah, even though you are an infidel and unclean.' He directed his gaze to Prince Juan. 'I thought you were afraid of heights.'

Prince Juan laughed. 'You and I seem to be destined to crawl through windows and jump down,' he signalled. 'So I thought I might as well start practising.' He rose to his feet. 'This man will not awaken for some time.' He strode to the saddlebags and grabbed them. 'I'll not let go of these again,' he mouthed.

Prince Ahmed was touched. Prince Juan had overcome his terror to come to the aid of his friends.

Miguel snorted, groaned, began to stir. The point of Aaron's staff was immediately at his throat. He slurped, gurgled something, then his head slipped sideways.

Prince Ahmed turned to face Aaron Levi. 'We should fly before these robbers wake up,' he stated.

'They will be up too soon for that,' Aaron replied. 'The innkeeper is obviously a power in this area. Not for the good either.' His sharp eyes darted around the enclosure, then outside and to the upper storey of the building. 'No one has observed us,' he remarked. 'Let us just bind and gag them, then hurry away to Jaén.'

'Is that where you are heading?'

'Yes, but my real objective is Toledo.'

'Ours too,' Prince Ahmed declared impulsively.

'Splendid. You have horses, I have a horse-drawn buggy. Your two ladies can ride with me. I am travelling alone and modestly, in order not to invite thieves and robbers. I stopped here only for luncheon so my horse is still harnessed. Let us attend to these two rogues and be on our way.' He nodded towards the saddlebags, lowered his voice. 'I can guess why those bags are so valuable. Just for your information, I am one of the leading bankers in Spain. I shall introduce you to my partners in Jaén, who will accept your treasures and give you a letter of credit for their value, less their charges for the service. You will be able to draw on a letter of credit anywhere in Spain.' The sharp, dark eyes sparkled in the hot sunlight. He cocked his head to a side like a sparrow. 'Accepted?'

This was one wise bird. 'You have been sent by Almighty Allah,' Prince Ahmed declared, then paused. His heart tightened and a laugh escaped him. 'To action then, infidel. You talk too much. It has always been the way of your people since the days of your prophets.'

* * *

King Pedro had had to postpone his weekly meeting with Ruy de Vivar by several hours, because Maria de Padilla had been taken ill that morning with severe stomach cramps, vomiting, bleeding stools and a high fever. The Court physicians had been with her constantly, to relieve her with leeching, hot compresses and foul-smelling decoctions. Smitten by anxiety, because Maria was seldom seriously ill, the king had spent the entire morning in her chambers and only left her when she finally began to rest, the vomiting and cramps arrested and the fever on the decline. But the fear that he might lose her remained.

One glance at the gaunt face of his chief spymaster in the golden glow of the hanging lamps as the bony figure began to speak, told King Pedro that here was the purveyor of bad news.

'Sit down!' he commanded brusquely, and Ruy de Vivar gingerly took the seat opposite the mahogany desk and placed skeletal hands primly on his lap. His face looked more pinched than ever and he was obviously nervous.

'Give us your news from Granada before your routine report,' the king commanded. 'And come to the point. Have you taken Prince Ahmed?'

'Your Majesty, our assassin was uncovered, arrested, tortured and executed four weeks ago. It is reported that he died without revealing his identity or our plans.'

'Godsbody, how was he discovered?'

'Our conjecture is that someone in the palace knew him.' A knowing smile entered the mean, crafty eyes.

'You mean?'

'Yes, Sire . . . I regret to say the only person in Prince Ahmed's entourage who could possibly have identified the assassin was Prince Juan.'

The logic of the statement smote King Pedro. 'Fucking bastard!' he exclaimed under his breath, then realized that if Prince Juan was a bastard, he, King Pedro, had been cuckolded. He would normally have seen the humour of his exclamation, but it only irritated him the more today. 'You can send another assassin, can you not, only this time make it a real deaf-mute even if we have to mutilate the man and give him a big pension for his loss?'

Ruy de Vivar gave his wintry smile. 'Unfortunately, Sire, that would be to no purpose, because Prince Ahmed and Prince Juan escaped from the Gen al Arif tower some days ago and their whereabouts are unknown.'

'Shit of a potsherd. How did that happen?'

'Nobody knows, Your Majesty. Probably not even Prince Ahmed's guardian-tutor through the years, Abou bon Ebben, who died of natural causes the same night the escape was discovered. All the searches initiated by King Yusuf have produced not even a needle-point's evidence as to where the princes have gone or in what hole they are hidden.'

King Pedro frowned, pondering what he should do. He finally made up his mind. 'Keep your contacts in both Granada and Castile alert for any news, which should be brought to our notice immediately. For the present, we can only wait for the two princes to appear.'

PART II

Assassins

Chapter 14

For days now the three highways leading to the city of
Toledo had been packed with traffic. The north and south
highways converged at the Puente de Alcantara which
had been built by the Moors in 866 A.D. adjoining an
ancient Roman bridge. It had been destroyed by flood in
1257 and rebuilt by one of King Pedro's predecessors,
Alfonso X.

The crowds consisted not only of the trains of the
twenty-one princes and counts who had accepted King
Pedro's invitation to the tourney. They included distinguished visitors who were eager to witness the unusual
event: the people, to whom it represented a period of
fiesta away from their fields not yet ready for the summer
harvesting, tradesmen who had simply closed up shop,
artisans to whom it meant an opportunity for combining
work with play and the inevitable vendors. In short,
everyone was thronging towards Toledo.

King Pedro had selected a historic ground as the venue
for the tourney, the flat area east of the promontory on
which the San Fernando castle stood. The Spanish hero,
Rodrigo Diaz de Vivar, known as El Cid Campeador, had
once been the governor of San Fernando. The castle had
even been one of the domains of the Knights Templar,
the chivalric order that had turned to money-lending after
the fall of Acre and had finally been dissolved by Papal
edict thirty years earlier.

The arena was a rectangle, long enough for the galloping horses, the length exceeding the breadth by one-
fourth, as required by the rules of tournament. King
Pedro had caused gaily coloured pavilions to be erected

at its eastern end, for the contestants and their entourages. He himself, other royalty, judges, ladies and high officials would occupy the platform at the western end, which was closest to the city, on either side of which tiers of seats were provided for distinguished spectators. The contestants would battle each other from north and south, so no one would have the disadvantage of the morning sun in their eyes. The viewing public would be accommodated in enclosures on the north and south sides, behind barriers consisting of two beams, the lower reaching to the knees, with a span of four steps for attendants and soldiers who would prevent infiltration by spectators.

The city itself was already packed with men and animals, bringing the expected surge of prosperity to 'merchants and vendors, hostelries, stables and whorehouses, not to mention Bishop Eulogius's Holy Church and cathedral,' as King Pedro commented tartly to Count Gaston. The Alcazar was crowded with the more important visitors, while the royal palace teemed with the princely contenders and their retinues.

Anyone who wished to camp outside the city was permitted to do so, on payment of the king's fee, in a specially allotted area east of the arena. King Pedro had caused temporary water, bath and toilet facilities to be provided, all for an added fee, in what he knew would be a small city for about four weeks, where people were permitted to erect their own tents or shanties, with lean-tos against carts and wagons for those who did not want to reside in their vehicles. Areas had been set aside for those wishing to ply their trades, so that the facilities of the city would not be clogged. Vendors were already selling bread, salt fish, poultry, spices and prepared food like *paella*, short-eats, dried and fresh fruit and sweets. Dressed fowls slowly turned on spits above red fires, beef and mutton were being barbecued on glowing golden embers. The mixture of smells was unbelievable, piercing the dreadful stench that every wind brought from the public latrines. Rosaries, said to have been personally blessed by His Holiness the Pope, were being sold side by side with dirty pictures, icons, jewellery and trinkets. Clucking hens in wickerwork containers pecked at seed. Stray cats and dogs slunk around, searching for scraps of food, the dogs snarling at each other in the fight for possession. Black-robed friars sold absolution, pimps sold sin, red and white uniformed soldiers maintained order against pickpockets, thieves and beggars. A knife-grinder's stone creaked and crackled continuously, emitting sparks, a smith's hammer clanked on metal beside a glowing anvil, carpenters banged hammers, salesmen screamed their wares, children screamed their joy, babies wailed in a cacophony of noise so incredible that it reached across the river to the palace, causing King Pedro to remark acidly, 'When the people make *fiesta*, you can smell and hear them from a mile away.'

Yet King Pedro was well pleased, because the surge of prosperity meant more funds in his Treasury. Apart from his naturally acquisitive instinct, he was going to need the money to play a major role in the campaign against Granada; he could use that conquest as a stepping stone to the rule of all Spain, something that none of his ancestors had been able to achieve. As he confided to Maria de Padilla, the milling throngs out there, enjoying the discomfort and confusion, were really pawns in his power game.

Five mornings before the commencement of the tourney, the contestants made their appearance preceded by their trumpeters and followed by their suites, before a crowd that consisted not only of the important personages but burghers, their outer garments with three-cornered sleeves embellished by light border decorations, their shoulder-capes hooded. *Caballeros* sported shoulder capes with decorated borders, turban caps, which were very much in the vogue, trailing long stoles, or coronets for those of high rank. Other men of rank were distinguished by high-pointed hats and fur-trimmed cloaks.

Among the contestants were Knights of the various Orders. The single Knight of the Spanish Order of St James was distinguished by his white garment bearing a red cross, with a girdle, the mantle fastened by a cord, gauntlets and beret. Two Knights of the Teutonic Order wore black mantles with white crosses.

As a symbol of the advanced Castilian civilization, King Pedro had also caused a large clock to be erected at the east end of the arena. This was a *horologium* with wheels, but containing a device, based on the first of its kind installed sixty-five years earlier in St Paul's, London, which caused a bell to be struck on the hour. The usual sundials and hour glasses had been placed on either side of the clock against the possibility of the latter malfunctioning.

The brave display filled King Pedro, seated on the platform, with pride, for the like of it had never been witnessed in Spain. After making one circuit of the arena, each combatant displayed his armorial device and crest in the window of his pavilion. When the last contestant, young Prince Peter of Swabia, had concluded his display, the four judges, princes from Spain, France, Germany and Italy, whom he, King Pedro, had appointed from among his royal visitors, made their entry in state, accompanied by the king-at-arms, the giant Count Fernando with his *poursuivants*. Each of the judges, dressed in long, flowing garments, richly brocaded and jewelled, carried the symbol of his office, a white staff, without which he would not appear in public during the tourney, even at the entertainments. The king-at-arms, holding the banners of the four judges in his hand, then symbolically stationed himself before the pavilion allotted to the judges as a guard-of-honour, while the contestants submitted their armorial ensigns, crests and credentials for review.

The grand banquet and ball followed that night.

On the next morning, back in the arena, the judges inquired into the characters of the contestants. After they had given their approval, the ladies, visiting royalty, ambassadors and other important personages were admitted by King Pedro's command. Maria de Padilla led the ladies of his Court. Princess Beatrice, being the prize, would only appear on the day of the contests. Helmets and armorial bearings had been arranged in lines at the front of the platform and a herald proclaimed the names of the owners to polite applause. Any person objecting to a combatant would have done so by touching that person's helmet, which would then have been turned down by the squires or *poursuivants*. No objections were recorded, but had there been any, the judges would have decided the case on the next day, based upon evidence that the contestant had broken a vow, lent money at usurious rates, married a person of low estate, insulted a lady or failed to establish a right by birth to contest. A person of unestablished pedigree could, however, be admitted if a king, prince or other high-ranking person touched him with a sword or club.

On the third morning, the contestants, richly attired but with furled banners, entered the arena carrying blunted lances. They took the oath of the tournament, administered by the white-haired Prince Lorenzo de Medici of Italy, one of the four judges. They pledged not to strike an opponent below the belt, not to attack one who had been unhelmeted and not to inflict unfair blows; any contestant breaking this oath would lose his horse and weapons and be excluded from the lists.

The judges of the tournament then nominated the *chevalier d'honneur*, the knight of honour. King Pedro had arranged for Count Gaston to be appointed, no one being better qualified by knowledge, experience and proven integrity. He was given a gold-tipped lance as his symbol of office, after which the judges conducted Maria de Padilla of distinguished beauty, if not rank – and Princess Mathilde, who possessed both, to the *chevalier* and delivered to him Princess Mathilde's head-dress, which Count Gaston would carry on the lance during each contest. This head-dress, *la Mercy des Dames*, would be used by them, at their discretion, as a signal to a combatant who placed his opponent in jeopardy not to continue the attack. At the request of the lady, the *chevalier* would lower the lance if the attack was to cease.

The judges then proclaimed the basic rules of the contests. The assault weapons would be only the lance, terminating in a small crown to prevent entry through the visor of the opponent's helmet, and a sword chained to the belt, to prevent the need to dismount if it was dropped. All weapons would be examined before each contest. *Gambesons*, padded at the shoulders, arms and back, were to be worn above thickly quilted underwear, all beneath the armour, which would include a leather *cuirass* with a metal breast-plate and back-plate buckled together, metal thigh greaves, gauntlets and helmet.

The flanks of the horses would be guarded by bands of straw, drawn together with strings and attached to the pommel of the saddle, a crescent-shaped bag of straw protecting the steed's breast. All the bands of straw would be covered with trappings bearing the heraldic devices of the combatants.

The formalities proceeded smoothly, and King Pedro was well-pleased. He hoped that King Charles the Bad would win. When King Charles became his son-in-law, the combined might of Castile and Navarre alone could conquer Granada, but he would of course have the assistance of Aragon and Catalonia as well. Once he was firmly entrenched in Granada, King Charles would turn on the small kingdom of Catalonia, attacking from Castile's north-eastern border, and take it. Aragon would follow.

He, King Pedro the Cruel, would then no longer need an ally or a son-in-law.

They had reached Toledo twenty days earlier and taken up residence at a spacious Roman villa in a large estate outside the city, belonging to Aaron Levi.

Zurika, with whom Levi had developed a special friendship, adapted immediately to the life of the villa as if she had been born to it.

The plan which Prince Ahmed and Prince Juan had formulated made it unsafe for them to live in the city, where they might be identified and easily apprehended. Besides, they had already discovered on the flight from the Alhambra, that security lay in the countryside. Since they had proceeded directly from Jaén to Toledo, they had received no news whatever from Granada.

They learned of the tournament only the day after they arrived in the villa. Prince Ahmed immediately decided that the best way to rescue Princess Beatrice was to compete and win her as the prize.

Without divulging their identities, Levi introduced the two princes to his rich banker friends, who cashed some of the letters of credit. This enabled them to buy four magnificent war-chargers, two of them greys with the most beautiful, glossy white coats, white suits of armour, lances, swords and all the trappings needed for Prince Ahmed's participation in the tourney.

They returned that afternoon in a convoy of horses, mules, muleteers and porters, to be met at the entrance colonnade of the villa by Levi. His dark eyes registered unwonted amazement as he stood in the fierce noonday sun eyeing their purchases.

'So you really mean to go ahead with your plan. How

will you obtain permission to participate in the tourney when you are, in the eyes of the judges, only a heretic Moor?' Levi demanded.

'I am a prince of royal blood,' Prince Ahmed retorted, watching Levi's grooms leading the horses to the stables, while astonished servants carried the armour and weapons inside. He began interpreting the discussion for Prince Juan, now a habit with him. 'I expect that if I challenge the winner insultingly enough, he will be forced to accept.'

'But how will you establish your credentials?'

'Prince Juan has the rank to touch me with his sword. Having thus vouched for me, he can slip away while I enter the lists, because King Pedro would not want to have him arrested in public. This is the quickest and most decisive way to save Princess Beatrice, so we shall have to take a chance. I shall beat all the other contenders and win her hand. Merely to have her escape from the palace would not give any of us the permanent security that victory in the tourney would ensure.'

Levi glanced around, anxious to ensure that Zurika, whose feelings towards Prince Ahmed were obvious, was not around. 'You will marry her?'

'Certainly.'

'This is madness. I simply do not see how you will accomplish it. Besides, you will have to become a Catholic or she a Muslim.'

'Can you think of a better way?'

'No, but . . .'

'If I combine brains with daring and determination, Merciful Allah the All Compassionate will provide the means.'

'You mean Jahweh?' Levi interposed, lifting his bird-like face, the dark eyes twinkling.

Prince Juan grinned merrily. 'God,' he mouthed.

They marked off an arena in the flat parkland adjoining the villa. Here, Prince Ahmed practised tirelessly and vigorously for the joust, from dawn to dusk every day, perfecting his lance technique, first against dummies, then in action with Prince Juan, their encounters including swordplay on foot. As at the Alhambra, Prince Juan was good, but Prince Ahmed was a natural and could generally best him.

Observing the conduct of the preliminaries to the tourney, they selected the third night of the opening ceremonies for their first secret entry into the Toledo palace. This would give them a whole day and a night before the morning when the actual contests commenced, in case anything went wrong.

According to Prince Juan, the secret tunnel was an extension from the ancient Roman aqueduct that had once spanned the River Tagus. Located south of the Alcantara bridge, its mouth, hidden by dense bushes, weeds and undergrowth, was beneath the Puerta de Dolce Cantos, once a fortified bastion. The tunnel continued underground going up hill until it reached the palace, where it ran within two false walls made to look like a single wall and led up two long flights of steps to the ladies' quarters. At that level, it lay between two of the ladies' suites, the queen's on one side, that of the chief princess on the other, access to each suite being through a small moveable slab on either wall which was in reality a hidden door.

Disguised as countrymen, dressed in black, they wandered around what was now tourney town that night, enjoying the crowds, the music and dancing, all of it completely new and fascinating to Prince Ahmed. It was well past midnight when the fever of the festivity began to wane, with people making for bed. They then began threading their way south along the highway, past the *Puente*, with the darkened Castello San Fernando to their left, until they came to the remains of the old Roman bridge.

It suited their purpose that the arena, tourney town and the continuing activity were well north of the *Castello*. A quarter moon had long set behind the Alcazar, making it a huge dark hill-mass surmounted by the black outlines of the palace and other buildings, each topped by four corner spires and chimneys, with an occasional rectangular mosaic of golden windowlight. Further down, the pinnacle of the cathedral thrust its eminence into a midnight blue sky, devoid of stars. The near-ravine of the highway, running between two hill features, was pitch-black and completely deserted at this hour. The ceaseless gush, splash and gurgle of the river and a distant sizzle which reflected the winding down of the wakefulness of town and city, were part of the total silence.

They paused at the dark relict of the old bridge. Prince Ahmed tensed as Prince Juan jabbed a finger repeatedly downwards. This was where they would make their way down the dark river bank and swim across. Prince Ahmed had never been taught to swim until ten days ago when Prince Juan had shown him how to float in the stream that ran past the villa. The plan was that they would float, stroking sufficiently to allow the river to take them down to the tunnel entrance on the opposite bank.

Could he make it? The thought of drowning was more chill than the prospect of the dark, cold water below him.

The clip . . . clippety-clop . . . clop . . . clippety-clop of hooves on the cobbled highway jarred on Prince Ahmed's senses. Who could it be? A night patrol? Fear churned in his guts. He fought to bring it under control. Remembering that his companion was deaf, he laid a hand on Prince Juan's arm, pointed in the direction of the sound, indicated that several horsemen were approaching from the south. He gave Prince Juan the agreed signal. They stepped back to the highway. Prince Ahmed's heart began thudding against his ribs.

* * *

Princess Beatrice had been alternating between hope and despair. Hope from the *Ballad of Horn and Rymenhilde*, despair at the harsh reality of the tourney that had finally overtaken her. Life was no longer a romantic ballad. How could she be rescued at the last moment by a handsome young prince who was not in her life and did not even know of her existence? Unless one of the twenty-one contestants proved to be the man of her dreams, which was extremely unlikely.

She had fallen into a fitful sleep after her mother had kissed her good night as usual, but had been awakened by the blare of palace trumpets announcing the midnight hour. That had been quite some time ago. She had tossed and turned beneath the blue silk sheets of her bed, flinging them aside from the warmth of the summer night, then covering up against the body-chills emerging from her apprehension. How could she give her virginity and her life to some strange man, probably King Charles the Bad if her mother was proved right? She had had a glimpse of King Charles the other day and the very sight of him had terrified her. How could a mother offer her only child to such a monster? And yet history was replete with these human sacrifices. Well, she would take her own life if need be and hope that the Blessed Virgin Mary would intercede on her behalf to get her into Heaven. After all, had she not led a virtuous, blameless Christian life?

Could she escape? Her eyes drifted to the far wall which held the panel that opened out to the tunnel. Both her mother's suite and hers had these panels that opened out to the tunnel which had been created by the Moors after they took over Toledo, to save their *harem* women if invaders ever took over the citadel. It was supposed to lead under the river out to the open countryside, but she did not know for certain. No one but the two royal women had known the secret, handed down only to each queen and the oldest princess, until she shared it with Prince

Juan nearly five years ago so he could continue visiting her after she was cloistered by her father.

The very thought of a long inky-black tunnel, infested with rodents, reptiles, possibly bats and foul vermin, was almost as terrifying as the fate worse than death which awaited her from the outcome of the tourney.

And if she did get through, how would she exist? She could take her jewels with her, but where would she go? To a convent perhaps, donating the jewels in exchange for sanctuary? Tonight, she did not have such courage. Could she summon it if the event was actually upon her and she was betrothed to the monster, King Charles? She did not know. The unknown had become more terrifying than a known fate, however dread.

A quiet, but insistent knocking on the entrance door of her bedroom brought her instantly alert, her heart beating faster. Who could it be at this hour? She froze the scream that boiled up in her throat.

The drunken revelry in the Great Hall had been unbridled because there would be no feasting tomorrow night, when everyone would retire early to bed to be fit and fresh for the combats which would commence the following morning. Though well into his cups, since it was long past midnight, King Pedro had some moments of clear-eyed sobriety as he surveyed the twenty-one candidates who, in order of rank, crowded the huge Spanish mahogany table that served the Great Hall of the Toledo palace. Their faces flushed with wine, they ranged from a young blond, blue-eyed, clean-shaven Nordic king of slender build, through swarthy, dark-haired German and brown-haired French counts, to a bald-headed minor Italian king, from the thin tall King Philip of Catalonia to the bull-like King Charles the Bad. Many of them had come merely for the fray, though hopes of being Prince Regent of Castile some day was no mean reward. King Pedro knew whom he would want for a son-in-law.

'Why then did you decide to hold the tourney, Your Majesty?' Count Gaston, seated on his right as the *chevalier d'honneur*, his gold-tipped lance of office carried by the footman standing behind him, had eaten and drunk sparingly as usual. King Pedro marvelled at the uncanny perception that had led the Count to pick up his searching glance and his conclusion. The question would normally have been an impertinence, which Count Gaston would never be guilty of, but the two of them had drawn close enough to each other for such frankness.

'It ensured that no ally would be lost to us, which would certainly have occurred if we had merely chosen some convenient king and announced a betrothal.'

'And the Princess Beatrice finds the idea of the tourney romantic perhaps?'

King Pedro's eyebrows lifted. '*En verdad*, we . . . er – do not know,' he replied softly. 'We assume . . . er . . . that any young princess would find the idea of having contenders for her hand joust to win her romantic, but her views had no bearing whatsoever on our decision.' The idea of consulting Princess Beatrice's wishes had never even occurred to him. With anyone else, King Pedro would have shut off this line of discussion, but having discovered that Count Gaston frequently opened up new avenues of thought to him, he had decided against discouraging the question. 'We are as cruel and despotic beside the family hearth as we are with the national family,' he added with a mock-ferocious grin.

'You will then face the appalling fate of all cruel despots, Sire.'

Observing the twinkle of the black eyes in the hatchet face, King Pedro realized for the hundredth time that he could never fathom what went on behind the mask of well-bred amusement. 'And what may that be, *Chevalier*?' he inquired.

'Your good deeds are not the least gripping. They pale into insignificance before the atrocities. Yet it is these good deeds, like the tourney, that will be recorded by history. I should imagine that King Herod must be turning in his grave each time he is remembered for having built the Temple of Jerusalem or the great sea-wall that created the Tyre harbour rather than for the innumerable grisly murders he committed.'

King Pedro's guffaw rang above the din of the room. He slapped the table. The wine goblets rattled, but no one even looked in his direction. What was one more drunken guffaw in the hundreds that had been rocking the Hall?

King Charles leaned forward inquiringly. 'What hash . . . um . . . hash . . .' Unable to articulate the word, he tried another approach. 'What did our clever Sh . . . Chancellor say?' He hiccupped and reached for his wine goblet.

'That it is more important to be remembered by history for cruelty and,' King Pedro looked pointedly at King Charles, 'badness, than for good deeds.'

King Charles cocked his head to one side, considering, but gave up, the effort too much for his fuddled brain. He wiped red winedrops from his beard and stared moodily into his goblet.

The man may turn ugly, King Pedro decided. 'You do not approve of despots?' he inquired of Count Gaston.

'As you are well aware, Sire, I neither approve nor disapprove of anyone or anything. I should imagine, however, that the only way for a despot to have his misdeeds recorded as heroic by history is to commit them with propriety. This is the least his people deserve. They are more accustomed to calamity, invariably being its recipient from Nature or from their rulers, than to creating history themselves. Despots, on the other hand, inflict two calamities on their subjects, the first when they are born, the second, ironically enough, when they die.'

'We must think on that one.' King Pedro's attention was distracted by a lugubrious wail from across the hall. A middle-aged prince with broad Germanic features, whose name he had forgotten, had begun weeping aloud, his face broken up in an expression of sorrowful disgust. 'What is wrong with him?' he demanded, surprised.

'He is in the fourth of the seven stages of drunkenness, Sire,' Count Gaston replied. 'Jocose, bellicose, amatose, lachrymose.'

'And the other three stages?'

'Adipose, varicose, comatose.'

'Good, good. But he now looks as if the first sound he ever heard as a baby was the passing of his own wind. Ha! ha! ha!'

'That is Prince Karl. He has much to be sorrowful about in his cups. Sober, he is reputed to be a sinner without conscience, except on Sundays when his conscience does emerge, but only so it can sleep late.'

King Pedro nodded amused agreement, glanced at King Charles, now glaring around the table. 'Our brother, your master, King Charles resents his competitors.' He knew a moment's qualm, lowered his voice. 'We worry lest he takes to the field right here and now, especially against King Philip of Catalonia whom he loathes. Any impropriety tonight would disqualify him from participating in the tourney.'

'You should not permit worries to arrive at mealtimes, Sire. It is like allowing creditors into one's privy.'

King Charles gave the lie to this statement. He rose to his feet with a roar, his chair crashing behind him. Huge knuckles placed on the mahogany table, his expression was so ugly that the babel of sound in the hall died down to a chill silence. Everyone, drunk or sober, stared at him

281

in astonishment. A departing attendant dropped a silver dish with a clatter-clank that was ignored.

'We can beat anyone in thish . . . thish room!' King Charles cried. 'Why wait for the day after tomorrow? To fight by the rulesh . . . rulesh . . . whatever! . . . ish for pop . . . pominshays. We shallenge anyone to resh . . . wreshtle with us?' He glared around with bloodshot eyes, bull-head swivelling until his gaze came to rest on the tall King Philip, two seats away from him. 'Ah, the Catalonian! You want to wreshtle?'

Before King Pedro could decide what to do, King Philip rose slowly to his feet, to tower over the bull-like King Charles. 'We will take you on in any kind of combat,' he declared in his deep tones. 'With or without weapons, mounted or on foot.'

The tension in the hall was so physical, it was like the smell of nitrate in the air before a fireworks display.

This drunken idiot could ruin the carefully laid plans of months. Even as King Pedro gripped the table to intervene, the chair on his right scraped. Count Gaston stood tall beside him. 'The combat phase of the tourney begins the day after tomorrow,' he declared quietly, in pleasant tones. 'King Pedro's hospitality has perhaps made us all move the hour-glass forward. There will be no fighting tonight.'

Chapter 15

He had held his breath at hearing the horse's hooves, his heart beating rapidly. Now he exhaled quietly, consciously steadied his heartbeat, gripped Prince Juan's arm and drew him back to the highway. The clatter of hooves grew louder, drowned the rush-flow-splash of the river. Peering through the inky blackness, Prince Ahmed tried to distinguish the displacement of air that would tell when the approaching group was close enough.

It was Prince Juan, his vision vastly improved as Nature's compensation for his loss of hearing, who first detected the moving mass. He immediately teetered drunkenly forward. Prince Ahmed followed suit, shambling from side to side. He broke into a Spanish song, alternately mumbling and gusting the words.

> 'On eager, romantic feet
> I walked along Maria's street
> It was plastered with urine and swill
> Pig's offal the gutter did fill
> I stood 'neath her window and sang
> Of a love that never would stop
> Her voice through my serenade rang
> "Aqua va!" And she threw out her slop.'

'Whoa!' The leader of the group had seen the two weaving figures. The smooth unison beat of the canter broke up as the riders slowed to a trot, then came to a halt, the leader but a few feet away now. The sudden silence was broken by the creak of leather, the snort of a horse and the stamp of a single hoof.

Through slitted eyes, Prince Ahmed detected that the

leader wore the uniform of a captain of the king's guard. He wove his way to the man, peered up. 'Ah, Maria, beautiful Maria, you have appeared at your window,' he cried.

'Get out of our way, you stinking drunk,' the captain growled. He raised his riding whip.

'Aqua va! Aqua va!' Prince Ahmed shouted. 'Maria is throwing out her slops.' He grabbed Prince Juan's arm, pulled him to the side of the highway just in time to avoid the downward slash of the whip.

'Forward!' The captain's arm pointed. The clatter of hooves broke through the stillness again. Prince Ahmed counted ten riders trotting past him. Only when the beat of the trot changed to a canter and the moving mass vanished into the blackness did he release his hold on Prince Juan's arm. They had escaped the king's patrol.

They hurried back to the relict of the bridge. Prince Juan leading this time, they went slipping and sliding down the bank, slithering to a stop only when they were almost at the water's edge. Prince Juan removed his shoes, placed them on the bank, lowered himself into the river.

Prince Ahmed stared at the dark water. Panic seized him. He began shivering and trembling, broke out into goosebumps. His brain screamed to him, Turn back and flee. He finally understood Prince Juan's fear of heights. Recollection of the escape from the Gen al Arif brought Princess Beatrice's face before his mind's eye. Skin like snow on the Sierra Nevada touched by the pink of the setting sun, hair like spun gold, eyes more blue than summer skies. If Prince Juan could overcome fear, so could he. Drawing a deep breath, he removed his shoes, placed them on the bank, turned his back to the water and lowered himself into it. He lay on his back, relaxing, then kicked off. As the flow of the river began carrying him downstream, he began using his arms and legs, as

Prince Juan had taught him, to propel himself towards the opposite bank.

The water slowly seeped through his clothes, chilling his body. Though drifting downstream, it was on a diagonal course towards the opposite bank. The steady movements of his arms and legs helped ease the cold. He stared sideways at the dark outline of the bridge, then up at the deep vault of the starless sky. Water splashed in his eyes, stinging. He tried to wipe it away, started to sink. Panicked. Merciful Allah help me. He got a firm hold on himself. Relaxed.

His head banged gently on a rock. He lowered his feet, found no purchase, wildly searched for the river-bottom and began sinking again. His bare feet touched a slimy rock. He slipped in his eagerness but finally found solid ground. Standing waist deep in water, he sucked in great gulps of air. He turned to face the bank. Prince Juan was already there, a few feet upstream. He clambered up.

Prince Juan found the hidden entrance to the tunnel with ease. They tugged and heaved at the slab of rock guarding it. Within moments the black tunnel yawned before Prince Ahmed. A noisome stench of droppings, fur and rodents smote him, followed by the scitter-scurry of feet and the whirr of wings. A bat flew out within inches of his face. Dear Allah, what a fearsome hole of Hades.

Prince Juan led the way inside, paused, fumbled along the side wall, croaked his satisfaction. He thrust something into Prince Ahmed's hand. It was metal, smooth and cold to the touch. He held it up against the pale rectangle of light from the tunnel's entrance and discovered that it was a flare.

He heard the scrape of tinder, saw the spark, watched it become a small steady flame. When the flare was lighted, Prince Juan grabbed it and began leading the way. Bats hanging from the low roof flapped away in the blackness, but in the flare's light, Prince Ahmed found the tunnel a little less loathsome. The noxious air was a mixture of coolness and humidity. The harsh odour of resin from the smoking flare only made its stench more foul. The tunnel was narrow, just wide enough for one person to proceed along it, straight uphill. He noted steps a little way beyond; the steepest parts of the tunnel were obviously served by steps. The Romans of old must have forced the water up the hill by the sheer force of its flow.

The floor of the tunnel became littered with droppings and dead rodents, the stench unbelievable. Prince Ahmed's flesh curdled and his skin crawled when something soft on the slippery floor crunched beneath his bare feet. An enormous rat, recently dead. Vibrations of disgust shot from his feet through his body. This was what Princess Beatrice faced for her escape route.

Long minutes of slow progress ended in two long flights of steps. Prince Juan came to a halt before a blank wall and turned left. They had arrived. His heart beating more rapidly, Prince Ahmed watched his fellow Prince place the flare on a metal sconce. The most dread moments lay ahead.

One thing that had irked Prince Ahmed came to the forefront of his mind. Prince Juan had insisted that he should enter first so as not to alarm Princess Beatrice, but would immediately have Prince Ahmed join them, so he could explain their plan to her, which would take less time than if Prince Juan wrote it down. He would then leave Prince Juan to spend a little time with his sister, return to the tunnel and wait behind the sliding door. That was understandable, but what bothered Prince Ahmed was the promise he had made that if Prince Juan were discovered in his sister's bedroom, he, Prince Ahmed, would flee and somehow return to rescue the princess. The possibility of having to desert a comrade at a moment of need was so detestable to Prince Ahmed that his mind found its release in an inconsequential question. Where had the bats gone?

The knock on the entrance door to her suite had terrified Princess Beatrice because the hour was after midnight. It had never happened before and she connected it with the premonition of disaster she had been experiencing all evening. She quickly assured herself that the ladies' quarters of the Toledo palace were inviolate and, besides, the knocking had been gentle, even respectful. Since she always kept the door unlocked any visitor who intended harm could simply have walked in.

Composing herself, she rose from the bed, donned her white dressing gown and walked swiftly across the room to her mirror, where she smoothed down her blonde hair. Her eyes wandered to the blue-robed statue of the Blessed Virgin and she murmured a prayer for protection.

Once at the door, she placed a cheek close to it and inquired, 'Who is it?'

'It's me, Teresa, Princess. Pray forgive my intrusion, but I desperately need to talk to you in private.'

Princess Beatrice resisted a natural urge to question the hour. Teresa was a buxom young woman from Barcelona, daughter of a fisherman. She had come to Toledo with a young dancer, named Lopo Reyes, to better her lot. Lopo had been killed in a knife fight, leaving Teresa destitute, so the parish priest, Father Dominic, had helped her obtain menial work in the palace kitchens. With her passionate nature, evident in the flashing, dark brown eyes, the texture of her olive skin and masses of wavy black hair, Teresa had risen swiftly from kitchen wench to be lady's maid. It was rumoured that this was largely due to the influence of the *major domo* of the palace, Ramon Castro, a reedy man of over sixty with a large wife and a larger family, to whom Teresa secretly granted the favours of her lusty body. Princess Beatrice did not really care how Teresa had improved her lot, because the woman was unfailingly pleasant, obliging and efficient.

Teresa slipped through the open doorway. Dressed in the white-frilled black palace uniform, she was obviously distraught, her face flushed, eyes red, their lids swollen from weeping.

Princess Beatrice's heart went out to the poor woman. 'What's wrong, Teresa?' She laid her hand on a plump shoulder. 'Come, sit down and tell me.' She led Teresa to one of the ante-room settles cushioned in white velvet.

'I could never sit down in front of you, my lady princess.'

'Of course you can.' She gently forced the woman on to the seat, drew up another settle for herself. 'Now tell me all about it.'

Touched by the kindness, Teresa burst into tears. Princess Beatrice waited until her sobs died down, took out her white linen kerchief and proffered it silently to the woman, who accepted it with a rueful smile and dabbed her cheeks and eyes.

'I would be dismissed from the palace, probably whipped, if you told anyone that I visited you,' Teresa began.

'You came because you knew I would never tell anyone.'

'Yes, yes, my lady. You have always been so kind to me that I knew you would not report me.' Teresa paused, sniffed, handed back the kerchief, wiped her cheeks with the back of her hand. 'I'm in serious trouble, my lady.' She hesitated, then the words came out in a rush. 'I'm pregnant.'

'Holy Mother Mary!' Unused to the ways of the world, this was a totally new situation for Princess Beatrice. What did Teresa think she could do to help? 'How did it happen?' she inquired lamely. 'I mean, I know you are not married. Who is the father?'

Teresa looked down, reflecting. 'Señor Ramon Castro,' she said quietly, without looking up.

Princess Beatrice's mind began to whirl. Pregnant by a married man and a palace official at that. The poor woman was really in trouble.

As if reading her mind, Teresa interjected, 'I have told Señor Castro, but he swears the baby is not his, that I have been playing with other men and am trying to trap him. I wish there was something I could do at least to make him listen. I should never have given my body to a married man, especially one with children of his own. Can you not at least help me find some way in which he would support the child, my lady?'

'I shall help you more than that,' Princess Beatrice declared fiercely. 'My mother can get you to a convent when your time comes and after you have the baby, you shall return to work for me.'

Teresa fell on her knees, took one of Princess Beatrice's hands and kissed it. 'Thank you, thank you, my lady princess. I knew you would help me. I shall be in your debt forever. May the Blessed Virgin reward you.'

She had barely finished speaking when Princess Beatrice heard the knocking on the bedroom wall. Tap, tap . . . tap, tap, tap . . . tap, tap . . . tap, tap, tap . . . For a moment, she wondered what it could be. Then the truth hit her with the force of a battering ram. The knocking came from the secret tunnel and it was Prince Juan's signal from the times when he used to visit her, the one source of warm comfort in a cold world. Her brother was actually here! How? How on earth had he escaped from Granada? No matter. He had to have come to rescue her. She removed her hand from Teresa's grasp, leapt to her feet. The young woman stared at her, puzzled.

'I must . . .' Princess Beatrice began, then stopped instinctively. Caution warned her that Teresa should not know about the tunnel or Prince Juan's return. 'We shall talk about this further in the morning, Teresa. Try not to worry for the present. Go back to your room now and sleep.' She helped the young woman to her feet, propelled her gently towards the door.

Tap, tap . . . tap, tap, tap . . . tap, tap . . . tap, tap, tap.

Teresa paused in her stride. 'That . . .' She stopped abruptly. A knowing look came into her eyes.

Holy Mother of God, she thinks I have a lover. Princess Beatrice was almost ready to tell Teresa the truth, but caution intruded once again. 'Go now, Teresa,' she commanded. A new expression on Teresa's face, as if she were the equal of her mistress in wanton conduct, filled Princess Beatrice with unease.

She waited until the door clicked shut, remembered with pity that Prince Juan was now deaf and dumb. She gathered up writing materials from a drawer of her escritoire, hastened to her bedroom, closing the door behind her. She laid the materials on a table.

Tap, tap . . . tap, tap, tap . . . tap, tap. Her heart began pounding.

She sped to the wall and pressed the panel so Prince Juan could enter.

King Pedro sat back in his chair with a muttered oath. Count Gaston was challenging his own king. How had he dared to do it? No matter, for the Basque would find a way to save the tourney from being destroyed by this drunken bull when everything had gone perfectly so far. Better the count intervene than he, King Pedro, so for the present he would merely watch the play.

Charles the Bad had swung round to face Count Gaston, total disbelief on his flushed face. All sounds had died down in the hall, even the most drunken guests sobering at the drama unfolding. 'Wha . . . What did you shay?' King Charles demanded incredulously.

'I said there will be no fighting tonight, Sire. I would respectfully remind everyone here that the tourney does not commence until the day after tomorrow,' he smiled. 'Tomorrow in fact.'

A roar of rage escaped King Charles. His face contorted with fury. 'You . . . you . . . our subject . . . our dog, dare to interfere?' His anger had sobered him. He stepped sideways to move towards the count. King Pedro held his breath.

'I did not address you either as your subject, your chancellor, or your dog, Sire.' Something cold and commanding in the deep voice made King Charles pause. A pleasant gaze locked into King Charles's, Count Gaston stretched a hand sideways, clicked his fingers at the footman standing behind him, then beckoned with them. 'I am speaking as the *Chevalier d'honneur* of the tourney, which commenced four days ago and will not end until tomorrow night. If you disobey my lawful request, you insult and dishonour the ladies, whom I represent, thereby forfeiting all right to participate.' He firmly gripped the gold-tipped lance which the trembling footman extended to him. King Pedro exhaled loudly. This was better than any play.

King Charles's stare turned to puzzlement. His eyes crossing in an effort to dissipate the vapours in his brain, he tugged at his black beard, snorted. 'Ha!' He paused. A cunning gleam entered the pig eyes. 'You are the *Chevalier* tonight and even a king must obey you.' He spoke quietly, but red sparks had flared in his eyes. 'At the end of the tourney, you shall be answerable to your king. Godsbody, so you shall.' His mouth twisted in a sneer. 'For the present, you can hide beneath the ladies' skirts!'

Count Gaston stood his ground, smilingly refusing the insult. King Pedro could not help but admire the quiet strength of the man. Why, oh why, could he not have the count in his own service? Someday perhaps. 'I shall never

291

be answerable for my conduct as *Chevalier* even to my liege lord,' Count Gaston replied. 'Or to anyone for that matter, save the two ladies whom I serve. My conduct towards you, my king, as your subject, has always been exemplary, I venture to say, whereas my conduct as a human being, towards God, is frequently questionable, which is why I beg you, my liege lord, not to prejudice your right to participate in the tourney.' An amused smile creased his hatchet features. 'As for hiding behind the ladies' skirts, Sire, what more gallant and satisfying a refuge can any man find?'

A bellow of laughter ran through the hall. King Charles the Bad looked around him, drunkenly decided to join in. Relief swept through King Pedro. A strength capable of ignoring an insult, a deft turn of humour, a willingness to assert the integrity of office, had eased an ugly, even calamitous situation.

King Charles looked around for the chair he had sent crashing. His footman sped forward and placed it upright again. King Charles grabbed his wine goblet. King Philip resumed his seat.

'A toast!' King Charles shouted, almost sober momentarily. 'To the *Chevalier*!' Count Gaston alone remained seated, while everyone, including King Pedro, sprang to their feet, raised wine goblets. 'To the *Chevalier*, God bless him!'

They drank deeply of the red wine, banged their goblets on the mahogany table, resumed their seats. Only King Charles remained standing. 'You dislike cats, do you not, *Chevalier*?' he demanded.

'Not my favourite animal, Sire,' Count Gaston responded amiably.

'Do you like what you see under those skirts?' King Charles roared with laughter this time and sat down, obviously well satisfied.

* * *

292

The passing days had puzzled Zurika. She had enjoyed the journey from Jaén to the villa, in spite of the tearful and heartbreaking parting from her grandmother, Pilar. It was the first time that they had ever been separated. At least Pilar had been able to buy a small house on the outskirts of the city, with Prince Ahmed's help, and would have a secure, decent home at long last which Zurika could visit on the way back from Toledo. Meanwhile, each passing day had brought new excitement and drawn her closer to both Prince Juan and Aaron Levi. For once, she had friends, men she could trust who would protect rather than molest her. It was a totally new experience for Zurika and by the time they arrived at the villa, she had decided that she would sacrifice her life if need be for either of these two men. As for Prince Ahmed, whom she loved with all the passion and fierce loyalty of her gypsy origins and background, there was nothing she would not do for him either, but she simply could not get close to him. While unfailingly courteous, considerate and charming towards her, he never made any move to show her any feelings of love. What had happened to the young prince who had kept a regular tryst with her dancing every single evening?

She had just woken from her sleep tonight to the realization that the hour was well past midnight. Prince Ahmed and Prince Juan had left in the evening to visit tourney town. She knew they had still not returned, because if they had, she would have heard them in the adjoining rooms. She had never been parted from them for so many hours since the day they fled the Alhambra together. Could they be in some sort of trouble?

The night was warm and she found herself sweating beneath her silk nightgown. She began to toss and turn. She glanced round the room, warm with the glow of silver hanging lamps that remained lighted through the night. The room was large and smelled of musk from two silver

293

incense burners on a gilt table at its far wall. The white flagstone floors were covered with pink and white rugs, which Aaron Levi said he had brought from a place called Venice. The walls were hung with oil paintings of ladies in groups, done in dark browns, whites, pinks, deep reds and golds.

Imagine me, Zurika, the gypsy girl, sleeping in this luxurious room on this comfortable bed with a pink canopy above it, down pillows and pink silken sheets! Yet the thought brought no comfort tonight. She decided that she simply must talk to Aaron Levi, who worked in his library poring over his account books and reports until long after midnight, needing no more than three or four hours' sleep.

She rose from her bed, slipped on her blue robe, reflecting that she had taken readily and naturally to the ways of life of fine ladies, in which the two princes and Aaron Levi had instructed her. She still had much to learn, but she would become the mistress of it all and make Prince Ahmed proud of her. When he became King of Granada, she would become his chief concubine. He could marry, take on a queen, fornicate with her or any other woman of his harem, but she, Zurika, would be his one love. She would slit the throat of anyone who tried to displace her in his affections. As she made for the door and unlatched it, she laughed aloud at the realization that in her heart she still remained a fierce gypsy woman.

Aaron Levi's library was at the opposite end of a wide verandah that opened on to the *atrium* or central court-yard in the middle of the residence, the villa being built like a fort behind its front colonnades. She had never disturbed Aaron Levi at his work before, so it was with some trepidation that she knocked on the brown oak door.

'Who is it?' Aaron's quavery voice called, the sound faint through the solid door.

'Me, Zurika,' she shouted.

'Come in!' She could sense the surprise in his voice.

As she entered and shut the door behind her, Aaron Levi rose to his feet. Concern showed in his gnome-like face beneath the inevitable black *yarmulke*. Did he wear this headgear to bed? Then she noticed with alarm that his eyes were covered with two circles of glass in a frame held together by a wooden support on the bridge of his hooked beak of a nose, and strapped to the back of his head.

'What is wrong, Señor Levi?' she cried, pointing. 'Your eyes . . . what have you done to them?'

A smile creased his face, revealing white teeth. He fingered the frame of the contraption with his right hand. 'Nothing is wrong, my child. I would say that these set right what age has made wrong. They help my old eyes to see better by making the images of writing larger, which is especially important when one is dealing with accounts. They are called reading eye-glasses.' He removed the eye-glasses, placed them on his desk, gestured towards the chair opposite it. 'Sit down please and tell me what brings *you* here at this hour.'

She sat on the edge of an oak chair upholstered in black leather. 'What will they think of next?' She nodded towards the eye-glasses, stifled a yawn. 'One of these would help my grandmother, Pilar.' She grinned, suddenly feeling more at ease. 'If she could read!'

He lifted grey eyebrows, then sat down. 'A good thought, worthy of philosophers who are constantly searching for truths that do not exist.'

Her eyes widened in surprise. 'Do you believe that there is no truth then?'

He sighed. 'I find truth in my one God, Jahweh, and in my religion, which directs my life and all I do in my existence, like working, eating, sleeping,' his smile became mischievous, 'and enjoying you. As to whether

295

these are really truths or not to others and even to me, I neither know, care about nor contemplate.'

'H'mmm.' She had a glimmering of comprehension. 'Nothing is real, is it?' She was thinking of Prince Ahmed's feelings for her.

He grew serious. 'I do not even conjecture so far, my child.'

The conversation suddenly became too heavy for her. 'Who gave you those – what did you call them, eye-glasses?'

'They were invented about seventy-five years ago by a genius, an Englishman called Roger Bacon, who inciden-tally also invented a substance called gun powder that may one day destroy the world.'

She glanced curiously at the large oak desk at which he was seated. It was covered with leatherbound books. Two of them open before him contained black writing and figures in a fine, manuscript hand, the work of his clerks and accountants who lived in the rear quarters of the villa. None of the figures would have made sense to her, since she could barely read or write, though Prince Ahmed had begun teaching her on the journey and Aaron Levi had found her a tutor who visited the villa daily.

The lowing of a bull from the nearby pasture disturbed the stillness. 'Ah! The bull is concerned about something.' The dark eyes twinkled. 'What is your concern?'

'Señor, the two princes have not returned yet. I couldn't sleep, so I came to you. Where have they gone? Could they be in trouble?'

A strange look flitted in his eyes. 'They are not in any trouble, my child,' he assured her. 'They have gone to the tourney town to scout the land for the tournament in which Prince Ahmed hopes to participate the day after . . . no, it is tomorrow already.'

'Why can't Prince Juan go directly to the palace? After all, he is the king's son.' All this had been explained to her before, but it was a means of getting to what had finally surfaced in her mind as the real cause of her concern.

'No king wants a deaf-mute son,' Aaron Levi explained patiently. 'If Prince Juan appears openly in the Toledo palace, he will be cast into the dungeons.'

'What will happen if Prince Ahmed wins the tournament tomorrow?'

Aaron Levi reached out and toyed with a stylus. His pause and the continued lowing of the bull suddenly irritated her. 'Prince Ahmed will win the right to ask King Pedro any boon and he will ask for Prince Juan's restoration,' Aaron Levi finally stated.

'I overheard the two princes talking this afternoon and they mentioned something about Prince Juan's sister, a Princess Beatrice. I think they want to rescue her because she is imprisoned in the ladies' quarters of the palace. Is that not so?'

He became very still, looked down at the stylus in his hand, while the odour of his rich scented oil reached her. 'They certainly want to rescue Princess Beatrice.' He sighed. 'She has suffered almost the same fate as Prince Ahmed did all his life in the Alhambra.'

'Does this make her and Prince Ahmed two of a kind?' she demanded, jealousy flaring in her.

'Not necessarily.' He stroked his chin, still avoiding her eyes.

'What will they do, after they rescue her?' Why was Aaron Levi avoiding her gaze?

'Presumably Prince Juan will remain in the Toledo palace and Prince Ahmed will,' he paused, shaking his head, 'take Princess Beatrice to Granada.'

'No . . . o . . .oo!' The anguished cry was torn from her fearful heart as she sprang to her feet, hot tears of rage and pain in her eyes.

He rose, came swiftly around the table to her side and

laid a gentle hand on her head. She could feel it willing peace into her but it could not ease her torment. 'We are all prisoners of circumstance, my child.' He began stroking her head. 'You were a prisoner of the gypsy caves and Prince Ahmed rescued you. Prince Juan was a prisoner of the Alhambra dungeons and, worse, still remains enchained, though Prince Ahmed rescued him too. Now it is the turn of the Princess Beatrice to be rescued, and you must help in that endeavour. It is one of the reasons why we are in this life, to help those who are afflicted.' He reached for her chin with his free hand, tilted it gently up and sideways so he could look at her.

He was the first man to touch her, but no part of her responded to the paternal affection.

'I shall never help,' she burst forth, wiping her nose with the back of her hand, large brown tear-brimmed eyes gazing piteously at him. 'If Prince Ahmed, *my* prince, takes Princess Beatrice, I shall kill her.'

He shook his head sadly. 'You are a prisoner again, my child, the prisoner of your passion.'

As he waited to follow Prince Juan through the narrow doorway that would give entrance into Princess Beatrice's bedroom, Prince Ahmed's heart began pounding at the prospect of seeing his vision of beauty at last, of speaking to her, hearing the voice he knew would be melodious.

After months of danger, of waiting, hoping, wondering, striving, it was going to happen at long last, a miracle of faith and, yes, he knew the word at long last, love. All his life he had been starved of love, so it had been easy to thrust aside any thoughts of this moment by concentrating on what was leading to it. His occasional moments of wondering how Princess Beatrice would respond to him had been few and far between, because he was convinced that she was *kismet*, his destiny. He recognized too that the years of barren, austere discipline had brought a strange, unexpected reward, in that they had fitted him perfectly for the role of rescuer.

A flicker of anxiety at the possibility of being caught in the female quarters of the palace, a crime more heinous than murder, was extinguished by the protesting of the entrance panel as it slid open, grind-squeaking after long months of disuse. He ducked to follow Prince Juan through the entrance, his breath trapped in the upper part of his throat.

In the dim light of the single hanging oil lamp that was lit, he saw the back of Prince Juan's black-clad figure, the sides of a white robe and above one shoulder a mass of wavy, blonde hair. Princess Beatrice was in her brother's arms, her head against his shoulder, murmuring incoherent words of concern which Prince Juan could not hear. 'My poor, poor Juanito. What have they done to you?' Her voice was subdued silver-gold, her compassion for his affliction obviously greater than any relief at his presence to help her. How wonderful!

Prince Ahmed could only see that the princess was slender and tall. As he breathed her honeysuckle scent, trickling through the sandalwood incense perfume that hung on the air, quiet ecstasy seeped through his being. She was perfect.

Prince Juan finally released her, turned to gesture towards Prince Ahmed, smiling. He saw her then in the exquisite completeness of her beauty, and his breath caught. All that he had imagined from the miniature was nothing before the living, vibrant being, hair like spun gold, delicate bones, skin the snows of the Sierra Nevada tinted by the first pink of the setting sun, eyes . . . oh, those large, luminous blue eyes, startled now at seeing someone else besides her brother. Dear Allah! The air spun around him, stopped abruptly as time stood still.

For the first time in his life, Prince Ahmed felt awkward, a mortal in the presence of divinity, for her beauty was surely divine. He bowed low, came erect to find her eyes had widened. 'I am Prince Ahmed, the only son of King Yusuf I of Granada and probably still his heir.' He paused, enraptured by a strange unwavering look of recognition on her face. 'I have come with your brother, Prince Juan, to rescue you, if that is your desire.'

'Horn!' she whispered.

He did not understand. 'Horn, Princess?'

'Yes, Horn.' Her voice was still low. She shook her head in disbelief, the waves of long golden hair shimmering. 'I shall explain later, but please go on. Tell me your plan.'

Her eyes never stopped searching his face, his wide shoulders, slim waist, then back to his own eyes, the head always shaking in disbelief while he explained the plan. 'Prince Juan, at great risk to himself, will accompany me to touch my shoulder with his sword in token that he, as prince of the most royal blood, vouches for me as a worthy contender at the tourney,' he concluded. 'I shall win the jousts and you will be free.'

His eyes searched her face for some token that she would then accept him, but found none. Disappointment left a curiously empty feeling in the pit of his stomach, but his love made him continue confidently. 'If I do lose, Prince Juan and I will still come here through the tunnel after midnight tomorrow to take you away. The tourney over, everyone will be feasting and celebrating, so it will be a good time for you to escape. We will have fast horses waiting on the highway and the remaining hours before daylight will enable us to place a sufficient distance between ourselves and Toledo to render us safe from pursuit, since we have arranged for relays of fast horses to take us to Granada, where you will finally be safe from all you have endured.' She shook her head yet again in disbelief. 'Horn!' was all she breathed.

'You agree, Princess?' he inquired, still puzzled by the repeated word.

She nodded.

'I shall go back into the tunnel now and wait by the entrance panel, so your brother and you can have a few minutes together. Please close the panel after I leave and keep your reunion brief, for you will, by Almighty Allah's grace, have all the time you need very soon.'

He smiled, bowed, turned and ducked back into the tunnel landing.

'I thank God and the Blessed Virgin,' he heard her say softly. 'And I thank you, Horn.'

Somehow he understood at last and his being filled with joy. She was *kismet*. She would belong to him, as he belonged to her.

The panel creak-squeaked back. He was left alone. The resin-sick odour of the lighted flare had become perfume to his nostrils.

Thoughts, plans, hopes whirled around in his mind as past fear intruded, now that the dream was reaching reality. She was a Christian, he a Muslim. How would they reconcile the difference? Would she convert? If he won the tourney, would she and her father King Pedro expect him to become a Christian. Never! He would never give up his religion.

Never? An absolute word, the true result of which only Allah knew. A thought spun from the back of his brain to its forefront like a whirling top. Love existed before either Christianity or Islam were created. Love would find the way.

At first it did not register, so engrossed was he in his thoughts. Then it penetrated. A loud knocking within Princess Beatrice's bedroom, followed by her cry. The crash of a door followed. The princess screamed. A command was shouted, feet pounded, a harsh male voice rose above the din, all of it muffled.

Dear Allah, Prince Juan had been discovered.

301

Chapter 16

Was it an eerie silence rather than a sound that had awoken him? Suddenly awake and alert, King Yusuf directed swift eyes around his bedchamber in the Alhambra palace, wishing for once that the lamplight were brighter. Nothing stirred in the rosy glow of the four lamps lighting the chamber, part of the three thousand scented lamps burning night and day in the palace. No intruder stalked the white marble floors covered with huge burgundy carpets patterned in pink, white and green flowers within a black oval frame, nor crouched behind the divans or the low filigreed marble tables, their tops inlaid with mother-of-pearl mosaics. The ivory and gold ornaments in the wall-niches, the rich Flemish tapestries adorning the walls were undisturbed, as they had been when he had fallen asleep, alone, several hours ago.

His huge divan bed suddenly felt warm in spite of the coolness of the smooth gold silk bedsheets and cushions on which he lay. It was going to be a hot summer. In the days of the Moorish Empire, the rulers had spent the summer months in the north where it was cooler. He flung aside the covering sheet, dropped a bare hand over the side of the divan to relax his body.

It would not be long now before he would be summering in Pamplona. He had received word from Fez, where King Abu Hassan still ruled, that his brother in Islam was now ready to avenge his bitter defeat eleven years ago at the Battle of Salado, which had ended his successful foray into the eastern Mediterranean region of Spain and in which his greatest general, Abdul Malik, had been killed. Thirty-one days from now, at the end of the Christian calendar month of July, fifty thousand Moorish troops would cross over from Morocco to Algeciras and advance to Granada to commence their *jihad* against the infidel Christians.

King Yusuf was still elated at the news. Perhaps he would find his son, Prince Ahmed, when he took Toledo. The prince must be there, since he had fled with that deaf-mute, Prince Juan. King Yusuf had absolutely no news of the two fugitive princes. Despite his most widespread inquiries, they had vanished like eagles over a mountain top. How could they have done it? Could they be dead, somewhere in the wilderness? His stomach cramped at the thought. What good would his conquests be if he had no heir to succeed him? And without a legal heir, the possibility of his being assassinated multiplied with every hectare of land he conquered. He feared no threat from Abu Hassan, who, being interested only in expanding the territories of Islam, in rape and in plunder, posed no threat to the future ruler of Spain. It was the enemies within the palace that King Yusuf feared. His Prime Minister, Farouk Riswan, the man who had once helped him gain the throne, had of late become conspiratorial. Tall and gaunt, with a skeletal face and the pale brown eyes of a fox, Farouk Riswan surely had his own ambitions, now that there was no legal heir to the throne of Granada.

King Yusuf had realized over the past months that his decision to isolate his son from the world in order to prevent his experiencing the distinctive emotion of love had been worse than wrong. It had been disastrous. He also knew now that, in denying Prince Ahmed love, he had deprived himself of it as well. His own horoscope should have been examined nineteen years ago, side by side with that of the newly-born Prince Mo-Ahmed al Kamal!

Now he was left with nothing but *jihad*, conquest, the

hope of attaining Paradise in consequence, or reaching it instantly by being killed in battle for the holy cause. His life had become curiously empty. Not all the great achievements of his reign could fill it. Mariam, the child-wife he had loved most of all, who had in turn adored him, had died suddenly of a seizure. His son had fled the palace and he had not even had the satisfaction of executing that old fool, Abou bon Ebben. Almighty Allah must be punishing him for something. Or was it the Jew's curse reaching out to him from across the centuries? And yet, the astrologers were all in agreement that this was one of the best periods in his life. Astrologers, bah!

At that moment, the sickly smell smote King Yusuf's nostrils. He knew instantly what had awoken him, even as the cold, slimy thing, taut as a whipcord, crawled on the back of his right hand. The instinct of danger made him freeze, slanting only his eyes downwards to his hand.

His gaze became transfixed with horror when it fell on the asp.

Princess Beatrice gazed in consternation at the men storming into her bedroom. When she saw her purple-robed father, the king, leading them, her heart sank. The two red and white uniformed guards accompanying him she could understand, but what was Ramon Castro, the *major domo* doing with them? Trembling before the rage in her father's eyes, she looked down, awaiting the breaking of his wrath.

'So you are entertaining your family tonight?' King Pedro demanded. The quiet sneer in his voice was more deadly than any outburst.

She continued looking down silently.

'Answer us!' the king shouted.

'Yes, Your Majesty.' She had to force out the words.

'How did he get in here?'

Suddenly realizing that she had to give Prince Ahmed

time to get away, she allowed her eyes to drift to the door through which her father had just broken in.

'Lying slut.'

He raised a massive hand to strike her but, scared as she was, she did not flinch.

'Gurg . . . gurg,' Prince Juan went, stepping forward between the king and her to take the blow.

'You fucking deaf-mute, you would defy us?' the king roared. His hand swung down, thudded against Prince Juan's head, sent him sprawling sideways.

King Pedro turned towards the guards. 'Seize him! Into the inner dungeons with him. And not a word to anyone, if you value your lives.' He watched the two guards stride to the unresisting Prince Juan, grab him by either arm and literally haul him out of the room. 'If one word of this gets out, you will all be flayed alive and hung out for the ants to devour!' he roared after them. The door clicked shut. He jerked a massive head at Ramon Castro. 'Thank you, *major domo*, for having brought this . . . this betrayal promptly to our notice.'

'It is the girl, Teresa, whom we must all thank, Your Majesty.' Ramon Castro had a dry, parchment voice. 'She came here a little while earlier to see whether all was right with the princess, who had been weeping all evening and unable to fall asleep. Despite the late hour, the princess received her in the ante-room, which aroused Teresa's suspicions. These were confirmed when Teresa heard a knocking within the bedroom and noted that it had agitated the princess. Suspecting that there was an intruder in the bedroom of whom the princess was aware, she sought me out in my quarters immediately. Fortunately, I have been sleeping in the palace these days,' he bared yellow teeth in an unctuous smile, 'the better to perform my duties at this most important time for all of us in Toledo, indeed in our entire kingdom. As you know,

305

I thought the matter to be of sufficient urgency to warrant Your Majesty's immediate and personal attention.'

She had been betrayed by Teresa, the young woman towards whose plight she had been so sympathetic! Princess Beatrice went chill, then numb with shock. Was this the way of the world? No gratitude, no honour. Were all people like this, or was it just the privilege of the underprivileged to sink so low? Why had Teresa done this? Obviously to curry favour with her lover and somehow get him to accept responsibility for the unborn child.

'You shall be amply rewarded for this, *major domo*.' The words confirmed Princess Beatrice's conjecture before King Pedro paused. 'You realize how important it is that this entire matter be kept a secret,' he growled. 'Impress this need on the girl. What did you say her name was?'

'Teresa, Your Majesty.'

'What was Prince Juan doing here tonight? How did he get in?' King Pedro demanded fiercely of Princess Beatrice. Receiving no response he slowly nodded a grim head. He kept a menacing gaze on her. 'Leave us now, *major domo*, so we can find out,' he commanded Castro, and the door clicked shut. King Pedro's fierce eyes flew to the wall which held the panel through which Prince Juan had entered. Only he shared its secret with her and her mother. Her heart stopped beating, her breath caught. Prince Ahmed could still be waiting behind the door.

With Princess Beatrice and Prince Juan obviously in mortal danger, Prince Ahmed's first instinct was to batter on the sliding panel, demanding entrance. The folly of such a move immediately emerged, however, leaving his brain cool and clear as mirrored water. Emotion rippled in. He should at least remain where he was, without deserting a comrade. But then the need to keep his oath to Prince Juan intruded. Wisdom caused him to grab the flaming torch from its socket and swing round towards the steps. The torch sputtered and spat as he hastened down, the odour of resin strong in his nostrils. The muffled roaring of a man in the bedroom began to ebb before he was halfway down. Bathed in sweat, he became conscious of his own odour of fear-sweat.

As he sped along the narrow tunnel, his brain became suspended above a torn, anxious heart, brain and heart moving along on two parallel lines, with him in between: fear of pursuit, the need to get away fast, racing thoughts as to how he could rescue Princess Beatrice. He barely noticed the dead rodents, scurrying feet and dreadful smells of defecation and rotting animal corpses. Crowded by his thoughts, the roar-flow and splash of the river reaching his ears told him that he had arrived at the tunnel entrance. He made for the lighter patch of the opening. Once there, he used the little torch lever to extinguish it and placed it back in its socket. Suddenly blind in the instant blackness, he stumbled out, tripped on a stone, prevented himself from falling with outstretched arms placed on the ground.

He would not replace the rock that guarded the tunnel's entrance, in case he needed to use the tunnel again. How were Princess Beatrice and Prince Juan faring? The question agitated him. Dear Allah help them.

The cool, clean air outside was healing as an *imam*'s blessing, but only physically. Guilt and fear prevented him from enjoying the midnight blue sky above him, the scent of eucalyptus from tall, dark trees and the rustle of branches before a breeze. He stood awhile, breathing deeply, clearing the noxious air from his lungs. He scanned the highway for swift waves of its darkness that would announce a pursuit from the palace gates.

He clambered upriver along the rocky bank until he reached a point about twice the distance from the dark outline of the Roman bridge. Floating across from here, he would be going downstream again and could hit the opposite bank near where Prince Juan and he had left their shoes.

This time, in spite of his fear of water, he welcomed its cold, tumbling embrace. As he floated, propelling himself diagonally across the current, plans began criss-crossing his brain, more clear than ever now. His head struck a rock. Sharp pain jerked him back to the reality of the present. He propelled himself round, slowly dropped his legs. Blessed relief, his feet touched firm ground. It did not matter that he was soaked to the skin again.

Thanks be to Thee, Almighty Allah.

He stood on the bank, breathing deeply, the air cold to his distending nostrils. His eyes immediately fell on his shoes. He sat down on a rock and put them on. He rose to his feet, noticed Prince Juan's shoes. His breath caught. He picked up the shoes, held them to his chest. They were cold and hard as the dungeons of the Alhambra palace which he had once been permitted to visit when he was still a boy. His throat tightened with anguish. He lifted his eyes to the unfeeling heavens and swore an oath before Almighty Allah. He would rescue Prince Juan or die in the attempt.

Chill horror froze King Yusuf I only for a second. Then his panic fled. Eyes still slanted sideways at the asp, he calmly assessed what he should do. One move, the slightest move, and the snake would strike with the speed of lightning. He held his breath. Someone had introduced the snake into his bedroom, knowing it would seek the warmth of the bed. An old trick of assassins.

Let the reptile come, his instinct told him, but prevent it from striking. How? Body coiled around his arm, the head was now at his elbow. Sharp, eager eyes darted over the top of the bed, the tongue flickered. Could he hypnotize the creature? Stupid thought. What should he do?

The answer came in an instant, out of nowhere.

His left arm was beside him. Allah be praised, it was not under the covers. He fixed his mind on the elbow joint. Desperately holding his upper arm still, he bent the lower arm at the elbow. Keeping it totally relaxed, slowly, ever so slowly he raised it until the fingertips almost touched his shoulder. The asp had stopped its cold creep on his bare arm, appeared to be surveying him with its head slanted. Some instinct had warned the creature of danger.

Keeping his body relaxed and perfectly still, King Yusuf inched his hand towards the snake, allowing it to move almost of its own volition, even keeping his mind blank. When his hand was close enough, he stopped. He was bathed in sweat. Pray Allah, his hand would not slip.

In one lightning move, he gripped the asp's neck. It struck on the instant, but too late. King Yusuf's hand held it with the strength of desperation. The obscene little mouth opened. The tongue forked out, remained rigid. The slimy body tightened on his arm in a desperate reflex, then writhed, struggling to break free of King Yusuf's deadly grip. The king began breathing again, in great gasps. Sweat broke out anew on his face and body. Jaws clenched, eyes almost popping out of their sockets with the constricted effort, he kept squeezing ferociously, desperately willing strong fingers to the base of the palm. The reptilian body finally went limp.

Breathing heavily with sheer relief, King Yusuf sat up, uncoiled the evil thing from around his arm. Almighty Allah had saved him. His mind flickered to Queen Cleopatra of Egypt who held an asp to her bosom when she wished to die. But how did a North African asp get to Granada and enter the royal bedchamber?

Someone in the palace wanted to kill him.

* * *

Although he was cold sober now after the night's drinking, King Pedro was still finding it hard to control his fury.

He was one of those who know immediate rage at being crossed, but years of ruling the nation had taught him to hold it in check. Kings should never respond to the emotion of the moment. Once he had control of himself, however, and the need for wisdom or cunning had abated, the anger would return, multiplied for having been held in check, like caged flood-waters through a broken dam. Then the cruel desire to wound would surface.

An added reason for retaining his composure now was a warning instinct. Others besides his son, Prince Juan, must be involved. If so, it should be easy to capture them too.

Then the possibility of an actual plot against him struck King Pedro. What more logical than that the seemingly Christian Prince Juan was the spearhead of a plot to assassinate him and succeed to the throne? Such a plot could have Moorish backing, freedom being Prince Juan's reward.

The answers lay in the tunnel behind the secret door. Besides him, only Maria de Padilla and their daughter, Princess Beatrice, knew of its existence. How and when had Prince Juan discovered it?

His suspicions brought the need for caution, restrained the expression of renewed fury. Tightening the tasselled belt of his robe, he began striding decisively towards the panel in the wall.

'No! No! *Padre*, no!' Hands together in supplication, tears streaming down her cheeks, Princess Beatrice flung herself between him and the panel. He paused, surprised at the interference. The young woman was distraught, her long golden hair dishevelled. 'I beg you not to enter the tunnel,' she insisted.

So Princess Beatrice was also involved in the plot.

Suspicion crashed into certainty, released his innate cruelty. With one move of a massive arm, he swept his daughter away from him, sent her spinning sideways. A cry of pain escaped her, brought him fierce satisfaction.

He pressed the spot in the wall. The panel began to move. As he gazed into the darkness of the landing, the acrid stench of burnt resin smote his nostrils, total silence reached his ears.

'You think there are others in the tunnel, *Padre*.' Prince Beatrice's voice came from behind him. It was so quiet and calm, the texture and accent so much that of his beloved Maria de Padilla that it made him pause. The dim shaft of light from the bedroom fell on the outlines of the unlit torch on its sconce, the other sconce empty.

'You could place yourself in mortal danger by entering the tunnel alone.' He was astonished at the quiet command in her voice. She sounded like a seeress. Was this really his daughter speaking? The raging flood waters of his anger died down to a simmer. 'You wish to check as to whether there were others with Prince Juan. We must indeed assume that there are others, but why risk your life before an assassin's dagger in that miserable stinking tunnel, where you could bleed to death alone and no one the wiser? In which event, history would pity you.'

The words struck home. He swung around. 'We shall get the guards,' he growled. 'But we thank you for the warning.' His eyes fell on her. She lay half-reclining against the wall from his blow. A red blotch flamed on her white cheek. It was the expression in her eyes that transfixed him. An indeterminate blue in the lamplight, they were so deep, unafraid, so fixed and cold, as to be eerie. Dimly he comprehended that he should never have struck her. She had never been subjected to physical violence before. He had no regret for it, but could not escape the knowledge that he had lost what little he had of her forever. Memories of her childhood intruded,

311

romps in the royal nursery, a laughing child riding on his back while he pretended to be a horse, a contented Maria de Padilla quietly looking on. And were lost too, as her voice, that of the child who had suddenly grown up, broke the spell. 'If you summon the guards, Sire, you will have defeated your own need for secrecy. My brother did come to visit me. He only wanted to discover how you would react to the return of a mutilated son.' She jerked her head at the writing materials on the desk. 'As you can see, we had no time for questions and answers, but Prince Juan would never plot to overthrow you. He is too gentle and saintly and, yes, too strong for treachery.'

The truth of her words smote him. He strode to the desk, examined the blank writing material, nodded his satisfaction. 'How did he know the secret of the tunnel?'

'He used to visit me regularly through it after you so . . . cruelly . . . imprisoned me in these quarters. He is the only human who really loves me.'

'Your mother loves you,' he cut in roughly.

'Forgive me for contradicting you, *mi padre* and Sire, but you are wrong.' An open smile, with no laughter in it, revealed white teeth. 'My *madre* loves you so completely that there is no room in her heart for any other love. Her love and loyalty for you transcend those she gives to God.'

He gazed at her in astonishment. She had touched him in the one place that was totally removed from wisdom or cunning, anger and cruelty. Maria de Padilla, the one all-consuming love of his life. His link with heaven and earth and the life hereafter. He was glad to have independent confirmation of Maria's love for him, especially from their child. 'She would sacrifice anyone, including you, for us?' His statement was a half-question.

'*Ciertamente*. Did she not sacrifice me to your desire to have me wed to someone who could help you achieve your royal goals?'

312

Detecting bitterness in her voice, he recalled Count Gaston's question. Have you consulted your daughter's wishes? It was too late now. Besides, a king must do what he has to do. He abruptly changed the subject. 'Why should we not summon the guards?' He realized that time was flying. Was his daughter deliberately delaying him so Prince Juan's comrades could get away? And yet something told him he should listen to the girl. A tiny flutter-crackle above him made his eyes flicker to the nearest hanging lamp. Tiny insects, scorched by the flame, dropped inside it.

'The success of the tourney is vital to Your Majesty.' Her voice became even more compelling. 'You have spent far too much time, energy and money to risk any loss of repute, especially at this time. If word gets around that your only son, once your heir, now a deaf-mute, escaped imprisonment by the cruel Moors only to be cast into your dungeons, it would not only ruin the entire tourney, but many of the crowned heads of Europe who are here to witness it would revile you.' Her voice turned harsh and bitter. 'They would not merely say that you are cruel. Their envy of all you have achieved as a ruler and the magnificent preparations you have made for this event, unsurpassed in the annals of Spain, would impel them to hold you to scorn. They would also call you stupid for consigning Prince Juan to the dungeons instead of seeking his co-operation to elicit important intelligence he must have of the Moors, their defences and their territories, against the time when you will be marching against them.' She paused. Her blue eyes, totally without fear, exuded a cruelty that made him shiver involuntarily.

'You yourself threatened the guards and the *major domo* just now with the direst punishment if they betrayed the events of tonight to anyone. Would you rather have yourself flayed alive instead, with honey poured over your skinless body, on an anthill, because it was you who betrayed the secret?'

Utterly dejected, Prince Ahmed collected the two horses from the stables near tourney-town, where Prince Juan and he had left them. He rode back to Aaron Levi's villa, leading the second horse with a saddle as empty as his heart felt at his comrade's plight. The starlit summer night had turned chill, but he was certain that the chill came from within him. He passed no one as he clattered along the deserted highway, the horses' hooves crisp in the silence, for by this hour of the night even roisterers had headed for their beds. The only sound was that of his mind, madly churning around for a rescue attempt and finding none.

He was so preoccupied with these thoughts that he almost passed the tall wooden gates of the high-walled villa gardens which loomed to his right through the darkness. He reined his mount sideways, edged it alongside the gates, drew his sword and started hammering with the hilt. His horse snorted violently, clearing its nostrils. Presently, a glow of torchlight appeared above the gates and a sleepy voice on the other side of the gates shouted, 'Who is it?'

He gave the password for the night: 'Conquistadore', and was rewarded by the squeaking of bolts and the rattle of a chain, followed by the creaking of the gates. A dark figure, clad in a black cloak with a hood above it, stood framed at the open entrance. The lighted torch flickering high in his left hand revealed a pointed staff held threateningly in his right.

The man recognized him, lowered his staff. 'Welcome, *señor*. You are rather late, aren't you? Been out on tourney-town, eh?'

'*Buenos dias*,' Prince Ahmed responded, for it was already a new day.

314

Still leading the riderless mount, he walked his horse through the open gates. He clip-clopped over the cobbled courtyard, past the little lodge, while the gates creaked shut behind him. The avenue ran straight to the villa, which had been built on a hillock. Its dark mass was framed against the deep blue of the night sky, above the two regular lines of dark trees, which he knew to be Italian cypresses, flanking the avenue. He reined in before the entrance colonnades running across the front of the villa. Two grooms, who had obviously been awaiting the return of the guests, rushed up to greet him. They betrayed no surprise that he had returned alone. One of the men helped him to dismount while the other led the riderless horse away. He walked through the colonnade and along the roofed entrance walkway to the door of the villa. The great carved wooden doors swung open before he could knock. A white-robed attendant wearing a black *yarmulke* on his head bowed to him.

'My master awaits you in his study.' As he took Prince Ahmed's cloak, the hawk-nosed servant's smile was white between black moustache and beard.

To Prince Ahmed's utter surprise, when he knocked and entered the study, Zurika was seated with Aaron Levi. She rose at the sound of the opening door and bowed low to greet him, while Aaron remained seated, as befitted his age.

'Zurika!' Prince Ahmed burst out as the door clicked shut behind him. 'What are you doing here at this hour of the night?'

'Where is Prince Juan?' she demanded, instead of answering his question. Her deep brown eyes had turned fearful. 'Has he gone to his room?'

He shook his head wordlessly in response, gulping to ease the ache that had started again in his throat.

'Please sit down, Prince,' Aaron Levi quietly bade him.

He took one of the two settles opposite the desk, gestured to Zurika to resume her seat.

'Where . . .?' Zurika burst out hysterically, a sob in her voice.

'You must be very tired, Prince,' Aaron Levi interrupted. 'Would you like some wine? Your clothing is wet too. Did it rain in the city tonight? Take your time and tell us what happened.' He paused, forced his mischievous smile. 'Oh, I forgot, you are forbidden liquor. How about some pomegranate juice, or some more water?'

'No, thank you.' Prince Ahmed was touched by the old man's obvious desire to put him at ease, although he must have his own fears at Prince Juan's absence.

'Is he dead?' Zurika was on the verge of tears.

'No.'

'I thank God and the Blessed Virgin Mary.'

'And I thank Jahweh,' Aaron added seriously.

Always impatient with people who launched into lengthy stories, holding back the most important facts, Prince Ahmed came directly to the point. 'He was captured by the king's guards while visiting his sister.' He went on to give details of all that had transpired that night, including the secret of the tunnel, for it was best to involve them fully since they would be his allies.

They listened without comment, the only interruption being the croak of a bullfrog from one of the ponds outside.

He had barely finished when Zurika turned to face Aaron and burst out, 'This was why I could not sleep tonight, *señor*. I had a premonition of evil. Poor Prince Juan has been moved from an Alhambra dungeon to one in the Toledo palace. We must rescue him before his father has him killed.'

Aaron Levi nodded slowly. 'But how?'

'Yes indeed, how can we rescue Prince Juan?' Prince Ahmed reiterated, helplessly. 'I have gone round and

316

round every possibility a hundred times without a conclusion. The dungeons must be too well guarded.'

'Perhaps we can buy the prince's release with ransom money,' Aaron observed thoughtfully. 'My banking colleagues tell me that King Pedro is in great need of funds for the forthcoming campaign against your kingdom, Granada, which he would like to dominate.'

Prince Ahmed was shocked. The Christians intended invading Granada! Adversity seemed to be piling up on him. It was too much. This was surely one of those periods of his life when the stars were crossed for misfortune. For a moment he wondered dismally what luck he would have in the joust. Then the reflex of his fierce resolve took over. Almighty Allah, having brought him this far, would carry him through to success, so long as he made each calamity a stepping stone to triumph with courage and determination. But he felt curiously lost without Prince Juan.

'Oh, it is supposed to be a great secret,' Aaron Levi responded. 'I am only aware of it because King Pedro demanded loans from my banker colleagues to support the campaign. But more of that later. Let us concern ourselves with Prince Juan for the moment. As I see it, the king is hardly likely to pay attention to any offer for the release of Prince Juan until the tourney is over.'

Prince Ahmed brightened. 'When I win, I could beg Prince Juan's freedom as a boon.'

'And then what?' Aaron Levi suddenly grew serious.

Up to now they had all delicately avoided the subject of Princess Beatrice. Prince Ahmed glanced at Zurika before answering, but she seemed lost in serious thought. 'Prince Juan and I had always assumed that when I won the tourney, we would be permitted to return to Granada as a matter of honour for King Pedro, when we requested it in the presence of the royalty, nobility and his own people.'

317

'I have not wanted to ask this question earlier, because Prince Juan and you are grown-ups with minds and resources to make your own decision,' Aaron Levi stated. 'The tragic event of Prince Juan's capture and incarceration, however, makes it essential for me to try and temper your reckless head-strength with a calm appraisal. Supposing you lose?'

Prince Ahmed was nonplussed. Neither Prince Juan nor he had ever considered the possibility of his losing. 'If I lose, surely I would still be accorded the honour due a combatant,' he began slowly. 'Tourneys, as I have been informed by Prince Juan, are governed by strict rules of honour, dignity being accorded to both victor and vanquished.'

Aaron Levi grunted, lifted his chin and stared down his beak nose at Prince Ahmed. 'Your father, King Yusuf, took the son of King Pedro prisoner and mutilated him. Why should King Pedro not reciprocate with King Yusuf's son? After all, is not reciprocity the basis of all diplomacy between nations?'

'Prince Juan was captured in battle. Tomorrow's event is a tourney.'

'You make a good point. Granting it, who will now touch you with his sword to vouch for your rank and fitness so you can actually participate?'

'That presents a problem with which I have been jousting,' Prince Ahmed smiled faintly at the word, 'since leaving the Toledo palace. I have decided to declare myself a prince and heir to the Granada throne. I am well fitted by rank, station and the absence of any ill-repute to stand on my own as a challenger.'

'By the rules, you are a heretic Muslim.'

'And you are an infidel Jew,' Prince Ahmed snarled back, giving way to frustration at last.

Aaron merely grinned. 'A heretic Muslim and an infidel Jew making common cause at the moment.'

'They should be able to do so without calling each other names.'

'I did not call you the name, Prince. I merely pointed out what you would be to King Pedro. You on the other hand . . .' He shrugged bony shoulders.

Prince Ahmed knew instant contrition. He alone had levelled the epithet when he had so much to be grateful for to this old Jew. 'You are right and I am sorry. Please forgive me,' he begged.

'You have been through much. You are becoming overwrought.'

'Nothing should be too much for good manners, courtesy and gratitude.'

'Spoken like a prince. We are family here and need no gratitude, but good manners and courtesy are more essential within a family than with the outside world. Do you not agree?'

'Prince Ahmed shall take part in the joust by saying who he really is,' Zurika suddenly intervened.

Prince Ahmed and Aaron Levi both turned to look at her simultaneously, their attention commanded by the quiet certainty in her voice.

'You, Prince Ahmed, will reveal your rank at the joust, then challenge only the victor, offering your life if you lose,' Zurika proceeded, as if she were in a trance. 'That they will not refuse. And if they do, the victor would have to urge it or be dubbed a coward.' Her eyes drifted to Aaron Levi. 'You once showed me plans of the Toledo palace, *señor*. You said they were given to you by the man who drew them up for King Pedro when you gave a loan to the king to build some improvements. Do you still have them? They must show where the dungeons are located.'

Aaron's grey brows creased in puzzlement. He pushed back his black *yarmulke* to scratch his forehead. 'Why do you want the plans?'

319

'In our gypsy lore, there is a tale of a dancing girl who rescued her lover from the dungeons of a Moorish king's palace.'

Prince Ahmed knew the story. It was but a fable, yet an absurd hope sparked within him and his brain, no longer weary, began to work furiously on translating the fable into reality as he listened to Zurika unfolding her plan.

When she had finished, he glowed with admiration for her. Not yet fully comprehending the nature of love, it never struck him that if the plan did not work, he might still marry Princess Beatrice, when Zurika, his friend and helpmate, would suffer the tortures of the damned.

Chapter 17

The day of the tourney had arrived. Prince Ahmed lay
back in the warm water with which the wooden bath in
the privy area attached to his bedroom in the villa had
just been filled, trying to compose his thoughts. Though
dawn had not broken, the first cooing of doves, the
occasional hoarse caw of a rook and the chatter of
magpies were just beginning. Peaceful sounds from an
outside world. In his immediate world, the lapping of the
sandalwood scented water against the sides of the tub
each time he moved and the barely perceptible scrape of
the scrubbing stone wielded by Simeon, the fair-skinned
young Jewish protégé whom Aaron Levi had allotted to
serve him and be his squire today, were gentle reminders
of turmoil and suspense.

Today's tourney would decide his destiny, perhaps the
future of Spain. After he had slept a few hours following
his return to the villa from the tragic mission to the
palace, Zurika, Aaron Levi and he had spent the rest of
the morning and afternoon going over Zurika's plan. This
included a visit by Aaron Levi, accompanied by Zurika,
to the palace, for whatever scouting could possibly be
done and a bribe by one of Aaron's banker colleagues to
a highly placed guard captain for a palace pass and
information as to the guard roster. He had not gone with
them, but slept for three hours before practising assidu-
ously for the joust, concentrating on skilful manoeuvrings
of his white charger to avoid the thrust of an opposing
lance, of his body to allow the lance to glide off it, and
charging the wooden dummies that had already been set
in place, to shatter lances.

Whatever he did, he could not erase the nagging concern at Prince Juan's fate and its possible consequences for Princess Beatrice. The one comforting thought was that King Pedro would not harm the princess, because she was today's prize, and he would see this beautiful lady again today. He would rescue her somehow; her fate should someone else win the tourney filled him with even fiercer determination. He was fit and ready for the fray, having forced himself to eat well in the face of the dismal prison slops which Prince Juan would be forcing himself to swallow, and had slept well for eight hours, so that his body felt relaxed and rested.

The lapping of the water brought to Prince Ahmed's mind the ceremonial bath before knighthood. Abou bon Ebben had insisted that he read the manuscript of the old French poem entitled *Hue de Tabarie*, written about a hundred years earlier, which had given an accurate description of the rites to be observed for admittance to the dignity of knighthood. He went over details of the poem in his head.

Hugh, Prince of Tiberias, is a prisoner of Grand Sultan Saladin. The sultan agrees to allow the prince to return to his native land on condition that he delivers a ransom to the sultan, which he is given three years to collect. Just before Prince Hugh leaves, the sultan requests that Prince Hugh, as a knight, confer on him, the sultan, the dignity of knighthood.

Since the sultan is an infidel, Prince Hugh at first objects. When he finally yields, he makes the sultan go through the several rites, acting not in his princely capacity but by virtue of his knightly status.

He dresses the sultan's hair and beard, then takes him to a bath, which he must leave only when he is free of depravity and cleansed from sin, like a child raised from the baptismal font; he must thereafter unfailingly practise honesty, courtesy and benevolence, and must earn the regard of all men. He then lays the sultan on a bed, saying, 'This is a symbol of the bed of rest in paradise, which is attainable through chivalric demeanour and is denied the unrighteous.'

When the sultan rises from the bed, Prince Hugh dresses him in white linen, enjoining him: 'This is the sign of the cleanliness in which you shall keep your body in this life, if you wish to be received by God.' He invests the sultan with a scarlet cloak: 'This colour represents the blood you must be ready to shed at all times in the service of God and in defence of the church.' He places shoes on the sultan's feet: 'This black covering of your feet must ever remind you of death, of the earth from which you have been fashioned, to which you shall return. Therefore cherish no pride, which is unbecoming in a knight, rather adhere to simplicity and singleness of purpose.'

The sultan rises. Prince Hugh girds him with a white cincture, repeating the injunction of external cleanliness, adding that the sultan's body must remain in virgin purity, free from every pollution and licence, which he should especially abhor.

Prince Hugh fastens the gilded spurs on the sultan's feet: 'You shall be swift and spirited as the charger pressed by spurs, in the race to serve God and perform your chivalric duties.' He hands the sultan the two-edged sword: 'One edge is for your self-defence, the other must always serve to protect the poor from being the downtrodden of the rich, the weak from mistreatment by the strong.'

Finally, Prince Hugh covers the head of the sultan with a white cap, saying, 'Thy soul shall be clean and spotless as this head-dress, unaffected by cravings of the flesh, thy soul which must be surrendered to God on the day of judgment so it may enter paradise.'

Prince Hugh withholds the final ceremony, the accolade, from the sultan, which was normally given by tapping the shoulder three times with a sword, followed by a blow on the face to remind the new knight that the knight bestowing the honour was charging him with the duties of his high rank. Prince Hugh avers that, being a prisoner, he cannot bestow the accolade on the Sultan Saladin, but he charges the sultan with fulfilling his knightly duties of acting with justice, courtesy and piety and of being charitable to the poor.

In the face of such requirements for knights, would he, Prince Ahmed, be admitted to the lists? The dignity of knighthood was conferred in Europe on all qualified young men when they reached the age of twenty-one. In Spain, the age was twenty. He, Prince Ahmed, was only eighteen. The conferment did not always require elaborate ceremonial. Kings often conferred knighthood, with or without the accolade, on the field of battle, so their men would perform more heroically.

And the selfishness of people who wielded power could prevent his participation in the tourney today. Those like the white Christian kings of Spain who least practised the knightly virtues were the most likely to raise objections to a lack of qualifications in others, however well-born. Perhaps they needed such hypocrisy to remain in power, substituting legal interpretations of laws, customs, traditions and ceremonial for the cardinal knightly virtues and genuine strength.

Seated next to her mother, Maria de Padilla, in the ladies' enclosure on the west side of the arena, Princess Beatrice was torn by many emotions, some of them quite conflicting. Yet she maintained the outward composure to which she had been trained through the years, an extension of the elegant lines of her clothes, over which the court dressmakers had laboured many a day. She wore a long, flowing, sleeveless white satin robe with a three-inch border of gold silk studded with pearls. Held in place above her breasts by a huge mother-of-pearl clasp, the robe spread along her shoulder bones beneath a necklace of three strands of pearls that followed the line of the robe instead of circling her throat, the effect of which, the chief dressmaker had said, was to accentuate the long, swan-like shape of her neck. The gold of the robe's border was a perfect match for her shiny gold hair hanging down behind her in free waves to her waist, from the coronet of pearls around her head. Her ankle-length dress was of sheer silk embellished only by six single rows each of three pearls, running down its centre to the gold shoes on her feet.

'You look absolutely virginal,' her mother had said when she had surveyed her in her palace bedroom that morning.

A virginal offering to my father's ambitions, Princess Beatrice had reflected bitterly beneath her appreciative smile, the Vestal virgin being sacrificed to barbarians for the good of Rome. Yesterday had been a day of unbelievable turmoil for her. Not being used to late hours, she was not merely sick at heart from the sad events of the previous night, but also exhausted from the unwonted physical, mental and emotional strain of preparing for the tourney. Pity for Prince Juan, excitement at having met the prince of her dreams and certainty that Prince Ahmed would somehow rescue her, however, dominated her abhorrence of the event ahead and its dire consequences for her. Unable to sleep or rest, she had spent much of the day kneeling on her *prie-dieu* praying to God and the Blessed Virgin for the safety of her brother and the pagan prince with whom she had fallen in love and for the strength to accept any fate that might befall her, which she would gladly endure to secure the safety of the two princes.

'You cannot bargain with God,' the Blessed Virgin had reminded her gently.

'Then I beg of you to give me all I desire, Holy Mother.'
The blue-robed statue had merely smiled.

She had slept well last night though, the sleep of sheer exhaustion and had felt more rested by the time she awoke. As she walked with her mother down the palace corridors, she had been conscious of the admiring glances of the courtiers, guards and attendants they passed. She heard the faint gasps at her beauty without satisfaction. The rich decor of the wall murals, paintings, pedestals, statues and ornaments filled her with wonder. It had been over four years since she was permitted these areas and all of it seemed new, incredibly rich and very ornate to her. Underlying it all was bitterness at the thought that she was finally being permitted freedom from the sequestered walls of the ladies' quarters only to face the greater bondage of being literally sold to the best contender at the jousts.

She and her mother shared a carriage drawn by four white horses. Once the royal carriages, headed by that of her father, King Pedro, preceded by the cavalry escort, cleared the eastern palace gates and entered the broad avenue that circled the entire city and headed towards the Puente de Alcantara bridge across the River Tagus, a distant din, which came from the new tourney-town, was foregrounded by the cheers of the people who had lined the streets for a glimpse of royalty and its inevitable splendour, rising above the rattle of carriage wheels and the clatter of horses' hooves on the cobbled street.

Her first impression of the world outside the palace was of noise. In addition, for the first time in her life she was experiencing the dreadful odours of slop, defecation and rotting garbage. Holding her ambergris-scented pomander to her nose, she gazed at the tall green cypresses lining the avenue with the blue vault of heaven above, its fleecy white clouds soft with silence, dimly perceiving what man had done to God's creation.

Tourney-town and the arena had brought to her mind the tower of Babel, though this did not diminish her interest in everything about her. Royalty dressed in the most gorgeous finery filled their enclosure, while her father looked simply magnificent, a great ferocious creature, dressed in cloth of gold and purple, glittering with rubies and amethysts, his golden crown giving him added majesty.

The ladies seated in their separate enclosure were dressed in more subdued colours, her mother in blue, Princess Mathilde in dove grey, providing an elegant contrast to the peacock-feathered men who strutted about.

Princess Beatrice's seat was between those of her mother and Princess Mathilde, the two *Grandes Dames* of the tourney. The only male in the enclosure was Count Gaston, the *chevalier d'honneur*, dressed in full armour. The count's dark, haunted eyes while he was bending down to bow over the hand she extended to him, had stirred Princess Beatrice. She had sensed compassion combined with respectful appreciation in his glance and instinctively felt that he was on her side, a man she could trust. She liked the clean lines of his hatchet face, with its dark moustache and pointed beard. He was the Chancellor of King Charles the Bad, the contestant she feared most. If she did not take her own life and had to submit to King Charles as the victor, would she not have a friend in Count Gaston?

She was seeing men in the mass for the first time in years. They did not impress her. Any one of them could be her enemy. When the twenty contestants had been formally presented to the two *Dames* and herself, there was not one that had not caused her to shudder; even the golden-haired Danish prince and the dark-visaged Swabian count were potential rapists and despoilers. At this stage, utter loneliness touched her spirit and a soul-weariness settled over her whole being. She was alone in the black void of a noisy crowd on a day of silver sunshine, with the stink of dust and distant night soil mingling with scents of gardenia, musk and myrrh. Somewhere within that void, the knowledge of Prince Ahmed hovered, extending a ray of hope, a shaft of brilliant reality from its despairing depths.

While all the other ladies seemed to glow in the contests, Princess Beatrice, hating violence, felt violated. Was all of it for her? The unseating, the wounding, everything short of death? And yet the unique scene unfolding before her was fascinating. She might never see the like again. She could not resist moments of pride that all of it centred on her.

The tourney commenced immediately the platform enclosure allotted to the ladies was filled. Count Gaston, holding his symbol of office at the top of his lance, mounted a white horse and left his place to accompany the four judges, also on white horses, on their ride round the lists to inspect the preparations for combat. A space in the centre had been corded off and the tourneyers stood on the opposite side of it. Count Gaston placed his lance of office in a slot on the ground in front of the ladies' platform and rejoined the judges. All five men then rode into the central space, where one of the judges removed Count Gaston's helmet and rode back to place it on his lance. The judges then withdrew to their own platform, while Count Gaston's escort rode into the space and took their places behind the count.

The tourneyers, who had been divided into two to represent challenges and acceptances, now drew up in battle array, facing each other at opposite ends of the cords dividing the lists. Their standard bearers beside them bore a colourful display. Their mounted attendants, in light body armour and helmets, carried the shafts of lances behind them, with foot attendants in the rear.

Heralds placed in the intermediate space of the divided lists proclaimed masters and events. As each name was announced, trumpeters immediately sounded fanfares that reached for the skies. The crowds began roaring in anticipation, the contestants shouted their battlecries, brandishing their swords. All of it made a most fearful din.

Suddenly, Princess Beatrice was struck by a totally new aspect of the tourney. It was all so utterly stupid. Without even the dignity of real battle, why did men have to wear fancy dress and behave like mummers?

Count Gaston cavorted his white horse, raised a gauntleted hand. In the hush that gradually settled, the braying of a mule and the bleating of a goat in the distance jagged the air.

The king-at-arms, a giant count named Fernando, also in full armour, rode up on a black charger. He reined in his mount and proclaimed the rules of the tournament in stentorian tones. At the direction of the judges, he thrice repeated the order to cut the cords dividing the lists. Each standard-bearer called out the *mot de guerre* of his master. The trumpeters jointly sounded a long fanfare for the first part of the event, the tournament *en masse*, in which the two parties at opposite ends of the lists would charge each other.

The battle began with the thudding of fierce hooves.

At this point Princess Beatrice closed her eyes. She simply could not bear to witness the ensuing violence. She knew that whenever a lance was properly aimed and struck the opponent's body, the lance shattered and the opponent was unhorsed. Sometimes both combatants shattered their lances and unhorsed each other, to return with fresh lances for a second charge. Any combatant who was unhorsed or did not shatter his lance was considered beaten.

As the morning wore on, Princess Beatrice heard the

names of the victors announced. This she did not want to shut out, for her entire life depended on it. She kept wondering when and whether Prince Ahmed would appear. She had faith that he would, as surely as Horn had emerged to rescue Rymenhilde.

Zurika was dressed in her red and white dancer's costume, tight at the breast and waist, flaring to a full skirt with rows of scallops ending at calf-length. Carrying a wicker hamper in hand, she marched into the palace with all the self-assurance of the gypsy, using the pass Aaron Levi had obtained to gain entry, her mission ostensibly being to give the prison guards a special treat of food and wine from the palace to compensate for what they were missing at the tourney. As she, Aaron Levi and Prince Ahmed had conjectured, the Toledo palace was virtually deserted this morning. Even the sentry details were sparse, consisting mostly of ancients, those at the gates being obviously morose at missing the fun outside.

Once within the palace gates, she cut across the gardens towards the northeast side where the dungeons were located near the main guard quarters, thus avoiding the guards in the palace itself, who would have been more alert. She reached the small prison building which contained the stocks without even being challenged again. The palace dungeons were reserved exclusively for high-ranking political offenders, while the main prisons in the city had their own cells and dungeons to house common criminals.

The squat, single-storey white-washed structure was surrounded by a high wall, the northern and eastern sides of which were part of the main palace walls. It was only mid-morning, but the air was already warm. She could imagine the discomfort of prisoners and guards alike when the heat of the afternoon struck, because no breeze could penetrate these walls. The suffering of the inmates of the dungeons, including poor Prince Juan, was unimaginable.

She was beginning to sweat by the time she knocked on the huge, iron-ribbed doors set into the western wall. There was no response. Was the prison unguarded? She knocked again, more insistently this time.

A metal latch on the door clicked open. 'Who are you?' a hoarse voice growled. 'What do you want?'

A swarthy face, framed in the small opening, glared at her. The sight of tangled black hair and hot, red-rimmed eyes brought the true reality of her mission to her, turned the sweat cold. Only the most ruthless guards would man this prison. The only persons who knew of her presence here, Aaron Levi and Prince Ahmed, had no access to the palace. Terror struck at her entrails and her legs went weak. She half-turned to run away.

The thought of Prince Juan at the mercy of such wretches steadied her. 'I am a messenger of goodwill from the palace,' she responded boldly. She placed the hamper, which was beginning to get heavier by the moment, on the ground.

The red eyes surveyed her, took in her figure, stripped off her red and white dress, making her feel naked. 'What goodwill is there in this miserable world, least of all in palaces?' He smirked hideously. 'Unless you have brought it between your legs.'

His coarse words enraged her. She wished she could draw her long knife, her father's knife, and slice off his filthy tongue. Her courage fully restored by anger, she pointed at the hamper. 'I was not sent by the king to cater to your gutter mind,' she spat out, then paused, controlling herself. 'When you see what the palace has sent you, your faith will be restored.' As her anger subsided before the demand of her mission, fear returned. She longed to be back in the safety of the gypsy caves in Granada.

331

Other than the threat from Majo, she had never needed to know the fear of men before.

'And who would be sending us good things from the palace?' the man inquired, his glance now suspicious.

'Whoever directed me must have done so on the personal orders of the king, who may have a reputation for cruelty towards those who oppose or offend him, but is full of compassion for his own.'

'What do you have in there?' There was less suspicion in the voice now, but its surliness was obviously natural to the man.

'Bread and cheese, capon pasties and two flagons of good red wine.'

'Good enough, but why were they sent through you, a woman, young and alone?' The red eyes flamed. 'And pretty withal.'

'Because all the male kitchen help and guards have gone to the tourney, leaving behind only a small staff, and the few remaining males are required for sentry duty.' She stamped an impatient foot. 'But enough of these questions. If you do not let me in I shall take the hamper back and you will be answerable to your fellow guards and to my masters.'

'All right, all right. No need to get nasty. A wight has his job to do.' The face disappeared. Lifted hasps clacked, drawn bolts screeched and a small wicket door to her left swung open.

She bent down, picked up the hamper. The guard held the door open for her to step through. She paused to survey her surroundings. Dressed in the white pantaloons of the prison guards' uniform, the man's tunic was open at the chest revealing a mass of crinkly black hair. He was as burly as he was swarthy and his body stank of stale acid sweat. He made a mock bow, one hand to his heart, the other outflung as she stood before him. 'I am Corporal Miguel Pedro, your humble servant. This way, milady.'

He came erect, grinned maliciously, revealing discoloured teeth, eyed her with open lust. 'Such a tasteful morsel too.' The door creaked shut, the bolt screeched again, the hasp clacked.

The fear in her stomach turned chill. Here she was, shut in a small white flagstone courtyard shaded by two green chestnut trees, with a man who obviously lusted for her body and, if the information Aaron Levi had obtained was correct, three more guards besides. Her one security against rape would be their belief that she was a palace servant. Otherwise, they could murder her and no one would be any the wiser. Instinct warned her to nip any aggression in the bud. She drew a deep breath, quieted her heartbeat and faced the corporal squarely. 'Look, *señor*, I am a poor girl with a job to do, just like you. Why don't you attend to your work and let me do mine?' She paused for effect. 'Besides, I am not here just to deliver food and wine. I'm a dancer too and have been commanded to entertain you and your fellow guards, who will certainly not approve your delaying their food, drink and entertainment.'

To her relief, the lechery left his eyes and he idly scratched his chest, reflecting. 'I will take you to Sergeant Villejo,' he said. 'Follow me.' He headed for the door of the low building, the front room of which seemed almost bare through the grilled windows.

She followed his clacking steps, conscious of the sun on her face and its white glare on the flagstones, fearful of entering the enclosed building. A fly buzzed at the tip of her nose and she shook it off with a toss of her head. A bird whistled from one of the chestnut trees. Then they were at the door, the reek of Pedro's sweat more penetrating.

The door creaked open. 'A young *señorita* to see you, Sergeant,' Pedro announced. 'Says she is a dancer, sent by the palace with food and wine.'

She stepped into the shade of a small room with a low roof supported by black rafters, its whitewashed walls discoloured. The floor had been swept clean, but the air smelled horribly of feet encased too long in boots. The furniture consisted only of a few settles against the walls and a plain deal wood table opposite her, at which a small man dressed in the prison guards' uniform sat with his feet on the table, biting his fingernails. Her first impression of his face was the luxuriant ginger moustaches. Small mean eyes, almost yellow, widened at seeing her. Obviously more interested in her body than her mission, he continued surveying her from where he sat, then began nodding slowly.

This was a ferret perpetually in rut. Zurika sensed real danger from him. She had already received her quota of good men from God and the Blessed Virgin in the two princes and Aaron Levi: had the time now come to pay for it? Once again, the thought of Prince Juan gave her strength. I am a gypsy, she reflected fiercely. I can overcome these sex-craved men with my instinct and cunning. But the fear remained.

'My name is Carmenita,' she declared, feigning boldness. 'You must be Sergeant Villejo.' She placed her hamper on the floor and took out the pass she had tucked into her right sleeve. 'I have been instructed by my master, the *major domo*, who I understand was acting on the command of His Majesty the King, to bring you and your men food, wine and entertainment.' She cleared her throat. 'His Majesty is extending this bounty to all those who have to remain on duty for him, while everyone else is at the *fiesta*.'

He made no reply, merely continued staring at her with unwinking yellow eyes. Ignoring him, she squatted to open the hamper, noticed the huge bunch of keys hanging from a nail in the wall behind him. Excitement shot through her. The keys to the prison, the cells and the dungeon! She raised the lid of the hamper, reached for the two small-necked, clay flagons of wine, stood up and placed them clattering on the table, followed by the container of food, stacking the bread and empty platters beside it. The aroma of baking from the bread was somehow reassuring after the disgusting stink of the room.

Corporal Pedro made a sideways dart towards the food. Sergeant Villejo raised the sole of a swift foot, thrust him back, then lowered both feet and leaned forward. 'Time enough for the food,' he declared quietly, his eyes still on Zurika. His voice was thin and dry, ominous. 'Let us first taste the wine.' He leaned forward, reached for the flagon nearest to him, removed the stopper. He grasped the handle, palm outward, raised the flagon, inverted it and drank deeply. '*Bueno*!' he exclaimed, replacing the flagon on the table. He smacked his lips, wiped red wine drops off them with the back of his hand. 'Your turn next, Pedro.' He nodded towards the flagon.

The burly guard looked lecherously at Zurika. 'I can't wait for it, Sergeant.' Zurika shuddered at the implication.

Sergeant Villejo grinned. 'That will come in good time.' He stretched a hand to fish out a capon pasty, held it between thumb and forefinger, surveying it. He sniffed. 'Smells good, but a young cunt smells sweeter.' He deliberately avoided looking at her, ran a tongue suggestively over the pasty, crunched it, smack-slurped, flakes of pastry dropping on the table.

The flagon went glug, glug, glug as Pedro, his head back, literally poured the red wine down his throat.

Zurika's own throat was dry, her chest tight. Her mind was caught between the rapid beat of a panic-stricken urge demanding immediate action and the calmer reasoning of her instinct. She had to get the men drunk. Not just these two animals, but the other three guards as well. There was more safety in numbers, because one of them

335

might start a fight over her and she could dart for the keys. Once she set the prisoners free, she would have allies and the blessing of confusion.

How could she get the other three guards to come out when the sergeant and Pedro seemed well content to eat and drink by themselves?

No sooner had the solution struck her than she set it in motion. Legs apart, hands on hips, arms akimbo, head tossed back, slightly to one side, she began a *cante jondo*, a deep song, the high, tremulous notes emerging from her throat resounding through the small room like golden bells. Pedro stopped with the flagon in mid-air, spilling red wine on his hairy chest. Sergeant Villejo paused in his crunching, his open mouth revealing a mess of food.

They both listened.

She felt the old thrill at holding captive those who heard her sing or watched her dance. For the first time that morning, she felt free and in control. Now, she would prevail. She closed her eyes and sent her notes sliding, fragmented, occasional sharp quavers reflecting piercing cries, *saetas*, arrows of song, carrying their swift message of love, sadness and loss to the hearts. She was no longer in the Toledo palace, nor on the Sacred Mountain that held the gypsy caves opposite the Alhambra palace. She was a messenger of the heart to the heart, both the giving and the receiving heart.

The last notes died down as she fell silent, their echoes still resounding faintly in the small, silent room. She opened her eyes, knowing that they were wet with tears, seeing nothing until the clapping of hands at the door leading inside the prison drew her attention to the three guards who had quietly entered the room and were standing side by side, facing her. Her plan had worked. They had answered the summons of her song. All three men were dressed in their black and white guard's uniform. One of them was short, round and bald-headed.

336

'My name is Carlos,' he cried. He had a high squeaky voice. 'You sing like a nightingale.'

The second man, lean and cadaverous, with sunken cheeks and glittering black eyes in a death's head face, merely grunted an introduction, 'Tonio.'

The last guard was a handsome devil, small-waisted and tall, built like a male dancer. The trim, dashing moustache and a scar on his right cheek were accented by pale blue eyes, fixed and staring, which sent a shudder through her. 'A singer worthy of the royal court,' he declared in soft, gentle tones. 'I am Pepe Ruiz. Shall we fuck?'

Zurika couldn't believe her ears, but the sergeant merely gestured towards the table. 'We shall have these first. Then we shall take turns fucking her.' He nodded slowly, the ginger moustache seeming to flare sensuously. 'Since I am in command here, my turn first.'

Zurika's heart sank again. Then the recollection of how she had held them with her song brought courage. If she had done it with her song, she could certainly do it with her dance. 'You will also have to watch me dance before you start any of that nonsense,' she stated boldly. She clapped her hands, stamped a foot, *golpe*, then went *punta*, *talon*, toe, heel. 'Come now, *señores*, first the food and the wine.'

To her delight, all three men started towards the table. Pepe Ruiz was first at the flagon. He drank deeply, placing himself so those pale blue eyes could continue to stare at her. He was the one she should try and set against the sergeant, she decided, yet he would also be the most dangerous of the five.

She allowed them to finish all the food and drink most of the wine, joining in their ribald jokes to divert them by pretending to be one of them. Her eyes flirted with each in turn, giving them the promise of her body, while her soul was sickened, smirched by what she was doing.

Surely God and the Virgin Mother would forgive her, because all of it was for Prince Juan.

When all five men were more than slightly drunk, she decided that the time had arrived.

She clapped her hands sharply, holding them erect, right palm on left beside her left cheek, stamped out a *golpe*. 'Are you ready for my dance, *señores*?'

'No!' Pepe Ruiz's voice was a quiet explosion. 'I am only ready for the fuck.' He drew a deep breath, flung aside the piece of cheese he held in his hand, wiped his mouth with the back of it. 'You can dance to the beat of my cock inside you. It is larger than a donkey's.'

'Just a moment, Pepe Ruiz,' Sergeant Villejo shot in. His chair crashed to the ground as he rose to his feet. 'Rank has its privilege. I go in first.'

She had taken the initiative too soon. She had failed. Trapped in this small room with five men who would rape her repeatedly, her mind swung this way and that, desperately seeking a way out. Finally she found it. 'Listen, *señores*, for your lives depend on it,' she countered, keeping her voice steady. 'I was sent by the *major domo*. He knows where I am. If I don't return soon or if any harm befalls me, you will answer for it.'

'Yes indeed,' Pedro echoed. 'We could be in real shit.'

'Un-unh.' It was Pepe Ruiz's voice, so certain that Zurika could not help staring at those merciless eyes. He shook his head slowly from side to side. 'All we have to do is to tell the *major domo* that you came here, delivered the food and wine, sang and danced, for all of which we thank him and his thoughtful royal master right royally,' he sneered, the scar making him look positively evil, 'then left.'

'But the bitch will tell on us,' Tonio protested, more voluble than he had been so far.

'If we let her leave.' Sergeant Villejo had obviously hooked on to Pepe Ruiz's line of thought.

'This is the prison,' Pepe Ruiz interjected, very, very quietly. 'The dungeons are here, the torture chamber, even the gallows.' His ice-cold eyes drank in Zurika's body. 'She will never leave here.'

Chapter 18

King Pedro surveyed the scene with satisfaction. Everything was working out as he wished. Two hours after the combat commenced, the initial contests between the groups, involving the best of three charges in each case, had eliminated all but six participants. Their jousts against each other had left the massive King Charles the Bad of Navarre and the tall, dour King Philip of Catalonia as the finalists. Both kings had proved themselves to be doughty fighters, King Charles by sheer ferocity and brute strength combined with cunning, King Philip by skill with his lance and expertise as a horseman.

The lists had been cleared, the two finalists had rested in their tents and now faced each other at opposite ends of the arena, backed by their squires in shining armour, standard bearers with bright banners, richly dressed heralds and pink-cheeked trumpeters. Both kings, in full armour, had been hoisted on to their horses. King Charles had selected a great black charger for the occasion, King Philip was mounted on a tall bay. Even from that distance, King Pedro could not help admiring the glossy coats of the animals over powerful muscles beneath their saddlecloths. King Charles's horse, seemingly impatient at the straw stuffing at its chest, kept tossing its head, but the rider controlled it in a very relaxed way with a gentle left hand on the reins and powerful legs.

King Pedro's excellent organization included sweepers and cleaners, who darted in after each contest to clear away the debris of shattered lances, scattered straw and horse droppings. Only the green grass, worn and scuffed by the hooves of charging horses, showed signs of the intense activity. The tiers of the royal enclosure were riotous with the colours worn by his distinguished guests. The ladies' enclosures to his right were a study of elegance and beauty. The applause and laughter of the vast crowds packing their stands across the arena told of a happy people representing a conglomeration of races, whites, brown Moors, black Africans. Each wore their own national costume, displaying great mosaics of colour, greens, browns, blues, reds, whites, topped by different head-dresses, the black *yarmulke* of the Jews, the red *fez* of the Muslims, even the tall *mitres* of priests of the Greek church. He could distinguish a red-cheeked baby, finger in its mouth, in the arms of an obviously Castilian matron, a tall, dignified *caballero* in a high black hat, two small boys wrestling each other. A blue sky ruffled by fleecy white clouds, the hungry cawing of a flight of rooks overhead, poised to streak down for scraps of food, the smells of hot earth mingling with the scents of the ladies and horse urine, all of it was Castile. Castile was Spain. Only by such unity as he had achieved today could his Spain be expanded to the oceans on its eastern, southern and western borders.

Time and again that morning King Pedro had known floods of pride into the reservoir that had been created once the tournament started. The entire event had proceeded smoothly and he had received such unstinted praise from all sides, visiting royalty, nobles, ambassadors and prelates, that it had left him glowing.

The chubby-cheeked Bishop Eulogius was seated on King Pedro's right, as the representative of His Holiness the Pope. Dressed in a deep purple cassock, the gold mitre on his head, he had modulated his normal cheeriness to suit the occasion, but the mischief remained. 'Would Your Majesty like a wager as to who will be the winner?' the bishop enquired. His blue eyes, barely perceptible beneath the crinkling of their folds and lids, were a thin line of merriment. Yet here was the one man who could undermine the unity he was creating.

King Pedro sensed the bishop's mischief. The bishop well knew that his king wanted King Charles to win. 'We shall accept your wager,' King Pedro declared, then proceeded without naming the prize. '*You* shall be the winner.' His guffaw drew eyes in his direction.

The mitred head was thrown slightly back, before a giggle escaped the prelate. 'You are really cruel, Sire, to deprive me of victory in a wager when I cannot triumph in the joust. As you know, I have no interest in any prize you may offer, only in ultimate victory.'

You had better not be interested in my daughter, you fucking peasant, else I'll have your balls, whether you have any or not, King Pedro thought with a flash of natural savagery. 'We shall have to arrange a contest of some sort in which you can participate and achieve not only the elation of victory but also a suitable prize.'

'And what would my prize be, Your Majesty? Holy fires?'

'Certain desirable maidens.' King Pedro guffawed again, then turned his attention to the arena at the sound of trumpets. Yet the thought of Bishop Eulogius with his demand for Inquisition nagged. If King Charles the Bad emerged as the winner of the joust, the unity of all the peoples of Castile and Navarre, Catalonia and Aragon was essential. Most of these people were Catholic, and so he would need the support of Holy Church as well, but he also had loyal Moors and Jews in his army and the administration. Bishop Eulogius posed a serious threat.

The giant king-at-arms, Count Fernando, once more in the centre of the lists, ordered the royal trumpeters of the tourney to sound their fanfares. When the echoes died down, he called upon the heralds of each contestant to proclaim their lords once more.

Since King Philip was senior to King Charles in the

length of his reign, his group had been placed to the right of the royal enclosure. How do small men produce such loud voices, King Pedro wondered as King Philip's herald, a diminutive creature with an absurdly loud voice, proclaimed, 'Oyez! Oyez! Oyez! Hear All Ye Your Majesties, my lords and all men present that the noble, the mighty, the puissant ruler of the kingdom of Catalonia and all its peoples . . .'

Shit of a mule! All these titles for the ruler of a kingdom of half a million people! Impatient for the battle to start, King Pedro deflected his attention to an itch in his neck, which he scratched with a stubby forefinger. A sudden rawness at the back of his nose and a tickle in his throat could herald a cold. He raised his face to the sun. He had been told that direct sunlight could stop a cold. It was beginning to get warm in the arena, bringing to mind his son, Prince Juan, enduring the heat of the palace dungeons. Serve the little Christian prick right. Why did he have no paternal feeling for Prince Juan, the product of his loins? Was it because Prince Juan was also the product of the womb of the woman he hated, Queen Juana? Or was the prince a constant reminder of a past infidelity, when he wanted to be true to his love for Maria de Padilla, the one decent thing in his life, even though the conception had taken place before he coupled with Maria? Ah Maria! His eyes drifted sideways to the ladies' enclosure. He had placed her so that he could see her at all times. Maria, totally aware of him as always, looked towards him instantly and met his glance. They smiled at each other, the intimate smile of two lovers. He looked away only when the trumpets blared again.

The heralds had ended their announcements, the contestants' trumpeters were sounding their masters' calls to arms, bray clashing against bray to announce the coming clash. The king-at-arms and his entourage cantered away. Count Gaston rode up, the lance of office in his hand with

343

the helmet poised on it. Grooms helped him off his horse, led it away. The count walked up and took his stand behind the two *Grandes Dames*.

The mounted contestants faced each other across the lists, motionless in the silver noonday sunlight from the sheer weight of their armour. The din from the crowds hushed. A single trumpet sounded the charge.

One moment the two men were still, lances levelled, the next their mounts jerked, then moved smoothly into action. A lumbering walk increased to a trot, moving faster than the canter. The thudding of quick hooves in discordant unison were soon throb-beats pounding to the approaching clash. The chargers reached full gallop. The beats merged into a continuous drumming.

King Pedro eagerly watched the points of the lances approaching each other. Closer and closer. He held his breath. King Charles's mount had suddenly swerved to the left. King Philip's lance point followed. King Charles immediately swerved again, so well to the right this time that King Philip's lance point was impeded by his own horse's head, passing King Charles's body harmlessly. King Charles's fantastic piece of horsemanship nearly brought King Pedro to his feet. King Charles's lance, accurately directed from an angle that only a man of an enormous strength of arm could have encompassed, caught King Philip in the chest, shattered. King Philip was thrust back and sideways to the right. His left foot slipped from its stirrup. He tried desperately to keep his balance, but his movements were at odds with the charging of his mount. He began slowly toppling to the right. Then his bay seemed to leave him behind, leaping ahead in continued gallop, sweat gleaming on its bare flanks. King Philip crashed to the ground.

The thunderous shouts of the crowd rolling across the arena overwhelmed the applause from the royal enclosure, the ladies' hand-clapping and the cheers of the nobility.

'*Bravo!*' . . . '*Fantastico!*' . . . '*Viva Charles!*'

King Charles rode on, gradually reigning in his great black. King Philip remained motionless in the dust, a huge crumpled heap of armour, shining in the sunlight. His squires rode up. King Charles slowly circled to meet them.

'He does not move!' Bishop Eulogius remarked, a tremor in his voice. 'Is he dead?'

The still, armoured figure on the ground stirred.

'No! But he will not fight again today,' King Pedro asserted. Excitement was cascading within him. His plan was working.

Bathed in a cold sweat, King Yusuf's first instinct after he had killed the asp had been to pull the bell-rope that hung over his bed and summon the guards. Some inner caution had, however, kept his hand poised in mid-air before reflection made him lower it. Whoever had placed the asp in his bedroom had intended that the snake, seeking the warmth of the bed, should kill him. The asp was not native to Granada. Each time he looked at it during the rest of the night, an untidy coil of brown whipcord on the red and black Persian carpet covering the pink marble floor beside his bed, a shudder escaped him, the small gaping mouth with its deadly hidden fangs caused waves of nausea.

There was no way in which the presence of a foreign snake in the royal bedchamber of the King of Granada could be an accident. He was well accustomed to facing death on the battlefield, the royal standard making him a highly visible target to the enemy, but this insidious creature told of a cunning, perfidious master. Who could it be?

Among all those who controlled access to his bedchamber, only one might want him dead, his tall, skeletal Prime Minister, Farouk Riswan of the pale brown eyes and the gaunt and bitter look, the man who had caused his predecessor to be murdered, so he, Yusuf, could ascend the throne. He had been forced to keep Farouk Riswan as his Prime Minister to prevent disclosure of the plot, but had greatly curtailed the latter's powers. So instead of being the power behind the throne, Riswan had remained its footstool. Yes indeed, the Prime Minister would cause history to repeat itself, having him, King Yusuf, killed in order to place another nominee on the throne, making sure this time that it was one he could really control. Who could that choice be? Certainly, it had to be one of the royal family.

On the other hand, the assassination attempt could well be a Christian conspiracy. Word had been received by his Chief of Spies in the Granada palace that King Pedro the Cruel was secretly preparing for war with a united white Christian alliance to back him. A cruel and ruthless foe, King Pedro had everything to gain from assassinating the King of Granada, incidentally wreaking vengeance for the mutilation of his son, Prince Juan.

For the umpteenth time since Prince Ahmed fled the palace, King Yusuf regretted having followed Abou bon Ebben's advice years ago and confining his son to the Gen al Arif tower of the Granada palace. Where could the young man be at this moment?

He, King Yusuf, should meet cunning with cunning. First the dead snake must be removed surreptitiously. Second, he must pretend that he was unaware of the attempt, to lull his would-be murderer into a sense of false security. He would therefore reveal the incident only to the castrated deaf-mute Tarif, whom he had taken into his immediate service after Prince Ahmed fled, because it somehow gave him a sense of closeness to the son he had lost. Tarif had proved himself to be so gentle, loyal and dedicated that King Yusuf had appointed the man his personal servant. The bell-rope would have summoned other staff. He would wait for morning, when Tarif would arrive, always the first to attend the royal bedchamber every morning to prepare him for *subh*, the morning prayer, as Tarif had once done for Prince Ahmed. Since he himself did not know the sign language, immediately he made the decision, he had risen from his bed and written a missive for Tarif stating what had occurred and giving him necessary instructions.

He slept only fitfully, impatiently awaiting the gentle music that heralded his every dawn, but each time he awoke his contemplation became increasingly melancholy. He had been a good king. Himself a poet, he had devoted himself to painting and sculpture, architecture, literature and science, and yet he had also achieved the first victory over the white Christians since the shameful ten-year non-aggression treaty following the defeat of the true believers at the Battle of Salado in 1340. He had given Granada a running water supply, with mosques and free education in every village. He had brought law and order to the country and ensured efficient local government. Had he been guilty of spiritual arrogance when he extended and embellished the Allah Hamra palace? If so, was the curse of ibn Nagralla, the other Yusuf, reaching out to him? What then was the benefit from all his endeavour? What had it really achieved?

When Tarif arrived and saw the dead snake, his face registered complete shock. Ever the trained servant, however, he quickly recovered. Yusuf silently pointed to his missive. Tarif scanned it, bowed, gave the hand to heart, mouth and head oath of secrecy it required. He had then carried the snake away in a litter basket.

During the entire morning, King Yusuf, accompanied as usual by his Prime Minister, proceeded about his royal business, but with a curious listlessness. He alternated between wanting to remove the man summarily from office and sending him to the torture chamber for a confession, but his innate sense of justice prevailed. 'We shall attend *zuhr*, the noon prayer, at the palace mosque,' he advised in an aside to the Prime Minister while conducting his public audience in the great hall. 'Let there be no special arrangements made.'

'But, Sire, you are sovereign of the realm.'

'No buts.' He forced a smile through his black moustache and beard. 'We are all one in Almighty Allah's realm.' His dark eyes pinpointed deliberately and inscrutably the gaze of the Prime Minister. 'Whether it be king or Prime Minister, saint or,' he paused for emphasis, 'would-be assassin.'

Something passed through the pale brown eyes, but he could not really catch it. Still, he had fired his warning arrow. It might at least drive the enemy underground, like an evil snake into its pit, for the present.

The public audience over, King Yusuf suddenly became obsessed with a desire to relive the past. 'We shall walk through the palace alone,' he declared. 'And go directly thereafter to the mosque for *zuhr*.'

He started his walk in the great forecourt of the palace. One hundred feet long and over eighty feet wide, it was paved with white marble, decorated at each end with light Moorish peristyles, one of them supporting an elegant gallery of fretted design. Along the mouldings of the cornices and on various areas of the walls, escutcheons, ciphers, cerific and Arabic characters in high relief gave the mottoes of the monarch-builders of the palace. Along the centre of the courtyard, an immense tank bordered by hedges of roses received its water from two great marble vases. He could not restrain a sigh at seeing the roses. How many times, in the days of bliss, had he picked a single rose for his Mariam. How her large brown doe-like eyes would light up when he presented it to her. He could hear her unfailing murmur of delight as a pain in his heart. The inner sound of heart pain, his constant companion.

'This single rose picked for me by the ruler of my heart is more precious than all the roses of his kingdom,' she always said. He had never failed to await the words breathlessly.

He stopped before a dark red rose, a budding virgin, half-opened. He bent to inhale its dewy, velvet fragrance, fought back his tears.

Such purity bestowed by Almighty Allah on man, who used it as a base to concoct evil.

He went from the warm silver sunshine of the court of the *al beerkah* under the shade of a Moorish archway to the Court of Lions, acknowledging the obeisance of attendants, the scimitar salutes of guards and the lowered spears of sentries with repeated fingers to heart, mouth and head. If anyone thought it odd that the king should be without his retinue, they gave no sign. They would not dare! He walked around the beautiful alabaster basins shedding their sparkling diamond waters, soothed by their incessant splashing lightly disturbed by a breeze. He inspected the twelve lions casting forth their crystal streams. Now why did he pause to do that, as if he were bidding each of them farewell? He recalled the words of the poet, Ibn Gabirol, from centuries away with sadness:

> And there is a full sea, matching Solomon's sea,
> yet not resting on an ox,
>   but there are lions, in phalanx on its rim, seeming to
>   roar for prey; these whelps
>   whose bosoms are like wells gushing forth to water
>   the myrtle garden, fragrant from its white blossoms.

He recalled his awe when he first saw these creatures as a boy and they seemed so much alive. Why sadness?

One of the dozen gardeners cleaning the fountains was

a dark, squat, ageing Moor, his bald head gleaming with sweat in the sunshine, whom he had known as a boy. Iqbal had been a young gardener at the time. Now he was an old gardener! King Yusuf suddenly felt ancient.

He paused frequently along the red and green tiled walkway that served all four sides of the marble courtyard, to look at the arcades of open filigree work supported by slender gilded pillars of white marble. Such elegance and graceful good taste.

He passed through the hall of the cavaliers and the richly adorned portal that gave entrance to the Hall of the Two Sisters, where a storm of heady scents, sandalwood, frankincense and myrrh, greeted him. Great Nubian eunuchs, armed with swords and spears, each of whom gave him silent salute as he approached, guarded this territory forbidden to all men save him.

What were their thoughts, these black eunuchs? Why was he on this solitary journey through his palace when he could be within those latticed jalousies, enjoying the attentions and favours of his *harem*, dozens of women at his command, ranging from northern Europeans with skins as white as the snows of their native lands to onyx-black Africans, even a brown-skinned Indian? Short, tall, plump, obese, skinny, flat-chested, full-breasted, the old and wrinkled retired from the active service of doing nothing all day. Most of the women were adept at the sexual arts, for whenever an inexperienced virgin was introduced to the harem, the chief concubine made it her duty to teach the young woman all she should know. A few suppressed giggles told that he was indeed being observed from behind the lattice curtains, probably even craved for, many of the women being lusty. He must surely be a disappointment to them, for he had sex only when his testicles told him they needed to be emptied, and the ottomans and couches within the *harem* held his body only about once each week. He enjoyed the sensations, but merely as one would enjoy scratching an itch. There was none of the deep-soul satisfaction that his unions of love with Mariam had unfailingly brought them both.

The silence that fell as he walked upstairs into his Mariam's quarters, obviously commanded by word brought ahead that he desired to be alone, was broken by the strumming of a Middle Eastern lyre, a sharp-gold voice chanting nasally, the tinkle of silver anklets, the chink-ching of finger-cymbals.

In Mariam's quarters, as always, he encountered a new silence, the silence of the grave. He had commanded that the rooms be left unoccupied. No one was even to enter them, except for cleaning ladies each morning. Yet Mariam's laughter rang in his ears every time he came here and her warm, husky voice uttered her soft endearments to this day, for his ecstasy ending with the utter misery of longing that could never be fulfilled.

The scent of musk-perfumed water emerged from Mariam's personal, private privy. Though no one used it, the three spigots running water, one hot, one cold, one scented, were turned on daily at his command.

Everything in the rooms was as it had once been. The king could decree existence, but not even an Emperor could command life. Only memories remained. However vivid, they were but a mirage caused by the barren sun of his present life that left him dry as the desert sands. For him, the real water of life lay only in the distant oasis that was Paradise.

The floors of pink marble, covered by great carpets of patterned green and white, Mariam's favourite colours, held their matching couches and pink cushions. The gold braziers on white alabaster stands still emitted grey wisps of jasmin-scented smoke. The low filigreed ivory tables contained their gold salvers, even the sweetmeats. The walls were still adorned with their great coloured tapestries depicting peaceful scenes from the Granada countryside. The one of a stream gently flowing through a pastureland on which brown and black cows grazed, with snow-capped mountains for a background, was his favourite. The wall-niches contained jewelled ornaments from many lands. Some of the gold vases, encrusted with rubies, emeralds and sapphires, were worth a king's ransom. He made for the open windows. It was like looking through a ravine. Across the confines of space between the palace buildings, narrow in comparison with what lay beyond, the valley of the Darro slept, bathed in silver forenoon sunshine.

Take the sun from the sky, Almighty Allah, for since Thou didst take my beloved away, why do I need the sun?

The high nasal voice of the *muezzin* calling the faithful to *zuhr* rang through the air.

> '*Allah is the Greatest*
> *I bear witness that there is no God but God*
> *I bear witness that Mahomet is the Messenger of God*
> *Come to prayer*
> *Come to virtue*
> *Prayer is better than sleep*
> *Allah is the Greatest*
> *There is no God but God.*'

King Yusuf turned and hurried to keep his *zuhr* tryst with God. At that moment, he uncannily knew why he had undertaken his sentimental journey.

Her breath in her throat, stricken by terror, Zurika could only pray piteously to the Blessed Virgin. Her body tautened. As if in answer to her prayer, the handle of the long knife at her waist pressed against her ribcage brought back the desperate ferocity of the cornered animal. Sergeant Villejo was only two paces from her now.

'Go for it, Sergeant.'

'Hurry, I can't wait for my turn!'

'Do you want me to hold her down, in case she struggles?' This last was from Corporal Pedro Cruz.

Prickles of cold sweat broke loose over Zurika's entire body but the moment her hand grasped the wooden haft of the knife, its solid feel sent courage up her arm and through her being, meeting a red-hot rage that misted her eyes. With a great cry, she drew the knife, saw the sergeant's pale yellow eyes widen for an instant, before they slitted. He half-crouched, brought his arms to waist level, gestured inwards with inviting fingers. 'Come on, slut!' he gritted through clenched teeth.

'Here sergeant, *amigo*, you need help?' Out of the corner of her eyes, she noticed that Corporal Pedro had an upraised settle in his hand. 'I can brain her.'

'No!' The red moustache bristled. 'I want to take this wildcat alone.' His eyes bored into her. 'Come on, bitch!'

The stink of his body sickened her.

She went into a half-crouch herself. Teeth bared, she held the knife at waist level, as she had seen the gypsy knife-fighters do. Her gaze intent on his, she jabbed forward, feinting. He made no move. He was obviously experienced. She thrust, feinting again. He blinked this time, then blinked once again, this time as if to clear his eyes. He shook his small, red head once in a quick jerk, then once more. His crouched body swayed slightly. His outstretched hands began to grow limp, the fingers slackening. He moved his hands up with an effort, began blinking rapidly. He exhaled hugely. His breath smelled horribly of garlic and wine. He began teetering on his feet. Pepe Ruiz sprang forward to hold him up.

A thrill of triumph shot through Zurika. The drugged wine was beginning to work at last.

'Arr . . . you . . . arr . . .' The slurred words told her that Corporal Pedro Cruz too was succumbing to the drugged wine.

Now only three guards remained. It might be a few more minutes before these men, who had started on the wine later, came under its influence. She would fight them all if need be, fight to the death. But would it take too long before they collapsed? The very thought of bestial male organs sickened her.

Help me, Blessed Virgin.

I shall keep myself intact for you my beloved Prince Ahmed. I shall save you even if I am raped, my dear friend, Prince Juan.

Frantic thoughts.

When Corporal Pedro Cruz began crumpling, Tonio had darted towards him and tried to hold him up. 'Hey, *amigo*, what's happening?'

Only Carlos remained free. Should she leap and attack him, kill him so only two would be left? To her joy the answer came. Carlos blinked stupidly once, then again, passed a dazed hand over his eyes. He looked at her, comprehension dawning. 'You bitch. I shall . . . shall . . .' He moved forward but his limbs had lost momentum. Hate-filled eyes glazing over, he slowly sank to the ground.

Tonio gave a great gasp and let his burden go. It hit the ground with a soft thud. He stared uncomprehendingly at it awhile, then his eyes crossed, lost their focus as he collapsed.

Pepe Ruiz alone remained on his feet, daring her with a quiet simmering rage that churned her guts. 'I see what you have done, you harlot.' He nodded slowly. 'If it's the last thing I do before I die, I'm going to fuck you.' His pause was deadly. 'Oh, I'm going to fuck you to death.'

In one quick motion, he flung the sergeant's body away as if it had been a doll. Terror streaked through her at his demoniac strength. Could she hold him at bay?

'Come on then,' she hissed.

He leapt for her suddenly, with the speed of a mountain

lion. His left hand chopped inwards and sideways at her knife wrist. Excruciating pain shot through her arm. The knife clattered to the floor. Then he was on her, pushing her against the wall with such ferocity that the breath left her body. His fiendish strength brought a flash recall of Majo. Then she was fighting her assailant. Slobbering lips sought her mouth. His breath reeked. She started sinking slowly down the wall to avoid his face, her hands seeking the ground to break her fall. Her right hand fell on something solid.

The knife. Thrilling, she grasped it. Her sweaty palm slipped. Pepe Ruiz was pushing her sideways and down now. His right hand came across sharply. The stinging slap sent stars through her brain. She nearly blacked out.

Another tremendous slap, back-handed this time. Blinding lights shot through the black sky of her senses. Her desperate palm feverishly groped for the knife handle, found it.

'Take me!' Some instinct of cunning made her say the old words and relax.

'Ha! I knew you wanted me, rutting bitch.' He eased his body.

She whipped her hand sideways, plunged the knife into his side with maniacal fury. Just between the ribs and the hips. The long blade sank in. Deep. Fierce joy shot through her.

Ruiz groaned, drew his breath in a great gasp. His jaw slackened, his mouth flew open.

She mercilessly jerked out the blade. His shrill scream of agony rent the air. His foul breath contrasted sickly with a sandalwood scent he wore. His hands clawed viciously for her throat but lost their power. His lungs sought vainly for breath in great rasps. His body went limp.

Zurika rolled him over sideways. He lay there helpless, contorted face up, blood gouting from the gaping red hole in his black tunic, stricken eyes still glaring their hatred at her. She raised the knife aloft. 'See this, vile pig!' She plunged the knife into his stomach, exulting in its smooth drive. His shriek rent the air, echoing in the confined space, music to her ears.

She lost all control of herself, plunged the knife again and again, his body jerking before each wild thrust. 'Take that . . . take that . . . for every woman you raped!' Her shrieks of hate mingled with his anguished screams.

She suddenly realized that he was lying still. Knife upraised, she stared uncomprehendingly at his sightless, staring eyes. A sob escaped her, then another, and another, uncontrollably. Sweat streamed down her face; spit drooled from the side of her mouth. 'How do *you* like being fucked, you bag of bloody shit?' she moaned.

The eyes, staring upwards, came into focus. She slowly took in the gaping wounds, the body she had mutilated. A great shudder ran through her. Her bloodied knife-hand remained poised over him.

I have killed a man, a human being. I have committed a mortal sin. Will I have to remain in Hell forever? Holy Mother of Jesus forgive me.

The cry of a wounded animal escaped her, shattered the silence. She flung the knife across the room. It hit the wall behind the table, clattered to the floor. Her eyes followed it in horror, fell on the keys.

Awareness of her mission returned. A deep, deep, heartbroken sigh escaped her. She shuddered, started shaking violently.

Presently, she brought herself under control. Her gypsy instinct assured her that she had done right. She rose resolutely to her feet, made for the keys on leaden feet. Numb, she held them in her hand, just staring at them. She drew a deep breath, started for the prison door. She stumbled, trod on the knife. The steel blade, even the haft, was bloodstained. A piece of white gristle made a hideous scar on the red blood.

Revolted, she retched, tasted bile and the morning's porridge. Only the weight of the keys in her hand brought back resolve. She transferred them to her left hand, picked up the knife.

She walked over to Sergeant Villejo's limp body and deliberately wiped the knife on his white pantaloons. That would be a reminder of his own escape from death when he and his three men awoke from their drugged sleep, that and the corpse of the man who had spilled out the blood.

She replaced the knife at her waist, beneath the blouse, then walked resolutely to the entrance door of Prince Juan's prison-dungeon.

Chapter 19

As the tourney proceeded, Princess Beatrice had become more and more fearful. Battle had followed battle, joust had succeeded joust and yet there was no sign of Prince Ahmed. Save for the fact that she had actually seen him two nights earlier and the grim knowledge that Prince Juan was languishing in the stinking dungeons, she would have wondered whether the Horn of her dreaming even existed, except as a figment of her forlorn imagination.

And now, King Charles the Bad had won the tourney. The victory was so clean cut that the intercession of the two *Grandes Dames* was unnecessary.

As King Philip's retinue gathered around him, he stirred and was helped to his feet. King Charles slowly reined his horse sideways, turned to face his own heralds, trumpeters and equerries who were riding up to him. Beneath the shade of the awning, Princess Beatrice began to sweat with apprehension.

The giant king-at-arms, Count Fernando, trotted into the lists followed by his aides. He beckoned to King Charles to ride alongside himself then turned to face the royal enclosure. The cheering of the crowds subsided. The royal trumpeters sounded a fanfare. As its echoes died down, a great silence enveloped the arena, in which a baby's wail and a goat's bleat sounded clearly.

'May it please Your Majesty King Pedro, sovereign lord of the great kingdom of Castile and royal patron of this tournament, to permit Your Majesty's King-at-Arms to declare its winner,' Count Fernando thundered.

'It does indeed give us great pleasure, valiant King-at-Arms,' King Pedro responded. 'Pronounce your verdict.'

358

'The winner is . . .'

The blare of a single trumpet from the entrance to the arena cut across Count Fernando's words. He paused and turned his head towards it in astonishment.

Princess Beatrice's heart began beating rapidly. Following the Count's gaze through the glare of the bright noon sun, she observed a small group of figures that had emerged at the entrance to the arena. A trumpeter clad in white rode a white horse, repeatedly sounding the fanfare. He preceded two heralds dressed in gold cloth, also on white horses, followed by a single flag-bearer with a furled flag. A horseman in full armour, also riding a white steed, a great war-charger, came next, followed by an esquire similarly mounted and bearing an upright lance.

'Horn has come for me, I thank Thee Holy Mother Mary!' Princess Beatrice breathed. Her heart seemed ready to burst with excitement, joy and relief.

The entire crowd gazed in silent astonishment at the extraordinary spectacle. The trumpeter whipped back his trumpet smartly from his lips, held it in the ready position at his right hip, broke into a light canter. The rest of the group followed suit, keeping pace with him.

They came to a halt before the king-at-arms. Count Fernando recovered from his shock and gazed at King Pedro for directions. The king raised a palm signalling Count Fernando to use his discretion. All round Princess Beatrice, the ladies were jittering questions at each other. 'Who are these people?' . . . 'Are they part of the tourney?' . . . 'What magnificent horses!'

Princess Mathilde leaned forward. 'Is not this interruption a trifle odd, dear Madam?' she inquired of Princess Beatrice's mother. 'Was it prearranged as a sort of circus?'

Maria de Padilla shrugged helplessly. 'This is a surprise to all of us.'

Princess Mathilde half turned to Count Gaston. 'Could

it possibly be that we have yet another contestant here?' she inquired, a hint of irritation in her voice. 'Our dear King Charles is already the winner under the rules of the tourney and should be declared as such. Will you see to it, *chevalier*?' Her voice had become imperious. She wielded her grey dove feather fan slowly. 'The heat of the sun has become rather trying. Once the winner is announced, we ladies can get back to the comfort of the palace. Will you not rescue us?'

'I would gladly do anything for the comfort of the ladies, Princess,' Count Gaston declared gravely. He did not seem to be put out by the interruption, was his normal composed self. 'But it would be easier for me to attempt to remove the sun for your protection than to interfere with the protocol of the tourney. Count Fernando is the competent authority and any final decision on unexpected events rests with His Majesty King Pedro.'

'Who are you?' Count Fernando thundered at the newcomers. 'And how dare you enter the lists?'

'It is enough that I have dared,' the youthful voice of the man in armour boomed out through his helmet. 'I am now in the lists and I challenge the winner.'

'You are precluded from doing so by the rules of tourney.'

The questioning murmurs of the vast crowd were now punctuated by an occasional shout, a jeer, hoots. Someone crowed, 'Cock-a-doodle-doo . . .' in derision. Princess Beatrice could not distinguish where their sympathies lay, but conjectured that they were with the newcomer since his presence meant yet another fight.

'Rules made by man can be altered by man. Only the rules of God are immutable. If the rules of the tourney do not permit it, the winner should be bound by his own rules of honour to accept my challenge. Else shall he be dubbed craven.'

An angry roar from King Charles the Bad blasted the

air. 'We fear no man. We accept any challenge, even that of an upstart. See to it, Sir King-at-Arms.'

'Then it only remains for you to present your credentials, Sir Stranger in White Armour.' Count Fernando sounded relieved. 'Prove to us that you are of worthy birth and character.'

Princess Beatrice's heart contracted with fear. It was a crucial moment. Prince Ahmed might be rejected. He would then be scorned, perhaps imprisoned, even put to death, for though he was of royal birth, he was an infidel and a heretic. The full impact of his courage struck, astounding her. Here he was, heir to the throne of Granada, who could have led a comfortable life with an assured future, risking all of it and his life for her and Prince Juan.

'By all that is holy, the man deserves to be allowed to compete for right royal courage alone,' Count Gaston murmured.

The odds Prince Ahmed faced suddenly filled Princess Beatrice with awe. This youth, this foreigner, this infidel, was virtually alone against the vast throng assembled around him, including royalty, nobility and common people. At that moment, she knew beyond doubt that she loved Prince Ahmed and would follow him to the ends of the earth, to serve him in poverty or riches, peasant hut or palace.

An expectant hush descended on the multitude and the spectator stands, broken only by a hacking cough from one of the visiting princes. Princess Beatrice gazed at her father. His anger replaced by scorn, his mouth had twisted viciously. But when Count Fernando looked questioningly at him, he slowly nodded his approval. 'King Charles will teach the upstart stranger a lesson he will never forget.'

Princess Beatrice eagerly watched the newcomer slowly raise his visor. His face was in the shadow of his helmet, the sun being directly overhead, but the dark, handsome profile made her breath catch.

'A very handsome man,' Princess Mathilde remarked. 'H'mm, regal too, but so *young*.'

'Obviously a foreigner,' Maria de Padilla snorted.

At a signal from Prince Ahmed, his trumpeter whipped back the trumpet to his lips, sounded a fanfare with a Moorish strain. Before its last note died away, the standard-bearer unfurled his flag. A sudden gust of warm wind whipped it. Princess Beatrice's exclamation was hardly an echo of the great gasp that went up from the entire throng.

The flag was green, with a silver star and crescent at the top right hand corner. The flag of Islam.

Whispers began in the ladies' enclosure. 'The infidel flag' . . . 'How dare he?' . . . 'Who is he?' . . . Princess Beatrice heard Bishop Eulogius angrily declaiming, 'Accursed heretic! Sire . . .' The rest of his words were drowned as the murmurs of the crowd rose to a crescendo.

Count Fernando was nonplussed only for a few moments. He raised his gloved hands for silence, his giant figure dominating the scene. The noise died down. 'Declare yourself, your rank and station.'

'I am Prince Mo-Ahmed al Kamal, son of King Yusuf I, ruler of Granada, by his wife, a princess of royal lineage, the natural daughter of the King of Morocco. I am heir to the throne of Granada.'

Gasps, murmurs, shouts arose.

'Infidel!' . . . 'Heretic!' . . . 'Blood-brother in Islam.' '*Alla-hu-Akbar!*' The last had to be from *Mude'jar*, Moslem Moors living in Christian territory, perhaps even from the *Moriscos*, converted Moors.

'You are not qualified to compete in this tourney for the hand of a white Christian princess,' Count Fernando asserted. 'You are no knight but a barbarian.'

'I do not seek the hand of the Princess Beatrice, only

the right of combat against the best of European chivalry and the release of the princess to wed whomsoever she chooses. For that, if I lose, I am prepared to forfeit my life.'

Oh dear God, Princess Beatrice thought piteously, he is offering his life for me.

'Insolent brown bastard!' King Pedro ejaculated.

Princess Beatrice's heart sank with the realization that her champion did not seek her hand. He does not want me. Horn does not want me. Tears sprang to her eyes. Perhaps he is spoken for to another lady. He may even be married already. No matter. I shall follow him, and even become his concubine, so long as he allows me to practise my Christian faith in his *harem*.

Count Fernando was taken aback. 'What says my royal master?' he inquired of King Pedro.

'Let his religion be no bar to your assessing his right to participate,' King Pedro responded smoothly. He turned towards Bishop Eulogius who had reflexively reached out a restraining hand, but had held it back, as touching the monarch was a liberty. 'Do not worry, Eminence,' he said in lower tones. 'Our champion, King Charles, will make mincemeat of this puling boy. Before the day's end, with the action we have set in motion in Granada,' his ferocious grin had a cruel twist to it, 'the climate should be right for our own . . . er . . . tourney!'

'Who vouches for you?' Count Fernando demanded of the challenger.

With a flick of his wrist, Prince Ahmed veered his white charger, rode up to face the royal enclosure. The stamp of a horse's hoof was lost in silence. To Princess Beatrice's surprise, Prince Ahmed's gaze locked into her father's eyes. 'The prince who was to vouch for me has been most cruelly and unjustly imprisoned. I look to his royal gaoler to vouch for me in his place.'

Another great gasp rose from the crowd. King Pedro

lumbered to his feet. 'Never!' he shouted. 'How dare you, the offspring of a savage barbarian who so foully disfigured our only son, turning him into a deaf-mute, seek our endorsement? You have come uninvited and disrupted our proceedings. Now stand on your own merits and be judged by our king-at-arms. Count yourself lucky that the rules of the tourney prevent us from having you seized and hanged.' He sat down, growling in his throat. 'When the tourney is over, we shall have his circumcised prick shoved in his mouth,' he ground out savagely.

Prince Ahmed swivelled his charger back. Princess Beatrice marvelled at his skill as a horseman. 'Then the royal king whom I challenge to combat will surely vouch for me, unless he is afraid of defeat.'

With a great roar, King Charles clapped spurs into his horse's flanks. The great black charger jerked, then seemed to leap forward in spite of the weight it was carrying. King Charles drew his sword, held it high, directed his mount at Prince Ahmed. The horse sped to the centre of the lists.

Blessed Jesu, he intends hacking my beloved to death. Princess Beatrice sprang to her feet, stifling the 'No . . . o . . .' emerging from her lips. O sweet Jesu, help my Horn.

Count Gaston muttered an oath.

Prince Ahmed stood his ground calmly, made no attempt to defend himself as King Charles's charger kept pounding towards him. Closer and closer. Princess Beatrice held her breath in horror.

At the last moment, King Charles swerved to the left, touched Prince Ahmed's shoulder lightly with his sword as he passed. 'We have vouched for this heretic!' he bellowed. Galloping past the group, he circled widely to the wild cheering that erupted from the crowds and reached for the sunlit heavens.

* * *

One may pray anywhere on God's earth, provided the place is clean. 'The whole world has been made a mosque for me,' the Prophet said. When King Yusuf hastened downstairs and joined his entourage at the entrance courtyard of the palace to proceed to the grand mosque for *zuhr*, he wondered why he had selected this particular mosque today.

It was a great rectangular building, with minarets at each corner and facing in the direction of Mecca, *quiblah*, due east. When King Mohamed ben Ahmer embellished the Alhambra palace a hundred years earlier, he had also improved the grand mosque. A simple ascetic, who wore coarse linen, he had ruled for forty years and avoided the curse of the Jew.

There was no mistaking the timeless beauty of the mosque, though it was crowded at this hour with the throng of worshippers performing their ablutions around the water tank and fountain at the centre of the great white marble-floored courtyard, from the boundary walls of which the white blossoms of hedges of flowering orange trees scented the air.

Ablution before prayer, commanded by the Prophet, was symbolic. King Yusuf and his aides, mingling with the other worshippers, washed their hands to erase all evil deeds performed, their mouths of unclean words uttered, especially falsehoods against the principles of Islam, their faces in order to present to God the removal of weakness and incidental aberrations, seeking His pardon for sins. Finally, they washed their feet for having strayed from the righteous path, pronouncing *niyyah*, avowal of the intention to remove all impurities and to accept perpetual prayer.

As he performed his own ablutions, King Yusuf also marvelled at the oneness of Islam and the equality of all those in its single brotherhood which could make a human being of a king. He paused to gaze appreciatively at the semi-circular row of rock *breccia*, columns of red, yellow and brown jasper, white and red porphyry, rising to a height of fourteen feet. Intent on their own worship, no one was taking note of him, not the grey-bearded, wrinkled-faced ancient with the skin of a dried brown grape, his bald head glistening with sweat in the noonday sun, nor the dark, cleanshaven giant Moroccan, probably a visitor to Granada, towering over everyone else, nor the chubby-cheeked, barrel-waisted Arab, obviously a trader, the dark slits of cunning eyes peeping from the folds around them.

Followed by his aides, King Yusuf passed into the shady portals of the mosque, just one of the crowd surging in. He was greeted by a mist of frankincense from the hundreds of lighted lamps filled with perfumed oil. He stopped before *mihrab*, the octagonal recess with seven sides of white marble, roofed with a great marble block, carved underneath in the form of a shell, which was the niche for prayer. To the right of the *mihrab* was the *nimbar* or pulpit, on which the *khatib* or spokesman would stand to address the congregation. On the pulpit was an enormous jewel-studded Koran of ivory, ebony, aloe and sandalwood.

Every mosque is a simple building, with nothing to distract the worshipper. Yet the interior of this mosque was an exquisite composition. Floors of multi-coloured mosaics, tiles and marble supported a delicate forest of pillars of earthy, vari-coloured stone, their pathways of stretching lights from the lamps, with as many doors beyond as there were rows of columns, all supporting a high roof with no visible ceiling unless one looked up and distinguished the sculptured, enamelled and gilded cedar wood and larch.

King Yusuf covered his bare head with a white muslin square and knelt in silent prayer at the *mihrab*, buttocks on heels, forehead to the cool white marble floor, as his subjects were doing around him.

'O Divine Allah, we have been told that Thou wilt inflict Thy punishment on whom Thou wilt, but Thy mercy encompasses all things. There has to be much evil in a ruler's life else he cannot fulfil Thy dictates of rulership. I have endured pain, punishment and mental torture in this life, all of it Thy *taqdir*, not merely that the seed of man and woman should produce a human being, but that each human being should act thus and so pre-ordained by *kismet*, destiny. The manifestation of Thy *taqdir* has been in the suffering I have endured from the loss of my Mariam. I have also paid a heavy price for playing Thy role with my son, Prince Ahmed, trying to alter the shape of his own *kismet*, and with Prince Juan by cruelly robbing him of the faculties Thou didst bestow on him at birth. Yet, O Allah, whatever tortures and punishments I caused to be inflicted on people seemed right at the time.

'Today, I do not know which of my actions was caused by duty as ruler of my people appointed by Thee and which performed by Yusuf, a human being following his own selfish dictates.

'I pray Thee to grant me Thy divine Mercy and take me, when my time comes, into Paradise, so I can once again be with Mariam who was my blessing and has been my punishment since she died, for . . .'

The sharp agony beneath his left shoulderblade threw him downward with a great gasp. His body wrenched sideways, his head slithered on the white marble floor, his mouth twisting. As the blackness began enveloping him, he was conscious that his assassin had fled.

The curse has struck me for having played God. This white floor will be stained with my blood. But its marble is cool . . . cool as . . . ah, Paradise.

* * *

Having bribed the guards, Prince Ahmed had watched all the encounters between the contestants from the entrance to the arena with interest, studying their styles and techniques. He had devoted special attention to King Charles and King Philip when they began to emerge as the finalists and particularly watched King Charles in the last joust, after which he had sped to the little grove between the palace and the arena where his small entourage awaited him with his armour, the lift to mount him on his horse when he was fully armoured, the wagon and all the horses. He had planned to use the grove as a base for escape should the situation demand.

Having returned to the arena, mounted on his white charger Amir, he had issued his challenge and now faced King Charles across the glaring sunlight that bathed the lists, noting his opponent's giant size and his skill as a horseman. He had already conjectured what tactics King Charles would adopt, but his mind was bright and sharp swordpoint alert to act reflexively against whatever surprise moves the king might make.

Thus far, he, Prince Ahmed had achieved his purpose; now if only Zurika had been able to proceed as planned, all would be well. He deliberately cast aside all fears for Zurika and Prince Juan to concentrate solely on his present task. How much he had grown up, especially during the last two days of crisis, since fleeing from the Alhambra palace. Silently thanking Almighty Allah, he prayed for Divine strength and support in the battle ahead.

The heralds of each contestant had proclaimed their masters; his trumpeters had responded to the fanfare of King Charles's. As he lowered his visor, he noted with surprise that, though there had been but a stony silence from the royal enclosure and that of the ladies, a great many of the watching crowds were cheering him, infidel though he was. He did not care a fig for the attitude of royalty, for when his eyes fell briefly on his lady, Princess Beatrice, she had given him back a quick glance before he veered his horse away from the front of the royal enclosure which told him of her feelings. She would be cheering secretly for him. He fixed the physical image of her firmly in his mind and only his princely training kept him from looking towards her again and again for a renewal of that first glance. While he prayed to Almighty Allah, she would be praying to her God to help him. Two supreme beings on my side, he thought whimsically for a moment, so how can I lose? Hot and sweaty in his armour – for while Toledo was much cooler than his native Granada, he did not enjoy stewing in a steel container – he now directed his total attention to King Charles.

The royal trumpets' call to arms resounded through the warm air. He felt he could literally hear the hush that fell over the arena, making more sharp the odours of oil and metal from his armour that mingled with the outside smell of parching soil and grass.

The king-at-arms lowered his sword, clapped spurs on his horse to clear the lists, took his position to the side of the royal enclosure, facing the contestants.

A single trumpet sounded the charge. Prince Ahmed levelled his lance, relaxed the reins slightly, eased his seat, applied light pressure with his legs. The white charger responded to the aids with precision. You and I shall achieve wonders today, dear Amir, Prince Ahmed thought, directing the charger to a trot, then a canter. He himself was riding reflexively now, his mind fully focused on the giant figure on a black horse, lumbering towards him at first then speeding faster with a smooth, easy motion. Within the silence of his helmet, Prince Ahmed's brain was bright as a sun's ray.

Both chargers achieved the gallop almost simultaneously. Prince Ahmed now concentrated on the point of King Charles's swiftly approaching lance. At a two-lance distance away, when the king veered left, as he had done with King Philip, a jet of exultation fountained within Prince Ahmed as he veered left too, avoiding the trap into which King Philip had fallen. His move made King Charles's lance swiftly drift away from its target for a split second. With superhuman strength, however, he deflected it back at the prince. Too late, Prince Ahmed had already swung his mount to the right.

The point of Prince Ahmed's lance found his opponent's chest, shattered. Beaten off balance by his own tactic, King Charles teetered on his saddle, while Prince Ahmed let go his broken lance and shot past, knowing he had unseated his opponent.

But how badly?

The great thud that reached his ears, followed by the quickening beat of the hooves of a horse freed of its burden, gave the answer even before Prince Ahmed circled his charger widely and rode back. King Charles lay still in the dust. The larger they are, the heavier they fall. A reflexive jerk of a greaved thigh told Prince Ahmed that the fallen king would not rise, but was alive. The joust was over. He had won in a single charge!

Now Prince Ahmed faced the most decisive moment. What would King Pedro do? He raised his visor and gazed hopefully towards the entrance to the arena. Before the onlookers could react to his victory, a roaring had arisen there. His heart quickened in triumph at seeing the mass of humanity racing through the entrance, shoving guards aside as if they were debris before raging flood-waters. In the centre of that mass of long, unkempt hair and tattered clothes, was the blond head of a horseman. Now Prince Ahmed's heart leapt. It was Prince Juan. Zurika had accomplished her mission.

King Pedro was on his feet, roaring commands that could not be heard in the din. Count Gaston had left his place behind the *Grandes Dames* and was moving towards the fallen body of his ruler in the lists. The palace guard was closing in round the royal enclosures and that of the ladies.

There was no time to lose. Prince Ahmed sped his charger towards the ladies' enclosure. Princess Beatrice had caught his eye, divined his intention. Rising swiftly to her feet, she descended to the green grass, clambered over the fence and sped towards him, ignoring the screams of other ladies.

As he drew near her, Prince Ahmed slowed his horse, bent as low as his armour would permit, his right arm extended. Princess Beatrice grasped it and sprang upwards, timing the move perfectly. He swept her up with the strength of desperation. She teetered. His arm felt as if it was being jerked off its sockets. Then he had hoisted her on to the saddle in front of him and his charger was gathering speed. One arm still around her, Prince Ahmed grasped the reins with both his hands, dug fierce spurs into Amir's flanks.

The noble steed responded once more, broke into a fast canter. As he approached them, the bedraggled crowd of released prisoners parted to make way for him. Gaunt, emaciated faces, unshaven, filthy, creased with suffering, extended brightened eyes and bony hands to him. The stench of unwashed bodies and dried excreta nauseated him physically, but there was thankfulness in his heart. These were his saviours, these poor innocents, these hardened criminals, these victims of King Pedro's justice. He became conscious that Princess Beatrice had settled comfortably against him. He wished he did not have his armour on, so he could feel the warmth and softness of her body.

Then he was alongside the dumbly laughing Prince Juan, who had turned his horse around. Soldiers with halberds were beating on the prisoners to sweep them off the arena. Cries, groans, screams and imprecations tumbled into the welter of confusion, as Prince Juan and he rode side by side towards the arena's entrance.

A louder roar and a series of crashes made Prince Ahmed glance to his left. Above the sea of matted, white, grey and dark hair, the black *yarmulke* of Jewish prisoners, the shiny helmets of guards and soldiers, he could see that the watching crowds had broken loose from their enclosure and were raging into the arena, laughing and screaming, to join the fray.

For a moment Prince Ahmed was nonplussed. Why should these people intervene on his behalf? Then the truth struck him. This was no intervention. The hot-blooded Spaniards loved a fight, especially against authority. Now they were wading into the king's men with gusto.

Pounding hooves thundering beneath him, Prince Ahmed led Prince Juan until they reached the entrance of the arena. To his horror, a line of footsoldiers, in black tunics and white pantaloons, steel halberds levelled, stood ranged across the entrance gates. They were obviously part of the army swiftly cordoning off the whole arena. Prince Ahmed's heart contracted, but without a moment's hesitation, he clapped spurs on his charger again, set Amir at the silent line of standing men. His eager eyes sought the grim faces for one that might be wavering at his move. They fell on a fair, beardless boy, scared, unaccustomed to battle. He set Amir for the boy. The dark eyes widening with fear told him he had found the weak spot. The boy's halberd wavered. He swept past it. The boy stumbled, leapt to get out of the way of the charging horse.

Prince Ahmed swept through the gap, shouting fiercely back at the screams and curses of the other guards. He recalled his cavalry instructor's words: In a mêlée, the man who decisively takes the initiative wins.

Then his charger was through, fierce hooves clattering

on the cobbled highway. He risked a quick glance back. Prince Juan was closely following him. A prince indeed!

His eyes fell on Princess Beatrice's golden hair. He breathed her scent of honeysuckle at last. Bred almost in a convent, she too had responded fearlessly, with quick intelligence and decisive action. What a princess! What a queen she would make.

Without pause, they made for the hidden grove where Prince Ahmed knew that Zurika and Aaron Levi would be waiting with fresh mounts and the wagon. The crane to lift him off his horse was already there.

Chapter 20

He sat back on the curved wooden chair, elbows resting on its oak arms. The glow from the hanging lamps did not comfort him tonight, while the reek of burnt oil was merely irritating. As for the paintings of bullfights, he was repelled by them, that of the matador administering the coup-de-grâce to a great black bull being a special reminder of King Charles the Bad's downfall at the hands of a Muslim matador from Granada, probably possessed of the same slender, agile build as the real matador in the painting.

King Pedro the Cruel had been alternating between fury, gloom and disbelief during all the hours following the debacle in the arena that afternoon. The back of his head ached and his jaws hurt from his habit of grinding his teeth when he was in a rage. He slid back his chair, stretched out massive legs. 'Fuck everything!' he growled unpleasantly.

With Bishop Eulogius, dressed in purple, seated across the great oaken desk, the words and the scene would have taken King Pedro back to the night when it all started, except for the presence of Count Gaston, immaculate in white, seated next to the prelate and for the bishop's seething anger. What should be done had been discussed extensively with all his guests during the dinner that night which he had originally planned as a celebration to crown the royal tourney. He had retired to his study after heated debate, covert slights and the postponement of any decision for a full assembly tomorrow.

'A white Christian princess, a virgin, abducted by a black Moor,' the cleric fumed for the umpteenth time.

His chubby cheeks were unusually flushed, his angry eyes no longer slits in the folds around them but wide pebbles of blue ice and he was not incanting his words. The man is a racist, King Pedro decided detachedly. 'How could we have let it happen, Sire? The heretic should have been seized the moment he entered the arena. I mean, the sheer effrontery of it is an insult to every white Christian. We should burn all unbelievers at the stake.'

I am facing one of the gravest crises in my life and all you can think of is a thrill for your feckless, fuckless penis while you watch people burning at the stake, you little prick, King Pedro thought savagely. He needed to direct his anger somewhere tangible, but wisdom prompted him to hold back its expression.

'I submit that we need cool judgment rather than fire and brimstone policies at this time of grave crisis, Your Majesty,' Count Gaston intervened smoothly.

Of all the distinguished guests, the count had been the most calm and understanding. Most of the other arseholes had been critical and condescending. King Pedro knew they were probably thinking that if he could not control Toledo and the Castilians, he was not to be trusted at the head of a large crusading Christian army. They would also consider his defeat last year at the hands of King Yusuf of Granada and that his deaf-mute son, Prince Juan, was on the side of this young Moor, Prince Ahmed. What a stinking mess!

'His Majesty had done all that is humanly possible in the face of a most unexpected and extraordinary event,' Count Gaston continued. 'His troops quelled the disturbance and the royal party was safely evacuated without anyone being hurt. Over a hundred of the rioters were seized and promptly hanged on His Majesty's orders. Their corpses are even now swinging on improvised gibbets in the arena as a public warning to others. I for one shall recommend to my master, King Charles, that we support His Majesty King Pedro in any immediate steps he may decide to take. As for any invasion of Granada, I submit that this is not a time for rushing into vengeance but for sober planning. After all, Your Eminence, was it not the first white Christian martyrs in the arena that faced the hungriest lions?'

King Pedro knew a flash of gratitude for the support from the hatchet-faced Basque, an aristocrat in more than name. 'We thank you, Count, for your support at this most trying time,' he declared. 'We shall nonetheless make vengeance our first priority.' He ground out the words. His eye fell on the painting across the room and it suddenly occurred to him that he had been so preoccupied with arrangements for the tourney that he had not played monster for quite a while. Perhaps that was why the people, having forgotten his cruelty, had invaded the arena for a fight. Well, the hangings would have brought them to their senses. More executions would follow when his secret agents headed by Ruy de Vivar had finished their work. 'Months of most careful planning, vast sums of money spent on a spectacular event that was turned into a fucking farce by a beardless Muslim boy and his associates who ridiculed and humiliated us before the elite of Europe's royalty and nobility.' His gorge started to rise. 'Why, we shall be held in contempt by all peoples and throughout history.' He could have groaned aloud at the prospect. He shoved forward his chair, grating on the marble floor, thumped the solid table so hard that it rattled. 'What else remains but revenge?' He was glaring at Count Gaston now. 'What else can restore our reputation throughout the world?' And yet he knew that he could not as yet permit Inquisition. Everything had seemed so harmonious just a few hours ago; now all kinds of conflict were suddenly swirling around him. 'Can you imagine how the accursed Moorish kings of North Africa will laugh when they hear the news?' His blood began to boil again and his face turned purple with fury. God blast those responsible, including his son, his only son who had turned against him. He would add to Prince Juan's mutilation. He would castrate the father-fucker, then cut off his cock. The mere contemplation of such punishment eased him somewhat, but he longed to hasten to Maria de Padilla's bedchamber where he could forget his troubles.

'My master lost the joust,' Count Gaston reminded him. '*That* is the most significant circumstance of the tournament. He will have to live it down. If he had won, matters would have turned out differently. So I beg you, Sire, to proceed with wisdom and restraint. Meanwhile . . .'

'You would exercise restraint while a white Christian virgin is probably being raped at this very moment by a black barbarian Moor,' Bishop Eulogius snarled, betraying such an unwonted rage that King Pedro began to wonder whether it was not being deliberately put on. 'What is important now is to take advantage of this mortal insult offered to all white Christians present at the tournament and advance white Christian unity,' he raised a pudgy pink hand, but not in blessing, 'and extract the direst vengeance on all heretics.'

'Your Eminence, this afternoon's events had nothing to do with heresy,' Count Gaston protested. 'Where is the rape? I personally saw Princess Beatrice jump the barrier and leap on Prince Ahmed's horse of her own accord.'

Bishop Eulogius flushed, controlled himself with a great effort. 'I shall respond to you point by point, Chancellor.' He was calmer now, intoning again. 'First, heresy is not limited to thoughts, words or deeds against our faith. The Moor's actions were a heresy against our time-honoured traditional codes of conduct.' His pudgy cheeks shone with his beam of triumph. 'Next, it was not the white Christians but the heretics who surged into the arena and battled His Majesty's soldiers for over two hours. I myself saw Moors and Jews in the mêlée. It was *they* who made a mock of his Majesty's authority and delayed pursuit of the culprits because priority had to be given to protecting the royal parties. The accursed miscreants could not have timed it better if they had been part of a major plot, which is still a possibility, with Jewish money behind it.'

'You have no evidence that it was only heretics who waded into the fight,' Count Gaston retorted. 'I saw many white faces and they seemed to be enjoying the fight.'

'Jews!' Bishop Eulogius asserted. 'Jews, Moriscos and Moors. All non-Christians humiliating our blessed sovereign.'

This prelate prick is trying to needle me into doing his will, King Pedro thought, more calmly. Count Gaston's words had given him food for thought. He was in an ugly situation and he had best proceed with cunning. 'Our wife, the mother of the princess, is distraught,' he temporized. 'She cannot understand how she could have carried such a wanton ingrate in her womb.'

'Her ladyship did not do it alone!' Count Gaston reminded him boldly. 'If you will forgive my presumptuousness, Sire, the daring initiative displayed by the Princess Beatrice is more the product of what bred her than of where she was bred!'

King Pedro could not restrain a laugh. 'We had not considered that the event offered us some credit,' he declared. His headache eased a little from his first laugh since noon. He thought rapidly. 'You are right, Count Gaston. We shall proceed in a manner that will achieve our ultimate goal and still bring us the satisfaction of revenge, which may well wait until it can be extracted to the last headless corpse, when it will be even sweeter for the delay and its increased dimension.'

'And exactly how will you proceed, Sire?' Bishop Eulogius inquired, his blue eyes frost.

'In a manner that will satisfy everyone concerned,

including you, Eminence.' King Pedro was suddenly in control of himself and the situation. 'First, let us analyse the position.' He paused, raised his huge head. 'Our meeting with our royal guests earlier tonight ended with denunciations and expressions of outrage which afford us neither support nor a plan of action. We have concluded that the white Christian rulers outside Iberia are totally unconcerned about the fate of the white Christian princess.' He nodded his head. 'Especially when that princess has a commoner for a mother. We know how these birth-proud European bastards think. Now that hope of ruling the kingdom of Castile through victory in the tourney is no longer open to them, they will go home and throw their blue blood in our face, boasting that they lost nothing but marriage to a commoner who fled with a Moor. Since all those who lost would have called the grapes sour anyway, it matters little to us. Fuck them all.' He lowered a forefinger, glanced at Count Gaston as if inviting him to do the deed.

'Quite so, Sire,' the Chancellor averred, declining the offer.

'And yet, if you revive Reconquista with the support of Holy Church, none of these Christian monarchs can openly refuse their support,' Bishop Eulogius thrust in, 'which was why you wanted them here in the first place.'

'*En verdad*. We shall preside over the conference we have called for tomorrow morning and attempt to forge a Christian alliance to restore our religion,' piously the king crossed himself, not giving a fart for sincerity, 'throughout the Iberian peninsula. They can hardly refuse that, can they, Eminence? We shall tie them down to specific areas of support and timing of their assistance to fit in with our plan.'

'When will you invade Granada, Your Majesty?' Bishop Eulogius demanded, persistent. 'And why should we not make this a European crusade instead of merely an Iberian one? After all, are we not opposing the Muslims again?'

King Pedro raised a restraining hand. 'All in good time, Your Eminence. In order to make a decision, we need to consider the basic factors involved.' He gripped the edge of the table with both palms, leaned forward. His brain was working with precision again. He would not go dashing alone against the Moors, as he had done before, to suffer more defeat and humiliation. He must first forge an alliance of all parties, including this little prick whose constant reference to the virgin princess had disgusted him, but whose support as primate bishop of Spain was critical. 'Our cavalry is already pursuing the fugitives though they had a two-hour start. We presumed they would head for Granada.' He grinned ferociously, lowered his voice. 'They may well be heading to a situation of chaos of our creation,' he asserted conspiratorially. 'It is possible that the Moorish kingdom is without a ruler at this very moment.' His grin widened. 'If our plan has seen fruition, Prince Ahmed, the heir, will walk into a kingdom without a ruler, and we should attack it sooner rather than later while it is weakened by internal conflict as to the succession.' He noted the admiring glance of the bishop with satisfaction. 'Strike first, then get the insolent Moor,' he concluded.

'Has Your Majesty also despatched pursuit troops along the eastern and western highways, since the fugitives may have made a detour before heading for Granada?' Count Gaston inquired.

'We had thought of that, but concentrating our effort on the direct highway was a chance we had to take in the interest of speed. If the fugitives have indeed detoured, our troops can ascertain this along the way and, having gained distance on them through being on the direct route, will be able to intercept them at the intersections of those highways with that leading to Granada.'

'Sire . . .' the prelate began.

'Just one moment,' King Pedro interrupted the interruption. He was convinced that Bishop Eulogius would not want the fugitives intercepted, so that the war against Granada could escalate more quickly, attended by Inquisition and the opportunity for him to become primate of regions beyond Iberia, when he would seek to be appointed a cardinal, even the prospect of being elected Pope. 'Count Gaston is right. We must not confuse speed of pursuit or lust for vengeance with the objects of Holy Church. Vengeance is mine, I shall repay, saith the Lord.' He crossed himself piously again, enjoying the barely veiled discomfiture of the prelate. 'Pursuit of the fugitives is a purely personal matter. The establishment of Holy Church is one of religious principles.' He paused, eyed the Bishop into silence. 'In order to formulate our plans, it is essential for us to know who was behind these . . . these . . .' he held back a sputter of returning rage, 'these infamous actions.' He paused, glanced at the door of the study. 'Just before we adjourned here from dinner, we received a report as to who was really responsible from the head of our town brotherhood. For your information, Count, his name is Ruy de Vivar and he claims to be a bastard descendant of our hero, El Cid Campeador. De Vivar's *Hermandad* organization is so efficient that he was able to obtain the necessary information in a matter of hours. We asked him to be in attendance outside, so he can give you both his news at first hand.' I have not lost my cunning, he reflected sardonically as he reached for the bell-rope. I need Navarre and Holy Church for my purposes so their representatives may as well become personally involved tonight.

He inclined his massive head graciously as the thin bald man with the thin, bald face entered and made a deep salutation. When the door closed behind him, it wafted the scent of amber from his usual tight-fitting brown tunic.

381

'This is Señor Ruy de Vivar, a descendant of our great hero, El Cid.' King Pedro nodded towards the prelate. 'On our left is Count Gaston, Chancellor to King Charles of Navarre. The hour is late, so please come directly to the point.'

Ruy de Vivar bowed low. 'I am honoured,' he stated as he came erect, his smile wintry as ever. 'My lords, my inquiries have disclosed that the entire plot – it was no less – to . . . er . . . remove the princess,' he had obviously decided against saying 'rescue', 'was the work of three men and a young girl.' His smile turned vicious, his mouth twisting. 'One of the three was a Jew, whose only son we had mistakenly beheaded, on the orders of His Majesty, several years ago for a crime he did not commit. The father, who had no other family, has since lived for the Jewish tradition of vengeance.'

'What is this Jew's name, *señor*?' the prelate demanded.

'Aaron Levi.'

'The banker?' He paused. 'I knew the Jews were behind this,' he added, vicious with triumph.

King Pedro observed with wonder that the prelate continued to be more concerned with the punishment than with the crime. 'He is one of the wealthiest men in Europe. Why would he risk all his wealth and possessions on such an enterprise?' he inquired.

'We have already told you, Eminence. Vengeance. An eye for an eye, a creed as ancient as the Jewish race. He obviously determined this was all he had left in life. You take my son, I take your daughter. Vicious justice.'

King Pedro was hard put to hold down his wrath, which had begun to boil again. 'He owned a villa near our capital, from which the entire operation was carried out,' he interposed.

'Did you say, owned, Sire?' Count Gaston had picked up on his use of the past tense.

'Yes, owned.' King Pedro bared his teeth savagely. 'We

have had the villa burned to the ground and have confiscated the land into our Treasury.' He lifted his head at Ruy de Vivar. 'But we interrupt you. Pray continue.'

'Prince Ahmed and Prince Juan were the other two leaders of the plot,' de Vivar stated. 'We have been unable to establish a motive for their actions, except for the romantic one of a brother's attempt to rescue his sister from his father, with his good friend assisting him.' He smiled apologetically. 'Madness perhaps, but you know your Spanish people, Sire. They will say that the rescue was to save a daughter from a tyrannical parent.'

'Fuck them all and fuck what people say,' King Pedro burst out savagely, but he could not avoid a moody stare.

'And what of the young girl conspirator, *señor*?' A hopeful note had entered Bishop Eulogius's voice. 'Was she an experienced siren or . . .'

'A fucking virgin?' King Pedro interjected brutally. 'How the fuck would we know when we never fucked her?' He restrained his anger. 'It was she who rescued our son, Prince Juan, from the palace dungeons to which we had consigned him night before last when he was intercepted while . . . er . . . attempting entry into the ladies' quarter. All we know from the four prison guards when they recovered from drugged wine she gave them was that she was an accomplished singer and claimed to be a dancer as well. She ended up a murderess, brutally and repeatedly stabbing the fifth prison guard. She was probably a gypsy, so *there's* another target group for your Inquisition.' He noted the split-second widening of Bishop Eulogius's eyes at his use of the word, which had been deliberate.

'Against the gypsies too, Sire?'

'*Ciertamente*,' King Pedro's eyes glowed with rage. 'Every single fucking race that insulted us shall be punished.' He shot a warning glance at the prelate. 'But only at the right time and place. As for the savage slaying of our prison guard, we have already sentenced the woman to death.'

'As you have just told us, Sire, this young woman drugged four guards, obviously as part of the rescue plot,' Count Gaston stated. 'It is the killing of the fifth guard that puzzles me. The savage mutilation would appear to indicate insensate rage. Could it not be . . .?' he ended with a shrug of slim shoulders.

'It does not matter a fart! She killed one of our guards. For that, she shall die.' King Pedro noted the blank look in Count Gaston's dark eyes, felt a moment's irritation at being silently criticized, then realized that he needed the count on his side to obtain King Charles's fullest co-operation. 'All your concerns come within our sole purview and shall receive full and just consideration.' He shoved his chair back, stretched out his tree-trunk legs, jerked his head for de Vivar to continue.

'As your Majesty is aware,' de Vivar's beady eyes twinkled maliciously, 'Lord Joram and Rabbi Azar are the two leaders of our Toledo Jewish community. They are appalled at what Aaron Levi has done and disclaim any connection with him, except that he owned the letters of credit that provided Prince Ahmed with the funds to buy the horses, armour, wagons and equipment necessary for his plan. Fearful of reprisals, Lord Joram has agreed to make available all records relating to Aaron Levi and I shall have them delivered immediately to Your Majesty. I am afraid, however, that the Jew cunningly transferred most of his assets elsewhere a few days ago, doubtless in anticipation of today's events. There is still considerable wealth here, however, that should substantially enrich the royal Treasury even if it cannot compensate for the loss of a child.' He raised a bony hand as if in benediction.

'All this fucking Jew's possessions throughout Castile shall be confiscated,' King Pedro growled.

'But I understand he will remain extremely rich through

his possessions in Granada, Portugal and abroad,' de Vivar responded.

'There are other ways in which we can break him,' King Pedro countered viciously.

'Inquisition,' Bishop Eulogius suggested with unfailing monotony.

King Pedro, in control of himself again, the headache having vanished, ignored him. 'As for the major issue, we shall, in consultation with our immediate allies, our brothers of Navarre, Aragon and Catalonia, accelerate the date of the invasion of Granada. We shall fund the operation by making a special levy on all Jews for the crime of their fellow-Jew, this Aaron Levi, besides offering a substantial reward for his apprehension, from the confiscation of his remaining assets in Castile.' He thought that rather neat.

'What of immediate Inquisition, Your Majesty, to fire our troops with religious zeal?' Bishop Eulogius persisted.

King Pedro bared his teeth evilly. 'That too will come in good time, when we have all the money we need from the Jews and stand before the walls of the Alhambra.'

'When do you hope to commence the invasion, Sire?' Count Gaston sounded concerned.

'Within thirty days, so we can take Granada before the winter rains.'

'If you will forgive me for saying so, Your Majesty,' the prelate intoned loftily, not looking the least like a penitent, 'you are following the lead of your illustrious predecessor, King Alfonso VII. He had the resoluteness and thrust of the Castilians, which enabled him to turn defeat into victory. You will recall his disastrous defeat by the Moors in 1195.' He gave Count Gaston a scornful glance. 'Partly because the Leonese backed out on him at the last moment. He subsequently persuaded His Holiness the Pope to declare his initiative a crusade and call on international volunteers. So in the battle of Solosa seventeen years later he was joined by Navarre, Aragon and Portugal, León once again being conspicuous by its absence.' The glance he gave Count Gaston this time was met by an amused smile. 'The Christian forces thrashed the Moors, ending their domination of our peninsula.' He beamed at King Pedro.

'So what is the point of your history lesson, the facts of which we are well aware?' King Pedro demanded irritably.

'Ah!' A sermonic pink finger was lifted and lowered. 'The Moors are well-nigh unbeatable when they embark on holy war, but they have always proved themselves weak in defence against our Spanish Christian soldiers, each of whom is the superior of the Moor in stubborn will, individual drive and boundless energy, each soul possessed of a constant heroism and an epic faith which provides a chamber of inner strength. How can you draw on these virtues, Sire? As King Alfonso did, by opening the door of Christian faith to the divine goal of Reconquista, which desperately needs a symbol.' The pink finger was raised again. King Pedro resisted the urge to whip out his knife and chop it off. It would look pretty silly lying on the oaken desk while its bloody stump remained bereft and bleeding. 'That symbol is Inquisition, the blazing fires of heretics' stakes.'

'Your Eminence, I would remind you and His Majesty that the first essential to a crusade is unity. The kind of unity which was not forthcoming from León for King Alfonso is available today.' The count's dark eyes had suddenly turned hard. 'One of the conditions of our support is that we have such unity. It is only whenever all Christian kingdoms combined that we defeated the Moors. Never forget too that the converted Moors and Jews are our most productive people. They have their own reservoirs of economic support. They are better agriculturists, engineers, tradesmen and manufacturers of the leather goods, armour and swords we badly need for our campaign. Their lands are more fruitful, their material wealth greater. Their civilizations are superior to ours technically, economically and even intellectually. Let us therefore harness them to our cause, to provide a tangible base from which our white Christian troops can launch their crusade.'

'Heresy!' Bishop Eulogius thundered.

'Truth!' Count Gaston countered calmly.

King Pedro could already see cracks in the foundation of Christian unity. 'We shall permit Inquisition at the right time and place,' he repeated.

Count Gaston's jaw set. 'Your Majesty, I submit to you with the utmost sobriety that the Christian world is united by faith,' he stated passionately. 'What is it then that makes each component part of that world Spanish or French, Italian, German or English, solid, cohesive, bonded? It is patriotism. Nations are neither territorial, linguistic, nor cultural, nor are countries any longer one tribe, one race, one kingdom or one religion. Nations and countries are spiritual. I beg you not to take any action that would fragment the Iberians into Castilians, Aragonians, Catalonians, Leonese and men of Navarre, into Christians and heathens, Moors and Jews who pay one half our taxes but to unite us all under your banner as Spaniards seeking to establish one single, beloved Spain.'

The defeat of King Charles the Bad in the joust had been a real shock to Princess Mathilde. She had always regarded him as being physically invincible. Seeing him lying prone in the dust had not roused sympathy but anger against him. Unseating from a high horse was symbolic to her and went beyond the shock of seeing a certain winner lose. She had grown so accustomed to her protégé winning all the time, not just in tournaments, riding competitions and hunting, but in the jousts of politics she had engineered in order to expand his future, that she had wondered during the course of that afternoon whether King Charles was not a loser. Had affection for the lonely boy that still resided in him clouded her judgment?

The question had jolted her. Too much was at stake for both of them to permit a mistake. Each time she pondered on it, she experienced the strangest feeling of emptiness. Like King Charles, she had grown unaccustomed to defeat since those long days of her own uncertain future. There had been no such errors when she depended only on herself.

Did she love King Charles less because of his downfall? The answer was a clear no. Love was the base from which her plans for him emerged and that had not been changed. What she was contemplating objectively was the subject of these plans, setting aside all emotions, so that she could succeed in the struggle to survive and survive better than others.

When she had finally made her decision, after much thought, it was based on the answers to simple questions. Why had she wanted King Charles to become an Emperor in the first place? It was so she could wield power from behind an imperial throne, the power she never had, the power that would make it unnecessary for her ever again to be at the mercy of others as she had been since her betrothed had died. Did it matter to her who was the titular head of the Empire? No, it could be a scarecrow dressed in regal robes and wearing an imperial crown for all she cared. Then, why not Charles? Indeed, why not!

She had managed to receive King Charles in her suite at some time every evening or immediately after dinner ever since they had arrived at the Toledo palace for the tourney. So tonight, she had missed their meeting. Now, never one to place the rules of decorum before her needs, believing that it was not what you do but how you do it that matters, she had taken an unheard-of step by calling on the king in his private chambers.

In the golden light of hanging oil lamps that made the pink marble floors glow, she found King Charles propped up on the white silk cushions of a huge four-poster bed, the carved gilt headboard of which ran all the way up to a frilled satin canopy of darker gold. The door to the bedroom had been left open in the interests of propriety, and Countess Isabella, her chief lady-in-waiting, sat decorously conversing with two of King Charles's medical attendants in the small sitting room on a high-backed chair placed where she could see the whole bedroom. The smell of astringent lotions, rubbing oil and unguents in clay containers crowding a gilt side-table dominated. Topped by a night cap with a tassel King Charles's huge bulk and bull-like face seemed oddly incongruous, even slightly comical.

She had been announced by the liveried royal attendant, had made her salutation and then sat on a gilt chair placed for her beside the bed.

When they were alone, to her surprise, King Charles, propped high on the cushion, muttered very simply, 'We lost,' and hung his head.

He sounded so like a little boy that her woman's heart went out to him, evaporating most of her anger. 'You lost a battle, you shall win the war,' she countered fiercely. 'Always remember that it is the final victory that matters.' She became imbued with the need to reassure him and herself. 'You will experience reverses, but . . . you . . . shall . . . be . . . Emperor some day.'

'How shall we live through the shame of defeat?' He seemed to be talking to himself. 'We have always been the champion.'

This was a different Charles. Did he lack the more basic depths of character that it takes to sustain defeat? Had his fall liquefied his brain? Impatience began mounting within her. She resisted the urge to admonish him that he had lost because he had been utterly stupid, repeating a tactic he had used less than a half an hour earlier against another opponent. 'All those you have defeated in the past, including King Philip, have lived through it,' she responded quietly. 'Risk of defeat is one of the hazards of any contender and it is no shame to lose. The bad element of defeat is when you allow it to defeat your purpose. A true champion always rises from the bitterness of defeat to rekindle the fires of triumph.' She could not help adding, 'God give you the grace to accept victory as if you are accustomed to it and defeat as if it were victory.'

'The girl,' he muttered. 'What will she think of me?'

Her eyebrows arched in astonishment. 'What girl?' she demanded before it dawned on her that he was referring to Princess Beatrice.

'The princess, the prize.' He still seemed to be speaking to himself.

Had he become deranged by his fall?

'She is more beautiful than I dreamed,' he muttered. 'Pure white, pure virgin. So young.'

The truth hit her. This rapist, this stud, this animal whose brute sexuality was one of his most attractive features in her eyes, had fallen in love. So young, pure white, pure virgin, he had said. What was she, Princess Mathilde, then? Old, smirched, used? For the first time ever, she faced her age and the taint of some of her own past sexuality and it brought shame, rejection, inferiority sweeping through her from obstacles of her past she could not overcome. Could it have been King Charles's preoccupation with victory the moment he saw Princess Beatrice that caused his defeat? She recalled that last conversation in the Pamplona palace when she and Charles had pledged fidelity to each other even if he were married. That concession had been based on the assumption that King Charles truly loved her alone. Now, jealous rage and shame flamed within her. How dare this . . . this churl in a peacock's feathers treat her as if she was some spiritual harlot! At that moment she hated King Charles. Only breeding kept her from leaping on him and clawing his eyes out.

She breathed deeply to bring herself under control. Many a princess had been a harlot, but not she. All these years, she had bent kings to her will without ever giving them her body. She was no harlot but a princess of royal blood and a survivor through sheer character and wisdom. She had fought all her secret battles objectively, with no emotional involvement. She had permitted herself emotion towards Charles since his early boyhood, her unfulfilled mother instinct reaching out to him. He had finally grown up to juvenile emotions. She simply had to let go. Dimly she realized that, even if she stripped herself of the involvement, she could still use King Charles to achieve supreme power.

A still small voice within her questioned. Would you continue being able to manipulate him if he took an intelligent, ambitious woman with whom he was in love for a queen? Would such a woman permit him to be your pawn? What would you do then?

The answer came back clear as the crystal morning dews of Pamplona on green grass. Destroy the woman.

'Godsbody, my loins ache for her, my heart craves for her. Have I lost her forever?' He had even dropped the royal plural before his singular attachment. What a peasant he was at heart!

'Perhaps,' she stabbed, deliberately cruel, then twisted the knife. 'At this very moment she is probably coupling with the victor, Prince Ahmed.'

A low growl escaped him. 'I had intended killing the black Moorish bastard anyway, but if he has taken my girl, I shall cut off his genitals and stuff them in his mouth.'

391

Here was a man of no class or distinction when it came to his sexual organs, but what had she expected from a rapist murderer? Certainly more than these infantile screechings, for she had respected the rapist in him. She despised the idealist lover. 'You should pursue the fugitives yourself, capture Prince Ahmed and do just that to him,' she advised. Then hatred of her rival possessed her, brought vindictiveness and cunning. 'Whether Princess Beatrice has coupled with the Moor or not, promise me that you will deliver her to me so I can punish her for what she has done to you.'

He looked at her directly for the first time. The hot eyes had turned red with anger, his face thrust forward though he had no neck. 'That we certainly shall,' he growled. 'We certainly promise.'

This version of Charles, the King, she could respect more, but the hatred of him and Princess Beatrice remained. She would never forget this night.

Meanwhile, she had not even inquired about his health!

She could not deny that she was shattered when she emerged from King Charles's suite and proceeded down the palace corridor, with Countess Isabella at her left and slightly to the rear. What a dreadful day it had been. The devastation of her hopes when King Charles tumbled on to the dust had culminated in the moments she had just experienced. Some deeper part of her, she guessed it was a wounded heart, lay crumpled in the dust. The real pain would come later. And as always they would never know.

Yet the very advice she gave her protégé applied to her. There were always setbacks in the course of a victory. She would use hers as spurs for the ultimate triumph. She had one advantage tonight. She could now be ruthless with the man who would take her there, King Charles. Throughout her entire life, even when she was a child, no one had ever suspected that she was so easily hurt, least of all King Charles. She would remain the charming, poised, well-bred Princess Mathilde, without a care in the world.

It somehow lightened her spirit when she saw Count Gaston approaching, obviously on the way back to his own quarters.

He stopped when he saw her, bowed deeply, betraying no surprise at her presence there so late at night.

'Ah, Chancellor, what a pleasant end to an unusual day.' She extended her ivory fan studded with glittering diamonds towards him. 'An added reward to us for having dared to invade the sacred precincts of the Toledo palace's male temple.'

The hatchet face broke into its charming white smile. 'How can it be an invasion, Princess, when you are the high priestess of beauty?'

'You can be so gallant so late at night?'

'Such truth about you is ever gallant, madam.'

She warmed towards him. Here was a man with whom she could converse. 'You know Countess Isabella of course.'

He bowed slightly in the Countess's direction. 'Who does not?'

Her lady-in-waiting actually simpered. Why could she not have had someone like Count Gaston as her protégé? The answer was very clear. Such a man was no one's front. Count Gaston would always be his own person. He reminded her somewhat of her father, Count de Beauvais, whom she had adored. With her mother dead at childbirth, her father had spent a great deal of time teaching her, his only child, all he knew, though she had her tutors in languages, history, politics, mathematics, equestrianism, even fencing in her earlier years. Then, just as she came to know her father as an adult, he had to send her away. It had hurt deeply and she had never gone back, even in memory, especially as her father died immediately after she left home. Recollections of dinner by firelight, the hunting dogs lazing beside the fireplace, sometimes returned.

'You are returning after dinner, Count? Did you enjoy your meal?'

He threw back his head and laughed. 'What would you say if I answered, yes and no? That the Castilian food is not as spicy as our Basque dishes?'

'I would believe you.'

'Etiquette demands a sober scorn for veracity, Your Highness.'

'To be sober last thing at night betokens unctuousness, don't you think? The least one can do to display contempt for the day is to be drunk at its end.'

'Well put. Sobriety last thing at night exposes one's calling, while grumpiness first thing in the morning disguises a peasant disposition.'

'People should teach their children how to live of good cheer and die of drink.'

'There is nothing that the children of today can be taught by their parents. Once upon a time, children were supposed to be nice and innocent. Nowadays they are not even nice.'

As her laughter rang down the side corridor, she noticed the huge, gilt-framed oil paintings of King Pedro's predecessors and ancestors lining the wall.

Ever perceptive, Count Gaston followed her gaze. 'The disadvantage of such portraits is that they perpetuate the afflictions of one's family and nation,' he remarked drily. 'To answer your first question, however, I am not coming directly from the great dining hall. After dinner, King Pedro, Bishop Eulogius and I adjourned to the king's study, with me merely standing in for my royal master.'

'What decisions did you reach?'

He shot a glance at Countess Isabella standing patiently beside her. 'More importantly, King Pedro and I curbed the impatience of his Eminence for an immediate, all-out effort to rescue a white Christian virgin and avenge the insults to our white Christian rulers.'

Somehow she was thankful for his light-hearted treatment of the subject of the white Christian virgin. 'I suppose Bishop Eulogius was all blood and fire for a Holy War without pause for planning?'

'King Pedro and my master had already done much of the planning. We shall not proceed precipitately.'

'I shall use whatever little influence I have with our King Charles to hasten the day.' Even the astute Count Gaston could never have guessed that she meant the day of reckoning for Princess Beatrice.

Chapter 21

Night had fallen with the suddenness of mountain country. The moon had struggled vainly to appear before being smothered by black clouds that left its glow barely visible. The pressure of sharp slopes on either side of the highway made it darker than ever, so they had to reduce their pace, the only lights being from the flares carried high by the outriders and the dim lamps on either side of the wagon.

It was midnight now and Prince Ahmed eagerly scanned the sides of the road for a suitable place to halt for a few hours, straining his ears for the sound of water which the horses needed.

Having taken command of their flight from Toledo, Prince Ahmed had Princess Beatrice and Zurika ride with Aaron Levi in the closed black two-horse wagon, which was large enough to accommodate all their baggage, including the suits of armour, their clothes and food supplies for the journey in hampers piled on its roof and in a rear compartment. He and Prince Juan rode in front of the wagon, immediately behind four trusted Spanish mercenary outriders hired by Aaron Levi.

Simeon, the young Jewish attendant Aaron Levi had allotted to Prince Ahmed, rode immediately behind the wagon followed by four more Spanish mercenaries. Eleven fully armed men should be capable of dealing with any brigands they might encounter along the way.

Riding at a fast pace along the deserted stretches of the highway during the day, to distance themselves from the inevitable pursuit, they had always slowed down to a sedate pace when they passed through inhabited areas to avoid attracting attention by any appearance of haste. Although Prince Ahmed knew from the curious glances of peasants and townsmen they encountered that a group such as his would be noted, his hope was that many other similar groups would be following on their way home from the tourney.

Just weeks ago Prince Juan, Zurika, Aaron Levi and he had ridden this same highway on their way to Toledo. So much had happened since the drastic change he had made by fleeing the Gen al Arif tower, to alter the whole course of his life. Dimly he registered it as a lesson for the future. Once the ship of one's life leaves its home port and the voyage begins, changes, sometimes drastic from violent storms, become inevitable. Now here he was heading back to Granada with a beautiful young princess who had won his heart and for whom he had become responsible. Many were the times that he had to exert all his willpower not to drop back on some pretext just to catch a glimpse of his snow maiden, Princess Beatrice, who must be melting from the summer heat inside the closed wagon ventilated only by air-slits. The vibrance of her body against his, even through his armour, as they raced together from the arena, still made him tremble each time he recalled it, while the discreet glances they had exchanged between the time they arrived at the grove and their departure in flight had made the entire adventure, all the risks, the danger, worthwhile.

The countryside seemed different to him this time and he realized the truth of what his military instructors had instilled into him. If you expect to return through unfamiliar territory, always look back while you are advancing, for that territory appears different, sometimes unrecognizable, seen from the other way round.

Even while they were racing through the long deserted stretches between the villages, hamlets and townships he had noted again with a sense of awe the immense naked solitude of southern Castile's canyons and ravines. Scoured escarpments bared their wounds streaked yellow, saffron and orange, relieved by hillsides carrying green pine, oak and dark scrub on their backs. When he breathed the fragrance of chestnuts distilling a sweet aroma into the clean air, he had been glad that Prince Juan could enjoy the sights and smells, though he could hear neither the woodsman's axe nor the yapping of dogs chasing the horses' hooves, nor the birdsongs rising above the clatter and the trundle of wagon wheels.

They had been fortunate at the two stops they had made. Would they have the same luck with this, more important, stop? The first time had been in the late afternoon, at a small meadow littered with green herbs and yellow daisies, beside a gurgling, splattering rivulet, the second at an ancient stone fountain, covered with greenish moss and tiny lichen white as lamb's fleece, pouring out crystal water. No one had disturbed them at either place, where they watered and rubbed down the horses, stretched their own limbs and fed and rested for an hour. The peace of the surroundings had touched Prince Ahmed through the thick veneer of restlessness that kept impelling him to be up and away from the danger of pursuit.

Although none of the people they passed had displayed any special curiosity about them, this did not mean that they had gone unnoticed. Questioning by the pursuers would soon reveal that they were on the highway heading towards Granada. Would the king's cavalry stop for the night or press on? Prince Ahmed himself was beginning to feel drowsy, the effect of a long, tiring and suspenseful day. He noticed that Prince Juan kept drooping in the saddle. Two nights in the dungeons did not exactly leave a man full of energy. Aaron Levi was bearing up remarkably well, considering his age, but then he never took more than a few hours' sleep each night. Princess Beatrice had been sparkling at the stops, but Zurika had been quiet, thoughtful and withdrawn. Though sensing that something serious was wrong, Prince Ahmed, being totally unused to women, could not determine what it was and kept wondering why the normally friendly girl was cool towards the princess. Jealousy being unknown to him, he ascribed it to the natural reaction of a gypsy girl who had to deal with a princess for the first time in her life.

The jingle of bells, tiny gold drops wending through the night, heralded the approach of a train of muleteers. Rich voices were raised in an old song wafted around a winding bend in the highway.

> 'A woman is like your shadow.
> Pursued, it runs away,
> Ignored, it follows you.'

The lanterns of the mule train soon appeared, a small procession of little rectangles of yellow light evenly spaced in the darkness, like those carried by choir boys during one of the Christian festivals he had witnessed in Toledo. The muleteers edged to the side of the highway, without slackening their trundling pace, to let the wagon pass.

'*Hola!*'

'*Buenas noches!*'

Friendly voices called out greetings as they passed the train. Swarthy, bearded faces gleamed in the semi-darkness, cheekbones briefly highlighted. The odour of mule sweat and dung remained after the last mule clip-clopped by.

When he first heard the ripple of the stream, it reminded him that he needed to wash well before dawn, to resume their flight. He had observed *subh*, the morning prayer, at the villa only that morning – it seemed to have been in another lifetime. As for *zuhr*, the early afternoon prayer, *apr*, the late afternoon prayer, *magrib*, observed after the sun sets and before its red glow in the west disappears and *isha*, the night prayer, he had offered these in his heart while riding though he was not on his knees and facing Mecca. Had not Almighty Allah declared through his Prophet, 'All the world is my temple'?

Prince Ahmed called a halt, seized a flare from the nearest outrider. A wheel-rutted track, probably created by woodsmen's carts, led into a grove. He rode beneath dark cypress trees until he came upon a shallow stream gurgling over pebbles. He splashed across the water and entered a small, grassy glade. It was an ideal spot. Though lying so close to the highway, the meadow could accommodate the men, horses and the wagon, well hidden from the outside world.

Zurika had followed the gypsy dictates of loyalty to family and friends when she had embarked on the adventure that she had suggested in the first place, to rescue Prince Juan. Concentrating on the task at hand, she had simply ignored what would follow once the rescue was effected. She was, however, fiercely jealous as only a gypsy could be and fearful of any association that Prince Ahmed might have with any other woman. Only when she arrived at the grove near the tourney arena to await the arrival of the two princes and Princess Beatrice, did it dawn on her that she might have risked her life and her virtue in a scheme that would rob her of the most precious hope in her life, to become Prince Ahmed's concubine.

When Prince Ahmed rode into the grove holding Princess Beatrice, the doubt became certainty and jealousy ripped her heart. A closer view of the dishevelled but elegant princess, her snow white skin, golden hair and beautiful figure, sent hideous blood spewing forth from the wound. Its pain enraged her.

In haste to flee the grove, Prince Ahmed, who had not known all the horror Zurika had endured in the prison, only thanked her briefly while having his armour removed. When he learned the truth, he was profuse in his praise, during their first stop, but by then the damage had been done, especially because Zurika, ever watchful, had become sickened by the glances he had exchanged with Princess Beatrice. Zurika had alternated between bitterness, despair and rage during the flight. Now only an insensate rage remained. The princess, seemingly impervious to her attitude at first, kept asking questions to which she had given monosyllabic replies, but had finally given up and concentrated on conversations with Aaron Levi, between dozes in the dank heat of the wagon. Zurika realized that the Jew had noted her stony silence with concern, for he kept smiling at her through the semi-gloom of the wagon and even reached out to pat her hand lightly a few times.

Under any other circumstances, the grove which Prince Ahmed had selected for the night's rest would have seemed idyllic to Zurika. The clouds had lifted and the sky, lightened by the glow of a yellow waning moon, was a deep shade of blue, sparkling with stars, the traveller's cross, hanging low in the south, visible through a break in the dark cypress trees and the mountains beyond. But the gurgling of the stream, the whisper of winds in the upper branches of the trees, the odour of fried mutton from their meal and the acrid smells of horse sweat and wet leather brought Zurika more pain than joy. She would have enjoyed it all, if there had been no Princess Beatrice to ruin her communion with her beloved Prince Ahmed. She was unaccustomed to reasoning beyond the immediate present.

The two horses had been unhitched from the wagon, the shafts of which were now held up by posts. The wagon and all the horses, rubbed down and supplied with hay-bags, were placed in the centre, protected by the men, who, having eaten, had rolled up in their blankets around the glade. Zurika and Princess Beatrice were to sleep on cloaks near the wagon. Prince Ahmed's solicitude for Princess Beatrice's comfort turned Zurika's jealousy into a forest fire, destroying reason and good sense, surging towards destruction.

Aaron Levi must have guessed her feelings, for he took her elbow and drew her to the other side of the wagon. 'You are obviously distressed, my child,' he stated quietly. Being shorter than her, his dark eyes gleamed up at her through the gloom, the hooked nose lifted, his white hair a pale halo beneath his *yarmulke*. 'What ails you?'

She knew that he had guessed the truth and his solicitude only infuriated her the more. 'Nothing! Nothing, *señor*,' she muttered, quickly shaking dark locks from side to side.

'You must realize that while all of us are accustomed to the discomforts of travel, this is Princess Beatrice's first exposure to it. She has led a very sheltered life in . . .'

'Not like a common gypsy,' she spat out under her breath.

The dark eyes filled with compassion. 'No one of Jahweh's creatures, especially those whom we love, is common, my child.'

Her misery, the hurt in her heart, seemed to explode at the reminder of love, but she kept it in check. Compressing her lips, she held back the hot, harsh words that rose from within her. '*Buenas noches, señor!*' she said, turning away abruptly to stride to her blanket and cloak. Aaron Levi's sigh followed her, a blessed instant like a cool wind on a warm day, unwelcome because she was shivering with the ague.

She lay on her cloak gazing up at the starlit sky. Princess Beatrice's breathing filled her with an obsession to stop that life flow, gleefully to watch the white face turn red,

402

then purple, the blue eyes bulging, all of it hideous even after death overtook the victim. Was that murder? Had she not killed a man just that morning? The pain within Zurika mounted, became insensate rage producing an overwhelming compulsion to destroy everyone and everything within sight as causes of her anguish. Mad screams began welling up from her chest. She gripped her cloak tightly, fought them back. Calm followed, a calm as hard as ice-covered rock.

Princess Beatrice was more beautiful than any other woman Zurika had ever seen before. The words of an old ballad kept hammering in her ears. It was about a woman so beautiful that

> . . . when she went in to hear Mass,
> The church danced in the light . . .

She simply could not shut them out, until she finally hit on a plan, perfected it. She should have been bone weary and sleepy. Instead, she lay awake, her mind bright as the stars, alert as the keen night air, waiting.

Up to now, Princess Beatrice had lived a sheltered, secluded life. Her world had suddenly turned topsy-turvy. Last night she had slept, fearful of the morrow, between silken sheets, on her safe bed in the warm, scented royal quarters of the Toledo palace. Tonight, she was lying with a brown blanket between her and hard open turf, covered against the cold by a black cloak, watching the first stars prickling through a clouded sky. Yet she was at peace for the first time that she could remember. What then was this vague apprehension lying within her, its source the young gypsy girl Zurika sleeping beside her?

Princess Beatrice had sensed Zurika's coolness the moment the girl had been presented to her near Toledo. Every effort she had made to converse with Zurika had been met with brief, non-committal responses, or a stony silence.

At first, she had ascribed this to the shyness of a young person, obviously not of noble breeding, meeting a princess for the first time, but as the day wore on, she had discerned the coolness turning to animosity and had deduced that it was directed at her personally. When the animosity had turned to silent hatred after their first halt on the flight to freedom, a hatred so palpable that it stifled Princess Beatrice within the hot, dark confines of the closed wagon, she realized that it was indeed directed towards her and her woman's instinct told her that its cause was Prince Ahmed's solicitude for her. Zurika was jealous. The gypsy girl might have risked her life to save Prince Juan from the dungeons, but she was not prepared to accept a rival to her own obvious feelings for Prince Ahmed. If mere suspicions so enraged her, what would happen when she finally discovered that Princess Beatrice also loved Prince Ahmed?

Why was it that her joy at the escape from the imprisonment of years had to have some drawback?

Princess Beatrice had been so worried by Zurika's attitude that she had drawn Prince Juan aside during their second halt and conveyed her feelings to him by signs. With his usual sensitivity, Prince Juan had already picked up on the situation but, while assuring her that he would watch out for signs of danger, he reminded her of his debt to Zurika, who had risked her life and modesty to save him. Just two days in the dungeons had left him looking worn and haggard, so he did indeed have much to thank Zurika for.

Would Prince Juan be able to keep awake to avert any move the wild gypsy girl might make against her that night? Possibly not, so she herself had best stay awake, though utterly weary. As she lay back, however, her eyelids became heavier. She wished there were wedges that could force them open. Her last conscious thought was a whispered prayer. '*Oh Blessed Virgin, thou hast saved thy virgin child from a fate worse than death, now save her from death.*'

Sitting up against the cushions of his great four-poster bed, King Charles the Bad stared at his new visitor inquiringly. Following Princess Mathilde's departure, his brain had slowly cleared. Though he had just talked to the princess, he could not remember what he had said, but something about the conversation had created a lump of disquiet within him.

'Godsbody, does it take being unseated from our horse for us to receive high-ranking visitors at an ungodly midnight hour?' he questioned the chubby Bishop Eulogius seated on a gilded chair by the gilt step-ladder that served the high bed.

The prelate's cheeks rose and his blue eyes vanished into their folds as he smiled his most disarming smile. 'I am sorry to intrude and beg you to forgive me, Your Majesty, but as you well know, the work of God brooks no restrictions of hours, by day or night, even with the highest personages.' He smoothed his purple robe over plump thighs. 'In bearing the cross of the religious at all times, we often risk the wrath of kings and leave it to their compassion to deal gently with our trespasses.'

King Charles eyed his visitor thoughtfully. He had never conceded the divine right of the Church over the State. He knew from his spies that this Bishop Eulogius loved his creature comforts, including his bed and a display of virgin flesh before he fell asleep most nights. The bishop was also reported to be a man of unyielding ambition, ruthless in its realization. He would not be here tonight unless he had something critical to discuss, something he could not or would not mention to his own king, something for which he would risk King Pedro's being informed of the visit at such a late hour. Ah, King Charles had it. The man needed an answer to his question that very night.

He decided on a blunt approach. 'What do you have in mind, Your Eminence?' he demanded. 'We are sure that you are not here at this ungodly hour to inquire about our health or wellbeing, except to the extent that it can serve your . . . er . . . holy purposes.'

Bishop Eulogius's smile grew cherubic. 'How well you discern our priorities, Sire. Please be assured that our solicitude for your health as a person matches that of our concern for you as the ruler of León y Navarra, but each exists side by side in separate dimension and we are here at this . . . er . . . devil's hour to address you as a ruler, since the needs of Holy Church have to be addressed without delay.'

Cherubim and Seraphim, ruler and individual existing side by side in one person, King Charles reflected sourly. A nice concept. He should be angry, but he was not disposed to react with violence even in his thoughts, because he had concluded that Bishop Eulogius needed to make common cause with him after the day's events. He, King Charles, gave not a fig for Holy Church, though he contributed his tithes, but if he could use the Church and this plump prelate for vengeance against that Moorish bastard and to secure Princess Beatrice to his bed, he would listen to anything at any hour of the day or night, whatever the state of his health. Why, he would even ally himself with the devil to achieve personal ends that went beyond past political ambitions. 'Since we have been confined to our bed, you must have more information than us as to what transpired today and how it all happened,' he asserted. He sat up higher on the cushions, adjusted his night-cap. 'Prithee, tell us all you know.'

'I have just come from a full briefing given by His Majesty, my king,' Bishop Eulogius intoned. He sniffed

406

at the stink of asafoetida from the table of medicines and unguents that punctured the sandalwood perfume from the incense burners and raised a scented pomander to his nose. 'Here is the full story as King Pedro has been able to uncover it, Sire.'

His voice assuming its normal incantation style, mellow gold as the lamplight, he detailed the facts, which he claimed to have just learned.

King Charles listened to the bishop's tale in amazed silence. Though he found parts of it incredible, simply told it was so complete that it did not require any questions, and by the time the prelate lapsed into silence, King Charles knew that the man was here because he was disappointed in his own king's lack of response to the demand for Inquisition. Did the bloodthirsty little maggot imagine that he could be wafted to the Papacy by the smoke clouds billowing from the stakes of his victims? The Papacy must be the bishop's ultimate object, but side by side with that, there had to be another. What had the bishop said about his health just now? That it existed in another dimension. For the prelate, the highest office, for Eulogius the man, what? Intense gratification from seeing Jews, witches and non-believers tortured? If so, why? And why fire? What was Eulogius the man trying to burn out of his system? His vengeance at rejection by women, except when he bought them, symbolized by witches because the witchcraft of womanhood had never been his to possess?

King Charles's brain was becoming confused. Such deep analysis was not for him. He depended on Princess Mathilde and Count Gaston for that. Besides, his limbs were aching tonight and his pride lay in the dust. For himself, King Charles preferred to fight with the sheer cunning of instinct, devoid of analysis. 'You are obviously here because you feel we can be of help to . . . er . . .

Holy Church, where others have failed to respond,' he declared. 'And you need an immediate answer.'

The bishop clapped pudgy hands in feigned applause. 'You are so wise, Your Majesty. Forsooth, you combine wisdom with . . .' You nearly said Invincibility, but thought better of it, you sod, King Charles thought, strangely without rancour. He would have to accustom himself to the fact that he would not be addressed as invincible again until he had reinstated his invincibility. '. . . divine grace,' the bishop ended, beaming.

'Prithee, proceed with your request,' King Charles bade him shortly.

'As I have already made you aware, I myself, speaking for Holy Church, would have preferred Inquisition, Sire, but my earthly sovereign, in his . . . er . . . God-inspired wisdom has decreed otherwise.' He sighed. 'And he alone has the earthly power to decree the heavenly Inquisition.' He savoured the last word between his small, curved red lips. He sighed again, more heavily this time, leaned forward in his chair. 'But we can make a beginning, you and I, Sire.' His voice had become intense, though he had dropped it. His blue eyes were pinpoints of ice. 'If you make common cause with Holy Church today, you will have earned her gratitude for tomorrow.' His glance was significant.

You have guessed my desires and are offering to become my ally. If you are prepared to turn against your own king, it has to be in order to fulfil your personal desires. You are clever too, more cunning than a weasel, for your offer is couched in such terms that I have to infer your intent so that you remain unincriminated. You are a dangerous man, evil too I perceive, for you have the power to corrupt. How can I use you for my own ends?

King Charles opted to use silence as his own ally. He waited for the bishop to proceed, carefully avoiding the gaze of the blue eyes by staring into space with a pretence of bemusement due to his physical condition. He was soon enjoying his visitor's discomfiture at the failure to elicit any response.

'While my king alone has the power to decree Inquisition,' Bishop Eulogius proceeded, more hastily now, 'any member of the Holy Orders can declare a person to be a witch. This dancing girl could only have overcome five hardened prison guards, even murdering one of them, by witchcraft. While she is under sentence of death, I propose declaring her a witch so that when she is apprehended she will suffer all the penalties inflicted on those of her abominable profession.'

Hardened though he was, the words chilled King Charles, but he withheld any reaction. Here was a woman under sentence of death. He, King Charles, was man of the world enough to conjecture that she had probably fought the five guards for her own life and virtue. Had he not himself had a few experiences with that sort of woman, some of whom had fought with the desperation of cornered beasts, stimulating him the more, but undoubtedly in self-defence? Now here was this little prick wanting to defecate on a corpse! Oh well, each to his own . . . What difference was there between his revelling in the physical domination of a rape and the enjoyment derived by the prelate from the means he would use to kill someone already under sentence of death? None whatever, yet he disliked and distrusted this man whose personal yearnings were overcoming his discretion. 'What do you want of us?' he inquired abruptly.

'Your support when I issue the edict of the Church against the gypsy girl on my return to the cathedral tonight and speed the soldiers of Christ along the southern highway to claim the young woman when she is taken prisoner by the king's cavalry.' He licked pink lips. 'I need the backing of any Christian monarch.'

King Charles did not give a gypsy's curse for this

obscure wench. The only woman of any importance to him now was Princess Beatrice. What Bishop Eulogius requested was little enough price to pay for fulfilling his own lust and love. It was an easy exchange, a young woman to be burned at the stake for a virginal princess whom he, King Charles, could burn up in bed!

It was later than usual when King Pedro strode into Maria de Padilla's bedchamber that night. For the first time since he had become intimate with her, a hint of anger in his heart was directed against her. Fearless though he was, it frightened him, made him feel isolated and alone.

She greeted him at the door as usual, but the delicately-skinned oval face seemed drawn and the grey eyes were curiously blank. When he took her soft body in his arms, it was pliable as always, but lacked something of its vitality, all of which brought his anger to the surface.

Obviously sensing the change in him, she stiffened, drew away and walked quietly to the canopied bed.

The anger flashed, exploded. 'So you too are walking away from us, like your daughter,' he roared.

She stopped, trembled, turned slowly to face him. In the golden lamplight, he could now see that she had been weeping. 'May I humbly remind you, Sire, that Beatrice is *our* daughter,' she said firmly.

This was a mistress he had never known before. The pain in her eyes only infuriated him the more, made him want to turn the knife in her wound. 'Motherhood is always a fact, paternity can only be an opinion,' he growled, lowering his voice so that the words could penetrate rather than engulf her. She winced. It gave him cruel satisfaction. 'We repeat, *you* have just walked away from us for the first time ever, as your daughter ran away this noon. How could you have bred such a traitor in your womb?'

Anger flashed in the grey eyes, something of steel

gleamed in them that startled him, before she resumed her normal submissive gaze. Sensing the submission to be assumed for his benefit, he could not help wondering how much of it in the past was real. The question drained him, left him strangely empty, as if once solid ground under his feet was being eroded.

'Yes, my lord, may I respectfully remind you that the tourney was *your* idea as to how to use *your* daughter, as you thought her at the time, to achieve your ends. It was Your Majesty that decided to keep Beatrice virtually a prisoner after she attained maidenhood, so she could be made to marry a man of your choice, one who could help achieve *your* goals. As a good mistress and mother, I brought Beatrice up in the ways of Holy Church and gentlefolk, ensuring that seclusion until *you* decided that she should be present at the tourney, vulgarly displayed,' he flinched at the words, 'like a leg of ham at a contest in a market fair. She used that freedom to escape from the prison Your Majesty had created for her. How can you blame me for what happened?'

This was indeed a Maria he had never known to exist. It made him pause, searching in a memory suddenly fuddled by time, drink and doubt for the truth. Surely it had been Maria, not he, who had conceived of Charles the Bad as the best possible husband for Beatrice so that he, King Pedro, could then take over the resources of the kingdom of Navarre and proceed to a unification of white Christian Spain under his, King Pedro's rule? And had it not been Maria who suggested the joust in the first place, so that the choice could be made without angering and shaming other eligible princes?

The king was so accustomed to integrating other people's advice into the appearance of his own decisions that the answers to the questions eluded him. Godsbody, this was not the Maria de Padilla of his life, but a strange woman with blank grey eyes and large breasts with brown

411

aureoles beneath a pink sheer-silk nightdress. He did not know how to cope with her. He was an enraged bull, with lowered head but not knowing which way to charge. Though tempted to buffet her, some deep instinct held him back with the knowledge that if he did so, he would end up beating her to death. Regardless of the present situation, his own future survival as a person depended on her. He was Pedro the Cruel to all save her. Now he was bursting to be cruel to her too, to punish her, but the soft, gentle Maria was a woman of incredible strength and he had to control his mad desire.

'Madam,' he declared grimly, his mind made up. 'Whoever may be responsible, a situation exists which only *we* can solve.' His innate majesty, always absent with her, reasserted itself. 'We intend doing so immediately. We shall ride out tomorrow at the head of *our* army, in pursuit of *our* daughter.' He noted her widened eyes with satisfaction. 'This means war before we are quite ready for it, but the decision is *ours* and ours alone. You will undoubtedly be affected by its consequences!'

He noted her blanch before he turned and walked back through the doorway, heard her sob. He paused to listen to her piteous plea. 'We have always lain together these sixteen years whenever you were in this palace, my lord. I beg you do not leave me now, when I need you most.'

Cruel glee mushroomed within him as he slammed the door behind him and strode away.

412

Chapter 22

She waited until she could hear Princess Beatrice relapse into the regular deep breathing of sleep, interspersed by the heavy snores from the guards. The total stillness of the campsite itself, beneath a clear sky sparkling with stars, was accentuated by the occasional creak of a branch settling through the night. The rustle of leaves before a light wind brought the odour of horse urine, dung and sweat to her nostrils. The earthy smells took her back to the stench of human defecation that used to disgust her in the cliff caves opposite the Alhambra palace. She remembered her grandmother, probably sunk into a deep sleep in Jaén at this very moment and the memory made her pause in her fierce purpose. She had come so far since those days, should she by a single act throw away all that she had achieved since leaving the caves?

Why had she left the caves? A slight slurp from the princess, now fast asleep, provided a quick answer. She had wanted a princess's life, but her dream had been to find it with a prince. She had found the realization of that dream in Prince Ahmed. To her, love was possession. This snoring princess with the white skin, blue eyes and golden hair had shattered it. The anger surged back, more all-consuming for having paused those few moments. She would destroy them all. She did not care if she was destroyed in the process.

She quietly moved her cloak aside. Holding it in her right hand, she half rose and surveyed the scene. Nothing stirred. Even the sentries must have fallen asleep. Cloak in hand, she placed her left palm on the blanket warmed by her body and levered herself to her feet, still peering intently around for any sign of wakefulness.

She donned the cloak, began walking towards the horses flatfooted, in the manner she had been trained as a gypsy, to avoid sound created by weight pressure if she tiptoed. If anyone saw her, she would pretend that she wanted to ease herself. The darker figures of the animals were soon etched through the gloom in a circle around the tree, heads drooped. She had an inconsequential thought that they were fortunate creatures to be able to sleep standing. A ghostly sound echoed overhead. She froze, heart pounding. Was it a demon? Tu-whit, tu-whoo . . . It had only been the hoot of an owl.

Glancing around to make sure that no one had wakened, she eased between the two horses, reached the tall tree to which they had been tethered and silently unhitched all the reins. She had decided on a bay which one of the outriders had been using for herself, because it was slender and looked fast. It awoke to her touch, and nuzzled her with a cold wet nose. She grasped its bridle, backed it slowly out of the circle till it was close to the wagon.

Now was the most dangerous part. One false move, one unexpected sound and the entire camp would erupt. She let go the bridle, held her breath. True to its kind, the bay lowered its head and started nibbling the grass.

She moved to her blanket, paused to look down at the figure of the princess. A dizzy urge seized her. She drew her knife from her waist. She would plunge it again and again into that still form. Had not her father given her that long-bladed knife for her protection? Was it not to be used against her enemies? Was it not just yesterday the blade had tasted blood? This creature sleeping so peacefully had destroyed her life. This was the real enemy.

She raised the knife aloft. She could not bring it down.

414

An invisible vice held her wrist. She was powerless against it. She teetered on the edge of uncertainty. Harsh reason intruded. Her hated enemy might scream before dying. The camp would awaken and she would be unable to destroy everyone and everything.

She slowly lowered the knife, replaced it at her waist.

She turned away, grasped the blanket and thrust it inside the wagon. She reached for the tinder-box stored in the little compartment of the wagon. With a firm hand she struck the spark, watched the yellow-red flame from the small taper. When it was steady, she applied it to the blanket. In moments, the dry wool caught fire, began to crackle lightly and blaze. She steeled herself to wait until the wood of the wagon caught fire, then seized a spare blanket from inside the wagon, applied it to the flame, ran with the burning blanket and flung it at the horses.

The animals screamed, panicked, backed away from the tree, began to bolt. She grasped the reins of the bay, mounted bareback and rode away, followed by cries of alarm from the sentries and the pounding of the fleeing horses' hooves.

She reached the highway, turned left and headed back north in the direction of Toledo and the pursuit of the king's men.

Prince Ahmed had been sleeping on a blanket not far from the wagon. He emerged from the depths of an exhausted sleep, subconsciously aware of the urgency to come awake, like a diver rising to the water's surface. The shrill whinnying of horses, stamping hooves, the shouts of guards made a foreground to yellow flames and smoke from the wagon. A reek of burning wool discoloured the pure mountain air.

The king's men had arrived! His first thought was for Princess Beatrice's safety. He grasped his sword and leapt to his feet, eyes feverishly searching the area by the wagon where Princess Beatrice had been sleeping. She stood close to the wagon, gazing at the flames in horror. He rushed up to her. She turned, saw him and fell into his arms. He held her close. Her body was warm, soft. Her heart beating against his chest quickened his own heartbeat.

Sanchez, a bearded, heavyset guard came running up.

'Is it the king's men?' Prince Ahmed questioned sharply.

'No, *señor*! It was the young woman. She released the horses and rode away on one.'

'What? Why would . . .?' Comprehension dawned, brought shock and horror.

'She did it because she hated me,' Princess Beatrice stated tonelessly.

The need for action dominated. 'Quick!' Prince Ahmed commanded Sanchez. 'Get the bucket. Bring water from the stream. We must put out the fire.'

'What good is a wagon without horses, *señor*? Let us go after the animals first.'

A shrill squeal resounded through the grove. Prince Ahmed turned swiftly in its direction. A rearing horse was silhouetted against the lighter dark between two clumps of trees. The figure of a man clinging desperately to its rein was half-hoisted into the air. Prince Ahmed cried out a warning. The horse's lashing hooves came down with a sickening thud-crunch on the man's head. The body remained poised for a split second before crumpling to the ground. The horse's hooves followed. Whinnying sharply, it took off in the direction of the highway.

Prince Ahmed released Princess Beatrice. 'Stay here!' he commanded.

Sanchez following, he ran to the still form of the guard. He knelt on the cold turf. Even in that dim light he did not need a close examination. 'His skull is smashed,' he muttered, shaking his head.

'He is – was – Leon, only nineteen years old,' Sanchez stated hoarsely. 'He came from Barcelona seeking his fortune to support his grandmother. God's curse on the woman who killed him.'

The reference to a grandmother reminded Prince Ahmed of Zurika's grandmother, Pilar. Prince Juan and Aaron Levi and he had treated the crone and Zurika with such loving kindness. Was this how she repaid them? Was it a gypsy trait to be ungrateful, devious, vengeful? But why vengeance when Zurika had risked her womanhood and her life only that morning to save Prince Juan? For a moment, the complexities of the world overwhelmed Prince Ahmed. He longed for the peace and calm of his boyhood years, alone in the Gen al Arif with Abou bon Ebben. He bowed his head with unidentified grief, said a silent prayer to Allah to receive the soul of the infidel Leon into Paradise.

'Prince!' It was Aaron Levi's voice.

Prince Ahmed glanced up to see the gnome figure of the Jew, accompanied by the taller Prince Juan and the slender Simeon, emerge through the darkness from the direction of the highway. They had obviously been chasing the horses, so he, Prince Ahmed, had been the last to waken. The realization shamed him, and shame brought resolution. Never again! 'We must plan what to do next,' he declared, signalling to Prince Juan with deft fingers. He eyed Aaron Levi helplessly. 'But why would Zurika want to do this?'

The eyes straddling the hooked nose were barely discernible in the gloom, but there was no mistaking their sadness. 'The ancient emotion of the lover, more fiercely expressed with passionate tribes, jealousy,' he replied sadly. 'It can consume all that is good, regenerating only what is left in the human soul, evil.' His grey head moved slowly from side to side. 'I should have known this would come. I should have questioned Zurika more, advised her when we talked briefly before she retired last night. I glimpsed the dark outline of the demon's figure within her, but I ignored it.' He hung his head.

The emotion jealousy was totally new to Prince Ahmed. It had only been recently that he had even identified the emotion love. 'You mean Zurika loved me?'

'Yes.'

'Why would anyone want to destroy a loved one? Surely love makes one want to serve, to protect, to sacrifice one's life if need be for the other.' Prince Ahmed was repeating what he felt for Princess Beatrice, what had gripped him from the first moment he had seen her miniature portrait.

Thoughts reeled from him, fresh new birth.

Love, the torment of one, the felicity of two, the enmity of three. Ah, the enmity of three!

The charm which draws two birds together uniting them with unfathomable empathy, creating happiness to be with each other, misery to be apart.

The great mystery and principle of the life force, the intoxication of youth, the sober delight of age.

As the bird sings to its love, the beetle woos its lady in the dust, the peacock proudly bares its tail at sunset when it dances to its drab peahen, so shall I approach my love . . .

In those moments of fear and despair, within the confines of a dark grove, the truth of love finally reached Prince Ahmed from within him. And set him free.

All the unidentified tumults he had known now focused on the word love. He loved and was in love, free at last of the manacles and chains of ignorance forced upon him by his physical captivity. Almighty Allah had driven him and Princess Beatrice to each other. A resolve seized him, maniacal in its intensity. He would save Princess Beatrice and have her as his mate forever.

He caught Prince Juan's gaze. 'We must forgive those who hurt us,' Prince Juan signalled. 'If thine enemy smite thee on one cheek, turn the other. Let us act without anger, hatred or rancour.'

Surrounded by gloomy guards, they sat beside the warmth of the burning wagon, barely hearing its occasional spit and sputter, to discuss their next move.

'All right then, we are agreed,' Prince Ahmed finally declared. 'We shall split up into two groups. We will divide the blankets and food rations between us. Having no horses, Señor Levi, Prince Juan, Princess Beatrice and I will take to the hill-country first and head for Granada. You guards will scatter and make your separate ways back to Toledo, carrying only sufficient money for the journey. You will receive ample rewards from Señor Levi's banker friend, Lord Joram, in Toledo upon presentation of the documents the *señor* will give you.' He paused. 'No purpose will be served by our attempting to destroy evidence of our stay here, because Zurika knows the location and will lead the king's cavalry to the site. She obviously hopes that by betraying us she will be forgiven all her actions of yesterday, if her part has been uncovered. We shall leave as soon as you have given Leon a Christian burial.'

A chorus of assent was his response.

What Prince Ahmed had not divulged even to Aaron Levi, Prince Juan and Princess Beatrice was his plan for avoiding pursuit on the journey to Granada.

Though it was well past midnight, Farouk Riswan, who normally slept only for about three hours before dawn each day, awaited his secret visitor in the inner chamber of his small mansion adjoining the Alhambra palace. The man, known only as Mizra, being the Prime Minister's chief spy, had direct access to the mansion through the secret entrance of a cleverly disguised trap door beneath one of the flagstones of the outer courtyard and a tunnel which led to a movable panel in the chamber. Farouk Riswan had created this entrance many years earlier, to receive his spies and to serve as an escape route as well should he ever need it.

Having raised King Yusuf to the throne after arranging the assassination of the latter's brother, King Mohamed IV, the Prime Minister had decided bitterly that King Yusuf was abandoning him because the king wanted to clear the way for Prince Ahmed, his son and heir. He feared no doubt more assassinations from his Prime Minister, including that of Prince Ahmed, in order to retain power.

Long before Prince Ahmed escaped, creating in effect a vacancy in the succession, the Prime Minister had sent out feelers to King Pedro of Castile, offering to have King Yusuf murdered so that he could place Prince Saad, the king's nephew, on the throne as a puppet under King Pedro's suzerainty. In return King Pedro would have to assure him, Farouk Riswan, virtual rule over Granada as a satellite of Castile. Castile's defeat in the battle against King Yusuf's army had cooled these negotiations, but a few months ago, Pedro had sent a secret emissary requesting acceleration of the assassination. Prince Ahmed was also to be a victim, and the Prime Minister was to have Prince Saad appointed his puppet king. Once in control, the Prime Minister was to do nothing to prepare Granada for King Pedro's planned invasion, and when King Pedro took over Granada, Prince Saad, the titular ruler, would have to take orders from his Prime Minister, who would work directly under the Castilian King.

The plan suited Farouk Riswan perfectly, but his first problem arose when Prince Ahmed fled the palace.

Nevertheless he had gone ahead with the assassination of King Yusuf, using this same Mizra as the dagger-man.

Prince Saad, whom Farouk Riswan had selected as his puppet, was a portly young Muslim with a better knowledge of wine and women than of government and a greater proclivity for being ruled by both than for ruling a country.

It followed that a major problem had arisen upon King Yusuf's death. The Council of Princes and the Assembly of Mullahs had joined together and taken an unexpected stand in favour of the regular Muslim custom of hereditary succession. The Prime Minister was instructed to publish notices throughout all of Spain to track down Prince Ahmed at any cost and bring him to the throne. Just that morning, the princes and mullahs had appointed a Council of Regency consisting of three princes, with Prince Saad as the titular head, to govern Granada in the interim. Prince Saad was permitted to live in the Alhambra palace, and Farouk Riswan would remain as Prime Minister, without special powers. Now all he had to look forward to was the day when King Pedro would take over his kingdom of Granada.

He glanced at the ornamental gold hourglass on its shelf of filigreed white marble at the far end of the small chamber that served as his study. It was almost time for Mizra's knock on the panel door. Kneeling, bony rump on heels, before the low table, its top a slab of black marble littered with official parchment, Farouk Riswan caught a glimpse of himself in the ornate mirror adorning the wall above the hourglass, noting with amusement that his hunched skeletal frame, clad in his customary flowing white robes and red *fez* cap, combined with a gaunt face and hooked nose to make him resemble a great bird of prey. At sixty-five, he was accustomed to the way he looked. He had always sought power to compensate for it, making up for lack of brawn with cunning.

Two taps sounded on the secret panel, so light that they could have been mistaken for night noises of the building. The Prime Minister rose to his feet, padded towards the panel, drew aside a large green and white tapestry depicting a scene in a Persian marketplace and gave the answering three knocks. When he applied light pressure on the panel, it slid silently outwards.

A ferret of a man, complete with red ferret moustache on wizened ferret features and dead eyes of the lightest brown, stood framed in the dark entranceway. He removed his red *fez* on seeing his master, revealing a small shaven head. Mizra never stepped inside the chamber. All their discussions were conducted where the Prime Minister could merely drop the tapestry and conceal the entrance in the event of an unexpected intrusion.

'You have news of importance?' Riswan commenced without ado.

'Indeed, lord Prime Minister.' Mizra's voice was surprisingly deep and mellow for one so small. His smile was a baring of discoloured teeth, but the dead eyes gleamed with triumph. What kind of man was this, the Prime Minister wondered, with no family, no friends? Well, they were two of a kind. 'We have located Prince Ahmed in Toledo.'

Elation sent blood pulsing into Farouk Riswan's head. 'Great news, praise be to Almighty Allah. You know exactly where he is staying.'

'Yes, lord. He, the deaf-mute white prince and a gypsy girl named Zurika are living just outside the city in a villa owned by a wealthy Jew named Aaron Levi.'

'Ha!' The Prime Minister smelled his own bad breath, and found it inoffensive. 'A Muslim, a white Christian, a Jew and a heathen gypsy. A great combination of Omniscient Allah, but what are they doing in Toledo?'

'What the princes do all day apparently is practise jousting.'

'To what end . . .?' The truth struck him. 'Ha!' Bad breath again, still inoffensive to him, but Mizra winced. 'The white Christian prince intends participating in the tourney.'

'If so, he has already participated, lord, since the tourney was this . . . er . . . last morning, but to what end would he desire to participate, lord, when the offered prize is his step-sister's hand in marriage? And why would Prince Ahmed expose himself to the danger of being apprehended, imprisoned and perhaps even mutilated in retaliation for Prince Juan's sentence from our late . . . uh,' Mizra coughed lightly in embarrassment, 'revered King Yusuf. The principle of reciprocity operates in diplomatic relations between all countries.' He grinned, a ferret baring its teeth.

The Prime Minister pondered that awhile. 'Perhaps he desires to re-establish himself in his father's eyes, as a worthy successor to the throne, even though deaf-mute.'

Mizra's decayed-teeth smile was cynical. 'On the other hand, this may be a deep, dark plot of Prince Juan's to entrap Prince Ahmed and have King Pedro wreak vengeance on him.'

Farouk Riswan shook his head. 'You spies are all alike. Always expecting the worst from people.' He paused. 'I have been told that Prince Juan is a model Christian, practising the doctrine of love in response to hatred.' He thought briefly. 'Prince Ahmed must be eliminated without delay. He must never return to Granada, except as a corpse.'

Zurika could make out the highway fairly clearly from pale patches of moonlight gleaming on the worn grey cobblestones, but she held her horse to the slow canter she had learned was easiest on the animals for a long journey, her entire attention focused on distinguishing the roadway. The world around her was a deserted place,

haunted by dark patches of shadow from branches overhead, and she a devil-ghost riding gleefully to the drum-
beats of hoof-clatter. Should not her horse have been a
black, rather than a bay, when her soul blazed with
devilish glee at the havoc she had wrought and the disaster
she would bring to those who had hurt her heart? She had
some money and jewels wrapped in a cloth belt and her
long-bladed knife at her waist. The future would be good
for her, somewhere in Toledo. She did not need either of
the princes or the Jewish merchant to make a life for
herself.

She had ridden steadily for several miles when she came
to a great looping bend. A gust of thin, cold air from the
open valley below assailed her nostrils. She sneezed
violently. Her grip relaxed momentarily on the reins.
Responding instinctively, the bay began a forward surge.
She sneezed again and the horse suddenly stretched out
its neck. She lost a rein. Sensing freedom, the bay swerved
in the opposite direction. Zurika began sliding sideways.
A thrill of fear shot through her stomach. She released
the other rein, leaned forward, desperately grabbing the
animal's neck. It snorted, swerved back on to the highway. Unused to riding, Zurika's throat ran dry, her breath
caught. Still slowly slipping, she panicked. She had best
slither right off, rather than risk being thrown.

She deliberately landed on her back. A gasp escaped
her. Relieved of its weight, the horse surged forward,
hooves slithering before they crisped to a quick rhythmic
clatter.

For a moment, Zurika lay there, thinking she had been
paralysed. She tested her legs. They were functioning.
She placed her palms on the cold cobblestones, levered
herself painfully to her feet. She swivelled her head
around, moved her limbs. Except for soreness in her
rump, she was intact. She took a few steps forward. She
had suffered no serious injury. Arms akimbo, she stared

along the highway dismally listening to the sound of hooves fading into the distance. She swore at the horse.

Holy Mother of Jesus, why did you let this happen to me? The thought was involuntary. Her resolve remained inflexible. The king's cavalry could not be far off in its pursuit. Grasping her cloak more closely against the chill, she began trudging along the side of the highway, alert to hide if anyone came her way. She did not relish the idea of using her knife against any more rapists.

The stark dark outlines of tombstones and graves appeared to her left. She was walking past a deserted cemetery. Thoughts of demons and ghosts intruded. She resisted the urge to bolt up the highway, forced herself to walk at a steady pace, resolutely fighting down the mounting terror each time her mind conjured a ghost.

She walked for over two hours at the same pace, meeting no one, before she heard a faint rumble in the distance. At first, she thought it was thunder. As the sound grew louder, it separated itself into the untidy clatters of a body of horsemen. Her heart leapt. The king's cavalry.

Fear spawned its memory in her belly. Supposing the soldiers tried to rape her? Her steps automatically slowed. For a moment, she was tempted to turn and flee. Then bitter rage overcame all else. Surely she would be safer in the open countryside with a large body of men, commanded by a responsible officer, than she had been with those beasts in a small room of the palace prison. She nonetheless grasped the hilt of her knife. It brought reassurance.

For the first time she faced the realization that once the fugitives were caught and punished, the present pattern of her life would be ended. She had two alternatives for the future. She could return to grandmother Pilar in Jaén or find work as a dancer in Toledo – perhaps the king would offer her a post as one of the Court dancers as a reward.

The increased drumming of hooves beckoned as an outlet to her bitterness. She began to run towards it, a bird sucked by a squall. The riders first appeared round a bend in the highway as a dark mass. She moved to the centre of the road. Feet firmly spread, she stopped and raised her hands.

The four outriders, riding abreast, were only yards away when they saw her.

'Ho . . . o . . .!' Arms were flung up signalling to those in the rear. The outriders stopped so close to her that she could smell their horses' breath.

'Who are you?' The man at the right centre shouted. 'And what the devil do you mean standing on the highway like that? You could have been run down and killed.'

'As you can see, I was not run down and killed,' she declared boldly. She made her tone imperious. 'Take me to your captain, for I have news of the greatest urgency concerning your mission.'

'Who d'you think you are, a lone woman emerging from the darkness and giving us orders? Are you a slut or a ghost?'

Before Zurika could reply, quick hooves on the cobblestones brought a horseman emerging through the gloom. 'What is it, Sergeant?' The voice was that of one accustomed to command.

Zurika's pulse quickened as a tall, bearded man on a tall grey reined in to her left. 'I presume you are the captain of this troop, *señor*?' she inquired, ignoring the lead horseman.

'Captain Carlos Montoya at your service, madam.' The man's voice was deep and cultured. He was obviously too well bred to betray any surprise at this apparition. 'What may we do for you?'

426

'You are in pursuit of the fugitives from the tourney, are you not, *señor*?'

His lips tightened. 'We certainly are.'

'I escaped from their group about two hours ago in the hope of meeting you.'

Once again, he betrayed no surprise. His grey nodded its head, champed at the bit. He relaxed its mouth with easy hands. 'Do you mean you were with the Princess Beatrice and the two princes?'

'Yes, *señor*. I was in the service of a Jewish merchant named Aaron Levi who provided the horses and the wagon for the escape. Totally unaware of what was happening, I was caught up in the events. When I discovered the truth during the course of our flight, I decided to escape. Being a loyal subject of our king and wanting no part in such plots, when the party took their first break for the night in a grove about six miles from here, I waited till everyone was asleep, stole one of their horses and rode away. I have no experience of horses, however, so the wretched animal threw me. I started walking in the hopes of meeting the pursuit.'

He eyed her thoughtfully. 'Did the fugitives not awaken and pursue you when you left?'

She smiled smugly. 'They couldn't. I freed all their horses and even set fire to the wagon before I fled!'

He nodded. 'You are a remarkably resourceful woman. I know your story is true in part at least, because your horse preceded you and we caught him.' His teeth shone white through the beard. 'We have also learned along the way that your party consisted of a wagon and about a dozen horsemen. We don't have a moment to lose. If we speed on we should catch up with the group before dawn. I'll have my orderly bring up your horse . . .' He paused, inquired casually, 'by the way, what colour horse was it?'

'They called it a bay.'

He raised a hand in acknowledgment. 'You can ride

alongside me and tell me your whole story while we continue our pursuit.'

'Señor, I have rendered a valuable service to the king regardless of whether you capture the fugitives or not. Will you give me the assurance of his protection and a reward?'

'Your desire for a reward is understandable, but why would you need protection?'

Zurika became confused. The protection she had really wanted was from her own crimes of yesterday. 'Er . . . we all need royal protection,' she volunteered lamely, then brightened at a flash of inspiration. 'The princes and the Jew have cause now to hate me. They might tell lies about me to wreak vengeance.'

'I cannot speak for His Majesty,' Captain Montoya responded gravely. 'Remember, *señorita*, that while there is always punishment for misdeeds, there is never recompense or reward for doing what is right.' Had he sighed? 'Such is life. You will have to place yourself in King Pedro's hands.'

As they rode along, Zurika told Captain Montoya the story she had made up. She had been brought to Toledo as a housekeeper from Jaén, where her grandmother lived, by Aaron Levi. On his instructions, she had accompanied the party to the grove near the arena that morning. No, she was not the mistress of any of them. She answered the captain's questions equally glibly.

The distant crowing of roosters in some remote village heralded the dawn, which had begun breaking across the night sky in a veil of grey and pink clouds shot with the gold of the approaching sun. Seeing it, Zurika realized that she was bone-weary. She had not slept for over twenty-four hours.

The first people appeared. A goatherd and his little boy, both enveloped in their dark blankets, directing their

428

goats to the side of the road with crooks and clicking tongues.

'*Buenos dias!*' The exchange of greetings brought daylight back to the night's life span.

Smallholders, spades in hand, on their way to the rare patches of cultivation in the desolate area, called out, '*Buenos dias!*'. . . '*Buenos dias!*' Hands to forehead in salute. New life to the earth.

A brown-robed friar, bag slung on broad back, staff in hand, plodded on leather-sandalled feet, resuming his pilgrimage to some shrine. '*Buenos dias!*'. . . He made the sign of the cross in blessing. God's life that never ended.

As they drew closer and closer to the former campsite, tiredness began to diminish Zurika's resolve. The first doubts arose. Had she done right? How could she be thus to people who had been so kind to her? Aaron Levi, the gentle Jew whose very gentleness came from incredible strength; Prince Juan of the sensitive soul, her teacher and friend, who had always been so understanding; even Prince Ahmed, because of whom alone she had escaped from the prison of the cliff-caves. Could it possibly be that Prince Ahmed was not really in love with Princess Beatrice, that he was merely rescuing a princess as he had once rescued a gypsy girl?

Ah, Princess Beatrice of the soft white, blue eyes, golden hair, poised carriage. Jealousy and hatred blazed anew.

The splash of the stream, a wisp of smoke, the smell of burning told her that they had reached the campsite. Her stomach clenched, she did not comprehend why, as she pointed silently towards the rough track leading off the highway. Female Judas, her conscience hissed. Be quiet, she commanded it fiercely.

Captain Montoya raised a hand, signalling the troop to come to a stop. The clattering dwindled down to a silence broken only by the rippling of the stream, the stamp of a horse and the snorting of animals blowing cold air from their nostrils. 'Lead the way!' the captain commanded Zurika. He half turned in the saddle. 'You men remain here. I shall go in alone with the woman. The fugitives are probably far away by now, but I want to take a quick look at what they left behind.' He nodded to Zurika.

Zurika walked her horse down the little slope, through the trees to the tiny meadow within the grove. She was alert now, but her emotions were mixed. She reined in at the edge of the campsite, took in the remains of the wagon, blackened and mutilated by fire. Some parts of the wood still glowed red. Three suits of armour were spreadeagled on the grass like the remains of the dead on a battlefield. The charred remains of a blanket lay by the tree to which the horses had been tethered.

Shame at having betrayed friends and enemies began to mount within Zurika. What did Sweet Jesu, who died on the cross for those who harmed him, think of her? What would the Blessed Virgin . . .?

'Ah, *Dios* . . . Ah, *Dios!* . . . What have I done?' Screams welled from her throat, resounded in her head and rent the air, echoing through the grove. The reins released, her horse dropped its head and started cropping grass.

Captain Montoya waited impassively until her screams subsided into sobbing and she finally fell silent, an occasional involuntary whimper jerking from her chest. 'Well may you weep,' he said in low tones. 'You are an extremely foolish young woman. Your actions have probably destroyed any chance we had of overtaking the fugitives. While they had horses, they would have stuck to the highway. Now, they are on foot and could be anywhere in this wild countryside, with at least four hours start on us.' He shook his head. 'You have to face your immortal soul for having betrayed your master and his

430

friends.' There was contempt in his voice. 'I shall detail four men to remain here with you while you rest. You will then be escorted by them to Toledo to face the king's justice.'

Chapter 23

King Pedro was delighted at the reactions of the other white Christian rulers in the Iberian peninsula – still his guests in the Toledo palace – to the news that the lead elements of the Castilian army were leaving that very day to attack Granada. Both King Charles the Bad of León y Navarra and King Philip of Catalonia made instant recoveries from having fallen off their (high, King Pedro reflected sourly!) horses and called on him to assure him of their support. King Philip would return immediately to his capital, Barcelona, to prepare his troops, while King Charles would send Count Gaston back to Pamplona for the same purpose. King Charles himself would accompany King Pedro in pursuit of the fugitives. Things seemed to be falling into place again. As for Bishop Eulogius, he was ecstatic.

Count Gaston would escort Princess Mathilde back to Pamplona. Once there, having ordered an army corps to move to Cordoba, he would proceed without delay at the head of a cavalry unit along the western highway in case the fugitives had crossed country to approach Granada by that route. Once the Castilian army reached Jaén, the Christian forces would attack Granada on two fronts. King Pedro's only concern about the plan was King Charles's insistence on staying behind in Toledo to join the chase of the fugitives, on the grounds that the personal insults he had suffered from Prince Ahmed demanded immediate vengeance, and Bishop Eulogius's plea to be allowed to accompany them.

As for King Philip, once he reached Barcelona, he would despatch a small fleet towards Alicante, where it would anchor and remain in readiness to attack Granada from the east coast at the appropriate time, the contact point again being Jaén. King Philip would also send a contingent of cavalry through Valencia to head west for the eastern highway and intercept the fugitives further south. Only when the main forces of all three were in position would the attack on Granada commence. Meanwhile, King Pedro's secret was that Farouk Riswan would have King Yusuf killed, after which he and Prince Saad would deliver Granada to him without the firing of a single arrow. It was vital to King Pedro's plot that Prince Ahmed should never reach Granada.

Now here, seated across the oak desk of his study after breakfast, was King Alfonso IV of Portugal, also wanting to join the enterprise: not wanting to be left out of a crusade, King Pedro reflected cynically. He had always felt an affinity with this ruler. An older man than himself, King Alfonso had succeeded to the Portuguese throne in the year 1325. He had been married to Princess Isabel but had fallen in love with one of her ladies-in-waiting, Iñes de Castro, creating a situation similar to King Pedro's own with Maria de Padilla. This morning, having slept alone in the palace for the first time in years and not enjoyed it, King Pedro had decided to make it up with his beloved Maria before he left Toledo.

King Alfonso was enormously broad and short, with a barrel chest and peculiarly flat features relieved by a hooked nose above a dark brown moustache and sharp black eyes. Dressed in a green velvet tunic, the sleeves with jagged edges, the whole embellished by three enormous gold chains, he looked more like a pirate than a king, yet his deep voice was pompous.

'Your Majesty, Portugal can be an invaluable part of your present plan, which has softened our earlier reluctance to be part of a huge single Christian army. Through this plan, the product of your ingenuity, each king will be able to act independently, so our concern regarding who should lead has abated. With Portugal advancing against Granada from the west, we will present the heretic Moors with yet another front.'

The pompous tones of the Portuguese king displeased King Pedro. 'While we appreciate Your Majesty's offer of help, especially as it comes from a white Christian brother, it would duplicate an approach from the west with that of Navarre.'

King Alfonso raised and lowered fingers glittering with gold and emerald rings. 'Ah, but Your Majesty would have two advantages from our . . . er . . . co-operation.' He smiled, revealing large, white teeth. 'First,' he raised a forefinger, 'we can get to the fugitives from the west sooner than Count Gaston. Second,' the middle finger joined the forefinger, 'we could also send a fleet with our main body to Cadiz to attack Granada on its narrow western border.' He stroked his moustache, a triumphant expression on his face. 'Divide our forces and rule Granada, eh?'

King Pedro liked the idea, but who would do the ruling? The answer could come later, but King Alfonso's plan would further reduce the risk of Castile's suffering another ignominious defeat. 'We thankfully accept Your Majesty's gracious offer. Let our staffs work out the details. Your commanding general is of course here and should talk to our own Chief of Staff immediately?'

King Alfonso nodded. 'What news of the fugitives, Your Majesty?'

'Reports have them heading south along the eastern highway,' he responded shortly. He could not wait to get his hands on Prince Ahmed. Cruel gurgles of delight bubbled within him at the thought of the tortures he would inflict on that Moorish prick.

* * *

Prince Ahmed had suggested that the guards scatter into the countryside initially, rather than take immediately to the highway, even singly, and risk being stopped by King Pedro's cavalry. 'Allow them a few hours to pass, then proceed north along the highway to Toledo and your homes,' he had advised. As he had intended, having circled north, he and his group reached the Toledo highway at dawn the following day. Admiration had been added to Prince Ahmed's love for Princess Beatrice. Especially during the hours of darkness, when they had walked and stumbled through the mountain country, she had bravely and cheerfully endured every hardship of what for her was a totally new experience. She was the ideal woman and he would be proud to make her his wife and queen.

They now stood on a rocky eminence shrouded by trees, looking down a naked yellow escarpment at a sharp bend in the grey cobbled highway below, devoid of life beneath the stout branches of oak trees draped over it. Prince Ahmed stared at the scene. Other bends to the south revealed parts of the highway for a mile or so, but the north to their left was obscured by the mountainside. Would it be safe to use the road?

The sky was overcast with grey-white clouds, so while the earth was light, the sun was only visible as a burnished silver glow just above the distant horizon. Below the highway, the land dipped down into a valley through which a narrow stream meandered, a barely visible silver-black ribbon between the dark green branches of an olive grove. To the left, he could detect a field of sunflowers, grown for their oil, which had begun lifting their faces to the sun. A tile-roofed *hórreo* or grain store, with a cross at one end, at the edge of larger patches of what had to be maize and corn, was the only building in sight. Mountain goats grazed on the poor grass of a plateau. A flock of wild ducks wheeled southward. His stale sweat was the only impurity. He could do with a perfumed bath.

'What do you think will happen to Zurika?' he inquired of Aaron Levi, standing beside him, a gnome beneath a black *yarmulke*, firmly grasping his staff.

Prince Ahmed's anger at Zurika's betrayal had abated, but he could not forgive her the privation and danger to which Princess Beatrice was now exposed. Since the Muslim code of vengeance did not extend to women and children, it was easier for him to feel sorry for Zurika. He, Aaron Levi and Prince Juan had debated this frequently during the course of their journey through the wilderness the previous day. Hot words had erupted from him at first, while Aaron Levi had maintained a noncommittal silence. Prince Juan, on the other hand, with his sweet, Christian nature, had never once expressed any feeling of anger towards Zurika, only the need to continue loving her.

Aaron Levi sighed. 'I'm very much afraid that she will have met the pursuing cavalry,' he responded. 'She will lead them to the campsite, after which, having no further use for her, they will send her back to Toledo, where she will not be treated as a heroine but as a common criminal.'

'How so?' This was an aspect that Prince Ahmed had not discussed with them yesterday. 'Surely she can make up a story that would free her of any guilt . . . er . . . a poor servant woman merely obeying her masters but finally exposing the truth through loyalty to her king.'

'When she reaches Toledo, she will be a public figure.' Aaron Levi shook his grey head sadly. 'Regardless of her story, she will be identified by the surviving prison guards whom she drugged and that will make her a murderess. You don't know it yet, Prince, but in life one can't expect any reward for doing one's duty, except for the satisfaction within one's spirit. On the other hand, failure to do

436

one's duty or the committing of a crime unfailingly brings full punishment.'

'Is life like that?'

'That is how man has made the social order.'

'Almighty Allah has made the social order.'

'Jahweh!' Aaron Levi exclaimed reflexively. He smiled. 'As a practising Jew, I should think no further than I have been taught, but how can I ignore what I have observed these many years? Almighty Allah, Jahweh, the Christian God, whichever you believe in, is the substance of Creation. Within Creation, we have countless entities, including the sun, the earth and the puny creature we call man. For each such entity there are good and bad effects, but only as each reacts to causes. The birds of the air and the beasts of the field are free to build their nests and lairs, migrate with the weather, but all this is instinctive. It happens without conscious reasoning or planning. Man, of all these entities, appears to be the one that can create its own order. Thus man is the slave of the order he creates, some through instinct, some by deliberate forethought, some merely the by-product effects of causes over which he has no control.'

'What about justice, right and wrong?' Prince Ahmed demanded hotly.

'All human concepts,' Aaron replied soberly. 'So they are only as valid as the desire or ability of human beings to use or control their own products.' He turned to face Prince Ahmed, his dark eyes intense. 'Do you find anything akin to human concepts of right, wrong and justice in the universe? Is it just that the sun, the giver of light and life, should also produce drought that destroys man and beast, tree and shrub?'

Angry retorts based upon Islamic teachings rose to Prince Ahmed's lips, but he held them back. Suddenly, these moments seemed to him part of Almighty Allah's divine will, with Aaron Levi an ancient soul sent to clear his mind, guide his thinking, make his heart more tender. Timeless moments indeed. 'Are you saying then that in the realm of the Almighty's creation, humans who are a part of it experience good and bad effects from its constant changes for their own good?'

'A bird can, if it is strong enough, fly before a storm that would destroy its nest or a man's home. Destruction, however, applies in more senses than one, for the thoughts, words, deeds and feelings of man can destroy his home even while the building stands. Right, wrong and justice are the stuff of man's creation, of man the god of the Universe of his lifespan. These concepts serve him, so he thinks. In the final analysis, however, each of us has to live by the stuff of our own creation, the produce only of our individual reality. Regardless of the teachings of my faith, deep inside me I know that each of us must live by the standards we have set up for ourselves, which are really based on whatever wisdom to survive that we possess. So we should follow these standards, not because they are inherently right or wrong, but because if we do not, we destroy ourselves through the good and bad effects of God's creation on our bodies, minds and hearts.'

'All that you say is blasphemy. It offends the teachings of Islam, which tell us that each one of our actions, the minutest of them, is the will of Allah.' Prince Ahmed uttered the words, but he felt no anger towards the little Jew gazing so intensely at him.

'Then we both blaspheme, Prince,' Aaron Levi stated quietly. He grinned mischievously. 'I with my words, you with your thoughts.' He paused. 'Yet, why should my words conflict with the teachings of either of our faiths?' he resumed soberly. 'For all of it still remains the will of the Creator.'

'I must think . . .' Prince Ahmed broke off as a faint sound reached his ears. He immediately identified it as the clip-clippety-clop of distant hooves, crisp in the clear dawn air. His pulses quickened; his gaze darted south. Five figures on horseback had cleared a distant bend. A few seconds later, they were hidden by the pleat of a hill.

Princess Mathilde rode astride her grey Arab charger instead of side-saddle, not to assert her equality or diminish her femininity, but because she enjoyed the greater sense of balance that the seat created, enabling her to be more comfortably in motion with her mount. She had been severely criticized for it by the dowagers of the Pamplona court in the old days, most of them undoubtedly jealous of her youth, looks and charm, she guessed, but in the process of time people had come to accept it and even to admire her considerable riding skills at the competitions in which she frequently beat the men.

She had insisted on riding the grey back to Pamplona rather than use her coach because she had come to enjoy Count Gaston's company. Moreover, the grey went rather well with the elegant grey riding clothes, a full-length robe flowing over pantaloons, and her silver hair! The count certainly matched her in elegance with his customary white silk tunic and velvet hose.

Freshly disillusioned by King Charles the Bad – the poor love-lorn lout had insisted on remaining in Toledo to accompany King Pedro's army because of his infatuation with Princess Beatrice – she found Count Gaston mature, charming and a gentleman. He even made her wonder whether she needed plots any longer. Why should she not settle down to a relaxed existence? Why should she not start with herself?

This was their second day out and they had resumed their journey before dawn to make the most of the cooler hours of daylight. The entire party consisted of one hundred cavalrymen, one half of whom rode as advance guard, with her and Count Gaston immediately behind them, followed by a convoy of royalty, noblemen and noblewomen, courtiers, ladies-in-waiting, others who had attended the tourney, on horseback, in coaches or wagons, their staffs and attendants with the baggage train. The second half of the cavalry escort brought up the rear.

'The promise of another beautiful sunny day, Count Gaston,' Princess Mathilde observed above the clatter of hooves and rattle of wagon wheels. She nodded towards the shiny glow of the eastern sky. 'I must confess that part of me should have been born a male, for I enjoy being with men in uniform. I adore the smell of horse sweat and wet leather. I love the *esprit-de-corps*.'

'You might like it under these idyllic circumstances, Princess.' Count Gaston glanced sideways at her, his hatchet face creased in a sombre white grin. 'But what of battle conditions, with the cries of wounded men, bloodied uniforms, the stench of unwashed bodies and rotting corpses, when the odours could rise higher than the *esprit-de-corps*?'

She wrinkled her nose. 'Must you intrude reality into my dream? Can you not leave me with my illusions?' She smiled to rob the questions of any offence.

'War is no illusion,' he replied, growing quite serious. 'Since our present journey is a prelude to war, we should all fully comprehend its realities.'

'You do not approve of the decision to invade Granada?'

'Such decisions are not mine to approve or disapprove, Princess, but I do have the God-given right to disapprove of war as a concept, even while my duty commands me to undertake it to the fullest at the command of my king.'

She realized that the count had held his views on war for some years. Now, for the first time, he faced the need to subordinate his personal attitude to his duty as a subject.

The realization drew her closer to him, brought a touch of his inner sadness, so she could have reached out in turn

440

to touch his hand, except for her background and training, her own reality! 'While others will exult in the blare of trumpets, to you they will sound like a death knell,' she said instead, her voice low.

A quick glance revealed his appreciation of her understanding but he made no comment. Not expecting any, she deftly changed the subject. 'Which raises the question – undoubtedly more soul-shaking! – of how long you think it will be before you stand at the borders of Granada.'

He must have picked up her motive for his eyes crinkled again. 'According to my present plan, we should reach Pamplona five days from now. I have allowed two days for issuing the necessary orders and for staff planning of the move of the army corps. But it will, of course, be relatively simple to organize the advance cavalry unit, so I can leave on the seventh day. Is that not what you really want to know?' His gentle expression robbed the words of any conceit.

'Yes,' she readily responded, then deliberately changed the subject. 'I understand that our army corps will consist of twenty-five thousand men?'

'Yes, including all arms of the service.'

She suddenly realized that she would miss Count Gaston. Was she falling in love with a man who had been virtually a stranger to her less than a year ago? Heaven forbid. And what of her promised fidelity to King Charles? That had gone out with his other dirty laundry. 'How long will it take the entire force to reach Cordoba?'

'I estimate one week of fairly hard riding.'

'So King Alfonso will be ahead of you?'

'Possibly.'

Out of the blue she realized with surprise that the pall of her jealousy and hatred of Princess Beatrice had begun to lift. 'Will I see you after we get to Pamplona?'

'I'm going to be very busy.' She experienced a stab of

disappointment. 'But one can always make time for what one wants to do.'

Could it be that he loved her? A long sideways glance at his hatchet features told her that the walls around his innermost being would keep it aloof from anyone forever.

Sensing Prince Ahmed's urgency, Aaron Levi had fallen silent and was peering towards the south. 'It is only at such times that I regret my age,' he muttered. 'These old eyes . . .'

The figures reappeared round the next bend. 'Almighty Allah!' Prince Ahmed whispered.

'Who? Who are they?' Aaron Levi inquired urgently.

'A woman bound to her horse, riding between two Castilian cavalrymen, with one more ahead of her and one behind. I cannot make out who the woman is, but it must be Zurika.'

Aaron Levi banged his staff on the ground. 'I knew it. I knew this would happen.' He paused, then suddenly gripped Prince Ahmed's arm. 'We must rescue her.'

'What? She betrayed us woefully and you want to risk our lives for her? Never!'

He felt a hand on his arm. Prince Juan had come up silently. 'It is Zurika,' he signalled positively. His blue eyes were pleading. 'We have no time to lose if we are to save her.'

'She is getting what she asked for and deserves.' Prince Ahmed's anger had created a curious hardness within him, implacable as one of the granite cliffs soaring behind them. 'As soon as they pass us, it will be safe for us to proceed to Granada.'

Prince Juan's face tightened. 'She rescued me from the dungeons,' he signalled. 'Even if she had not, the code of the *caballero* dictates that I rescue any woman in need, whatever she may have done to me.' He nodded towards the ribbon patches of the highway. 'There they are again. The prisoner is indeed Zurika.'

Even before he shifted his own gaze towards the highway Prince Ahmed had heard the clippety-clop-clip-clop of hooves. The approaching party had rounded another bend. Stubbornness gripped him. 'I say we do nothing,' he growled decisively.

'Then I shall have to make the attempt alone,' Prince Juan responded, quiet determination in every gesture.

Fury seized Prince Ahmed. 'What?' he demanded.

'Prince Juan will not be alone.' Prince Ahmed turned, incredulous, towards the quiet, dry voice of Aaron Levi. The Jew banged his staff again for emphasis. 'I have probably lost more material possessions on this enterprise than you, Prince,' he asserted coldly. 'My only recompense must be noble conduct of the sort which my religion does not call for towards an enemy.' He turned towards Prince Juan, gesturing. 'Let us plan how we shall do it.'

The sound of hooves became muffled. The riders had vanished around another bend.

Aaron Levi was taking sides against him. Prince Ahmed's fury knew no bounds, before cold inspiration contained it. 'You do that and you will be placing Princess Beatrice in jeopardy,' he stated flatly, signalling with deft fingers for Prince Juan's benefit. Smiling in triumph, he folded his hands across his chest, awaiting their response.

'Only because I shall be joining them in the attempt.'

Prince Ahmed swung round in shock. Princess Beatrice had come up unobserved. She had obviously heard all that had transpired. Her eyes were not angry, but pleading. 'My brother has reminded us of the code of the *caballero*,' she stated quietly. 'Although you have not taken the *caballero* oath, you are a prince. Your oath is implicit in your birth, which demands that you rise above normal mortals, including yourself when necessary.'

Beneath Princess Beatrice's pleading was love for him,

soothing cold water putting out the fire of anger. 'You are right, noble Princess,' he declared, marvelling. 'But you must not expose yourself to the danger of our rescue attempt. Aaron Levi, Prince Juan and I will handle this alone.' The clatter of hooves rose again. He glanced down, noting the spacing of the cavalrymen this time. 'We do not have a moment to lose.' He thought swiftly, surveyed the terrain, then turned to them excitedly. 'I have a plan. We must quickly work out . . .'

'Pray excuse me,' Princess Beatrice interposed. 'But there are four of them and only three of you men. I insist on joining you.'

Prince Ahmed marvelled again, this time also at an authority in her voice which brooked no contradiction.

She should make her break for freedom as far away from Toledo as possible, Zurika had decided. Her unexpected fate had finally brought her face to face with reality. She was a young gypsy girl in a world that was totally strange to her. How naïve she had been. The grave danger of her situation brought the realization of how secure she had been with her friends. As the clouds of the desire for vengeance dissipated, terror took over. In Toledo she would be identified by the prison guards, who would make up their own story about the events of the fateful morning. She would be tortured for the truth, which could terminate in her telling lies to end her suffering and enter the peace of death. What a terrible, terrible mistake she had made, but for which she and her friends would be well on the way to Granada by now.

The soldiers had not body-searched her, so her long-bladed knife remained at her waist. The four cavalrymen whom Captain Montoya had left behind had treated her with unfailing courtesy. Except that her feet were bound beneath the horse while she rode, she could have been a gentlewoman being escorted by four soldiers. Corporal

444

Ramirez, who rode in front, was a tall, gangling man with a long droopy grey moustache and sad brown eyes. The two men on either side of her, Angelo at her right, José to her left, were both lean veterans, while Pedro at her rear was bald beneath his high cavalry cap, his face round and wrinkled. Zurika rather suspected that Captain Montoya had selected these veterans because they were trustworthy family men who would not attempt to molest her. They seemed in no hurry to get to Toledo, contenting themselves with making their horses walk or trot slowly. They had slept in a wayside herder's cottage last night and she missed the regular baths to which she had become accustomed at Aaron Levi's villa. Today, she smelled like a mountain goat.

Though they were proceeding at a slow pace, they would still be near Toledo by nightfall. She must make her move soon, before people began to stir. To her right, the rising sun was a glow in the east, a silver sheen above the horizon. The valley below must be inhabited, an olive grove, patches of cultivated field, even a *hórreo*. She glanced to her left. The hillside rising sharply above the trees lining the highway would have to be her escape route.

Still at a walk, they rounded a deep bend. Sunlight fractured the shadows of dark oak branches overhead, creating dappled patterns on Corporal Ramirez's uniform and the rear of his black horse, whose gait reminded Zurika of the back of a deliberately seductive woman.

It was instinct more than the faint swish that made her turn in her saddle. A croak escaped Pedro before she saw the rope loop tight around his neck. He released the reins to claw at his throat, but was lifted up and off his saddle, while his well-schooled chestnut walked on as if nothing had happened. Pedro remained dangling in the air as if he were on a gibbet, clawing wildly now at the rope around his neck.

445

What in God's name was happening? Could it be bandits?

The rest took place simultaneously. Two silent figures dropped on Angelo and José, bore them to the ground, while their horses whinnied, reared, then, lightened of their loads, kept walking on.

A woman's scream sounded at their front. Zurika's gaze darted to the white-clad figure with dishevelled hair that had dashed on to the highway from the cliffside. Recognizing Princess Beatrice, Zurika's heart began to thump. This was a rescue attempt. Corporal Ramirez, with one swift backward glance, sent his black leaping towards the figure. He reined in his horse beside it, leaned over, grabbed.

Red rage at seeing Princess Beatrice, regardless of her mission, erupted within Zurika, blinding her. She dug fierce heels into her horse's flanks. It surged forward. She drew her knife from her waist, brandished it aloft, forgot all else.

He was sufficiently young to have made a quick recovery from his fall in the joust, so the past day of cantering south along the eastern highway had afforded King Charles so much time to think of Princess Beatrice that he had become obsessed by her. Each time he imagined her tall, slender body, the narrow waist beneath full breasts flaring out to shapely hips, he mentally stripped her to imagine the delight of rosy limbs and a golden pubis. He lusted for her at such times, but this did not mar romantic thoughts of wooing her, to have those large blue eyes melt into his. He imagined her saying, Oh Charles, you are *so* Bad, but what a delightful brute.

He had never felt this way, even as a youth.

Riding his black charger to the right of King Pedro who was mounted on a tall bay, and with the purple-robed Bishop Eulogius on a small grey Arab to his left, King

Charles took in King Pedro's bull-like face and marvelled that such a one could have fathered an exquisite being like Princess Beatrice. What would the product of his own mating with Princess Beatrice look like? Should not pride and his position prohibit marriage to someone who had run away with an infidel? Well, even if Prince Juan's presence with the fugitives did not excuse the guilt, he was King Charles, the man who made the rules. Why, he could even make a saint of a fornicating donkey!

They had left Toledo late the previous afternoon with the advance elements of King Pedro's army, consisting principally of cavalry units. Having bivouacked for the night in a string of adjoining valleys, they had resumed their journey at dawn. King Charles was sufficiently alert for the question to surface in his mind. 'How is it that Your Majesty's army could move out so fast?'

King Pedro threw back his head. His laugh rang out above the dense clatter of hooves. 'Our army has been ready to move at short notice for months,' he asserted. His tone indicated that he was not willing to say more.

'His revered Majesty is always in a state of readiness,' Bishop Eulogius incanted, beaming. 'Especially for fornication!'

'Except when he is confronted by his favourite scheming bishop collaborating secretly with his favourite scheming son-in-law to be,' King Pedro growled. 'We refer to the declaration of the gypsy girl Zurika as a heretic behind our backs.'

'Godsbody, we thought Your Majesty would applaud our action, by drawing any opprobrium for the declaration on our own self,' King Charles protested, lying. 'The girl should be apprehended and burned as a witch.'

'She has to be captured first, then tried,' King Pedro demurred, without conviction.

'Trial by ordeal,' King Charles suggested.

'No, no!' Bishop Eulogius protested. 'She must be

447

burned at the stake . . . er . . . once she is found guilty by my ecclesiastical court.'

Zurika swung her mount to the left of Corporal Ramirez, the long knife upraised for the plunge into Princess Beatrice. But some deeper instinct suddenly made her slow the bay. In an instant, she dropped the blade and shifted her grip. Holding the point between thumb and forefinger, she raised the knife again and flung it straight and true as she had been taught in the gypsy caves.

It found its mark. The gangling Corporal Ramirez jerked violently, loosening his grip on Princess Beatrice. A cry escaped her as she fell on the highway. The corporal lost his rein, began slipping off his horse, the knife sticking out obscenely from his neck.

Zurika reined in her horse. What had made her change her mind? Surely it was God and the Blessed Virgin. She felt clean again. Exulting now, she circled her bay. Prince Ahmed and Prince Juan had grounded their opponents and were sitting astride them, while Aaron Levi was climbing down the tree from whose overhanging branch Pedro still dangled by the neck. She came up on the side of Corporal Ramirez's riderless horse and grabbed its rein, ignoring Princess Beatrice who was struggling to her feet. 'You saved me, Zurika,' she declared thankfully, no sooner than she had come erect.

Within minutes, the group were reunited with a horse for each, no questions asked of Zurika and no recriminations. Zurika marvelled at these people. Her own gypsy folk would have slit her throat at the betrayal.

They dumped the bodies of Corporal Ramirez and Pedro over the side of the hill, Prince Juan saying a prayer for their souls. Then they trussed and gagged the two unconscious guards and placed them on the side of the highway.

'The poor men did not know what struck them,' Prince

Ahmed exulted. 'They must have thought the heavens opened up to drop thunderbolts.'

Zurika was thrilled that his glance included her, free of rancour, pleasant even. The ugly question intruded, Is he grateful to me for saving his beloved?

'You saved Princess Beatrice, Zurika,' Aaron Levi echoed the sentiment to her dismay.

'We are all most grateful to you,' Prince Ahmed declared shortly.

'I betrayed you all, yet you saved me from torture and death, my lords. How can I ever repay you?' Something broke loose in her. She began to weep uncontrollably, her body racked by sobs.

'Say no more about it,' Aaron Levi commanded.

The faint rattle of wagon wheels overlaid by voices raised in animated conversation arose above her sobs. 'We have no time for weeping,' Prince Ahmed broke in, his voice deliberately harsh. 'There are people coming. We do not have a moment to lose.'

Chapter 24

The spy Mizra had offered to lead the assassination attempt on Prince Ahmed personally immediately he learned of the reward Farouk Riswan had offered. 'This is too important an assignment to be left to amateurs, Lord,' he asserted. 'I shall lead it myself.'

'A very worthy decision,' the Prime Minister had replied, knowing the truth. 'Go with Almighty Allah.'

Having carefully considered the available choices of professional assassins, Mizra had selected three men. None of these would depart from Granada. He would pick them up at Jaén, Baéza and Ciudad Real, along the way. This had several advantages. Firstly, the assassins would not know each other. Then, they could be easily disposed of once the assassination attempt was successful, to prevent their blabbing or trying to blackmail him. Thirdly, he could therefore keep the entire reward for himself. Finally, by proceeding alone from Granada, he would not arouse the attention that a band of men, however small, might create.

He had slept for four hours following the interview with the Prime Minister before heading north on horseback. When he saw Abdul at the Alhambra mosque during morning prayer, he knew that Almighty Allah had blessed this venture. He and Mizra looked like twin brothers. Abdul, who was visiting from Jaén, had readily accepted the assignment. By dawn that day, two small, insignificant grey Arabs with dead eyes fronting coolly murderous minds, were halfway to Granada's northern border with Castile.

* * *

They had delayed one week in the mountain wilderness, safely hidden in a cave, before Princess Beatrice, whose back had been hurt by the fall, was well enough for them to resume their journey. A tiny hidden spring served the cave which must have been inhabited in early times. No one disturbed them, the only signs of life being the inevitable hare, which Prince Ahmed and Prince Juan were able to trap for the food they could cook without fear of discovery. 'Your Spanish epigram, *dar gato por liebra*, serve up a cat instead of a hare, the great deception, certainly does not apply to us!' Prince Ahmed had jokingly signalled to Prince Juan the first time they ate hare. He found himself enjoying the semi-nomadic life experience, the impatience to push on having worn off immediately it became necessary for them to pause for Princess Beatrice's sake, so he could truthfully assure her that her disability was affording him a much-needed holiday.

The time of peace and rest, especially from the tensions and strenuous events of the past three days, was good for them all. They never went near the highway, so were unaware of what had happened to the dead cavalrymen and the other two whom they had spared. Prince Ahmed was certain that the latter would have been rescued with no more injury than hurt pride. The two princes and Zurika travelled long distances to forage for food each night, Zurika displaying an inborn prowess at stealing eggs, tomatoes and fruit from the occasional farmyard with an uncanny ability not to disturb the watchdogs. They slept by day, when Princess Beatrice and Aaron Levi, who had slept during the night, kept watch.

Prince Ahmed found living in the mountains even more exhilarating than walking or riding through them. Cool beauty and vast silences were disturbed only by the sounds of nature, such as high winds and an occasional bird call. Even the howling of wolves at night was balm for the soul. They missed only their baths, having to keep their precious water source for drinking and the minimum needs of hygiene. Though cleanliness was not a characteristic of many of the poorer people of Spain, all of them, even Zurika, were addicted to it.

'Jews and Muslims bathe regularly,' Prince Ahmed, a mischievous glint in his eyes, had signalled to Prince Juan on their first night in the cave. The deaf and dumb prince had wrinkled his nose at his own high odour, his affliction having improved his other senses. 'Your mendicant Spanish monks have long considered the antithesis to be desirable, venerating physical dirt as the test of moral purity and true strength. They dine and sleep year round in the same woollen habit, to achieve that highest odour of sanctity, a foul stench which is the height of their spiritual ambition. Why, many of your saints are even painted sitting in their own excrement! The common people follow suit. So why be offended by your saintliness, Prince?' He smiled openly, to show he was joking.

'I'm no saint!' Prince Juan had responded with a grin. 'Nor of the common people,' he added. 'And I suggest that you never forget what the great Roman orator, Cicero, said of us Spaniards. "If God were not God, He would be the King of Spain and the King of France would be his cook," to which I would add that the King of Granada would be kitchen scullion, so long as he remained clean of body as required by his Muslim faith!'

Prince Ahmed clapped him affectionately on the shoulder. They had fallen into an easy bantering of insults as they drew closer.

When they had lost their horses in the meadow, they had taken only as much baggage as they could carry, principally the money and jewels belonging to Prince Ahmed and Aaron Levi, which they carried in belt pouches, a change of clothes, some toiletries, flint and tinder for making fires. Princess Beatrice had exchanged the finery she had worn to the tournament for one of Zurika's plain garments, with two of the gypsy girl's skirts and blouses for spare, one of which she later returned. They looked a ragged bunch. The horses they had captured were equipped with cavalry saddlebags containing food and toilet articles. 'The Castilian army has not only provided us with mounts but also with the comforts of home,' Prince Ahmed remarked drily to the others.

When they left the cave, the prince led them down the southern slopes of the naked mountain range at a leisurely pace, reasoning that they should allow Captain Montoya and his cavalry squadron enough time to draw well ahead, reach the Granada border and return without success.

'Shall we be passing through Jaén?' Zurika inquired as they were leaving.

'If all goes well,' Prince Ahmed replied cautiously.

'Could I visit my grandmother there?' Zurika inquired.

'If we do make it to Jaén, you may wish to remain there awhile, joining us in Granada later.'

Circling wide to the west, then south, they plotted their course from the movement of the sun by day and the stars, especially the traveller's cross, by night. Aaron Levi revealed a surprising knowledge of astronomy.

The seemingly endless region of *meseta* plains of central Spain were new to them all. It was one thing to cross the *meseta* along a highway, quite another to travel across country through its featureless miles. Most of it Prince Ahmed discovered to be akin to his conception of the Arab desert lands. Avoiding the small townships, what people they encountered were mostly farmers who, for their own protection, lived in clusters of houses surrounding a small church, travelling considerable distances in consequence to their individual fields, olive groves and orchards. The heat of the *meseta* was scorching by day, but the reward came at dusk, with the silhouettes of farmers, on muleback or on foot, against the glowing western sky, producing the notes of their slow songs, ancient as the land, which recreated the slow motion of their ploughs cutting into a hard, bare soil.

Their hopes soared on the fifth day, when they forded the Guadalquivir river, which had shrunk under the summer's intense heat. They were now closer to the Granada borders and should hit the highway soon, so they proceeded with greater caution. When they reached the slight eminence, Prince Ahmed directed the two ladies to remain sheltered with all the horses at the bottom while he, Aaron Levi and Prince Juan walked to the summit to scout the area beyond. They reached the top and gazed eastwards, taking care not to be silhouetted against the skyline. Prince Juan, with his uncanny sight, was the first to spot the long, straight stretch of the old Roman highway, from the slight eminence on which they stood. 'There it is!' he mouthed, pointing. Prince Ahmed followed his hand to focus on the highway. His breath caught. Moving figures dotted the straight line as far north and south as his eyes could see. 'Men on horseback!' he muttered, as if his normal voice could have carried that far. 'Almighty Allah! This is a whole army on the move, heading south. Who could it be?'

'It is the Castilian army, heading for Granada,' Aaron Levi replied soberly. 'My associates warned of this.'

'How could they have got here so soon?' Prince Ahmed demanded in amazement, unconsciously signalling with his fingers for Prince Juan's benefit. 'Could they have left Toledo *before* the tourney?'

'My father moves with the speed of lightning,' Prince Juan responded. 'Yet even he could not have got here so soon unless he planned the expedition weeks ago.'

'This means war,' Prince Ahmed stated slowly. His initial deflation was swiftly followed by anger. 'I must get to Granada at once to help my father and my people.'

'But how?' Prince Juan questioned. 'We can hardly use the highway.'

'We must turn back, cross the *meseta* and take the western route.' Prince Ahmed's blood quickened. He recalled his father riding out to do battle against the Castilian king, leaving him behind, angry, frustrated, the hope of the future dying with the echoes of the Moorish war-trumpets in his ears. This time, sword in hand, he would ride into battle. He stared at Prince Juan. This man should be his enemy. Sensitive to the slightest change, Prince Juan's gaze met his, reading his every thought. Their glances locked for interminable seconds, blankly for the first time.

Prince Juan finally shook his head sadly. 'I shall not join in a war against anyone,' he signalled. 'Least of all against you, my friend Prince Ahmed, and your country.'

'Do you not feel for your own country?'

'Spain is one country. We should not be fighting against each other, making ourselves the prey of foreigners, as we have done throughout history because of our internal divisions.' Prince Juan's fingers paused. 'Besides, I am a Christian and cherish higher principles than war. If my enemy smites me on one cheek, I must turn the other.'

'And I am a Muslim,' Prince Ahmed flamed back passionately. 'I believe in world Islam to save mankind. Granada is the seed from which Islam can sprout again to become a gigantic tree, spreading its magnificent branches through Spain, all of Europe and eventually the world, far beyond the horizons to which it extended two centuries and more ago to include the entire space between the great Western Ocean and the Indian seas. I am of the soil of Granada. It is being threatened by those who would seize it. They are the mortal enemy. I must leave everything, everyone and thwart their evil designs.'

Aaron Levi shrugged bony shoulders. Prince Juan

merely looked at Prince Ahmed, the blue eyes glistening sadly. 'What is your wish?' he finally gestured.

Prince Ahmed's mind was finally made up. 'I shall leave you all immediately and proceed alone to Granada by the fastest route possible.' Suddenly, his heart became bleak with near despair at the thought of parting from Princess Beatrice. Almighty Allah would have to be her protector. 'When I reach the Alhambra, I shall prevail on my father, who will undoubtedly be grateful now for my return, to command all the border guards to give you safe passage into the kingdom and to escort you to the safety of our palace, even though war may rage around us. I suggest that the four of you make for Jaén, avoiding the Castilian army. As we know, *Señor* Levi has powerful connections there and Zurika can take you to her grandmother's house, where you should be safe.'

'You are right,' Aaron Levi responded. 'I suggest that we race south over the *meseta*, parallel to the highway, and cut into it when we are well ahead of the comparatively slow-moving Castilian army.' A sparkle in his dark eyes revealed excitement. 'I want you to know, Prince, that I am grateful to you and all others who have brought back life to my existence!'

'One thing you must be careful about,' Prince Ahmed warned. 'Captain Montoya's cavalry may be ahead of you when you cut into the road. Do not get trapped between the two enemy forces.'

Mizra, the spy turned assassin, had reason to believe that Merciful Allah was blessing his enterprise. First, he had not had to go all the way to Jaén to meet Abdul. Next Abdul and he had easily met Rauf, a slim, slight, youthful-looking killer, the most ruthless of them all but with the same dead eyes, at his usual vegetable stand at the Baéza marketplace three days later. Rauf had readily accepted the assignment and the offered reward. Finally, late on the fifth afternoon, the three of them had been stopped and questioned on the highway, before they got to Ciudad Real, by a Captain Montoya leading a squadron of Castilian cavalry, as to whether they had passed a group of fugitives from King Pedro's justice. Mizra naturally had no news to give, save lies, but with the skill of the professional he had been able to extract all the information he needed from the captain.

This changed everything. The hunt had become more difficult, but Mizra was not going to give up the opportunity for wealth such as he had never dreamed possible. He could retire, though he probably never would, because he loved and needed the suppressed excitement, the sense of power, the feel of controlling the destinies of others and the thrill of the kill that his work afforded. In this last, he was no different from the others. They too lusted for murder, especially young Rauf. Mizra knew him to be a killer by instinct who was unique in that he derived sexual pleasure from the kill, experiencing an orgasm each time he plunged a dagger into a victim.

After his encounter with Montoya, Mizra proceeded north along the highway to the campsite. Merciful Allah was still on his side, for two days later he and his comrades crossed the advance elements of the Castilian army. Mizra demanded to be conducted to the captain of the lead squadron, pretending that he had information to impart. Giving bogus information of no value regarding a wagon they had passed along the way, thus putting the Castilians off the track, Mizra not only learned of the ambush and the rescue of Zurika, but also of the exact spot at which the event had taken place.

Both Mizra and Abdul were trained trackers, but where were the tracks? What would they do if they were in Prince Ahmed's shoes. Since he was unaware of the events in Granada, least of all his father's death, Mizra

457

reasoned that Prince Ahmed would make a wide detour in the mountain region, then try to hit the highway again.

Occasional horse dung, scour marks where hooves had slipped, once trampled bushes, clearly marked a trail which the fugitives had made no attempt to conceal. When they discovered the cave, Mizra's blood quickened. The trail was obviously warm. What had caused the delay? Had the fugitives merely rested there for several days, or was one of them wounded? Mizra accelerated their pace.

Now, in the pale light of evening, they had paused at the top of a low incline. About half a mile away, three figures were silhouetted against the skyline of a slight eminence. 'Look at those three figures. One of them must be our target,' he commented.

Rauf's keen eyesight picked out two more figures and five horses at the base of the eminence. He pointed. 'Women,' he stated laconically.

Mizra's thrill was followed by his usual icy calm before the kill.

When the two princes and Aaron Levi returned, their grave faces warned Zurika that some new calamity had befallen them. She listened to what they had to say with an outward calm that hid a fast-beating heart. After Prince Ahmed had finished speaking, she did not know whether to be glad that he would no longer be near Princess Beatrice during the foreseeable future, or sorry that she herself would be separated from him. The terrific problem she faced was uncertainty. She could only guess at what was going on between Prince Ahmed and Princess Beatrice, so the questions beat into her brain with the thud of miniature battering rams. Are they hiding their love for each other or are they merely friends? None of the group had even once referred to her betrayal. Was she being treated with gentle, well-bred condescension?

In spite of everything, she remained grateful to Prince Juan and Aaron Levi, loved Prince Ahmed and continued to hate Princess Beatrice.

'If I may be so bold as to venture an opinion, you are right to proceed alone, my lord prince,' Zurika remarked when Prince Ahmed finished speaking. Her eyes tried to penetrate the approaching darkness which was laying a soft purple-pink mantle on the earth as if the future lay there. Two buzzards flew overhead on slow wings in the direction of the highway, scavengers heading towards the human scavengers, she thought, surprisingly devoid of any feeling of outrage that Granada was being invaded. Whoever ruled Granada, it mattered not to the gypsies, whose life never changed.

Suddenly a chill premonition gripped her with its question. Would she be the victim of human buzzards? It left her incredibly sad and lonely. 'Are you leaving immediately?' she inquired of Prince Ahmed.

'Indeed, I must.' He seemed surprised at the hopelessness of her tone.

The wisdom of an ancient people gripped her. 'It is as well,' she stated. 'We ourselves should lie low until the entire army of Castile has passed, however long it takes, then proceed to Jaén!' Impulsively, she reached for her waist, drew her precious knife, proffered it to Prince Ahmed. 'You will be travelling alone, Prince. I pray you take this for your protection.' She had finally stripped herself of her one security.

'I have my sword and dagger . . .' he began, then changed his mind. 'It is your father's knife, so I accept it with great humility and shall hold it safe for you. You have taught me how to use it. I pray that I shall never have to, until I can return it safely to you.'

Princess Beatrice was stunned by the news. The thought that Prince Ahmed would be departing immediately left her bereft and speechless. She looked at him with tearful eyes, then quickly glanced away into the distance to avoid revealing her feelings. *If Prince Ahmed truly loves me, how could he leave me for anyone or anything?* The age-old question kept hammering at her brain till her temples began to ache. She resolutely held down her heightened breathing to avoid sobbing.

Was Prince Ahmed really Horn, or had she been mistaken? She made up her mind. 'I mean no offence to you, Zurika,' she smiled at the gypsy girl, 'but when we get to Jaén, I should like my brother to enter me into Saint Benedict's Convent there, so that he and Aaron Levi can be free to go.'

'You want to become a nun?' Prince Ahmed demanded.

She was thrilled by the note of consternation in his voice, but she forced herself to remain aloof from him in her heart. 'No,' she responded. 'I only want a place of refuge where I will not be anyone's responsibility,' she gave Prince Ahmed a cold, pointed look, 'nor impede the aims of princes.'

Prince Ahmed's pain at her remarks brought her no reward, only a stab at her conscience. This young man had risked his life for her. Was this the way to show gratitude, especially when she loved him?

Suddenly remorseful, Princess Beatrice gentled her glance. 'I mean, there is much that you men have to do at this time,' she added lamely. 'Zurika will be with her grandmother in Jaén. Only I am a passenger. I do not wish to remain anyone's responsibility. Each of you has done enough for me. It is time I looked after myself. Be assured that I shall be safe and secure in the convent.'

'But, but . . .' Prince Ahmed floundered, 'you will be exposed to the danger of discovery all the time.'

He sounded so anxious that Princess Beatrice restored him back to his role of Horn in her mind! 'The Reverend

Mother Euphrasia is the Superior of the convent. She is a first cousin of my own mother, Maria de Padilla. They have always been very close to each other since they were little girls and my mother has sent many a gift and generous donation to the Convent through the years. No one but Mother Euphrasia need know my identity and she would sacrifice her own life rather than betray me.'

Prince Ahmed blinked. 'But suppose you somehow fall into the hands of your father?' he persisted. 'He may marry you to King Charles the Bad.' A note of pleading had entered his voice.

Princess Beatrice observed the red sparks in Zurika's eyes and trembled. Would the gypsy girl strike again? Had she erred in divulging her plan to stay in the convent? 'That risk is always present, wherever I may be, until I finally get to your kingdom,' she declared, feigning self-assurance. Yet the mere mention of King Charles the Bad made her shudder with dire foreboding.

Mizra and his two companions had eased their horses behind the cover of a heap of rubble immediately they saw their quarry. Having spotted a clump of dead scrub not far from where the two female figures waited with the horses, Mizra decided to make for it, the better to observe the group and, if possible, hear what they were saying. 'I'm going to crawl over there,' he pointed to the clump of scrub. 'If they spot me, which I doubt,' he grinned his self-confidence, 'don't intervene, because I will make up a good story. They are not going to suspect a lone Muslim whereas three might make them concerned. They have obviously made for the highway hoping to have a clear passage to Granada. They could not possibly have imagined that an invasion of Granada was under way. I must try and find out what they are planning.'

'Are you sure this is the group?' Abdul questioned. 'You have never even seen this Prince Ahmed?'

Abdul was always cautious. 'That is what I'm going to find out.' Mizra's gaze shifted to Rauf. The young man had drawn his assassin's dagger and was running a forefinger over its sharp edge. Incongruously, his dead expressionless eyes had a dreamy quality from the feel of the blade which made even the hardened Mizra shudder. Allah prevent this man from being my enemy, he thought, before I kill him.

Accepting Rauf's silence as assent, Mizra snaked his way with expert skill, like a giant lizard, flat on his belly, one leg, then the other, bent at the knee then sliding flat up to waist level to lever him forward. The attention of the women was focused on the top of the eminence, so their backs were turned to Mizra and he reached his objective unobserved, being safely in position by the time the three men returned to join the women.

Mizra listened to the conversation, which carried clearly in the still air of the *meseta*, with interest. The Castilian army was proceeding along the highway. The darker young man, who was indeed Prince Ahmed, was to go west alone. The other two men and the women would wait just below the west of the eminence until the rearguard of the Castilian army had gone by, then follow it to Jaén where the princess would go to the Benedictine Convent. Her brother would leave her there and proceed with the Jew to Seville, where the Jew had friends who would assist them to get to Alhambra. Mizra knew the convent fairly well, but Abdul, being from Jaén, would know it better. As he slowly snaked his way back to his companions, Mizra had what he modestly considered a brilliant inspiration.

Abdul's eyes came alight with admiration when Mizra imparted his news. 'You are fantastic!' he exclaimed, keeping his voice low. 'When you crawled, you looked

462

like part of the *meseta*, brother. If I had not known you were there, I would never have spotted you.'

'It only takes practice,' Mizra replied, pleased at the praise. 'You will yourself to be a part of the earth, taking your mind totally away from your objective, excluding any thoughts, because they can connect with your quarry. The mind apart, it's just a matter of controlled agility.' He glanced beyond Abdul's shoulder. 'Like that snake over there which you have not become aware of because it has not seen you!'

Abdul swung around immediately, reaching for the knife at his waist. Mizra observed his alarm with amusement before the snake slithered away.

Rauf, on the other hand, had made neither comment nor movement. 'Your plan, brother?' he demanded quietly, sharpening the long blade of his knife on a small honing block, to and fro, to and fro, with methodical precision. Mizra shuddered again at the assassin's quiet menace.

'Like our quarry, we must split forces,' Mizra stated, forcing himself to eye Rauf steadily. 'You and Abdul will follow the party heading for Jaén while I pursue Prince Ahmed.'

Rauf's cold eyes turned deadly. 'The reward is for Prince Ahmed's death.'

'Abdul knows Jaén better than the Holy Koran. Can you imagine the reward King Pedro will give to have his son, the Jew and the girl Zurika delivered to him? We shall all share both rewards.'

Rauf pondered this for a moment, saw its logic and nodded. 'Which means we have to deliver them alive?'

Mizra shuddered for the third time. No orgasm for you, prick. 'Undoubtedly,' he confirmed.

'And Prince Ahmed?'

'Dead.'

'I would rather take him then.'

463

Was there going to be a dispute here? It was time to assert his authority. 'My master' – he had not divulged who it was, he never did – 'will only deal with me. He will even take my word that the deed has been done. Only I can receive that reward and give you your share.' He waited coldly for the words to sink in.

'Supposing something happens to you out there alone in the *meseta*, or Prince Ahmed kills you.'

'That is the beauty of the plan, brother, for Abdul and you would then at least be able to claim the reward from King Pedro. Besides,' his black-toothed grin was evil, 'there will be an added reward for you because of Princess Beatrice.'

Rauf's thin eyebrows lifted. 'From her father?'

Mizra's expressionless face concealed his triumph. 'No, from her suitor.'

'Who may that be?' Abdul demanded.

'The loins of King Charles the Bad of León y Navarra ache for her. He will pay handsomely if you help him get her to his bed.'

How do you follow a single rider in open *meseta* country during the daylight without betraying your presence? How can you do it after darkness falls, when you cannot even see your quarry? These were the two problems that Mizra faced. In recent years, he had been more the master spy than the assassin, but even his earlier experiences of tailing quarry had been confined to cities and towns. If Prince Ahmed chose to ride fast, the pounding of Mizra's own horse's hooves in pursuit would betray him. Worst of all, since Mizra did not even know precisely where Prince Ahmed was headed, he could not even pick him up again if he lost him in the darkness.

All this made Mizra's task incredibly difficult. He came to a quick decision. The deed had to be done tonight. He would tail Prince Ahmed at a safe distance until dusk, then close the gap, get within striking distance and gallop in for the kill.

Count Gaston's departure from Pamplona had left a curious vacuum in Princess Mathilde's life, which had begun when her purpose ended, when Charles the Bad, the rapist who took anyone he desired, by force if need be, turned into an adolescent lost lover over Princess Beatrice. The protégé who had sworn to love no one but her, whomever he might have to marry for convenience, had failed her.

Since returning to the Pamplona palace, she had puzzled in her mind as to whether the curious emptiness she felt, which so frequently brought physical tiredness, depression and listlessness, was occasioned by her heart or her head. Had she depended on King Charles the boy and the man as the central male figure in her life, or was her need for him only the product of her ambition to create and rule an empire so that she would be totally secure for the first time in her life?

Something new had been stirred in her by Count Gaston since their ride back from Toledo. What it was she couldn't quite identify, nor did she wish to. I'm a mature woman, she told herself, too old to discover that I have fallen in love with a man whom I can never have. Yet she had to admit that the return journey from Toledo had revealed to her something she had missed throughout her life, the reliable companionship of a man who was her match in maturity, intelligence and sensitivity. In spite of being terribly busy after they reached Pamplona, Count Gaston had visited her daily before he left at the head of a cavalry column on his assignment against Granada. They had never discussed anything intimate, only shared experiences, yet the intimacy had been there. They were two of a kind, meant for each other. But they would

465

never have each other, due principally to the count's reclusivity of spirit with anyone save God.

Several days had elapsed since the count had departed, yet the aura of his presence, the image of his dark, brooding eyes carved into a hatchet face but ever ready to light up with laughter, remained with her. Strangely, late evening became the time of greatest loneliness, this being when she used to have her daily talks with King Charles. These talks had taken place unfailingly through the years, but they were no illusion, despite the betrayal. Having finally decided that she would not support King Charles in his ambition to become the Emperor, she paid the price by missing the purpose that had supported her life.

Seated in the favourite chamber of her suite of rooms, she ran nostalgic eyes around her, recalling that her Charles, as he had been then, had provided her with the means to renovate the quarters after he became king. Though comparatively new, the gilt love-seats upholstered in black and white striped satin to match the marble floors and the white Flemish carpets seemed as ageless as the large painting of Prince René above the mantelpiece, while the soft golden glow of the crystal glass lamps, which had just been lit, was as transient as she was upon this earth. How much longer did she have to live?

'I have lived too long,' she whispered to herself. Unless Prince René was waiting for her, she had nowhere to go after she was dead. People went wherever their beliefs took them and she really had no beliefs as to an after-life.

Her eyes drifted to the dark outline of the chestnut trees beneath the walls of the balconies that thrust out from the three great windows of the chamber. The scent of sandalwood from the incense braziers suddenly became heavy, then overpowering. She needed fresh air. She tried to get up and make for the nearest balcony. She did not have the power to rise from her seat. She wanted to, but could not. Her whole body and the seat seemed fused into one, her legs were powerless.

The pain began at the top of her upper arms, just below the shoulder bones. It spread like a fire to her neck, meeting lungs, clamping her chest from the inside. Oh merciful God, just one breath. Nostrils dilating, mouth open, she clawed vainly for air. The red haze of her brain was shrouded by blackness. Through the excruciating agony, her spirit smiled. She finally knew her belief in the after-life: it was not where she was going that mattered, but to whom.

'*René, mon chéri*,' she whispered soundlessly.

Chapter 25

Prince Ahmed said his evening prayer as he rode through the *meseta*. His heart was heavy from having left Princess Beatrice and being without Prince Juan, Aaron Levi and Zurika for the first time in months. They were his friends and all his life he had never had real friends except for his attendant, Tarif. He had often wondered what had happened to Tarif. Would he ever see the deaf-mute again? When would he meet his beloved Princess Beatrice next? Once again, his future was uncertain. He soon reached a dismal state of mind.

Holding his grey to an easy trot through the slow darkling air, Prince Ahmed recalled that the future had always been uncertain for him. Even when he lived in the security of the Gen al Arif tower, he was always gazing through the dusk of the present into the darkness beyond that was his future. He had had no control over his present, his future or his destiny. Was this the will of Allah? He was the same again now, when everything had seemed to be working out for him, heading for the security of his father's kingdom with his friends and his love, Princess Beatrice, he had run into an invasion of the very kingdom that he had hoped would be his sanctuary.

None of these doleful thoughts diminished his acute inner sense of awareness. He had developed this in the Alhambra palace as a boy, to permit himself the secret freedoms of the prisoner he undoubtedly was against discovery by Abou bon Ebben and the deaf-mute eunuch attendants and guards. That sense had been heightened by the events of the past months and especially the last three weeks.

With approaching darkness, the sounds of the plain had died down into the hush before night sounds emerge. Was it his ears that had caught a tiny chink above the slow drum of his own mount's hooves, to the right and behind him? It had registered because it was a sound that had no place in the *meseta*. His mind snapped out of his morbid contemplation and his body froze before a warning of danger, but his brain emerged dagger-bright and sharp.

Resisting the urge to look back, alert ears scanning behind him, he slowed the grey to a walk, then abruptly reined it in, glancing quickly to right and left, pretending to search the terrain. He was rewarded by the tiniest, single drumbeat behind him, ended on the instant.

Danger warnings sizzled through him. He was being followed by a single horseman, not just followed, but tailed. Why a single horseman? Was it a scout from the Castilian army? Hardly likely. A bandit perhaps? A chill went through him at the thought. Here he was, alone on the unknown *meseta*, being tailed by an enemy who not only knew the territory but had the initiative. Brigands were known to infest the vast solitudes of Castile, searching for prey. He resisted the urge to clap his heels into the grey's flanks and bolt away. Fighting down his fear, he deliberately replaced it with a cold, hard knot of ferocious determination. His brain began working cool but fast. He would play the intruder at his own game. Relaxing the reins, he gently squeezed with his thighs. The grey responded automatically, moving forward.

Prince Ahmed's hand reached for his dagger, then moved away. A dagger was useless except in close combat. He unobtrusively loosened his sword.

Within moments, he heard the sudden pounding of urgent hooves behind him. He wheeled the grey almost on its rear legs to the left, then dug fierce heels into its flanks. The trained cavalry horse shot forward like a bolt from a catapult. He heard the whine-whizz of a scimitar slicing through the air, felt the breath of the blow on his neck, but not the stroke. An icy thought registered. The attacker was left-handed. Wheeling his horse in a wide arc to the left and rear, Prince Ahmed charged towards the attacker, who had wheeled right, obviously to make another pass convenient to his sword arm. Gripping both reins in his left hand, Prince Ahmed reached for his waist with his right hand.

Would he be able to draw Zurika's knife in time. He slowed his mount, desperately slid one sweaty hand to his waist, grasped the blade instead of the handle. He drew the knife, slid his fingers to grip the point between thumb and forefinger as Zurika had taught him to perfection so recently. He raised his arm, aiming. The assassin had almost passed him. Allowing for the rider's speed, he flung the knife, heard its impact, then a gurgle. Fierce exultation surged through him. Gripping the reins with both hands, he spurred his horse to greater speed, then drew his sword and made another wide circle. The assassin had toppled off his mount, but his foot was caught in a stirrup. The horse slowed, then stopped. The rider dangled beneath it, still as a sack of grain. Prince Ahmed dismounted and threw his reins over the grey's neck. Sword drawn, he swiftly scanned the *meseta*. Nothing stirred. Only a snort from the assassin's bay disturbed the stillness.

Alert for danger, Prince Ahmed approached the fallen assassin. A groan told him the man was not dead. Drawing nearer, he noticed the bald head, the red fez fallen on the bare soil a banner that sent a shock through him. This was a fellow Muslim. It was doubly imperative that he find out who had sent the man, why he had been tailed and attacked. Sword at the ready, he squatted beside the assassin's body. The knife protruded grotesquely from his neck. Rasping sounds were emerging from his chest. Red blood, pumping from the wound, distorted agonized groans. 'Who are you?' he demanded. 'Why did you attack me?'

'I . . . beg you . . . in Allah's name . . . cut me loose . . . lay me down. I . . . am in . . . agony.'

'Only after you tell me what your mission is and who sent you.' No pity, only ruthless hatred.

'Farouk . . . Riswan paid me. I kill your father.' The voice dropped to a whisper of anguished breath. 'Dead . . . dead.' He gulped, face contorting. 'Farouk sent me . . . Mizra, kill you. I . . . I . . . get Abdul . . . Rauf . . . help me . . .' The words trailed off into a gurgling sigh. A spasm contorted the body before it went limp. Mizra, whatever his other names, was now a corpse. Ahmed glanced around quickly, withdrew his knife from the dead man's neck, wiped it on the bloodied robe and replaced it at his waist, silently thanking Zurika.

So his father was dead. Prince Ahmed could find neither pity nor regret at the news. Thoughts flashed in a second. He had never known his father except as the king who had imprisoned his own son almost from birth and had mutilated Prince Juan for life. As he squatted there, everything fell into place. Almighty Allah was indeed looking after him. The fate of Mizra, self-confessed assassin, was now in Almighty Allah's hands. But he had mentioned the names of two other men, Abdul and Rauf. Where were they? Prince Ahmed sprang to his feet, glanced alertly around. Only two bob-hopping hares met his gaze. If there were other assassins present, they would have attacked by now. He relaxed.

Although he did not know Farouk Riswan personally, he had heard of the Prime Minister from Abou bon Ebben as being a man of insatiable greed, ambition and ruthlessness who had helped place King Yusuf on the throne by arranging for the assassination of King Yusuf's brother. Why had the Prime Minister hired an assassin to kill the king of Granada? Why had he sent assassins to murder the rightful heir to the throne? The answers were obvious. Riswan had a rival contender or nominee whom he could manipulate as the successor.

What a catastrophic situation. Granada must surely be in chaos without a proper ruler. Now it faced an invasion. He regretted that he had not followed the Castilian army to obtain intelligence as to its strength, but he had assumed that his father's spies and patrols would have provided the fullest information. Now the urge to get to Granada became all-consuming.

The thought of the other two assassins intruded again. The prospect of spears and knives at his back, a dagger in the kidneys or stomach, sent chills up his spine. He must hurry away. Not all the tenets of Islam regarding the disposal of dead bodies of those of the faith moved Prince Ahmed. His one thought now was to escape an unseen death.

He replaced his sword, said a quick prayer of thankfulness for the knife, for Zurika and for her father who had given her the knife. He freed Mizra's stiffening foot from the stirrup, let the lifeless leg fall to the hard, barren soil of the *meseta*. The small robed body lay in a heap, face upwards. How many people had the assassin murdered? Vultures, buzzards and hyenas would feed on him now.

He remounted his horse, made a swift decision. He would throw Abdul and Rauf off the scent. Instead of heading towards the traveller's cross which had appeared pale beyond the twilight air, he swerved his grey to the right. With many a backward glance, he proceeded towards Cordoba.

It was only after he had travelled for an hour that he realized, with a chill up his spine, why the other two assassins had not been with the dead man.

* * *

Four days later, at dusk, Prince Juan, Aaron Levi, Zurika and Princess Beatrice reached the outskirts of Jaén, unaware that they were being followed by two assassins. They had gathered from snatches of animated conversation at an inn that the whole city was agog with news of the arrival of the Castilian army and the impending invasion of Granada. Factions already seemed to be forming, with the sympathies of many Moors veering towards their brothers in Islam, causing Princess Beatrice to worry about her father and her own native kingdom. King Pedro and King Charles were said to be quartered south of the city, having declined an invitation to occupy the old palace. Jaén was to be a rendezvous for other forces as well.

Having agreed that they should first get to the Benedictine convent, which was located to the north of the little cottage that Zurika's grandmother Pilar had bought for herself, they rode in pairs at an unhurried trot so as not to attract attention. Princess Beatrice, with Aaron Levi at her right, followed Zurika and Prince Juan, all of them holding to the left side of the road. It came to Princess Beatrice's mind that this cobbled highway, called the Via Augusta, had been built centuries earlier by the Romans, extending from Rome to Cadiz. Traversing it on horseback now, instead of in a closed wagon, she marvelled at the monumental work which she had only known as a fact of history. How had the Romans accomplished such miracles? It must have been through their vision, their knowledge that fast communications were essential to hold an empire, their skill in harnessing labour and material even in the most distant outposts, their courage, fortitude and perseverance in completing any work however long it took. In consequence of such roads, Roman citizens were protected wherever they lived. '*Civis Romanus sum*,' I am a citizen of Rome. A Roman had only to say the words and, if he was violated anywhere in the Empire, the legions would march.

'*Buenas noches!*' A passing *caballero*, obviously taken by her looks, saluted Princess Beatrice as he passed in the opposite direction. Strange how he could single out a pretty face in the middle of a highway crowded with people on horseback, in carriages or wagons. Like them, most of the vehicles were hurrying to get to the gates before they were closed for the night and only pedestrians could enter by using the 'needle' gate. Only two red-fez-topped men on camel-back and sundry pedestrians were going in the opposite direction.

With his uncanny instinct, Aaron Levi picked up her thoughts. 'It took the Romans to come thousands of miles to build this road,' he said. 'Our own Spanish people, like the dashing *caballero* who just greeted you, are much more interested in love, music, the arts and single combat than in such long-term creations. Being the most passionate race in the world, the Spanish have no time for either prolonged wars of conquest or long-term development.' He sighed, shaking his head. 'The people of my own race, on the other hand,' he nodded towards the two black-cloaked figures, *yarmulke* on head, staff in hand, whom they were overtaking, 'do not indulge in histrionics. For centuries they have been as fierce and dogged as any race in the defence of Zion. Here in Spain, however, the majority of us Jews pursue more pedestrian professions than war. We are agriculturists, industrialists, artisans and,' he grinned charmingly between his grey moustache and beard, 'that euphemism for moneylenders, bankers!'

'My mother often told me that my father, King Pedro, has a great fondness for your people,' Princess Beatrice volunteered impulsively. 'He considers you to be the backbone of Castile, indeed of all Spain.'

Aaron Levi frowned. 'We Jews are aware of this, and yet, with due deference, His Majesty has also had to bend with the wind of the Catholic Church. Only recently, he has . . .' Aaron Levi hesitated and, even before he completed the sentence, Princess Beatrice knew he had decided to say something different. 'Only recently, he has been under great pressure from the Catholic Church, in the form of Bishop Eulogius, to recommence persecuting us Jews and even subjecting us to Inquisition.' His face was as sombre as the gathering darkness.

'How do you know this?'

'We have our sources,' he replied briefly. A horsedrawn wagon trundled by, its driver erect on the high seat, ignoring the world around him. 'That wagoneer must be a Moor,' he stated, changing to a safe subject. 'Note his shaven head and dark colouring.' He paused, nodded ahead. 'I always find that the dim lights of a walled city create a mystique.' He pointed towards the glow above the black silhouettes of buildings, etched with golden squares and rectangles of light from high windows, that spread across their vision. 'Does it not give you the feeling of returning home even if the city is a strange . . .'

He stopped abruptly at the clatter of urgent hooves. A masked horseman came dashing along the verge to the left of Princess Beatrice. Before either of them could recover from their surprise, the rider grabbed the nearest rein of Princess Beatrice's horse, jerked at it so firmly that the horse reared.

Shock rendered Princess Beatrice lifeless. The reins slipped from her nerveless fingers. She began sliding to the left. The stranger had already released the rein. Before she could fall, in one swift movement, he gathered her by the waist with his right arm. She felt the steely strength of him. Then he dug cruel heels into his horse's flanks.

'Raise the alarm and you will all be discovered,' the masked man yelled over his shoulder to Aaron Levi.

Princess Beatrice came to her senses, started to struggle.

'Stop fighting!' the man gritted. 'My name is Rauf. I come from Prince Ahmed. He sent me to save you from an ambush that has been set up ahead.'

The name of Prince Ahmed sent thrills through her. She immediately ceased her struggles. 'But you left my friends to their fate.'

'The ambush is by King Charles's men, who are not awaiting your friends but are after you alone.' He paused. 'Will you get up in front of me now?' A grin revealed white teeth. 'I'm not a very big man and you are not exactly light you know, so this position is most uncomfortable!'

His levity eased her suspicions, though she somehow could not warm to him. What he said made sense. After all, how could such a stranger have known about King Charles the Bad? 'Why the mask?' she inquired.

'Do you think I want to be recognized?'

That made sense too. She clambered up in front of him as they rode, their backs to the city. He smelled like a camel's breath, incongruously inlaid with a vestige of sandalwood. They soon hit the highway once more at a point not much further north. Passers-by merely gave them curious glances as they emerged like ghosts from the gloom. Since most people were still headed for the city, they soon had a clear passage and Rauf made good speed. Princess Beatrice tried to look back, but her view was blocked by the rider's body. 'Where are my friends?' she demanded.

His chuckle was guileless. 'Don't worry. The Jew is following us. The other two will undoubtedly do likewise. You will all be reunited soon.'

'And Prince Ahmed?'

'He is waiting for us further up the highway, not far from here.'

True enough, she heard the clatter of cantering hooves behind her. Imagining Aaron Levi bumping in the saddle, she felt curiously comforted, more so when her own riderless horse came alongside.

The stranger maintained his fast pace until the crowds on the highway had dwindled to an occasional stray pedestrian. He then cut away to the right along a dirt road.

'Where are we going?' she demanded.

'To where Prince Ahmed awaits you.'

'But he has headed directly for Granada?'

'He changed his mind for love of you.'

Exhilaration shot through her; joy suffused her being. Oh dear Virgin Mary. O sweet Jesu, you have answered my prayers.

Zurika's quick ears had picked up Aaron Levi's shout above the sounds of the highway. 'The *señor!*' she cried, reining in her horse and swinging round in her saddle, a hand gripping Prince Juan's arm.

Though he could not hear, his heightened instincts made Prince Juan instantly twist round and he could not miss seeing Aaron Levi's upflung arm and distress. Without a moment's hesitation, he veered his horse around, signalling to Zurika to follow, ignoring the annoyance of a man trotting up on a mule, legs flapping, whose path he crossed. Zurika backed her horse to the side of the road, eyes feverishly scanning the highway. A man on horseback, holding a struggling woman by the waist, was arching away across the fields, followed by Aaron Levi. The woman's horse, freed of its rider, kept rearing and bucking with shrill neighs. Prince Juan plunged off into the fields to join in the chase. Vaguely Zurika heard the bewildered questions tumbling from the onlookers. '*Quién?*' . . . '*Qué?*'

Princess Beatrice had been snatched. By whom?

Zurika's first reaction was one of alarm for her safety. Then came fierce elation. Her rival had been removed from the scene. Why should she join in the chase? Why did she not keep on her way and get to grandmother Pilar? But some deep-rooted loyalty of gypsies for their comrades swiftly took over. She urged her horse off the highway, ignoring the questions that were being flung at her. Unable to assist the victims or to satisfy their curiosity, these people would proceed on their respective ways. One or more would report the incident to the guards at the gate, who would shrug it off as perhaps the action of a lover seizing his beloved from the clutches of a tyrant father and her brother. For the rest of the people, this would merely be an incident for conversation. Such was life. People never wanted to be involved.

Barely conscious of her whereabouts, Zurika followed the three horses and the fourth riderless mount back on to the highway. By the time she reached the dirt road which the kidnapper had taken, she noted that Princess Beatrice was not struggling. Prince Juan and Aaron Levi were not far behind. Surely the stranger could not be a friend. They were fugitives. They had no friends.

Zurika followed the track. It led away from the highway for some distance before entering the gloom of a grove of olive trees, where Zurika lost sight of the others. It was so dark here she was unable to distinguish the road except from the curving avenue of light-coloured boles of olive trees. The grove ended abruptly near an open gate. A small field lay beyond ending at a tiled white cottage, its two front windows faintly glowing with yellow light.

Aaron Levi and Prince Juan had reined in their horses side by side at the front entrance and were gazing around in puzzlement. Princess Beatrice and her captor had vanished. Zurika reined in her horse. Aaron touched Prince Juan's arm and pointed to the left of the cottage. Prince Juan drew his sword, circled his horse in that direction, while Aaron Levi, staff at the ready, circled right.

A terrible mistake, Zurika's gypsy blood screamed its warning in every vein. Whoever it is wants you to split up! She dismounted, flung her reins over the saddle, began walking stealthily towards the right side of the cottage. Strange whizzing sounds, croaks, the neigh of a horse and the stamping of hooves brought memory flooding back. The sounds were fresh-familiar, but she could not identify them. Rounding the side wall of the cottage, she saw a large barn well to the rear of the house, set beneath dark trees in a smaller field in which cattle drooped and a couple of goats gazed stupidly in her direction.

She immediately spied the two dark figures, and two riderless horses, and knew what had happened. The kidnapper had ridden his mount straight into the barn, where he had disposed of Princess Beatrice. Zurika's terror mounted. Dear God, not more violence. The kidnapper and a waiting accomplice had just used lassoes to noose Prince Juan and Aaron Levi and drag them off their horses. Her friends were two heaps lying prone on the grass.

Everything had happened so smoothly and fast, these kidnappers were surely experts. Her one hope was to escape and somehow rescue her comrades later. She turned to flee, tripped on a stone and stumbled. She reached for her knife. It was not there. She had given it to Prince Ahmed. She sprang to her feet and sped towards her horse. She gripped the reins and flung herself on to the saddle, the pounding of feet on gravel behind her panic-alarms in her ears. Heart thudding against ribs, she dug fierce heels into the horse's flanks. Unexpectedly, it shot forward, leaving her behind. She fell with a thud, the breath knocked out of her. Eyes closed in pain, she placed her palms on the brown soil, trying to rise.

Sweet Jesu save me. Her silent, despairing cry was lost in the thump of a man's body upon her. The breath was knocked from her body. A swift hand found the vein in her neck. She smelt the man's foul odour before losing consciousness.

PART III

Auto-da-Fé

Chapter 26

The wooden door of the tiny room swung violently open. Princess Beatrice's shock turned to terror when she saw the massive frame of King Charles the Bad in the dim light of the oil lamp hanging from one of the wooden rafters supporting the low roof.

Last evening, she and her three companions had all been captured by two men whose names had turned out to be Rauf and Abdul. The most striking thing she had noted about them both was that they had dead eyes, which made her shiver with fear. The first night had been one of unbelievable discomfort. The four of them, trussed up and gagged, had been dumped on bales of straw in the loft of a barn. Apart from the terror of her situation, squeaking rats, scuttling insects, fleas and the dank odour of damp straw in the total darkness had brought their own horrors.

They had been given a dinner of bread and cheese, and their gags removed to permit them to eat, but one of the two men had always been present to ensure that they did not converse. Thereafter, the captors had taken turns on guard at the door of the barn, the only advantage of which was that the prisoners could attract their attention whenever a call of nature made its demands. Princess Beatrice's own two visits to the outhouse, which stank so hideously that she had difficulty using it, had revealed no habitation near by.

Princess Beatrice had reflected wryly that the person least affected by the surroundings must be the afflicted Prince Juan. The torment of uncertainty, however, was equally shared. What did their captors intend for them?

The question remained unanswered when Princess Beatrice was conducted alone to the cottage well before dawn the next morning. Contrary to her fears of molestation or rape, her gag and bonds were removed. She was taken to a tiny room furnished with a truckle bed, a rough deal table, two stools and a commode. She was provided with water in a wooden tub, a comb, brush, mirror and some toiletries. She was even given one of Zurika's changes of clothing and the morning meal of dried fish and a sweet orange. All this was done in the most sinister silence.

Why had she been singled out for special treatment? She dreaded the answer. The men were going to return her to her father in good shape, for a huge reward. She became convinced of it when she heard Rauf ride away shortly after the crowing of roosters and the bleating of goats announced daybreak.

More answers were provided that afternoon when the thumping of hooves and Rauf's soft voice interspersed with sharp commands announced the arrival of soldiers. She resisted the urge to scream for help. To her surprise, the newcomers left without even entering the cottage, but not before she noticed through a tiny chink in the window that the riders wore the uniforms of Bishop Eulogius's personal bodyguard. They left shortly afterwards, taking Zurika and Aaron Levi with them.

Why only these two? Why not Prince Juan and herself? And why Bishop Eulogius's men? Why would the bishop want a Jew and a gypsy girl? The questions kept thudding in her brain but confirmed her fear that she and Prince Juan were being kept for delivery to their father. How could she save herself from the fate that would inevitably mean marriage to Charles the Bad? Prince Ahmed had saved her once. Would he come again? That was too much to expect. How was he faring? Was he safe? She had to cling to the belief that she would somehow be rescued to combat the madness of panic that kept sweeping through her. She alternated between forlorn hope and abject despair during the entire day, never ceasing to blame herself for the plight of the others, frequently falling on her knees and praying to God, sweet Jesu and the Virgin Mary.

Late that evening, when Princess Beatrice knelt once again on the bare floor to pray, she could not help remembering her elegant *prie-dieu* in the Toledo palace. Did she want to go back to its security?

That was when the door of her room burst open.

She rose to her feet, staring in abject terror at the barrel-chested King Charles standing in the doorway, massive legs spread, arms akimbo. Dressed in purple and gold, he still looked like a ferocious bull. In an instant, the reason for the special treatment accorded to her dawned starkly on her. She was not to be delivered to her father but sold to King Charles. From him, there would be no escape. Even prayers would not help now.

King Charles must have sensed her fear. Strangely, his expression softened and he bowed low, right hand to heart. 'You are safe now, Princess,' he assured her, his voice gentle.

What was happening? Was she being saved from death by this known beast to meet a fate far worse than death? 'You will conduct us back to our royal father then, Your Majesty?'

Instead of replying, he produced what he had been holding behind his back. It was a huge bouquet of red roses. Flowers in hand, King Charles moved forward, closing the door of the room behind him. He paused before her, bowed low again and proffered the flowers to her. 'These roses are red because they are blushing with shame before your beauty,' he said gruffly, but with a catch to his voice.

Amazed by this poetic statement, she teetered on the edge of uncertainty. This man, rightly called the Bad, was a known rapist. His only use for women, as Princess Beatrice's attendants had gossiped, was to satisfy his bestial lusts. Now here he was acting like a choirboy in love! Not knowing how to react, she resorted to graciousness. 'Your Majesty expresses sentiments that are as noble as his mien.' She made a deep curtsy, accepted the bouquet, held it to her nose and lightly breathed its dewy fragrance. It helped dissipate her fear, but she avoided King Charles's amorous eyes.

'Then it remains for you to come home,' he declared, his voice suddenly hoarse.

'Your Majesty, I would rather enter a convent in Jaén than return to Toledo.'

'We were not referring to Toledo but to our palace in Pamplona,' he asserted gently. 'We wish to marry you.'

Amazement made her raise her gaze to his at last. The tenderness in his fierce eyes stunned her. 'But that is not my home, Sire,' she replied weakly.

'It is from now on. We won your hand at your father's tourney. The accidental victory of one who was not qualified to enter the lists counts for nothing.' A savage note had crept into his voice. 'We are here in part to extract vengeance from the Moor for that insult. The judges of the tourney finally declared us to be the legal winner. Just this afternoon your royal father confirmed their verdict by signing and sealing a royal edict. Having won your hand, beautiful princess, we shall now escort you to our palace, where we hope to wed you, but only after we have won your heart.'

He sounded so humble, yet so dignified, she did not know whether to laugh in his face or cry for him. Yet for the first time ever, she felt she was in command of a situation. This rabid sex maniac truly loved her. Surely then he would understand her own love and listen to her plea for Prince Ahmed's safety. 'Your Majesty is aware that I fled the tourney and my heritage with Prince Ahmed of Granada,' she began.

'But you had your brother, Prince Juan, and others to chaperon you at all times, did you not?' Had a note of anxiety entered his voice?

'*Ciertamente*, Your Majesty. And I would have you know that Prince Ahmed never once made any attempt on my person.'

'He was probably unable to do so because your modesty made you take proper care. Otherwise, you can never be sure how these barbaric Moors might act.'

'Prince Ahmed is no barbarian,' she protested.

King Charles's eyes flashed red points of fire, their sudden change of expression astonishing. 'You would defend your abductor?' he demanded, his voice a low growl.

It never dawned on Princess Beatrice to heed the warning. 'He was not my abductor, Your Majesty, but my champion and my saviour.'

The massive jaw dropped. He stared at her in disbelief, then kept jabbing a stubby forefinger at her to emphasize each word. 'You . . . accept a heathen Moor . . . as your . . . champion?'

She lifted her chin. 'Proudly, Sire.'

The upraised arm swung, backhanding her across the cheek. Stars shot through her head in a flash of excruciating pain. She went sprawling sideways. Unable even to think, she placed a palm on the cold floor, began to raise herself up. Before she could open her eyes, he had flung himself on her. 'You fucking slut, you have opened your legs to a heathen. Now open them for me!'

For a split second, she noted that he had omitted the royal plural. Then his weight began crushing her, driving the air from her lungs. A stifled scream escaped her. She beat at his chest with impotent fists.

'Scream your fucking head off, you whore. You are a

487

whited sepulchre like your mother.' His hot, slobbery lips wet her face, seeking her mouth. His free hand tore her blouse away. As her breasts spilled out, shame entered her spirit, erasing the will to fight. His manhood pressed against her pubis. He reached down roughly and moved her skirt up.

Oh Horn, save me!

Into the dark haze enveloping her, sharp pain pierced her womanhood. Ah . . . ah . . . ah! She had been despoiled.

'O Merciful God! O Blessed Virgin! . . .'

She shrieked once, began to go limp, but not before she endured the obscene in-out-in movement defiling her.

Zurika and Aaron Levi had been escorted to Jaén by the bishop's guards. She had never seen the purple-robed bishop before, but now learned that his name was Eulogius. As the closed wagon into which the two of them had been bundled clattered through a paved courtyard, Zurika had observed that they had entered a monastery in Jaén. She could not identify the order, nor did she care. Why were they being escorted to the bishop's residence instead of to King Pedro's headquarters? She could sense that Aaron Levi shared her concern, though he said nothing. The presence of two guards in the wagon had discouraged conversation, but the Jew had maintained a cheerful exterior. It had been an inspiration to her to do likewise. After all, the gypsies had much in common with the Jews. Both their tribes were persecuted.

The wagon ground to a stop. The monastery doors were opened throwing a shaft of golden light onto the walkway. As she alighted from the wagon, Zurika observed a great paved courtyard lit by flaming torches, surrounded by dark green cypresses lined up like soldiers on parade along the high front and side walls. The austere three-storey building on the fourth side was patterned with rectangles of pale golden light from closed windows. They entered a well-lit entrance foyer through high wooden double doors. There Aaron Levi was directed by the guard captain to remain while she was escorted down a wide white marble-floored corridor covered by a red carpet with brass sconces carrying tapers lining austere white walls. They turned right through an archway at the end of the corridor and mounted two floors of a wide staircase also covered by a red carpet. Here they turned right again and doubled back along another wide corridor to wooden double doors at its far end. This floor represented a different world. The corridor carpet was far richer, the wall-sconces were of gold, the tapers were sunk into crystal containers and deep red mahogany stands supporting beautiful alabaster statues of saints lined the walls.

The guard captain knocked respectfully on the door.

'Enter!' The faint voice that reached Zurika's ears was sonorous, bringing to mind a church service.

The captain opened one of the doors. 'The prisoner, Your Eminence!' he announced, gesturing to Zurika to enter.

As the door clicked shut behind her, Zurika had a vague impression of a spacious chamber with a balcony opening out to the front courtyard below, rich carpets, gilt furniture with plush red velvet upholstery, crystal glass hanging lamps and marble statues. Then her eyes fell on the figure standing at the far end of the room.

She had expected him to be tall, hawklike, stern. Here, instead, was a short, plump figure clothed in purple, with chubby pink cheeks and eyes that were obviously blue, even at some distance. She bobbed an awkward curtsy.

'Come here, my child.' The prelate's voice was as gentle as his expression was cherubic.

As he watched her move towards him, a strange look entered his eyes. 'You are of extraordinary beauty, virile,

489

but virginal,' he commented when she paused before him. His eyes roved slowly over her figure, savouring every curve. She became uncomfortable for the first time. Was this a priest, and a bishop at that? His blue eyes moved back up to hers. 'Are you indeed a virgin?'

The shocking question brought a flush of shame to her cheeks before her anger began to mount. She stared at him levelly, without speaking.

He sensed her mood, for the blue eyes turned to ice. 'You are in an extremely dangerous position, gypsy girl, and only I can save you.' He paused. 'You are a proven murderess and therefore exposed to the Castilian king's justice. You are also accused of heresy and witchcraft, which is why you are here as the prisoner of Holy Church. I have claimed prior rights over you and His Majesty King Pedro has graciously consented to concede his own sovereign claims to those of Holy Church. Do you understand what I am saying?'

Fear had erased Zurika's anger as he spoke, chilling her whole being. She looked down. 'Yes, Eminence,' she responded, using the title which the guard captain had given the bishop.

'If you satisfy Holy Church, it will use its influence to save you from the claims of the laity. Do you understand *that*?' His voice had remained soft, level, slightly husky, incanting.

'I do.' She hesitated. 'How do I satisfy Holy Church?'

'Ah! I am glad you are seeing reason.' He reached out a chubby finger to touch her cheek. 'What a beautiful, beautiful maiden! You have not yet answered my question though. Holy Church requires virgins for their purity and freedom from the sin of copulation, as did the Romans of old with their Vestals. I repeat, are you a virgin?'

Could there be some justification in what the bishop was saying? Had she misjudged him? After all, were not virgin nuns the brides of Christ? 'I am a virgin,' she replied, her voice low, briefly meeting his gaze.

'Ah, how desirable!' His glance became positively lustful. There was no mistaking it. Zurika was hard put to control her trembling, fear giving way to mounting anger. This little hypocrite of the Church was no different from Majo, worse because he was a bishop.

'Take your clothes off, virgin, and display your purity to Holy Church.' The sexuality in his voice was the same as that in Majo's eyes. Fury replaced all else.

He reached out both hands, one to touch her cheeks, the other to raise her chin.

She spat in his face.

He had drunk a flagon of wine to bolster his courage when he rode to Princess Beatrice as a suitor. Her rejection of him had caused an unexpected explosion. So overcome had he been with disappointment, hurt and anger that the desire to punish her overwhelmed him, and in an instant, Charles the lover had reverted to Charles the Bad. So he brutally sawed away at her unconscious body, animal noises escaping him. He lusted so much for her as the replica of his mother that he lost his erection only after he had come the third time, the last in her rear, through which he tore. He lay atop her for a full minute, panting, sweating. He wiped his slobbering mouth with the back of his hand, his eyes triumphantly absorbing her pure beauty. Godsbody, how exquisite. She was indeed a youthful replica of his mother. In taking her, he had well and truly fucked his mother-bitch.

He rolled off her, rose to his feet and began pulling up his breeches. Ironically, the sight of her bruised face as he looked down on it brought adoration back and recalled the hopes of romance. The red roses scattered on the bare floor and tiny stains of red blood discolouring her petticoat and bare thighs shattered those hopes. What had he done? The devil in him, allowed free abandon through the years, each new dissolute sexual act breeding on the last and providing its cumulative effect for the next, had taken over, swept away his future. Tears sprang to his eyes. A great animal cry escaped him.

He gained control of himself. She had no right to defy him, least of all to throw a lover in his face. He hastily completed his dressing. A greater truth suddenly smote him back to sober reality. What indeed had he done? He had raped the daughter of his ally the King of Castile, the heiress to the throne, in their very kingdom. A terrible deed, fraught with dread consequences. Here he was, alone on foreign soil with only a handful of men, against King Pedro's entire army. He could be arrested and killed.

He had to escape. Should he flee to the western highway, join Count Gaston and return to Pamplona? It would end all his plans for the future, a terrible price to pay for a few minutes of lust, but at least he would have his life and his kingdom. He wondered what Count Gaston's reactions would be. And Princess Mathilde's. Well, fuck them all. He had fucked the girl. He would take the consequences. She had no right to reject him. His eyes drifted back to Princess Beatrice's face. Was she worth it? He could not find the answer, but he had always battered his way through the consequences of his misdeeds in the past and would do so again. Should he kill her, laying the blame on the kidnappers? An attractive solution.

He bent down to seize her slender white throat, but native cunning reasserted itself. The unconscious woman could never divulge what had happened to anyone. Let her live. He might still be able to use her for convenience and she could still ensure his union with Castile.

Suddenly he knew what he had to do.

He strode out of the room, closing the door carefully to

avoid anyone seeing inside the room. The little ferret-faced man named Abdul stood by the entrance door. He made a quick genuflection then stood up rubbing his hands together unctuously. 'Your Majesty is satisfied?'

'Not really,' King Charles replied shortly.

'The princess will go with Your Majesty?'

'She is no princess.'

'What?' A dangerous glint entered his eyes. 'Do we not get our reward?'

'*En verdad*, that you shall, regardless. You saw two boxes containing gold and jewels, did you not? We shall have our guards bring them to you. One at a time, so you will not quarrel over the spoils.' He bared his teeth in a grin. 'The first box is for you. It contains some money as well, which you should hide from your comrade.' Divide and fucking rule them, he thought savagely as he walked out into the gloom, acknowledging Abdul's repeated farewell genuflection with an upward flick of his wrist.

He had taken the precaution of having only two people accompany him from Jaén. Colonel de Villa was his personal aide, a most trusted bodyguard commander. The captain's personal and loyal trooper carried the two metal boxes. Both instinct and reason had told King Charles to maintain total secrecy, so even King Pedro might not know that he had found Princess Beatrice until he could announce her acceptance of his suit. He thanked his stars for this wisdom. As he walked to his horse, he noticed the other kidnapper leaning negligently against an olive tree, honing a sharp knife. A cool, dangerous one that, from the aura he emanated.

'We were fooled into coming here,' King Charles informed Captain de Villa briefly. 'These two men are idiots. They have wasted our time, but the reward shall still be theirs. Take the first box into the house, close the door and give it to the man named Abdul.' His grin was as wolfish as he felt. 'Having thus fulfilled our promise to him, wait until he is occupied opening the box. Then use your sword to kill him, but soundlessly. Leave the box behind when you come out again. Then take the other box to the man leaning against the tree and kill him too. You can then bring both boxes back with you.'

Captain de Villa was a big muscular man, well used to his monarch's ways. He bowed deeply. 'Your Majesty's slightest wish is my command.' He straightened up, took the larger metal box from the trooper, strode inside the house and closed the door behind him.

The other kidnapper had straightened up, the tip of the knife now held carelessly between thumb and forefinger. King Charles knew the significance of that gesture. He smiled pleasantly at the man, nodded towards the trooper. 'Our captain will personally give you the second box.' He turned casually and walked up to his tall bay. He grasped the reins, swung into the saddle, slowly gathered the reins and waited. He heard the door of the cottage open and close. The man called Abdul had met his fate. Without looking in any direction, King Charles gave his horse the aid. The animal moved slowly forward. He had barely reached the gates when he heard frenzied screams of fury and pain from the second assassin. Captain de Villa was fulfilling his task well. A sword thrust through the stomach was the most agonizing form of death.

No one, other than these two trusted men, would know that King Charles the Bad had visited the place. Princess Beatrice, free to continue her escape, would never betray the secret.

The underground monastic cells of old had an additional use for prisoners of the Church. The stench of urine and excrement reached Zurika at the top of the steps leading down to them. The reek of fear-sweat from the poor fettered wretches confined in the cells and the horrible odour of dank straw awaited her at the bottom, mingled with their occasional groans and cries. Her stomach blanched with fear before relief eased it at being thrust into the same cell as Aaron Levi. He shook his head in disbelief when Zurika told him what had transpired.

'So he will have his revenge,' Zurika concluded. 'He said that he would not have me confess under torture because this might bring me royal clemency, nor will he have me go through trial by ordeal as a witch in case I drown. He will try me himself tomorrow as a heretic, at an *auto-da-fé*, find me guilty and sentence me to be cleansed by fire. He wishes to see me roast at the stake, enduring the tortures of the damned. His parting words were, "The fire should also dry your spittle, so you shall not have any left to direct at me while you are slowly dying." He is more than a madman, he is evil, Satan on earth.'

'How did you respond?' Aaron Levi's voice was low.

He knows me so well, he knows that I did respond, Zurika thought with an access of fierce joy. Someone in this sick world knows who I am. 'Yes, I did reply,' she reaffirmed. 'I told him that spittle existed only in the mouth, but it was ejected from my spirit. Even my dying spirit would hold him in contempt.'

'Wonderful! What did he say then?'

'Nothing, he merely stared at me,' she lied. She could not bring herself to tell him that Bishop Eulogius had promised her, in bland, sonorous tones accompanied by a most cherubic smile on a face in which the blue eyes were frost-cold, that she would first watch Aaron Levi roast before the flame was applied to her own pyre.

She could have spared herself the compassion for less than half an hour later two guards strode in and thrust a rolled parchment bearing impressive seals at Aaron Levi.

The Jew took the document to the bars of the cell, donned his glasses and read its contents aloud in the dim fitful light.

'I, Thomas Eulogius, primate bishop of all Christian churches in Spain, by virtue of clerical powers vested in me by Holy Church combined with lay authority granted by His Majesty King Pedro, sovereign lord of Castile, do hereby proclaim and declare that penal proceedings have been instituted against Aaron Levi, a Jew, and Zurika, a gypsy, both with no abode of record and will be heard by a duly constituted Court of Holy Church on Tuesday the second day of August in the year of Our Lord thirteen hundred and fifty-one and that you, the said Aaron Levi, and you the said Zurika of no last name, are herewith bound over, when the customary bell is rung to signify the hearing of criminal matters, to appear on the morning of the same day at the plaza in front of the town hall of the City of Jaén, there to hear the charges against you and to await such verdict and sentence as may be handed down by the said Court.'

He scanned the document again, shrugged his shoulders and turned to Zurika with a sad smile. 'These so-called courts do not even permit us to speak in our defence,' he stated softly. 'It is the end of the road for both of us, I'm afraid. My own road has been both long and interesting, so I have no regrets, for I have even bloodied a king's nose.' He paused, the smile gave way to a sigh. 'But you, my child, you are so young.'

She recovered consciousness to find Prince Juan bending over her, bathing her forehead with a wet linen. Where was she? Recollection crashed in and would have swept her away into its maelstrom of horror had it not been for her brother's presence. Had she only dreamed of the torture she had endured? Soreness and ache within and around her womanhood and her rear told her otherwise.

Dear God, dear sweet Jesu, Holy Mother, I was raped and brutalized by a man who brought me flowers.

Even while her outer mind was numb, her inner mind was slipping into frenetic desperation, though without comprehension. Prince Juan's gentle hands and gaze, his boundless compassion, helped maintain her sanity. She reached up, touched his hands, held their palms to her aching forehead. 'Do you know what happened?' She mouthed the words. He nodded slowly, tear-filled eyes on her nonetheless holding a hypnotic compulsion for her to remain calm.

'How did you get here? Where are the kidnappers?'

He released his hands gently, began gesturing with deft fingers. 'I was left behind in the loft when the bishop's soldiers seized Zurika and Aaron Levi this noon and took them away. They probably had no use for me. The man Rauf then bound my hands and feet. He started to gag me, but realized that it was unnecessary and threw the gag away.' He smiled wryly. 'Guessing that I would be left alone till nightfall, I managed to loosen my bonds sufficiently to roll to a thin, exposed metal edge of the loft ladder. I sawed myself free, went to the door of the barn and was about to slip out when a man, accompanied by two others, rode up with Abdul. It was after dusk by now. One of the newcomers, carrying something, went into the cottage with Abdul, while the other remained outside. I noticed Rauf leaning against a tree, silently watching. I thought with despair that they had come from our father to take us to Jaén. The newcomer emerged from the cottage in about half an hour. He then mounted his horse and waited while one of the other men, an officer in uniform, carried a box inside the cottage. He came out in less than two minutes, alone and emptyhanded. The leader began to ride off, but the officer took another box from the remaining man and gave it to Rauf. As soon as Rauf grasped it with both hands, the officer drew his sword. Rauf dropped the box, but was too late. The blade went into his stomach, making him writhe in agony until he died. A sword in the stomach is one of the most painful of deaths.' He gazed sadly at her. 'I wish I had known what was happening to you.'

'You could not have saved me, beloved brother.'

'I would rather have died in the attempt.'

She was moved to her depths. She touched his cheek. 'Then Abdul too must have been killed inside the cottage,' she mouthed with gestures.

'Yes. He had been run through with a sword. His body is lying in the next room. After Rauf was killed, the officer went inside the cottage and brought out the first box. He and the other man rode away behind the leader.'

'It was Charles the Bad who raped me,' she mouthed with bitter vengeance.

His gasp was a croak. He had never seen Charles the Bad but he knew the king's reputation. His face broke up piteously. He nearly broke down completely.

Princess Beatrice knew she had to take over if they were both to survive. She had to treat the rape almost like something horrible that had happened to someone else. The time of grief and trauma would surely come, but for now she had to thrust all else aside to get to Prince Ahmed – not Granada, but Prince Ahmed, whom she desperately needed. She suddenly felt a great calm, resolute decision having taken over the writhing in her brain. 'King Charles does not dare confess to having done this foul deed for fear of the wrath of our father and all of Castile,' she reasoned to Prince Juan. 'He will never even speak of it. Neither must we. I shall now wash, my beloved brother, and we shall leave this accursed place, spend some time at the convent in Jaén. As soon as the opportunity arises, we shall disguise ourselves and head for Granada. There is no longer any security for us with our father or in Castile. You and I therefore have neither country, nor home. Only Granada is left to provide us with both.'

'You and I need no tangible country or home, beloved sister,' he responded, recovering his self-possession. 'We are of the universal family of Christ. Why should we be the victims of a kingdom's boundaries when we belong to God's boundless kingdom?'

A torrential rainstorm which she could hear from her cell only as a continuous sweep of muffled sound somewhere outside its walls had brought increased physical oppressiveness to the foetid air, adding to Zurika's mounting terrors. She had begun her life in the stench and oppressiveness of the cliff-side cave: was this how she would end it, from a stinking, noisome cell? At least the caves had access to God's free air outside. Grandmother Pilar's predictions had promised her a prince. She had found one only to lose him. What was it that had lurked behind the prince in the flaming crystal? She would give up any prince, anything at all, to have her grandmother's comforting arms around her and the stench of stale clothes and unwashed body in her nostrils.

The outcome of the *auto-da-fé* was certain. Zurika's heart fluttered with panic. What would it be like to have the first flames of the fire licking at her body? Oh God in heaven, what of her face, her eyes, her hair. Would she go blind before she died, so she could not even look at God's earth one last time? Would she be blind when she arrived in heaven, purgatory or hell? Surely God would send someone, an escaped Prince Juan, a returned Prince Ahmed, to rescue her. Forlorn hopes from certain despair. Would Grandmother Pilar learn of the event and come to witness it? Zurika prayed that she would not.

With his usual uncanny perception, Aaron Levi picked up her thoughts. 'I'm afraid we must abandon all thought of a rescue or reprieve,' he said gently, his smile sad through the gloom. 'It is more important for us to reconcile ourselves to what is going to happen.'

'Oh *señor*, I'm so terrified,' she whispered hoarsely.

He reached out bony arms to her and she dragged her manacled self to him, over the stinking straw. His frame was skeletal, bore a faint scent of sandalwood beneath the acid dank of unwashed body and sweaty clothes, but she could feel warmth from his slow-beating heart. He held her firmly, but not tight. It was the first time in her life that any man had held her, as far as she could remember. She had the sad thought that for this alone it was worthwhile to have come to such a moment. He held her in silence, but she soon began to feel his calmness and serenity being willed into her. An indefinable peace began entering her being. He placed a gaunt cheek against her hair, its touch more tender than that of her grandmother's gnarled hand.

'I should have told you this when we first met,' he began. 'Or at least that night in the library, when you were so heartsick.' He paused, reflecting. 'The time never seemed right, yet it is never too late. Perhaps Jahweh decided that this moment would be better because tomorrow you will most urgently need to remember what I'm going to say.'

She stirred against him. What could he have to say that was so important? The stink of fresh human defecation smote her nostrils, bringing with it a memory of the cave. She shuddered involuntarily. Some poor wretch in an adjoining cell groaned, another let out an unearthly shriek, then started to whimper.

'You must calmly accept what you cannot change, however fearful the calamity. Every moment of your life can be a happy one to the real you.' He was speaking slowly and clearly. 'That happiness is really serenity, which is not something that exists moment by moment, but is a living, continuing entity from the essence of creation. It is not just a force we have to draw from, but one that we are *in*, if we so choose. Do you understand, my child?'

'I understand your words, *señor*, but I am an ignorant

gypsy girl and cannot feel this force you speak of, still less how I can draw from it, even if it does exist.'

'Ignorance, not knowing, only exists in the realm of mankind which has created it. All living creatures, even those that are so tiny we cannot see them, have true knowledge.' He sighed. 'I fear that man alone has lost that knowledge in the murky caves of his own creation.'

'Tell me what you mean in simple words, *señor*.' She suddenly sensed she was on the threshold of a great discovery that could help her in this dreadful situation.

'When you observe creation, you only witness or know of its movement, which is continual change.' He was speaking even more slowly so she could understand. 'Storm and tidal wave, drought and flood, thunder, lightning, the rain which is pouring down outside, the lives of men, including those in this prison, of animals, birds, fishes, plants, trees, the life forces within rocks and rivers, oceans, and mountains, all of it circles continuously around each entity and the entities within the entities which possess the serenity of the essence of creation.'

Suddenly she thought she understood. 'Like the continuing passion that creates the dance?' she questioned excitedly. 'When I dance, all that I portray, whether it is by the movements of body, limbs and eyes or the joy, sorrow and longing in them, comes from something within me which exists all the time, even when I am not dancing, and is exciting by its very serenity, continuing even after the dance is ended.'

'Exactly.' The single word softly spoken conveyed untold pleasure. 'There is an inner you, therefore you can be continuously serene. An ancient people have called it *prana*, so I shall use the word. If you live within your *prana* all the time, without interruption, you can experience pain without being affected by it.'

'How may this be, *señor*? Pain is pain. Sorrow is sorrow. These are ever with us.'

'Indeed, but they do not have to be *of* us, my child. What is pain? It is something experienced by you, is it not?'

'Yes.' She dimly perceived that her effort to concentrate on what he was saying had caused her present terrifying circumstances to be set aside.

'Pain is of the body, mind and spirit, all of it experienced in your mind. First you have pain of body. You know it can be relieved by medicines which dull certain centres of the mind so that the message of pain is not received, creating the same effect as when you faint. Where then is the pain?'

'It is there . . .' Her brain was white and bright, even aching with the desire to understand. 'No, perhaps it is not there if the mind does not feel it,' she stated excitedly.

'Precisely.' She sensed the glowing of his being. 'You have had pain at times from your dancing too, have you not?'

'I have.'

'It can be excruciating when the dance is over, sometimes that same night, or when you wake up in the morning. As the day progresses, however, you find that you have lived with it, functioned through it, at times hardly conscious that it is there. This is because pain is not the centre or the core of your physical life but merely a part of it. It is within the core that you can find unfailing inner serenity, unconsciously sometimes. Why then should you not reach for it consciously all the time and live in it?' His arms tightened around her. 'Even when your body is being consumed by fire.'

'Is that possible?' she inquired in wonderment, yet reaching desperately for his truth as a lifeline from horror and despair.

'Certainly. How else did your saints achieve martyrdom with more than fortitude, with joyous ecstasy, like your

502

Saint Eulalia when she was tortured and finally burned at the stake?'

Hope was a rill inside her, slowly fountaining. 'Of course,' she whispered, the truth as daylight within her. Somewhere she had heard the words, the truth shall set you free. She had only understood them to mean discovery of a lover's infidelity to free oneself of him. Now she knew its real meaning.

'Then we have pain of mind,' Aaron Levi continued. 'This is either caused by the body, which we have just spoken of, or by circumstances. Fear, apprehension, uncertainty, ignorance as you just called it,' he paused for emphasis, 'rejection by others, especially loved ones, their actions and words, their deeds, which are thoughtless with evil effects when done deliberately to wound. These are among the sources of our pain of mind, are they not?'

'Yes, señor.' Young as she was she had experienced much of it these past days.

'Pain of mind can be the result of our own and other people's acts and circumstances on the one hand and our own state of mind and how we react to those acts and circumstances on the other. We have no control over much of what happens around us, but we can always control our reactions, if we remain in the security of our real home, the *prana*, which is our true link with God. So the storms of life and circumstances can swirl around us, powerless without affecting the *prana*, the refuge from which we can control all pain instead of allowing it to control us. We can even combat adverse events, guide our lives from the cool serenity of the source like a good general from his base, directing troops and resources more effectively than if we allow ourselves to be embroiled in the adversity.'

'Like being in a convent,' she remarked.

'Yes indeed, but beyond that, being at peace even when the persecutors, rapists and murderers enter the convent

503

desiring to desecrate it and you. When you arrive at that stage, you will be immune from torment.'

A deep gratitude seized her. 'I cannot thank you enough for the precious gift you have given me, *señor*.' She turned in his arms and kissed his wrinkled cheek. 'I comprehend without knowing. What I do know is that I now have something more precious than life. I have truth.' She paused, thinking. 'There will be the times of terror, but I know that this will help me until my body ceases to exist tomorrow.' Her voice turned fierce with her resolve. 'Even if it be not the truth, I shall cling to it and it shall be my refuge and strength.'

'The truth of each moment is the reality of each moment.'

This she did not understand, but she fell asleep quietly in his bony arms, lulled by the faint beating of his ancient heart.

Chapter 27

He had elected to remain with his army encamped on the plain immediately south of Jaén, for King Pedro the Cruel preferred to live as his troops did in the field. He rather enjoyed the freedom of the army camp, the camaraderie and revelry with his nobles. Yet luxury travelled with him in his connecting pavilions, so he did not mind the indeterminate period during which he awaited word that all allied forces were in place, the arrival of Count Gaston's army corps at the northwestern border of Granada, the troops of the Portuguese army commander in place on the western border and confirmation that King Philip's naval force was positioned offshore and his small Catalonian land force on its way to Jaén.

King Pedro's one frustration was that he had not been able to fulfil the only cause of his haste in moving the Castilian army south, which was to catch up with the fugitives. Each day without further news than the near-miss attendant on the misfortune that had befallen Captain Montoya's guards frustrated him the more.

He blamed the gypsy girl and the Jew for making the escape possible and had been in no mood for justice or mercy yesterday, when Bishop Eulogius requested and obtained from him a signed and sealed royal warrant giving Holy Church priority in its claims for the bodies of these two villains. Even though he recognized that the crafty prelate was timing his plea well, King Pedro's hopes of apprehending the fugitives had finally been extinguished. On the plus side, the grant of this warrant meant that, having already transferred certain land fiefdoms to the bishop, he would be honouring his earlier pledge, of which the pudgy cleric had had the effrontery to remind him, to provide virgins and Inquisition as well in exchange for the support of Holy Church in the invasion of Granada. Why should he, King Pedro the Cruel, care if two criminals received neither justice nor mercy from the bishop? Perhaps the girl Zurika was a virgin. Whether or not she submitted to the prelate's sick desires, he, King Pedro had 'delivered' a promised virgin. The joke was that his concession was only theoretical, because the fugitives had obviously escaped to Granada, and he, King Pedro, had given the little prick of a bishop all of nothing!

When he received the request for an audience early that morning from his master-spy, Ruy de Vivar, whom he had included in his royal train to assist in tracking down the fugitives, his hopes had risen and he had agreed to receive the man immediately.

Unusually for summer in this part of the country, heavy rain had beaten down on the pavilion roof all night. It was just about abating when de Vivar was ushered in and made his deep bow. While somewhat cooling the torrid heat that, being from the more temperate north, King Pedro and his courtiers had found most trying, the rain had brought a high humidity that laid a thin veil of wet on linen and made bare feet squirm against the sponge of leather slippers and damp red Venetian carpets.

'You may wipe the rain from your face,' King Pedro bade his visitor.

'Thank you, Sire. By your leave.' De Vivar removed a brown linen square from the pocket of his brown tunic, the usual amber scent of which had been extinguished by the damp air.

'We hope you have more for us than this gloomy weather,' King Pedro stated.

'We are getting closer to the fugitives, Sire,' de Vivar assured him, fingering the bridge of a thin, aquiline nose.

'The gypsy girl and the Jew,' he appeared to be sneering at the very mention of lowly races, 'have been apprehended.'

King Pedro leapt from his gilt settle in delighted surprise. 'When? Where are they? What about our son and daughter? And that Moorish prick, Prince Ahmed?' Observing de Vivar about to rise in deference, he resumed his seat.

De Vivar raised a bony hand. 'To answer your questions in the order you asked them, Sire,' he replied precisely. 'The two people were apprehended last night in the barn of a cottage a few miles north of the city. Apparently, they were delivered to Bishop Eulogius's men by two Moors who had taken them captive. I am attempting to reconstruct the details, but there is no trace as yet of Prince Ahmed, Prince Juan or Princess Beatrice. Meanwhile, Bishop Eulogius will try his two prisoners for heresy at an *auto-da-fé* this morning in the town hall plaza. It is a foregone conclusion that he and his Ecclesiastical Court will find them guilty and sentence them to public execution.'

'What? The bishop has no . . .' King Pedro cut himself short. He had been tricked by the plump little prick of a prelate after all. Bishop Eulogius must have known that the two fugitives had been located before he requested and received the royal warrant surrendering his, King Pedro's, sovereign rights to the two bodies. Fuck the bishop! He would summon the pervert immediately and take over the prisoners.

'Apparently Bishop Eulogius obtained prior jurisdiction over the two accused by Your Majesty's gracious surrender of sovereign rights.'

De Vivar's words were a reminder to King Pedro of the need to proceed with caution in order to avoid a confrontation with Holy Church at this point in his invasion plans and to prevent the people from thinking him an opportunist who could not make up his mind. 'Can the whereabouts of our son, daughter and the Moorish prince not be ascertained from the two prisoners?' he temporized.

'They have refused to talk, Sire.'

'Torture them until they do,' he growled in response.

'Apparently such is not the intention of Holy Church, which is only concerned with matters religious.'

'Religious indeed!' He resisted the temptation to add that Bishop Eulogius's only religion was the worship of virgin bodies. 'What can we do?'

'As your Majesty well knows, I have no partiality for gypsies or Jews, blacks or heathens, but public executions such as the bishop will undoubtedly decree are more likely to divide than to unite the Castilian people at this time, the only favourable factor being our distance from Toledo.'

Either way he, King Pedro, stood to lose. 'The Spanish people will even accept the public execution of a turnip, so long as it is occasion for a *fiesta*,' he retorted sourly. As always, he decided to accept the *status quo* and batter his way through any consequences, but he suddenly longed for Maria's sage counsel. 'We shall keep away from this event, to which we will undoubtedly receive an invitation shortly, on the pretext that we are indisposed. You must ensure through your network that judiciously placed people in the crowd spread word among those who support *auto-da-fé* that we are responsible. Those who are offended by it should be told that Bishop Eulogius is entirely to blame and we had no part in it.' He would bide his time and make the bishop pay for making a fool of him. For the present, he would present a pleasant face, allowing the cleric to believe that he was unaware a deception had been practised on him.

'I shall certainly do that, Your Majesty.'

'You personally have no news at all regarding the other

fugitives?' the king inquired abruptly, desiring to change the subject.

'None whatsoever, Your Majesty. When we have discovered exactly where the gypsy girl and the Jew were captured, we shall have a precise location from which to launch our investigations. I assure Your Majesty that it is only a matter of time before we will uncover our . . . er . . . royal quarry.'

The peace of the convent in Jaén was so tangible that it had touched Princess Beatrice's heart the moment she stood outside its locked gates with Prince Juan the previous night. Once inside, the horror of the rape she had endured continued to seem like someone else's experience. Having stabled their horses at a nearby inn, they had reached the convent so late that the great wooden entrance gates set into the high ivy-covered walls closing the entire property were locked and barred. The ancient lodgekeeper who peered through the Judas latch had finally agreed to permit them entry only if Mother Euphrasia personally approved. It was apparent that the nuns were taking no risks with an entire army encamped in and around the city.

Mother Euphrasia had received them in the parlour. She proved to be a petite religious with delicate features, milk-white skin and green eyes, whose sparkle could not disguise her air of calm authority. She smelled of skin scrubbed clean with soap. Once she was convinced as to who they were, she not only welcomed them but even invited Prince Juan to stay in the small entrance lodge, readily agreeing to keep their identities secret. She would introduce them to the sisters, quite truthfully, as the children of a cousin in Toledo who were on their way to Cordoba, but had sought the security of the convent until the Castilian army moved south.

The convent was served by an entrance courtyard

dotted with pines and junipers, through which a short roadway led directly to a stone chapel. Around a square central flagstone quadrangle were dormitories and cells with cloisters, all in several small buildings and linked to the refectory and the kitchens by internal corridors. Thirty-three nuns, dressed in the black and white *capucha* and wimple, twelve novices in simple white and several orphans, most of whom did the menial work, resided here.

Princess Beatrice was allotted a vacant cell. It had a bare floor, a small truckle bed and a little stand, the top of which served as an altar, complete with two small candles on either side of a blue and white clay statuette of the Blessed Virgin, at which she had knelt and prayed.

'*O Virgin Mother, I am no longer a virgin but I still pray to Thee to succour me in my distress. The Heavenly Father had some divine purpose in making me endure the hell of rape's torment. Perhaps it was to teach me not to be arrogant about my virgin state. Regardless of the reason, I beg Thee to give me the strength to rise above this calamity, to treat it as an opportunity and not an affliction.*'

The religious were noted through Europe for giving sanctuary to those who needed it without ever betraying them, so Princess Beatrice felt totally safe at last. Being completely exhausted in body, mind and spirit, she had fallen into a deep sleep, from which she awoke only when the chapel bell rang for the morning *Angelus*.

Where am I? What am I doing here? The soreness in and around her womanhood, the sharp pain in her rear and the ache of her inner thighs provided their own sick answers. Her gorge started to rise. She gripped the side of the mattress to stifle the hysteria mounting within her. She broke into a cold sweat. Wild eyes sought the doorway, fell on the statue of the Blessed Virgin, were arrested by its calm. She had determined not to think about the horror. Long moments passed as she struggled for control. As the peace of the Convent began to enter her soul again, the unseasonal rain that was pouring down outside somehow helped her cast aside the dread hell's brew while the continued pealing of the mellow summons to prayer . . . ding, ding, ding . . . dong, dong, dong . . . ding, ding, ding . . . brought calm again.

The morning devotions and a simple breakfast of bread, cheese and fresh milk concluded, Mother Euphrasia invited her and Prince Juan to her private parlour for a long talk. They had barely begun their conversation when a visitor was announced by Sister Agnesia, a jolly buxom nun who had hastened into the room, her round face flushed with suppressed excitement, a parchment scroll in her hand. 'Forgive me this intrusion, Reverend Mother, but we have just had a messenger from His Eminence the Primate Bishop Eulogius with news of the utmost importance.'

Mother Euphrasia smiled tolerantly. 'Speak, Sister,' she said. 'Important news from His Eminence is only second to news from His Holiness. We are honoured, though you sometimes have trivial news of great urgency.'

'We are all commanded to attend an *auto-da-fé* in the plaza opposite the town hall this morning,' Sister Agnesia announced. 'Two heretics are to be tried. If found guilty, they will immediately be purged by fire. The large stakes are at this very moment being planted on the open ground just south of the city and brushwood is being piled six feet high around the stakes.'

'By whose authority has the event been proclaimed?' Mother Euphrasia inquired, a note of hesitancy in her voice.

'Bishop Eulogius himself has decreed it.'

'He is the primate bishop of Spain,' Mother Euphrasia stated firmly. 'Next to the Holy Father, he is our link with Heaven. Why, he might even become the Holy Father some day.' She had surely noticed Princess Beatrice's look

511

of revulsion. 'If Holy Church has decreed it, there must be good cause for the trial, my child. We shall all attend.' She stared compellingly at Princess Beatrice and Prince Juan. 'You too.' Her eyes returned to Sister Agnesia. 'Who are the heretics?'

'I did not ask, Reverend Mother, but they must be named in that scroll. The bishop's messenger mentioned that one of them is an old Jewish man and the other a young gypsy girl.'

The world reeled around Princess Beatrice. Was there to be no end to her afflictions? She had arisen from one calamity after another, only to be smitten down by the next and the next. Now this. Her heart screamed its horror. Why, God? Why? *I would rather endure rape's torment a thousand times than have those I love harmed. Is it that I bring misfortune to others? Have I not brought evil to my mother, my father, my brother, Prince Ahmed and now this ultimate torture to Aaron Levi and Zurika, who would never be facing death but for me?* An anguished cry rang from her breaking heart before everything went black.

At dawn they were served a miserable slop of cold rotten pottage, consisting of pork, chick peas and cabbage. Zurika was in no mood for food, but ate at Aaron Levi's insistence, to build up her strength. White *sambenitos*, gowns and mitres of penitence, were flung at them by a surly guard with a brusque order that these be donned.

By the time they were hustled, despite their fetters, to the rear courtyard, the rain had ceased and bright sunlight hurt the eyes. A tumbril with slatted wooden sides to which a tired-looking grey nag with a drooping head was harnessed awaited them. Two of the bishop's guards hoisted them into the wagon, in which they sat on a floor laid with faded yellow straw. Headed by mounted guards, more riding behind, all dressed in the purple tunics and white nether-hosen of the bishopric, the open wagon proceeded through the gates onto a busy road.

With the guards clearing the way, they soon hit the main street. The babble of voices interspersed by an occasional shout and the screams of children became deafening as they rattled over the grey cobbles, at a slower pace now because of the increased crowds. Although this street was wider, two- and three-storey houses overhanging on both sides made it seem more congested, while an open water drain flowing lazily grey-black down the centre contained the stinking offal and debris over which pigs snuffled and dogs growled. The appalling stench made the cliff-caves of the gypsies, with their ready access to fresh air outside, seem heavenly to Zurika, and yet the rain-washed blue heavens contrasting sharply with scattered white plumes of clouds were no different from those above the ravine of the Alhambra.

Most of the people were in festive mood, being gaily dressed in greens, reds and blues with many black and white *mantillas*, red fezzes and black *yarmulkes* evident. Zurika wondered what the fiesta was about until someone pointed at the tumbril crying, 'Look! Look! The heretics!' She then realized with sick surprise that the *auto-da-fé* was the *fiesta*, she and Aaron Levi the principal players. For once in her life, her role in a *fiesta* would not be to dance.

'Shitty heretics!' . . . 'Foul scum!' The expletives soon came hurtling at them from all sides. A stone rattled against the side of the wagon. Tomatoes followed, splattering red.

'*Aqua va!*' The cry from a balcony was followed by night soil from a chamber pot, splashing its vile mess on them. Zurika looked up furiously through the urine dripping down her face. The plump, grinning visage of the dark-haired matron on the second floor was evidence that she had flung the contents deliberately. The woman shook the empty chamber pot in the air at them as if it were a victory banner, shrieking vituperation that was lost in the welter of crowd-screams.

'People have to do such things, work themselves up to a bestial fury, to justify their enjoyment of such an event,' Aaron Levi remarked quietly, wiping the slime off his face with a linen cloth. The crass cruelty of the act, despoiling her body that was due that very day to suffer the ultimate obscenity, caused Zurika to lose the iron self-control she had been exercising. She and Aaron Levi were alone in a hostile, merciless world. His philosophy would not alter their fate. Chill terror entered her bones. She began to tremble, then to shiver uncontrollably. Only a supreme effort of will from some reserves of gypsy pride enabled her to hold back her shrieks, to restrain the insane desire to tear her hair, gibbering with fear, bitterness and rage. What place did gypsies have in this dreadful world? Or Jews?

The utter dread that gripped her, reaching down to her bowels, became so overpowering that she let go of their contents. Dear God in heaven, I am soiled by others from outside and by myself from within me. Where can I go for relief? How can I escape from this bog of human droppings? She tried to rise, but was held down by her heavy fetters. Frustrated, in cold despair, she spat at the woman. It helped.

Aaron Levi placed a quiet hand on hers. He removed the soiled linen from his tunic, began tenderly wiping her face. Within the taunts, threats and derision of the crowd swirling around her, the Jew's tenderness created an island of peace. When he had finished wiping her face, he laid a hand on her cheek, turned her head to him and held her gaze with dark, compelling eyes. 'There is no dignity in death,' he stated. 'Only in the manner of our dying.' His gnarled, dry hand reached for hers again, held it firmly. The tangible calm he exuded vibrated through

514

her like the compelling first notes of a guitar drawing her to dance. She relaxed. 'Dignity!' he added quietly. 'All you and I have left, that no one can take away, is dignity.'

She stifled the spurt of a thought. You are old and have lived your life to the full, while I am young and should have all of it ahead of me. When she stood up to dance before any crowd, she was no longer a lowly gypsy, one of a desperate race. The dance she put on was an act, but it came from her innermost being, giving her dignity, a place of honour with her audience. Today, she would put on the greatest act of her life.

The guards quickened their horses' hooves to get the tumbril safely through the jeering mob, away from the clutching hands. If she could have danced for these pigs, they would have been cheering her instead. Contempt for them filled her. She lifted her head. She would never allow such cannibals to rob her of her most divine possession, her dignity.

The plaza was packed with people, but a gap had been cordoned off by guards on foot leaving the way clear to two wooden platforms. The one to Zurika's left, she guessed, was for the inquisitors and dignitaries, who would arrive in procession. The platform to her right was bare except for two stools, but it would soon be surrounded on three sides by guards with spears.

'Peace and serenity in your being, with courage and dignity their clothing,' Aaron Levi murmured. 'We will have to listen to a sermon, oaths, abjurations, reconciliations and spurious pleas to us, the obdurate, for relaxation towards the secular authorities.' She did not understand some of the words but gathered their meaning. His bony face wrinkled more as he smiled, the hooked nose twitched with amusement. 'All extremely boring! As for the reading of our sentences, they will be interminable, though they can be summed up briefly, in five words, You shall die by fire.' His dark eyes became hypnotic. 'Reach

515

now for the inner core of your being, my child. Never let go of it.' His fierce determination and willpower were the more compelling because the words were so calmly spoken, he could have been advising a child not to be afraid of bathwater.

Zurika fell under his spell, gazed at him fascinated. The ugly, screaming, stinking world around them shrank to non-existence. Gypsy and Jew became one in unity of courage and dignity.

They were completely separate now from the surrounding tumult, which she no longer heard, having at last entered the peaceful eye of the storm swirling and snarling around them. 'I may not get another opportunity to say this to you.' The words emerged from Aaron Levi clear as dewdrops, his voice no longer dry. 'If there is a heaven, you and I will arrive there together. Being with you will be my heaven. If there is no heaven, the hours we have known together, especially these last ones, will have been my heaven on earth, for knowing you has been the ultimate heaven of my long life. I love you, my dear child.'

Her breath caught in a sob. 'The one thing I did in my life that was of heaven, godly, was to dance,' she trembled. 'My one sorrow is that I never danced for you, *señor*. I love you and I promise to dance for you in heaven.'

A wide balcony on the town hall, fronting the plaza, had been reserved for the nuns. Mother Euphrasia had agreed that Prince Juan should not accompany them, and Princess Beatrice, who insisted on going, would wear a white veil so as not to be recognized, especially if the two kings were present. Prince Juan had slipped away before they left the convent. It had seemed to Princess Beatrice that he had something in mind, but she realized dismally that it could never be to organize a rescue attempt.

Standing in the gloomy interior between the black wimples of Mother Euphrasia and the senior nuns, Princess Beatrice could see the entire plaza, even the empty wooden platforms beneath them. When the tumbril heralded by the bishop's guards rolled into the plaza, she was appalled by the jeers and obscenities of the crowd thronging three sides of the platform. Were these Christians? The wagon came to a stop. Her heart clenched with pity and horror when Zurika and Aaron Levi, manacled and chained, were roughly helped down. They were so dirty, bedraggled and weary-seeming she could have broken down sobbing. The palace training of years held, however, but she had to close her eyes to prevent a blackness from overcoming her again. *Oh God, Oh Blessed Virgin Mary, Oh Sweet Jesu, forgive me. I did not know what would happen. I would rather have suffered the tortures of being King Charles's queen, the isolation of becoming a nun, I would have endured torment and death rather than have it visit these poor innocent people. How will I ever atone for this evil? Oh God, I did not know, I simply did not know what I was doing.*

She opened her eyes. Through blinding tears she saw the cross of the Church on the opposite side of the plaza, the naked Jesus wearing a crown of thorns hanging from it, the spear at his side.

The cry that rent Princess Beatrice was all the more pitiful because it was only in her heart.

'. . . so Lucifer was consigned by Almighty God to darkness in order to reveal light and was allotted a leading place in the *theatrum mundi* . . .'

'. . . The devil prevents victims from confessing their crimes, especially witchcraft and heresy . . .'

Glittering snatches of words, uttered in a voice of incantation, were penetrating the dark numbness of Princess Beatrice's brain.

'. . . We shall not afford them the gates of pardon which would release them from the transient fires of this earth before they enter the eternal fires of hell and damnation . . .'

The voice was the more fearsome because of its calm, sonorous tones and the dread hush of the crowd. Somewhere a pigeon cooed. Others echoed it, but the inexorable voice went on.

'. . . A person who has surrendered to Satan has no free will . . .'

'. . . By virtue of powers vested in us, the true representative of Holy Church, granted by God on this occasion through his secular ruler in Spain, King Pedro . . .'

'. . . We hereby sentence you, Zurika, a witch of no last name, and you Aaron Levi, a heretic whose sinfulness has been expressed in foul deeds against our noble ruler, King Pedro, to death at the stake. The sentences shall run concurrently, with the exception that Aaron Levi's shall be carried out first, so that the said witch, Zurika, may behold the evil she has wrought and witness the power of Holy Church over Satan. You shall be taken to the execution ground immediately, which has been prepared outside the southern walls of the city of Jaén, and there put to death without delay . . .'

A shriek rent the air, disturbed the stillness of the sonorous words. Princess Beatrice gazed in amazement as a grey-haired old crone, staff in hand, burst through the crowd and hobbled towards the sunlit platform on which the dignitaries were seated while the purple-robed Bishop Eulogius delivered the sentence. If the crowd had been hushed before, it was stupefied now.

'You no have right kill my granddaughter, Zurika,' the woman screeched. Princess Beatrice realized with a shock that this demented creature must be Zurika's grandmother, Pilar. In an instant she knew what Prince Juan had had in his mind when he left the convent. 'She be good girl, good Christian, say prayer, worship Virgin Mary, Blessed Saints, Peter, Paul, Sweet Jesu and God Father. Zurika know nothing about witch. I, her grandmother, Pilar, look after her many year, since her father die. You no can . . .'

'Take that woman away,' Bishop Eulogius cut in, his voice no longer sonorous but icy as the high mountains in winter. 'If she does not take care, we shall punish her for contempt of these proceedings and against the judges of Holy Church.'

Princess Beatrice could actually see the faded eyes of the old woman flash, so terrible was her anger, as guards dragged her away.

'I curse you, I curse you. Some day I have revenge on you . . .' The rest of Pilar's ranting was lost in the babble of the crowd, which seemed strangely sympathetic towards her.

'Revenge . . . I curse you . . . revenge . . . God send you terrible . . .' The words echoed in Princess Beatrice's brain and made her shiver.

Princess Beatrice had absolutely refused to witness the executions and Mother Euphrasia had not insisted after her first admonition, 'It is important for us to witness the tortures which the damned suffer in this life so we can take care not to endure them ourselves throughout eternity, my child.'

Fortunately, she and Prince Juan had made no mention to Mother Euphrasia of their connection with Zurika and Aaron Levi, revealing only Prince Ahmed's participation in Princess Beatrice's escape from the tourney. Even so, Princess Beatrice was horrified at Mother Euphrasia's calm attitude towards the executions. It reminded her of her own mother, Maria de Padilla's, total devotion to her father, King Pedro, regardless of right and wrong, compassion and love. Mother Euphrasia was equally blindly devoted to the Church.

Prince Juan, who had been present at the executions as an act of desperate loyalty, briefly told Princess Beatrice what had happened after the trial.

Both Aaron Levi and Zurika had gone to their deaths silently with remarkable dignity.

Not a sound had escaped the victims, a bubbling Sister Agnesia had added. But a final shout from the heretic Zurika when the brushwood around Aaron Levi's stake had begun to flame proved they were both of the devil: 'You shall meet me in heaven, *señor*, and I shall dance for you there.'

When Pilar watched her beautiful, beautiful Zurika licked up by the flames and slowly engulfed in billowing grey smoke, her ancient heart broke. Her ward, her love, her *queridisima* who had been the central part of her life since her son, Zurika's father, had died in the knife fight, was gone from this world forever. All that remained for Pilar was her revenge. Her hatred of Bishop Eulogius knew no bounds. She wanted a slow, slow torturous death for him before he entered the torments of the eternal Hell to which she would consign him.

Pilar knew the rites, but never before had she practised black magic.

She hobbled directly back from the executions to her small, single-roomed cottage set within a tiny plot of land on which she had been growing vegetables just outside the city walls of Jaén. Going directly to the wooden chest that contained all her ritual materials, she sorted out the effigies, the black wax candles, the menstrual blood, all the other necessities of her craft, readying them for the midnight hour. She sat on the bench and began her powerful incantations, for once to Lucifer and his minions alone, repeating them over and over again so that the words would hammer away at the evil spirits like flowing water eroding stone until they responded, and breaching any protective wall of Christian ritual that might surround Bishop Eulogius and protect his black, evil heart.

When the midnight hour approached, she lit the black candles, placed each in one of the white circles she had drawn on the floor and lay across the worn bench ready for the ultimate cursing.

'O powers of Darkness, O powers of the Evil One, Satan, Fire, Damnation, O powers of Hell, guide the vile, obscene body of Bishop Eulogius to your blackest, tortured Death, for his soul is already one with you . . .'

And the most powerful plea of all:

'If you need my ancient, wrinkled body, this bag of white hair and bones to crunch on, this tired soul unto eternity, as a reward for granting my demand, take all of it too, so long as you take the soul of Bishop Eulogius to eternal Hell, for I would gladly endure its tortures. Amiah. Hell shall be my reward not my punishment if I can witness this evil man's torment . . .'

Chapter 28

He had barely reached the outskirts of Cordoba when the gossiping owner of an inn at which he had stopped for the noon meal broke the shocking news to him. The city and the entire area west of it was occupied by an army from León y Navarra, waiting for orders from King Pedro to attack Granada. It was rumoured that the King of Portugal would also invade Granada, at its western border. The menace to Prince Ahmed's kingdom was complete. Meanwhile, Cordoba was thriving from the huge influx of visitors, but 'Almighty Allah placed my humble inn on the wrong side of Cordoba,' the innkeeper stated dolefully.

He had opted for a settle at a common table on the verandah of the inn, where the meal of *paella marinera*, which did not contain the forbidden pork, was served. Lost in his own bitter thoughts, which shut out the jumble of voices and languages around him, he became enmeshed in the blackness of a despair on which the glaring sunlight on the dirt courtyard outside cast no light.

Having made good speed on his own so far, Prince Ahmed had hoped to reach the Alhambra palace before the end of the week. Once there, he would assert his right to the throne and search for Princess Beatrice, whom he intended marrying whatever the extremist *imams* might say about his consorting with an infidel Christian, and give her, Prince Juan, Aaron Levi, who had sacrificed so much, and Zurika, complete security at last. He had, however, looked forward to spending an hour or two in Cordoba. Described by Arab historians as 'the jewel of the world', Cordoba was one of the great legacies of the former Islamic rulers, being the oldest of the Arab civilization centres in Spain before it gave place to Seville under the onslaughts of Christian rulers from the north and finally to Granada. Apart from its magnificent palaces, Cordoba contained about 500 mosques, including the Great Mosque inaugurated by Abdul Rahman I, over 1000 baths inside and outside the city, which had probably helped save it from the ravages of the Great Plague, more than 100,000 residences for the people and 50,000 more for officials, court favourites, military chiefs and other members of the government. Four hundred years earlier, during the reign of Caliph Alkahem II, its library had contained some 400,000 manuscripts. The city's streets were paved and lighted; its water came from the mountains through an aqueduct and it was also the acknowledged scientific centre of Europe at this time, a leader in medicine, botany, chemistry, physics, mathematics, astronomy and geography, all based on a thriving economy from agriculture, industry and a commerce made accessible by boats sailing up the Guadalquivir from the seaport of Cadiz.

Now Granada seemed to be blocked by Christian armies at all the regular border crossings. Prince Ahmed was tempted to weave his way through, but abandoned the idea, which meant eluding guardposts and patrols spread over several miles. Would Cordoba always remain for him merely this collection of spires and minarets in the distance, glittering in the haze of the late afternoon sunlight, the unreachable reality, the dream unfulfilled? Somehow the vital need to head back east, thereby missing his longed-for glimpse of the magic city, signified all Prince Ahmed's shattered hopes and brought him to his lowest ebb. The reality he faced was indeed terrifying. Here he was in enemy territory, virtually surrounded by enemy forces which stood between him and the sanctuary of his kingdom. Worse, the kingdom, being obviously divided and without a real leader, was completely vulnerable. Would there be a Granada, a kingdom for him? Within weeks it could become Christian territory unless its forces were marshalled to repel the attack long enough for traditional help to arrive from the Moorish kingdoms of North Africa. He recalled Abou bon Ebben mentioning something about 100,000 men, was it from Morocco? He was sorry he had not listened more carefully, but it had not seemed important at the time to one who was so much a prisoner in the Gen al Arif that he had even been denied a place beside his father, King Yusuf, in the strike against Castile. Was that in another lifetime?

Had he been right to leave his birthright on an errand of sheer gallantry, to escape from imprisonment only to go to the rescue of a fair maid? Had that been irresponsible of him, unworthy of the heir to a throne? If he had remained in Granada, the throne would have been secure for him and the kingdom would have remained undivided. Perhaps his father might never have been assassinated if he had been available to succeed. Guilt! Guilt!

All the same, he had to admit that, having once seen the picture of Princess Beatrice, he simply could not have acted any differently. Dimly he recognized that it was cause and effect, a host of causes, most of them discernible, and their multitudinous effects, many unidentifiable. The real *kismet*, destiny, irrevocable, inexorable.

His thoughts were distracted by a snapping and snarling. Two mangy dogs were fighting over a scrap of bone in the sunlit glare of the brown courtyard. While they bared fierce teeth at each other, a third dog sneaked up and ran away with the bone. It amused him at first, but then the lesson began spinning in his brain. He had been too direct in his own approach. He had imagined that if he headed for Granada through Cordoba, the rest would follow. Absolutely not! He should be as circumspect about getting to Granada and once he reached it, as he had been when he fled. Sneak in and seize the prize. That was the message Allah had just given him through these three mangy dogs.

The presence of a Navarrese army here, which had brought him up short, had also to be a sign from Allah. Yes, that was it, Almighty Allah had guided him, even when his earlier actions might have been irresponsible, to bring him to this afternoon of hot, Cordoba sunlight. He would follow the Divine purpose. He was destined to be the saviour of Granada despite all the terrible dangers threatening it and him. Becoming Emperor of all Spain would follow.

The conclusion brightened him. He began planning his moves, delighted to discover the native cunning that was part of his own legacy.

Go back the way you came had been his deduction from Almighty Allah's message. He had acted on it, retracing his horse's steps eastward, then south along the route of his escape from Granada. Once he crossed the steep ravine that was part of the border, he had felt safe at last. How ironic it was that he could finally stop looking over his shoulder when he had been doing just that the other way round only months ago! But traces of the reactions of the past months remained. He caught himself looking over his shoulder though there was no longer any need.

Although the journey from the border to the Alhambra had been relatively safe, he had no illusions as to what awaited him the moment he surfaced in the palace as the rightful heir. The hand of Farouk Riswan who had murdered his father and sent the assassins after him would strike. Farouk Riswan, Prince Saad, who was reported to head the government and their supporters would come after him instantly, needing to strike well before he advanced his claim. His one hope was to strike first. He had made his plan accordingly.

Four days after he left Cordoba he entered the capital through its main northern gates without even being stopped. He had been appalled at the total lack of security throughout the country in the face of invading armies at its borders. Even the people on the highway had not seemed over concerned; their life went on as usual.

He intended contacting Abou bon Ebben in the tower, unless the old tutor had been executed on the late king's orders for allowing the imprisoned heir to escape, and Tarif, the old, black deaf-mute, whose loyalty to him was unquestionable. He would discover from these two men what princes, noblemen and officers supported the legitimate succession. He would contact such loyalists and initiate the action he had conceived.

In the golden light of evening, he finally stood once more in front of the slab of rock on which Zurika had first danced for him. The scent of cypress was the same, but the Sierra Nevada mountains beyond, devoid of snow, were purple black, the sky pale blue above them. It brought forcibly to his mind that it was Zurika who had altered the entire course of his life, pulling him away from the poet's frenzied ecstasies that had once even caused him to ejaculate before a graceful tree to a more normal state. He recalled the past with a sense of wonder at all that had transpired, at how much for the good he personally had changed, tinged with regret that in the months since his escape from the Gen al Arif he had not written one single poem, not even for Princess Beatrice though she had become the central figure of his life. Why? There had simply been neither time nor mood.

The rapping of a woodpecker drew his attention to the jagged dark granite of the escarpment. It suddenly seemed to him that the black slab of rock was a stage and he the audience. The woodpecker's knocking ceased, abruptly, as if it had fulfilled its purpose. The earth became hushed, the evening sunlight wrapped warm around his chilled body. He stared at the rock, hypnotized like a bird before a serpent. In the golden light of evening a female figure slowly materialized through warm air that had miraculously turned to heavenly colours.

Dear Allah, what exquisite beauty. Olive skin, tight drawn over fine bones, soft mouth, red as pale rosebuds, dimpled cheeks. The eyes, the dark-brown sultry eyes, latent with passion, were the soul of all sorrow, the throb of a smile. *Golpe*, stamp . . . *punta*, toe . . . *talon*, heel . . . *punta* . . . *talon* . . . She began to dance. He eagerly sought her beautiful eyes. Black disappointment fountained within him, surfaced to fill his entire being. He could not connect with her gaze. Why not? Was it, as before, because her back was to the evening sun, her face in shadow. No, this time her entire attention was focused elsewhere.

Dear Allah, Zurika is not dancing for me but for someone else.

His eyes shot in the direction of her gaze. The figure of a man materialized, seated on a ledge of rock. Staff in hand, he was facing Zurika, one leg bent, the other slightly straighter, shoulders hunched, head thrust forward in rapt attention. An ancient, clad in a dark robe. Even before he saw the black *yarmulke* on the grey head, Prince Ahmed identified the long, narrow features, the hooked nose straddling wrinkled cheeks. Zurika was dancing for Aaron Levi. The moment he realized it, the vision broke in a flash. Prince Ahmed was left staring stupefied at a bare slab of black rock in the empty golden air of evening, conscious of the odour of his own body covered with sweat.

His entire being consumed by the vision he had seen, the Prince stood motionless in the shredded sunlight beneath the dark green cypresses. What did it mean? Was his imagination playing tricks on him? Why? Had something happened to Zurika and Aaron Levi? Had they been captured? If so, had Princess Beatrice also fallen into her father's clutches – or King Charles's? The last possibility sent chills through Prince Ahmed. Dear Allah, please not that, I beg Thee.

The possibility of danger to Princess Beatrice brought back resolve. If she had been captured, he would rescue her once more if he had to take Toledo or Pamplona apart stone by stone. If she was married to King Charles, he would still take her for his wife, regardless of the laws of the Catholic Church, for Islam did not recognize Christian marriage.

For the first time since he parted company with them, regret at having left his friends overwhelmed all else.

His thoughts were interrupted by a gentle cooing. He glanced in its direction. The doves were perched on the upper floor balustrade of the tower. Mating may be a part of Allah's will, but now the Gen al Arif became a towering reminder of his duty to the nation and the danger of his mission. Casting all else aside, he concentrated on quietly approaching the base of the tower.

Once there, his breathing heightened by fear, he scanned the movements of the sentries on the palace battlements. The old gap remained. He timed it for his upward spring and grasped the floor-ledge of the balcony to his former rooms with unerring fingers. His muscles responding like strong, pliant creepers, he soon reached the upper balcony. He heaved himself up, body erect and resting on both palms placed upon the floor. His startled gaze rose to meet a pair of black, inscrutable eyes, staring at him. Terror gripped him.

Each passing hour of the days that followed the *auto-da-fé* had been a slow torture of self-recrimination and regret for Princess Beatrice. The tragic fate that had befallen Zurika and Aaron Levi overshadowed her own dreadful rape experience, making the latter less tragic. What, after all, was rape compared to death at the stake? Princess Beatrice was hard put to keep thrusting aside the overpowering temptation to relive the last hours of her friends, especially their time at the stake, in her imagination. How did the first heat of the brushwood, the crackle, the licking flames feel? It required a desperate need for self-preservation, more for the sake of those she loved, especially Prince Ahmed, rather than for herself, to hurl these thoughts aside, for when added to her own horror and frequent nightmares they would create the highroad to insanity.

Her strong will, combined with Prince Juan's understanding and Mother Euphrasia's obvious compassion, carried her through this terrible period and slowly brought her back to normal. What remained overt was her terrible shock at the blind support most of the nuns had given to the *auto-da-fé* and the cruel executions.

Princess Beatrice was therefore ready by the time rumour reached the convent, several days after the executions, that King Pedro's armies would be moving in a couple of days, to discuss the next move with Prince Juan.

The two of them had developed the habit of walking by themselves in the front courtyard every evening while awaiting the tolling of the bell calling to *vespers*, the sixth of the daily prayers. As always, this was a golden time of the day when the sun's torturing heat gave way to the lengthening shadows created by its own fading light. The calls of birds wending their way home across a paling blue sky or from their nesting green cypress and juniper branches drowned out even the soughing of a fugitive breeze that carried the first sweet tinges of honeysuckle to clear the air. The silver-fluted voices of children, which she had never heard in her Toledo palace prison, exulting in a last romp on the other side of the high ivy-covered wall before they were summoned inside their houses for supper, added to the peace around her. A sudden cooing of pigeons from the cote at the side of the convent building completed the smoothing caress of approaching nightfall, which gave her hope that she might find peace within her after all.

They stopped by common consent beside the boundary wall at the far end of the flagstone walkway and faced each other. They had developed a deep perception of each other's inclinations, felt very comfortable together.

'We cannot remain in the convent indefinitely even though we are more than paying our way,' she gestured. 'It is time for us to move on.'

'I had to wait till you were ready,' he responded, the blue eyes gentle.

'I know. You have been marvellous. I mean that. A complete marvel. You have made me realize that there is greater strength in supporting someone and leading from behind than in dragging them along.'

'One of God's missions for me was to help you in this way.'

They had both studiously avoided any reference to or discussion of the tragedies of the past weeks. 'Then I thank you and I thank God for you.' She paused. 'You must have heard the news that our father intends to commence his advance against Granada on all three fronts in a few days. You and I have always agreed that our only refuge is Granada, have we not?'

He nodded. 'Your own refuge is Prince Ahmed,' he replied serious-eyed. 'A place is not the refuge that a person can be.' He must have noted her puzzlement. 'For instance, the Toledo palace was no refuge for you and me, because our father was not our refuge either. So we had none. Our true refuge, I believe, is ourselves, but when there is another self loving us that we in turn love, then the union of loving spirits means a single refuge in each other.'

530

Her cheeks warmed with a blush at Prince Juan's first direct reference to her love for Prince Ahmed, then her breath caught with pity. Her beloved brother had to seek his own refuge within himself alone, for it was extremely unlikely that he would find any woman who would love him in this special way. Least of all would a woman of the necessary compassion and sensitivity be easy to find in the world of royalty and nobility, where there was so much false pride, selfishness and arrogance. She had only to search Prince Juan's face, however, to understand that for what he did not have, there was vastly increased strength in the chiselled features. 'It is time we planned to leave for Granada,' she declared bluntly, mouthing the words as she gestured.

'It is time we did more than plan,' he countered, his fingers denoting firmness. 'We should move immediately, to get ahead of the advance elements of our father's armies and obtain a clearer passage to Granada.'

In a flash she realized the truth of his suggestion. 'You have known this since we first came here?' she gestured, her eyes inquiring.

'Oh, yes.'

'Why did you not tell me before, dear brother?'

'You were not ready to move,' he repeated.

Tears gushed to her eyes. He could have escaped by himself, or forced her to go with him sooner, but he had waited because she needed him and he had exposed his own life to jeopardy once again just to allow her healing time. 'You are a true prince and *caballero*,' she signalled impulsively.

He looked away, embarrassed.

'When should we leave?' she inquired to ease him.

His response was decisive. 'Tonight.'

While each passing day had reduced King Charles the Bad's fear of discovery, it had also brought him an

531

increasing sense of loss. He had fallen in love with Princess Beatrice at first sight on the morning of the tourney. He had recognized this only dimly, because he had never loved anyone in this romantic way before. To him Princess Mathilde was just a mother figure. Now he simply could not remove Princess Beatrice from his mind, her oval face, pink and white complexion, the mass of golden hair framing those sparkling blue eyes. He had first noticed the grace of her carriage when she walked to her seat at the tourney and could easily recall the slim, tall body, the full breasts he had suckled, the narrow waist and flaring hips. The image of his mother, yes, but so youthful and fresh that he could also think of her in the most poetic terms. Uniquely for him, he had desired to woo her as a lover, win her and marry her.

What then had happened to turn him into a ravening rapist? She had rejected him for another. He had fucked her to punish her, the way he had lusted to punish his mother for her rejection of him in favour of his father. Now he abysmally regretted the rape.

It was evening and he was seated in his pavilion, adjoining that of King Pedro, gloomily staring at the plain south of the city of Jaén, when his chief attendant entered to announce that Count Gaston had arrived from Cordoba and begged an audience. Mention of the count brought Princess Mathilde and their strange 'love' affair more sharply to the fore of King Charles's mind. It was at this time of the day that he would begin organizing his schedule for their regular meeting. Today the recollection loosed more arrows of regret to pierce him at having lost Princess Beatrice forever.

Count Gaston's arrival must surely mean that the army group from León y Navarra was in place, representing one more step in the capture of Granada which was vital to King Charles's own plan to become the Emperor of Spain. As the chancellor stooped and entered the pavilion, he searched the count's hatchet face for signs of ill news. Finding none, he remembered that the man kneeling to kiss his hand never betrayed emotion.

He indicated a gilt settle opposite his chair. 'Pray be seated, Count, and give us your news.' As always he came directly to the point. He did not believe in false inquiries about a man's health or how he had fared on his journey, in this case from Pamplona to Cordoba and now on to Jaén. The count was here and that was enough.

'I have come to report to Your Majesty that our army group is in place, ready for the advance.'

'*Bueno*. You have acted with commendable speed. What about parade states, the health and morale of officers and men, weapons, supplies?'

'Excellent, Sire. All as planned.' He went on to give details.

'It is no more than we expected from you, Chancellor.' An upsurge of enthusiasm for his own cause mushrooming within King Charles brought the need to bestow praise. 'You are without a doubt the finest military leader in Europe.'

The ghost of the familiar smile gleamed briefly white across the black bearded lips as Count Gaston inclined his head. 'Always excluding Your Majesty.'

Fuck you, King Charles thought irritably. You are such a superior bastard. Do you even have to rise above praise? He had always used this man's talents for his own purposes but had never come to know him. Yet he vaguely recognized that Count Gaston had an inner humility that set him apart from whatever condescensions were extended to him. Trumpeters outside announced *vespers* in lieu of a bell. King and Chancellor rose to their feet, crossed themselves. King Charles wondered what Count Gaston's prayer was, or if he was even praying. 'Prayerful customs elevate man,' he remarked when they had resumed their seats.

'Then the Muslim people must also be in a state of supreme elevation, Sire,' the count responded drily. 'Though perhaps to a lesser degree than Catholics who have seven calls to prayer where the Muslims have only five.'

'Damn you, Count, is this a time for philosophy?'

'I beg your Majesty's pardon. I was merely maintaining your conversation.' The count paused, black eyes suddenly intense. 'And I venture to suggest that your present observation is very timely since we are now poised to attack the Muslim stronghold.'

As always this bastard had confused him. Some day . . . he promised himself, knowing that the day would never dawn because Count Gaston was irreplaceable while any harm to him could set up a Basque uprising. 'You sound as if you have reservations about our plan,' he ventured instead.

'I always have reservations against war, bloodshed and physical violence unless it is necessary to defend oneself or to protect the weak and oppressed, Sire. You are well aware of my views, but they have not and will not alter my loyalty and diligence to Your Majesty's cause and to the responsibilities you have vested in me.'

'We never had an opportunity to discuss this venture,' King Charles granted. 'Do you think it is unwise or immoral? You may speak freely.'

'Morality is the responsibility of each individual, so I do not waste time assessing it in others. Wisdom is another matter, but there again we are dealing with decisions already taken and I do not waste time evaluating *faits accomplis* except where it is necessary for future action.'

'What concerns you then?' King Charles was roused by more than curiosity, by interest. He had missed Count Gaston's sharp intellect in recent weeks.

'The entire campaign is unnecessary, Sire. It could also

be tactless and a vulgar expression of the ambitions of the Castilian king. As for the inclusion of Holy Church, with the direct presence of Bishop Eulogius to give this invasion the guise of a Reconquista crusade, it is sheer hypocrisy.' A grim note entered the count's voice. 'I understand that the gypsy girl and the Jew were captured and have been burned at the stake after a sham *auto-da-fé*. I would not have advised Your Majesty to be a party even by association to such a savage act.' His voice shook slightly. Oh, so you can at least display outrage, King Charles thought inconsequentially. Well, it makes some part of you human. 'We are not barbarians to offer sacrifices to the gods before we set out to war.'

Count Gaston's expressions gave King Charles the uneasy feeling that his own secret ambitions and plans for betraying King Pedro eventually were suspected by the chancellor.

'We understand your feelings, Count, and share them,' King Charles lied. 'You must have been told that Bishop Eulogius alone was responsible for this . . . er . . . monstrous deed and that our brother King Pedro and we ourselves were conspicuous by our absence from the atrocities.'

'Bishop Eulogius will pay the price for his actions.'

'How? Do you imagine that God will punish him for what was meant to advance the Christian cause in Spain?'

'God will punish him, Sire, but not through direct action such as striking the bishop dead or even hauling him before a judgment seat. I do not believe that God acts like human beings to deliver justice or mercy. Rather, God operates through inexorable laws of cause and effect. In the most simple terms, Bishop Eulogius's actions are the effects of heredity, his own personality and his environment. His first step towards inhumanity must have been taken long ago, a little boy insecure with his peers plucking off the wings of flies to compensate.'

'Ha!' Dimly King Charles perceived from his own childhood that the count's words could apply to him as well. 'Go on!' he commanded.

'Each little action through the years was a cause multiplying this syndrome doubly rather than in regular progression, as the years went by. Today, Bishop Eulogius has reached a stage that even the little boy of old might never recognize. He is no longer a victim of others but of a total self he has created by his actions. The desire to be secure amongst his peers at all costs has been promoted to the burning need to be pre-eminent, even burning others to achieve that end. We ourselves have become the victims of his desires, as he drives towards his own endeavour, ignoring wisdom and restraint. His very presence here in what will soon be a war zone reveals that abandonment of restraint, since he is risking his life for the purposes that drive him. The horse and wagon are driving the driver.'

'What do you think is his ambition?'

'I believe he wishes to be made a Cardinal, then Pope.'

King Charles's eyes widened. 'What? How could he possibly . . .?' He lapsed into silence, contemplating this new factor, wondering how he could put it to use. Obviously he should ally himself with the bishop. Ah, he had it! *This* was why King Pedro was allowing the primate so much latitude. The Castilian ruler was cunning. This was yet more evidence that he certainly aimed to become King of all Spain, then Emperor. Well, he, King Charles, would dispose of King Pedro at the appropriate time. 'You may be right,' he conceded, reverting to the subject under discussion. 'Do you consider that Bishop Eulogius's punishment will be failing to become the Holy Father?'

'If Bishop Eulogius does attain his goal, Sire, he will destroy himself by being an UnHoly Father!' Count Gaston observed sombrely. 'But I expect his actions to bring him to some dreadful end before he gets that far,

536

probably at the hands of gypsies, Jews, Moors and other so-called heretics whom he has mortally offended.'

'You wish it for him, do you not?'

'No, Sire. I do not waste spiritual energy on such wishes.'

The trend of their discussion suddenly made King Charles desire the presence of Princess Mathilde, so he could obtain her views on these events as well. 'We wonder what Princess Mathilde's reaction will be?'

Something in Count Gaston's expression when the chancellor raised his eyes again caused King Charles a spurt of concern.

'Did you say "will be," Sire?' the count inquired.

'*Ciertamente.*'

'Have you not heard the news?' The sombre note in Count Gaston's voice matched his expression.

'What news?' King Charles was alarmed now.

'Princess Mathilde is dead.'

'No . . . o . . . o!' King Charles held back the animal cry of anguish that nearly escaped him. Nostrils dilating with the effort, he half rose, struggling for control before speaking. 'We had not received the news,' he finally said, flopping back on his seat. 'This is so . . . so sudden. How did it happen?' His voice was hoarse with emotion.

'As I have been told, the princess suffered a heart attack shortly after we returned to Pamplona and I had left again with the advance guard of Your Majesty's army group.'

'A terrible, terrible loss.' That was King Charles's eulogy.

'Indeed, Your Majesty.'

There was no one now. King Charles had shared his very soul with Princess Mathilde since he was a little boy. No one else knew him. She had plotted for him, placed him on the throne, guided him . . . He was a little boy lost once more. How dared she leave him?

Long moments of abject misery elapsed before his natural aggressiveness reasserted itself, as it had always done even during his boyhood. Fuck it all, he would find someone to replace Princess Mathilde. Even as the determination surfaced, light dawned on King Charles as if bright sunshine had instantly replaced a black, bleak night. He clicked mental fingers. That was it. Princess Beatrice would be the replacement. She would become his soulmate. He would woo her and win her for his wife. It would not only be a far, far better relationship than he had known with Princess Mathilde, for after all Princess Beatrice was the daughter of Maria de Padilla who had reformed King Pedro and been all things to him, but it would also provide him, King Charles, with the most direct route to the throne of Castile, as Princess Mathilde had planned.

How could he mourn Princess Mathilde's death when it paved the way to his future without any possible emotional interruption or embarrassment? He had spared her some moments of memory. It was enough. He would now proceed with his own life. He never took the time to think of God, or even to wonder whether God existed, but Princess Mathilde's death at this time had surely sprung from some Divine will.

In a flash, King Charles became elated. Now it only remained for him to find Princess Beatrice by fair means or foul.

Chapter 29

With the first shock of seeing the dark eyes above the balcony wall, Prince Ahmed nearly lost his grip on the ledge. In a trice, however, he recognized the face and then he nearly let go again, this time through joy.

It was Tarif, even more wrinkled perhaps, but still his man. Tarif, the black face wreathed in a smile of recognition.

'Tarif!' he exclaimed, forgetting that he was addressing a deaf-mute. He heaved himself higher and clambered on to the balcony. A tear moistened the hand that Tarif knelt to kiss. 'How are you here at this time to greet me?' He was gesturing with quick hands now. It was like old times again.

'I knew that my lord prince would return some evening, so I have kept vigil here daily at this time. I have missed my lord.'

Prince Ahmed's eyes grew moist. 'I missed you too, my helper and friend.' He had never regarded Tarif as a servant. 'I have much to tell you, but that must wait. I presume the Gen al Arif tower is unoccupied.'

'Yes, lord.'

'And where is my teacher, Abou bon Ebben?'

'Dead.' The word was mouthed without emotion. 'He died of a heart attack in the presence of your father, the king, on the very night you left.'

The cold hand of sadness clutched at Prince Ahmed's chest, but grieving would have to wait. 'Can we talk here without fear of interruption or discovery, or should we move inside?'

'Here would be better, lord.'

'My father was murdered, was he not?'

Tarif nodded slowly.

'Who was responsible?'

'The common talk is that it was at the instigation of Prime Minister Farouk Riswan.' Tarif paused, seemed to make a decision. 'You too could be in danger, lord, now that you are back. These are evil men.'

'I know.' Prince Ahmed began probing for information, knowing that Tarif's replies would be honest. He discovered that Prince Saad now occupied the palace, where Farouk Riswan spent most of his time from early morning till late at night, governing Granada from behind the scenes, slowly eliminating the conservatives who had demanded a customary succession.

'Even though you are in grave danger, your return is most timely for our kingdom, lord,' Tarif finally ended.

'Only if my plan succeeds.' He eyed Tarif compellingly, reached out a hand to grip one bony shoulder beneath the white robe. 'There are groups in the capital then who are loyal to the true succession and must hate the new regime?'

'Of course, lord.'

'Who is their leader – I mean the strongest, the most resolute man?'

'Captain Husain of the First Cavalry Regiment. Your royal father trusted him so well that he selected the captain to pursue you and Prince Juan on the night you escaped.'

'Where does Captain Husain live?'

'In the Alcazaba, the palace barracks. His regiment has retained the honour of providing the palace guard. As a matter of fact, he is on duty in the palace this very evening.'

Prince Ahmed's pulses quickened. Almighty Allah was surely on his side. 'No one in the palace, except for those

540

who served in the Gen al Arif, knows me by sight. Even Prince Saad and Farouk Riswan have never seen me, nor has Captain Husain. How can I convince the captain of my identity?'

'I shall vouch for you, lord, as will certain others of your household who were loyal to your father and will be loyal to you.' He glanced down at Prince Ahmed's right hand and his face brightened. 'Besides, you are wearing the royal ring.'

Prince Ahmed had forgotten about the signet bearing the family seal of the Nasrids which his father had sent him on his thirteenth birthday. Yet his whole future and that of Granada might depend on the word of a deaf-mute palace servant. How ironic. 'I thank you, Tarif, and I accept your offer with great humility and appreciation.' He gazed deeply into Tarif's eyes. 'I shall not forget, but how can you bring the captain here without arousing suspicion?'

Tarif's black leather cheeks creased into a smile. 'We shall use the underground passage, Prince.'

'What underground passage?'

'The Gen al Arif is connected to the main palace by a secret passage of which my lord prince was not made aware.'

'You mean there is an entrance other than the public one from the Alhambra below?'

'Yes, lord. It leads from the south side and was intended exclusively for the use of your royal father. Even Abou bon Ebben did not know of its existence. I knew of it because King Yusuf confided the secret to me in case you ever needed it.' He smiled. 'Your royal father was right!'

'He never used the passage,' Prince Ahmed could not help interjecting bitterly.

'I am sorry,' Tarif gestured, his dark eyes filling with tears.

Prince Ahmed reached out to clap his hand on a bony shoulder. 'You should not be, my friend. I merely did not know a father, whereas you lost your voice, your hearing and your manhood and the architect and others who built the underground passage lost their lives at my father's command so they would not betray the secret.' He paused, his gorge rising, and began to shake his head as the conclusion dawned on him. 'All for me,' he whispered, fighting back tears of horror. 'So much cruelty, so many lives, to keep me in ignorance of love and make me a worthy heir.'

Tarif had departed to find Captain Husain after assuring Prince Ahmed that no one would venture into his former quarters. The knowledge of how many had suffered for him had brought an inflexible resolve that he would not betray his people. He would prove himself a worthy heir.

He became charged with excitement, though some fear intruded as he wandered slowly from room to room, nostalgically pausing at a painting here, an ornament there. The musk-scented lamps, which were never extinguished even by day, remained lit, so he was able to see everything even after the dark shadows of evening started to lengthen outside. Everything was as he had left it, down to the manuscripts in his study and the writing materials on his desk.

Through all his fear and apprehension, Prince Ahmed began to experience relief at being back in clean, comfortable quarters, combined with a sense of having returned at last to where he really belonged. He could only hope that Princess Beatrice, Prince Juan, Aaron Levi and Zurika were not being exposed to discomfort on their way to Granada, which they should reach shortly. If they were in the city already, they could wait for him to surface publicly before declaring themselves.

His steps were eventually drawn to the window of his

study from where he had first seen Zurika dance. The flat slab of black rock was empty, the mountains far beyond them purple beneath a rosy pink haze of sunset skies. Doves cooed from dark cypress branches beneath him, the sound melding with a breeze that soughed through the leaves. What had his vision of an hour ago meant? The question was swept aside by thoughts of Princess Beatrice. It was in these very quarters that he had first beheld the miniature painting of her. It would not be long now before she would be alone with him in this very room and at this very time of day, gazing at this very view. Or into each other's eyes? He actually trembled at the prospect.

He sat at his former desk facing the doorway of the study and waited. Almost one hour passed and night had fallen before he heard the click of the entrance doors and the duet of clicking riding boots and padding sandals on the marble floors. He stood up, stepped away from the desk and drew his sword, just in case.

The man who stood at the open doorway was surely Captain Husain. Noting Prince Ahmed's naked blade, a glint of amusement crossed his cleancut face. He was a fine figure of a man, of commanding personality and haughty demeanour. Well over middle height, with broad chest, wide shoulders and narrow waist, his body seemed to have been poured into his red cavalry tunic and tight white pantaloons, making the great curved scimitar in its silver sheath at his side seem an ornament rather than a weapon. His features were regular, with a fine straight nose, beetling black eyebrows, trim moustache and no beard. His olive-skinned cheeks, the right bearing the scar of a sabre nick, were contoured tight, the chin cleft. His eyes beneath the red fez with a small plume on the right side were brown and penetrating. He stood at the doorway, surveying Prince Ahmed keenly, making no attempt either to greet him or to enter.

Finally he seemed satisfied. 'At least you look like a

prince,' he stated flatly. 'If you really are, you can assume that I am addressing you as Your Royal Highness.'

Prince Ahmed was amazed at the greeting, but pleasantly amused as well. This was a strong man, a man of steely courage, one whom he instinctively trusted. 'At least you look like a cavalry captain,' he retorted, smiling. 'If you really are half the man my royal father obviously thought you to be, you can assume that I shall bestow many a title on you!'

White teeth flashed as the fine lips parted in a smile before the chin was lifted in a laugh that bellowed through the room. 'At least you have a royally high wit,' the captain riposted. 'That is a saving grace even if you are an imposter.'

'Come in and sit down, Captain,' Prince Ahmed invited, indicating a gilt ottoman at the side of the desk. He glanced at Tarif, hovering in the outer room. 'You may close the door and wait outside,' he gestured the deaf-mute.

'You summoned me,' Captain Husain stated when the door had clicked behind Tarif and they were seated. 'I do not wish to be guilty of treason, you understand?'

'Perfectly.'

'For that reason and with no disrespect, I need to ask you many questions in order to satisfy myself as to your identity. More important than the question of treason is the security of the country. If you are indeed Prince Ahmed, we can look to a better future and I shall serve you with my life if need be, but if you are an imposter . . .' The glint in the brown eyes, hard as tourmalines, spoke more than words.

'I respect you for that. You may ask me any questions you like. I welcome them. Let me, however, first establish good faith.' He raised his right hand, middle finger extended. 'This gold ring bears our family seal. It was sent me by the late King Yusuf, the father I do not ever

544

recall seeing, on my thirteenth birthday. Tarif will remember.'

Captain Husain squared his shoulders. 'First, would you briefly tell me the story of your life from your earliest recollections until this moment?'

Prince Ahmed gave him such details as he felt would establish his claim, omitting only the sexual parts, but including the seance with Pilar, Zurika's dancing and the tourney. His listener proved attentive as a hawk above prey, displaying a flicker of interest only when Prince Ahmed told of the final cause of his rebellion, being bred to war and trained to battle but unable to ride with the troops when the trumpets sounded for the foray into Castile. The questions Captain Husain asked were designed to check details, about Abou bon Ebben, the other tutors, the layout of the Gen al Arif tower and especially the events on the night of the flight from Granada, with some of which he was familiar from the briefing given him by the king. They revealed a tough, incisive mind, leaving Prince Ahmed with a curious feeling of uncertainty and discomfort. His whole future was in this man's hands.

It took over an hour before they both relapsed into a thoughtful silence echoed by the quiet around them. Captain Husain seemed to be studying the carpet. Finally he raised level eyes at Prince Ahmed. 'I accept your identity,' he declared. 'What are your orders, Your Royal Highness?'

'Can you find ten officers in your regiment who would be fearless and resolute in implementing a plan of action I have conceived?' Thanks were not necessary with this man.

'Yes. And many others besides.'

'And these men would follow their orders without question?'

'To the death.' The brown eyes flashed, the dimpled

chin jutted out resolutely. 'We are the First Cavalry Regiment, the King's Own. We have been without a king for too long.'

A thrill of exultation ran through Prince Ahmed. He leaned forward, elbows on the table. 'Here then is the plan.' Even as he outlined it, he realized that Captain Husain's simple, direct request for orders had been a test. The cavalryman would have hesitated to give even the legal heir to the throne his support unless he was convinced that the claimant was not depending on others to hoist him to the throne.

As he proceeded, he detected Captain Husain's increasing interest even though there were no visible signs of it. 'Do you have any questions?' he finally inquired.

'None whatever, Your Royal Highness.' Prince Ahmed noted the repeat of his title with relief. 'It is an excellent plan, lucidly presented, which I will work with you to implement.'

'Would you tell me now the names of the other principal officers who will join us?'

Captain Husain ran a thumbnail beneath his black moustache. 'The most important of all is Colonel Ismail, who commands the First Cavalry Regiment.'

A thrill, this time of hope, went through Prince Ahmed again. 'That would ensure for us the loyalty of the entire regiment?'

'Absolutely. We also have Major Raschid the second-in-command and Lieutenant Wahid our crack squadron commander. The rest of the group of ten will be sergeants.'

'Good.'

'When do you desire to put the plan into operation?'

'Tonight.'

They had discussed a hasty departure with Mother Euphrasia. They did not want her to have to tell any more lies, so informed her that while Prince Juan was in the city that afternoon he had run across a group of people from Toledo, one of whom was known to him, who were travelling to Cordoba well before dawn the next day. Rather than inconvenience the nuns by leaving at such an awkward hour, they would spend the night at the residence of people known to another of the group and proceed with them.

Mother Euphrasia appeared to believe their story, but a fleeting expression in her eyes convinced Princess Beatrice that she did not. After an early supper, they parted from the sympathetic Mother and the other nuns on the most affectionate terms.

The ancient lodgekeeper was out, so Princess Beatrice used the lodge to disguise herself as a boy, wearing one of Prince Juan's black tunics, with white nether-hosen, her hair coiled up beneath a cap. 'You look such a pretty boy,' Prince Juan had gestured, smiling. 'Especially now that your sunburn from the *meseta* has peeled off!'

Having secured their horses, they rode openly through Jaén at dusk along the highway to Granada. Princess Beatrice had found the convent to be a sanctuary. Now she was back again in the turmoil of life symbolized by jostling crowds, loud voices, the shouts of vendors, raucous laughter, creaking wagons and the clippety-clop of horses' hooves. It was the city's noisome smell, however, especially the acrid odours of urine and sweat from human bodies that triggered off a return of fear and horror. The recollection of the rape suddenly became vivid in her mind as if a window had been flung open. She closed her eyes in an effort to shut out the images, but they would not go away. Hard put to it to stifle a scream, her fingers tightened instinctively on the reins. The horse jerked its head and took off down the street, scattering screaming people in its path. Princess Beatrice lost the reins, but the sudden movement wiped out the ghastly image in sufficient time for her to grasp the martingale strap and prevent herself from falling off. The horse lengthened its stride, while the princess reached for the reins again, dimly aware that Prince Juan was following. Having regained the reins, she quickly brought her mount under control again. Breathless with fear and from the sudden exertion, she reined in the horse, glancing ahead of her through the red-gold torchlight. Two approaching horsemen had halted, obviously to avoid her approach. The entire scene around her, the crowds, the wagons, the shouts melted. Her attention focused only on one of them, the bull-like face of King Charles the Bad, her rapist.

The arrival of Count Gaston with the report that his army was in place, combined with advance information that the Portuguese force was expected to reach the Granada border the next day, had put King Pedro in excellent spirits. The situation had called for a celebration in his dining pavilion, where he and King Charles usually supped together. He had invited Bishop Eulogius, to whom he had given no indication of his true feelings regarding the duplicity the bishop had practised on him in regard to the gypsy girl and the Jew, and Count Gaston to attend.

The pavilion, lined with pink silk and lit by two crystal oil lamps hanging from the centre pole, was luxuriously furnished, with a huge red and white Flemish carpet on the worn grass, a refectory table of polished oakwood and heavy oak settles. The table was laden with silver dishes containing capon pasties, rissoles made of shredded figs, almonds, pears, dates, dried ling and haddock, lenten *ryschewys*, beef marrow fritters and miniature pastries of cod's liver. The odours of the roasts and spices were most enticing. King Pedro, seated facing the entrance to the tent, was dressed in brown, Count Gaston in his customary white sat on his left, the purple-robed Bishop Eulogius at his right.

King Pedro glanced at the sand-clock on the oak side-board. 'Our brother King Charles is late,' he observed, nodding towards the open entrance. Through it, he could see some of his troops, who, having had their dinner, were seated in knots around the plain. Despite the summer heat, one group had built a campfire. A guitar strummed, a high tenor voice was raised in song.

> 'O young jealous girl of my soul
> You make music of light and of darkness
> Stand closer, so close by my side
> Then stand completely within me . . .'

The music was so clear in the hush of dusk that King Pedro imagined it wafting up to the deep blue sky, pricked by the first stars, on its way to heaven.

'No matter, this excellent Cadiz sherry-wine shall be our consolation.' He seized his silver goblet and drank deeply, explaining, 'A mere sip will hardly compensate for the absence of our brother!' He wiped his mouth with no more apology for his lack of grace towards a wine that should have been sipped. Fuck that anyway, he thought silently and pleasantly. I do not drink wine for its taste or flavour, but because I enjoy what it makes me feel, though tomorrow morning could be another matter.

'Surely it is the imbibing of good wine that matters,' Bishop Eulogius commented in sycophantic tones, 'not the method of doing it.'

'A blessed sacrament?' Count Gaston queried, an ironic glint in his dark eyes.

'Ah, sacrilege!' the bishop retorted, raising pudgy hands in mock horror and sipping his own wine to allay it.

'No more sacrilege than worshipping good wine, Your Eminence,' Count Gaston retorted.

King Pedro guffawed. He smacked the table with an open palm, rattling the goblets. 'Well put, Chancellor.' As always, he liked this man, especially for taking on pimps like the primate bishop, apart from his own king. He grew serious in an instant. 'We had hoped to discuss the timing of our advance on Granada with our brother,' he added, deliberately changing the subject so he could discuss the move while he was still sober. 'Do you know your master's whereabouts, Count?'

'No, Sire, but I understand that he left the encampment on horseback with his aide-de-camp, without giving any explanation.'

'Probably gone to one of the bawdy houses in the city,' King Pedro conjectured. 'He could easily have a wench from our comfort corps brought to his pavilion, but he probably needs a change.' He reflected a moment. 'Well, if that is the case, he might be gone till dawn. Since you are in command of the Navarrese army group, Chancellor, can you not speak for your king?'

'I believe so, Your Majesty.'

'When is the earliest that your forces can be ready to advance?'

'They are ready, Sire. Our advance elements are on notice to commence moving within an hour of receiving orders.'

'Good.' King Pedro had been getting bored with the inactivity in Jaén. What no one other than Ruy de Vivar knew was that he was also awaiting confirmation from the Prime Minister of Granada that the borders would not be defended against his advance, word of which he had received that very afternoon. He wanted to end the campaign quickly, take over Granada and return to his Maria in Toledo, or better still, have her join him in the Alhambra palace. He had received a most loving letter from Maria only that morning, confirming his own view that nothing and no one should come between them. The promise of a visit to the Alhambra would be a fitting reward to her for the reconciliation. 'Who will give the order?' He already knew.

'My king, of course, but I assume that I will carry his word to Cordoba.'

They discussed plans for the move of the two armies, liaison between them and the final encirclement of the Moorish capital. 'Our spies report that the ruling clique in Granada has made no moves to assemble their forces and advance,' King Pedro continued. 'We believe they will accept a siege of the capital, hoping for help from their brotherhood in North Africa. How long would it take you to get back to your headquarters, Chancellor?'

'Two nights and three days, Sire.'

'When can you leave?'

'At first light tomorrow.'

King Pedro rubbed his palms together. 'Excellent. We shall commence our own move four days from now, at dawn. Since it appears unlikely that the Moors will risk open battle with us, the arrival of our combined forces outside the walls of Granada need not be perfectly coordinated.' He raised his goblet. 'Here's to hellfire and damnation to our enemies,' he cried.

'Here's to victory for Reconquista!' Bishop Eulogius echoed lifting his own goblet.

'To the triumph of righteousness!' Count Gaston toasted.

From as far back as he could remember, Charles the Bad had been given to acting on impulse, which was why he had so frequently been disciplined by his mother. As he trotted his black horse beside Colonel de Villa's bay, heading for Jaén through the gloom of night, Charles the Bad knew he was doing it again. Act like a prince and you will end up a king, Queen Joanna used to admonish him. His reaction, even as a little boy, had been, what good is acting like anything, when I am not a mummer but a prince? All I want is to be *me*. As a bigger boy, after he had learned swear words, he used to think, often savagely, fuck that and fuck you too, *Madre*.

No sooner had he determined, during his conversation with Count Gaston, that he would win Princess Beatrice for his wife, than he also decided to leave that very night for the cottage where he had raped her, without divulging what he was about to anyone except his aide-de-camp, Colonel de Villa, who would accompany him once again. The huge cavalry colonel was the only person he trusted for this kind of mission. His absence from the camp would be noted by King Pedro only when he failed to turn up for dinner. A king, least of all a guest king, did not ride off into the darkness on his own, but he cared not a fuck for that. He was Charles the Bad, his own man, acting like himself. He had tried to follow the demands of protocol as a guest in the Toledo palace, but it had been tiresome and life on a campaign should certainly not make such demands. If it did, well, fuck that too!

He had commanded his attendants to bring him and Colonel de Villa some food and wine from the officers' mess tent, since it could turn out to be a late night, also two unlit oil lanterns. He did not quite know what he would find in the cottage, apart from a couple of rotting corpses which were probably still where they had been left, or where else he would pursue his quest, but the cottage was the logical place to begin.

Colonel de Villa, a huge figure towering on his left with the two lanterns hung across his saddle, had the password so that they would have no trouble getting back into the camp. By the time they left the campfires behind them and trotted towards Jaén, the lights of the city were glowing in the blackness beneath a deep blue sky. The air was clear, but the warmth of the day hung over the earth. The highway was practically deserted at this hour except for some pedestrians who would get into the town through the 'needle' gate.

The colonel had previously obtained a pass from the chief police officer in Jaén for the *Hermandad* confederation of towns to which Jaén belonged and they had no trouble having the main gates opened by the police sentry to let them through.

'Entering a town at night reminds me of walking into a house from desolate darkness,' King Charles confided to the colonel as they trotted up the flare-lit main street. He needed to make conversation to keep eagerness for the success of this mission from affecting his mind.

If Colonel de Villa was surprised at the somewhat poetic turn of speech, he gave no indication of it. King Charles knew him to be a laconic man of action, more endowed with loyalty than with imagination. True to form, he merely inquired, 'Why, Your Majesty?'

'It was dark and almost deserted on the highway outside the gates. Here, the streets are lit with flares and with the glow-falls of lamplight from open doors or windows. Note the crowds: the gaily dressed are those on a festive evening, the more homely attire is that of people heading back to their hearths and kitchens, all of them a diverse family.' He nodded towards the dark figure of a man emerging from a tavern on pliant knees. 'See, we even have the family drunk. And look at those women in their black outfits and white *mantillas* hurrying for their visit to the church confessional after having served supper to their own families.'

'I see, Your Majesty.' It was obvious that Colonel de Villa did not see.

Nor for that matter did King Charles himself find the simile appropriate any longer. 'Jaén is laid out in four squares, like most other cities,' he observed, deliberately changing the subject as they passed the street of eating houses, branching out of the highway to their right. He could see the fires above which roast fowl and pork slow-turned on spits. Surely the succulent aroma reaching his nostrils, through the stench of sewers and rotting garbage, signified home, but what did he, a king, know of homes, having lived in a palace all his life? Yet King Charles was enjoying the informality of the outing so much that he had to resist the urge to dismount and stroll with the crowds.

They were riding so purposefully that pedestrians, mostly vague figures with faces in shadows, kept skipping out of their way. The diversity of races was greater here than in Pamplona, with more Moors in their fez caps, Jews with black *yarmulke* and foreigners. King Charles could not help noting a giant Nubian, dressed in a gaudy robe of bright green with a gold border, incongruous against his black skin. The man walked alone, though he was loaded with gleaming gold necklaces, his sheer bulk obviously a defence against footpads.

A small convoy of three rattling carriages led by footmen carrying flares crossed them, heading from the centre of town. A wealthy family out for a formal occasion, he conjectured. Ordinary people leading ordinary lives. He could appreciate them objectively, but he needed more than an ordinary life. They rode through the main square, thronged with people, the town hall to their left, the church with its prominent cross a dark silhouette against the night sky, to the right.

'This is where the *auto-da-fé* was held, Sire,' Colonel de Villa volunteered, breaking his silence.

'Did you attend?'

'No, Sire.' The colonel's tone expressed his disapproval of the event more forcefully than words.

Beyond the square, the highway narrowed somewhat, but they were followed by the hub-bub of voices. A clatter of approaching hooves on cobblestones rang above the din, heading straight towards them. A horse and rider were approaching them at speed, between pedestrians who were leaping out of the way. King Charles's hand instinctively reached for his sword hilt.

'A runaway horse, Sire!' The colonel exclaimed, reining his mount slightly to the left.

King Charles automatically followed suit. The rider quick-clopped past a golden flare. King Charles's eyes fell on a youthful face partly shadowed by a cowl. For an instant they looked into terrified eyes. 'Godsbody!' he growled. 'Why do these young people not learn to ride before they take a horse onto busy streets? It's like mounting a woman before you know how to fuck.'

The horse was, however, slowly being brought under control, without any assistance from another cowled horseman who had been closely following the runaway. 'They need no help from us,' he added. 'Let us press on, for we have more important work to do.

As they trotted past the two riders, something began to gnaw at King Charles. He tried to identify it, but in vain. It was over half an hour later, when they were outside the town once more, heading along the dark highway towards the cottage, that the truth hit him in a blinding white flash. The eyes of the young man on the runaway horse! They were not those of a young man, but of a woman.

He wheeled his mount around. 'Follow me!' he shouted to the colonel. Digging fierce heels into the black's flanks, he galloped back towards the city.

Where could Princess Beatrice have stayed since he left her at the cottage? The question flailed at King Charles the Bad's brain as he sped back to Jaén through the dark. It must have been in the town, because she could not have entered Jaén on horseback after dark. The cowled horseman following her was surely Prince Juan. Where was Prince Ahmed? God, how he hated that fucking Moor, hated him so much that he could feel his hands around the Moor's neck, squeezing, squeezing, watching the frightened eyes pop out, then slicing away the genitals so the bastard knew what had happened before he died.

Where were brother and sister heading? Was it to some place in town, or were they leaving it? The guards at the gates would open them for anyone wishing to leave the town, entry alone required a pass. He could easily check with the sentries when he reached the northern gate as to whether a man and a woman on horseback had left. A flash question intruded. Could the horseman accompanying Princess Beatrice have been Prince Ahmed? King Charles doubted it. The assassins had made no mention of a Moor being in the party. Since the gypsy girl and the Jew had been captured and executed, it had to be Prince Juan. Where to find his quarry? He wished he had Princess Mathilde to advise him, but she was dead.

Questions kept scraping King Charles's brain raw even after the northern gates creaked shut behind him after their re-entry to the town. Where to find . . .? He concentrated on the single question as they started trotting down the highway . . . and stopped abruptly as the logical answer struck him with hammer force. He clicked mental fingers. Princess Beatrice had spoken of entering a convent just before he fucked her. A Christian girl seeking refuge would turn to a convent. There was only one convent in Jaén, of the Benedictine order. Facts came rushing into place. He recalled King Pedro mentioning this convent in passing as one of the institutions which his mistress, Maria de Padilla, supported due to some family connection with the Mother Superior.

As luck would have it, just at that moment a citizen police patrol of two uniformed men, carrying stout staffs, emerged from a side street. 'Ask them the way to the Benedictine Convent,' he directed Colonel de Villa.

* * *

Captain Husain returned to the study in the Gen al Arif accompanied by three officers, whom he had obviously convinced that the man he was taking them to was indeed Prince Ahmed, heir to the throne. He introduced each of them in turn. Colonel Ismail, a trim, bird-like man, with alert black eyes straddling a small, beaked nose, a grizzled beard and the slightly bowed legs of the life-long cavalry man, was obviously accustomed to command. Major Raschid and Lieutenant Wahid might have been twins, both being fair-skinned, burly men with round faces, bristling, black moustaches and grey-green eyes. Captain Husain had assured Prince Ahmed that, to avoid any risk of attracting attention, he had not brought the sergeants, but they were standing by to follow orders.

Sitting at his old desk in the study in the golden glow of sandalwood perfumed lamplight, Prince Ahmed was experiencing a curious division of reality between the past many years when he was a student prince seated at this very desk, in bondage, and the present when he was freely conspiring to overthrow an existing regime. The desk at which he sat facing the officers occupying settles drawn up immediately opposite him was a sort of physical link between past and present.

'I regret I cannot offer you any refreshment, gentlemen,' Prince Ahmed stated after the usual pleasantries were ended. He smiled faintly. 'But as you have gathered, I am somewhat restricted in my ability to play the host tonight.' His gaze swept each one of them in turn. 'I am looking to you to rectify that omission, so you can be assured of such courtesies in the future!'

He could tell from the expressions on the faces of the men that he had struck the right note, a touch of levity instead of the smother of fierce exhortations. It had come out naturally, but he made a mental note to use the technique in future. 'I am assuming that you are satisfied as to my identity and my rightful claim to the throne of

Granada, else you would only be here to arrest me.' He smiled, then quickly sobered. 'Our country faces more than a crisis of succession today, it is at its most perilous moment in history.' He surveyed the men questioningly.

'Agreed, Your Royal Highness,' Colonel Ismail commented. 'According to my reports, the Castilian army will soon leave Jaén. Meanwhile our rulers have done nothing except send a feeble plea to Morocco for the help promised your royal father under different circumstances. All of us here are convinced that the present regime in our kingdom has made a pact with King Pedro to permit him to take us over so they can rule more freely under his suzerainty than they can at present under the Council of Regency.' He glanced around him and received nods of assent.

Prince Ahmed was appalled. Such treachery? Why should he doubt it? 'Will King Abu Hasan of Morocco respond favourably to what you call a feeble plea?'

'I believe he will. As you are undoubtedly aware, the North African rulers have traditionally regarded Granada as a buffer against Christian incursions across the ocean as well as a staging post for *jihad* throughout Spain. Besides, they have past defeats to avenge.'

'I for one am certain that the emirs will help only those who organized the murder of their brother caliph,' Major Raschid interposed, 'to ensure a succession on the throne other than from your royal Nasrid dynasty. With your return, however, we have a greater assurance of support as well as continuance of the Nasrid rule, which all of us in this room are agreed is to our kingdom's advantage.'

'I thank you, gentlemen. We are indeed going to need help from our allies, though it galls us to have to seek it. The threat to Granada's borders does not come from the Castilian army alone.' Prince Ahmed deliberately kept his voice level. 'An army from León y Navarra has arrived in Cordoba. Ships from Catalonia are expected to land forces on our coast and it is possible that Portugal will attack us from the west. This is a well-planned Reconquista and we are beset on all sides.'

'Merciful Allah!' the colonel exclaimed. 'This makes double traitors of those in power here.' He paused. His black eyes glittered fiercely. 'United, we can take on all comers, however heavily outnumbered we may be, as the Holy Prophet did before us and our long line of Arab sultans, such as Yusuf ibn Ayuub, Sal-eh-din, the Conqueror.'

'You are right, Colonel,' Prince Ahmed responded. 'Like our forebears we shall look to Almighty Allah for help.' A grim note entered his voice. 'But the strength, resolution and speed of action must come from us, as Allah's instruments, all of which require strong, united leadership.'

The moment of truth had arrived. The four men looked at Prince Ahmed silently for orders. 'We must first deal with the enemy within,' Prince Ahmed asserted. 'I have first-hand evidence that Farouk Riswan had my royal father assassinated.' Why were public figures always assassinated when lesser mortals were merely murdered? 'I personally killed the man whom the Prime Minister had sent to seek me out and have me murdered because I am the legal heir.' He gave them details of his encounter with the assassin, Mizra. 'More currently, as you have implied, Colonel, the neglect of the interim government to gather intelligence as to the invaders' moves and to take effective measures to defend the country, and possibly the intent to deliver it to the enemy for their own ends, is treason.' He earnestly surveyed each one of them in turn. 'Gentlemen, I ask you what under Islamic law or the laws of any country, is the penalty for these offences?'

'Death!' they hissed in unison.

'Here then is what I propose we do.' He outlined his

559

plan, then added, 'If you do not wish to participate, you are welcome to leave and I shall not hold it against you.'

A hush fell on the room as each man pondered his role and doubtless the consequences of failure.

Captain Husain took the lead. 'I am with you, Prince. My life and fortune have always been available for Granada.' His gaze was level, the cleft chin jutted out. 'From this moment, you, my lord, are Granada.'

'I agree,' Colonel Ismail stated. He glanced questioningly at Major Raschid and Lieutenant Wahid. They both nodded. 'It is done then, Your Royal Highness. When do we commence the operation?'

Prince Ahmed rose to his feet, clapped his hand on his sword hilt in a deliberately dramatic gesture. 'Right now!'

Chapter 30

King Charles the Bad did not wish to divulge his identity and pretended to the ancient lodge-keeper of the convent gates that he and Colonel de Villa were emissaries from King Pedro.

'A fine time for anyone, least of all a king, to send emissaries, especially to a convent,' the old man quavered through the open Judas latch. 'You look more like a pair of ruffians to me. And what be the nature of your business?'

'We shall tell that to Mother Superior,' King Charles grated, holding back his temper.

'And what excuse can I give my Mother Superior for disturbing her at this hour? Shall I say that a pair of cut-throats from the street want to come in and rob her?'

'Cut-throats don't ride fine horses,' Colonel de Villa interposed soothingly. He made his horse cavort. 'See!'

'A fine show indeed,' the old man was obviously unimpressed, though perhaps a little more convinced, 'but we are not looking for circus performers tonight.'

An inspiration flashed through King Charles. 'Tell your Mother Superior that King Pedro has sent us on an urgent mission connected with the young deaf-mute man and the young woman who were in the convent several days and left tonight.'

A stunned silence told King Charles he had hit home. 'Wait outside!' The old man snapped the latch back in place. The clack of his sandalled feet receded.

They waited an impatient ten minutes before the bolts were drawn and the gates creaked open. Lantern in hand, the lodge-keeper closed the gates behind them and

561

hobbled ahead, taking his own time to reach the front doors. 'You can leave your horses here,' he said. 'Hope they don't urinate or mess the place. It's me that has to clean up.'

They were ushered into the parlour by a bustling nun in black and white habit. A petite woman also clothed in black and white introduced herself as Mother Euphrasia. She indicated two high-backed chairs across the bare flagstone floor and drew up a similar chair to sit in front of them. In the steady golden light of tapers on the wall-sconces, the mother looked clean, scrubbed pink and alert, especially for such a late hour. King Charles introduced himself as Count Charles of Huate and Colonel de Villa by his own name. Though they were alone in the room, he sensed other nuns hovering nearby.

Mother Euphrasia came directly to the point. 'To what do I owe the honour of this meeting, *señores*?'

'We are here at the command of His Majesty King Pedro to discover the whereabouts of two persons to whom you gave shelter recently,' King Charles responded.

'The convent affords shelter to many, my lord Count. It is one of our missions.'

'I am referring to a young woman and a young man from Toledo.' Noting the tiniest hardening of the blue eyes, he plunged in. 'The young man is a deaf-mute.'

'There are no such persons here.'

She was prevaricating. 'They may not be here now, but they left this evening.' King Charles could not keep the growl from his voice.

'We are not given to providing strangers with information as to our guests or wards,' Mother Euphrasia stated frostily.

'I am here on a mission for your king.' The words had a warning note. Unaccustomed to being crossed, King Charles was getting impatient with this bitch.

562

'I certainly owe allegiance to our King, my lord, but my first allegiance is to God. I belong to His estate, Holy Church.'

Mother Euphrasia's strength only infuriated King Charles. 'Have a care, madam,' he grated. 'We can have your convent taken apart and you imprisoned.'

'You may take the convent apart, but it is only a building. No one can take Holy Church apart, not even the devil. As for imprisoning me,' her smile was contemptuous, 'I am already imprisoned in the service of Our Lord.' She paused, eyed him with level blue eyes. 'Besides,' her tone became sweet, 'I doubt that your master, King Pedro, would permit such actions, especially at a time when he needs the support of Holy Church for Reconquista.' She rose to her feet. 'Under the circumstances, therefore, I see no reason for prolonging this conversation. The lodge-keeper will open the gates for you. *Buenas noches, señores.*'

King Charles was on his feet in an instant, contrite for once. There was no point in trying to intimidate this woman. He needed her, so he should woo her sympathy instead. 'I beg your pardon, Reverend Mother,' he said humbly. He held up a placatory hand. 'Please sit down and I shall tell you the truth.'

Something in his voice and expression made her resume her seat. White hands folded on the black habit, she looked at him expectantly.

He began pacing the room, conscious that he should not lose face with Colonel de Villa, but determined to do whatever was necessary to obtain the information he needed, desperately now. 'I did not wish to divulge my identity for reasons which you will find obvious. I am King Charles of León y Navarra.' He gestured towards the colonel, 'And this is my aide-de-camp.' He smiled. 'His name at least is correct.'

Mother Euphrasia betrayed no surprise, made no attempt to greet him as a king, merely waited.

He paused in front of her. 'My outburst just now,' he deliberately avoided using the royal plural, recognizing that a more personal note would better suit his purpose, 'was the product of love, which has turned a part of this mature ruler into a callow youth. Please forgive me for it.' She did not respond to his placatory grin, became more watchful. 'You are aware of the tourney held recently by King Pedro at which the prize was the hand of Princess Beatrice in marriage. I was determined to win the tourney, but at that time, the prize was merely a necessary and useful incident to me in the alliance between our two nations. Then, on the morning the tourney opened, I saw Princess Beatrice for the first time. I was immediately smitten by her beauty, her purity and obvious goodness. I fell in love for the first time in my life and have been pursuing her ever since, to the extent of accompanying my brother King Pedro with my immediate entourage on his advance against Granada, while my chancellor led my army down the western highway to Cordoba, where it is now quartered. Far from harming Princess Beatrice, it is my earnest desire to make her my queen and to nurture, cherish and protect her for the rest of my life. I love her so much that I would even ensure safe passage for her brother, Prince Juan, wherever he may wish to go, regardless of her father's wrath.'

As he went on to give her the entire story with complete frankness, her face had gradually softened. 'Your confession – it is no less, coming from a proud king – does you more honour than your earlier attitude.' She hesitated, reflecting. 'The identities of Princess Beatrice and her brother, Prince Juan, are known only to me. Everyone else in the convent believes them to be relatives of mine visiting from Toledo until the royal army moves against Granada, before proceeding to Cordoba. Since you know so much already, I might as well tell you that both of them left the convent this evening.'

'Where were they headed, Reverend Mother?'

'It would be wrong of me to divulge that to you. Even though I have not sworn to maintain secrecy, confidentiality was inherent in the grant of sanctuary to them. I hope Your Majesty will understand.'

He did not wish to understand, but he knew better than to express himself forcibly again. 'At least tell me this,' he pleaded. 'Are they headed for Granada?'

'I cannot tell you.'

'Reverend Mother,' he declared earnestly, 'do you not realize that if Princess Beatrice goes to Granada, she will be at the mercy of infidel Moors, especially Prince Ahmed, who obviously has designs on her virtue since he would never marry someone of a faith other than Islam? The princess is young and naïve. Her brother is a deaf-mute, reportedly a good Christian and therefore extending his trust even to those who maimed him for life. Help me, I beg you, to save these young people from themselves. At least tell me whether she and her brother are making for Granada, for I ask it,' he deliberately made his look reverential, 'in God's name.' Since he had no reverence in his make-up he was enjoying the feel of moulding the strong nun like clay.

Mother Euphrasia looked down for a few moments. King Charles could almost hear the thump of his heart as he waited in suspense for her reply. Finally she looked up at him. 'They are indeed going to Granada, Your Majesty.'

To Princess Beatrice's relief, the sentries at the south gates permitted her and Prince Juan to leave Jaén without asking awkward questions. Dropping her voice to sound as much like a young man's as possible without straining and giving herself away, she had explained that she and her brother lived in a villa not far from the city, had been delayed visiting relatives and must get back because her brother had suddenly lost his voice from a sore throat.

'Worst thing for a sore throat is to expose it to the night air, even in summer,' the police sergeant advised, before letting them through the gates. 'Get him home soon.'

'You have really grown up these past weeks,' Prince Juan signalled her, guiding his horse with knees alone as they walked their mounts away through the night. 'I cannot believe that you are the sister I knew in the Toledo palace, leading such a protected, secluded existence.'

'When one is confronted by life and especially by the evil it contains, one either grows up or perishes,' she responded soberly.

Her words released the horror of the rape again in her mind. As she fought to overcome it, Prince Juan drew his mount close enough to enable him to reach out and grasp her hand. You are such a sensitive soul, my brother, you know what I am feeling. The perception comforted and strengthened her.

Prince Juan had spent a lot of time in Jaén scouting the dispositions of the Castilian army. Having also located and studied maps of the region in the town hall, he now took the lead in directing their horses east in order to skirt the eastern flank of the army before crossing the Granada border, then heading west for the highway again. The region had been notorious for bandits, but he had been advised that the presence of the Castilian army had driven them away.

A huge, pale yellow moon arose about an hour before midnight to light their way through the lonely, barren countryside.

One hour before midnight, which was the time for changing the palace guard, Tarif, carrying the lantern he had used to guide the officers to the Gen al Arif, led Prince

Ahmed, Colonel Ismail, Major Raschid, Captain Husain and Lieutenant Wahid through the trap door at the south-eastern end of the Gen al Arif on the long walk along the secret tunnel. The air was dank and foetid, the gloom so overpowering that the lantern illuminated only a small radius around it. The flight of slithery steps leading down below the ravine seemed endless to Prince Ahmed. It forcibly reminded him of the tunnel below the Toledo palace to the ladies' chambers, which Prince Juan and he had negotiated to reach Princess Beatrice. Had that been a lifetime ago? Where were his beloved princess and his dear friends? He resolutely cast thoughts of them aside to concentrate on his immediate purpose as they proceeded cautiously downwards in single file. The air became colder, closer and more humid. The only sounds in the chilling silence were the pad of their footsteps and the occasional squeak of a rat.

After what seemed an age, the steps ended and they proceeded at a quicker pace. The sounds of their breathing interspersed the skittering of tiny feet racing ahead of them, the squelch of an occasional small skeleton and the dreadful stench of rodent fur, rotting flesh and defecation, the only difference from the Toledo tunnel being the absence of Prince Juan and the acrid odour of the flaming torch. Prince Juan had been the flaming torch that guided him to the radiance of Princess Beatrice, Prince Ahmed reflected poetically. The tunnel had not been used for years and he resolved to remove some of its veil of secrecy and have it thoroughly cleaned and provide it with better lighting. Palace tunnels were always useful escape routes from invaders, especially for women and children.

It was nearly midnight when they started to climb interminable steps again and finally stood before the secret door at the northwest side of the Alhambra palace.

The moment of truth had arrived. Prince Ahmed's

heart began to thump in his chest. Just ahead of him lay glory or death.

It was midnight before King Pedro staggered through the pale yellow moonlight to his sleeping pavilion adjoining the dining tent. Bishop Eulogius had begged to be excused two hours earlier, but Count Gaston, steady on his feet, though having matched King Pedro drink for drink, was escorting him. The sounds of the camp had died down, but drunk though he was, King Pedro could feel the remains of its vibrance, like the continued hiss of flares after their flames had been extinguished.

He paused at the open entrance flap of his sleeping pavilion. His personal attendant, old Sanchez, having nudged two pageboys who were sleeping on the rug awake, came solicitously forward, made obeisance. King Pedro waved him back with an impatient hand. He turned round to face Count Gaston, noted through a half-haze that the hatchet face seemed softer in the moonshade. 'Your m-master h . . . has . . . has not returned ash yet,' he observed. 'We hope no . . . hic! . . . harm hash come to him.'

'Never fear, my lord,' Count Gaston replied confidently. 'King Charles is very capable of looking after himself.'

'Ish he often given . . .' He belched royally, grinned. 'Brought back the good taste of food,' he commented.

'A belch is not to be sneezed at, Sire?' The count's black beard and moustache parted in a grin.

King Pedro slapped a huge thigh, laughed uproariously. 'We like your wit, Count Gashton. You should join our Court as Shan . . . Shan . . .,' unable to mouth the word he gave up, 'join our Court and . . .'

The sound of hooves pad-pounding on dirt interrupted him. He gazed in the direction of the sound. Two horsemen materialized through the flare-light of the avenue that had been created to serve the royal pavilions.

Count Gaston's keen eyes quickly identified the riders. 'Ah! It is my royal master. Returning safely from the hunt, Your Majesty, as I said he would.'

Before grooms rushing up as if they had been awake for the event could help the riders to dismount, both men swung off their sweating horses. The grooms led the mounts away.

King Charles lumbered up to them. 'Our dear brother and our chancellor have lain awake for our return! How thoughtful!'

'On the contrary, we are only here at the end of our dinner chay . . . chalebration,' King Pedro responded, still sore at the lack of consideration on King Charles's part. He was not so drunk that he could forget the possible consequences of any harm having come to the ruler of the adjoining kingdom. 'You mished . . . mished a great meal and shplendid wine which comforted us so much we did not mish . . . miss you.'

'Ho! ho! ho!' King Charles pointed a finger in King Pedro's direction. 'Our brother is witty even at midnight.' His face grew serious. 'It is fortunate that Your Majesty is awake and in full possession of his faculties at this hour. We only left your gracious presence so unceremoniously because we had word of the fugitives.' He paused, scanning King Pedro's face for a reaction.

He got it. 'Godsbody!' King Pedro swore, vaguely conscious that he was using King Charles's favourite expletive. 'Where? When? How? Where are they?'

'We have no information as to the whereabouts of the Moorish bastard, but your son and daughter left Jaén tonight, heading for Granada.'

King Pedro was so stunned that he became sober on the instant. 'How do you know this?' he demanded.

'Our sources must remain confidential for the present,

569

Your Majesty, because we have sworn not to reveal them, but we verified from the *Hermandad* police sentries at the south gate of Jaén that Prince Juan and Princess Beatrice passed through on horseback about three hours ago. We pursued them along the highway for about ten miles, but they seem to have vanished into the *meseta*.'

King Pedro instinctively looked towards the figure towering behind King Charles, Colonel de Villa, as he knew the man to be. The aide-de-camp nodded verification respectfully, a certain stiffness suggesting that his king's word needed no corroboration. 'Well, our brother king,' King Pedro said at last, after innumerable questions, 'let us find these runaways and, if you are of the same mind, you shall have our daughter's hand in marriage.'

'Nothing would please us more.'

King Pedro was amazed at the earnestness in King Charles's voice. This man with as great a reputation for badness as he himself had for cruelty must be really in love with his daughter. What did he see in the young woman? Did she seem more desirable because she had slipped through his hands? How could he, King Pedro, turn this to his own use? He grew thoughtful. 'We might even have a change of heart about our son, Prince Juan,' he volunteered, testing.

'Why, Your Majesty?'

The sharpness of King Charles's voice brought King Pedro back from the euphoric world of romantic love to the stark reality of political ambition. King Charles had betrayed himself by the single question. He did not want Prince Juan to succeed to the throne of Castile and might even kill Prince Juan to prevent it. 'A Christian prince could act as an adviser to you and our daughter when you succeed us on the throne.'

'If we marry your daughter, Count Gaston will remain our adviser, so have no fears on that score, Your Majesty.

You may not be as ready as we are to forgive Prince Juan the dreadful humiliation he has heaped on Your Majesty.'

You are a cunning bastard, King Pedro reflected. 'A good choice,' he conceded aloud.

'We now request Your Majesty's approval to ride on for Granada posthaste to capture the fugitives before they reach Alhambra.'

'We have planned to move four days from now, after Count Gaston has had time to join Your Majesty's army corps in Cordoba,' King Pedro protested, quite sober now, his speech no longer slurred.

'We recommend riding for Granada ahead of the armies, Your Majesty.'

'You would ride alone?' It might not be such a bad idea for King Charles to ride on ahead, King Pedro reflected, for the border would not be denied him, but a suitable escort would be essential.

'Indeed we would, Sire, but our plan is to send our aide-de-camp, Colonel de Villa, post-haste to Cordoba to alert our army group to advance immediately, so that Count Gaston may accompany us on this vital mission.'

King Pedro glanced at Count Gaston. The hatchet face was impassive. 'You should take an escort,' he suggested.

'We are hoping that Your Majesty will detail a hundred men from one of your cavalry regiments to accompany us.'

'An excellent idea! When will you leave?'

'At dawn.'

As he had planned, Prince Ahmed entered the private audience hall of the Alhambra palace alone, without knocking, shortly after midnight. To his intense relief, the passage from the exit door of the tunnel, along the lamplit verandahs and hallways, to the private audience chamber had been almost ceremonial, because of Colonel Ismail's presence. Guards saluted deferentially, even if they wondered what the Colonel was doing in the palace at that hour of the night.

The Colonel, Major Raschid, Captain Husain and Lieutenant Wahid had immediately sent for the six sergeants to report to the huge entrance foyer of the king's quarters, known as Mirador de la Daraxa, without delay. They had arrived at the double from the Alcazaba within ten minutes, giving Prince Ahmed time to survey the Mirador, which he was seeing for the first time. This was a long, narrow, rectangular room with a circular foyer that gave entrance to the complex of gardens and buildings known as the Gardens of Daraxa, the living quarters of the palace, including the harem. He had been told by Abou bon Ebben, who had often described the palace to him, that this complex led to the tower of the Peinador de la Reina overlooking the valley of the Darro, where his mother had once lived. That tower had been kept unoccupied by his father, who had frequently wandered through the empty rooms in memory of his dead love. Such deep sentiment. Why would such a man ignore his living son who occupied another tower just across the ravine? The unasked question, as always, hurt and still baffled Prince Ahmed.

The Mirador was an exquisitely decorated chamber, with wide arched windows on one side overlooking the gardens and apartments below. Its walls had lofty arches above the windows as well, soaring to the high cupola, with painted carvings beneath each arch backgrounded by intricately patterned wooden fretwork. The panelled walls were a mosaic of blues, greens and red with white borders. Intricate poetic inscriptions of Arabic script lined each projecting column. The white flagstone floors were patterned to look like marble and were covered by huge Persian carpets of colours matching the mosaics. Ivory and gold ornaments enriched every niche and alcove, chaste in the golden light from the crystal lamps exuding frankincense perfume, in contrast with the ornate walls and columns.

All of it, far exceeding even the luxury of the Gen al Arif tower, suited Prince Ahmed's taste and he found himself responding to its lavish, extravagant decor. It was far removed from the many nights past when he had slept in the open countryside with a saddle for a pillow and fast-soiling blanket for cover.

Would he lie between silken sheets again tonight or in a shroud?

The question released a tremor of apprehension as he noted the arrival of the sergeants and flung open the door at the right side of the circular foyer that led to the king's private chamber. He paused at the entrance, had a brief background glimpse of pink marble floors overlaid by a rich Persian carpet before his whole attention became focused on the two men.

A huge, obese figure at the far end of the chamber was clad in cloth of gold and glittered with jewelled necklaces. Immense rump on heels, knees on the seat of the dais-throne behind a rectangular ivory-topped coffee table, this was undoubtedly Prince Saad. The tall, cadaverous old man occupying a settle to his right must be Farouk Riswan, the Vizier. Prince Saad had a heavy-jowled face with thick red lips and beady black eyes, the heavy lids of which had opened wide in anger at the intrusion. He exuded such a tangible aura of gross living and sensuality that it was easy to see why he was the pawn of the Prime Minister, austerely clad in white, with the death's-head face of a predatory bird and the dark, evil eyes of a vulture. The bony chin jutted up questioningly at the unannounced visitor, at whom he stared.

The entrance door clicked shut behind Prince Ahmed. He made no move to advance, merely stood with his back to the door, silently contemplating the two men, who seemed now to be surveying his own simple attire, pink-coloured tunic and ballooning pants, with no jewellery, red silk fez-cap.

Prince Saad concluded that he was no one of importance. 'Who the devil are you?' he demanded, his voice a gurgle emerging from his short, fat neck. 'And how dare you enter unannounced?'

'I am Prince Mo-Ahmed al-Kamal, legal heir to the Kingdom of Granada,' Prince Ahmed replied quietly.

Prince Saad's heavy jaw dropped. A stupefied gasp escaped him. Farouk Riswan's downward gaze above his skeletal cheeks remained transfixed, but his eyes told of a brain working fast and furious.

'I have come to claim my birthright,' Prince Ahmed continued suavely. 'I am sure that you gentlemen will support my claim as soon as you have verified my identity and will ensure the restoration of the legal succession to the throne of Granada, thus ending all doubts and uncertainties of the interregnum.' He raised his right hand to display the signet ring.

Farouk Riswan lowered his chin and Prince Saad raised his lower jaw back into place. They exchanged a quick glance, followed by a swift nod.

'Come forward, Prince Mo-Ahmed,' Farouk Riswan invited in a parchment-dry voice. 'As you know, neither of us has ever seen you before and,' the smile creasing the wrinkled sides of his eyes and displaying yellowed teeth was positively evil, 'it is not customary for claimants to the throne of any kingdom to appear at midnight, like Al-ad-din's genie.'

Prince Ahmed strode forward and paused before the coffee table. Neither of the men had made any move to rise in greeting.

'Tell us, Prince Ahmed al-Kamal, as you claim to be, how did you get through to these very private quarters? Have you an armed retinue?'

Having anticipated the trick question, Prince Ahmed

gave his trick reply. 'I had been given a plan of the palace by my former tutor, Abou bon Ebben, so I knew all the secret ways into it. Once inside, I showed the guards my signet ring and stated that I had been summoned by you both to attend a private conference alone.'

He smiled. 'Your security is very lax, Prince Regent and Prime Minister, and will require tightening.'

A flicker of anger registered briefly in the Prime Minister's eyes. 'Did you reveal your identity to the guards?'

'No.'

'So you are completely alone?'

'Yes.'

'Insolent dog to have intruded on us!' Prince Saad interjected. 'You shall be taken to the dungeons and tortured.'

'No, Prince Regent, he shall be taken to the dungeons and executed immediately,' Farouk Riswan intervened blandly. His gaze became piercing. 'Whether you are indeed Prince Ahmed al-Kamal or an imposter, both the Prince Regent and I deem that your presence in this palace tonight, indeed in the kingdom of Granada, constitutes a threat to national security.' He turned his head towards Prince Saad. 'Do you not agree, Prince Regent?'

The jowls flopped vigorously. 'Indeed I do. He is obviously deranged, whoever he is. Having already lost his head, what does he have to lose when the executioner removes it?'

So this was the type of person ruling his kingdom. Anger boiled within Prince Ahmed, but he gave no evidence of it. 'You would murder me in cold blood, as you had my father assassinated?'

'Certainly.' The Prime Minister did not deny the accusation. Instead, he sounded as cold and calm as if he were graciously acknowledging the bestowal of some gift. 'Was King Yusuf's death not poetic justice considering that I had a band of Christian assassins kill his brother, the fourth Mohamed, in order to elevate your father to the throne?'

'And you sent assassins after me as well.'

Another flicker, this time of something Prince Ahmed could not identify, crossed the evil eyes. 'They caught up with you?'

'Yes, but I escaped.'

'Pity.'

'Why?'

'They could have saved us the tiresome duty of your execution tonight.' For all the emotion he showed, he could have been talking about swatting an intruding fly. 'But enough of this talk.' He reached for the tasselled gold silken bell-rope hanging beside the throne.

'I am to be executed without a trial?'

The Prime Minister paused, his hand gripping the gold silk. 'You have already proved yourself guilty of stupidity, the worst of all crimes in anyone aspiring to rule.'

'How so?'

'By coming here alone.'

'Capital punishment for capital stupidity?'

'Precisely.' He tugged sharply on the bell-rope.

Silence fell on the room, except for Prince Saad's heavy breathing. The door opened. Captain Husain stood at the entrance. He saluted, ignoring Prince Ahmed. 'You rang, my lords?'

'Yes,' Prince Saad replied angrily. 'How did this dog of an intruder get into this room?' He paused. 'And what are you doing here at this hour?'

Farouk Riswan lifted his stern grey brow, pointed an accusing finger. 'What indeed?'

Captain Husain ignored the first question. 'Inspecting the guard, Prince.'

'Take this man away and have him executed,' Prince Saad commanded.

'You have not explained how this intruder got in,' the Prime Minister interposed icily.

'Through the entrance door, I presume,' Captain Husain retorted, then quickly shifted ground. 'Do you really command me to take this man away and have him executed?'

'Certainly,' both men declared in unison.

'Without a trial?'

'He has already been tried and found guilty.'

'By whom, my lords?'

'By your Prince Regent and your Prime Minister,' Farouk Riswan declared, finality in his parchment voice. He waved the back of an impatient hand to indicate that the audience was over. 'Enough of this foolery. Just carry out your orders.'

'But you are not a competent court, my lords. Under Muslim law . . .'

Prince Saad interrupted him with studied patience. 'This man is insane.'

'Under Muslim law, a man accused of a crime, especially of a capital offence, must be tried by a competent court. If he is judged to be insane, he is the victim of Almighty Allah's will and, having been punished already through Allah's curse of insanity, must be committed to a proper hospital for the insane since he is not responsible for his actions. That, my lords, is the law I have sworn to uphold.'

'We are the law,' the Prime Minister declared. A note of unmistakable menace entered his voice. 'If you refuse to carry out our commands, you, Captain Husain, shall be at the receiving end of the executioner's blade.'

Captain Husain smiled, shifted his glance towards Prince Ahmed. 'Do you, who have remained un-named so far, have anything to say about this extraordinary situation?'

'Captain Husain!' Prince Saad shouted. 'You obey

our . . .' He stopped abruptly before Captain Husain's white-gloved hand, calmly upraised.

'These two men, namely Prince Saad, the Prince Regent and Farouk Riswan, Prime Minister are the real criminals,' Prince Ahmed stated quietly. 'They have just confessed to me that they arranged for the murder of our late King Yusuf I and sent assassins to kill the heir, Prince Mo-Ahmed al-Kamal.'

Captain Husain's seemingly pleasant disposition instantly turned to steel. 'Is this true, my lords?' he demanded, frost in his voice.

'It is none of your business, you pitiful mongrel of a cavalryman,' Prince Saad roared. He hesitated, dropped his voice. 'Yes, it is true,' he asserted with deadly quiet. 'You see, Captain, Prime Minister Farouk Riswan and I are men who create our own laws. We punish anyone who harms or crosses us and therefore the kingdom we govern with summary execution. So be warned.' He swivelled his huge head towards Farouk Riswan. 'Is that not so, Prime Minister?'

'We are the law,' the Prime Minister repeated. 'We have wasted too much time on this farce already when we have heavy affairs of state to settle.' He flipped the back of his hand towards Captain Husain. 'Take him away!'

'Guards!' Captain Husain shouted over his shoulder.

Colonel Ismail, Major Raschid and Lieutenant Wahid clacked in side by side through the open doors, followed by six huge sergeants. They marched into the chamber and ranged themselves on either side of Prince Ahmed.

Prince Ahmed half turned towards Colonel Ismail, who was immediately to his right. 'You heard the self-confessed evidence?' His voice was cold as hail on the high mountains, each word crystal clear.

'Yes, my lord prince.' Colonel Ismail spoke for all the cavalrymen.

Prince Saad began clambering to his feet, while Farouk

Riswan became motionless as a corpse. Prince Ahmed noted their consternation with savage glee. 'You have had the best direct evidence required by any competent court, confessions to instigating murder, confessions to conspiring against the State, boasts of treason. Do you acknowledge me, Mo-Ahmed al-Kamal, to be your lawful king?' Prince Ahmed's voice sounded as solemn as he felt.

'We do.' There was not one dissentient voice.

Colonel Ismail stepped forward smartly and turned to face Prince Ahmed. He knelt and kissed the prince's hand. 'I do acknowledge you, O King, and swear eternal fealty to you as long as you govern Granada and its kingdoms wisely and with justice.' He rose to his feet.

'The ruler of an Islamic state has the power, given by Almighty Allah, of life and death over his subjects. Our first act as the ruler of Granada is to declare these men, Saad and Riswan, guilty of murder, of conspiracy against the kingdom and of high treason. We sentence them both to be executed this very night in the palace dungeons.'

Chapter 31

Prince Ahmed was now King Mo-Ahmed al-Kamal, or Mo-Ahmed V as he had proclaimed himself. Seated on the dais-throne just vacated by Prince Saad, King Mo-Ahmed spent the rest of the night, until just before the summons to morning prayer resounded faintly ouside, planning with the Council of Regents, all of whom had been hastily assembled for the security of the realm.

Despite the rash suggestions of some hot-head princes and an imam, wildly enthusiastic at the turn of events, that an all-out *jihad* should be commenced immediately against all the invading forces, wiser counsel finally prevailed. The first priority was to send fast emissaries to King Abu Hasan for the promised 100,000 men. Emir Salim, a senior ambassador well known to the King of Morocco and the latter's first cousin, was selected to head the embassy and, on the new king's directive, would depart just after dawn. King Ahmed anticipated that these reinforcements would now definitely be despatched because Granada had a secure succession and therefore a Treasury willing and able to pay for the mercenaries, on whom Granada too had largely depended for over two hundred years.

By the time he attended morning prayer in the mosque where his father had been slain, the kingdom of Granada was on the way to rapid transformation. News travels fast, especially within a city. The brotherhood of Islam, crowding around the forecourt fountain, acclaimed him as the Chosen of Allah.

After a quick inspection of the Alhambra palace, his first ever, King Ahmed deliberately selected the Sala de la Barca for his all-important conference with the military chiefs of the Granada army. This was a long narrow chamber which accommodated the eighteen-foot table of the Regent Conrad of Tyre, purchased and brought across the seas one hundred years earlier by his ancestor King Mohamed II. The Sala provided access between the Court of Myrtles and the Hall of Ambassadors. Seated at the centre of the table with his back to the Hall after *zuhr* and breakfast, King Ahmed had a soothing view of the silver waters in the slender stretches of the long, central pool of the Court of Myrtles through a handsome arched doorway, the intricate carvings of which matched those of the Sala's exquisite wooden ceiling. Security was maintained by huge, armed guards in red and white uniforms, tasselled red fez on their heads, scimitars held in both hands, points on the ground, posted at close intervals but well out of earshot, around the entire Court and the Hall.

The bearing and demeanour of the twenty uniformed men who sat around him at the table, many of them emirs, princes and nobles, showed that his father, King Yusuf, had chosen his commanders well.

General Saldin, seated at his right, was the Commander-in-Chief. A burly, grizzled infantryman, he had not only led the successful strike against Castile, but had fought at the Battle of Salado ten years earlier and was a veteran of many previous campaigns. General al Afdal, the cavalry commander, on Prince Ahmed's left, was tall and slim. The thin scar of a sabre cut running down the left cheek of a hawk-face and iron-grey moustache gave him a dashing appearance. Among the other more important chiefs were the rangy General Farouk commanding the Archer brigades, General Zahir, a man of enormous height and girth, the artillery chief, the small, wiry General Hakim of the Corps of Engineers and the Alhambra Fortress Commander, General Iqbal. The only fat officer in the group, except for Colonel Rafik, the plump

Paymaster General, was appropriately in charge of the Service Corps, General Deen.

Having appointed Colonel Ismail to take charge of Civil Defence with immediate promotion to the rank of General, and Captain Husain, now a Colonel, as his personal chief-of-staff, King Ahmed had commanded them both to be present.

After a few pleasantries, King Ahmed, conscious of his youth and inexperience but determined to show these veterans that he was a capable leader, came directly to the point. 'We are all here today facing one of the gravest crises in the history of our kingdom. We shall not waste time on lamentation, recrimination or exhortation. You gentlemen represent the only hope of our subjects for freedom and independence from a foreign yoke. With the help and guidance of Almighty Allah and our own ingenuity, courage and resolution, we shall prevail.'

As he looked earnestly around at the intent faces, their hands tapped the table in applause. 'We are with you, Revered Majesty.' General Saldin's quiet voice spoke for them all.

Knowing that he had struck the right note with these total strangers, who already had some idea of the enemy movements, King Ahmed proceeded confidently. 'First, we must announce a few measures besides those of which you are aware. Since we are in a state of war, we hereby declare martial law throughout the kingdom. Under these circumstances, the appointment of a Prime Minister would be superfluous and could prove inhibitive to the military. We are therefore transferring all functions of the Vizier to General Saldin with immediate effect. His headquarters and staff will take over all the Prime Minister's departments and carry out all the latter's existing civilian functions.' He glanced at the General.

'*Malik* . . . Sire!' The general seemed at a loss for

words. He rose to his feet amid a murmur of approval, bowed low and resumed his seat.

'The next important civilian post is that of the Royal Treasurer. We are removing Emir Deen from this post, since his conduct even during our late father's lifetime has been suspect and anyone handling money must be like,' his eyes twinkled, 'the sultan's wife, above suspicion. We are delegating these functions to our Paymaster General, Colonel Rafik, who is promoted with immediate effect to the rank of General.'

Colonel, now General Rafik took the news in his stride, rising and bowing low. 'I shall serve Your Majesty with more than pride,' he declared, 'with honesty.'

'Gentlemen, please be aware that these appointments are made only for the duration of the emergency. We shall not perpetuate military rule because we desire to govern a free people.' The tapping of the table indicated unanimous approval of his policy. Delighted at the response, but aware that men of ambition could exist even in this elite group, he proceeded. 'When we have won, if General Saldin has performed well, as we know he will, he will have the option of transferring from the Army to the office of Prime Minister, which we would be honoured to offer him. The same applies to Col . . . General Rafik.' He paused, solemn eyes drifting over each man in turn.

'To address the question of planning,' King Ahmed continued. 'Our first essential is a knowledge of relative strengths. We have sparse intelligence as to the enemy. From all we have gathered on our journey here, we roughly estimate the combined Castilian/Aragon armies, soon to arrive at our northern gates, at sixty thousand men, including all arms of service, the Navarrese force which will approach from the northwest at twenty-five thousand and the Portuguese at ten thousand. With the Catalonians from the east, we can assume a total enemy strength of one hundred thousand men, more or less. Our own army, as reported to us this morning, consists of thirty thousand, twenty thousand of whom are within the city, the remainder dispersed throughout the kingdom. We are therefore outnumbered five to one.' His smile was totally confident when he gazed around the table this time, inviting comment.

General Iqbal, the broad-faced, black-bearded fortress commander, was the first to respond. 'History is full of deeds of valour performed by people of the True Faith and even infidels besieged and heavily outnumbered, Your Majesty. Some of my colleagues and I were discussing our situation just this morning and we recalled the infidel Isabella, of Toran in the Holy Land, who at the age of fourteen defended the city for five days with only eighteen men against fifteen hundred of the men of Yusuf ibn Ayuub, Sal-eh-din, the Conqueror.' He revealed white teeth in a deprecating smile. 'I do not say this to digress, but because it strikes me that the defence of Alhambra is the base of our success.'

'The key to Isabella's feat was resolution,' General al Afdal, the cavalryman, interposed. 'After all, eighty knights under King Richard the Lion-Heart of England rescued three royal ladies including his wife from the entire Muslim garrison at Acre. So we are all agreed on the required essentials of character. His Majesty obviously has plans which he will depend on us to perfect and fulfil.' His nod at General Iqbal robbed the words of offence. 'My colleague is right, however, for Alhambra is the base we must never surrender and from which we can take the offensive. Pray deign to proceed, Sire.'

'You have endorsed our own appreciation of the situation, full details of which we expect you to have before us by sundown tonight, though we will launch certain initiatives immediately after this conference. Your joint report shall be in the classic form based upon our object, which is to destroy the enemy. It shall therefore contain factors affecting the attainment of the object, such as relative strengths, topography and even phases of the moon, with conclusions to be drawn from each factor: courses open to the enemy, courses open to us and your final plan.'

They had all been through military school. If they were surprised at his academic knowledge they certainly seemed delighted with it. 'Excellent!' . . . 'Tremendous!' were among the swift comments, respectfully offered.

'We now call upon General Iqbal to inform us briefly as to the present state of readiness of Granada for a siege of several months.' He paused, raised a palm. 'You may all remain seated while you make your reports.'

The gaunt-faced, cross-eyed General Iqbal cleared his throat. 'I had anticipated your question, *Malik*.' His voice was gravelly and his grey eyes turned even more inwards with concentration. 'The first essentials of a besieged community are food, water and shelter for both the civilian and military populations. I am glad to report that, thanks to the Merciful Almighty for abundant crops and your prudent royal father who made use of the ten years of peace to provide the means to store them against the elements, whether human or of Nature, we have sufficient stocks of food to last us for six months, much longer if rationed, which I recommend we should do immediately rather than awaiting dire necessity.'

King Ahmed nodded his agreement.

'The same should apply to water,' the general added. 'As you are doubtless aware, the underground reservoirs of the city are fed from the mountains and our peculiar location assures us of a safe supply.' He paused. The grey eyes were uncrossed a little as he relaxed. 'As for the distribution of both food and water, the present systems can continue even during a siege, since the core of the city is sufficiently far removed from the reach of any enemy artillery bombardment not to be affected by it.' He grinned deprecatingly. 'I mean, we are not in the same position in this regard as Toran or even Acre in the Holy Land. The people can therefore go about their normal lives except during times of actual attack, even at night. Though our oil stocks are plentiful, I recommend immediate rationing of this item as well.'

King Ahmed could only assume that the cross-eyes were being directed at him for a response. 'We do not intend remaining in our City like rats in their holes,' he declared. 'The plans you gentlemen present to us this evening will undoubtedly include how we can defend ourselves and also launch counter-attacks. What about our military supplies?'

'If Your Majesty will forgive me, should we not first be informed as to our fire-fighting capabilities?' It was the enormous Artillery General Zahir who intervened. 'Many a stout defence has been destroyed by fire.'

'We have adequate sand supplies, fire-beating canvas and demolition implements stored along the walls and at key points in the city,' General Iqbal stated. 'I recommend that we appoint someone completely reliable and efficient such as Prince Gamal to be Civil Defence Chief to organize civilian fire protection and ambulance squads so that the military can be relieved of these responsibilities.'

'An excellent idea!' King Ahmed commented.

'As for military supplies, our artillery lines the walls, but we should increase the munition stocks of rocks, stones and the like immediately to create adequate reserves. I shall organize this with General Zahir's help today. Bows and arrows are in plentiful supply, as are uniforms, armour, swords, pikes, lances and spiked clubs. We do need more horses for General al Afdal's cavalry, so he should send patrols throughout the countryside to bring in at least one thousand more horses before we are encircled.'

'Greek Fire!' King Ahmed shot at the artillery chief.

'Your Majesty?' General Zahir shifted his bulk on his settle, puzzlement in his eyes.

'It is not taught in our military school, General, but when we had our Middle East history lessons from our former tutor, Abou bon Ebben, he spoke of a most effective weapon of our brotherhood whether investing forts or defending them. Even non-combatants can use this weapon. Leather bladders are filled with a mixture of boiled sulphur, wine dregs, petroleum, crystallized salt and gum of Persia. Launched from catapults, or by hand at closer range from slings, the weapon *naffatin* sends the naptha arcing into the sky, emitting a white phosphorescent light which is intense even at noon and therefore frightening. The substance flames on impact and cannot be brushed away, smothered or doused, except with vinegar, of which we have plentiful supply, do we not?' He glanced at General Deen whose jowls shook in the affirmative. 'This will protect us against retaliation in kind and we are sure the enemy will have no vinegar except that which is their substitute for blood!'

The laughter that rang through the chamber lightened its atmosphere. King Ahmed sensed the approval of the generals even before General Saldin commented, 'A brilliant idea, Sire! I have heard of it, but never thought to use it.'

'Your illustrious namesake, Sal-eh-din – may he be at peace in Paradise – used Greek Fire effectively,' King Ahmed commented. The situation was not as hopeless as he feared it might have been. He could not help a glow of pride at his father for having brought Granada to this state of readiness side by side with enormous social and economic developments. King Yusuf had thought of everything. Now it was his, King Ahmed's turn. Thanks be to Almighty Allah that the entire military leadership

587

had remained loyal to the legitimate succession and the freedom of the nation during the interregnum.

He waited until the lively exchange of information by the generals, which, to his dismay, had obviously not taken place since his father's death, had abated. 'We have discussed defence, gentlemen,' he volunteered. 'Now let us talk of the offensive. More elaborate plans must await your detailed submissions this evening, but we insist that cavalry strike forces be detailed to leave immediately for the northern border to harass the advance elements of the Castilian army.'

Knowing that, with the wide detour they were making, they had to move fast if they were to reach the Alhambra ahead of the Castilian army, Princess Beatrice and Prince Juan rode through most of the first night, heading east with short stops for resting themselves and the horses. They slept for only four hours the following afternoon in a convenient grove of stunted Spanish oaks, sweltering in the torrid heat, but grateful for the longer rest. When they resumed their journey that evening, they kept moving, now making south. Shortly after dawn the following morning, they crossed a deep defile and conjectured that they were finally within the Granada border. Feeling safer at last, they soon cut directly west, making for the main highway. They rested again during the siesta hours, this time on a broad ledge below an overhanging escarpment. That night, they got their first hours of sleep during darkness, holing up in a deserted barn.

Having made it a point to keep mainly to the hilltops, avoiding the skyline, they had met no travellers, the only local inhabitants being herdsmen grazing their flocks on the rare plateaux that contained scrubby green grass. They had descended to the lush, fertile valleys below only to avoid difficult terrain and to buy food and water for themselves and their horses from the occasional small farmhouse, where questions really did not matter and were in each case stilled by a gold coin.

Princess Beatrice found the appearance and character of the people of Granada different from those she was accustomed to in northern Castile. The settlers here were mostly Moors and Moriscos, generally of swarthy countenance and hospitable disposition. She and Prince Juan were so sunburned by now, their golden heads so bleached, that only their vivid blue eyes made them look dissimilar to the local population, but even the eyes could have placed them as being of Berber extraction.

Late that evening, still heading due west, they mounted the crest of a high hill side by side and paused at its bare summit. Prince Juan suddenly gurgled with excited speech that would not emerge in intelligible form, ending in a glug-gibber. Princess Beatrice's gaze, following his shaking finger, met what could have been a dusk-scene from any high country along their travels. The setting sun cast the shadows of mountains before them on the valley below. The sky, except to the west, was a pale, sombre blue, against which barren hill and rugged mountain were sharply etched in greeny-purple shades of varying hues. A flight of rooks slowly circled the valley below them, preparing to land on their tree-top nests for the night. The silence was so total that even a breeze dared not whisper. She suddenly comprehended the unity of the earth in all its disparity.

But that was not what Prince Juan had spied. His finger pointed at the grey ribbon of the main highway stretching below them, half-way down the hillside, following its contours. A little further south, over a silver-grey stream, it crossed a bridge, at the entrance to which was a guardhouse. Elation filled her. This must be one of the bridges about which Prince Ahmed had told her, though not yet the one that he, Prince Juan, Zurika – oh Zurika! – and Pilar had encountered on their first night out of Alhambra.

Oh God, O Blessed Virgin, O Sweet Jesu, I thank Thee all for our deliverance.

Buoyed by the feeling that their luck had finally turned, Princess Beatrice gave her horse its head to descend the hill, but Prince Juan's detaining hand made her rein back. This time, his silent fingers pointed upwards at the higher hill across the valley to the dark outline of a small, square, squat stone building. What could it be?

'A watch-tower,' Prince Juan signalled. 'It is one of those carrying brushwood for the signal fires that announced our flight from Alhambra.'

Now Princess Beatrice picked up a sound to which Juan would be deaf, a faint rumble from the north of the highway, a sound that did not belong in the silence. She listened intently. The rumble changed to a roll, became a drumming. 'Horses,' she gestured excitedly to Prince Juan, indicating a bend where the highway disappeared on its journey north. 'Travelling fast,' she added.

'We should hide behind that clump of bushes and see what it is,' Prince Juan suggested.

They reined their mounts sideways, kneed them to where the bushes offered a screen from the highway. They had barely paused when the drumming suddenly increased to a clatter. A column of cantering riders, led by two men, emerged round the bend. Cavalrymen! Were they Granadan? Surely they could not be Castilian.

Princess Beatrice anxiously scanned the faces of the leaders. Suddenly, her stomach clenched, squeezing fear to mushroom upwards like a snake ready to strike. Her breath caught; bitter bile arose at the back of her throat. How could it be? This was Granada. Was there no escape for her from this monster. She would have recognized that dreadful bull-like neckless figure anywhere. King Charles the Bad had arrived.

* * *

As he slow-cantered round the bend, Count Gaston on his left, a bridge lay starkly before them in the evening light about half a mile away. King Charles the Bad pointed to it excitedly. 'Two more of those and we shall be at the Alhambra,' he declared. '*En verdad*, we shall surely run into our . . . er . . . quarry well before then.'

Count Gaston's answering nod was grim. 'As you can see, Your Majesty, we have been spotted by a single sentry from outside the guardhouse protecting the bridge.' He transferred the reins to his left hand, used his right hand to loosen his sword in its scabbard, observed men pouring out of the building. 'We may have to fight our way through, Your Majesty. You take the right and I shall take the left?'

'Agreed.' King Charles's wolfish grin was as ferocious as he felt. 'About time,' he exulted. In one swift movement his long sword gleamed in his hand. 'Pity those borderguards merely waved us on while our weapon cried out for Moorish blood!' A quick backward glance assured him that the cavalry was following in column of four. He seized his shield in his left hand, raised his sword aloft, heard the rasp of metal above the thunderous clatter of their horses' hooves. He pointed his sword at the bridge. 'Cha . . . ar . . . arge!' he bellowed and clapped spurs on his charger.

The guards were drawn up across the entrance to the bridge in two rows, pikes levelled. He counted ten in the first row, made straight for the centre at full gallop, roaring like a beast. He was rewarded by the flicker of fear in dark eyes above swarthy, bearded faces. He held his mount on a straight course until the very last moment, reined in just short of the pike thrusts, veered sharply right with a great rasp of shod hooves. The pikes wavered uncertainly, tried to follow him, got in each other's way. He spun left again, took the pike of the sentry at the extreme right on the horse's body armour. The weapon splintered. With a bursting thrill of delight, he rode straight at the sentry. He had an impression of a dark, brown-bearded face, eyes goggling in terror, heard the agonized cry as he charged over the body. The rear pikeman was so stunned he had no time to thrust his pike before the charger smashed into him. His shriek of agony mingled with the crunching thud of hooves. King Charles shouted in triumph and then he was through, pounding across the bridge, a laughing Count Gaston, who had obviously followed similar tactics, at his left. Horses whinnied shrilly behind them.

They reined in sharply together by common consent and wheeled around. The lead elements of the Castilian cavalry had simply smashed through the puny double defence line. Fallen men were screaming in agony, one whimpering, another sobbing, from the pounding hooves and hacking swords. Those on their feet were springing away from the destruction. Two men had simply leapt into the water below.

Within minutes they were all across the bridge, leaving its entrance strewn with dead and groaning wounded. They paused for the cavalry colonel to take a quick body count of his own men, check the horses. 'No casualties, Sire,' he reported saluting. 'Three troopers with wounds, all mounts usable in spite of some flesh wounds.'

King Charles could not hide his glee. 'God is on our side!' he cried, crossing himself with a piety he did not feel. He swivelled his charger expertly around.

Count Gaston's cry anticipated his order to advance. 'Sire, look!' A gauntleted hand pointed upwards to their right.

At the top of the high hill, a beacon blazed.

'There too, Sire!' It was the colonel's voice this time and he was pointing towards the next high hilltop to the south, on which another fire was beginning to blaze.

'What are those?' King Charles inquired of Count Gaston, though he already guessed.

'Alarm signals,' Count Gaston answered grimly. 'They will extend from mountain-top to mountain-top until they reach Alhambra.' His gaze was inquiring.

King Charles quickly considered the new development. Should he turn back? Never! It suddenly occurred to him that his whole life was at stake either way. If he went forward, he could be killed. If he retreated, his ambitions and his lovelife were over. Besides, King Pedro had assured him that the rulers of Granada were co-operating in what was for all practical purposes to be a surrender. 'It will take another day for a strike force to reach us from Alhambra,' he prevaricated. 'We shall proceed at least to the second bridge before turning back.'

It had occurred to him that if he could catch up with Princess Beatrice, she would be completely entranced by his courage and valour, caring and devotion to her. Penetrating deep into enemy territory where everyone of thousands was hostile to him in order to rescue her from pagans, yes, even a pagan lover, with only one hundred men, was a unique exploit that would resound through the halls of history. Minstrels would sing of it, fathers tell the story to the sons sitting on their knees by the fireside. She could not be far away now. She would forgive him the rape and marry him.

There was no time to be lost. 'Forward!' he commanded and urged his charger to a canter.

Princess Beatrice had watched the fight with horror. This was no tourney, but the real thing. The shouts, the screams, the shrieks of agony, the shrilling of wounded horses would be with her forever. *She could almost smell the men's blood.* Compassion for the fallen and wounded urged her to go to their aid, but she held back. There was nothing Prince Juan or she could do for them.

Why did people have to indulge in violence?

Through it all, however, she could not help a shiver of admiration for the courage and daring of Count Gaston and King Charles. She had kept glancing at Prince Juan. He had remained very still, lost in an inner contemplation, sadness in his blue eyes. Only when King Charles had assembled his men on the other side of the bridge did he lift his gaze, but it was to the mountain tops across the valleys. 'It took the second watch tower long enough to spot the first fire and light their own,' he signalled. 'But now since it is almost dark and the fires are more easily spotted, they will quickly extend to Alhambra, from where strike forces will be launched.' The fires began to flicker and rise, flicker and rise. 'They seem to have a system of signalling as to how many intruders are involved.'

She could not resist the question that had been pounding at her frequently for days. 'Do you think Prince Ahmed has reached Alhambra safely?'

He nodded his golden head in the affirmative. 'I do not have bad forebodings about him. I pray God he is safe.'

She pointed hopefully down towards the bridge. 'King Charles must have observed the signal fires. Do you think he will turn back?'

He shook his head and her heart sank. 'No. He is a stubborn man, not the sort to give up easily.'

'Forward!' The bellowed command reached them distinctly from below.

'He will go on until he is forced to turn back.' Prince Juan paused in his gestures. 'I suggest that we follow him, though not on his tracks. We could ride down to the river, find a convenient spot to ford it and try to catch up with him. It is essential to keep him under observation. If faced by a large enough enemy force, he will surely turn back and we can give ourselves up to the Granadans and request that they take us back to Alhambra.'

Her breath caught. 'And Prince Ahmed!' she whispered to herself. Hope had begun to blaze within her, heading for Alhambra like the fires on the hilltops, signalling an end to her own black night, carrying the message of love to her prince. *I am coming to you at last, my beloved prince . . . Horn. Oh Horn, it is I who am coming to you.*

Fierce resolve seized her. King Charles would be the beacon light to her love. She must never lose sight of the rapist. 'We will not ford the river, my brother,' she gestured.

He stared at her in surprise. 'Why not?'

'Because we will go over the bridge and follow King Charles along the highway.' She smiled as his eyes lit up. 'Will that not be simpler?'

They were finally on the move. Seated on his black destrier in hauberk and thigh greaves of black leather, since the presence of his entire army around him removed the need for full armour, King Pedro the Cruel had cause for satisfaction as the troops of Castile and Aragon marched past him in the pale light of a cool dawn. The sixty thousand men who had been spread across the plain to east and west of the highway were converging on it in orderly ranks based on plans evolved by his chiefs of staff the previous day. Bishop Eulogius and his chaplains detailed throughout the encampment had conducted a pre-dawn Mass, stressing the crusade on which they were embarking for Jesus Christ and His Holy Church against heretics, so most of the men, even those with colds, the ague, stomach ailments and blisters, seemed to be in a state of religious zeal.

While King Pedro acknowledged the salutes of the rank upon rank of his columns, Bishop Eulogius, seated beside him on a white palfrey, blessed the passing men, uplifted palm repeatedly making the sign of the cross. *I wish I could keep him here all day,* King Pedro reflected savagely. The unending line would extend for over twelve miles, and it would be hours before the bishop could canter up to his position at the head of the army. This is the mightiest force ever assembled by Christian Spain even if the Navarrese, Catalonian and Portuguese army corps are excluded, and so I, King Pedro, will go down in history for having achieved Reconquista singlehanded. He immediately rejected the still, small voice within him that whispered of Christian unity and the role of Bishop Eulogius and Holy Church. It was he alone that had risen above the ashes of the tourney's debacle to reach this moment.

Since it would take all day for the final elements of the convoy to pass him, the king had decided to receive the salute only of the cavalry regiments, which led the column in a brave display of coloured uniforms, trappings, lances with pennants fluttering, the banners of the regiments and the standards of the noblemen before racing to take his place at its head. The regiments of bowmen would follow, preceding the infantry led by the pikemen and spearmen, then the artillery with their siege machines, perriers, mangonels, catapults, battering rams and trundling horse-drawn wagons laden with ammunition and massive bolts. Each unit had its trumpeters and heralds, besides transport carrying tents and sufficient supplies to last one week. Then would come the ambulance units for men and animals, preceding the transport vehicles with sumpter horses and mules bearing huge supplies of food independent of such as would be commandeered along the way, clothing, weapons, spare horses and all the craftsmen, blacksmiths, carpenters, welders, ironworkers, with the paraphernalia and equipment of their respective trades. The comfort corps of women would come last with a protective screen of cavalry.

The sun was warm on his back and the nape of his neck when King Pedro wheeled his black to ride to the head of the column. He wondered for the umpteenth time what had happened to King Charles, Count Gaston and the one hundred cavalrymen. No news was good news, for it meant that the border was open and there was no resistance from the Moors. Once he seized Alhambra, he would fuck that treacherous bastard Farouk Riswan. He did not need a serpent even as a puppet. He was headed for vengeance for his defeat in battle and at the tourney. He would have Maria de Padilla design for him a new Imperial Crown.

It was evening the next day by the time King Charles the Bad, having rested for a few hours during the night, saw the outlines of the second bridge straight ahead of him in the darkling golden light. This must be a deserted part of the country for they had only passed a few wagoneers along the way. The guards were probably playing chess in the guardhouse to the left, because only two sentries casually manned each side of the bridge. That was odd. Had they not seen the signal fires?

While trotting on, the king quickly surveyed the topography. The bridge linked two hill features which sloped gently towards the highway. Both slopes were clothed with copses of dark cypress and wild oak, spreading from the tops of the embankments through which the highway had been running for the past half-mile. It was an idyllic scene of a peaceful countryside disturbed only by the smell now becoming a stink of his own unwashed body, the odour of horse sweat and the clattering of hooves on cobbles.

The two sentries had heard the sounds of their approach; they glanced up swiftly. One of them seemed to shout before they all raced for the shelter of the guardhouse.

So much the better, King Charles exulted. The Moors were cowards. He would have clear passage. He knew a moment's regret at missing a good fight, getting rid of some more of his venom towards all Moorish bastards. He seized his shield, transferred the reins back to his left hand. He drew his long sword, raised it aloft, then pointed it straight ahead. 'Cha . . . aa . . . arge!' he roared and dug his spurs into his horse's flank.

The animal responded with a will. The entire force thundered towards the bridge. There was no sign of any opposition. The sentries had vanished into the guard-house. King Charles roared with laughter. 'Cowards!' he mocked as he flashed past the building, Count Gaston, silent as always, beside him. He was half-way across the bridge, the cavalrymen following in close ranks, when his eyes, scouting ahead, saw it.

Where the highway ran between a low embankment, it was blocked by felled trees.

He reacted immediately, raised his sword high. 'Whoa . . . a . . . oo!' he bellowed. 'Ha . . . a . . . alt!'

He reined in his horse. By the time he came to a full stop and wheeled around, he was past the bridge, which was already crowded with riders in column of four.

A hissing overhead announced the first deadly hail of enemy arrows from both sides of the adjoining hillsides.

He had been king for two days which had been a whirlwind of planning and executive sessions with the military chiefs and senior civil servants, endless meetings with imams, princes and nobles and receiving delegations of townsfolk, tradesmen and organizations of every religion. He had not realized the variety of people a ruler had to deal with.

'There seems to be a committee for every aspect of life,' he had remarked wryly to Colonel Husain. 'We would not be surprised to be called on by the Honourable Society of Rats, bringing us gifts from the city sewers!'

'The only gift that rats can bring is the Black Plague,

Malik, and Allah forbid that they bring it to us.' Colonel Husain had paused. 'We are, however, ruthlessly eliminating all the human rats whom our late unlamented Prime Minister had started to install in key civil service posts. Fortunately, he could not infiltrate the army and did not have enough time to corrupt the entire administration.'

For the very reason that the royal routine was firmly established, the demands of protocol, of which King Ahmed was impatient at such a time, made life difficult for him. If there was a better way, he could not think of it. All these people had to meet and felicitate the new ruler. It was not merely his duty to see them, but he wanted to and a personal fondness for them had begun to stir within him. It made him realize with startling clarity that the worst effect of his father's imprisonment of him in order to shut off the fountains of love had been to deny his oneness with the identity of the nation.

He had elected to live in his father's chambers in the Daraxa, except that he would have nothing to do with the harem, not even to pay the mandatory daily visit to bestow gifts to the dozens of women there, many of whom would, he knew, be disappointed not to receive the royal favours, especially from one who appeared to be a virile young man! His only thoughts were of Princess Beatrice and he was glad of the excuse that he was busy, for a king was expected to use the harem for relaxation from the demands of the world.

So the two days had passed with incredible swiftness, from the time he arose before dawn to Tarif's ministrations till nearly midnight when he finally fell asleep. As the hours crept by, anxiety for Princess Beatrice and his friends had increased, especially after last evening when he had been informed of the watch-fire signals that told of one hundred or so foreign horsemen at the first bridge. He had immediately despatched two squadrons of cavalry and two of mounted bowmen on a mission to intercept and destroy. What could have happened to Princess Beatrice? The need for her had even made him visit his former study in the Gen al Arif tower before sunset yesterday, eagerly scanning the black rock platform on which Zurika had once danced. It was bleak and bare, the emptiness mocking him through rose-gold light.

You may be king, but I am no one, nothing, I shall bow neither to your command, nor your plea.

Now, on the following evening, he stared at the same emptiness willing a gypsy girl and a Jew to appear in the flesh, with a beautiful princess besides, her colour more beautiful pink-white than the snows of the Sierra Nevada, and a deaf-mute prince, all watching a gypsy girl dance. Only emptiness materialized, mocking him again.

His heart desperately reached out to Princess Beatrice, for she at least was tangible in his life. He grasped only a dread premonition, bringing sheer loneliness to settle on his being like a soiled grey shroud.

By evening, the head of the vast cavalry which King Pedro the Cruel led was only one-third of the way to the border of Granada. They had proceeded even through the gruelling afternoon sun because it was necessary to keep moving so that the tail end of the army could make the highway before nightfall. Mounted scouts racing ahead checked against surprise attacks, while marshals cantered up and down the column to maintain order. The foot-soldiers in particular suffered from the sun's heat, in spite of frequent line changes to permit those in the centre lines the freedom of marching on the outside.

'It will take us six days to reach Alhambra, probably three days longer to invest it before commencing our attacks,' King Pedro remarked to a red-faced, sweating Bishop Eulogius riding beside him. 'We hope the

Navarrese and Portuguese armies will also be in place six days from now.'

'Not to mention the Catalonians,' Bishop Eulogius intoned. 'Christian unity demands that all the Christian kingdoms are present at this historic event.'

Which will make you immortal, as well as a Cardinal and the Pope, King Pedro thought savagely. This fucking little prick always had to intrude himself and some equally trivial technicality! Tired after the whole day's march under a blistering sun, King Pedro was in no mood for such claptrap. 'We are favoured of God,' he commented. 'When we first rode out on the highway from Toledo, we merely led detachments of fast cavalry to catch up with the fugitives. Now we are leading what is perhaps the largest army assembled in Christendom since the Crusades.'

'Holy Church's complete faith in Your Majesty has led you to this event.' The primate pursed his little red Cupid's bow mouth, licked his dry lips. 'You will lead the military attacks on these heretics, while I, on behalf of Holy Church, shall lead the religious attacks which shall cleanse them with fire.'

King Pedro curbed his impatience. All that would be faced later. He turned his thoughts in other directions. How had King Charles the Bad and Count Gaston fared? Where were they now?

Neither prelate nor king knew a wrinkled crone had joined the comfort corps of the convoy. Pilar had made a quick sale of her cottage in Jaén at a reduced price. She had used some of the proceeds to bribe a wagoneer. She ignored his ribald comment. 'And what comfort do *you* have to give our brave soldiers?' The rest of the money in a little bag tied hidden around her waist, staff lying beside her, she rode inside the wagon with black vengeance in her heart.

Chapter 32

The bridge was a mess of groaning men slumped on their saddles or fallen on the cobblestones. Squealing horses, some with arrows sticking out of them like great porcupine quills, stampeded. Though at least ten men on the bridge were casualties, some beginning to retreat, the cavalrymen on the other side were pushing forward. A split second of consternation, then Charles the Bad reacted instinctively. Retreat was not only dangerous, it was foreign to his genius. He shot a glance at Count Gaston. The cool Basque, obviously of the same mind, nodded and smiled.

They wheeled their horses sideways in opposite directions, raised their swords aloft. The next hail of arrows hissed over them.

'For God and Holy Church. Ch . . . aar . . . arge!' They thundered in unison and plunged into the hillside.

'*La ilaha il' Allah*, there is no God but Allah,' came the answering cry. King Charles had a split second's recognition of the fundamental meaning of the conflict before he heard the four lines of cavalrymen who were not unhorsed leave the groaning wounded behind to speed forward. He was dimly conscious that the two right-hand lines were following him, the left-hand lines Count Gaston, before he charged from sunlight into shadows. The unexpected move took the enemy, who had been lined in the shelter of the trees to launch into the attack, completely by surprise. Long sword swinging, roaring like a maddened bull, King Charles smashed his charger into them. A swarthy veteran became a headless corpse, a beardless youth with terrified eyes crumbled with the sword point in his belly.

Dimly conscious that his men had spread out in line on either side of him, Charles the Bad was lost in the blood-lust of killing. Mounted men encircled him, but the trees were in their way. Red haze in his brain, but vision clear, he kept urging his mount forward. Swing!. . . Cut!. . . Lunge!. . . Chop! . . . Each move ending in a dead man. Again and again, endlessly. Men yielded or fled before his fury, blocking the path of those behind who were spurring to the attack. He was encircled time and again, but he hacked his way through.

The battle raged for half an hour before the pressure eased and he found himself in the open, gazing at a fleeing enemy. He paused, heart pounding from the exertion, breath rasping, and became suddenly conscious that his sword arm was aching. He deliberately brushed away the sweat from his face with the back of a gauntleted hand. The red mists cleared, but hatred remained, welling up, crying out, pursue the enemy, kill every one of the fucking bastards. Wisdom dictated otherwise.

Satisfied that the enemy had been routed in the single short fierce encounter, exulting at the outcome, King Charles sheathed his bloodied sword. The movement brought a spasm of pain in the exposed area of his hauberk, just beneath the left armpit. He touched it gingerly with the gauntleted fingers of his right hand. They came away red with blood. He had been wounded and had not even known it in the heat of battle. His inner tunic too was soaked. No matter. Time enough to attend to wounds later.

The Moorish cavalry had obviously ridden post haste from Alhambra upon receiving the fire signals from the hill-tops. This showed that, contrary to King Pedro's expectations, stout resistance would be offered from the capital. It could only mean that Ahmed, the Moorish prick – he would still cut off the bastard's cock some day and stuff it into his mouth – had reached the palace, ended the interregnum and installed himself on the throne. Princess Beatrice was obviously well on her way to Alhambra, but it would be suicide for him to keep up the pursuit with possibly thousands of Moors between herself and him.

His huge shoulders slumped. Had all these days of hideous risks and the fierce fighting been in vain? The instant answer was, Never! He had thrilled to the danger, rejoiced in the kill, which still vibrated through his entire body and transported his brain. He would find some other way of rescuing Princess Beatrice. Oh yes he would, but the present demanded its own sober action. He wheeled his mount around. Between the trees dead and wounded men lay scattered beside injured horses on the hard brown soil. Riderless mounts moved about uncertainly. A young Moorish cavalryman, his white tunic beneath the leather corselet red with blood, was crawling away from a fallen horse. Its two front legs vainly pawing the ground, eyes wide with pain, the whites showing terror, the grey finally staggered to its feet. Gleaming sword raised aloft, a ruddy-faced, black-bearded Castilian cavalryman rode up fast. One great swing and *thwack-grind-crunch*! A shaven head rolled. The body of the Moor remained still a few moments, then began to crumble.

King Charles's swift survey revealed three Castilians dead to over two dozen Moors. A good encounter. Now if Count Gaston too had had similar success, they could ride back to King Pedro's main body ahead of the pursuit with something achieved.

If only Princess Beatrice had seen him fight, she would have understood the difference between a man who was a man in a real battle and a puling boy in the make-believe world of the joust. By the time the story of this evening's engagement got around, he with but ten men would have defeated ten thousand! She would be thrilled by it. God, how he loved her! The sparkle in his blood suddenly carried through to his loins. What would he not give to enter her virginal body at this very moment.

He began threading his way through the approaching dusk, avoiding groaning Moors, all of whom were being slain by his troops. He had no personal taste for killing fallen men. It was a job that had to be done, but he preferred the thrill of hand-to-hand combat.

The faint drumming behind him did not register at first. As its intensity increased, alarm gripped his entrails. He knew what was happening even before he spun his horse around, drawing his sword.

The Moors had played a Tatar trick, pretending to flee only to wheel around and attack on both flanks.

Riding well behind King Charles the Bad and the Castilian cavalry, Princess Beatrice had been in a turmoil of mixed emotions, mostly dire, dominated by horror and dread. Charles the Bad, her rapist, was just a mile away and she was actually following him though his mission must be to seize her. Try as she might, she could not keep the rape from returning vividly to her mind. She had thought it dimmed to near extinction, but now it had come back with such starkness that she imagined the reek of King Charles's acrid sweat and stale wine remaining on the air he had just ridden through. She kept on reliving that first moment of his rage when she told him of her love for Prince Ahmed, the instant of stunned perception before he exploded into violence . . . the sharp pain of the vicious blows . . . the terrifying knowledge of his intentions before the sting of the blows turned to numbness . . . the begging for mercy . . . the sheer terror at realizing there would be none . . . the hopelessness . . . the crushing torture when he . . . when he . . . when he . . . She kept shutting out the recall, but it kept returning, like a series of paintings in a brightly lit gallery. She could actually see him in the dim lamplight of that tiny room, his vicious look, his brutal appearance. She heard the bestial growls emerging from his throat, gagged at recalling the terrible breath from his slobbery lips. Dear God, how the hateful feel of it all made her shiver and tremble. She simply could not believe that it had all happened to *her*, the sheltered Princess Beatrice of the Toledo palace who had never been exposed to violence of any kind, only to gentility and refinement. Yet the horror was hers. Right now.

For the very first time, the memory recurred. Prince Juan had picked up her thoughts with his uncanny perception. Guiding his horse with his knees alone, he had spoken to her. 'It was easier to forget while he was nowhere on the scene, but now he has returned to haunt you, *querida*. Do not let him, I beg you.'

The compassion in his blue eyes had brought tears to her own. She merely nodded her agreement. Any other response would have made her break down, sobbing, screaming.

'I understand. It is almost as if by following him, you are once more on the brink of its horror. All I can suggest is that you concentrate on the present. You are free of him . . . free . . . free.' His eyes became compelling. 'It will never happen to you again, I swear to you. I would kill you first. So put him out of your mind and concentrate on what lies ahead for us in Alhambra.' He had looked away quickly, well aware of the futility of any advice. One simply never gets over a rape, she had decided. One must learn to live with it.

As the evening deepened, they had closed the gap between themselves and King Charles's detachment. Though evening was the worst time, for that was when the rape occurred, Princess Beatrice found that just one day of struggling with terror and overcoming it had made her stronger than she had been after the many days when there was nothing visible to bring it back. They had slowed down just beneath the crest of a low incline of the highway, when they saw the bridge in the distance. Then it happened. Cavalrymen on the bridge halted abruptly, horses reared, their shrill neighs faint. Men fell. She reined in her horse without conscious thought, remained petrified as the scene unfolded. She barely heard glug . . . glug . . . glurp noises emanating from Prince Juan, came to only when she found her horse being dragged sideways. Her horse, its head up, was pulling against the rein that Prince Juan had grabbed to jerk it away from the highway. Only then did she comprehend that her pursuers were being attacked by Granadan forces. She regained control of her horse and her hopes soared. She and Prince Juan could join the Granadans after they put King Charles to flight and proceed safely to Alhambra. 'I thank Thee, O God, O Blessed Virgin, Sweet Jesu!' she silently prayed.

When they were out of sight on a low hill sheltered by trees, Prince Juan paused. Two battle scenes, one on each side of the highway, unfolded beyond the bridge. Princess Beatrice could hardly bear to watch, though much of the action was hidden by the green branches of scrub oak and cypress. She found herself torn by conflicting loyalties. To her surprise, deep inside her the Castilian element remained, supported by some instinctive bond with Count Gaston. As for King Charles personally, he was no Castilian and not all her Christian spirit could prevent her from praying that he would be butchered.

To her dismay, the Moorish cavalry began streaming away from the right-hand side of the highway. Minutes later, those on the left also took flight. Her heart went bleak. Were her hopes of getting to Alhambra safely to be dashed?

Prince Juan touched her arm. 'The Granadans have lost,' he signalled. 'But with the large numbers he now knows to be against him, King Charles will not proceed. He is sure to head back to the border. Let us leave immediately, so we can detour the bridge, ford the river further down and make for the highway again to try and reach it before dark. We will almost certainly have a clear passage to Alhambra now.'

As she swung her horse east, a faint drumming reached Princess Beatrice's ears. Intent on getting away fast, she failed to see the counter-attacks of the Moorish cavalry.

After the first moment of alarm, all the latent ferocity within him exploded. 'They are attacking again!' King Charles roared, swivelling his horse fully to face the charge. His voice, fractured through the trees, echoed. 'Kill the fucking bastards!' He drew his long sword, kicking his charger forward, but instinctively electing to fight within the obstructions of the brown tree trunks since his men were outnumbered.

The two lines of horsemen came up fast. He selected a huge leather-helmeted rider, wielding a scimitar, riding a grey. Sword aloft, he made directly for the cavalryman. He swerved at the last moment to the left of a tree trunk so the man could not use his weapon, reined in and brought his sword sideways in a tremendous back-swipe. It nearly came out of his grip as the blade sliced clear through flesh, gristle and bone, jarring his shoulder. He bellowed exultantly and charged again. He withdrew his weapon to thrust clean through the unprotected stomach of a stocky, snarling opponent. The clash of metal, the bellows and screams of enraged men, the snorting and whinnying of horses and the taste of blood in his dry mouth only maddened him. Lost in a frenzy, he hacked his way through the enemy, finally reached open ground only to wheel around and take the line of mounted men in the rear.

The Moors had reckoned without the ferocity of Castilians in battle. As dusk began to shroud the open hillside, they began streaming back along it, but not before King Charles had killed five more of them. The living would be back to harass the invaders along the highway.

His sword arm ached, his breath was tight in his chest, his wound was bleeding so profusely that he could feel its trickle soaking his undershirt. But the blood was sparkling again in his veins and its lust had not been fully satisfied. His instinct told him that the enemy would not attack again tonight. He had best gather his troops, count casualties and head back fast for the border, however tired they all might be. There definitely was no time to bury the dead.

He drew a deep breath. 'Back to the highway!' he roared.

By the time he reached the road, threading his way through the groans and screams of mortally wounded Moors fallen on the hard brown soil, with riderless horses darting hither and thither, confused, he counted over fifty enemy dead to only eleven Castilians. As his detachment began forming up in column of two behind him, a captain began to take a body count. Count Gaston's men started riding back. They too had driven the enemy away. Good. He scanned them anxiously for his chancellor's unmistakable figure. He subconsciously counted thirty-five Castilians before the count emerged, riding slowly. King Charles knew a tremor of joy. He had not realized how much he cared for and needed this man.

King Charles reined his mount sideways. Then he saw it. For a moment he could not comprehend what he was seeing. Battle hardened as he was, sick horror engulfed him. A sword hilt protruded from Count Gaston just above the hip, where his metal hauberk ended. The man must be in agony, barely daring to move. The breath rasped in his chest, sweat streamed down his gaunt cheeks, blood oozed beneath his metal hauberk. Yet he was seated erect in the saddle as if the weapon piercing him was just a part of his body.

King Charles made to draw out the sword, but Count Gaston held up a weak hand. 'If you . . . pull it out, Sire . . . I would die.' He paused, nostrils dilating with his deep, juddering breaths, smiled tiredly. 'I shall die . . . soon . . . but not yet.'

'Then why not sooner to end your agony?' King Charles pleaded. 'What is the point of living like this?'

This time the smile was a secret one, touching only the sides of the dark eyes. 'It is a pact . . . between . . . between,' a spasm of pain brought the words out in a whisper, 'God and . . . me. I must . . . not go . . . before my time . . .' Red blood dripped down from his nose, staining the black moustache. He slowly drew a white kerchief, wiped it.

King Charles comprehended that this remarkable man was kept alive and suffering by his implacable views. To pull out the sword would be akin to committing suicide. King Charles's mouth was dry, his chest ached, his throat hurt with the first real anguish he had felt for anyone. El Cid Campeador had ridden to battle with a spear in his chest so his men would know he was not dead, as a duty to his soldiers. Count Gaston was bearing his cross because of his duty to his God.

The bodycount revealed that twenty-seven cavalrymen had been killed, against over two hundred of the enemy, whose wounded were put to death or just left lying in red pools of blood. King Charles had his own wounded placed in two horse-drawn wagons which they found behind the guardhouse, the guards having fled.

It was nightfall before he led the sad, slow procession back on its way back to the border, Count Gaston swaying in the saddle beside him. They rode into the night in order to make certain they were not pursued. Count

Gaston spent most of the long, weary hours in a semi-conscious state, murmuring at times. King Charles could occasionally hear the name 'Ingemar' and comprehended that the count was communing with his dead love. Seven times he had to reach out to prevent the wounded man from falling.

Riding slowly through cool air beneath a deep, crisp blue sky glittering with stars, the clatter of hooves on the cobblestones a disharmonious harmony, King Charles discovered that his deep concern and admiration for Count Gaston, amounting to awe had brought a protectiveness, which could only have emerged from the wellsprings of love. Did it come from the same source as his love for Princess Beatrice? He did not know. All he knew was the intense pain of loving, for he did not want to lose Count Gaston, not because he would never find anyone to replace the chancellor, but because he loved the man. And it seemed as if he, King Charles, was losing his every love.

Around midnight, Count Gaston straightened suddenly in his saddle. 'It is time, Sire,' he stated in a firm, clear voice. 'Would you deign to halt a little while, so I can welcome our common friend, death?'

'Ha . . . a . . . alt!' King Charles's voice broke as he bellowed the order. The night took up the sudden sound, sent it echoing and re-echoing between the low hills. The clattering of hooves ceased, gave way to the creak of saddles; the wagons ground to a halt, the snorting of a horse was quickly stilled, as if men and animals understood the solemnity of the moment.

King Charles dismounted, made to help Count Gaston dismount. The Basque held up a demurring hand once more, his smile wan in the starlight. He drew a deep breath and swung elegantly off his horse. The wound was probably numb, but the pain must still have been excruciating. King Charles marvelled as he followed Count

Gaston's unsteady steps to the grass verge on the side of the highway.

Count Gaston turned with a smile. 'Pray be seated, Sire, so I may sit down too. As you can see . . .' his nostrils dilated, the skin of his face jittered, but he never winced. 'As I was about to say when I was so rudely interrupted by that boring boor . . . pain . . . I am . . . unable to lie on my chest . . . or my back . . . I beg your gracious leave to die seated . . . But your head must always . . . be above mine.' He smiled strangely. 'Only while I live.'

They sat cross-legged, facing each other. The cavalry-men remained in their positions, but King Charles was aware of their curious glances. There is no dignity in death, only in the manner of our dying, he thought dully.

Count Gaston lifted tired eyes to the heavens.

> 'Under the wide and starry sky
> Dig the grave and let me lie
> Glad did I live and gladly die
> And I lay me down with a will . . .'

he quoted from the anguish of some future poet. He straightened up. A gasp escaped him. 'Your Majesty, the play is over. You may applaud.' A long, weary, shudder-ing sigh escaped him. His body began slowly toppling sideways. 'Ingemar,' he said in a clear voice. He was dead before he hit the ground, elegantly.

A man goes where he believes he will go. Count Gaston had died as he had lived his entire life, with dignity. Even in mortal agony, he had never winced or uttered a single cry. Only his skin and the rasping breaths had told their story. He had triumphed over death by passing into it as calmly and elegantly as he had lived.

For a few moments, King Charles remained numb.

Then the roar of an animal in mortal pain escaped him, shattering the silence and solemnity of the night.

On the second morning, Prince Juan pointed out the sprawling walls with their turrets, enfolding the towers of Alhambra. Princess Beatrice gasped at the sheer beauty of it all and her heart began to thud with excitement. They had reached their goal at last. The remnants of the defeated Granadan cavalry had caught up with them the previous afternoon. The task of this cavalry group had been to seek out and destroy the enemy, but it also had orders not to pursue the enemy if it turned back to the border, but to strike and return immediately to Alhambra, which was sorely in need of men.

Princess Beatrice had identified herself and Prince Juan to the commander, Colonel Rafik, a typical dashing cavalryman with piercing grey eyes, taut features, a thin moustache and a lean, tight build. The colonel was in a dour mood, obviously disgusted by the loss of so many men and the fact that he could not turn defeat to final victory by pursuing the enemy, but he knew of Prince Juan's incarceration and escape from the Alhambra and had received specific orders from the king to look out for a Castilian prince and princess, a Jew and a gypsy girl and escort them safely to the palace.

'How did the king know about us?' Princess Beatrice had inquired, believing King Yusuf to be still alive.

Colonel Rafik looked surprised. 'King Ahmed was with you on the flight from Toledo, was he not?' he demanded sharply.

Princess Beatrice's heart leapt. Prince Ahmed was now king. Clearly he did not know about the executions of Zurika and Aaron Levi. Some of the joy left Princess Beatrice at recalling the tragic event. Yet relief remained that all indeed would be well. And she would meet her beloved prince . . . no, king now . . . no, Horn forever, in a matter of hours.

Her very soul was in the sigh she heaved. The grim fact of the Christian invasion was something she had to accept. Since it had to be, nothing mattered so long as she and Horn were physically together again. 'I take it that King Ahmed's father died,' she ventured to Colonel Rafik.

A grim expression crossed the commander's face. 'No, Princess, he was killed by an assassin's knife,' he replied, 'in the palace mosque, of all places.' He went on to give the fullest details of all that had transpired in Granada since the murder, the events following King Ahmed's return and the preparations for the siege.

So this morning, with a cool autumn breeze blowing from the snow-covered Sierra Nevada mountains, Princess Beatrice finally headed for the north gates of the Alhambra.

It was a lonely ride back for King Charles the Bad. His wound, which had been bandaged only after Count Gaston had been buried in a shallow grave 'under the wide and starry sky' with a rude cross to mark the spot, became increasingly stiff and sore. The towering presence of Colonel de Villa now riding beside him only aggravated his sense of loneliness. Princess Mathilde gone, Count Gaston gone, now only Princess Beatrice remained as the anchor of his life. He had to get her somehow and he would do so regardless of cost or consequences, he thought savagely.

On the second morning, he spotted the advance cavalry of the Castilian army in the distance, but it gave him no satisfaction. He would rather have been pursuing his love, Princess Beatrice.

Chapter 33

The Mexuar Court was the largest of the royal courts in the Alhambra palace, excluding only the Court of Myrtles. Located in the Mexuar complex at the western end of the Alhambra, it was the closest court to the public entrance square. King Ahmed had followed his father's practice of holding the daily audience in this court, not the least because of the rectangular pool in the centre, sparkling with silver water and ornamented by scallops on each of the four sides. The Court had floors of white marble, which was carried up the sides of the walls ending in patterned tiles, excluding only the western side which was wide open, like a deep portico.

As always, King Ahmed knelt on his throne, buttocks on heels, at the far end of the court, his immediate staff, including the acting Prime Minister and the Royal Treasurer, standing around him beneath the platform, which was tall enough for their heads not to be higher than that of the ruler. Except for a large space in front of the platform for those being granted audience, the court was crowded with princes, noblemen and courtiers in multi-coloured tunics, held by gold belts studded with gems, jewelled necklaces and arm bands, imams clothed in white robes, Catholic friars in brown, Jewish rabbis in black and suppliants in their best clothes.

This morning, King Ahmed had to hear a case in which Rahila, a widow, kneeling before him clad in the black robes and veil of *purdah*, had been robbed of a small bag of gold by a bailiff she had trusted. The man, named Deen, was a great pot-bellied Ethiopian, richly dressed in cloth of gold beneath a shiny black face. He had been acquitted by the *kadi*, the Muslim magistrate, on a technicality, having pleaded that he had no intention of taking the gold when the woman left the room, leaving the bag on a table in her house. His hand had shot out without his knowledge, seized the bag and placed it in his deep, inner pocket. Only when he reached his own house did he find the bag. Not knowing where it came from, he kept it. The *kadi* had merely directed him to return the gold, but the widow wanted more than reimbursement, she demanded justice, including revenge.

Conjecturing that the *kadi* had been bought, King Ahmed adopted an understanding tone with Deen. 'Is it your submission that you are not guilty, bailiff?'

Reassured by the king's demeanour – for after all this was a man's world, besides which he had paid a generous tribute to the Royal Treasury only yesterday! – a pudgy smile creased the bailiff's features. 'Yes, Your Majesty. I am not guilty.'

'Since the bag of gold disappeared from the plaintiff's residence there must surely be some guilty party?' King Ahmed questioned, smiling amiably.

'It was my hand that took the gold, *Malik*, not me.' Deen repeated his former defence, half-grinning now, sure of the outcome.

'Then you are saying that your hand is guilty?'

'Yes, lord.'

'And you are a witness to the guilt of your hand?'

'Certainly, lord.'

'Well, bailiff, I find you not guilty.' Hearing the widow's sob through her black *yashmak*, he knew a quick stab of pity. He paused. Deen's face was wreathed in a full grin. 'But we find your hand guilty.' He glanced questioningly at the defendant. 'Do you not consider that a fitting verdict?'

'Undoubtedly, Sire. Almighty Allah has blessed you with infinite wisdom.'

King Ahmed laughed pleasantly. 'Then we sentence your hand to one year's imprisonment in the public jail. You may decide whether or not to follow your hand. Further, you have given this petitioner a bag of gold, but your hand has not. If your hand does not make restitution, as required by our laws, of an additional bag of gold to the plaintiff at the end of its term in jail, it will be executed.'

He had barely acknowledged the murmurs of surprised approval that ran through the court, noting Deen's utter disbelief and dismay, when the crowd of onlookers parted and Colonel Husain, his chief aide, hurried through the gap. King Ahmed was already acquiring the ability to discern from the demeanour of any of those who approached him whether they brought good news or bad, except with Colonel Husain. The ex-cavalryman always looked as impassive as he had on the night of their first meeting.

The colonel rose from kneeling to him. 'Your Majesty, I beg an immediate private audience with you on a matter of utmost urgency.'

'With pleasure, Colonel. Shall we have the court cleared?'

'No, Sire, that will not be necessary. If you would graciously follow me to the Cuarto Dorado?'

'Certainly.'

As he followed Colonel Husain, King Ahmed wondered what the emergency could be. No, not emergency, but 'utmost urgency' were the words the man had used. And his aide was always precise in his language.

They passed through the Mexuar gallery, entered the Court of the Cuarto Dorado and turned left into the smaller Cuarto.

She stood at the far end of the room, radiant in pink-white beauty, with long gold hair and luminous blue eyes, Prince Juan smiling beside her. King Ahmed's heart was enraptured. He did not notice what she was wearing or that Colonel Husain had saluted and withdrawn, closing the door behind him. King Ahmed strode forward and took Princess Beatrice in his arms.

She was soft and yielding, clung to him desperately as he bent to kiss her lips. 'Horn!' she whispered, 'Horn, at last.'

After King Ahmed had embraced Prince Juan, Princess Beatrice recounted the story of their journey, including the tragic fate that had befallen Aaron Levi and Zurika. He cried aloud with grief then, his brow creasing, face twisting. She held him closely to comfort him. She excluded from her tale only the story of the rape. Her beloved had to be spared that cross which she would bear alone, but with the comfort of Prince Juan's sympathy.

Minutes of sweet communion passed before she remembered his duties. 'You must return to the audience, Your Majesty,' she declared firmly, gesturing for Prince Juan. 'Your people await you.'

'Surely they can await us a short while longer, when we, their sovereign lord, have waited a lifetime for you.'

Prince Juan grinned boyishly. 'Do not let her start telling you what to do, Your Majesty,' he signalled.

'I shall always be the voice of His Majesty's conscience,' she responded primly.

It was so good to be free at last, to laugh, even cry for Aaron Levi and Zurika, so long as it was with her beloved.

King Ahmed grew serious. 'We beg of you to marry us tonight,' he shot at her.

Stunned, she could barely speak. 'But, but, Your Majesty . . .'

'No "buts" in this kingdom, but me,' he teased, dropping the royal plural, then became serious again. 'The imam can marry us. We can have a Church ceremony later on if you desire it.'

618

'I have no clothes,' she wailed.

'The Court tailors will make you anything you desire.'

'Your Majesty is so compelling,' she protested. 'And what will your people say about your marrying a white Christian princess?'

'With a ruler, you should use the word "autocratic", not "compelling",' he suggested, then made his face stern. 'We would be autocratic with our people too, where our heart's desire is concerned, but the timing is perfect now. We have just ascended the throne following a confused interregnum. All the people, including princes, nobles and imams, need us. They would never risk another change so soon, especially at this time when vast enemy armies are approaching our gates.' His tone grew fierce. 'If they deny me, I shall abdicate the throne. I once left you for them. Now I am here for them. Besides,' he added cunningly, 'my marrying the heir to the throne of Castile will seem a great political alliance.' He paused. 'Beatrice, will you marry me?'

'I will marry you, beloved Horn. Oh, I will indeed. You are so cunning, I should be as lost without you as I was in Jaén.'

He allotted his mother's former suite in the harem quarters of the Daraxa to Princess Beatrice, so she could have her first bath in days, the only perfumed one since she left the Toledo palace, after which she could rest. The room he assigned Prince Juan adjoined his own bedchamber. 'Time both you non-Muslims had a bath,' he teased.

On the way back to the public audience in the Mexuar courtyard, King Ahmed, with some trepidation, confided in Colonel Husain his intention to marry Princess Beatrice that night.

To his surprise, the Colonel expressed hearty approval. 'After all, Your Majesty, even by Shi'a rules, you are entitled to *nika*, four wives of your choice and any number of concubines, so long as you look after all of them,' he asserted seriously, then smiled. 'There are also examples in Islamic history of rulers following the Sunni interpretation of the Holy Koran, which implicitly permits *muta*, other marriages, which our prophet too accepted.'

King Ahmed paused in his stride, laid a detaining hand on Colonel Husain's arm. The red and white uniformed guards lining the walls, spears at the rest position, glanced alertly at the interruption. 'Colonel Husain, I love Princess Beatrice,' King Ahmed declared, dropping the royal plural in his earnestness. 'Many rulers resort to political marriages to secure and expand their realms. I shall do no such thing. Princess Beatrice alone shall be my wife and queen, even though as a non-Muslim she will not have the royal title unless and until she inherits the Castilian throne of which she is the declared heir. She shall always reign alone as queen in the harem and in my kingdoms wherever they both may be, as she does in my heart.'

'God be with you, my king. You have had my allegiance as the ruler of Granada; your words make you a king in my own heart.'

The words, simply uttered by a proud, taciturn soldier who had deliberately chosen not to have a family so he could better serve his regiment, heartened King Ahmed. He made the public announcement of his decision immediately he resumed his seat on the throne. He spoke with sincerity, assurance and quiet determination, and the applause from all those present, including the imams, told him their approval was unanimous.

King Ahmed and Princess Beatrice were married early that night, before the Mullah-i-Assam in the small oratory of the Mexuar court. Having no relatives with whom he had had any association, the king kept the ceremony small and informal. Only Tarif, his first invitee, Prince Juan, who supported the bride, Colonel Husain, General Ismail, General Saldin, the army commander, General Rafik, the Royal Treasurer and Prince Ashraf, the Lord Chamberlain, were present.

The ceremony ended, his wife, glowing with the luminous beauty of the loved and loving bride, retired to her quarters, while the king, his heart beating with an excitement he tried hard to conceal, had a short dinner celebration with his guests, including at the table an embarrassed Tarif, to whom he bestowed freedom from servitude with the position of Royal Valet as a wedding gift. 'Your acceptance, Tarif,' he signalled the old deaf-mute, 'and yes, those tears pouring down your cheeks, are your own wedding gift to us.'

He had been impatient for the meal to end, yet back in his bedchamber, when Tarif began to disrobe him, fear intruded. He knew absolutely nothing about sex, nor did the virgin Princess Beatrice. Tarif had instructed him in what he had to do, but he became increasingly terrified as the minutes went by. Never one to flee an enemy, a part of King Ahmed simply wanted to run away.

'Forget about what you have to do, Your Majesty,' Tarif assured him. 'Forget about proving anything. True love bursts into bloom when a virgin man and a virgin woman make love for the first time. Just let your love flow in touching, kissing, caressing. Offer flowers to your beloved before you enter the shrine of her womanhood.'

The words helped King Ahmed set aside his fears. Wearing a white robe, it was still without great confidence, but more eagerness in his heart, that he strode through the lamplit corridors to his bride's quarters, escorted only by Tarif. He knocked on the door, barely noticing its exquisite ornamentation. His heart had begun to thud against his ribs.

'Come in!'

'Your golden voice opens the quiet doorway to para-

621

dise,' he declared immediately he stood at the open entrance. In anticipation of their first glance, he deliberately avoided looking within until the door clicked shut behind him. In the glow of lamplight, his eyes slowly wandered over the pink marble floors, covered by great carpets of green and white, supporting their green in matching couches with pink cushions. He breathed the gentle, jasmine-scented fumes from hanging lamps and gold braziers on their white alabaster stands. His searching eyes took in the huge, coloured wall-tapestries, but still could not find her.

His gaze sought the open arches. She was standing by the balcony wall, her back to the views of the black ravine of the Darro valley framed between dark hillsides under a starlit blue sky. She was dressed in a flimsy white robe, beneath which her tall figure glowed pink below golden hair hanging free to her waist. He took in the silhouette of generous breasts, flaring hips and full thighs with awe. What a perfection of colour and form. He sought her eyes. Oh, sweet Allah, those eyes almost blue-black in the half-light against the pink-white face, framed by the shining golden hair. How exquisite.

For a moment, he was the poet, seeing her without any sensation other than an adoration of beauty. Then his gaze merged into hers. The eyes! Those eyes he had discovered in a tiny painting. Eyes that had locked into his for the first time in her chamber in the Toledo palace, filling him with ecstasy.

Her gaze was luminous, virginal, compelling. His organ began to rise, expanded to a full erection. Drawn by her magnetism, he slowly advanced towards her, murmuring the words that arose in him.

'Angel of beauty and of grace
Our virgin states, your loving face
Make me your slave forever . . .'

'Oh Ahmed, my King,' she breathed. 'Oh Horn.'

From the sweet ecstasy of his adoration of her beauty, the flawless sight, the golden sound, the scent of musk, enshrined in the purity of God's creation behind her, holy lust emerged. He reached her, slowly embraced the smooth body with never a wrinkle on it. His organ swelled to bursting point. As he kissed her, instinct made him move his loins, gently thrusting, gently thrusting.

A cool breeze flew in from the valley, caressing them both as they stood there. She moved her pubis gently against his. Eyes closed, cool in the night light, warm in the body-shadows, vibrance began to dawn, thrilling his crotch. The slow quiver-fire reached into his eager-answering consciousness. She moaned.

Oh Allah, she *responds* to my *ecstasy*.

Ecstasy suddenly peaked, uncontrollable. He ejaculated.

As he had planned, King Ahmed was about to make his first major foray against the enemy just when they were settling into their positions in the flat lands, hills and valleys surrounding the capital. He would personally lead ten thousand cavalrymen in the assault that morning. He had slept every night with Princess Beatrice. He had prematurely ejaculated each night, falling asleep disgusted with himself.

This morning had been different. He had awoken well before dawn to find Princess Beatrice sitting up, coughing and retching into the gold spittoon placed beside their canopied divan bed. 'I feel sick in my throat,' she explained.

'It must be something you ate last night,' he suggested, alarmed. 'Shall I send for the Court physician?'

'No, thank you, beloved.' She noticed his concern. 'Do not be alarmed for the sickness is not from my stomach, but in my throat.' She smiled wanly. 'I shall be all right.

You do not need an ailing wife on your hands when you are about to go to battle!'

The artistic sensitivity that had seemed such a blessing so far had begun to lay its curse on King Ahmed. Young and inexperienced though he was, he longed to fulfil his bride and himself sexually and to give Princess Beatrice his child. Was it never to be? Each time he approached and held her, he ejaculated. She remained a virgin. Despite her patience and understanding, her assurances that having sex was not only in the act of physical union but in making love, King Ahmed developed more and more apprehension with each failure, as he regarded it.

Meanwhile, the passing days had strengthened the defences of Alhambra and the resolve of its people against the intelligence reports brought in by scouts of the advance of the Castilian army from the north, the Navarrese from the northwest and the Portuguese from the west. Only the south was free.

This was the seventh morning after his wedding. The advance Castilian elements of the enemy were reported to be only a few miles from the capital. Granadan fighting patrols had harried the Castilians every night, citizens' groups had sabotaged its supply train, but the unending juggernaut had rolled inexorably along to its objective.

When the *adhan*, the call to prayer for *subh*, resounded from the minarets at dawn, King Ahmed reflected sadly that this would be the last call that some of his troops, possibly he himself, heard and answered. He was more dejected than he would otherwise have been because he was worried by his wife's sickness. Would he return from a successful engagement only to find her dead? The possibility filled him with gloom, though he knew that everything became exaggerated at such a time. Supposing he was killed? He had left strict instructions that Princess Beatrice should be moved to the Gen al Arif tower with

Prince Juan. He had also provided for them both from his private treasury. But what if King Pedro succeeded in taking Alhambra? The Christian Princess Beatrice, daughter of a Christian king, heir to the kingdom of Castile, had married a pagan. Even her father would be hard put to it to save her from the wrath of Holy Church, especially the likes of the Bishop Eulogius, who was surely Satan on earth.

And then there was King Charles the Bad with his ambition to marry Princess Beatrice so that he could add Castile to his domains. The fact that Princess Beatrice was a widow would mean nothing to the Christians, because hers was not a Christian marriage. Even if it had been, a dissolution would be easy to obtain. King Ahmed recalled Isabella of Toran, heir to Jerusalem in the Holy Land many years earlier. She had been married to Lord Humphrey, but it had meant nothing to Christians like King Richard of England when she was forced to marry Conrad, Marquis of Monserrat, so he would become entitled to the throne of Jerusalem.

Princess Beatrice had told him fiercely last night that, rather than submit to that monster, Charles the Bad, she would kill herself and beg for God's mercy before the Judgment Seat. Though he did not want her dead, he could not help part of him being elated by the assertion. But, dear Allah, what a dismal prospect!

As he began performing his *subh* ablutions in the courtyard of the private oratory where he and Princess Beatrice had been married, he resolutely put all such thoughts from his mind while he pronounced to himself the *niyyah*, the intention of performing that ablution in order to cleanse impurity and accept prayer. He washed his hands, cleansing all the wrongful deeds of humanity, his mouth of all falsehoods against the principles of Islam, his face, to present to God a personality that had removed frailty and striven for purity. Finally, he washed his feet, seeking God's pardon for having gone astray.

By the time he entered the oratory and faced the direction of Mecca, *giblah*, at the semi-circular niche, *mihrab*, he was more than calm, he was serene, having dedicated the day's battle to Almighty Allah as part of *jihad*, Holy War.

They emerged through the city's northern gates in silver morning sunlight. Just ahead of him, the green banner of Islam with its silver star and crescent, to his right, the snows of the Sierra Nevada mountains glittering and shining, causing the sky to appear a paler blue. Blackbirds flew noisily overhead, puzzled by the unusual activity. Beneath the dank odours of the city, he could smell his heavy jasmin scent through his armour.

With enemy sentinels on the hilltops, there was no way in which he could take the Castilian forces by surprise. Soon after he and his four thousand cavalrymen began cantering rapidly along the highway, he heard the trumpets in the distance. A few miles later, he saw the enemy drawn up in line of battle along the level ground on either side of the road, cavalry well behind the two front lines of kneeling and standing pikemen, with gaps through whom the mounted men would charge: a classical defence posture providing for attack or counter-attack. He rather thought that the enemy cavalry would await his charge, for which the Moors were renowned, so that the pikemen could blunt it, causing severe casualties before counter-charging. It suited his overall plan this morning, a plan of which he fervently hoped the enemy would have no inkling.

'We hope our intelligence is accurate,' he shouted above the thunderous clatter of hooves to Colonel Husain, riding straight-backed beside him.

The dashing cavalryman guessed what he was thinking.

'It stands to reason, Sire,' he shouted back. 'The entire Castilian army stretches many miles along the highway. Such huge numbers are rather like a moving fort. They are best suited to open battle on flat ground, after assembling fully, or in siege operations. This morning, we are opposed by more than ten thousand of the enemy's advance elements.'

Ten thousand, the man had casually said! Over two to one, but the odds made no difference to him. A thrill of exultation mushroomed and filled King Ahmed's being. 'We are glad and proud to be riding beside you on our first battle, Colonel Husain!' he exclaimed involuntarily.

A smile lit Colonel Husain's normally enigmatic face framed by his helmet and cheekguards. 'I have ridden into battle often, Sire, with many a dear, valiant comrade,' he stated, his dark eyes completely sincere. 'But this is my finest hour.'

Still slow-cantering, when he gauged that they were nearing enemy bowshot, King Ahmed gave the command to his trumpeter.

The trumpet blared. 'Extend into open line!' Horsemen behind him began to fan out on either side. Other trumpets took up the call. King Ahmed reined in his horse while the squadrons galloped into place. Three lines each of one thousand men, with the fourth to reserve had been his order. He thrilled at the precision with which the manoeuvre was executed.

Colonel Husain picked up his thought. 'The enemy are already seeing that, though heavily outnumbered, we are a force to be reckoned with, Sire,' he shouted.

The first hail of enemy arrows hissed towards them almost before he finished speaking, and fell short.

'They are testing for range,' Colonel Husain advised.

The warmth of the sunshine began to penetrate King Ahmed's armour. 'Sound the charge!' he commanded his trumpeter. He lowered his visor, drew his sword and raised it aloft.

'*La ilaha il' Allah!*' The battle cry from one thousand throats burst upwards to the blue heavens.

He clapped spurs on his white battle charger, heard the enemy's answering roar. 'For God and Holy Church!' It was their God against Almighty Allah.

Even before he reached full gallop, the next hail of enemy arrows came whizzing down. King Ahmed took one on his shield. Somewhere to his right, a stricken horse whinnied shrilly. The charging line did not waver. The levelled pikes loomed, a vast hedgehog. He swerved, deflected a pike-thrust with his blade, took a youthful head on the run with the scimitar. He broke through to the open ground, heard the enemy trumpets blaring the charge. He wheeled with his men to take the pikemen in the rear as his second line of cavalry came thundering up. The earth shook with the pounding of enemy hooves.

King Ahmed went into a frenzy. Yelling, screaming, cursing, he took blows on his shield. He cut, chopped, thrust and slashed. Metal clanged, heads fell, bodies rolled, horses snorted and whinnied in pain. The red blood mist before his eyes soon matched his blood-dripping sword as he forced his way back through the pikemen, crossing his own charging cavalry. Caught in front and rear, the pikemen began to waver. Then his second line of cavalry broke through them to meet the pounding enemy cavalry charge on the open ground behind the pikemen. He led his own line back, filtering through his third line of cavalry. Blind to all else, he and his line of cavalry reformed and charged again. As always Colonel Husain was with him, the veteran cavalryman, bold, aggressive, protective.

The battle resolved itself into groups of his men fighting enemy cavalry, pikemen and bowmen. An hour later it still raged. The grass had been scuffed by hooves and feet. Dust began to rise. The glaring sun was hot. His eyes were half blinded with sweat. His sword arm ached. A twisting pain at his hip told of a wound. He did not know when or where he had received it.

Where were they?

Though completely engrossed in hand to hand combat, the question began to bother him.

Half an hour later. Where were they? Had they tried and failed? Had they tried and failed? Had they tried and failed? The question began to hammer in his brain. If they had, was it not time to retreat before enemy reinforcements arrived from the main body to decimate his men?

He had his answer at that very moment. The wavering of the enemy rear was so tangible it made his blood sparkle with renewed hope. The attacks he had commanded, sending out four thousand more cavalry in small groups last night to work round the highway and hit the enemy attack group a mile beyond its assembly point, were succeeding. His men had arrived and were pressing the enemy. The attack group was isolated.

From then on it was a massacre.

At noon he ordered his trumpeters to sound the retreat. Bathed in sweat, caked with blood, breathing heavily, he was still not the least weary, only vibrant. Weariness would come later, he guessed. For the present, he was still asparkle from battle and the lust to kill. Observing that Colonel Husain shared his mood, he reached out and gripped the aide's hand before urging his white charger back towards the capital. As his trot became a gallop, his trumpets behind him blared the retreat.

His cavalry squadrons broke off the encounter and reformed. As they followed him back to the Alhambra, they left a plain strewn with weapons and the dead, the wounded, the dying. Arrows and pikes sprouted grotesquely from maimed bodies. Horses lay on their sides, some on their backs, thrashing wildly with legs pitifully waving in the air. Riderless mounts galloped wildly around. Screams of agony, moans, whimpering, sobbing, the shrieks of men and the squeals of animals in death throes.

The foray had been a total success. He estimated that he had lost about two hundred men, dead or wounded, to about four thousand of the enemy.

He would send out a truce party to recover his wounded for treatment and the dead for a proper Muslim burial. The victory would not make the enemy turn back, but would merely delay them, giving more time for the Moroccan reinforcements to arrive and providing the invaders with a thunderous display of Moorish mettle.

PART IV

Councils of War

The War Council met every night after an early dinner, always spartan by King Ahmed's decree so that people of rank did not feast while the rest of his subjects were rationed. This hour of the day afforded more time for discussion without the cramp of subsequent appointments or events. The Council would review the results of yet another day's siege and plan the next day's and future moves. He would have had Prince Juan, who was well acquainted with Castilian strengths, strategy and tactics, attend the meetings except for his physical disabilities. So he made it a part of his routine to drop in on Prince Juan's bedchamber every night, after the War Council meeting, to brief, consult, spend time with a friend so tried, trusted and proven that, though a Castilian prince, he had a pass under King Ahmed's royal seal for free access throughout the capital as well as in and out of it, without question.

Following the meeting with Prince Juan, he would spend each night with his wife, Princess Beatrice, but he generally arrived in her chamber so tired and late that he did not have to endure the shame he had come to fear from his unfailing premature ejaculations, which had kept her a virgin in his eyes.

The third month of the siege was drawing to a close. Word had been received from King Abu Hasan of Morocco a month earlier that he would arrive with 100,000 men in the spring, after the winter storms had abated. Such a storm was raging tonight, its gusts whipping up the water in the central pool of the court. The twenty members of the Council seated around him in the golden glow of the sandalwood scented hanging lamps in the Court of Machucha, its far walls lined by giant guards, had fallen into the habit of chatting before he called them to order.

'I ran into Hadji Juyyuh this morning, Sire,' General Deen, the fat Service Corps chief announced. He covered his mouth with plump fingertips to stifle a belch. He probably fed better than anyone else.

'We did not know that the seer was back from Mecca,' King Ahmed responded. 'So he has finally earned the titled "Hadji". Did he have any difficulty getting back into the city?'

'Our southern gates still afford reasonable access,' General Iqbal, the Fortress Commander, stated. He sniffed from a bad head cold that suffused his face red and made his brown eyes bloodshot. 'Pardon me, Sire, but this cold is more deadly than our Greek Fire.' He turned and blew each nostril expertly into a gold spittoon that a thoughtful attendant had placed beside him, then wiped his nose with a white linen square he removed from inside his red tunic.

'General Iqbal should volunteer as our secret weapon against the enemy,' General Zahir, the huge Artillery Commander observed, stifling a grin. 'He could stand on the ramparts and . . . er . . . just blow the enemy away.'

The Fortress Commander joined in the good-humoured laughter that rippled around the table.

'It is remarkable how frequently General Deen happens to run into men whom he has invited to visit his quarters, Sire,' General al Afdal, the slim, moustached cavalryman, asserted dryly, taking advantage of the brief lull in the conversation. 'Since he is enmeshed by the science of astrology, one might conclude that such chance encounters "are written in his stars".'

General Deen's rubicund face turned even more red. 'Well . . . er . . . well, my colleague may laugh at my interest,' he began, then lapsed into an embarrassed silence.

'And what did the Hadji, your astrologer, have to say?' King Ahmed intervened, turning to General Deen.

'Your royal father . . . er . . . died after Seer Juyyuh left on his pilgrimage, Sire, so he did not afford himself the opportunity to read your horoscope. But he cast it immediately on his return to Alhambra two days ago. He has predicted a long and glorious reign for you.'

My father kept me a prisoner because an astrologer cast my horoscope when I was born and warned that love could be the stumbling block of a long and glorious life for me, King Ahmed reflected. I paid the price, but today, though not yet twenty-one, I am completely happy, loving my wife. 'Did he predict a son and heir for me?' he demanded, feigning a flippancy he did not feel because this was at the heart of the one question that bothered him: would his premature ejaculations prevent him from ever having children?

'Indeed, Sire. You will have a son and also a daughter.'

'His Majesty's long and glorious reign and his children will come from His Majesty's endeavours, not because of any decree of the stars,' General Saldin, the burly Commander-in-Chief, declared heavily. 'While I personally believe that the sun, the moon, the stars and the planets can physically affect our lives – after all, does not the full moon produce the highest frenzies in the insane? – I am also convinced that we should merely take care when heavenly influences are malign and push when they are favourable. No more.'

'Is it not possible that our taking care during times of adverse influence is what creates, aggravates or perpetuates the adversity?' King Ahmed inquired of him. 'Should we not always have the resolve to convert bad times to good and the prudence not to overextend in good times, lest bad times result?'

'A profound thought, Your Majesty,' General Saldin observed. 'I must think on it.'

King Ahmed directed his gaze to General Deen. 'And would you not agree, General, that any Court astrologer who does not predict a long and glorious reign for his sovereign might end up experiencing a quick inglorious death?'

He interrupted the ensuing laughter by rapping on the mahogany table to call the meeting to order. 'General Saldin, let us start the meeting with your report on the enemy's all-out assault today.'

'As you know, Your Majesty, the assault resulted in another failure. The operation commenced with a bombardment from the long-range artillery they call *malvoisin*, under cover of which assault forces advanced towards the ramparts. We kept their catapults, mangonels and archers at a distance with our own artillery, which has a greater range, and inflicted severe casualties on the advancing infantry. They then directed spearpoints of cavalry to try and breach our northern, western and eastern gates. Greek fire from our troops as well as civilians manning the ramparts, for which we must all thank Your Majesty once more, and accurate archery forced the cavalry to withdraw. A large infantry force, under cover of targes, then brought up three battering rams to the north gates, while bolder enemy elements took heavy casualties to reach our walls. They flung up ladders with grappling hooks.' He grinned. 'We allowed them to crowd the ladders, then hurled Greek fire at them, while huge boulders and heavy fire from our archers dealt with the battering rams. It did not take the enemy long to retreat. The entire assault lasted four hours. I estimate the enemy casualties to be several hundred dead and wounded, besides two score horses. Our own are but a few dozen men. It was not a good day for the Christians,' he concluded grimly.

King Ahmed glanced at General Iqbal. 'Your damage report, General.'

'About the same as with every one of their general assaults, Sire. As you know, these are predictable, one every Thursday morning, with unfailing regularity, perhaps as a sort of prelude to their fish-only Friday. Our firefighters always put out the fires with sand and water. A few buildings are damaged or demolished, none of any significance. Most can be rebuilt in short order. We collect their spent arrows for our own use, as they undoubtedly do with ours. Our food stocks remain adequate.'

'The infidels obviously think they can starve us into submission,' General Saldin interposed. 'They don't have a hope in their Christian hell of doing so.'

'Do you agree, Fortress Commander?' King Ahmed demanded.

To his surprise, General Iqbal grew thoughtful. 'I do have an area of grave concern, Your Majesty.' He paused, sniffed. 'One of the prime causes of anxiety in a prolonged siege is health and sanitation. When thousands of people are confined within a city's walls, sewage and garbage disposal become a major problem.'

'We do have our dumps for refuse, which we burn, and adequate scavenging services, do we not?'

'Yes, Your Majesty, but it is difficult to make people follow the rigorous rules for the personal disposal of garbage and excrement that are so essential in such a situation. Besides, we often have corpses stacked awaiting cremation. I have asked our Physician General to attend this meeting and bring to your royal attention a somewhat alarming situation.'

Gone was the joking Fortress Commander. A thrill of alarm shot through King Ahmed's body. Please, Almighty Allah, not pestilence to add to our problems. The entire War Council around him had fallen silent at the fears expressed by General Iqbal. 'Summon the Physician Gen-

eral,' he commanded the guard nearest the entrance to
the court.

Physician General Suby was a small, rat-faced Syrian
bearing a fierce red moustache like a banner. When he rose
from kneeling, King Ahmed gestured towards the vacant
settle opposite himself that was reserved for invitees. 'We
understand you have some concerns regarding the health
and sanitation of our capital, Physician General?'

'Indeed, Your Majesty, much to my regret.' Suby had
a dry voice and spoke in a monotone, with a dull lecturer's
delivery. 'Our problem is rats, black rats, which have
begun to emerge from their holes in increasing numbers.'

The chill silence of those around him seemed to reflect
the hollow feeling in the pit of King Ahmed's stomach.
'Perhaps the stacks of garbage to which General Iqbal has
referred attract the rats?' he proffered hopefully.

General Suby stroked one of his ginger moustaches.
'The rats die soon after they appear, Sire, and that means
a problem. Besides, they are all sopping wet when they
emerge.' He anticipated the next suggestion, 'And not
from the sewers.' He paused, his yellow eyes grim. 'Most
alarmingly, I discovered while on my way here that every
one of the rats has bled from the mouth.'

The silence of the grave fell on the room. All eyes were
fixed on General Suby with near-horror, each man
scarcely daring to face his conclusion. 'I personally saw a
huge black rat in the flare-light on the side of the main
street as I walked to the palace just now,' he continued,
his voice low. 'Its fur was drenched. I watched it move
uncertainly, stopping and starting to recover its balance,
until it suddenly spun round with a squeal and fell on its
side. Blood gushed from its open mouth before it died.'

Dear Allah, we have resolutely defended our faith.
Why are You about to inflict this Christian calamity on
Your Chosen?

* * *

It was with a heavy heart that King Ahmed walked back to the tower of the Peinador de la Reina. He was glad that Colonel Husain, who escorted him, was the silent type so that each of them could be lost in his own thoughts as they passed through the lamplit courts and corridors, deserted at this hour, even desolate seeming because of the immobility of the statuesque sentries standing guard.

Having had a long day, commencing with the attack on the capital and ending with the news that the Black Death might have hit it, King Ahmed was so ready for bed that he had sent word through a eunuch to Prince Juan that he would not be visiting that night. As for Princess Beatrice, should he alarm her with the terrible news? He decided that complete truth, however calamitous, was essential between her and him. Besides, it would be gossip on the streets by evening, when panic would sweep through the city. So he looked forward to lightening his private dread, deliberately unexpressed during the Council meeting, with her alone.

The major problem was the siege. If the Christian armies could be made to withdraw, the people of Alhambra would not panic so much. The chiefs had reported that, in other besieged cities smitten with the plague, the moment the gates were finally opened, people streamed into the countryside. Some believed that the disease was caused by changes in the earth's temperature creating southern winds, others that it was caused by corruption of the air, against the stench of which they carried scented flowers. Others yet thought the cause to be the raining down of frogs, toads and reptiles from the heavens, malefic planetary conjunctions or simply the wrath of God at sinful man. Somewhere deep in his mind, King Ahmed sensed that, though the Black Death might be viewed as the wrath of Almighty Allah if it did visit Alhambra, some good might be extracted from the calamity, be it only the physical cleansing of man. Being faced with such a dire event for the first time, he searched feverishly for a tangible cause of the outbreak other than the popular conjectures to date. Apart from the symptoms of the disease and its obvious contagion, the one common factor seemed to be black rats emerging from their holes and dying by the hundreds in public places. It would be essential to have the rats removed or burned by vigilance squads – with Greek fire perhaps? – the moment they made their appearance, so he would command that this be done.

That was as far as he got in his thinking before he arrived with Colonel Husain at the entrance to the Daraxa, the king's living quarters, beyond which no male could proceed except the king, such immediate members of the royal family as the king specifically approved and the eunuchs. The colonel kissed his hand and they bade each other the blessings of Allah for the night.

King Ahmed's gloom lightened at the prospect of being with his wife. He could relax at long last, discuss the situation and the cares of the day without any need to appear stoic and enjoy the blessed balance of a few hours of peace before facing the tribulations of the next day. He had planned to set out in the mid-morning after his regular public audience was over, on an inspection of the City with General Suby.

He was surprised at the tremulousness of Princess Beatrice's voice when she responded to his usual knock, the one . . . one, two . . . representing each of them and both, a loving routine they had established. Was she sick again? Dear Allah, not that in addition to all else, for it would hit him in the heart. Mouth dry, he rushed inside the chamber. She did not hasten to greet him from the divan on which she usually awaited him. She was not even seated on it. Looking around wildly, he saw her standing at the far end of the chamber where she had received him that first magic night of their marriage. She was leaning against the balcony wall beneath the central arch. Dressed in a warm woollen nightdress against the chill of the night, she seemed to be contemplating the rain pelting down so hard that it hid the mountains beyond the Darro valley below.

'What is wrong, *queridisima*?' He ran to take her in his arms, but she raised both palms to stop him with a single negative shake of her golden head. She had obviously been weeping.

'What's wrong, beloved wife?' he repeated. 'Are you sick? Is it something I have done?'

She shook a quick head many times. 'No, my beloved king, you are never wrong in my eyes. It is I . . .' Her voice trailed off into a sob.

'What?'

'I should have told you this before, but I was afraid to hurt you and that was wrong, for now I must hurt you even more.'

'What? What? Why should you have to hurt me?' He gestured hopelessly in his bewilderment. What was happening? Was he going mad?

'I was raped before I reached the convent in Jaén.'

'Raped?' At first he could not take it in. 'What are you talking about?' Realization dawned. His heart twisted. 'Who raped you? In Jaén, you said. Was it some common Castilian soldier? Where did it happen?' He moved towards her. 'Oh my poor darling. You bore this alone.' Outrage flared. 'I shall find the man who did it and flay him alive myself. For now, please let me hold you. Oh *querida, querida*, how you must have suffered!'

She slipped into his arms, weeping. He covered her pale, wet cheeks with kisses.

'You are so good . . . Horn.' She raised tearstained eyes to him. 'You mean it does not matter to you that I am not a virgin?'

He laughed low. 'How could it matter when I have not

even been able to reach your virginity. We complement each other, you the virgin ended, I the virgin not yet begun! And do you think virginity ends with the piercing of some veil inside you? No, no, no, my beloved. Each time I look at you, I see a virgin princess; each time I hold you in my arms you are my virgin love, and when I finally enter you some day, it is I who will receive your virginity. Yes, yes, both of us virgin, you and I.' His voice shook with tender passion. 'Indeed, it shall be so each time we mate, for the rest of our lives. That is how I feel about you.'

'Oh, Horn, Horn, you are so wonderful. I wish I could have given you the precious physical gift as well.'

'You have given me the precious gift of understanding my own sexual frailty. You will help me to overcome it, I know, and then we shall have Almighty Allah's greatest gift of all, the product of our union, our first baby carried in your virgin womb.'

'Oh Almighty God!' She pulled away from him. 'Is that what you really want? Our child from my virgin womb?'

'With all my heart.' A wisp of black cloud arose within him: he did not know why. The rain, accelerating, seemed to beat in his head. Dire foreboding seized him. 'Why?'

'I am already with child,' she declared simply, eyes fearful.

For a moment he could not comprehend what she meant. Then its significance hit him like a thunderbolt. 'You . . . are . . . pregnant?' He jabbed a finger to emphasize each word.

She nodded.

'From this rapist?'

'Yes.' The word came out in a terrified whisper.

'Who was he?' The words were a strangled croak.

'King Charles the Bad.'

'K . . . King . . . What do you mean? How could King

Charles have done it?' He was indeed losing his mind. He reached desperately for sanity.

He listened while she told him the whole story in quiet, steady tones, assuring him that Prince Juan could vouch for its truth. When she finished, he was smitten dumb. He wished he could tear his eardrums out to erase her words. He wished he were dead. Instead, his mouth was dry, his chest hurt, his head had begun to pound. His whole world had crashed.

Beaten down, deserted by God and man, how much can flesh and blood take in one day?

Anger began to form, to mount within him, a helpless rage such as he had never known before.

Dear Allah, I beg you not to let it explode. Help me in this at least.

'You should have told me before we were married,' he said, suddenly calm. 'You were not just marrying Prince Ahmed, but the King of Granada who owes a duty to his people. You caused him to betray his people.' He reflected further, cold sober suddenly. 'Besides, you have hidden this from me for three months now. So all our loving was based upon a lie.'

He turned around without looking at her and walked out of the chamber.

Alone in bed for the first time since his marriage three months earlier, he was spending a sleepless night. The lie . . . the lie . . . the lie . . . kept pounding into his head. The stark fact was that his wife had told him the truth only when she realized she was pregnant. If she had not been, he could have gone to his grave in ignorance. He was horrified at the rape, knew boundless pity for all Princess Beatrice must have endured since it occurred. Besides, how she must have agonized over whether to tell him. He loved her with all his heart and would love her forever. But the lie remained! And the truth had not been exposed to him from love but only when expediency demanded it.

Then suspicion reared its foul, scaly head like some vile prehistoric creature from a slimy swamp. If he had not unfailingly had his premature ejaculations, his wife could have hidden the truth from him forever, *pretending that the baby was his*, though she knew with certainty that Charles the Bad and not he was the father. Another hideous possibility arose, the twin creature of that other monster. Supposing the father was someone totally different, someone from the Toledo palace? After all, what *did* he know of Princess Beatrice other than the face she had presented to him, a lying face at least during the recent past? If she could hide one truth from him, why not some other more ghastly situation?

One deliberately hidden truth from Princess Beatrice had begotten the possibility of other more fearful lies in his mind. One vile suspicion in his mind had spawned other monsters. He saw this and fought desperately for hours to overcome the onslaught. His brain searched feverishly for dates of conception, of monthly periods, but met only fog. He felt so helpless. He had no knowledge of such things – only that a baby was born nine months after conception.

Should he check his wife's story with Prince Juan? His mind immediately rejected the temptation. That would be dishonourable. Each time this possibility hit, the idealistic lover within him shrank back in pain, but his most dreadful dilemma remained the giving of a bastard heir to his people.

And what could he expect from Prince Juan anyhow, his trusted friend who had betrayed him, knowing the truth and hiding it? He had conversed with the prince every night since he became king, had confided State secrets to him. How could Prince Juan have kept the truth from him like some arch-deceiver? A part of King Ahmed conceded that Prince Juan might also have been trying to spare him more terrible hurt, but how do you base either a marriage or a friendship on a lie?

He should cast personal considerations aside and think only as King Ahmed, confining his problems to his sense of duty as a ruler. He had been bred in the traditions of royalty. Abou bon Ebben and every one of his other tutors had dinned it into him that ruling a kingdom was not a one-sided treasury for the benefit of the monarch, but consisted of mutual duties and obligations between king and subject. He, King Ahmed, had a duty to be truthful with his people. He loved Princess Beatrice so much that, personally, as a free individual, he would have forgiven her even the lie, accepted the child, pretended to the whole world that it was his in order to protect his wife and ease her torture. It was King Ahmed who faced the obstacles. If the baby was a boy, it would be heir to the throne of Granada under both customary and Muslim law. If it was a girl and his only child, her husband would become king. How could he expose his people to a succession that did not contain one single drop of Moorish Muslim blood?

As for his wife, some deep instinct of faith in her and of the eternal purity of their love finally surfaced, won the battle against foul suspicions. Princess Beatrice would give him the same fidelity as he had unfailingly given her.

Many times during the night, Ahmed the man was tempted to go to his wife's chamber, hold her in his arms and accept the baby as his, to comfort her, putting her pain before his. Twice he actually went to the door of his chamber. But *King* Ahmed made him pause with his hand on the door-handle.

His whole world had indeed fallen apart.

Alone in her bed for the first time since her marriage three months earlier, Princess Beatrice was spending a sleepless night, alternately tossing and turning on silk and linen sheets that felt warm in spite of the coolness of the night and kneeling at her *prie-dieu*. It had a small altar on a shelf above it containing a blue and white statue of the Blessed Virgin Mary beneath a red and white crucifix on the wall. Her husband had insisted on providing her with these infidel symbols within a Muslim harem because he loved her so much, defying all possible criticism or consequences. And what had she done? She had crucified him on the altar of her deceit. None of the practical considerations that had seemed so vital three months ago mattered any longer.

The very first time she knelt before the Blessed Virgin, she faced the stark realization that she should have told King Ahmed the whole truth before she accepted his offer of marriage. The rain splattered and misted outside, but her mind was suddenly as clear as when silver morning sunshine lit the bedchamber instead of the golden lamp-light around her.

'*O Virgin Mother, what did you do when you discovered the awful truth that you were pregnant from the Holy Ghost, something no man would believe?*'

She knew the answer even before the gentle lady replied.

'*I told my betrothed, Joseph, all, and at first he cast me out, but he later forgave me and made the child his, even though it made him the laughing stock of his family and his community.*'

'*But Holy Mother, I am so young . . .*' She paused, remembering. 'You were even younger,' she whispered, not voicing the thought that so far as the Virgin Mother was concerned, she had had no choice.

A flash of lightning from outside lit the face of the Blessed Virgin, revealed a smile of knowledge. '*I know what you are thinking, my child, but the fact is simple. Youth and age are of man and beast. The truth is ancient* as the hills. Only the truth would have set you free. You will never know, nor will your husband, the answer to the question of whether you really hid the truth for yourself or for him, but it is you who created for yourself the punishment of this question which you will endure for the rest of your life. I bleed for you, my child, but I have no control over your decisions as to right and wrong, or their consequences.

The truth of the words hit Princess Beatrice with merciless force.

'At least there must be some hope for me in heaven, Holy Mother,' she wailed. 'Remember, I resisted the temptation which assailed me again and again to get my husband's seed into me somehow and make him think the baby was his, so he would not have to endure the tortures he is undergoing at this very moment.'

The Blessed Virgin's expression was most mild, but there was a hardness to her tone: 'For whose benefit were you tempted?' she demanded tersely. 'It is you who would have been saved much heartache and terror, embarrassment and despair if you had put such a vile plan into effect.'

'But did I not overcome the temptation? Should I not get some reward for that not only in heaven but on this earth?'

'At the gates of heaven, which shall be your first stop, as for every other dead soul. As for overcoming the temptation, I seem to recall that you had some slight help in making your decision from the person whose moral support you deceitfully sought to enlist on a few occasions, a rather shocked Prince Juan . . .'

'I wish I were dead!'

'But you are not.'

'I am not sure that I actually did wrong for such a terrible punishment to have been inflicted on me. Should one always come out with the truth just because it happens to be there?' She could not help some petulance emerging from the depths of her suffering. *'Should I tell my mother that her dress is horrid just because it happens to be ugly?'*

'Only if by telling her you can save her from some ill consequences through wearing it.'

Princess Beatrice thought that one out carefully. *'You mean that I should have risked hurting my husband because he was entitled to the truth in view of the decisions he was making. In other words, I owed it to him to give him the facts, even though they could cause him grief, because they had a bearing on his major decisions.'*

Lightning flickered through the chamber, a rumble of thunder followed, bringing the odour of burnt fireworks into the air. The eyes of the beloved Madonna remained inscrutable.

'You are so wise, Holy Mother,' Princess Beatrice declared involuntarily. *'I love King Ahmed so.'*

The face of the Virgin Mary lit up then. *'I am but a mirror, my child. The wisdom is yours. As is the love. Do you know what you must do now?'*

'Yes, Madonna.'

'I have seen you grow up from the praying child to the arguing adult. That is good, for it means you are now making your own decisions. Your large blue eyes are sunlight on the Mediterranean when they glisten with tears, my child.' The statue of the Blessed Virgin had the same gentle warm voice as of old. *'God gave you blonde hair, delicate features and a slim, tall body so you could look like the angel you are. I shall intercede with Our Father for you now that you have decided to do what is right.'*

Some time before the muezzin's call to *subh* the rain abated. Somehow it helped, but not much. By the time he made his way to his usual public audience, he was composed, but his eyes were grainy, his body felt fevered and his heart remained sick. To his utter astonishment, Colonel Husain, who was always at the door to the

Daraxa to accompany him, informed him that an old gypsy woman, named Pilar, had begged a private audience. Knowing the whole story of the flight from Granada and the return, the colonel had ordered that she be escorted into the corridor serving the oratory to await the royal pleasure.

What was Pilar doing in Alhambra? She should be in Jaén. How did she get here? King Ahmed's first reaction was, Oh no, I want to put the entire past where it belongs, behind me. Zurika's betrayal during the flight from Toledo created all this mess. I owe her and Pilar nothing. Quick reflection, however, brought recall that the old crone had helped him on two occasions, first when he was sick in his mind and she conducted her seance, next on the day of the flight from Alhambra, when she had awaited him with horses. He never forgot a favour. 'We shall see the woman now, on our way to the public audience,' he informed Colonel Husain. He directed his steps through the Mexuar towards the oratory. Staff in hand, clad in a black robe, she was seated on the pink marble floor, scratching herself. A huge black Nubian sentry, scimitar at the rest position, looming above her, made no attempt to hide his distaste.

As Pilar scrambled to her feet, King Ahmed waved the sentry away, indicating that he wanted to talk to the woman in private. He also requested Colonel Husain to await him in the audience court.

Pilar knelt and kissed his hand, then rose to her feet looking up at him with rheumy eyes. How gaunt she had become. Black hollows circled her eyes and her wrinkled cheeks sagged as never before. She gave the impression of one totally bereft until his eyes met hers. Something burned in those ancient eyes, something terrible, fearful, inexorable. What was it? Rage, bitterness, an unyielding purpose.

'You desired to see us,' King Ahmed stated. 'We have

649

granted you this private audience out of gratitude for the help you once gave us, firstly by removing a fog from our brain, then by providing us with horses for our escape from Alhambra to freedom.'

Pilar's toothless grin was sad. 'That a good time, lord. My Zurika with me.'

King Ahmed's eyes stung. 'Yes indeed, it was a good time,' he agreed wholeheartedly. Pilar would never know how good in comparison with the present. He gentled his gaze. 'How did you get to Alhambra from your cottage in Jaén, and what can we do for you?'

'I sell Jaén cottage and come with King Pedro army,' Pilar explained. 'I now live in cave I had before.' She paused, her glance sympathetic. 'I see great troubles for you, King, in crystal. Plenty trouble. Crystal say Black Death have come here.' She nodded slowly. 'But crystal also say you be all right.'

He had needed something like this to relieve his mind even a little. 'How much did you get for your house in Jaén?'

She grinned ruefully. 'Sell house very little money, to come with King Pedro army.'

'Why? Was it to end your days in the cave with your memories of . . . er . . . Zurika?'

Pilar's unblinking eyes suddenly blazed with hell fires of fury. 'I, Pilar, have only one reason live.' Her voice was trembling with the effort to control herself. 'Bishop Eulogius burn my *queridisima*, Zurika. He be Satan on this good earth. I bring him hell before he die. This be all Pilar live for now, then can die.' Her voice was shaking. 'To punish evil bishop, I even go hell, shouting joy, blessing God, Simon, Jesus, John, Mary.'

King Ahmed was stunned by the rage which had turned an ancient crone to a vibrant messenger of death. It was no use trying to deter or even advise her. 'How can we help you?' he inquired gently.

'You give me pass, come, go freely City gates to King Pedro camp, where Bishop Eulogius live.' She bared toothless gums in an evil leer. 'I do everythings then.' She nodded slowly.

'You shall have the pass under my royal seal immediately,' the king promised.

When she left the harem quarters that morning, veiled according to the rules of *purdah*, Princess Beatrice was calm but in despair. She was escorted by the chief attendant allotted her, a grey-haired matron named Farida who had served King Yusuf's queen and still disapproved of the departure from harem rules. Farida's displeasure was nothing new. Despite King Ahmed's approval, she had shown it from the very first time that Princess Beatrice and Prince Juan had met on their weekly visitations in the circular Mirador de la Daraxa. The rain had abated and a watery sunlight had begun to appear outside, but Princess Beatrice was in no mood to view beauty.

Her stern Muslim attitude notwithstanding, the motherly Farida seemed to understand instinctively that something was terribly wrong, and not just from Princess Beatrice's tearstained eyes and flushed cheeks. She cleared the room of the eunuchs and female guards and stood guard outside the Mirador so that Princess Beatrice and Prince Juan could talk alone.

Prince Juan had been very much aware of Princess Beatrice's terrible dilemma since she told him what she feared soon after she started getting morning sickness and her period became overdue. When thirty days had elapsed, she accepted the grim fact that she was pregnant. Now she knew how desperate the palace maid Teresa must have felt when she became pregnant from the *major domo* who denied paternity.

She had told Prince Juan that her husband could not

possibly have fathered her baby, leaving him to guess that it was a question of dates rather than the real cause.

Today, with his usual perception, Prince Juan immediately noticed her carefully covered grief. His blue eyes became luminous as they did when he felt specially loving. 'You told King Ahmed that you were pregnant, did you not?' he signalled.

She nodded silently, biting her lower lip to keep back the tears.

'And he knows it is not his child?'

She stared at him in dumb acquiescence.

'Are you sure the baby cannot be his?' He stared penetratingly at her. 'It is not just a matter of dates?'

'Yes,' she managed to whisper.

'I see.'

She knew that, incredibly, he comprehended how this could be, but true to his character, he never questioned what particular cause there might be, whether it was impotence or sexual deviation.

'Is he not willing to forgive you and accept the baby as his?'

'Prince Ahmed was most supportive, loving, caring about the rape. He even accepted the months during which I hid the truth from him, pretending, yes, pretending,' her tone grew fierce against her own guilt, 'that all was well. It is not my husband, Ahmed, but King Ahmed that cannot accept the bastard child.'

'No need for harsh words,' Prince Juan signalled. 'Any child is of God, regardless of the institutions of man.'

'I feel so terrible about myself.' She would have wailed if she had uttered the words aloud. 'I have such mixed feelings about the baby, brother. At times I love its little being within me which I am protecting and nurturing with my flesh, my blood and my body's sustenance. But most of the time I remember the monster that created it and am crazy with a desire to tear the baby monster from my womb.'

It was the first time she had declared herself so passionately. He reached out and gripped her hand. His fingers were large, warm and comforting. She wanted to break down and weep in a mixture of gratitude and utter desolation. 'What will you do?' he finally inquired, releasing her hand to form the words. 'I can see you have already made a decision.'

She told him. 'I shall need your help,' she ended.

He squared shoulders that had been slumping. 'I believe it is the right thing to do,' he responded. 'I shall indeed help you.'

Rather than call pointed attention to the grim possibility that a Black Death epidemic was impending in the capital, King Ahmed decided to make his inspection seem routine. He therefore rode his white charger, with no trumpeters to announce his coming, no escort, accompanied only by General Suby and Colonel Husain on either side of him.

Many people believed, as he had done, that it was because the Muslims were a clean people from the requirements laid down by the Prophet, that they had escaped the recent epidemic of Black Death which had killed over twenty million people in White Christian Europe. Just before they set off from the palace, however, General Suby had shown him a chronicler's report. The dire scourge had first struck China, before spreading westwards. 'India is depopulated,' the report concluded. 'Tartary, Mesopotamia, Syria, Armenia are covered with dead bodies. The Kurds have fled in vain to the mountains. None are left alive in Caramania and Caesarea.' So much for the immunity of Muslim and Jew alike.

As they trotted through the cobbled streets in the clear silver of rain-washed sunlight, it was difficult to imagine a black fate. Yet King Ahmed was hard put to overcome his despondence.

They paused by the Daralhorra houses at General Suby's insistence. He pointed silently to the side of the street, where two swarthy-faced Moorish boys, white teeth bared in mischievous grins, were holding up dead black rats by their tails in each hand.

'Drop those rats!' General Suby commanded sharply. 'Go home and wash yourselves thoroughly.' The boys dropped the rats, ran away, scared. Curious bystanders began to gather, three black-gowned women in *purdah*, a white Christian matron, a cowled, brown-robed friar.

King Ahmed stared aghast at the four little black corpses lying pathetically on their sides. They had bled profusely and their bodies were sopping wet. Counting nineteen more dead rats in the immediate vicinity, he exchanged a glance with Colonel Husain, who shook his head grimly.

An old man dressed in a grey robe came up, dragging himself jerkily, with a curious splaying out of all his limbs. I hope he has not recognized me, King Ahmed thought. Then he saw the man's dark eyes, peering upwards from a bent head. They were fever bright.

'Stop where you are!' General Suby commanded sharply.

The man paused uncertainly. King Ahmed watched curiously as the Physician General dismounted, threw the reins over the neck of his bay and strode up to the newcomer. He halted several feet away, began surveying the man. Puzzled murmurs arose from the crowd. 'Stand back!' General Suby directed them with an authoritative sweep of his hand. 'What is your name?' he demanded.

'Er . . . er . . . er . . . I don't know.' The dark eyes turned vague. 'I think . . . I think . . . yes, that's it. I am Mahroof the trader.'

'How are you feeling, Mahroof?'

'Not so good, Your Honour. I have pains everywhere since yesterday, especially in my neck.' He raised a wavering hand to touch the nape of his neck. 'I think . . . I think I was going to the hospital.'

'What about your groin?'

'Oh yes, yes. Swelling there too, lord. Buboes, you know. They have begun to bleed . . . plenty of pus too!' He paused. 'How did you know?'

King Ahmed's low heart sank into a bottomless pit.

'Almighty Allah!' Colonel Husain muttered.

General Suby slowly, cautiously circled Mahroof, pausing behind him to reach up and touch the nape of his neck. 'You had best get home and rest,' he advised.

He walked back to his bay, picked up the reins and swung back onto the saddle. King Ahmed glanced at him inquiringly.

'He had a hard lump, like a knob on a tree trunk, at the nape of his neck,' General Suby explained in a low voice. 'There can be no question but that we face the evil visitor, Black Death.'

Chapter 35

King Pedro was in his pavilion, being helped by his valet to dress for the evening meal, when he heard the high-pitched screaming. Seizing his sword, he rushed outside. Two burly guards in the uniforms of Holy Church, drawn swords in hand, were dragging an untidy old crone from Bishop Eulogius's pavilion. 'I gets you! I gets you!' the woman was screeching in triumph. One of the guards side-swiped her with his sword. She staggered, recovered, spat at him.

'You filthy bitch!' The guard swung sideways again with his sword, really hard this time. The crone was dashed to the ground. She sat up, screeching curses. Curious princes and nobles began emerging from their pavilions.

'Shut up!' The second guard suddenly drove his sword into the pit of the woman's stomach. She collapsed, sat up again, gazing down at the sword. 'I thank Thee, God!' She croaked, then stiffened in agony. Her eyes widened. 'Zurika!' She thudded back, lifeless.

King Pedro strode forward, waving away the royal guards rushing up from all directions and the princes, led by King Charles the Bad. 'Who is this woman?' King Pedro demanded.

'Was,' King Charles intervened.

'She somehow managed to sneak into the pavilion of His Eminence, Your Majesty,' the older guard, bloodied sword in hand, volunteered. 'We heard Bishop Eulogius's cry, rushed in and dragged her away from his pavilion.'

'You did well to kill her,' King Pedro fumed. 'How the fuck did she get here?' He looked at the bag of bones in its black robe. 'She must have been a witch. Any of us could have been killed.' He stalked into Bishop Eulogius's tent and was halted abruptly at the open entrance by a dreadful stench.

He gazed stupefied at the scene inside the pavilion. Clad in his customary purple, Bishop Eulogius lay slumped unconscious on his bed, a rough, filthy woollen blanket flung over him. Robe and blanket were stained with blood.

Body of God, what did this mean? Even the prelate's plump, cherubic face was disfigured with dark red blood and pus. Worse, the bed was strewn with the corpses of black rats.

Bishop Eulogius, his pallor ghastly, lay back on his bed propped up on red silk cushions. Wearing a clean white nightrobe and cap, his plump body made him look like a capon. King Pedro had commanded the bishop's guards to remove Pilar's corpse for burial. While the attendants had cleared away the dreadful mess in the pavilion and cleaned up the prelate, the royal physician had revived him.

King Pedro had told the princes, nobles and officers who had gathered that a demented woman had got through the lines. She had been killed and there was no cause for alarm. They should return to their pavilions. King Charles the Bad, who was closest to Bishop Eulogius's pavilion, was the only one to make any comment. 'Fucking pavilion stinks! We should avoid it like the plague.'

Reasoning warned King Pedro not to enter the pavilion. 'Your explanation of this extraordinary event, Eminence,' he demanded, standing at the open entrance.

'The old crone is . . . er was, a gypsy named Pilar, Your Majesty.' Bishop Eulogius was too breathless to indulge in his normal intonation. 'She was the grandmother of the gypsy girl whom our Church tribunal sentenced to death in Jaén for witchcraft and heresy.'

'You did so by trickery,' King Pedro responded, feigning cheerful acceptance of the deed. 'You wanted to feast your eyes on the virgin body of the gypsy girl, did you not?'

'Certainly, Sire.'

'When she denied you, she sealed her fate. You transferred your lust for orgasms through her to obtaining them from watching her and the Jew burning at the stake.' He was still pretending his usual pleasant understanding of the bishop's strange tastes. 'You can tell us everything and be sure of our understanding.'

Bishop Eulogius contrived a wan smile. 'You know us too well, Sire.' His look became conspiratorial. 'Indeed, we know each other too well.' He sighed. 'You may have heard that when sentence was being passed, the old gypsy woman approached the Church tribunal, cursed me and vowed vengeance. I did not take her seriously, even when she appeared so miraculously outside my pavilion this evening, pretending that she wanted to confess her sins to me and obtain God's pardon. Being a Christian and a member of Holy Church, I could not deny her, but what I immediately decided to do was first to grant the absolution she sought – she would not understand the Latin ritual – and then to have her tried as a witch and sentence her to death.' His childlike smile was almost back to normal. 'But first, I was curious to hear her story, especially as to how she managed to get from Jaén into the encampment and through our lines.'

Trumpets outside sounded vespers. The pavilion was darkening from the cool evening air. Bishop Eulogius sat up, crossed himself and repeated three Hail Marys and the Lord's Prayer. King Pedro followed suit, mumbling the words, eager for them to end.

'Ah, we can now resume with the peace of God within

us,' the prelate said. His eyes crinkled in the usual mischievous grin. He drew a pink comforter over himself and lay back on the bed. 'Where was I, Your Majesty? Ah . . . er, why do you not come in and sit down first?'

'We would rather not,' King Pedro replied. 'Er . . . we must hurry and change for dinner. Prithee, proceed with your story.'

'My story, yes. The old crone told me she lived in a cottage in Jaén, which she sold. She used the money to buy her passage to Granada in one of our comfort corps wagons. When we reached Alhambra, she slipped through our lines. None of our sentries cared about an old woman – gypsy at that – leaving the encampment. She returned to a cave she used to occupy across the ravine from the Alhambra palace.'

'Which was where she had lived all her life and where she brought up her orphaned granddaughter whom she grew to worship,' King Pedro conjectured.

'Your Majesty is so wise,' Bishop Eulogius commented.

'No, Eminence. People and life are so obvious.' He paused. 'So are you in spite of your deviousness and cunning.'

The bishop smiled openly. 'We are two of a kind, Your Majesty, and know each other so well.' He seemed to have recovered his strength.

'Go on!' King Pedro directed.

'The woman was known to Prince, now King, Ahmed. She had accompanied him, Prince Juan and her grand-daughter on the flight from Alhambra as far as Jaén, where the Jew, Aaron Levi, joined them by chance at an inn outside the city. The old woman remained in Jaén to buy the cottage, while the others proceeded to Toledo. The first Pilar knew of the return of her companions was when she had an unexpected visit from Prince Juan who had taken refuge in the convent there with Princess Beatrice. He informed her of the *auto-da-fé*.'

'So our brother King Charles was right, our son and daughter were indeed both at the convent!' King Pedro interjected. 'We shall find a way to punish the Mother Superior for having harboured them.'

'I would advise Your Majesty not to do so.' Bishop Eulogius's voice suddenly carried authority. 'You should not create divisions at this time, nor should you usurp the rights of Holy Church to deal with its own. Never fear, I shall hold a full inquiry into the incident.'

King Pedro nodded agreement. 'Pray proceed, Eminence.' He was anxious to hear the end of the story and be done with this farce.

'*Ciertamente*, Your Majesty. Knowing King Ahmed, this Pilar obtained an audience with him. She begged for and received a pass from him to slip in and out of Alhambra at any time.' Bishop Eulogius wiped a pale, damp brow with the back of a plump white hand. 'Her crystal told her of many things, she claimed, but her dire need was pardon from me for her insults and blasphemy. She kept up this pretence until the end. She told me very calmly that the only thing she had valued in life had been her granddaughter. She was sure I had tried to violate the girl – apparently she had also read it in her crystal. She had, however, brought me gifts. She reached in her bag and produced a handful of greyish powder, which she flung in my face. I know I screamed in pain. She reached into her bag again and I began to lose consciousness. Just as I blacked out completely, I heard her screech, "Vengeance! I seek vengeance for my *queridisima's* death!"'

King Pedro had reached the end of his patience. 'Zurika died a heroine,' he asserted heavily, 'safeguarding her modesty from a deviate pervert. She deserves a monument erected to her chastity. Maybe we shall still do it.'

Bishop Eulogius's shock registered with an opening of his little red mouth. He looked like a startled fish now, the blue eyes popping. 'Sire . . .' he began.

'We know each other too well, do we not?' King Pedro slashed in with a ferocious grin.

The prelate recovered, still thinking that he was dealing with the king with whom he had negotiated all these years. His blue eyes twinkled. '*Touché*, Sire.'

King Pedro decided to play the bishop's game a little longer. 'Prithee, proceed with your story, Eminence. The old woman obviously used her pass to get out of Alhambra, but how did she get through our lines?'

'The same way that she got into my pavilion, Sire. She claimed to be a penitent needing audience with me. She managed to win over the guards by telling a few good fortunes, after which it was easy for her to make her way through camp. Once she was well inside, why should anyone take notice of an old crone hobbling along on a staff? Also, no one could remain close to her for long because of the dreadful stench she exuded. She was treated as a joke, not a menace.'

'We suppose she also offered herself to you, Eminence, as a sinner who had practised witchcraft and blasphemy, who once she received pardon from Holy Church would welcome your sentence of death at the stake like her granddaughter? She too must have known you too well, Eminence.'

The chubby cheeks crinkled. 'Her crystal ball must have revealed much to her. To end the story, Your Majesty, she opened her bag; the foul stench nearly overpowered me. That powder she flung at me . . . I wonder what it could be? Anyhow, thank God for your royal physician, who revived me. He told me that my guards had killed the old woman.' His blue eyes became lecherous. He passed a pink tongue over red lips. 'I consider it a pity, Sire,' his glance became conspiratorial again, 'a view which I would only confess to you,' a knowing smile crossed his face, 'because we know each other so well.' He giggled.

'So I am your confessional, Bishop?'

'You have such a nice turn of wit, Your Majesty. Come to think of it, you have always been my confessional. And we can both enjoy this moment because I have come through the encounter with the Old Witch of Vengeance unscathed.'

This was the moment. He, King Pedro, was Cruel. King Charles was Bad. Bishop Eulogius was evil. He had his own vengeance to wreak on this presumptuous peasant who had clawed his way to high places. *En verdad*, he had many a score to settle with the little prick of a prelate, the last being for having outwitted him in Jaén. 'We have our own confession to make, Eminence,' he stated with feigned humility.

'How so, Your Majesty?' Bishop Eulogius smiled charmingly. 'Do you seek absolution for your sins?'

'No, but you have need to seek absolution for yours, Your Evil Eminence.' King Pedro literally licked his chops at the words he was about to utter. 'After you screamed and fainted on your bed, before the guards ran in and apprehended her, this Pilar flung the foul contents of her bag on you, blood and pus from a sick person, dead black rats, sopping wet and bleeding, and a blanket used by a dead man. You did not know of this because our attendants cleaned it all up before you regained consciousness.'

The bishop's eyes widened with shock. The glimmer of knowledge began to dawn. Horror intruded. 'That is why you are standing at the entrance there and will not come in?'

'Precisely.'

Stark terror filled the blue eyes. They began to bulge. The pudgy face cracked. Croaks emerged from a stricken throat. 'You mean . . . .?'

'Yes, Bishop Eulogius. We *do* mean.' His voice became as cruel as he felt. 'Our royal physician only expressed suspicion, but we are convinced of it.' It did not matter that he was not convinced. He fixed bleak eyes on the now sobbing prelate. 'You shall be confined to your pavilion from now on, Bishop Eulogius. No man shall enter it. The necessities of life will be left at its entrance. You shall perform all your alimentary functions,' he grew impatient at his own euphemisms, 'piss and shit, in this pavilion. Until you die, you shall live as those two innocent people you cast into the basement prison of the monastery at Jaén lived during their last night on earth, in your own filth and squalor. Vengeance has indeed found you out, you evil, miserable manifestation of inhumanity. You are a moral leper. Your actions alone may make it necessary for the Christian armies to withdraw, so we do not need you and Holy Church any longer. If we do withdraw, you shall remain in this pavilion as a physical leper,' he paused, baring feral yellow teeth, 'contaminated with the Black Death.'

He strode out of the pavilion to the music of shrill scream upon scream from the condemned Bishop Eulogius.

Dismal though the subject of the Black Death was to take to bed, it needed so much more discussion and planning than any other that King Ahmed made it the last item on the agenda of the War Council's nightly meeting. He had vested the entire responsibility for dealing with the epidemic in Physician General Suby and appointed the ginger moustached, feisty medical man to the War Council. If the atmosphere in the lamplit Court of the Machuca had always been serious and sober before, as befitted the military situation, it had at least been lightened by occasional levity. But now, while none of the generals would ever display fear, an undercurrent of gloom pervaded the meeting. It was one thing to joke at death on the battlefield or in action, another to laugh when the Black Death loomed.

'Your report, Physician General,' King Ahmed finally commanded.

There was tiredness around General Suby's eyes tonight. He was obviously working around the sand-clock. 'I regret to have to confirm that we do have an epidemic on our hands, Sire, minor at the present time and confined to the Daralhorra area, where there have been eleven reported deaths, but nonetheless an epidemic. I personally inspected every corpse and eight of them died of the Black Plague.'

'The usual symptoms?' General Saldin inquired.

'Indeed. Blackened skin with purplish blotches. Pustules on the body, swollen glands, buboes with blood and pus, unfailingly on the groin and at the armpits. There is no mistaking the symptoms. The other three men died from natural causes. I have directed that all the dead be buried without delay, no wakes or watches, just a simple religious ceremony. The problem is to get people to co-operate. The news has spread and most are in a state of near panic. The gravediggers have been performing well, and I can only hope they continue. I have arranged for a mass burial pit at a single cemetery and for open wagons to be available for relations and friends themselves to haul the corpses for burial, if the public services ever prove inadequate due to the large numbers of the dead.'

The hideous situation being objectively discussed seemed far removed from the beauty and elegance of the palace, yet it was here. King Ahmed's heart ached with grief. At this very moment people, his subjects, were dead or dying, most of them in mortal fear. If a man had the ague, a broken limb, or a battlewound, something could be done about it. If the enemy attacked, soldier and civilian would fight back. Now, everyone had powerlessly to await an event which was totally out of their control.

What with the news from Princess Beatrice and his chosen isolation from her, King Ahmed was hard put to avoid drifting into a permanent state of the blackest depression.

The curse of Yusuf ibn Nagralla, the Jew, is upon us. Why?

'What about those who are living but may have the symptoms?' General Iqbal had asked the question which King Ahmed had been framing in his mind.

'I have organized twenty physicians to conduct examinations in different sectors of the city. We have begun meeting at the hospital before the evening prayer to compile statistics and plan strategy. As of today, we have twenty-six active cases which we have identified. I instituted a programme of education this morning by briefing a selected group of imams and elders as to the early symptoms of the disease, the best measures to be taken to prevent its spread and the plans for burial. They are conveying these to the people with pleas that no one should panic.'

'What are the early symptoms?' The plump paymaster, General Rafik, shifted his bulk.

'The first signs are a splitting headache and a general feeling of weakness. Then come aches and chills in the upper leg and groin, a thick white coating on the tongue, rapid pulse, slurred speech, confusion, fatigue, apathy and an uneven gait. Soon blackish pustules appear. By the third day, swellings commence, especially under the armpit, on the groin and at the nape of the neck,' he glanced at King Ahmed, 'as Your Majesty will recall from the first victim we saw.'

King Ahmed nodded. 'A pathetic sight.'

'The swellings become buboes, full of blood and pus, frequently as large as eggs. Purple blotches appear on the skin from internal bleeding. Dreadful pain and brain disorder then brings what we call the Dance of Death. By the fourth or fifth day, wild anxiety and terror overtake the victim, followed by a sense of resignation as the skin blackens and the rictus of death, with gaping mouth, settles on the body.'

A chill silence settled over the chamber. The question General Rafik had asked was important, but King Ahmed sensed that some of the Council wished it had not been asked. General al Afdal, the dashing cavalryman, summed up that sentiment concisely. 'We never go into battle asking what the dead and wounded look like, Your Majesty. I for one am not going to look anxiously at my mirror or examine my body for signs of disease.' He shook his head, conjured up a devil-may-care smile. 'I shall face this enemy as I would any other.'

'Hear, hear!' General Saldin interjected.

General Rafik flushed. 'Your Majesty, I submit that we are not facing a cavalry charge,' he burst out angrily. 'Rather, it is an onslaught from the most dangerous, insidious foe known to man. I would remind my colleagues that it left over twenty million people dead in Europe just three years ago.'

'It's a question of attitude,' General Saldin flashed back, a bite in his voice. 'There is no dignity in death, I tell you, only in the manner of our dying.'

'You must know what the foe, death, looks like to cheat him.' General Rafik's voice had risen almost to a shout.

'We cavalrymen do not cheat . . .' General al Afdal began. He paused before King Ahmed's hand uplifted for silence.

'Gentlemen, we have had many spirited debates in our councils,' King Ahmed declared solemnly. 'That is expected from leaders who feel strongly about their commands and our overall position. But when we start to bicker about attitudes, we create a foe more deadly than the Black Death itself. We face the hideous buboes, the painful swellings, the foul patches, the disorientation of discord. We are all overworked, frustrated and tense with the problems that beset us. If we face these problems as brothers in Islam, with love for each other, we shall either overcome them or die nobly to meet again as brothers in Paradise.' His voice shook with the fierce determination surging through his entire being. 'Have no fear, gentlemen.' The words rang out with a new confidence. After all, he was the Chosen of Allah, the leader of these men and of his people. He had allowed himself to be smitten down by personal tragedy. That too he would settle, he decided in a flash, by visiting Princess Beatrice again tonight and telling her he would accept the baby and let all the world believe it was his; the right of his people to a proper succession he would deal with at the appropriate time. He did not even try to hold the passion back from his voice. 'We shall face our foes and, with God's help, we shall overcome them, each and all.' He glanced around the room, met nods of approval.

'I apologize to General Rafik for my remark,' General al Afdal stated.

'And I for mine,' General Saldin added.

'And I humbly apologize to Your Majesty and my brothers for my outburst,' General Rafik declared.

'Well then, gentlemen, let General Suby proceed with his report.'

He listened intently while the Physician General informed them of the exact situation as he could best assess it, the measures taken, advice as to rest, diet, cleanliness and to prevent panic, action to raise the morale of the people, isolate the afflicted and those exposed to the disease while ensuring that they were fed and looked after, not treated as lepers and outcasts by their terrified families and neighbours. 'For, as His Majesty has just reminded us, we are all brothers on this earth, even true believers and infidels.'

The idealism of this last remark jolted King Ahmed.

'Our physicians are the real heroes of this dread hour,' he asserted. 'They constantly expose themselves to the disease, treating friend and foe, true believer and infidel alike, facing the battle charge of the most terrible foe known to man with dedication and self-sacrifice.'

Another silence fell on the chamber, this one contemplative. 'We take our real heroes as much for granted as we do our loving parents.' General Saldin was voicing the sentiments of all. 'I for one do not have the courage to undertake such awesome duties as those being carried out so nobly by General Suby.'

A unanimous rapping on the table greeted his words. General Suby's yellow eyes glittered with tears. He brushed them aside with the back of his hand. Too overcome by emotion even to thank the Council, he simply went on with his report.

Utter relief from his decision regarding Princess Beatrice had restored King Ahmed's ability to think clearly from first principles. It was as if a fog had been lifted from his brain. A thought he had had the very night they had been told of the entry of the Black Death to the city, while on his way to Princess Beatrice's chamber, and set aside because of the terrible news she had given him, returned. He developed it on the instant. 'In our concern about the Black Death, we have ignored a very basic fact,' he declared, genuinely smiling it seemed for the first time in days. 'Bubonic plague is the enemy of Muslim and Christian, Jew and Gentile alike, in fact of the entire human race. Do you not agree that it is an enemy even more feared by the forces besieging us, because they have so recently seen its face?'

The beginning of comprehension on the faces of those around him lightened the entire atmosphere of the Court. General Saldin banged the table lightly with a clenched first. 'You are right, Your Majesty.' He thrust out his chin. 'You are so wise, the Chosen of Allah.'

'We thank you. Now it would appear that this scourge was really sent by Merciful Allah to save us if we but help ourselves. Word of it is undoubtedly on its way to King Abu Hasan, from his spies. He will never send us the promised help while the epidemic exists. He will resort to interminable postponements with renewed assurances that he does not intend fulfilling. And who can blame him? This also is to the good, gentlemen, because we have always had some apprehension as to the consequences of such massive support from any ally. Our own history is replete with examples of the escort taking over the caravan!'

'You are so right, Sire,' General Saldin interjected. 'Are you not suggesting that, just as the Black Death will intimidate our ally, it will cause our enemies to flee?'

'Precisely.'

General Saldin suppressed his excitement, but his eyes glowed. 'We should send an embassy to King Pedro tomorrow morning, to inform him of our plight.'

'He could merely think it the ploy of a beleaguered foe in peril,' King Ahmed responded.

'Perhaps we should invite King Pedro to send a deputation to the capital under guarantee of safe conduct, ensured by hostages,' General Iqbal suggested.

King Ahmed shook his head. He had already decided what should be done, but as always he was giving his advisers first chance of coming up with the solution. Now, receiving no other responses, he leaned forward, placed his elbows on the table. 'Four years ago, Christian merchants from Genoa and local residents of a town called Caffa on the Black Sea had a disagreement so serious that fighting erupted between the merchants' mercenaries and a local army led by a Tatar lord. While attacking the Christians, the Tatars were stricken by the plague. Moved by spite, the Tatar lord loaded his catapults with the corpses of those who had died of the disease. The Genoese became infected and sailed back to Italy.'

He surveyed the faces of each general in turn. None betrayed shock, only dawning comprehension. 'We are not concerned to spread disease amongst the enemy. We should never do anything so vile, even if it meant exterminating ourselves. But,' he raised a forefinger for emphasis, 'there is no reason why we should not deliver the news of our plight to the enemy in a dramatic fashion.' He turned to General Suby. 'You shall cause six corpses showing unmistakable symptoms of the disease to be selected, but only from families who gladly offer their dead for this purpose.' He directed his gaze to General Zahir, the huge Artillery Chief. 'You, General, shall select six catapults which you consider expendable and fire for distance at first light tomorrow. You will only get close enough to the enemy to make them notice your . . . er . . . deadly missiles, which you will fire immediately after morning prayer. It shall be our gift of thanksgiving to Almighty Allah!' He laughed. 'With such a gift, the enemy forces will hurry their retreat to their respective kingdoms.'

After the meeting, it was with an eager heart that King Ahmed bade farewell to Colonel Husain at the entrance doors to the Daraxa and sped to the tower of the Peinador de la Reina where Princess Beatrice awaited him. He would not talk to Prince Juan tonight. His wife should be the first to have the news of the change of heart and the high hopes of the morrow. With everything falling into place for the first time in months, he might even enter his virgin bride and lie with her in total fulfilment.

There was no response to his eager knock. With everything going so well for him, he was certain that she must either be asleep or in the privy. He opened the door and entered the chamber. His eyes sought the divan bed, roved eagerly to the balcony wall beneath the arches. No silhouette against the blue night sky and the black mountains beyond. At that instant, the feel of an empty chamber gripped him. It contained no aura of a living presence.

His mouth ran dry, his breath caught. Where was Princess Beatrice? He hastened inside. His eye fell unerringly on her writing desk. A neatly rolled manuscript lay on it. Even before he rushed to it, his heart was torn with a knowledge that spewed forth a greater emptiness, this time from within. He undid the white ribbon and unrolled the manuscript with trembling fingers. He raised it to the golden lamplight and read:

My beloved husband,
By the time the attendants bring you this letter, it will be tomorrow morning and I shall be facing my fate and my punishment for having hidden the truth from you and lived a lie.

My Brother, Prince Juan, and I are agreed that we have brought you nothing but ill fortune. This is not what anyone would want for those they love. A lover's role should be to sustain, to comfort, to succour, to create serenity and happiness.

Prince Juan loves you too, make no mistake about that, but he and I both erred grievously. Our desire to spare you pain came from love, as we thought. We now know that it was not love but selfishness that dictated our silence. God will punish us both for it, especially me, for I love you truly, more than my own miserable life.

We are leaving your capital by the same route, ironically enough, that my beloved brother and you yourself took to freedom. This time, he goes to slavery. So do I. We expect that when we return to our father, King Pedro, he will be appeased. So will King Charles, to whom I intend offering myself as wife. If I see in the future that this has helped you and your people, it will have been well worth the doing.

By some strange act of eternity, I love you and shall be as faithful to you on my marital bed, enduring its shame and torment for the rest of my life as I did that dreadful night on the hard floor of rape and bestiality.

You deserve better than one such as me, but you will never find anyone to love you so truly. I believe I was created for you from your fifth rib, my Horn.

Be with God, beloved husband, for that is how I shall think of you always. I shall pray daily for God to be with you. I have not given you anything tangible, except my tears, one drop of which has fallen here in proof, while I shall remain,

Eternally your very own,
Beatrice.

The cry of a wounded animal in pain escaped King Ahmed, tore through the night and was lost in the valley below.

Chapter 36

Having woken to the *matins* trumpets, King Pedro the Cruel was in a vile mood. He would skip the prayers today. He had spent most of the night in his dining pavilion matching King Charles the Bad drink for drink, so he needed curses this morning rather than prayers! He had not known whether it was to celebrate his final victory over Bishop Eulogius or to forget his fears that the Black Death was looming over his armies, but it did not matter, for he had enjoyed the revelry while it lasted.

Now, in the cold light of day, he reasoned that he had perhaps over-reacted in his concern about a possible epidemic, from the horror he had experienced when the plague hit Castile such a short time ago. The obscene things which the old witch, Pilar, had flung on Bishop Eulogius – blood, pus, dead black rats, a blanket – were probably meant to put the fear of God into her enemy, and to debase him, for Muslim cities had not experienced the Black Death. As for that little prick of a prelate, let him suffer thinking he was to die. Even if he did not die, let him remain in exile, a pariah and outcast. Even Holy Church would not run the risk of trying to support someone who might be smitten by the dread disease. Fuck Bishop Eulogius! Fuck Holy Church! Fuck everybody! God, how his head hurt. He was certainly paying the price for the carousing with the blare of trumpets echoing and re-echoing through his splitting brain, his mouth and chest parched and his bile-infused throat urging him to vomit.

He dunked his head in a basin of cold water which his valet had placed on the commode in his bedroom pavilion. 'Br . . . r . . .!' He shook the water violently out of his shaggy red hair like a dog newly emerged from a lake. His head felt clearer, the cobwebs swept from his brain. He glanced at his reflection in the ornamental mirror hanging from a tent pole. You still look like a red-haired, red-bearded monster, he told himself with satisfaction. A bath would surely feel good but he had had his weekly bath two days ago, when he returned from the sortie against Alhambra. He would get his valet, Garcia, to sprinkle some extra scent on his body when he removed his nightgown.

A gust of cool air swept through the pavilion. Someone had opened the tent flap. He turned towards the entrance. Garcia had entered and was bowing a narrow silver head to him.

'What is it?' he demanded impatiently. He never liked his routine disturbed, especially on a hangover morning.

'You have visitors, Your Majesty.'

'Visitors? At this unearthly hour? Tell them to go to the devil and return at a more godly time.'

'But, Sire . . .' The valet stood aside so he could see through the open entrance.

'Body of God!' This must be a nightmare. King Pedro rubbed his bloodshot eyes, blinked and looked once more. The world seemed to spin upside down and back again. He blinked once more and opened his eyes, wide this time. There was no mistaking the figures. Emotions whirled within him, but strangely the dominant one was relief. The search was over, for the hooded figures were those of his son, Prince Juan, and his daughter, Princess Beatrice.

By daybreak, King Ahmed had made up his mind. He made *subh* a special time of thankfulness to Almighty Allah for His divine revelations.

He had commanded that his white charger should await him at the entrance to the palace and that only Colonel

Husain should accompany him to the catapults that were to hurl the Black Death corpses at the enemy lines. They rode through semi-deserted streets to the rampart walls. Artillery General Zahir's huge bulk loomed beside the six great catapults. He came up to King Ahmed's charger, kissed the royal hand.

'Are you ready, General?' King Ahmed inquired.

'As ready as we will ever be, Your Majesty.' General Zahir's huge face broke up in a grin. 'We have tested for range, so the enemy will be alert to receive our next barrage.' He nodded in the direction of the six bundles, loosely wrapped in red, one beside each catapult. 'The wrappings will come free in flight, Sire.'

'A grisly task, General.' Suddenly King Ahmed had no stomach for the deed. These bundles had been living, breathing human beings just a few hours ago, mutilated by the disease, no doubt, but alive. Now . . . He tightened his stomach muscles, steadied his resolve. The corpses would be heroes in death, the saviours of their former compatriots with a place in Paradise. The deed had been conceived by him as the King of Granada. The order to execute it would be given by the King.

'Load the bodies!' he commanded.

'Bodies loaded, Sire,' the response came back in less than a minute.

'Prepare to fire!'

General Zahir echoed this order.

'Fire!' King Ahmed directed quietly. He had accepted full responsibility.

'Fire!'

A rattle, a creak, a tremendous WHUMP!, a clatter of recoiling wheels. The first corpse went soaring through the silver sunlight. Its wrapping began to unwind against the pale blue sky as it arced over the ramparts and disappeared.

King Ahmed calmly commanded the firing of each of

the corpses. When it was done, an icy cold lay within him. 'Let us ride to the north gate, Colonel.'

Colonel Husain expertly reined his huge bay alongside. King Ahmed urged his white charger forward.

The sight of his two children sobered King Pedro more than the cold water into which he had dunked his head. His immediate reaction was one of delight. Princess Beatrice especially was a strong reminder of her mother, Maria de Padilla, and it made him realize how much he missed his wife. He was also feeling a little jaded by camp life and sometimes longed for the comforts of the Toledo palace. Forgotten too was his dislike of Prince Juan. 'Fine hour of the day for you both to return home!' he declared gruffly. 'Well, do not just stand there, girl. Come in and give your father a hug.' He extended his arms to her.

She stared at him for a few moments, uncomprehending. Then tears welled up in her large blue eyes. She flew to him with a cry. 'Oh *Padre, Padre*!'

He held her close. Her body was cold from the morning air. Conflicting thoughts raced through him, the desire to protect struggling with the return of anger and the urge to wound. Her vulnerability surprised him, especially when he recalled the tough stand she had taken the night before the tourney when he had discovered Prince Juan in her quarters and the single-mindedness of her flight. Now here she was, sobbing her heart out, wetting his nightrobe unashamedly with her tears, while Prince Juan looked on with obvious delight. Fucking deaf-mute, he thought, but affectionately!

Presently her sobbing subsided. He gripped her by both arms, pushed her gently away and looked down into her tear-filled eyes, an exact replica of Maria's but in blue instead of brown. 'How did you manage to escape from the Moorish bastard?' he inquired.

Her eyes flashed.

'If you mean King Ahmed, *Padre*, he is not a bastard but my husband.'

'What?' The rage exploded. He flung her from him. Prince Juan leapt forward to prevent her falling. 'You dared to marry that heretic?'

'I *wanted* to marry him, *Padre*.' She stood straight and tall, chin lifted, her voice firm and strong, her glance unafraid. 'And I did. If you will please hear me out, I think we can achieve your objectives now that I am here.' She glanced towards the trembling valet. 'I suggest we do so in private.'

A steady pounding had commenced in King Pedro's head. For long moments he teetered uncertainly between rage and good sense. Finally, good sense prevailed. He jerked his head at Garcia in dismissal. The man hurried away. 'Come on in, both of you!' he directed. 'But what you say had better be good. Or else!' He left the threat hanging. The first shaft of sunlight hit the roof of the pavilion, a flight of rooks sailed overhead, cawing sadly. After the clean air from outside, the inside of the pavilion smelled of his slumbers. He indicated two gold settles and sat himself down on his bed. His groin itched. The reminder of buboes made him shudder.

'Your story!' he commanded Princess Beatrice briefly. 'I want the truth.'

She told him, gesturing the words for Prince Juan's benefit. Strangely for him, King Pedro listened with patience. Something told him that this was one of the most important events of his life. He displayed no emotion until she told him of the rape.

'King Charles did that?' he demanded incredulously.

'Yes, *Padre*.'

At first, he could not believe it. King Charles would not dare. Then he remembered the first occasion when King Charles had left the encampment at Jaén. That had been the same night Bishop Eulogius's man had seized the

677

gypsy girl. Princess Beatrice's story accorded with the facts. A low growl escaped King Pedro. Body of God, King Charles was just as evil as Bishop Eulogius. The fucking bastard had come into Castile, *his*, King Pedro's, kingdom, *his* kingdom and raped his daughter. The bastard had not even mentioned locating her. After the rape, he had not dared. But before? What a double-faced, deceiving scoundrel, the last person he would want for a son-in-law. The anger erupted, but not against his daughter. 'We shall kill that bastard!' he roared. 'We shall have his balls.' He leapt to his feet, grabbed his sword.

Princess Beatrice and Prince Juan rose up in alarm and blocked the entrance. 'Sire! Sire! I beg you not to act in haste.' His daughter held her stomach with the palms of her hands. 'I am carrying his child.'

For a moment it did not register. He was already halfway towards them at the pavilion entrance when the truth struck. He halted abruptly, stared at her, sword still in hand. 'What . . . did . . . you . . . say?' He emphasized each word.

'I am pregnant, *Padre*, from the rape by King Charles. You are to have a grandchild.'

His first grandchild a bastard? This must be some monstrous joke. 'Why not from your Moorish husband?' God Almighty, what a choice, a bastard or a half-breed!

'That is impossible.' She flushed. 'For reasons that I shall not explain to you.' The chin jutted out in the manner he had seen once before. 'You cannot kill the father of my unborn child.'

He saw the tragedy in her eyes and his cruel heart melted. 'You obviously have a solution to the problem,' he stated quietly. 'What is it?'

'You must make King Charles marry me and legitimize the birth.'

'That rapist?' Then he saw the sense of it. This was indeed Maria de Padilla's daughter.

'But you are already married.'

'It was not a Christian marriage, though I shall always be married to King Ahmed in my heart.'

He was used to marriages of convenience, but concern for her remained. 'You must loathe King Charles,' he suggested slowly.

'God forgive me, but I do, *Padre*. There are times when I also loathe what I am carrying in my womb. I shall, however, try to be a good wife and mother.'

'He may not want you.'

'Perhaps, but he desires the kingdom of Castile with all his heart.'

'You have thought of everything.'

She smiled wanly. 'I am your daughter, am I not?'

For Princess Beatrice these had been her blackest hours. Her heart was torn at having left King Ahmed. She loved him so completely. Would she ever see him again? She had made him suffer so much. How would her father react to having herself and Prince Juan back? How would she cope with King Charles's bestiality if he did marry her? The questions terrified her, but she had gone ahead with her plans determinedly for King Ahmed's sake. As a last resort, she could always take the veil. When she and Prince Juan had slipped out of the Alhambra palace the previous evening, going through the Gen al Arif tower and taking the route along which he and Prince Ahmed had once fled to freedom, using rope ladders, she had thought that her heart would break for she was heading for life imprisonment.

Now, amazingly, the father she had never really known had received Prince Juan and herself with kindness, so perhaps some good had come out of the nightmare of rape. It brought the glimmer of hope that she could somehow persuade King Pedro to withdraw his army and return to Toledo, a naïve expectation when dealing with huge armies and even more gigantic ambitions, but something to work towards.

After their meeting, King Pedro had directed her and Prince Juan to his dining pavilion. Seated on settles, they had watched a relay of liveried attendants prepare for the meal. White linen was laid on the table, with silverware and napkins. The scents of breakfast *mortrews*, boiled fish paste with breadcrumbs, stock and eggs sprinkled with pepper and ginger, spread on the side-board, with golden oranges, yellow melons and milk, did not interest Princess Beatrice whose heart was too heavy for food.

'People are aware that Bishop Eulogius has been confined to his pavilion with an armed guard over it,' she gestured to Prince Juan. King Pedro had informed them of the incident, evading her question as to why he had done so. 'I overheard one of the footmen conjecturing that the bishop has some infectious disease. I wonder what it could be.'

'An evil heart,' Prince Juan responded seriously. His Christian spirit did not extend to approving *auto-de-fé* or executions at the stake.

'Now, if only our father would confine King Charles also to his pavilion.' She sighed. It was a hopeless thought. She was in mortal fear of her first meeting with her rapist. The very thought of it made her want to vomit, but she would go ahead with her plan regardless.

King Pedro joined them for breakfast after he was dressed. Despite bloodshot eyes, a somewhat unkempt appearance and a hoarseness to his voice, he was in a mellow mood when he strode into the pavilion. 'We have requested King Charles to join us at breakfast,' he stated gruffly, directing a glance of understanding at Princess Beatrice. 'He does not know you are here.'

They helped themselves to food from the side-board and breakfast proceeded in well-bred fashion, as if no problems existed, with discussions as to the weather, camp and palace life. Princess Beatrice did her best to maintain a cheerful appearance. 'You were both in Alhambra yesterday,' King Pedro suddenly shot at her. 'You can give us the fullest details as to the enemy strength, dispositions and plans.'

'I was not privy to any of the planning, since I lived within the harem,' she replied.

'Surely King Ahmed shared his secrets with you?'

'There was never time, Sire. With the siege on, he was away from early morning until late at night.' A cunning thought intruded. 'What I do know is that the capital is manned and equipped to withstand many months of siege, since a huge Moroccan force is expected momentarily.' Sweet Jesu forgive me for stretching the truth.

King Pedro's red beard jutted towards Prince Juan. 'How about you, Prince? You were not confined to the harem.' He bared yellow teeth in a wide grin. 'Wish you were, eh?'

Princess Beatrice translated with her fingers and Prince Juan signalled back with an answering grin. 'He says he is deaf and dumb.'

'Clever! But he is not a eunuch!' He slapped his side and roared with laughter at his own joke, then directed bloodshot eyes to the open entrance of the pavilion, outside which the clamour of approaching voices had arisen. 'What the fuck is that?' he demanded of the *major domo*, Ramon Castro, who had hastened in and now knelt to him.

'An extraordinary event, Sire.' The man was stammering. 'Begging your pardon, but the colonel of the guard begs you to come outside.'

'Godsbody, can we not enjoy our family breakfast in peace?' King Pedro roared. 'Is this the price a king must pay? What is going on?' Realizing that he would get no more information from the trembling *major domo*, he kicked back his settle, rose to his feet and strode out.

The sun was now well risen and slanted silver light on the rectangular open green sward between the royal pavilions. A crowd of soldiers, mostly infantrymen, were gathered in a rough semi-circle talking to each other in hushed tones. A huge, burly Castilian colonel towered above an open horse-drawn wagon at the centre of the group. Two men stood guard over Bishop Eulogius's pavilion at the furthest end of the open ground.

The moment King Pedro emerged blinking from the pavilion, the colonel called the party to attention and saluted. The sudden silence was broken only by the murmur of voices from the neighbouring pavilions, the whine of a stray dog and the distant bleat of an encampment goat. A hideous stench smote him.

'At ease!' King Pedro commanded.

'Prithee, Your Majesty, what goes on here?' The rough voice was that of King Charles the Bad emerging from his tent.

Not pleased at the intrusion, King Pedro half turned towards the bull-like king. 'That is what we are about to discover, Your Majesty,' he stated, feigning courtesy. He turned back to the colonel. 'What do you have here?' He nodded towards the wagon, saw for the first time that it was loaded with naked bodies, all badly mangled and bloody. He counted six before erupting. 'Have you taken leave of your senses?' he roared, pointing a shaking finger towards the corpses.

'I beg your pardon, Sire.' The colonel remained perfectly composed. 'But it is the enemy who may have taken leave of theirs.' He gestured towards the wagon. 'These arrived in an enemy catapult bombardment from the capital just before sunrise.'

'Wha . . . at . . .?' King Pedro heard King Charles the Bad, now ranged alongside him, echo the question.

'It is the truth, Your Majesties,' the colonel responded quietly.

682

'What was the purpose? Is this a new form of Moorish punishment? Were these men our spies? Or is the enemy short of bolts and rocks for their catapults?'

'With the rocks only in their heads?' King Charles grinned.

'No, Sire.' A chill went through King Pedro at the colonel's sober tone. 'The bodies were shot from the capital in quick succession. There were no other corpses nor any other salvoes. If you would graciously step forward, you will note that while the hideous mangling of the bodies was inevitable from their bizarre journey, the men were already dead when they were loaded. We took time to ascertain that and decide what to do before finally bringing them to Your Majesty.'

'What would . . .?' The hideous possibility hit King Pedro in the stomach. He stepped forward to look at the bodies, laid neatly side by side face up. Beaten to pulp, they were gross, obscene in the clear sunlight. His eyes sought the groins, noted the bloody buboes mixed with pus. Terror gripped his guts, turned them to water. He drew a deep breath to regain control of himself. The truth of what King Ahmed had intended dawned on him.

'These men died of the Black Plague,' he declared quietly.

He heard King Charles's gasp ending in a croak. Frightened murmurs arose from the men. He held up a massive hand for calm. 'Silence!' he bellowed, looking commandingly at the circle. 'Listen, all of you. These corpses were despatched to us as a convincing message that the Black Plague has broken out in Alhambra. Now we warn you, that message shall not cause panic to turn into an epidemic in our ranks.' He fixed his gaze on the colonel. 'You, colonel, will ensure that these bodies are taken clear away from the encampment immediately and dumped into burial pits, along with the wagon and the horse which must be killed. Any man who has had physical contact with the bodies, other than the physicians, must be isolated.' He paused. 'Look to it now, while we for our part decide on our future course of action.'

He was hard put to it not to let his shoulders slump. His dream was ended, replaced by a nightmare of terror.

Fear of the Black Plague churned his guts even while the colonel was issuing orders to the men. Before he finished, King Pedro wondered what Maria de Padilla would advise and came to a quick decision. 'Will you join us in our dining pavilion?' he inquired of King Charles the Bad. 'Breakfast has been served there.'

Fear was written all over King Charles's face; the bloodshot eyes bulged with it, the neckless head with its shaggy black hair was slack on its huge shoulders. You are not only bad, you are ugly, King Pedro thought. On the instant, he made another decision.

King Charles followed him into the pavilion. He gasped at seeing Princess Beatrice seated inside. He stood stock-still like a wild beast at bay, clearly suspecting a trap. As Princess Beatrice and Prince Juan rose and bowed deep to him, King Pedro became finally convinced of the truth of his daughter's statements.

'Pray be seated all of you.' King Pedro's invitation was a command. King Charles hesitated a moment, grasped his sword hilt, thought better of it, pretended it was a natural gesture and took the settle nearest the entrance.

'Some food for the soul,' King Pedro declared, 'before Your Majesty feeds the stomach.' He eyed King Charles with suppressed rage. 'We are aware that you raped our daughter.' He kept his voice cold and impersonal. 'We should kill you for it with our bare hands, for such a vile, despicable act has never been committed in the annals of our history.'

King Charles leapt to his feet. 'We do not have to put up with your . . .'

'Sit down, rapist, and listen to us,' King Pedro gritted. 'You would not get further than the entrance to our pavilion before we cut you down.' He eyed the furious king levelly.

A silent battle of glances ensued. King Charles reluctantly sat down. 'What do you have to tell us?' he demanded belligerently.

'You have fathered a child.' King Pedro's tone was as brutal as he felt.

'Wha . . .?' The huge jaw slackened, dropped. The bulging eyes, surprised, shifted to Princess Beatrice, were lowered to assess her stomach. He noted the bulge with obvious distaste.

'We expect that you . . . er . . . make an honest woman of our daughter, redeeming your action, even though it is a little late to legitimize the bestial conception.' He was playing with this unsuspecting ruffian now. 'There is, however, one slight complication.' Cruelty made him pause in order to ensure that he had King Charles's undivided attention. He was actually enjoying the situation now. 'Not dreaming that she was pregnant, our daughter was married to the man of her dreams.' How he loved turning the dagger in the wound of this bastard's pride. 'King Ahmed of Granada is her husband. As you can imagine, this marriage throws a different complexion on the situation. It may be necessary to have an annulment, even though this is a non-Christian marriage. Of course, the world will never be sure of who the real father is.' His massive jaw jutted out. 'But we know, do we not, our brother?' He was almost purring now, watching King Charles's face work with confusion and fury. 'One thing is certain.' He smiled with his mouth, not his eyes. 'Princess Beatrice can no longer be heir to our kingdom of Castile. We shall be naming our son, Prince Juan, to succeed.' He held up a hand as a croak escaped Prince Juan, who had lip-read his words. He knew his son's reaction would be refusal, but he had to continue with his ploy. 'Do not thank us, our son, for you are a fitting heir,' he interjected.

'You . . . want . . . us . . . to marry . . . your daughter, when she has been married to a heretic, barbarian Moor and is probably bearing his child?' A massive clenched fist banged on the table, set the platters and silverware rattling. 'You must be mad.'

'Since you have not denied the rape, we were hoping you would do the Christian thing,' King Pedro responded mildly.

'You realize that this is the end of your dream of taking over all Spain?'

'For delivery to you? Why, King Charles, was that not a dream you shared with us so you could have the entire reality?' He shook his head from side to side amusedly. 'Did you really think you had us fooled?'

'We shall withdraw our armies immediately,' King Charles cried.

'And destroy Christian unity?' King Pedro demanded sweetly.

'Christian unity be buggered.'

'God buggered a Christian unity which He knew did not really exist when he smote Alhambra with the Black Plague. Most Christians will claim that God sent it to punish the heretics at long last, but at this moment we believe that it was His punishment on us Christians who took His name in vain to pursue our selfish personal ambitions.' His voice shook. 'As for you, make no mistake about it, you foul lecher. It is the punishment of Sodom and Gomorrah. You have revealed your true nature quite clearly to us. Do you believe for one moment that we would deliver our daughter's fate to one such as you? No! No! No! Never!' He pounded the table to

686

emphasize each word. 'She shall return to the convent at Jaén and bear her child, whom the nuns will look after, leaving her free thereafter to make any life she chooses. She and her bastard child will always be welcome in their real home, our palace in Toledo. As for your threat of withdrawing your army from the campaign, understand, King Charles, that the campaign is already over. We of Castile have the largest number of men on the field. We shall commence our withdrawal immediately, leaving our foes in Alhambra to face the far, far greater threat of the Black Plague.'

As King Charles stormed out of King Pedro's dining pavilion into the morning sunlight, he was in the grip of savage emotions, dominated by fury at the manner in which King Pedro had literally played with him and the insults heaped on him, especially in the presence of Princess Beatrice. This alone would normally have driven him to uncontrollable actions, but his instinct for survival had made him hold back. He was in the extremely vulnerable position he had originally feared immediately after the rape, an act that Holy Church and even his people would not condone. Seeing Princess Beatrice pregnant had somehow extinguished all the idealization of her he had conjured. The romance had died in a flash. This was no slender virgin of exquisite purity but just another pregnant woman. And he loathed pregnant women. They all reminded him of his pregnant mother, Princess Beatrice especially because of her resemblance to his mother.

He did not feel at all secure in this camp. Princess Mathilde and Count Gaston were dead. Yet all he wanted now was to get back to Pamplona, away from a situation where he did not issue all the commands, away from the hideous Black Death. Safe. That was what he wanted . . . to be safe!

687

Colonel de Villa, his huge aide-de-camp, awaited him in his pavilion. He barely acknowledged de Villa's salute before bursting out, 'Colonel, we shall leave this accursed encampment immediately for Pamplona.' Noting that the aide betrayed no surprise, he proceeded. 'You must be aware that the Black Death has broken out in Alhambra.'

'I just heard the news, Your Majesty.'

'Delivered by catapult?'

'A somewhat extraordinary mail, Sire, but most effectively delivered.'

'We shall ride ahead with the First and Second Cavalry Regiments, which are all we have in this sector. We desire to leave within the hour. Can they move that fast?'

'*Ciertamente.*'

'Send fast messengers to General Duke Conte in charge of our main body in the northwest to follow us within two days at the most.'

'Your slightest command is my life, Your Majesty.'

'Good.' At least he had this man mountain to give him loyalty. Love was a lot of mule-shit. When he got back to Pamplona, he would start fucking, whoring, raping again to his heart's content.

A high-pitched moaning and insane screams broke out from across the green sward outside. 'What is that?' he inquired.

Colonel de Villa's face turned grim. 'It is the primate, Bishop Eulogius, Sire. He has been confined to his pavilion in isolation since last night, on suspicion of exposure to the Black Death. I rather suspect that he has been given confirmation of the outbreak in Alhambra by one of his aides. He will be left behind to rot alone if the Castilian forces withdraw.'

'The primate, eh? No wonder he sounds like a fucking mad baboon.'

'He probably is, Your Majesty.' Colonel de Villa

sounded as if primate bishops who went mad were an everyday occurrence.

'He fucking deserves whatever hideous punishment is meted out to him by God and man.' King Charles crossed himself piously before remembering that he did not need such play-acting before Colonel de Villa. 'After all, he sentenced innocent people to death at the stake.' An inkling of his own sins pricked but was immediately set aside.

'I shall direct your attendants to prepare for the move and convey your commands to the officers without delay,' Colonel de Villa stated. 'I shall be back very soon.' He drew himself to his full height, towering above his sovereign. 'Will that be all, Your Majesty?'

'No, Colonel.'

Colonel de Villa tilted his head inquiringly to one side. 'Your command, Sire.'

'Fuck everyone and everything.'

'Very well, Your Majesty.'

He had just finished issuing orders for his commanders to assemble in his pavilion by noon and was seated on his favourite chair, thinking out his plans, when Ruy de Vivar was announced. As always, King Pedro gave his spy master immediate audience, alone. The bony de Vivar, clad in his usual amber-scented brown tunic, was visibly agitated for once, his low bow almost perfunctory.

This man was surely the bearer of ill tidings. When troubles hit, they did so in regiments. A tremor of apprehension ran through King Pedro as he indicated a settle. 'What is your news?' he demanded.

'First, Your Majesty, may I humbly inquire whether the information I received on my way to your royal presence just now is correct. Is our entire army indeed moving back to Toledo?'

'Yes.'

De Vivar brought skeletal hands together as if praying. 'God and the saints be praised for that, Your Majesty.'

'Why?'

'I have just received word that your half-brother, Prince Henry of Trastamara, has been taking advantage of your absence to foment a revolt amongst the remaining nobles.'

'The bastard!'

'That is his right by birth, Your Majesty.' The words were primly spoken through thin, compressed lips.

King Pedro clapped the arm of his chair, exploded with laughter. 'Well put, Spymaster.' He sobered on the instant. Ambition definitely had to wait. 'All the more reason to hasten our return.'

Immediately Ruy de Vivar left, King Pedro summoned Princess Beatrice and Prince Juan. The last few hours had brought so many dramatic changes that his brain was reeling and he needed to steady it. Never having experienced family before, he sensed that stability existed only within the confines of family feelings. Even when individual members of a family were separated, the critical factor was an indefinable seed, a divine germ, from which all support sprouted.

He had an hour of free conversation with his children, uninterrupted by command to his *major domo*. During this time, he learned more about them – Princess Beatrice 'translating' for Prince Juan – than he had in his entire life. Vaguely he realized that he was grasping something more precious than any kingdom.

He looked up in annoyance therefore when Ramon Castro reappeared tremulously at the entrance to the pavilion. 'What is it?' he demanded, hearing the commotion outside.

'You have a royal visitor, Sire,' the kneeling man quavered.

'King Charles?'

'No, Sire. King Ahmed of Alhambra.'

Princess Beatrice heard her father go 'Huunnh!' Mouth open, the yellow teeth showing, he looked like a bull just gored in the stomach. Then her heart started to beat wildly with fear. Yet she stared at the silver rectangle of the pavilion entrance, eager to gaze at the man whom she had thought never to see again.

King Pedro cleared his throat. She sensed from Prince Juan's stiffening that he comprehended what was happening. 'Has he . . . the king come with a large escort?' he demanded.

'No, Your Majesty. He has come alone.'

'Alone? You mean with his immediate entourage? Under a white flag of truce?'

'He has come completely alone, with no truce flag.'

Princess Beatrice's blood turned to ice. She knew her cruel father. He would seize her husband, imprison him, torture, maim and finally kill him for all the insults and humiliations of the past.

'What the . . . Hrrmp! Well, what are you waiting for, you oaf. Show him in!'

King Ahmed paused for a moment at the entrance to accustom his eyes to the shadows of the pavilion. Princess Beatrice's pounding heart flew out to him through eyes wet with tears. To her surprise, he knelt at the entrance to King Pedro, then moved lithely forward and kissed the king's hand. 'What does this show of humility mean?' King Pedro demanded roughly. 'You are a king too, in your own right, are you not?' He seemed puzzled and some of the rough, brutal edge had left his demeanour.

'We did not offer you homage as our sovereign lord.' The deep, mellow voice penetrated her soul, made her shiver. 'I, Ahmed, did so as your son.' He smiled. 'With

691

your permission, Sire.' He turned to her and held out his arms.

She heard a grunt of surprise from her father and Prince Juan's gurgle of delight. She flew into her husband's arms straight as a homing pigeon. He held her close, kissed her golden hair tenderly. He smelled of sandalwood perfume and the natural fragrance of his skin. Though he seemed cool, she could feel the thud of his heart against her breast. She had the absurd thought, please do not ejaculate, my husband.

'Very touching,' King Pedro sneered. 'But that does not absolve you from all the hideous misery you have caused, the wrecking of well-laid plans, the humiliation inflicted on us in the presence of the crowned heads and royalty of Europe. And now you have been foolish enough to deliver yourself into our power.'

She heard the words in despair, but desperation filled her with sudden determination.

She turned fiercely on her father, placing herself between him and King Ahmed. 'Whatever you do to my husband, you shall first do to me,' she cried.

Prince Juan came alongside, turned to face King Pedro.

'Even more touching!' King Pedro's bloodshot eyes were inflamed with anger. His cheeks twitched.

'Why do you not kill us yourself, with your sword, as you did all those men who came to rescue my mother?' Prince Juan gestured, with her translating.

King Pedro's hand went to his hilt. Princess Beatrice knew of her father's quick mood swings. For a moment, she feared he would draw the weapon and run Prince Juan through.

But King Ahmed gently moved her aside so that he was directly in front of King Pedro. 'We are face to face finally,' he declared. 'And the physical power is yours.' He grinned as the distant bleat of a goat intruded. 'Just as it is within the power of that goat to bleat.'

'Wha . . . aa . . . at!' King Pedro roared. 'What kind of a fucking jackass are you, to make jokes at such a time?' Then the humour of the words reached him. He gave his tree-trunk thigh a resounding smack and guffawed. 'You are no jackass,' he roared. 'You are a jesting son of a bitch.'

Princess Beatrice had been holding her breath. She released it now. She remembered her husband telling her how he had learned the trick of putting out fires with the cold water of light-heartedness on the first day he had met the officers of the First Regiment, Husain, Ismail, Raschid and Wahid in the Gen al Arif tower. It had helped him establish his identity more surely than protestations. He had done it again.

'Make up your royal mind, Your Majesty. Or do you claim that my late royal father was a jackass who wed a bitch? Hardly a compatible mixture, still less a biological possibility!' She marvelled at his complete ease – and he just turned twenty.

'Eh?' King Pedro gaped at him, then shook his head in disbelief.

'Regardless of my origins, I must respectfully request you to consider some facts.'

'So it is "I" not "We" this time,' King Pedro interjected. 'You keep slipping in and out of the royal plural like a lustful man inside a woman!' He roared uproariously with laughter at his own joke, slapping his thigh again. King Ahmed showed white teeth in a smile of appreciation. The atmosphere of the pavilion lightened. King Pedro's laughter died down, subsided with a couple of titters. 'All right, give us your facts.'

'You are aware that we face an epidemic of the Black Death in Alhambra?'

'How could we not be, when you delivered the news to us in such telling fashion?' King Pedro laughed again.

'I assume that you will now withdraw your forces?'

'Why should we? The Black Death has not struck us! We can afford to wait while your people die like flies.'

'You know as well as I do that you dare not run the risk.' King Ahmed's voice was firm, flinty as steel. 'If you remain here, you face a far more dread foe than Moorish armies. Your allies and your own men will desert you. All you will have left is a hollow purpose.' A grim note entered King Ahmed's voice. 'My commanders in Alhambra have been commanded by me to do everything in their power to spread the disease among your men and cause terror in your ranks.'

Princess Beatrice heard King Pedro's growl with alarm. Surely her husband was pushing him too far.

'This would not be to your advantage, for yet another reason.' King Ahmed paused deliberately.

Moments of silence passed on iron wings, while she held her breath again until King Pedro broke it. 'What the fuck reason can there be?' he finally demanded.

A flicker of contempt crossed King Ahmed's face at the obscenity. 'Your bastard half-brother, Henry of Trastamara, has been trying to raise the standard of revolt against you in northern Castile while you were away.'

King Pedro paled. So Ruy de Vivar's report had been absolutely correct. 'How do you know this?' he inquired belligerently.

'You and I both have spies in each other's kingdoms, do we not?'

King Pedro stared at him. 'Is that all you have come here for? Well, you have said it. But you are alone and unarmed. What is to prevent us from detaining you?'

'That is precisely what I came here for.'

King Pedro shook his red head like a bewildered bull. 'What in hell do you mean?'

'I came to offer myself as a hostage,' he half-turned and grasped Princess Beatrice's hand, 'in order to assure the safety of my wife.'

'Against us?' King Pedro growled.

'No.'

Princess Beatrice caught her husband's reticence. 'I have made my father aware of everything,' she interposed. 'King Charles is leaving for Pamplona, withdrawing with his army immediately. The kings of Portugal and Catalonia will surely follow. My father stands alone.'

'I came to protect my wife against King Charles.' The assertion was made with incredible assurance.

'How would your presence as a hostage ensure that?'

'Because I would remain in your custody as Princess Beatrice's husband.'

'Ho! ho! ho!' King Pedro pointed a derisive finger at him. 'You want us to acknowledge a heathen as our son-in-law? You must be having a hashish dream.'

'I am dreaming *your* hashish dream. Pray, consider. Your son-in-law will not be a heathen Moor but the legal ruler of Granada. With Prince Henry of Trastamara creating trouble within your kingdom, you, deserted by the kings of Aragon, León y Navarra, Catalonia and Portugal, will need all the allies you can get! As soon as you lift your siege and withdraw, Alhambra will open its gates and let our people flood into the countryside, away from the Black Death. Meanwhile, the plans we have devised to combat the spread of the epidemic will surely work. When this unfortunate period is over, you will have thousands of superb fighting men as your allies.' He nodded. 'You have experienced our mettle already. Besides, King Abu Hasan of Morocco will send over one hundred thousand men he has been recruiting to help us. You will then have the strongest, the most staunch ally in all Spain.'

'Who will kill me to get the Castilian throne added to his domains!' King Pedro sneered.

'That is a most unworthy remark, which I shall not

695

deign to answer. I am here, am I not, totally in your power?'

'You are aware that our daughter is pregnant.'

'Yes.' King Ahmed's voice was steady.

The cruelty showed in her father's expression. 'Bearing another man's seed in her womb?'

How terrible. She looked at her husband imploringly, not knowing how to comfort him.

'I am her husband and she bears my child.' The reply was firm and assured. At first, she could not believe her ears, then the joy bells began ringing within her. Nothing else mattered any longer.

Oh dear Virgin Mary, Sweet Jesu, Compassionate God, I thank all of Thee. I do not mind dying at this moment, but I prefer to live.

'We should all of us, as a family, keep the knowledge of what has occurred a secret,' King Ahmed proceeded. 'If I remain in Toledo as your hostage, though the husband of your daughter, no one will be able to cast stones at us,' surprisingly, it was King Ahmed's voice that became touched with cruelty, 'especially the royalty and nobility who are jealous of your wife, the Lady Maria de Padilla. They will never be able to allege that she bred a daughter who gave birth to what they would call a bastard child.' His voice shook with emotion. 'I would give my life to save the reputation of Princess Beatrice.'

'Why?' King Pedro inquired in shocked amazement.

'Because I love her and my sole purpose in life is to cherish her.'

'You would give up your kingdom for her?'

'Not gladly, but yes, I would.'

King Pedro's bloodshot eyes grew thoughtful, staring at King Ahmed as if they would penetrate his soul. Finally, he seemed satisfied. He nodded. 'We believe you,' he declared simply. 'We understand such a love.' He seemed to be talking to himself. He reflected a long while.

Princess Beatrice found the silence in the pavilion unbearable as she awaited his verdict.

'So you think you have won once again,' King Pedro murmured. His red-bearded jaw jutted out. He contemplated King Ahmed over wide cheekbones furred with red hair.

'If you say so, but all I originally sought was to win your daughter's hand. Now I seek a life with her.'

'You have taught us much today, but we cannot let you win.' With a sombre expression, King Pedro tapped the side of a massive thigh. 'Here is our judgment. Heretic, heathen, barbarian, you may be, but we will not be able to find a more worthy husband for our daughter on the face of this earth. We shall withdraw our armies from your territory immediately on executing a treaty of alliance with you today, so there can be peace between our kingdoms. You shall then be free to return to Alhambra with our daughter and our blessing.'

'Your Majesty, Sire . . .' King Ahmed stammered, at a loss for words for the first time.

Princess Beatrice ran to her father and clasped her arms around him. She could feel his rude strength and smell his high odour, but it did not matter because she also felt the thudding of his heart. He grasped her suddenly, held her close with a fierceness that took her breath away. Then he suddenly grasped her arms and released her.

'There are two conditions,' King Pedro cautioned and her heart sank again.

'What are they, *Padre*?' she inquired tremulously.

'First, as soon as the epidemic is over, Prince Juan returns to Toledo as our new heir to the throne.' He nodded towards her fingers. 'Tell him. Add that it will only be to give us security. We know that he will probably end up in a monastery, but that must come later.'

She translated swiftly. To her joy, Prince Juan nodded, adding, 'I shall miss you when I leave.' He had obviously been reading lips because he seemed to know all that had transpired. 'Tell my father that his generosity has won him back a son.'

King Pedro laughed at the response.

'What is the second condition, *Padre*?' she inquired, still anxious.

'You know that Holy Church will be furious about this cross-religion alliance. Well, fuck them.' She noticed King Ahmed wince again. 'Christian unity is over. To drive the lesson home to them,' he cleared his throat to hide emotion and she knew immediately that he was about to tell a lie, 'you shall bring our grandchild to Toledo as soon as the baby is old enough to travel. Your mother would love that too.'

King Ahmed strode to King Pedro, knelt and kissed his hand. Prince Juan followed suit.

Princess Beatrice, the only woman present, had the last words. 'You are a fraud, *Padre*. Your cruelty cloaks a loving heart.'

Epilogue

Within sixty days, it was clear that the Black Death had only paid a passing visit to Alhambra. People began streaming back to the capital from the mountains and the countryside to which they had fled for refuge once the siege was lifted. Despite his dedicated service, Physician General Suby had escaped the plague, as did all the other members of the War Council whom King Ahmed retained under the new title, Council of Rehabilitation, as his consultative and executive body to restore the capital to its former state. Freedom from military rule would come later.

On his return from the Castilian encampment, King Ahmed had moved Princess Beatrice, Prince Juan and himself to his former quarters in the Gen al Arif tower, ostensibly to free himself and his wife from the harem, but in truth to remove Princess Beatrice further from possible contagion.

Now the cold winter months had given way to the coolness of spring and nightingales sang once more in the palace gardens. King Ahmed had made it a point to spend time every evening with Princess Beatrice and Prince Juan in his study in the tower. He and Prince Juan would normally stand by the arched balcony windows. With Princess Beatrice, now beginning to show a definite bulge to her stomach, seated on a settle close to him, they would just quietly chat as families are wont to do, watching dusk fall and listening for the sounds of night dropping its blinds over the windows of the earth.

This was King Ahmed's time of peace and relaxation, free from the pressures of his royal duties. By tacit consent, the one topic they avoided was any reference to Aaron Levi, Zurika or Pilar.

'This is the best time of day for me,' Princess Beatrice repeated that evening. One of the sweetest things about family was this repetition, without fear of being reminded that the words had been spoken before. 'I know I have only a few more hours during which to hold up this double burden,' she placed light hands over her bulging stomach, 'before collapsing on my bed.' She paused, concentrating on her left hand. 'See, the baby has started kicking me already.' She looked at King Ahmed with luminous blue eyes. 'Feel it!'

King Ahmed had come to accept the baby without reservation as his own and was even helping her cast aside her occasional aversion towards it. He was reaping his own reward, because the sight of her swollen body moved him in a different way now and had helped him make some headway towards overcoming his problem of premature ejaculation. He bent over and placed a palm on her stomach. She directed his slender fingers. 'See . . .'

He felt the pulse of the life within her and marvelled. This was the stuff of creation. It did not matter who the father was. He gestured to Prince Juan to feel the baby.

His thoughts were interrupted by a frantic fluttering of wings. As he glanced in its direction, a white dove settled on the balcony wall. Its little breast heaving, the round eyes rolled, flitting from side to side in terror. His mind flew back many years and his eyes sought the heavens. The outline of a hawk, black wings spread like small sails against a blue ocean of sky, was heading away from its prey. He glanced at Prince Juan, knew without asking that they were both sharing again a confidence he had extended long ago.

A cackle reached his ears, followed by the mutter of strange incantations. Bewildered, he turned sharply towards the interior of the study, had the impression of a large glittering crystal on the marble table. The incantations continued, but he could not discover their source.

As a chill loneliness seized him, he swivelled round instinctively, frantic eyes searching the slab of rock. Sunlight chilled his warm body. The black rock was as empty as the distant snow-covered Sierra Nevada mountains, their white peaks tinged with the pink of the descending sun. The loneliness intensified.

A gasp escaped Princess Beatrice, a glug-glug croak emerged from Prince Juan. King Ahmed immediately knew where their attention was focused.

The familiar figure began to materialize on the black rock. *Golpe*, stamp, went a foot. His eyes roved upwards. A slim, tall body, shapely hips, tiny waist, full bust. The face of exquisite beauty. Olive skin, tight drawn over fine bones, soft mouth, red as pale rosebuds, dimpled cheeks. The eyes, the dark-brown sultry eyes, latent with passion, the soul of all sorrow, forecast when he first beheld them and since then endured, yet unable to erase the throb of a smile.

Punta, toe . . . *talon*, heel . . . *punta, talon* . . .

'*You gaze on beauty of young girl. No more you need trees and flowers. No more you need horse, sword, walls of tower. Now you have tree, flower, song of bird, perfume of blossom, power of horse and sword, all in one . . . young womans.*'

Had the voice emerged from within the study or out of the past from his heart?

This time, he knew whom Zurika was dancing for. Yes indeed, there was Aaron Levi, clad in a dark robe, seated on his rock, staff between his legs, one knee bent, the other half stretched out. Aaron Levi with his gaunt wrinkled face and deep dark eyes beneath a black *yarmulke*, a smiling Aaron Levi clapping out the rhythm with his hands.

He has learned to do that by watching Zurika dance in heaven.

King Ahmed was about to exclaim with joy when another figure materialized behind Zurika. A tall dark-robed man, black *yarmulke* on bald head, hawklike visage, square grey beard covering a lantern jaw, huge beaked nose straddling dark unfathomable eyes. Who could this be? King Ahmed was seized by horror. Zurika abruptly stopped her dance, frozen in the *punta* position. Aaron Levi rose swiftly to his feet. His staff now held in both hands, he advanced threateningly towards the new-comer, who immediately trailed away into nothingness.

Aaron Levi returned to Zurika, held out his hand. She grasped it, relaxed, stood firmly on both feet. Hand in hand, they turned to look at the balcony window. King Ahmed tried to call out but the words would not emerge.

'Oh, Blessed Virgin,' Princess Beatrice whispered.

'Oh, dear God, they are leaving us forever.' The words were a guttural croak, but incredibly they had emerged from Prince Juan.

They had begged God to help Prince Juan, King Ahmed knew, and God had answered their prayers. By some divine quirk, the job of maiming his voice had not been perfectly done. At this moment, Prince Juan had the miracle of speech restored, while King Ahmed was smitten dumb.

The sinking sun laid pink hands on the many white breasts of the Sierra Nevada mountains. Between them were only empty earth and air.

Postscript

King Ahmed embellished the Alhambra palace lavishly. He added a special suite for Princess Beatrice, but he became the prey of a conspiracy in 1359 A.D. He fled to Gaudex and then to Fez, taking Princess Beatrice with him and giving Maria de Padilla custody of their son. Prince Juan had meanwhile become a Benedictine monk and King Charles the Bad remained sunk in his exalted position as ruler of León y Navarra.

Three years later, amid the rejoicing of his people, King Ahmed returned to Allah Hamra as Granada's King. The exile had restored his humility. He ruled peacefully for thirty years.

Yusuf ibn Nagralla must surely have been baffled during this latter period. After all, thirty years is a long time for any spirit, especially a vengeful one, to be out of work!

Ahmed's son, Yusuf II, succeeded his father only to be poisoned to death. After the death of his son, Mohamed VII, the people placed his brother, Yusuf III, on the throne. The son who succeeded Yusuf was named Mohamed VIII; but he was a rude and arrogant man who was forced out of power in 1427, after ten years of rule, escaping to Malaga when the Christian King John II attacked Granada in 1431. Yusuf IV, placed on the throne by King John, died after only a few months. Mohamed VIII resumed the throne, but was imprisoned by his nephew, Mohamed X, who occupied the Alhambra in 1445. A hopeless ruler, he was deposed by Saad, a son of his father's cousin, the same year. When Saad died in 1483 Abdul Hassan, his son, succeeded him, but was driven out by Moham... XI, returning to power only to retire in favour of ...other, Mohamed XII. Betrayed to King Ferdinand ... Abu Abdulla Boabdil, Mohamed XII fled to Morocco.

Abu Abdullah Boabdil had hoped that King Ferdinand and Queen Isabella would place him on the throne of Granada but his hopes were dashed in 1490, when King Ferdinand demanded that he surrender the kingdom. In 1492, Boabdil was banished to Fez with the award of a fiefdom in Al-Bushara. Once more Yusuf ibn Nagralla had occasion to marvel and triumph at the effectiveness of his long-ago curse.

'You do well to weep like a woman for what you failed to defend like a man.' Thus did Aisha, mother of Abu Abdullah Boabdil, admonish her weeping son as he rode into exile from the Alhambra palace, ending Moorish rule.

Ibn Nagralla's curse was lifted when those whose professed doctrine was to turn the other cheek – even though most did not adhere to it – took over his *hisn*. But no Christian ruler dared to augment what existed, still less add to the wondrous beauty of his creation, which finally became deserted and desolate, save for the weeping, wailing spirits, the occasional laughter that haunted it. It lay tattered and forlorn until 1828, when an aesthete from a completely new country, America, rediscovered Allah Hamra. His name was Washington Irving and he worked devotedly to restore the Alhambra to its pristine grandeur.

Finding himself at last one with Jahweh, the Jew Yusuf ibn Nagralla was free to whisper the tale of Mo-Ahmed al-Kamal.